The Bright Unknown

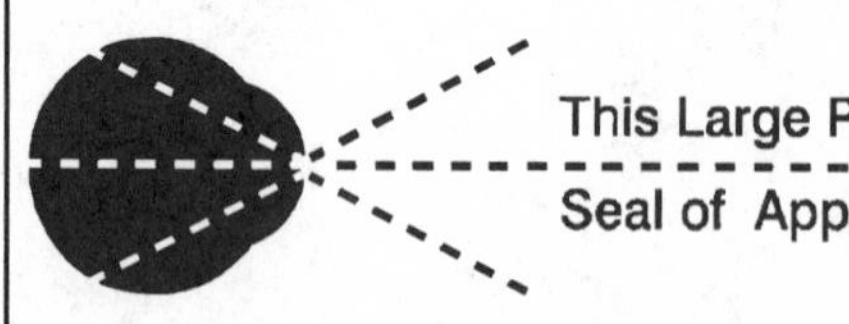
This Large Print Book carries the
Seal of Approval of N.A.V.H.

The Bright Unknown

Elizabeth Byler Younts

THORNDIKE PRESS
A part of Gale, a Cengage Company

Thorndike Press, a part of Gale, a Cengage Company.

Thorndike Press® Large Print Christian Fiction.
The text of this Large Print edition is unabridged.
Other aspects of the book may vary from the original edition.
Set in 16 pt. Plantin.

**LIBRARY OF CONGRESS CIP DATA ON FILE.
CATALOGUING IN PUBLICATION FOR THIS BOOK
IS AVAILABLE FROM THE LIBRARY OF CONGRESS**

ISBN-13: 978-1-4328-6754-6 (hardcover alk. paper)

Published in 2020 by arrangement with Thomas Nelson Inc., a division of HarperCollins Christian Publishing, Inc.

Printed in the United States of America
1 2 3 4 5 6 7 24 23 22 21 20

For Joann, my dear grandma-in-love,
and for Kelly, who understands so much

"I am out with lanterns,
looking for myself."

EMILY DICKINSON

1990
Gravel Paths

I'm not sure whom I should thank — or blame — for the chance to become an old woman. Though as a young girl, sixty-seven seemed much older than it actually is. My knees creak a little, but I still have blond strands in my white hair.

I have watched the world grow up around me. I was old when I was born, so it seems. Was I ever really young? I've been around long enough to know that *progress* is a relative term. What is progress anyway? A lot of damage has been done in the name of progress, hasn't it? But then I have to think, where would I be without it?

Not here.

There are a few other surprises about making it to 1990. We are still firmly living on planet Earth, the Second Coming hasn't happened, despite predictions, and devices like the cordless phone are at the top of many wish lists for housewives. Another surprise is that housewives aren't so common.

I haven't taken much to technology myself and still use a rotary phone. But I did receive a ten-foot coiled cord as a gift. Recently I heard a girl say the words *old school,* so I guess that's the new way to say what I am. There's something funny about having a new way to say *old-fashioned.*

When you have a childhood like mine, being considered out-of-date is a compliment and means I'm among the living. There were times I never expected to live to be this age. Many women of a certain age would love to move back the hands of time and remember the days of their youth. But I'd rather let them become as dull as my old pots and pans — they carry the nicks and dings from use over the years, but no one remembers how those wounds happened and the flaws don't make them useless.

When I step outside and squint at the June sun, I'm caught off guard by the brightness. The sun and I are old friends, and she greets me with a nod as I walk beneath her veil of heat. The walk to my mailbox that's at the end of a long drive has been part of my daily routine for years. Sometimes I amble down the natural path twice, just for the fresh air, but mostly to remind myself that I can. I don't take freedom for granted. The gravel drive almost didn't make it when we first moved in. My kids wanted us to pave it to make it easier to bike and scooter. But I didn't like the idea of a strip of concrete dividing the green mowed lawn of our yard from the grasses that grew wild and untamed on the other side of the driveway. That path between the feral and the tame is dear to me and too familiar to let go of.

The grit from the stones beneath my soles is a safe reminder of where I come from. Painful memories sometimes rise off other gravel paths — some narrow and dark, and others that weren't there till I made them with my own two feet. My driveway reminds me of the freedom I have to come and go as I please. Things were not always this way.

The mailman waves at me from the other side of the road as he lowers the flag of a neighbor's mailbox. I wave back and don't look before I cross. This road is as isolated as my memories.

I throw a glance inside my aluminum mailbox before I shove my hand inside. The occasional critter sometimes can't resist the small haven in a storm — and we had a doozy last night. The stack of mail looks lonesome, so I wrap my hands around the contents and pull them out. The arthritis in my wrist flares and I wince.

I shut the box, then turn back toward my home. A rubber band wraps a *Reader's Digest* around the small bundle of white envelopes and fluorescent-colored flyers. I flip through the mail to try to force out the throb that remains in my wrist. Electric bill. Water bill. A bright-yellow flyer announcing a new pizza joint in town with a coupon at the bottom for Purdy's Plumbing. The cartoon scissors that indicate to cut along the dotted line have eyes and a smile. I don't resist smiling back.

Underneath the pile is one of those big yellow envelopes. A bulky item inside carries the shape of something too familiar, but I don't want to name it. A chill washes over me. Shouldn't a woman my age be prepared for surprises? The last time this kind of bewitchment caught me unawares I was nothing more than an eighteen-year-old girl — frightened and alone. Learning too much all at once. Trapped inside gray concrete walls. Feeling the loss of my last bit of innocence, which had been tucked somewhere behind my heart but in front of my soul — guiding it, guiding me.

But I didn't lose myself in that Grimms'

fairy-tale beginning. My over forty years of marriage made me a survivor of unpredictability. I've crawled through the shadow of death delivering my babies — reluctantly inside the frightful walls of a hospital no less — and became a woman amending her own childhood through motherhood. But this envelope brings me a certain dread that I cannot explain. The contours of the contents. I don't want to open it, even though my entire life has been in anticipation of this.

I consider pushing the package into my apron pocket along with my garden shears and the one cigarette that's waiting to be smoked on my front porch — a habit I started in 1941 and stopped trying to quit in the 1950s. It is only one a day, you see.

But I'm seduced. I turn over the envelope. The name in the corner isn't familiar, but the town in the return address boasts that my nightmares are not dreams but memories after all. The handwriting appears businesslike and feminine.

My gaze travels to the center. It's addressed to someone I shed long ago — so long ago it's almost like that girl never existed. My mother, who'd been a lost soul, gave me the name — sort of. A question mark is scribbled next to the name — the post office doesn't know if it really belongs here. But it is me. This much I know, and I wish it weren't so. After a few deep breaths I pull out my garden shears and slip them through the small opening in the corner with shaking hands. How I do it without cutting myself, I'm not sure.

My suspicions are correct. When I tip the envelope over, a 35mm film cartridge falls into my hands. It's old, almost fifty years old, in fact, and it's warm in my palm. That eighteen-year-old girl named on the envelope cries a little, but she's so far under my concrete skin it doesn't even dampen my insides. I long ago wished I could forget it all, but the voices from my past are stronger than my present. What am I supposed to do now?

The resurgence of guilt, shame, and pain — the bards of my heart — croon at me. I toss the film roll and it lands on the edge of my gravel path between blades of grass.

Who sent it?

Where did it come from?

I look into the envelope and see it's not empty. Before I can bat away my impulses, I pull out the small folded piece of paper. The even and balanced script handwriting reads:

Brighton,

I have the rest of them if you're interested.

Kelly Keene

Kelly Keene. I don't know her. Why does she have the film from my dark years? I look back at the ground, and the cartridge stares at me as it lies prostrate there on the gravel and grass. The exhumed voices from within it speak in my ears. They've never been far away. They're always in the shadow or around a corner. A reflection in a darkened window. Their voices bend over my shoulder, their ghostly faces look into my arms full of children and grandchildren, and the memory of their smiles reminds me how far I've come and the strength it took to always take the next step forward.

And yet the whisper of voices also calls to mind a promise I've left unfulfilled. The burden of this guilt nestles next to my soul. Though shrouded in grace, it knows the entwining paths of peace and despair.

For decades I've kept these voices to myself. But this film begins the sacred resurrection of these forgotten souls, and with them comes the unearthing of my past.

1937
These Bright Walls and the Dark Story They Tell

The flossy gray clouds outside mirrored the blandness inside the walls of my home. The window made me part of both worlds. One I watched and coveted. The other I lived in. Neither was safe.

I flipped through the diary I'd received four years ago on my tenth birthday, and in each entry I noted the dreary weather on the top line. But I didn't need a journal to remember further back than that, since somewhere in the reserves of my mind I was sure I remembered the day I was born — and every rainy birthday since. On that first April morning the storm had pelted the window. The xylophone of sounds was muffled by the press of my ear against my mother's warm breast. I'd imagined all the details of my birth for so long that I was sure they were true, but I would never really know. And my mother would never be able to tell me about those moments because long ago her mind had hidden so well that no amount of searching could bring her back.

A sigh slipped into my throat. I swallowed hard, and the air landed like a rock in my stomach. I breathed my hot breath on the window, then traced a heart. My fingertip made a squeaking sound against the cool glass pane.

I focused past my finger. Not even a single speck of sun lined the edges of the trees in the far horizon across the road and field. A field I'd never stepped on because it was on the other side of the gates. I was told the grounds where I lived mimicked what neighborhoods looked like. Only I'd never seen a real neighborhood, so maybe that was a lie. The only green grass I'd ever stepped in was the grass that grew on the property of the Riverside Home for the Insane.

I smeared away the heart with angry fingers and lightly tapped the glass, making a dull *clink* sound.

I looked around behind me before opening the window as far as it would go. I grabbed the iron bars and pressed my face into the opening. I stuck out my tongue to catch a few raindrops. The coolness jetted through me.

"Girl," said a voice from behind me. I pulled back and bumped my head on the window frame. "If Nurse Derry catches you doing that . . ."

Nurse Edna Crane — Aunt Eddie, as she insisted on being called — had been in the room right after I was born, slippery and squirmy between my mother's thighs. It was Aunt Eddie who'd fixed in my mind the visions of my birth — the low-hanging clouds and the mist from outside crawling indoors and clinging to the walls like ivy vines curling to catch a glimpse of new life. Me. And to think it was in a place where life usually ended instead of began.

Aunt Eddie walked past me and shut the window. She grunted when she turned the lever at the top, then swore and stuck her finger in her mouth. The latch was fussy, I knew. I'd worked on loosening it off and on for an hour. I'd woken a mite past three when my mother began with her fit, and I couldn't find sleep again after that. When Mother had quieted, though, I'd tiptoed from our room and started in on the window knob. I hadn't broken the rule of not leaving the second floor, but I needed air. The dewy world beyond the window was thick with it. The fresh, rain-soaked whiffs were suffocated in the stale spaces of this place.

It was more than simply moist and dank and smelling like rot, more than the decay of daft dreams, more than misery joining the beating of hearts. It was death itself. The scattered remains of us — the barely living — our eyes, ears, hearts, and souls lying like remnants everywhere.

The older nurse squared my shoulders and tried to fix my hospital gown and hair. I knew, however, that I was nowhere pretty enough to be fixed. Weeds bloomed, but that didn't make them flowers.

"Your dress is wet, and how on earth have you already mussed your braid?"

My dress? It was a hospital gown, only Aunt Eddie always called it a dress. The sigh I'd swallowed away earlier whispered at me, begging to be released. I ignored it, and it flitted away.

"Got it caught in the windowsill. There's a nail." I pointed to the window.

"This won't do. When your hair's not done, you look like a dirty blonde at a whorehouse, but when it's all done and pretty — now, you could go to church with that kind of braid." She'd braided my hair before bed, but it was messy when I woke.

I let Aunt Eddie pull my French braid out and tried not to wince as she tucked the strands this way and that way. She combed down my fine flyaway hair and pulled it harder than ever, making slits of my eyes. To please her I smoothed down the gown — a used-to-be-white shift with snaps up the back, though a few had gone missing years ago. Nurse Joann Derry, whom I called Nursey, took it home one day and made it fit my narrow shoulders, since they were made for bony grown women. Their pointy, emaciated shoulders could keep anything up. Nursey did this as often as we were issued new clothing, which was usually once a year.

Last year she had to find me a different gown for a few days while she worked out the stain from my first curse from my issued one. I'd just turned thirteen. The saturated red mark on my gown and bed and the stickiness between my legs hadn't been a shock to me. Before my mother was sterilized — a procedure doctors thought would help her melancholia depression and psychosis — I was always the one to clean her up because Nursey was charged with nearly a hundred other patients and had little help. Nursey had given me Carol's gown; she'd died only the week before and was barely cold in the graveyard out back. Her family hadn't claimed her body. Now she'd just be C. Monroe on a small stone marker. Wearing a dead woman's gown was commonplace around here, but knowing who'd worn it last left me with the heebie-jeebies.

I'd stayed in bed for most of the first day of my curse, and my friend Angel had assumed I was dying when I wouldn't go out for a walk through the orchard and then to the graveyard where we'd memorized every headstone. Nursey gave him an explanation, though I don't know what she said. Later he told me she'd mentioned my burgeoning womanhood and hormones, something we'd learned about when she gave us a few biology lessons.

Nursey had believed my step toward womanhood deserved something special, and when she brought my institutional shift back to me, she surprised me by turning it into a real dress. Her smile lit up when she pointed out something called a Peter Pan collar and the ruffles at the hem. When I put it on I spun around like I did when I was little, before I understood that it wasn't normal for a child to live in an asylum.

I cried when the hospital administrator, Dr. Wolff, refused to let me keep it, claiming he'd already made too many exceptions when it came to me. Nursey said we shouldn't push our luck — whatever that meant. Luck? Me? Luck would be the chance to run away and buy myself as many ruffled dresses as I wanted and wear a different one every day. Maybe fall in love and get married. Maybe even be a mother.

Maybe. Someday.

By now, at age fourteen, I knew that being a resident of the Riverside Home for the Insane was not how everyone else in the world lived. But it had been my life since birth. None of the doctors' diagnoses — *feeble-minded, melancholia,* or *deaf mute* — could be used to describe me. I didn't even have a bad temper. All my friends had these labels, and I was familiar with them, but they didn't apply to me. Neither were they used on my best friend, Angel — he was just an albino and didn't see well.

My poor mother was bewitched with voices and demons, and my father never cared enough to rescue either of us — or even visit. He was our only ticket out of this asylum because he was our next of kin. But today, on my fourteenth birthday, the fresh air outside tapped on the windows, taunting me, willing me to make a run for it. But what about my mother? If I left, wouldn't I be as bad as my father? I didn't want to be bad.

"All done." Aunt Eddie patted my shoulders and spun me around to get a good look. My distorted reflection stared back at me through her pooling eyes. I was a plain girl with too big a name. It hung over my identity like the issued hospital gown drooped on my shoulders. But it was the only thing my mother had ever given me.

"Brighton."

Nurse Joann Derry's voice vibrated through the chilled, bleak corners. She came into the small dayroom. "Brighton Friedrich, young lady, where are you?"

"She's here." Edna pushed me past the patients who were filing in after breakfast.

The closer I got to the dayroom door and to the hall that led to the dormitory, the more I could hear Mother in an upswing of a fit. The wails beat my eardrums, and my heart conformed to the rhythm. She needed me. Rain and Mother's fits were like peas and pods that multiplied on my birthday.

Mother's groaning always began around three o'clock in the morning every year. Then, for the next few hours, she would go through the pains of labor and childbirth as if it were happening for the first time. But when she found no baby at the end of it all, she'd mourn this phantom loss. She'd scratch at the concrete walls so severely her fingernails would bleed, and if we didn't restrain her fast enough, she'd lose one or two. After years of pulling out her hair, her roots remained fruitless. If we didn't watch her closely she'd pick at the softest places on her skin — the insides of her elbows, her wrists, her breasts — till they bled. The white coats called it psychosis. She couldn't, or wouldn't, cope. They said they didn't know why, but I wasn't sure I believed them anymore. They'd hurt so many of my friends that I knew not to trust them.

As for my mother, I'd never known her any other way. Besides restraints, my presence was the only thing that helped her. Sterilizing her had not released her from this madness. Her hormones were not responsible.

The doctors depended on a few things to calm her. My presence and touch, even as a baby, was one prescribed method. But if I failed, Nursey had no choice but to camisole or restrain her to her bed or a chair or give her a dose of chloral hydrate. Insulin was the new Holy Grail for fits and mania, putting patients into a coma-like sleep for many hours to days at a time. But the injections agitated her and caused a dangerous irregular heartbeat. There had never been good answers for Mother.

Next door was the Pine View children's

ward. The nearby buildings were connected through a basement hall. At Pine View the patients were treated like animals — not so different from my ward. But here, I was safe. Or at least as safe as one could be in an asylum. Joann took care of me like a daughter. After my birth I'd been transferred to the children's ward, but Joann fought for me to be returned to Mother's room, promising to care for me. Nursey had only been eighteen years old then and not in a position to demand much, but the ward doctor, Sidney Woburn, was keen on Nursey and was known to give in to her requests. I would learn more about that when I was older — the wiles of a desperate woman and the web of deceptions.

But today, when I got to Mother's room, I saw several wrapped gifts on the rag rug that Mickey had taught me to make years ago to help my room feel less sterile. How I'd missed Mickey since her unexpected death a few years earlier. Her silvery hair always brushed against her eyelids, and her pink skin looked happier than her reality. On my bed, beyond a small stack of gifts and memories of Mickey, sat a cross-stitched orange cat pillow. Nursey had taught me how to cross-stitch on one of her many off-duty evenings. Those were the hours she would read stories like *Peter Pan* to Angel and me. I would cross-stitch, and Angel would just sit and listen. I named the orange cat Nana and secretly wished it was a dog instead — and that it was real. And that Neverland was real too. A tattered teddy bear Mickey had made from an old brown towel lay limply next to Nana. It was the last gift I got from Mickey.

Today there was also a small cake the kitchen staff must have baked. There was always a shortage of flour and sugar; someone had sacrificed for this cake. It sat on the non-hospital-issued nightstand. That nightstand got stuffed into a medicine closet whenever any official visits were made to see how well things were run. I would get stuffed into a closet, office, or somewhere too — I even had to crawl under a bed once with Nana. I wasn't allowed to be seen. I was used to the lie by now. However, since it was rare we had ward visitors, the farce game of hide-and-seek had not been played for years.

Angel, my best friend, who lived in the children's ward, was sitting on the floor by my bed. His gown looked extra dingy in comparison to his pale skin. His wavy, white-blond hair was mussed and stuck to his forehead. He looked up as we walked in.

His smile, even with yellowed teeth, gleamed, and his blue-red eyes looked toward me through what I knew to be blurry vision. I waved at him, and he waved back until my mother's animalistic moan jarred away my attention. Away from Angel and from all the small touches in my room meant to make me feel like a regular girl on her birthday. A regular girl. All I knew of regular girls came from books. But my fictional friends Heidi, Pollyanna, Betsy, Anne, Sarah — none of them had regular lives either. So perhaps there were no regular girls anywhere.

"Helen." Nursey rushed in and patted my mother's shoulder gently and gestured frantically for me to get closer. She pulled me toward Mother when I was reachable. "Helen, Brighton is here."

"Liebling." Her gravelly voice spoke this German word that I'd heard my whole life, though it had become seldom in these later years. My eyes wandered to the old stack of books under my bed where I used to have a German translation dictionary, hoping for some message from her besides these broken words. But the book had been stolen by a patient and ruined.

Mother's stringy hair, the color of rain clouds and sand, hung like dull curtains around her colorless face. She was not nearly blind like Angel, but still she did not see me. She always stared out into nothing. When I was a child I would sit so that our eyes were level, desperate for her to look at me. Once, her blue gaze lighted on me — though only for a brief moment. In my childishness I thought she might be waking up from this catatonic daze. A soft smile had crept over her stretched, dried lips, but her softness turned into terror and she screamed in my face. I never tried that again.

Today her eyes traveled around but never landed on anything. Mumbled whispers in a fragmented language clouded my thoughts, making it impossible to reason through this annual nightmare. I could only submit to it. Her arms reached out, and when no one handed her a baby, she pulled at her clothing and looked for an infant — me — beneath the single thin blanket. She was wearing no underclothes, which was typical for most patients, and she lifted her gown, searching, before she grabbed at her belly and groaned. Wilted and scarred skin draped on her like poorly fitted clothing. The shell my mother lived in had withered years earlier.

I hated my reality, but hated hers even

more. Surely she deserved better than living a life of lunacy. Surely she'd not been the sort of woman who had been so terrible in her right mind that losing it seemed a just punishment. And why had I reaped the consequence of her infirm mind?

As she went through another round of what she believed was labor, I thought of the tiny and beautiful woman she must have been when she was admitted — already pregnant and uncontrollable and entirely lost. She was just a pebble in the ocean. A raindrop in a storm. I used to ask after my history, but my curiosities were met with short, unembellished answers. Nothing that ever hinted at why my father hadn't returned for me. I knew nothing about this Lost Boy from Neverland, as I had come to think of him.

Joann was up and down the hall, leaving me to deal with my mother. I'd even started helping with baths and cleaning for the last two years — Angel had too. The staff in the children's ward pretended not to notice that Angel was absent most days, since it meant one less patient for them to care for — another allowance Nursey gave me so I could have a friend my own age.

She tried to give me some sort of life, though we had to hide it all from Dr. Wolff.

Patients were never supposed to be out of their wards like Angel was, but I also knew that little girls weren't supposed to be born and raised in a madhouse, though it was the only world I'd ever known. So allowances were made — as long as it didn't interfere with Nursey's duties, naturally.

A little later I let Angel open my gifts. Aunt Eddie gave me a new pair of underclothes — two pairs. Angel didn't flinch at the intimacy and handed them to me without shame. We'd shared so much together — too much, according to Nursey — but underclothes weren't much to us, except that we were glad to have them.

The next gift was a chocolate bar from one of the cooks. The smell alone took me out of these walls for a twinkling moment. "Here, take a bite."

"Mmm." Angel took the tiniest of bites and smiled. He always had a shy grin tucked into his mouth. I let my piece melt on my tongue until it wasn't there anymore; the taste filled my senses.

"You have one more gift," Angel's smooth voice reminded me. He held up a yellowed envelope with my mother's name on the front. *Helen Friedrich.* It was from Nursey. "Ready?"

Angel's hands carefully untucked the flap

and pulled out a small paper. "What is it?" he asked and held it close in an effort to see the details. He used to have a magnifying glass, but it had been broken to bits when he'd snuck it and a book into his ward. His nurses were ruthless — worse than Miss Minchin. At least Sarah Crewe had never been beaten senseless. Nurse Harmony Mulligan, on the other hand, had no problem administering a beating now and again. That had been months ago now and he had healed up, but he was sad not to be able to read well anymore. He could see well enough in the light, but darkness was nearly impossible for him.

He raised the thick paper to his eyes, but he had turned it the wrong way. The other side revealed eyes that stared back at me. My mother's eyes. I grabbed the old photograph from Angel's hands.

"Mother? It's a picture of my mother." A warm tingle swarmed and buzzed in my belly, but it was chased away by the chill that was always pocketed deep inside. I looked from the image on the paper to the skeletal woman lying flat on the bed. Though she hardly resembled the rounder and healthy-looking woman in the picture, this surprising gift took my breath away. I thought I might even resemble her a little

— her high cheekbones and jawline and maybe the soft almost-smile her lips formed.

"Up, up. Time for your birthday picture." Nursey walked in with her camera. She'd done this for years.

"Where did you get this?" I held the photo of my mother as I stood.

"Her file." She held the camera up to her eye.

I looked at the photo again. "I kind of look like her, don't I?"

Exasperated, she lowered the camera. "I have two floors to deal with today, Brighton. Let's go. We can talk about that later." She raised the camera again.

"Can Angel be in this one?" I asked her. She usually said no, but maybe not this time.

"Just you, Bright." She waved Angel away. He continued to smile as he obediently stepped aside.

I stood there, and the feel of the old photograph in my hand made me smile. After I heard the *click* I pulled Angel over. "Please?" I pleaded. My life wasn't much without Angel.

Nursey exhaled and waved him in.

Angel and I stood shoulder to shoulder. I looked up at my friend who was wearing a smile like a warm breeze — and the *click* sounded. Nursey threw me a look of frustration, then stuffed the camera back into her apron pocket and left the room in a flash. What did she do with the photographs? I had never seen any of them.

"Tell me about the photograph." Angel slouched on the bed with me.

I paused, contemplating, trying to take in every detail.

"It's so strange to see her like this. It's almost as if this is a storybook picture and not even real." I paused and shallowed out my gaze to tell him the basics. "She's wearing an ugly, long black dress and she's sitting on a chair. And —"

I pulled the photograph close to my eyes.

"And what?"

"There's a hand on her shoulder, but the photograph has been cut. I can't see who's there."

"Cut? I wonder why."

I ran my finger over the cut edge — it was clean, smooth.

In silence I took in the rest. The older woman in the chair next to her had dull eyes. The serious-looking man gripping the older woman's shoulders like he was trying to keep her still.

I looked so long I memorized it. I traced the length of it with my thumb. The fingernail I'd chewed off earlier mocked me. Nursey would threaten to put rubbing alcohol on it again if she caught a glimpse of it. I tucked it away.

My eyes returned to the hand on my mother's shoulder. The hem of the long sleeve at the wrist was similar to my mother's, and the fingers draped gently over her shoulders were thin and elegant. The hand belonged to a woman — a young woman. Who was she?

1928
An Angel to Watch Over

I looked back at Mickey as I began to run. She was smiling and waving at me. She'd just told me that I shouldn't be gone long. Her soft, warm hug had sent me on my way, out to the graveyard. I liked it back there — it was quiet, except for the birds. The building I lived in was never quiet.

My five-year-old legs were fast. Not long after I first started running out there, Nursey gave up trying to catch me since she and her helpers had so many others to watch. They couldn't catch me anyway.

The friends I lived with didn't even notice me. Mother never noticed either.

And Nursey knew I would come back. I told her not to worry. I did wish Mickey could come with me so she could tell me more stories. But if she or Mother or any of the others tried to run off, Joann would camisole them. I hated that. Nursey said I was different from them. They were a lot older, I supposed, and some of them talked to themselves. But I did that too, some of the time. Sometimes they screamed. But so did I. Some of them told me about visions they had, and they sounded a lot like the dreams I had at night.

Some of them were just like storybook mothers and grannies, though, especially Mickey. Since I didn't have any other children to play with, Nursey picked a few of the women for me to spend time with in my room. She said she'd chosen the best ones. Mostly Mickey and Lorna came. They'd tell me funny stories and read books to me and play games with me. Nursey always made sure that one of them was in my room with me for a few hours every day since I wasn't allowed anywhere else in the building. But outside I could be alone.

I looked back at the patients. Some of them were holding on to the rope that led them to the courtyard and our huge garden where we worked on nice days. Some of them walked on ahead without the rope. No one cared that I wasn't there. I was lucky.

Then I started running again. I liked the way the dry grass brushed my bare feet. The graveyard was the farthest away I'd ever been from the building. After Claudia from room 205 died, I wanted to know what would happen to her body, so Nursey let me watch the gravedigger. Ever since then I liked imagining the people who were buried there. Nursey said it was strange and used the word *morbid.* She wouldn't explain what it meant even after I begged her. But Mickey told me that it meant I was interested in learning about death and dying. It wasn't that I was interested so much as I needed to know where the body went, since Nursey always said they were in heaven and I wanted to know where heaven was. It was the ground.

When I was more than halfway to the graveyard I put my arms out like an airplane and sang the special song my friend Rosina had given me.

"All things bright and beautiful." I sang it as loud as I could, and because I only knew the first four lines, I just repeated them over and over. When I got to the last line I stopped and yelled it as loud as I could in the sky. *"The Lord God made them all."*

The Lord God was someone Rosina talked to a lot. Nursey did too, just not as nicely.

I ran again and was going so fast that I could feel my heartbeat speeding up. I liked the way that felt. Nursey told me that my heart pumped my blood, and the faster I ran, the faster it pumped. Now when I ran I imagined that every time my heart pumped in and out it was telling me to run like the wind. So I did.

But today someone was near a gravestone in the corner of the yard. I stopped running. It wasn't the big, old gravedigger. It was a small person, like me. But different. Like a pure white person.

An angel?

The word came into my mind as quietly as Nursey's *hush* when I was frightened. But I had to take a minute to remember what the word *angel* meant. I remembered that Joyful, the kitchen lady, had used the word *angel* a while back when she brought up some food. She was a nice lady and always pinched my cheeks, and she gave me a red ball for my birthday a few months ago.

"Better hope a bright and shining angel is watching over her, Miz Joann," she'd said one day. "You keep her close, you hear. If she got to be here, she deserves some protection from all this mess." I remembered how her eyes rolled to the sides and looked extra white against her brown skin.

Later I asked Nursey what an angel was. She told me that children had guardian angels who watched over them and kept them safe. She said that they were beautiful and so bright they would light up the sky. This person standing there was so white — I was sure it was my very own angel.

I walked toward the angel, and when I was close I waved. I could see that the angel was a boy because he was wearing a shirt and pants.

"You're beautiful," I said to the angel.

He was.

He tilted his head like he didn't understand.

The closer I got, the more I could see how bright the angel was. Maybe I was supposed to have been an angel, because my name is Brighton. But I wasn't bright. My skin was peach, and my hair was the same color as the gravy that Joyful served sometimes.

The angel looked at me, but there was something wrong with his eyes. He squinted them like he couldn't see well. I stepped closer. His eyes almost looked purple, but then they looked red and blue too.

"Can you talk?" I asked him.

"Who are you?" His voice was small and quiet.

"I'm Brighton Friedrich. I live in that big building over there." I pointed to it, and his eyes roamed in the right direction, but he squinted real hard. "Don't you see well?"

He shook his head and then looked at the

ground. I looked down too. The only color besides his eyes that he had on his whole body was dirt on his feet. I looked back up at him.

"Don't feel ashamed." I felt very grown up using the word *ashamed.* Nursey used it, but usually when she was telling me that I *should* feel ashamed because I'd broken one of her rules. "Maybe angels see better as they get older — you know, so they can guard over children."

He didn't say anything so I kept talking. "What's your name?"

He shrugged. "I don't think I got one."

"Didn't your mother give you one?"

"Don't have a mother either. Don't think so, anyway."

"No mother?" I gasped. Was it because he was an angel? "Whose room do you sleep in then? I live with Mother in room 201. That means we are on the second floor and the first room."

The angel boy started digging his toe into the dirt. "There was this one woman who used to sing to me a long time ago, but I don't know where she went."

"Maybe she's in heaven." I pointed at the graveyard. "So what do they call you?"

"The albino." He looked toward me.

"I don't think that's a real name. I'm going to call you Angel."

"Okay." He almost smiled.

"Until you are a grown-up angel with wings and can watch over children who need you, I'll watch over you." This was just about the most exciting thing that had ever happened to me.

"Wait till Nursey and Mickey hear about you." I took his hand and started leading him toward our buildings. "And Joyful."

"I know Joyful." He smiled again. "She told me once that she don't know how God made someone so light as me and so dark as her."

"I know who God is," I blurted out and stopped walking.

Angel raised his eyebrows. "You do?"

"Do you know the bright and beautiful song?"

"No. I don't know any songs."

I wrinkled up my face because I didn't know anyone who didn't know any songs.

I sang my song for him. "You're bright *and* beautiful."

"What was your name again?" Angel tilted his head; we were closer now, and I didn't mind how close he had to get to see me. It was nice to have a friend my size.

"Brighton."

"Maybe you're my mother, Brighton?"

"I don't think so. I'm only five. Mothers are usually older." I hated disappointing him. "What were you doing all the way out here?"

We started walking again. "We were outside to get our washing. I hate washing day so I ran away." His rubbed his wrists. "They'll probably strap me down in my bed again."

"They'll restrain you?" I stopped walking again and got real close. Yep. His eyes really were red and blue all at once.

"It makes me cry."

"Nursey would never put me in restraints. But Mother is restrained a lot and everyone else I live with is too — I sneak out of my room sometimes. Nursey said that it helps them calm down, and she lets me pat Mother. Why would you need to calm down?"

He shrugged and let out a big breath.

"Why do you run away? I love baths. Nursey brings the tub right into my room and makes the water nice and warm, and she reads a book to me at bedtime too."

"We just stand in a row next to the building and the aide sprays us. The water is really cold. It's so cold that my elbows and knees get stiff."

He wiggled his arms like a rag doll.

"Naked?" I asked, and he nodded. My heart felt funny — but I didn't know why. I had heard there were other children who lived near me, but I wasn't allowed to play with them. But this one didn't have a name or a mother or get to take real baths, and I wanted him to be my friend. I would ask Nursey to let him live with me.

When we started walking again I imagined Angel tied down in his bed. My heart started pumping fast and I wasn't even running.

"Brighton?" He took my hand in his.

"Yeah, Angel?"

"What's a book?"

1937
Dry Bed of Grass

Angel was the brightest person I knew. His skin was like the whitest moon hanging in a navy sky. Brighton would've been a good name for *him.* He was left alone at the children's ward door when he was just a tiny shining boy. Nursey said they guessed him to be about three when he was found.

Angel was albino. The only one at Riverside, and he was nothing like most of the other children in his ward. Neither was I. Like the women's ward, the children's ward was categorized in medical terms that I'd learned way too much about when I was young. The majority were children the white coats described as *mentally retarded* or *mongoloid,* but sometimes a blind or deaf child was admitted, or a runaway no one could handle in a real orphanage. Once a child displayed behavior that was deemed *unimprovable* or *imbecilic,* they were brought to Riverside.

Angel did become a guardian over some of the patients. Some of his nurses were kind because he was helpful and didn't give them trouble, but others were as cruel as a stepmother in a Grimms' story.

One afternoon we were in the graveyard and I took Angel's hand and traced his finger over the few dips and curves in an old headstone. For a long time we had tried to figure out what had once been etched on the ancient, cracked headstone. The impressions were so old and worn that unless you looked at the stone closely, it looked blank. We'd decided it was the oldest in the graveyard. It was sunken into the soft earth at an angle and reminded me of one of Mother's crooked teeth.

"It might be a *P*," Angel said and looked at me, his eyes a shade of violet in the afternoon light. The blue in the center of the red blended into an otherworldly color that was now as familiar as my own common blue.

I dropped his hand and slumped back into the dry grass. I tilted my head and squinted my eyes, trying to look real hard at it. Maybe it was a *P* — or maybe it was a number.

"We'll probably never know." I sighed.

He helped me up, and beneath the swirling of the not-quite-white clouds, we played our game. Over the years we'd memorized every etching in the gray stones in the graveyard — always just the first initial and last name. I called out, "H. Cochran," and Angel went searching with his walking stick to keep him from tripping over a gravestone.

"Found it," he yelled a minute later. He started the fictional biography. It was part of our game. "Her name is Hester. She's a mother and bakes apple pies for her children every Sunday." He smiled from the opposite corner. "Your turn."

From where I stood, *E. Ray* and *F. Moscrip* faced me. I closed my eyes and Angel yelled the name.

"B. Bender."

"B. Bender," I whispered and put my hands out to steady my first few steps. I'd have to go down four rows and then over six, and I would be at Bender. I cautiously stepped and winced when I forgot about the small hole in the dirt the exact size of my shoeless foot. I pulled it out and heard Angel snigger.

"I'm here," I called over my shoulder but kept my eyes shut — in case I was wrong. I knew I wasn't, though. I could hear Angel's feet brush through the dry grass between the small grave markers.

"Who is he today?" Angel asked, and I opened my eyes.

We flopped down on the grass, our faces to the sky. The April blue was thin, and the clouds moved faster now than when we'd first slipped through the basement kitchen and out the cellar doors. Both of our hospital uniforms rippled in the breeze. If anyone from the surrounding homes and farms on the outside caught sight of the two of us running through the graveyard, they wouldn't question why we were kept at a madhouse. What would happen if they knew the truth?

Still, we were luckier than most here; Nursey gave us small allowances of freedom. But when Angel turned eighteen he would be removed from the children's ward and put in the men's ward — and everything would change. That time was growing near. What type of plan we would need to keep this from happening, I didn't know.

If he didn't die within the walls of the men's ward, he really would go mad and I'd never see him again.

"Who is B. Bender today?" he repeated as he pulled the dry grass from the ground beside him and let the pieces rain over us.

"His name is Bartholomew. He's a carpenter. He's tall and has thick black hair."

"You always say black hair." He turned, facing me.

"I do not." I elbowed him.

I paused for a moment and looked up. There was a break in the clouds and the sun's rays began to pour over the edge, making the sky glow. I cupped my hand to shield the sun from Angel's sensitive eyes and held it there until the sun moved back behind the clouds.

I was always watching out for him. Only months after I met him in the graveyard, I found him at the bottom of the stairs in his own ward. I'd snuck in through the kitchen in the underground tunnel system, looking for him. He'd been lying at the landing for several hours with a broken leg. He still walked with a subtle limp.

"Okay, Bartholomew Bender was a carpenter, and on his daughter's tenth birthday he built her a dollhouse." I continued my make-believe.

I remembered a picture of a house in a newspaper wrapped around one of my birthday gifts. The caption said something about how it was being turned into a historical museum of sorts. I'd never been in a real house, but I often considered what it would feel like. I'd read fairy tales about houses made of candy and castles with servants. If I wandered through a dark forest and found a house, I wouldn't care what it was made of or how grand it was; I would just be glad I'd found a home. And I'd be glad if there was a glow from the window so that I knew someone was waiting for me.

"The dollhouse was yellow with a white porch. And when he worked —"

"He whistled. His favorite food was pork chops and pancakes with —" Angel added.

"Maple syrup," we finished together and laughed.

Angel and I had never had maple syrup, and no matter how much we tried, we couldn't imagine how it tasted — or how anything that came out of a tree could taste good. We'd never had pancakes either, but those were easier to imagine. We'd learned all about this in the books I read to the two of us. Nursey's work had gotten so busy she didn't read aloud to us anymore. Most of our books had been read so often the spines were broken.

Angel inhaled deeply as if he could smell the warm breath of a coming storm. He relaxed, and we didn't speak for several minutes. Our comfortable silence made me sleepy and content.

"Do you think we'll ever have families?" I didn't look at him, afraid he'd see the desperation in my eyes. "Maybe have a real house and maybe I would make apple pies for my children on Sundays."

"And maybe I could build a dollhouse for my daughter," Angel added. After several slow clouds passed overhead, he sighed. "I hope we get to, but . . ."

I took his hand that lay in the grass near mine and we were quiet together. My eyes roamed over the nearby stone markers and caught sight of one that I often avoided. It said *M. Randall. M* for Mickey. Kind. Warm. She loved me all the way to the end.

"I think my mother was invisible — maybe a ghost or something." His voice was velvety smooth like the skin of a peach.

I turned to look at my friend, confused. Dry, brittle grass poked up between us like little broken fairy towers. Angel rarely talked about where he'd come from.

My vision narrowed like a needle on his eyes, and I could only see the blue in the center. His eyes whispered to me, but the wind picked up and whisked his silent thoughts away. I would only catch his spoken words today.

"Invisible?" I said, trying to match the softness of his tone. I couldn't. My voice was low and throaty.

Angel looked up into the overcast sky and

closed his eyes to the brightness. It covered us like a dome, and the trees along the property line began to stir. Lightning flashed, but the low rumble that eventually followed was distant. I turned back to Angel. His cotton-white hair fell on his forehead and over one eye. I pushed it away.

"When my mother left me here, no one saw her come and no one saw her go."

1990
Overexposed

I gently rock the processing tray, waiting for the image to appear. The red light in the dark room and the smell of the developer as I anticipate the photograph all have the best effect on me. The dark room cradled and nurtured me in my midtwenties — as I became my own newly processed and developed person. A new life with images I had some measure of control over. Taking photos is one thing, but seeing them come alive in front of me, like something coming from almost nothing, reminds me of new life instead of death. Something so different from the world I came out of.

And now, even at my age, I still get a thrill when I walk into my dark room and, in the pitch black, crack open the canister and thread the film into the plastic reel and tank. It's a solitary job, and the quiet has become part of me. A different sort of solitary than before.

The developer in the tray ripples lightly on its own now, so I carefully let go. I watch the paper bloom into a photograph. It doesn't take long, which never ceases to amaze me. The gray slowly darkens into real edges until an image arises. Fifty years ago I saw my life through a viewfinder and now, like some sorcery, those fragments lay before me.

But like a passing rain, the image comes and then goes entirely black. I've overexposed and lost the image. I grumble a word to myself that I am glad no one else hears and flip up the light switch. I grab the negative strip again and my magnifier loupe. Am I exposing the right image? With anxiety and reluctance, I bend over and look at my contact sheet, using my loupe. This keeps me at an emotional distance. Seeing these images that I know so well is like being outside of myself. Usually these recurring pictures are held tightly within the confinements of my mind, but now suddenly they're free.

I hold my breath and let my gaze wash over the small image. The loupe magnifies it enough for me to see. The foreground and the subject are in focus, but the background is not. That isn't the one I wanted. I move to the next frame. This is the one. My breath catches, and my eyes squeeze shut.

I reach back and turn off the dark room light again. I flip back on the safe bulb, and the red glow anesthetizes me and I breathe evenly. I pull out another piece of printing paper from the sealed box and put it carefully on the enlarger. Then I return the negative to the enlarger, snap the light switch on, fit it so the image is straight, then check my notes on the exposure. I decrease it by half. It has to work this time.

I'm not in the dark room as often now since I quit teaching at the local art center. But my hands still move deftly — like they lived in this world to cure my own melancholy, slipping from one reality to another. It's hard to leave all you know. The retained scars and damage don't repair on their own. But when your hands can walk you through, eventually your mind and soul follow.

I expose the paper once again, then move it from the enlarger into the developer. I tilt the tub a little back and forth to get the agitation going again. Then I wait. Surely the exposure is close and this will reveal the photo I took when I was a mere girl of sixteen.

The image surfaces on the paper, and after about a minute I carefully pull it out and put it in the stop bath. My heart thuds against my wrinkled-up chest. I feel as young as, well, maybe a fifty-year-old, but my heart is still that teenager who held the viewfinder to her eye and the image in her cast-iron memory.

I put the print in the last tub to fix. The red hue in the room doesn't give me enough light to know if this is going to be a good print, but I can see I'm getting close. Closer than I ever thought I'd be.

I hear the phone ring through the thin walls of my dark room. It is probably Doc. That's what I call my husband — Doc. He finds it irritating but cute. I started it when he graduated almost forty years ago, and it's rare I use his name anymore. Names are slippery things, aren't they? I've been prone to nicknaming since I was a child. Nursey. Angel. Aunt Eddie. I did it with my own children. Martha Annabelle became Marty-Bell and Lucas John was L.J. before we came home from the hospital. Oh, hospitals, what wonder and awe and disappointment they offer. My Rebekah Joy never had the chance to be nicknamed or to come home. I trap that memory away and focus on the ringing phone.

I shake the names from my rattled brain, and after another quick glance at my newest print I turn on the light and walk out of the room. The light in the rest of the house feels brighter than it really is, and for several moments it's unwelcome. Brightness sometimes has that effect on me after so many years of darkness.

I scold the phone that I'm coming. It doesn't hear me. Only the birds through the open windows hear me. And they don't care.

The ring rattles my beige phone. It shakes the kitchen counter and my nerves.

"Hello," I say when the receiver isn't quite to my ear yet.

"Hi, Mrs. Friedrich?" An unexpected articulate voice cuts through my annoyance.

"Yes? Who is this?"

"My name is Kelly Keene." The articulation has ceased and stuttering has begun. "I-I wanted to see if you received my package?" She has a young-sounding, pleasant voice, but it doesn't keep my leeriness away. "Mrs. Friedrich? Are you there?"

"I received your package, yes," I finally say. "How did you happen to have it? And the others?"

There is silence. Is Kelly Keene as unsure about this conversation as I am?

"I-I'm calling from the *Standard* here in Milton." Her words are stammering yet rushed.

"So you're a reporter," I say flatly. So she

isn't after anything but a story, and I am not about to give her anything to talk about. I don't do sideshows. But my heart betrays me still and reminds me that this woman has my film, and for that I plan to make nice. "What's this about?"

"There's a town hall meeting next week, and I was calling to invite you." She pauses. "To personally invite you."

Her emphasis on *you* makes me squint, as if the tiny movement will make me figure out her intentions through the phone cord.

"Ma'am," the voice says. My pause is too long.

"I'm a little confused, Miss Keene. I don't live in Milton, but even if I did, since when does anyone get a personal invitation to a town hall meeting?"

"You're right." She hesitates for a moment, and I open my mouth to give her a piece of my mind for the cryptic package and the invite. What I really want are my film cartridges. They are my belongings. "There's a proposal up for discussion that I think will interest you. I don't want to make you uncomfortable, Mrs. Friedrich, but since you spent so many years at the Riverside Home for the —" She clears her throat and doesn't finish — but I do . . .

Insane.

"I assumed you might have an opinion about it being torn down to be made into a community center," she finishes.

"Please do not call here again, Miss Keene."

"Wait." I can hear her even though my hand hovers over the cradle of the phone. I put the receiver back to my ear.

"No one else knows." The young woman's voice is urgent and almost nervous. "I haven't spoken to anyone about you — about the photos or about your real name. I was asked to help catalog the items in the buildings. Mostly we found old suitcases and medical files. But then I came across the film . . . and a few other things."

She pauses as if she's trying to find the words. But I know there's nothing more intriguing and mysterious than undeveloped film. I am hard-pressed to see the wrong in what she's doing.

"I see," I respond. "Have you developed the other cartridges?"

"No — of course not," she says quickly. "I didn't think it was my place."

Okay, so I am dealing with a saint. Admirable. Maybe. I'm still unimpressed by anyone holding my cartridges hostage. But I want them more than I've wanted anything in a long time.

"Not much of a reporter, are you?" I gave up using tact a long time ago.

"Well, I'm not *really* a reporter. I answer phones." Her laughter is a little too honest. She's nervous, so I get direct with her.

"What do you want, Miss Keene?"

"I wanted to get your film to you."

"And why don't you just mail the rest?"

"I'd like to meet in person. And I think you might have an interest in what's happening with the buildings. Maybe you'd like to see them again — before they're gone."

I am not sure if she is intentionally trying to elicit guilt or if there is some hidden motive, but regardless, learning that the buildings are being torn down without a word from those of us who lived in them — my hand goes to my chest.

I tell her I'll think about it and then we say goodbye. And I will think about it. Though I can't see myself doing anything but requesting the film canisters from her, developing them myself, and adding them to my collection — a collection that may forever be in a secret album almost as hidden as my mental vault of memories. My mind takes a snapshot of what it would look like to have my pictures and life plastered all over the local papers — out there for everyone to see and read about. I don't know where to put that in the boiling cauldron of my brain.

I imagine my children learning more about me in a newspaper than I have told them. They know the general timeline of my life, but not the specifics. Not the dark parts. They don't know much about my mother, and what they do know might compare more to the somewhat innocuous Mrs. Clause, when really she was more like Rochester's wife. Only my closest friends, who are few, know these same facts. I suppose because I am well-adjusted, digging for more details never seemed necessary to them. Since most church and PTA ladies are happy with the veneer of our lives and not the underbelly, I've let them see the easy-to-understand parts of my life. But the truth is that many of the decisions I've made — like getting married, having children, getting an education — have been because I wanted to confront and outbrave what was expected of me. And I think I did that.

I hope my former photography students never have the same motivation for taking photos as I did all those years ago. I am not sure that the idea of snapping an image means the same thing to them as it did to me. To capture a moment in time that otherwise would be lost and muted was no small thing in the gray, dull world of my youth. I didn't take pictures to remember all the good things that happened in my life. To put them in an album. To share with others so they could participate in my reminiscing. I took pictures to document the evil that had been done. The moments in time no one wanted to live and that no one should've lived in or died in.

But to share them? They are too private. Too identifying. Too sacred.

1932
All Dust and Ashes

Mickey's gravestone was at the end of the row. A row I knew well.

A. Robinson.

E. Ward.

Then came *M. Randall.* Mickey Randall. My Mickey. The one who had taught me to jump rope, to read, and to be very quiet when any visitors were in the ward and I wasn't to be seen. The one who had given up her spot in Mother's room for me. One of the first to rock me to sleep. She'd been one of the many women who had been brought to the hospital because she was too sad to get out of bed and care for her own children. No one had ever come back for her. By the time I was born, she was over fifty and had spent over twenty years in the hospital. She was a fixture on the ward.

She was like me, though. Forgotten and left behind by someone outside of the walls.

"Ashes to ashes, dust to dust. Rest in

peace, my friend," Lorna from down the hall said. Her gown rippled in the sunny breeze, and I could see the form of her skinny legs.

"What does that mean?" I choked out. "Dust and ashes?"

My ears were hot and felt like what red looks like. They rang a little, so I focused on Lorna's mouth, which was moving — but why couldn't I hear what she was saying? I looked from Lorna's old, gray-hued face to my hand that was being squeezed by Nursey's. My nine-year-old hand looked so little in her red-chapped hand. My eyes traveled up from our hands, up her arm, to her white-cuffed sleeve, and then to her face. She looked at me, and I realized I couldn't hear her either.

My lungs inhaled and inhaled and inhaled. But I couldn't get enough air. My gaze rested on the turned dark soil in front of me. Mickey was under all that dirt.

She was in heaven now.

Nursey had told me that the morning before. I asked why, because I didn't understand what she meant. Rosina had explained to me that the graveyard was not heaven. So why would Nursey say that Mickey was in heaven? Then she told me things about souls and spirits and bodies and death. I didn't like it.

My chest ached. And I remembered that this was how Mickey died. She had an ache in her chest that was so bad that she couldn't breathe anymore.

I pounded my chest and felt all of my body full of sadness and gray stir up like a pot of Joyful's watery stew. My skin felt stretched under the strain of keeping all the ache inside. It needed to get out of me somehow.

But how? Would it eventually seep out of me — out of all my open spaces — or would it crack my skin open and give me those stretchy scars like Mother had on her belly?

Angel stood in my view now — between my eyes and M. Randall. He didn't need to say anything for me to hear him. He was crying and then my face was wet too and there was a lot of screaming and scratching and hair pulling — all things I did to myself.

Everything hurt if I quit and then Angel — who had grown much taller than me — wrapped himself so tight around me I couldn't move my arms. He pulled me down to the ground and wrapped his legs around me too.

At first I struggled, and Nursey tried to pull him off. I felt restrained, like I'd seen Nursey do to Mother. But when my skin wasn't tingling or ready to burst anymore, I realized the good Angel was doing. He was helping me — saving me — from exploding into all the dust and ashes Lorna talked about.

"Brighty." Nursey's voice finally cut through all my noise. "Slow down and breathe."

She said it like she thought I could just do it. But I couldn't. It wasn't as easy as all that.

"All things bright and beautiful," Angel began, quoting the song I'd learned long ago. It calmed me. By the time he was on his third go-around, I was able to breathe out the words with him as I was tucked away inside the arms of my guardian angel. Nothing could hurt me now.

1933
Misunderstood Brighton

I hadn't been outside in weeks. My view of the outdoors was masked by the cardboard and newspaper Nursey had put over my bedroom window to try to keep out the icy drafts. The hospital was always cold in the winter — colder than cold. The ice crystals formed in pretty designs on the inside of the windows, but it also made us all shiver at night. The outside light made the inside bearable, and without it all I had were these four walls. This left no space for the stench to seep out, so we breathed the air of what smelled like the dying remains of once free and joyful lives. At least the winter had a heavenly appearance, with its fluffy and white dreams cast everywhere. But also like heaven, it was out of reach to me.

I was ten now, so I knew the graveyard wasn't heaven. When people died, their bodies went under the ground but their souls went to this magical place called heaven. That's where people sang and floated around with the angels. Rosina said the streets were gold and the gate was made of pearls. It sounded as fanciful as Wonderland, but instead of the Queen of Hearts, God lived there. I asked her once to tell me what rabbit hole I needed to fall through to find it, and she said, "Only through death, *chica,*" and then she crossed herself. It made me wonder why we cried when somebody died and they got to go to heaven. Shouldn't we cry because we have to stay?

At least when it was this cold, mean old Dr. Wolff would allow the staff to provide old sweaters and bathrobes to the patients who wouldn't peel them off right away or destroy them — or pee on and soil them. Mine, as usual, was oversize, but it was warm. I still wasn't allowed out of my room much, but Nursey made sure that Angel could visit often — his nurses had to agree too. He would run through the basement tunnels, stop by the kitchen to pilfer a few bites of food, then come to my room. Mother was usually sitting in the dayroom or in some therapy, like the rest of the patients. So we had the room to ourselves. We didn't have anyone who taught us anymore. We just learned on our own now. And played games and made up stories, like what we would be when we grew up and what sort of house we'd live in someday. Our days were slower and slower when it was wintertime.

"Nursey's going to be upset if you keep pulling at that cardboard." Angel followed rules better than I did. "You ruined the first one and remember how cold you were until it was replaced."

I sighed and slumped down on my bed. He was right, as usual. He hunched over a book with his magnifying glass so he could read. He'd changed so much since we'd first met. He was so tall now, and his voice had plunged like a raindrop. It made him sound much older and smarter — like he actually knew what he was talking about.

Maybe he did.

"Remember when Betsy played in the snow?" I said and jumped on my cot, making it creak like Lorna's knees, upsetting his reading. When we read *Understood Betsy* recently I felt I'd found a friend. Betsy had had a strange upbringing too — not as strange as mine — but she eventually had a family. Maybe I would too.

"Nursey promised us we could on the first snowfall," he said.

"Do you think she'll actually tell us when it snows, though?" Nursey was more like a mom than Mother in a lot of ways, but I started to wonder about some of the things she told me, like that I couldn't leave this dirty hospital unless someone came to get me even when I was all grown up because of something called *laws.* Surely when I was older I could just leave. Angel too. Why would we have to stay?

"It's only November and I can see out my windows."

He put his fat science book down on our stack of schoolbooks. Besides science there were a few novels and poetry books, math, and a dull McGuffey Reader.

"I don't know why any of this matters if what Nursey says is true and we'll never be allowed to leave." This frightened me and made me feel like my body was full of tears and like I wanted to scream. Like all the sadness and meanness inside of me were wrapped together.

When Mickey died last year I'd had my first real fit. That's when things changed. I hated living at Riverside, and someday I would leave — no matter what Nursey said. I looked at Mother's empty bed and imagined leaving her behind. Or maybe she'd be in heaven by then. *H. Friedrich* would mark her spot. I took a deep breath.

Things were different for Angel and me

too after he'd wrapped himself around me like a camisole jacket and held me as tightly as he could. It felt safe.

Angel pushed our books to the back of the wall under the bed in the heavy silence my comment had created. He was around thirteen now, and while we'd seemed the same age for a few years, we didn't anymore. He wasn't scared like he had been when we met, and he smiled all the time now. But there was something in his eyes that was less playful somehow.

I understood it, really, but I stuffed it far down to my toes — otherwise I was sure Mother's sort of sadness would creep in through my skin and be my sadness too. I loved Mother, but I didn't want to be like her.

Angel slid himself out from under the bed and smoothed down his summer cloud hair. It fell on his even whiter forehead and to his nearly invisible eyelashes. He tilted his head to look at me, and I knew he wasn't sure why schooling mattered either.

But he gave me a smirk, then sat with me with his arm around my shoulders.

"If Nursey says schooling matters — even in here — then it does. Even with the laws, I think she'll get us out of here someday.

She'll figure something out," he said. "I think."

I didn't say anything. I was only ten, yes, but I wasn't sure I believed him. I did have fantasies of my father rescuing me, even though he'd never visited or written me. I didn't even know his name or what he was like. What would it be like to be with him instead of Mother? I didn't like to think on that too long, because she needed me. I was glad that every night I could see her thin form and know there had been a time when we were one. Maybe she knew me then.

"When we're adults, she'll help us get out, and Dr. Woburn does almost anything she asks." His hope kept him talking and smiling. "Surely he'll help if she asks."

"I've seen them kiss." My face wrinkled up.

"They've been kissing for a while. You're only now noticing it?" He lay back on the bed, so I did too, and we stared up at the ceiling.

"Do you think we'll get married someday?"

"To each other?" He sat up and his eyebrows reached his hairline.

"Gross." I slapped him and he fell back down next to me.

We were quiet for a moment.

"I think *they're* going to get married," I said.

A few hours later, Nursey breezed in after her shift. She sent Angel back, brought me my tray of disgusting dinner, and then I did what I did every night: I complained about eating alone. She reminded me that it wasn't healthy for me to eat in the ward cafeteria. "Remember when I had to pry a patient's hands off of you."

But that didn't stop me from remembering that everything had changed since Mickey's funeral when I'd had a fit. She was afraid I was becoming like them. Like the incurables.

It wasn't quite my bedtime when she tucked me in as tightly as a thin blanket could tuck. She sat on the edge of my bed, and her eyes were so big and blue, and I felt five years old again. It reminded me of how I used to tell her almost daily that I wished she was my mother. It wasn't because I didn't love my actual mother but because I knew if Nursey was my mother she wouldn't have to leave me every night and I would have a real home.

"Can you be my mother?" I asked her again, even though I felt guilty because I was old enough to know the answer.

"Brighton," she started.

"Never mind." I turned over and faced the wall.

The door creaked open — I didn't have to look to know it was Aunt Eddie bringing Mother. Nursey got up and put Mother to bed, turned off the light, and returned to me.

"You know I love you like you were my own." She rubbed my back.

"Why can't you take me home?" I turned to face her. "I know about adoption. I read the entire *A* encyclopedia."

"It's not that easy. And besides, I'm not married. A woman like me can't just adopt a little girl. And you're not an orphan."

I looked over at Mother. She was staring straight up at the ceiling. That wouldn't last all night, but it would for a few hours. She'd had surgery a few months ago that was supposed to help calm her. It was called sterilization. I knew it meant she wouldn't bleed anymore and could never have another child.

The surgery didn't change anything, though.

"I wish I was like other girls and lived in a real house with a real father and mother." This wasn't new.

I returned my gaze to Nursey. Her eyes were shiny.

"Don't marry Dr. Woburn."

"What?"

"You'll leave me if you do." My lungs squeezed tight.

"I won't ever leave you."

She said it like she meant it, but she didn't say she wouldn't marry him. My hand banged my chest, trying to force my breathing to calm.

"I won't marry him. I'll never leave you." Even though she whipped those words out of her mouth like a syringe of insulin to calm a patient, her eyes left mine. And her quiet was darker than the room.

Then Mother did what she rarely did anymore and began to hum. She was looking in our direction and even though she was just staring off into nothing, I knew she was humming for me. It reminded me of a lullaby, and the melody warmed the cold air as my breathing met the slow and even tempo. This mother of mine understood me better than anyone understood her.

1939
House of Lies

On the front of the Willow Knob building there hung a small balcony. A Juliet balcony. It was really just there for looks — a facade — and nothing like the one the real Juliet stood on, lighted with hope and romance. The house itself boasted a lie to any traveler on the road whose gaze fell upon the beautiful architecture. No one could ever imagine how the inside of the building didn't match the outside. But it was all lies. A houseful.

The balcony was between tall, white-shuttered windows that were supposed to remain unopened. But when the day waned and the sinking sun stretched its pink fingers along the floor of the otherwise gray hall, it summoned me to come and open those windows.

If Nursey caught me, she would do more than scold me. She'd refuse privileges, like limiting my visits to the dayroom to talk to the patients. Or disallowing Angel to come for a few days. If any of the other nurses or aides found me on the balcony, I would be threatened with solitary. Nursey wouldn't let it happen, of course — but I would be punished nonetheless.

But right now Nursey's shift was finishing and Nurse Wilma's was starting. She didn't care much for me and would not forgive my infringing on rules. But I heard at supper that she was in the hydrotherapy instead of my hall. So I slipped out of the dining room — a small freedom Nursey allowed now that I was sixteen. The veil between my world and a patient's was becoming thinner. And the more my independence grew, the more the routine of the life of a patient set in.

And, like any patient, I was not supposed to leave the dining hall early or be on the balcony.

The staff was afraid someone would fall, but the only way I could fall was if I jumped. But why would I want to jump, unless I wanted to die? In order to die I had to live, and I hadn't lived yet. But my thoughts did run in constant circles as I imagined how I might find a way out. Nursey didn't bring up a future outside of this building. I knew better than to believe that I had some magical father to rescue me or that Nursey would marry and then adopt me.

It was up to me — and Angel — to figure a way out. To find out how to get around the laws and rules and locked doors.

For now, though, rules didn't keep me from following the bright path from the setting sun that cascaded down the hall. I wiggled my toes that were bathed in that light and followed the trail like a fairy path that led me to the balcony. Everyone else was finishing their meal — a meager serving of sliced potatoes and a watery tomato gravy. We were so overcrowded that I wouldn't be missed right away as patients were dismissed to their rooms.

I pressed my right shoulder into the warped frame to open the tricky window. It rattled, and I looked around. I heard the shuffling of feet coming toward the cross section of halls. The patients' dismissal came quicker than I'd anticipated. With deft hands I pulled the window up far enough for me to slip through and then closed it, leaving an unnoticeable crack at the bottom that only fit my fingers so I could draw up the window when I was ready to come back in. I peeked my eyes around the edge of the window and watched.

"Daggum taters again." Flo's ancient voice eroded the air as she walked through the hall. At eighty-two she was the oldest on the ward. She was as together as anyone I knew and had only been admitted because her husband took up with a *floozy* — that's how she put it — and she'd tried to hurt him. She was as small as a person could be and she was always complaining about the food. "Soft enough to chew, though." I could faintly hear Flo smack her lips around her few remaining teeth.

Carmen's loud voice agreed. She was about three times the size of any other patient. She ate whatever tiny Flo didn't. While Flo fairly tiptoed, Carmen's gait was more of a waddle. I loved them both.

My mother padded along next, her eyes in my direction. She'd seen me even though her eyes hadn't met mine. Her thinning gray hair hung down like a curtain over the sides of her face. I brought my finger to my lips. Why I did this, I didn't know. Mother's words were like tattered rags tossed about a room, and they were always in German. Mother was an immigrant.

The photograph Nursey had given me on my fourteenth birthday flashed across my memory. Nursey had said little more than that it was in Mother's personal belongings and that the people in the photograph were my grandparents. I kept the picture close, in the soft space between the pillow and pillowcase, and pored over it every few days. In the two years I'd had it, it had aged a decade from all of my handling. But when I'd asked about the hand on Mother's shoulder, Nursey always said she didn't know.

Mother stood and stared as the other patients walked around her. When the aide came — another new one who would probably only last a few weeks — and took her arm to push her along, she pulled away. I winced when he grabbed her again. Her feet tripped as she resisted. Her face grimaced.

"Nein," Mother yelled. *No.* I knew this German word well. *"Nein."*

I turned away. I didn't want to watch. I watched every day. I watched when she pulled her hair out from the roots and wiped off her bloody fingertips on the walls. I couldn't do anything to stop her. The time I'd tried I'd ended up with the heel of her hand against my temple. I was six.

Every time they strapped her arms down on her iron bed frame, I could do nothing but watch. When she woke in the dead of twilight with her demons dancing between our beds and a curdling scream that could terrify the ghosts in the graveyard — I could only watch. Only watch.

Though I turned away this time, I could

still see her in my mind and hear her in my ears. I would always see and hear her, even when I was as old as Flo. Would I still be here then, in this place of concrete and disappointment?

I sank down and pulled my knees up to my chest. The flowering weeping willow's boughs reached for me in the summery breath. It called out to me. *Come to me. Let my delicate white tears fall over you.* I extended my hand, even though I knew the branches were too far away to let their beauty cry over me. When the wind flowed again, delicate white petals fluttered through the air and landed next to me. I gathered several in my hand and rubbed a silky pair together. I repositioned to cross-legged and put the petals in the trough my gown made, making it almost pretty. I fingered the petals' satiny texture and watched the willow stir in the wind and the veil of dusk that was slipping away to night. The low-hanging moon was tiny and insignificant, a reflection of me. It was almost invisible in the outlying hills. The blue hills became a jagged black, the outline etched against a burst of orange.

I wished the beauty could wash my memory and make me as bright as my name. These were the moments that kept my own mind in one place. Reciting the bright and beautiful song didn't help anymore, because there was little that was bright or beautiful about my life.

A voice spoke behind me — close to the window, above my head. I stilled but leaned my ear toward the window.

"Marry me, Joann." I recognized the voice as Dr. Sid Woburn's. He'd been the women's ward doctor for most of my life. He was half handsome. He'd been injured in the war and had a deep scar that ran the length of his forehead. He looked stern and unyielding, though I had to admit he was gentler than Dr. Wolff and many of the aides. He and Nursey had been sweet on each other for years. How many times had he asked her this question?

I'd overheard a great number of private conversations between them in my sixteen years. The older I got, the more important and serious these conversations became. Sometimes I heard the two discussing sex. My entire body warmed hearing their intimate words. I never intentionally listened in, but their conversations intrigued me. And this time I couldn't get away.

I risked a peek and saw him press in for a kiss.

"Bank's closed." Her hand went to his

chest. "You know my answer isn't going to change, Sid." Her sigh was so big I felt its weight. "I'm committed to her, and if we married . . ."

"She's almost grown — actually, she is grown. You've kept her safe and given her so much — even an education." He paused. His voice was soft and tender. "You've taught her how to cope with her life here. What more can you do?"

"It's not enough." A scuff of feet sounded and I squeezed my eyes shut, hoping it didn't mean they'd caught sight of me. "She doesn't deserve to be here."

"Come on, Joann." He hit the window frame. "Why are we talking about this again? She's sixteen, and you've given up your life for her."

Nursey was crying. "But I feel so guilty."

"Listen, you can't make up for her life here — or be responsible for her future. Eventually she's going to have to stand on her own two feet. You did what you thought was best."

"So I should be more like your sister? Feel no remorse for giving up Angel for a life of luxury?" she scoffed. "That's what you want, isn't it?"

Angel? His mother is Dr. Woburn's sister?

"We both know it was Howard's doing.

And my mother's. Cynthia didn't know better."

"You could've explained things." Her voice rose an octave. "She was just plain selfish."

"She'd have lost everything if she hadn't given him up — that's not Cynthia. And you know that no one says no to Howard."

"Oh yes, the good doctor. Dr. Howard Long." The words were doled out as though they tasted like ward food. "First do no harm, right?"

The quiet was even heavier than the conversation.

"I didn't pull you aside to upset you. I need to talk to you about something else." His tone had changed. It wasn't thin, edgy, and stiff anymore; it was soft and thick. "He's going to be transferred."

"Who?"

"Angel."

I didn't know how to take in everything I was hearing. Cynthia, Dr. Woburn's sister, was Angel's mother? And he was being transferred?

"Oh, Sid, you can't." She spoke almost as loudly as my heart was pounding.

"He's nineteen, and we need space in the juvenile ward. He's slotted to move to Orchard Row in the next few days." The resignation in his voice was a restraint around my throat.

"No." Nursey's voice dripped with venom.

He wanted to take Angel away? Orchard Row was so full that it seemed that the walls swelled with men. Over the years I'd learned all about the other wards. Like the women, the men had two wards, each sex having one designated for the most violent patients — many were convicts. However, in Orchard Row, the nonviolent ward was only a bit less dangerous. Packed tightly, so many men would never be safe. Their yard was fenced — not open like ours. We had looked through the wooden slats as children. Eventually we were run off by an oversize colored aide yelling at us, but we'd kept watch from a distance through our childhood and knew it was a place where nightmares were born.

"Orchard Row is the most overcrowded of all the wards. You know that. And it's too dangerous for him. Are you trying to get rid of him? Is Howard behind this?"

I was paralyzed. I wanted to punch something. I wanted to yell in agreement with Nursey. But I just sat there.

This was a death sentence.

When I heard a thud against the window above me, I peeked. Joann's back was flattened against it as Dr. Woburn's hands wrapped around her forearms. If either of them looked down, they would see my shoulder. I held my breath.

"Get rid of him? The boy is my nephew. I'm not that cruel." He let go of her and ran a hand through his hair. "Come on, Joann, he is years older than anyone in his ward. He's not a child anymore —"

"It's not his fault that most of the children don't live to be as old as he is. You know as well as I do that patients rarely age out of the children's ward — they die there. But he has a chance right now, and we both know it's because of Brighton. He's everything to her. He'd be dead if it wasn't for her. She's kept him safe. He can read anything I give him with a magnifying glass — he's so smart. Give them more time."

"More time for what? They don't have a future, Jo. No one is coming for them, and neither of them can legally leave on their own. We can't change those laws." Whispers like yells heated the air. "It's admirable that you've given them an education, but you've educated them for nothing."

My eyes fell shut. I pulled up my knees and wrapped my arms around myself. *For nothing.* All of this life was for nothing. I was nothing.

"I had to give her something. She deserves more than this. They both do." Her voice broke. "I was sure the laws would've changed by now. They are both mentally capable of leaving."

"The law says it's for their next of kin to decide. Angel's parents will never take him home and Brighton's father is a criminal and — well, he's — Besides, I don't know if they could survive out there. Imagine that. They don't know anything about the real world. Keeping them here is a kindness."

"Shh," Nursey whispered. "Someone's coming."

During a long pause I realized that the sun had relented and gone to bed and I was still out here. The moon had risen and enlarged, and the glittering stars were just beginning their twinkle. I didn't know how such beauty could exist in the moment I was most lost in my life. Was it taunting me? Or was there some hidden message within it?

I knew I needed to get back to my room before Nurse Wilma noticed I was missing. Maybe she already had. But I didn't want to leave this hiding spot. I wanted to hear more so I could form a plan to keep Angel out of the men's ward. But I felt paralyzed.

"Listen, quickly, before someone finds us

here. All of this is going to happen fast because the juvenile ward is being audited and we have to have everything shipshape — files and treatment plans. The state wants to make sure we're not spending too much money."

Audits weren't common, but they did happen now and again. I had been hidden on more than one occasion because of them.

"Just change his age." Nursey's voice was insistent.

"I'm done doing all that," Dr. Woburn half yelled. "This isn't the same as hiding Brighton. I could have my license revoked and never practice again if I keep hiding files or concealing patients or covering up for deaths. And Howard is part of the audit. He needs to transfer some children from his hospital here — they're more overcrowded than we are."

"Is that what this is really all about? You're worried that your brother-in-law will see Angel?"

"It's not about Howard. It's about the auditor. Dr. Wolff won't discuss letting Angel stay. He has to be treated like every other patient."

"But he's not."

"Joann —"

"Listen, let's just take them both out. We

can help them get jobs and —"

"Joann, stop. We'd both be fired and we'd never work in the medical industry again. There have been too many cover-ups over the years that would surface. What happened with Mickey alone would be enough to ruin my reputation. I'm not going to lose my — everything — over a few mistakes with patients." Dr. Woburn sounded angry now. "But the secrets end here. No more deceptions. He's being transferred."

The silence was like liniment, slathering a layer of numbness over me. His actions had killed Mickey? Flashes of her smile and husky voice surfaced. The warmth of her lap and the sadness in her eyes.

"When Angel was brought here, his grandfather was a ward doctor and his uncle was a resident doctor," Joann spat back. "All these lies. I won't stand by this."

"You've told plenty of lies. Don't become self-righteous now. We both have a lot to lose, so you have a choice. Do you want Brighton to know all you've covered up? Do you want to lose her?"

"Fine, move him," Nursey barked.

I heard someone approaching and the voice of an aide. And then they were gone and I was alone. All the weeds they'd just sown in my garden sprouted and the air was crowded with them.

I stared at the night sky bursting with sparkling constellations. The summer I was eight Mickey taught me all about them. The Crux was my favorite because it was small and hard to find and only showed up for a short period. The presence of the little cross of stars comforted me. It reminded me of me. Small and, unless the stargazer knew exactly what to look for, easily overlooked.

Somehow I was able to slip back to my room unnoticed. Whether it was luck or the God Rosina prayed to, I wasn't sure. All that mattered was that I wasn't caught. But as I curled up in bed, I couldn't sleep. The confessions and private words replayed in my mind over and over again. As soon as I'd almost fall asleep, I'd startle awake. I'd seen plenty of seizures over the years — would the sanding of my heart and senses cause the shuddering to start? Would this be how my own life of insanity began?

Patients often made up entire fictional worlds to lose themselves within. How nice it would be to lose myself in some wonderland. If I had to be trapped in the back acres of my mind, a false world would not be worse than my reality. But would it free me of all this confusion and disgust and the burden of being a prisoner? No.

All I could think of was that I had to rescue Angel before he became just another patient like Mickey. He was all that mattered now.

1939
Bright-Yellow Canary

A tremor of anxiety woke me the next morning. Angel. He was all I could think about. I couldn't let go of what I'd heard. As much as I loved Nursey, I'd do whatever it took — even if that meant losing her. The air in my lungs was so heavy.

I pulled myself up to sit on the edge of my bed, my thin blanket rumpled around me, my clammy skin and breathlessness catching me off guard. I'd never started a morning like this.

I tried to settle my mind on my surroundings. The voices of the patients moving toward breakfast. The shining morning sun outside. Mother having kept her gown on — uncommon and good.

She was still. And dressed. And so quiet. My breathing improved by a degree.

Nursey rushed in. I turned my back toward her to make my bed. I didn't know what to do or what to say to her. I focused on my breathing as I smoothed and tucked the thin sheet.

"You're not ready for breakfast yet. And you haven't taken your mother to the toilet. If she doesn't go soon, she's going to soil the bed. What's going on with you? You know we depend on you," Nursey scolded but didn't wait for an answer. "Also, there's lice on the ward. Nitpick your mother right after breakfast or we'll have to shave her head again."

A nearly annual occurrence.

I didn't respond. I couldn't even look at her, afraid of what my face would say.

"Bright?" Nursey asked again with more than a sliver of annoyance in her voice. "Brighton."

"What?" I spun to look at her.

Nursey's hands were on her hips. Her bright-red lips were pulled into a straight line. Behind her blue eyes hid secrets about me. I turned away and folded up my threadbare green blanket and put it on the bed.

"I know how to take care of Mother. Don't harp."

After taking a moment to narrow her eyes, she left. I led Mother to the toilet, washed her face, then set her gown to rights. I tried to ignore the demons egging on my anger, but I couldn't stop thinking about Angel's fate. I sat Mother on the bed and pulled a brush through her hair, which was more pieces and patches these days.

She began to hum. It was an older tune from long ago.

I turned her to look at me, and she didn't resist. I often tried to find where she'd gone inside her eyes. Her eyes roamed above to the cracked plaster ceiling and then to the peeling wallpaper. Then her head tilted to look at me — not just toward me. She stopped humming and took a long breath and pursed her lips.

I squinted my eyes at her as if it would help me decipher her better. My ears and soul knew her every groaning; it was her language. But something was different just now. She was trying to say something. Even as I went from standing to sitting, her gaze followed my movements. Her eyes held mine.

I didn't — couldn't — say a word or even breathe for fear of interrupting whatever was happening. The stirring of her mind? A memory? A real word about to be spoken for me?

"M-m-ma —" she stuttered, holding the open sound like a long note. Not guttural. Not wild. Not base. She was trying to speak to me. "Mm-ma-mar—"

"The canary whistles. The mine is safe." Lorna's giggly voice roamed from down the hall into my room. Nursey called her schizophrenic, but I called her my friend. The repetition of words made me turn toward the door. She poked her freshly shaven head inside. Her facial features appeared too big for her chiseled, gaunt frame. "The canary whistles. The mine is safe." Then she ran off, repeating her words.

She only spoke in riddles now and always with a wide-eyed and clown-like smile.

The canary whistles. The mine is safe.

I didn't know what she meant. Probably nothing. Only then did I realize that Lorna had pulled my attention away from Mother. I snapped my head around and was flooded with disappointment. Mother's blank and distant expression had been restored, and she'd flown back to her faraway place, humming an off-tune melody.

I waved my hand in front of her. "Mother? What were you saying?"

My pleas, silent and spoken, were so numerous over the years they'd become like another organ inside of me. My heart. My stomach. My bowels. My pleas.

I grabbed her shoulders and shook — and not very gently.

"What are you doing?" Nursey unleashed

my grip.

"She was trying to talk to me." I yanked away from Nursey and kept my eyes on Mother. I lunged back and my fingers clasped her bony shoulders, but she remained a rag doll. "Mother, what were you saying? Please." My eyes electrified with coming tears.

Nursey pulled me away again.

"What are you going to do if I don't stop? Move me to another ward? Like Angel?" I said it with all the venom I could muster, but as soon as I did, I knew simply blurting out what I'd learned was not wise. Her grip remained, and I didn't pull away.

There was no injection so poisonous as the revealing of deceptions. Her eyes widened and her cheeks paled and grayed like the walls. Even her made-up lips looked pale. A deep swallow traveled down her throat. She loosened her grip and kept her hand on my arm, as though she couldn't entirely let go.

"You don't know what you're talking about." Her words were spoken with the weight of a feather.

"I do so. I know about Angel and Cynthia and Dr. Woburn. I heard everything."

Her breathing grew labored. Was she going to faint? But now that I'd started I couldn't stop.

"Stop the transfer or I'm going to tell everyone everything I know. He killed Mickey," I said through my teeth. I'd never spoken like this to Nursey, or to anyone.

Her face went blurry in my vision and a surge of panic rushed from my stomach to my ears. I needed to say these things to her, but my breath and words were all mixed together. My hand went to my chest as if it would help my breathing.

"You can't think that I would ever let anyone hurt Angel. And Mickey was an accident."

"He covered it up," I said between gasping breaths. "I'll tell anyone who will listen."

Without warning, she tightened her grip and began dragging me down the hall. I'd observed this, of course, numerous times. How she'd break up fights or deal with someone refusing treatment. But never me. She'd spanked me once and then immediately apologized for doing it and never laid a rough finger on me again.

"Nursey, stop," I yelled, and I pulled as hard as I could. "Stop. You're hurting me."

She stopped walking suddenly and my feet fumbled, making an effort to remain upright. "You do not blackmail me or Sid," she said in a low, faltering voice that sounded like it shook more from anger than worry.

My strength and breath were returning by measures.

"He'll die if he goes to that ward. You said that yourself. If you don't stop them from taking him, I'll blab it all. The aides aren't loyal to you. I'll tell them to tell the newspapers." I knew enough about newspapers spilling big stories because we always had old ones on the ward to read but mostly to sop up filth when no one was around to clean.

I got my feet under me and was within a few inches of her face, though I was a half foot shorter. I tried to keep my voice steady to counter my mounting fear.

"You don't make the rules, young lady. I do." She pulled me into the dayroom and into an empty restraint chair.

I knew what was coming. I'd witnessed it so many times in my life. Before I could even try to get away, Nursey put my wrists into the restraints. Cracked, scratchy leather straps. Then she told Nurse Wilma to shave off my hair. My hair. My hair was what Nursey always said separated me from the patients. No one else had time to grow theirs long like mine because it was shorn off almost yearly because of lice. Mine wasn't, though.

How often had Nursey said that I was *her* girl. That I was her long-haired, precious little girl. That I wasn't a patient. But that was no more.

I tried to shake free from her grip as she buckled my wrists in, but this place — this prison with its weapons and hold over all its patients — I couldn't get free of it. I always wondered why patients stopped struggling so quickly. Why didn't they fight harder? But now I knew why. The restraints were so tight it hurt worse to resist. My skin twisted against the clutch of the old leather and metal, but I kept pulling. I growled and tried to bite at Nurse Wilma when she came at me with scissors to first cut off my nearly waist-length hair. My arms wouldn't budge, but my ankles hadn't been secured yet. I kicked Nursey in the shins before she pulled my legs tightly into the straps.

"I don't have lice," I screamed. "Nursey, don't do this. Don't let him kill Angel like he did Mickey."

I repeated my words over and over, sounding crazier than Lorna. Maybe I was. Maybe Nursey had been wrong about me and I was no different from them. Right then I didn't feel any different.

This was the moment I went from being

cared for and protected to being a patient along with my mother and so many others. Silky strands trailed down my arms and my head chilled. My hair was gone so fast — and so was the life I thought Nursey had created for me. Would this be an annual occurrence for me from now on?

Dirty clouds of hair littered the space around my feet. And none of it was a part of me anymore.

I didn't know when I stopped struggling, but at some point I did. I didn't feel the razor run across my scalp; I only felt the closeness of Nurse Wilma's hot and soft body that smelled of night-shift sweat. The stench made my stomach jerk and sputter, but there was nothing inside to come up.

Lorna was still chanting about the yellow canary and that the mine was safe. But I knew she was wrong. The mine wasn't safe, and we were all going to die here. Panic filled me while the restraints squeezed my arms and legs. The room was full of other patients, but none of them could help me. Then Mother walked into the room and stood near the chair. Even though her eyes didn't seem to see me, she must have sensed something was happening to me. She rarely came out of the room on her own.

My breathing heightened and I started to

scream. Nurse Joann, that's who she was to me now, told me to stop, but when I wouldn't she cupped her hands over my mouth and the back of my neck with such steadfastness I couldn't even try to bite. All I could do was listen to all the other voices and sounds in the room. But no one could hear me.

1939
Deliver Us from Evil

Nurse Joann pushed me into solitary confinement before my hair had even been swept from the floor. *Solitary confinement.* I repeated the phrase over and over again in my mind and occasionally whispered it, letting it mingle in the damp air around me. This had never happened before.

As a little girl I'd danced and twirled and recited poetry for the nurses and patients at Joann's request, to show off. I wasn't a *patient.* I was their doll to dress up and play with. I was everyone's daughter in one way or another.

But what Nurse Joann had done changed everything.

My face had memorized the press of her hand over my mouth. I had been made silent. Would I ever be unmuted? Would anyone ever know that I was living here, in this place? And what about all the others?

I had been sitting on the cot for hours

since a porridge for breakfast had been brought. The cot's itchy blanket was in a ball behind me. The toilet in the corner was small and filled with weeks-old filth that made the tiny room smell of waste. The brick exterior wall was cold and moist to the touch.

I'd resisted every inch of Nurse Joann's pull toward the two solitary rooms. I'd hit, kicked, and scratched. But it made no difference. She even had to release another patient just to stuff me inside.

Not long after, poor Rosina was put in the other. She was praying now as she had been for hours — quoting the Lord's Prayer in Spanish. She'd taught it to me years ago, telling me that I needed some religion. The words came back to me and I said them with her. Together in our separate rooms. Joann told us to stop. So I yelled louder. Until I got to *"Y líbranos del mal."* I didn't move on from that line but repeated it over and over. Louder and louder.

"But deliver us from evil," I began to yell in English to make sure she understood.

I didn't know the context of this prayer. But what it had to do with this place, I knew. Maybe Nurse Joann was evil. Dr. Woburn too. If he was willing to put Angel in the men's ward because of an audit, he was evil. If he had a hand in the death of patients, he was evil. Angel would die in that ward. I had to tell someone what I had learned. I didn't care if that meant Joann would lose her job too and leave me. All I cared about was Angel.

"Y líbranos del mal," I continued to yell. "But deliver us from evil."

I yelled those words until my throat hurt.

"Stop saying that," Nurse Joann repeated as loudly and as often as I said Rosina's sacred words.

Once Rosina was released, the words were only whispers, and the small square window in the door showed only the open and empty room opposite me. I had no companion. I was alone. I hated being alone.

Joann silently delivered a small lunch on my second day. She placed it on the cot next to me.

"Are you ready to be rational?" she asked. I answered by flipping over the tray full of food. Refusing to eat was what patients did. And I was a patient now.

The late-afternoon sun filled the broken glass and barred window. It was set high in the brick wall. It was small but big enough that if I could get up to it I would be able to see across the lawn toward the children's ward. It had taken all my angry-patient strength to push the iron bed frame under the window. Maybe I could see Angel. Maybe if he knew I was in solitary he could convince Joann to let me out. But how would he know? Maybe I would never see him again. Maybe I would be bald for the rest of my life. And cold. And unloved. And worse — unheard.

My toes curled around the damp, cool bed rail. Since I wasn't tall I had to stretch, and when I could finally see out the small window, I nearly let out a hoot and holler. But my feet tired quickly, so I had to take breaks from watching and waiting for any sign of Angel.

I memorized every part of my view of the children's ward. There were bars on the windows, but in the glow of the sun they were nearly invisible, making the building look almost approachable. It was a smaller building and had peaks over the windows that reminded me of houses from storybooks. But I knew better. I knew that the inside front door had claw marks from the children who had tried to escape.

Footsteps sounded in the hall. Someone was coming. Maybe Joann had changed her mind. Maybe she would let me out now. Maybe she would tell me that she'd saved Angel. Maybe I would tell her that I would not reveal her secrets.

But that was a lie. I would tell anyone if it meant that I could save Angel.

I hopped off of the bed rail and stepped to the square window in the door. The hole in the thick door was large enough for my arm to fit through — I'd tested it out as I'd seen other women do on many occasions. But now I peered through it and saw Wilma. She told me to go away, and I stuck my tongue out at her like I'd done since I was three.

But it was the woman behind her that caught my attention. Our eyes met, hers dark brown and mine blue. She was small and sad. Her hair was a disarray of deep chestnut curls. I'd never seen curly hair like that. The palms of my hands went to my scalp. I slapped it, and the sound was so strange I did it a second time. But my eyes never left the new patient.

We got new patients all the time, and every patient started in a solitary room — usually for two full days, longer if they were aggressive. This was a new girl. Who had sent her here? Had the doctors told her family that she'd get better in here? Had anyone told them that this was a place to die more than live? The soul first and then, many years later, the empty body. I'd seen it too many times. I could feel my own soul fluttering, desperate to leave my shell, to leave me behind and go on to somewhere better.

Would this new young woman die here? Even though I didn't know her, I didn't want her to. I could see that she was close to my age. This was unusual. She looked away from me and cried as Wilma unlocked the solitary door. The hospital gown fit on her body better than on many patients. That wouldn't last long. She would lose her healthy weight fast.

After Wilma's footsteps faded away, the girl began screaming and weeping and calling for her mother. I put my ear in the small opening in the door. This grief was something new to me. Usually the women cried incessantly for days and spoke to the spirit of a baby who had died or pleaded with their husband. Often tears would turn to anger and anger into more treatments, more pain, more madness, and always more loss.

But her calling and crying for her mother with such deep sorrow was unexpected.

"Psst. Hey, hey," I said in a loud whisper. "It's all right."

She continued to weep with a mournful sound that I'd never heard before. Sad, not mad.

"Hey, lady. Don't cry, please." I tried to

say it sweetly. I wanted to help her. I wished I knew her name. "I'm Brighton. Please don't cry. We can talk — if you want."

The weeping slowly quieted, and I thought she may have fallen asleep.

"We can talk through the little window in the door. Are you there?"

It was another long minute before there was movement through her square peephole. I could see one of her eyes. We stared at one another without a word for so long it seemed like we'd aged.

"What's your name?" I finally asked.

She didn't say anything. All I could hear was the constant din of the hall leading to the dayroom. Maybe she didn't hear me.

"I'm Brighton. I live in room 201 with my mother." Maybe just introducing myself would help.

"Your mother?" I could see part of her face through the doorway cutout now.

I nodded. "Yes. My mother."

"You were brought here together?"

"Sort of." I almost had to laugh. "She was pregnant with me when she was brought here."

She didn't respond right away. I could hear Lorna yelling at the top of her lungs about not letting the bedbugs bite. Was it that late already? I turned to look out the window. It was black. I rushed over and stepped up on the bed rail to look out. All I could see was the glow from a few children's ward windows. I would watch again tomorrow.

I returned to the door.

"So you were born here?" she asked.

"Yes."

"You grew up here?" Her voice rose up at the end. "How old are you?"

"I've always lived here. I'm sixteen."

"You don't sound —" She paused, and I knew why.

"I don't sound insane — mad — crazy?" I suggested and couldn't help but smile a little.

"Yeah," she responded. "Isn't that why everyone's here?" She paused. "That's why I was told I was here."

I shrugged, even though she couldn't see it. Maybe? I didn't know anymore. There was so much jumbled up in my mind, and the line between clear-mindedness and lunacy didn't seem as obvious as it used to be.

"What is lunacy anyway?" I questioned. Many women had just been considered mere inconveniences to their families, though others had such erratic behavior it would have been dangerous not to get help for them. If the doctors didn't know what to do except to tie them down, how would a husband or parent know what to do? But if they came with sickness at any level in their minds, the longer they stayed, the worse it got. This wasn't where people were cured; it was just another type of prison.

"Right. Lunacy," she said like she was thinking of far-off things.

"What's your name?" I asked.

"Grace. Grace Douglass."

"Did your husband leave you here? Did your baby die? Or did you try to hurt yourself or someone else? Do you only cry and not eat?" All the reasons I'd heard flew out of my mouth. "That's why most of the women are here."

"You ask a lot of questions." Her voice was so friendly my heart started to swell. Would this Grace Douglass be my friend?

"My husband didn't leave me here." As she spoke each word her voice sobered. There was a long pause. "My parents did. And I don't have a baby — but my parents are afraid it might happen."

"Oh." I knew what she meant. "So that's why you're here?"

The pause continued so long I almost repeated my question.

"There's more. Mother says I'm too ambitious and Father thinks I'm fanatical about things like photography and travel. And I love the wrong kind of boy. That doctor said it was moral insanity." The sadness in her voice formed a bridge between us.

I leaned my forehead against the door. I didn't know what she meant about loving the wrong kind of boy. How many kinds were there? Mentally disturbed was the most common diagnosis, but I was very familiar with the term *moral insanity,* though I didn't understand that in her case. She was the youngest I'd seen admitted for it.

There were plenty of patients on my floor I was sure would not survive well outside these walls — not that they were doing any more than surviving here. My mother was one. Lorna too, though she hadn't always been as bad as she was now. The ones who needed help with the basics of life or who would hurt themselves or others if given the chance were the ones who could use help from a doctor — but this hospital offered only nightmares. In the dictionary *asylum* meant an offer of protection. There was no protection here.

Sisters Rosina and Carmen weren't insane; they just couldn't speak English when admitted. After their parents died they'd become homeless. Their howling in grief and begging for food were a nuisance to the neighborhood, and without anyone to claim responsibility, they were sent here.

Too many stories. Too much sadness. My shoulders slumped under the weight of it all. My chest heaved. I focused my breathing to be regular and steady. I wanted to keep talking.

"How old are you?" I finally asked.

"Eighteen."

We talked until Wilma yelled at us to sleep. But before that Grace had told me what it was like to go to school. About a woman named Agatha Christie who wrote detective novels. About her camera in her bag that was taken from her when she arrived. She told me about circuses, traveling to England, and kissing boys. All through the small square window. When she talked about those things, her voice shone as bright as the moon and I felt more alive than ever.

I fell asleep with all the images she'd gifted me. They swirled, raced, and spun in my head until it became a real world deep within me. The prettiest, brightest world I'd ever known. Why had Joann never given me these images? What fantastic things Grace had seen. What a life she'd led. And now she was here with me.

The last thing she said before we both

retreated to our cots was what I had begun thinking of constantly.

"Do you think we could escape — if my parents don't come back for me?"

That would mean being without Mother. Escaping had been on the fringes of my mind since I'd received the photograph from Joann on my fourteenth birthday. What Joann probably thought would satisfy some curiosities spurred on a desire in me to leave. Before that, the idea of leaving didn't seem real. My maternal attachment to Joann had filled so much of me. But not anymore. Things were changing. And now I had Grace.

The light was bright through the window in the wall when I woke the next morning. I squinted. I heard a door slam and yelling filtered through the broken glass of my solitary window. I jumped up and stood on the bed rail again. There was Angel.

"Angel!" I yelled through the bars and broken panes. His eyes roamed, looking for me, and I knew he would not be able to see so far away. But he would know it was me. "Angel, up here. I'm in solitary."

The door flew open and hit the wall behind it. Joann stood silhouetted in the hall light, her nursing cap casting a bullhorn-like shadow on the wall.

"Brighton, stop."

I looked at her and then back outside again. Angel was being escorted away, but he was still looking for me. And I was all too sure about where he was being taken. Madness and desperation boiled in me. My hands grabbed at the bars and I pulled myself up higher. I screamed and yelled, and when the broken glass cut me, I didn't care.

As he was being taken away with a man on each side of him, I continued to call for him.

"Get down from there." Joann was pulling me down. My feet couldn't find the bed rail, so my tumble was painful and hard against the concrete floor. I groaned for a moment but got up as quickly as I could, my shoulder and hip aching.

"Leave me alone." I moved to a corner and had my fingernails splayed like claws. The way we looked at each other reminded me of the time Joann — Nursey then — taught me about bulls and how these men would master them with a red cape. Which one of us was the bull? Which one of us was the master?

Then I heard a car motor. I stepped back onto the bed rail before Joann could grab me, kicking her in her middle. She swore and doubled over. A black car with silver edges had driven up. I watched as a man in a suit and a white doctor's coat exited the car with Dr. Woburn. Was that Angel's father? Several other men were with them, each with white coats and clipboards.

"Brighton," Grace's voice called from her room. "What's happening? Are you okay?"

She kept asking, but I was looking in the direction Angel had walked. I couldn't see him. He was lost in the fog that hung in the air. Suddenly I felt a sting. My body involuntarily flinched, and I turned toward Joann just in time to see her pull a syringe from my thigh.

Insulin.

She'd just injected me.

Would I ever see Angel again?

And what about Grace?

What about me?

Rosina's God, deliver us from evil.

1990
Black, White, and Bright

The black-and-white photograph of Joann Derry doesn't look newly developed. The white frame isn't yellowed or curled at the edges, but the film is so old the developing and printing have set off the varied shades of black in a yellowed glaze. Some details have been eliminated, but nothing my memory can't conjure. I carefully pin the new print on the drying line along with a dozen others that have turned out. Not all the images I took have been printable. I was a budding photographer then, with a lot to learn.

I try not to study the photos as memories — not just yet — but only as a photographer. While photos only take minutes to process, my insides will take longer. But thoughts sneak in and I remember taking this photo. It's an entirely different world, but I remember it like I am that girl right now, holding that late-thirties-model Kodak camera. In it, Nurse Joann is closing the back of my mother's hospital gown. Joann's exhaustion is evident — the sag of her jawline, the hunch of her shoulders, the deflation of her spirit. My breath catches in my chest, and as hard as I try, I can't look away. The image holds me captive. This is what I didn't want right now. I just wanted to have the prints, not relive the madness.

But the photo has become a siren and I am not turning away.

Mother's stringy hair cascades down her back, and my stomach shudders at the pointy narrow shoulders. Mother is suddenly so real to me I am expecting her to turn around, point her bony finger at me, and remind me that this was all my fault. Everything that happened the year after this photo was taken was all my fault. Maybe instead of Mother turning it'll be Joann and she'll inject me with insulin again. After a minute of staring I realize I'm rubbing my thigh and I stop. The burden of forgiveness is heavy.

She had loved me. She'd taught me to tie my shoes, to read — and when I asked her about sex, she told me. Now, as a mother myself, I realize what it meant for Joann to do these things and be this person to me. She gave me everything during those long, bleak years, had given up so much, but she had also taken much from me. She'd kept secrets — secrets that revealed the darkest pieces of my life. She is why I am Nell and why I've been Nell for so long. I don't want to be anyone else.

An hour or so later the phone rings again. I rush out of the dark room a second time and grab the receiver. The balm of my husband's voice settles in the old wounds newly opened. He tells me about the child psychology conference and that California feels like another country.

"You'll never guess what I am doing today." I haven't used our small home dark room in years. I tell him about the film canister and the phone call from Kelly Keene. I tell him I have no idea what I'm supposed to do.

I know he's nodding his head. He often does this when on the phone with the parents of his patients.

"I don't know what to do. You know how I feel about that place and . . ." *Who I really am.* I can't finish my sentence, not even with him, even though he knows all my secrets. Some of the things surprised him, but he doesn't shock easily. "It's just been so long and I thought I was past all of this."

"What do you want to do?" He's using his

doctor voice. I know Doc isn't going to tell me what to do, though. He never does. He lets me talk and think until I decide for myself.

"I want my —" A cuss word taunts me as it sits in the pocket of my cheek, but then I think better of it. I swallow it back. "I want my film cartridges, of course."

"But what do you really want?"

"Don't use your doctor voice with me." I don't say it angrily but more as a reminder. Sometimes he doesn't know he's doing it.

"Nell." His voice rests against my tense insides and softens me. "I can come home. I can be on a plane by morning."

Would this help? Or is this something I have to figure out by myself?

"No," I sigh. "Grace and I made a promise to each other about those pictures."

"You haven't talked about her in a long time." I hear the smile in his voice. "So you're going to go meet this Kelly woman and maybe — go back?"

The pause after this question could last for years as far as I am concerned. And because my husband doesn't rush anything, he waits until I am ready to speak.

"I think I have to." I realize then that I'm holding the latest photo I exposed and processed. Angel's face is staring up at me, and my breath hitches.

The idea of dragging all of that out again with another person — this stranger, Kelly Keene — makes my stomach want to rid itself of everything I've eaten today. All of it is going to end up in the trash can if I don't get control over this. There will be too much to trudge through. Our children know just enough, but they would never consider for a moment that my first eighteen years nearly shredded anything good out of me — because I never let it seep into my mothering. Oh, how I worked and worked to be the mother I wished I'd had. But in every filled milk glass and tuck-in with a kiss I knew my own buried faraway mother would've wanted to be that mother also. It made me stronger to think of her and know that there was a reason I did what I did.

"Are you still there?"

I blink and shake my head. My mouth is open, but nothing comes out for several long moments.

"I'm here." I sense the surge of strength fighting against the shock of everything Kelly Keene is bringing to my life.

"You are who you are because of those years. I've never wanted to change you, even if that meant taking it all away." He always knows how to talk to me. "If you need to do this, I'll support you, but be careful."

I'm nodding without saying a word. My eyes burn, but I won't close them. I don't want to squeeze any of the tears out.

"I can come home. This conference will happen again next year," he offers again.

"No. It's okay." I inhale so deeply I think my lungs might pop like an overfilled balloon. "I know you should be there, and I'm a big girl." I chuckle and exhale all at once, and look back down at that bright boy who saved my life over and over so many years ago.

Only after I assure him that I'll be careful does he tell me he'll call me tonight and that he loves me, and then we hang up. I return to the dark room, but before I hang the Angel picture on the wire with a metal clip, I eye it a bit more. My building is in the background. The back door is held open with a small rock so we can get back in. Angel stands in the foreground. It's a little blurry, but when I bring the picture close, I can smell the dried grass and fresh breeze and hear the choir of birds that sang to us about our future.

That boy was more than simply the subject in the photograph — he was my everything in those dark years.

"Angel," I whisper to myself. I lift my

hand and touch the image of the skinny boy in white standing there with his wide, innocent smile and eyes that played between red and blue. He didn't know what was coming yet, and it breaks my heart again.

I need to see it all again. To remember it and to be close to it once more before it's all gone. Buried dust and ashes. I am not ready to let go yet. But I am ready to find those buried souls and love them and remind anyone who will listen that the invisible still exist.

1939
Heaven Backward

"Y líbranos del mal." I turned to yell it at Joann. While I still had control over my body, I kept repeating the line of prayer. I understood now why Rosina did it. Why she couldn't stop once she got started.

"Deliver us from evil."

I reverted to English to make sure Joann knew what I was saying. I wanted her to know what I believed about her. Evil. This place was evil. The walls were a hell made out of brick and mortar. But instead of heat from the hellfire, there was a constant chill and dampness in the air.

The sting from my feet slapping against the cold floor radiated up to my thighs and hips. Then everything started happening in slow motion. I pulled my arm away from her grip. Her pretty and perfect fingernails scratched against my skin. My own were bitten and torn. Claw-like nails were a weapon against out-of-control patients.

Joann began to blur.

Her words, "Sorry, my love," were drawn out and felt like dandelion fuzz in my ears.

I took a wobbly step away from her. One step back and into the corner of the small room. She had her hands out to me, splayed, and her mouth was moving, but I could feel the insulin rush through me now. Her voice didn't sound like her. A voice somewhere repeated my name. Whose voice was it? I looked around for it.

I looked back at Joann's face — it went from two to four back to one. She really had lied to me my whole life — but now I knew the truth. We weren't the same, she and I, like she'd always said we were. She'd told me for as long as I could remember that she and I weren't like the patients. That we had our minds and they didn't. That we could learn and be rational and they couldn't. There were too many truths and lies braided tightly in these thoughts.

She wore her white nurse's cap on top of her light-blond styled hair. The magazines I'd stolen described the hairdo as *coiffed, sleek, sweeping,* and I could see all of those words in the beauty of Joann's hair. My hand moved in slow motion up to my scalp, and the stubble rubbed against my palm. I was a patient. But Joann, with a face that looked like the magazine ladies, was not.

Her white uniform fit her well, and I looked down at my gown. Long. Loose. Soiled. Old. Likely had been worn previously by a now-dead patient. It wasn't even mine. It was just the one that had been handed to me the last time the laundry came through. This one hung well below my knees, down to my calves, and had room enough for two or three of me.

She had freedom.

I had nothing.

"Can you hear me, Bright?" Joann's words started cutting through the insulin. "I'm so sorry. I'm so sorry."

I wrinkled up my brow. My mouth frowned. I could feel it now.

"I hate you," I whispered.

The twitch in her face indicated surprise. I was surprised myself. I didn't like the way the words tasted in my mouth, but they were true in that moment. And then I fell, and no one caught me.

I gave in to the insulin and my mind lingered only on how my muscles went from tense to relaxed and how good it would feel to sleep.

But it was the kind of sleep where voices could be heard. Joann apologized over and over, telling me she didn't know why she'd done it. She was afraid and exasperated and didn't know why I wouldn't just stay the little girl who trusted her.

That little girl was gone.

She may as well have been dead.

I heard Mother too. Was I in my room? She wailed and thrashed and made all the familiar sounds. And a few times her sounds seemed to try to form my name. I was alone for so long, left in the dark, and I didn't know where everyone had gone. So far away. How long this went on, I wasn't sure, but slowly there was a fold of light in the corner of my mind and Mother was there. I think I said *Mother* but my mouth didn't move, so I must have only thought the precious word. But the woman in the fold of light didn't look like Mother. Similar but different. She was warm and glowing and whole. She smiled at me, and the glimmer in her eye was so different from how she usually looked at me.

"Mother?" I asked.

She just smiled and waved and twinkled at me. She wasn't wearing a hospital gown; instead, she was in clothes I'd see in Joann's catalogs. Her rounder, soft features invited me to come closer, but when I couldn't, I realized I was in restraints. I was camisoled. I struggled and screamed, but something was in and around my mouth. With every muscle I tried to push, pull, and stretch, but nothing worked. Heat and dampness formed in the crevices. There was no release.

Did this last for minutes or months? My mind and body were equally taxed. I wanted to leave my body. I pleaded with my soul to fly away and leave the rest of me behind. But my soul had wrapped around me, holding me together like glue, while the camisole ripped me apart. But slowly I gave in. I stopped struggling. I let go.

Joann's voice and Mother's humming returned then.

"Brighton," Joann said with a spark of urgency. "Wake up, my darling."

Darling? She wasn't allowed to call me that anymore, just like I'd never call her Nursey again.

My mouth was dry and something was still in it. I tried to speak. A mouthpiece. Was I really at risk of swallowing my tongue? Had I had a seizure? It was removed as if Joann heard my silent request. My tongue felt large and thick, and when I felt the vibration in my throat, I was relieved that I could still make a sound.

"Brighton, open your eyes," Joann commanded as nurses did when trying to wake patients from an insulin stupor. "Open your eyes."

My eyelids fluttered. The light was so bright I winced. Was this what Angel experience when in the sunlight? I tried to shield my eyes with my hand, but the camisole held me down. Panic rose in me when I realized that it hadn't just been in my subconscious but that I was actually restrained. I pulled harder and could hear Joann telling me to calm down so she could unbuckle the camisole but making me promise to stay under control. I nodded my head. I didn't think I'd have the strength to fight anyway.

She sat me up, and my body felt loose and free of any bones or muscles inside. Joann deftly unstrapped the camisole, and my ears were cued to another voice. It was far away, but I had to remember why it was familiar.

"Grace," I said. Then coughed. My throat and mouth so dry. But I had to try again. "Grace."

"Who?" Joann asked, confused. She tried to keep me in the bed as she pulled away the camisole and placed it by my feet. I pushed her away, but my arms were like the Jell-O Joyful served, and my legs were strapped to the bed rails.

"My legs," I said. Joann let go of my arms and loosened my legs. I swung them over the side of the bed, only to fall as soon as I tried to stand.

"My legs," I repeated. They were numb and growing tingly. I wiggled my toes and then my ankles while Joann tried to explain that it was just my circulation.

"You have to forgive me, Brighton," she pleaded, hanging all over me. "That shot wasn't meant for you. You know I always keep one with me, just in case. You were out of control. I didn't know what else to do."

She continued, and I let her talk without responding. I wasn't considering whether or not I could forgive her; all I knew was that I needed to get to Grace. I needed to help Angel.

"Forgive me, Brighton," Joann said on her knees, her head bowed on the bed next to me.

I contemplated little on her request as my legs gained strength.

"Where's Angel?" My voice chilled the room further.

She shook her head as black streaks from her makeup made pathways down her perfect creamy skin.

"We can talk about him, but you have to forgive me. Please forgive me." She reached for me again, and because I had nowhere else to go, I stood on the small cot, my legs nearly buckling.

Which was harder — the tile beneath her knees or the very tissues of my heart? Forgiveness was something so dearly connected to forgetting, and I wasn't sure the former could happen without the latter. It was like asking the broken window to repair itself. Everything she was saying, the way she was desperate to touch me, all the tears she was shedding made my soul and stomach wind up together. My hunger was only satisfied feasting on my hurt and anger toward Joann. Maybe it would change someday, but maybe not.

"Where is Angel? What have they done to him?"

She didn't answer but kept crying.

"Answer me," I growled at her. I had learned that from a patient long ago — to use my voice like that. That woman was dead now.

"Brighton, you don't act this way. This isn't you." Joann tried to wipe the wetness from her face, but it only smeared the blackness across her no-longer-perfect cheeks. "Come down and let's talk."

"How am I acting?"

Joann blinked and looked away from me.

"Am I acting insane? Tell me, Nurse *Joann.*"

I emphasized her name. This wasn't the same woman who had mothered me over the last sixteen years. That woman never would've injected me with insulin. This was not the woman who had read *Aesop's Fables* and *Little Women* to me. Oh, to be a character in those stories and not be me. Not be Brighton. Not be shorn. Not be brittle-souled and lost.

Then I heard a voice coming from Mother's cot and looked at her, and the sight of blood pulled me toward her on my weak and wobbling legs. Her arms were bleeding. This was what she did to herself when she was agitated.

"Mother, what happened?" I asked and moved to sit next to her on the bed.

"I know," Nurse Joann said behind me. I ignored her and grabbed the damp cloth that had been draped over the footrail of her bed, already stained with blood.

I carefully turned Mother over and welcomed the stare of her blank eyes. The look was familiar — though something did flicker behind her eyes when she saw my shorn head. Like she noticed the change. I forced my grimace to a smile. I wanted to put her at ease.

"Mommy." Tears rushed to my eyes when the word spilled from my mouth. When was the last time I'd called her that? "Let me clean you up."

Slurred words escaped her mouth, none of them intelligible. But I knew they were happy sounds. Not the ones she made when she was being dragged to hydrotherapy or forced to swallow powdered water that she knew would sedate her. I knew her sounds, and I knew what she was saying. She was happy to see me. She'd missed me.

I gently wiped her arm where the scratches still bled. She relaxed into my touch. Her free arm rested on my knee, and her fingers thrummed gently against my skin.

"You're so good with her." Nurse Joann's voice broke.

I forced myself to continue my even strokes and not look at Joann. The woman whom I'd seen as a second mother my whole life had betrayed me. The coolness of my scalp was a constant reminder. A shiver fell like water from my head down my back.

"Please don't hate me," Joann whispered. "I didn't mean — I was scared."

I finished with my mother and helped her sit up at the edge of her bed. After I carefully slipped her head through her gown and helped her arms through, I finally turned toward Joann.

"*You* were scared?" I wanted to hiss at her

like Lorna. My words started out quiet but grew to fill every space of the room. "How do you think I've felt since I was six and realized that living like this isn't normal?" I gestured around me. "That other children live in homes with a mom and dad and sisters and brothers. They go to school. Eat dinner together around a table. Sit in front of a fireplace and read together. I live in a lunatic asylum with women considered insane and incurable — if they weren't crazy when they came, they are now. None of us can leave. We're all trapped. I'm trapped."

I felt dizzy and squeezed my eyes shut to gain back my balance. I opened my eyes and found Joann wide-eyed with a hand out, as if to calm me.

"I've done the best I could with your circumstances. I haven't taken other jobs — better jobs — because I love you. I've put so much on hold. Even pushed Sid — Dr. Woburn — off, for goodness' sake."

"Dr. Woburn." I shook my head. "He's a murderer, and I'll tell everyone."

"Stop saying that. No one will believe you anyway. I haven't gotten married and I haven't had the family I've dreamed of because I wanted to be with you. As long as you're here —"

I cut her off. "As long as I'm here? Where

else can I go? I'm stuck here."

She stopped speaking, her mouth gaping open for several long moments. "I know."

The tremor that went through my heart was like a battle cry from deep inside. I was unprepared to hear her agree that I was trapped. And telling me that she'd given up a future family because of me only compounded my reality. But if she loved me so much to give everything up, then why cut my hair and throw me in solitary?

Why camisole me? Why torture me?

"You don't know what I've kept you from," she continued. "I kept you from the children's ward, insisting that you being near your mother was the best thing for her. That might've been true then, but really it was because *I* fell in love with you. I wanted you for myself. I was a silly eighteen-year-old, barely old enough to be a nurse here. But you —"

She stopped and cleared her throat. The heavy pause wrapped around me as tightly as the camisole had been.

"Look at what you did to me." I pointed to my head. "And then solitary — and —" I pointed at my bed where the camisole and the restraints lay.

"You threatened to ruin us — me and Sid." She spoke in a grave whisper. "We would both lose everything."

"I've already lost everything," I yelled. "Actually, I haven't lost everything. I've never had anything. All I have is the shell of a mother and Angel. And you were ready to let Dr. Woburn take him away from me. Where is he?"

"You know where he is. You didn't give me the chance to fix it. And I haven't left your side since —"

"Was he really taken to Orchard Row?"

Like a dam breaking, tears rushed to my eyes. My throat constricted. My hand went to my chest to steady my breathing. Had she really just said Angel was in the men's ward? My eavesdropping on nurses and aides had taught me that even the non-dangerous men's wing had a weight and height requirement for male nurses and aides. The men could be so violent they had to be handcuffed for basic medical assessments.

"I've been at your side for three days. And there was the audit and —"

"Three days?" I leaned against the wall and finally looked at Joann and took her in. Her hair was in disarray and her cap was askew. Her white uniform was covered in stains. Sweat marks lined her dress under her arms. I'd never seen her look so unkempt.

Suddenly my mind jumped to the new patient.

"Where's Grace? The girl in the other room in solitary."

"The new patient? She's still in solitary." Joann's dismissal of Grace, her lack of concern, stirred my anger.

"Get Grace out," I pleaded. "Why is she still in there? New patients are usually in solitary for only two days."

"She bit Wilma," Joann snapped.

I nearly broke out in a smile. She had spirit, and she wasn't afraid. I liked her even better.

"Get her out, Joann," I insisted. "I still have a lot I can share about Dr. Woburn. Does everyone know Angel's his nephew?"

"Don't," she whispered and shook her head.

I slowly got up from Mother's bed. My legs were gaining strength. Joann followed me like an unwanted shadow.

I held the hall railing and started to walk down the hall like I had bones older than dirt. My feet slid in something wet. I got my bearings again and kept walking. I had to get Grace out of solitary. And I had to figure out how to get Angel out of Orchard

Row. If I had to tell every aide and every nurse who passed through here that Dr. Woburn was Angel's uncle, I would. Surely that would uncover other secrets. I wouldn't let this go until Angel was safe and out of Orchard Row. Even if that meant I'd never leave these four walls.

Joann kept following me, and when I turned to look at her, our gazes fixed. I heard a loud motor idling near the building, and I shuffled as fast as I could while still holding on to the hallway rail. Joann followed me into Carmen's room, and we looked through the barred window.

A white bus was parked in front of the children's ward. I watched as twenty-two children exited the bus. The rickety bunch walked in a ruled line, their wrists held by a rope to keep them straight. The front door of the children's building remained shut, and all were ushered around back where they would be bathed. Bathed. Angel had told me all about what it meant to be bathed. None of them could've been older than ten or eleven. Some fought the rope and were immediately chastised by a uniformed attendant who had stepped out of the bus ahead of them.

Now there really wouldn't be any room for Angel.

Farther down the foggy hospital road and then off to the left was the men's ward — Orchard Row. Two two-story buildings connected by a hallway, and they were still overcrowded. Bars on every window — every window broken or completely shattered. Glass littered the ground around the buildings. Angel was in there. Right now. I grabbed my stomach.

"I need Grace," I told Joann as I stared out the window.

I heard her keys jangle as she walked away. The door squealed when it opened, and I shuffled out of Carmen's room and stood in the hall, waiting. Grace rushed out of the room and turned toward me. Even though she'd never seen my whole face, she knew who I was and she ran to me. She held me, and I felt her thick curls against my shaven head. Her touch felt warm and familiar somehow.

Finally, I had a sister.

1939
Doorways

I woke the next morning with a weight in my soul and the feeling I was being watched. I opened my heavy eyelids to see him. Angel. A sheen of light fell over his complexion. Glowy and spirit-like. I looked toward Mother when I heard her moaning in her sleep. Then I looked back at the figment of Angel. He was still there, and his smile twinkled in the morning sunrise. I blinked — was he real or had I moved into the dark unknown of a melancholy mind and would believe now and forever that Angel was present, no matter where he really was?

"Good morning." Angel waved.

I waved and mouthed *Hi,* but no sound came out of my mouth.

Joann breezed in with a medication cart. She looked cleaner than she had the day before.

"You're awake, I see, Sleeping Beauty," she said without much tenderness. She was marking up a clipboard. "Angel, have you told her about your release?"

"You can see him too?" I asked.

"See him?" Joann started pulling Mother into a sitting position.

"Angel."

"Brighton, are you feeling all right?" She came over and started to reach her hand out toward me, but I pushed it away. I didn't want her near me.

"Angel, is that actually you?"

The figure of Angel laughed, and while it seemed inappropriate given where we were, it was the best sound I could've heard.

"It is you," I yelled as I jumped out of bed and wrapped my arms around him. He winced and I pulled back. He held my arms and looked down at me with that smile I would never forget.

"Did you think I was a ghost?" He rubbed my arms.

He laughed a bit more, but I saw tears fill his eyes. My empty heart filled up with them.

"You're hurt, aren't you? They hurt you," I said and began pulling at his shirt.

"It doesn't matter." I didn't let him get away with that, and checked him over like any nurse or mother would. His middle looked like a watercolor painting — covered in purple and blue bruises.

"He was in the infirmary within the first twenty-four hours," Joann said as she walked Mother out of the bathroom and then handed her off to an aide who, with several other patients, was heading for breakfast. "Broken ribs."

"I guess they didn't like me." Angel shrugged.

I looked over at the door, but Joann was already gone.

"This is all her fault," I said. "Joann knew this would happen. You're lucky to be alive."

"She's the one who got me released."

"I had to blackmail her," I told him. I'd tell him the whole story later. "You wouldn't have been there if it wasn't for her and Dr. Woburn."

"If it wasn't for them, we'd probably be dead," Angel countered.

I paused long enough to take in the truth that he was safe. For now.

"So she got you *released.*" The word surfaced. That was the word that had been used, wasn't it? "So you're leaving?"

I stepped back.

Angel wrapped his arms around me. So gently. So carefully. The kind of delicacy we both needed.

"I'll never leave you." He smoothed a

hand over my bald head, and I suddenly felt very naked. I shied away for a moment, but he didn't let me step away. "It'll grow back."

I nodded.

Then Angel told me all the details about how he was released to work with the groundskeeper, Mason. He would be a patient working, not a real employee, but the work was full-time. He would be given a small closet in the basement to sleep in for now. He would be busy. Very busy. But he would be safe from Orchard Row.

There was delivery in this. Had Rosina's God heard my groaning and utterings?

Then I told him everything I'd overheard — it all seemed like years ago. His mouth pulled into the widest grin possible. Why was he smiling? I had told him about all the lies and what I knew about his mother and that Dr. Woburn and Joann had known all of it all along.

"Dr. Woburn is my uncle," he said with awe in his voice.

"He's a liar, Angel. Isn't that more important?"

"Brighton, I have an uncle. I have a mother and a father who are alive." He stood and chuckled and turned in a circle until he faced me again. He held me closely and looked down at me. He'd grown so tall, and I'd stopped growing at least a year ago. The way he looked at me reminded me of the way I'd seen Dr. Woburn look at Joann. His hands were warm and held me gently. There was something new in this moment.

I could almost see all of his thoughts and questions churning in his head. They weren't the ones I'd expected. Where was his anger? Where was the hurt?

"Angel, Joann has been lying to you — to us — about your family our whole lives." I pulled away from him and took a step back.

"I know, but I can't get angry about it. Just knowing something — anything — about where I come from makes me happy. Makes me feel like" — he shrugged — "like I'm someone."

I watched my friend as he laughed and exuded a happiness I wished I had. His red-blue eyes scanned through the window toward the children's ward — where his father had been the day before.

"Why aren't you angry at them?"

"Are you angry at your mom when she hurts you? Do you hate her because she has turned away from you countless times?"

"That's different."

"But she's hurt you, Brighton. And you still love her."

"Of course." This wasn't the same thing at all.

"I've been wanting to know something — anything — about where I came from for as long as I remember, and now I know a little bit about myself."

But none of them care. I wanted to yell this, but I didn't. But I did speak firmly. "Dr. Woburn is more worried about his job than your life."

"And you are more worried about your life than Nursey's," he returned.

"Don't call her that," I said quietly, but deep down inside I was jealous that the nickname still sounded sweet in his mouth. It was bitter in mine. "And Joann has everything. Why do I need to worry about her?"

He stepped away, and his pale face grew slightly pink.

"She's given up marriage and children for you. She might've made some bad choices, but the choice to love you has kept you alive. That's what Nursey has done."

Our eyes locked for several long moments, and I could tell we weren't going to see things the same. He wasn't wrong, I knew that. But there was still so much wrong that had happened, and I had a feeling that something she'd done, a secret she'd kept, would be the reason I would never get out.

"Angel boy, where are you?" Joyful's voice was as sharp as a sparrow's call and as warm as a hug all at once. She loved Angel and me.

Our stare broke when I heard her voice vibrating through the narrow gray halls.

"I'm here," he said, turning toward the open door, "in Brighton's room."

"I been looking for you for ten minutes, boy. I ain't got time for this," she scolded. The whites of her eyes grew. "Now, come on. I got your uniform ready."

He'd always had this sense of glowing to him because of his albino skin, but the glow I saw now was different. He reached out and squeezed my shoulder. "Be happy for me, Brighton. Maybe I can sneak us some extra food." He lifted his eyebrows in excitement, then he left.

I watched him. From now on he wouldn't look like a patient, he'd look like a worker. I had suggested Joann do something to get him out of the men's ward, but now that it was happening, I was nervous about how this might change us.

The lines had been blurred.

All the patients had jobs. Gardening and harvesting in season, peeling potatoes, sewing gowns for the patients and shrouds for the dead. Cleaning and laundry every day. Those who were capable were given tasks for several hours of the day. But there were plenty of patients who weren't able to do any of these things and who didn't do much more than stand around the dayroom or lie in their beds and move from therapy to therapy. There wasn't much for them to do but exist and survive.

I forced a smile as Angel waved goodbye for the day.

An aide had walked Mother back as far as the door and told me she needed washing. I could smell that she'd soiled herself in the few minutes she'd been away. Mother walked to the bed and sat. I knelt in front of her. She raised up her hand and put it on my cheek, and her eyes searched my face for a moment. Her bald head had transformed her in such a strange way. I didn't want to look at her, but I did. My bald head had transformed me too, only in different ways.

"Mother?" I whispered. "It's me, Brighton."

Her first finger lightly tapped my face a few times. A gentle touch from her was not something I often got. The leftover pieces of my heart tried to right themselves, only to find that too many pieces were missing.

"Mother." The morning's yellow sun cascaded through the broken windows; the rays cast light across my arms and spanned across her face. The image of the sun on her face made me imagine things I had always wished.

I imagined her walking through our little house to my bedroom some sunny morning. There would be a light breeze pushing against my lacy curtains. She'd sit on the edge of my bed and put her hand on my shoulder or my back and rub in circles. She'd gently push my hair back and wake me for school. She'd say my name, Brighton, a few times, like a pretty whispering song made of feathers and clouds. I'd slowly wake up and I'd say, "Good morning, Mother."

When the slap came across my cheek, I was unprepared, having fallen into my own Wonderland. I was back in my reality, and I wanted to run away.

Angel learning a sliver of his own history after living his whole life knowing nothing somehow made me feel less known. Would I ever be known? Would Angel?

Dr. Woburn mentioned my father. A convict. What had become of him? Would I ever have a future outside of this building? Would I get the chance to love someone and get married? No, I would be here for the rest of my life. There would be no husband, no children, no life — unless I escaped.

"Brighton?" Grace stood in the doorway, looking around like she wasn't sure if she was supposed to be here. "I was walking by to go to breakfast."

I barely recognized her. Her mounds of thick dark curls were gone. Her head was as bald as mine.

"Your hair." I breathed the words, unnerved at my shock. I'd relished her normalness, and now she looked like the rest of us.

She smoothed a hand over her scalp, then shrugged her shoulders.

"I guess they were nervous about the lice after all," she said, then turned her gaze toward Mother's bed. "Is that a straightjacket?"

"They call them camisoles here." I gestured toward the restraint lying over the foot of her bed.

"So this is your mother?"

My gaze returned to Mother.

"Yes," I said with a voice laced with disappointment, and my palm touched the place she'd just slapped.

"You look like her."

I looked at my mother. We were both bald

and imprisoned. But so was everyone on the ward. We were all the same now.

Grace didn't leave the doorway, almost like she was afraid to approach my mother.

"We need to find a way to escape," I said.

"I don't think I'll be here long enough to worry about that." The truth in that hurt.

"But no one is coming for me." My eyes were fixed on Mother so I didn't have to look at Grace. I didn't want to see how pathetic I looked in the reflection of her eyes.

"Then I'll come for you."

And then there was hope.

1939
UNDEVELOPED

A shift had happened. No longer was I a protected little girl who had been born in a shroud of bad luck. No longer was I given time toward any education and separated from the rest of the patients. Everything had changed. Like a tree drops leaves, like a mower cuts down long grass, like a shot of insulin subdues an anxious mind, there was a before and an after in my life now.

It wasn't that Joann ignored me or cared nothing for me. I disallowed any closeness — though chastised by Angel — and maybe she realized things had changed too. A waxing or waning season, I wasn't sure. But to me she seemed tired and her resilience low. After years of devoting her energy toward me, on top of her regular duties, perhaps now she felt tired of it all. Even me.

Besides the uniform, the contrast between her and the patients grew less and less. Her hair, always neat, was less styled, her lips less red, her cheeks less rosy. Her eyes darker. Her skin more ashen. I saw the signs of someone's soul entangled in melancholy, and I wasn't sure how my own soul was affected by it, but I knew somehow it was.

Was it my withholding of forgiveness, or was her guilt ruining her? It was hard to tell. All I could think about was Grace and Angel, wondering if it was possible to escape, and how. *Escape.* Breathing the word itself seemed preposterous. Grace had no reason to believe she would be left at Riverside long term, and she was sure she would find a way to have me released as soon as she got out. She said if the police knew how we were treated, they wouldn't keep me locked up here. She was sure of this so I believed her.

Angel came to visit when he was able to carve time away from his new duties. And Grace — she was like no one I'd ever met. She was from *out there.* From the real world. Of course, Rosina, Carmen, Lorna, and all the other women from my floor had also come from there, but she was different.

The other ladies had been at Riverside for as long as I had, or longer. The world they'd known had passed away and a new one that sparkled and sang had arrived — or so Grace told us. Grace was also my age, the youngest admitted patient I could remember. And she wasn't plagued with melancholy or paranoia, though she'd been given a diagnosis that said otherwise by doctors, so she could tell me everything I'd ever wanted to know.

Grace was vivacious and filled with stories. The other women had long since lost whoever they might have been before Riverside. When you're treated like a worthless piece of flesh, eventually you believe it. I had seen it happen over and over. The original person disappeared. Someone new was born in their place. It didn't take long before they became unrecognizable.

I knew this was why Joann had made me keep my distance from the rest of the patients for so many years. It had been for my good. Cutting my hair had not been, nor had solitary or the insulin injection.

Joann still pleaded daily for forgiveness. But I only spoke to her to ask for privileges for me, Angel, and Grace. I knew she'd give in to win me back. And I was too hurt to consider the alternative.

I didn't ask for much, but Grace and I wanted her camera back, along with some film. All patients had their belongings taken from them and put in the attic to be returned upon their release. She'd brought her camera, having no idea where she was being taken.

At first Joann said no, citing rules and regulations. But a few days later she handed us half a dozen cartridges with the reminder that I needed to remain silent about the secrets I knew and that neither the camera nor the film could be seen by any doctor. If anyone found out we would end up in solitary or worse. And any photographs we took would be destroyed. We agreed. It wouldn't take many photographs to prove the poor treatment and care we received. Grace would sneak these out and be able to share them to help Angel and me.

It didn't take long before the snap of the camera box began to pull me from my own dark moods. The trapped image of light inside the little box gave me hope of something unknown waiting to be discovered. Grace's Kodak had been a gift from her parents and now it was like a gift to me. I didn't know how it did what it did. And how with a push of my finger I could capture what I saw, images that before could only be captured in my memory.

The only photographs I'd been in were the ones Joann had taken each year on my birthday. And she'd never shown me those. Now here I was on the other side of the camera, with my eye to the viewfinder. The camera had quickly become even more to me than it was to Grace. It felt like a part of me, and since one of Grace's roommates was prone to taking things apart, the camera stayed with me.

The camera helped me see things differently. I saw the truth about so much my eyes had merely glanced over before. I saw the dust in the corners, chipped plaster. I traced along the room, and my mother filled the frame. She sat with slumped shoulders and her gaze on the floor. Her hair was spiked in various places, and because she'd pulled out so much of it over the years, it only grew back in patches. I scanned over to Grace. She waved and giggled.

Her hair had also started to grow, and the curls formed like corkscrews against her scalp. My life had changed since the day my hair was cut off and I was stuffed away, out of sight. It was Grace's voice that I'd begun to hear inside my head, speaking to me in a way I'd never known before. Learning about a whole world of things I'd never even heard of before.

Grace taught me about how important light was when taking photographs. She talked about shadows and framing and how all of it was affected by the light that streamed in. She told me to think about the pictures of starlets in magazines and showed me how to capture the glint in the eye.

Then Grace posed like a fashion model, and we both laughed.

"I'm going to take it." With a gentle press, the button clicked.

"Brighton." Joann walked in and helped my mother stand up. She was going to see a new doctor today who was visiting from New York. He was assessing certain patients regarding a new procedure called a lobotomy. "You know you're not supposed to have the camera out when we have a doctor on the ward."

There was an ache in my heart because she now carried an edge to her voice. I knew that blackmailing her to get my way had been wrong, but I didn't know how I could've done anything differently. I would always do what I could to help Angel and Grace. But that didn't take away the pain held in the cavern between Joann and me.

When Joann walked away with my mother, I pulled at Grace's robe and gestured for her to come with me. "Come on."

"Where?"

"We're going to get a photograph of hydrotherapy."

"You devil." Grace winked as she took my

hand, and we tiptoed to the other hall. Photographs of any therapies were, of course, against Joann's rules.

"I can probably get one through the broken window," I whispered to her, pointing at the door.

Grace nodded as she kept an eye out for any nurses or doctors.

I had to go on my tiptoes to see through the window. It was filled with the usual patients. Ghosts of vapor and hope rolled around the room. Eight porcelain tubs were stuffed with patients lulled into complacency, only their heads poking through the bathtub covers. Streams of steam escaped through the broken window above us. Oh, to be steam.

With a snap of my finger I'd captured all the forms of water. Water in the tubs. Steam hanging in the air like curtains. Ice in the water cups the barely present nurses drank while inside. And now the forms of the patients were held hostage in the box in my hand. Doubly captured. Would anyone ever know them and who they were? Who they were to me? Would anyone know me? Did their families remember they'd left them here to decay?

I felt a sense of urgency to pull out the film from inside the camera so I could see it again. To see how the mixture of light had cast upon the thin, dark strip of plastic. It was the light painted upon the dark that created the image; darkness vanished when the light touched it. Was light powerful enough to rule the darkness within our reality? I had slowly stopped believing it. Slowly stopped believing that any plan Grace might have upon leaving Riverside would work. Grace's family was not my next of kin, and there was no guarantee that she'd get out or that she could help my release if she did. All of her assumptions suddenly sounded like a fairy tale.

"I'm never going to see these pictures." When the words left me, the weight of them fell from my thin body.

The moaning of the hydrotherapy patients grew louder — like mourning.

"What do you mean? What about our plan?"

I shook my head slowly in response and stared at the box in my hands. I'd pushed this truth so far back in my mind that I'd forgotten it existed. None of the staff would ever allow these photographs to be printed. Joann would never allow Grace to take the film out of the hospital with her. Why had I fallen for her idea? Joann was only pacifying me. No wonder she'd given in so easily. She knew she would make sure the film was destroyed. The real world would never know how an out-of-control patient could be stuffed inside a solitary room, strapped in a water tub, or secured to her bed, all for the convenience of the staff. It surely wasn't for the healing of the patient. The patients might be left moaning like that for days.

Acknowledging that I would never see the photos I'd taken suffocated me as badly as the camisole had a few weeks ago. Without the miracle of an escape, I would never see the real world Grace spoke of and no one would ever see the hell I lived in. Like the images in the camera, I would never be known without the door being opened.

1939
Patient

I stayed in bed the next morning. I couldn't get up. My body wasn't stronger than my mind. All I could think about was spending the rest of my life here — at this home for the mad. I was almost seventeen and knew so little of what eighteen-year-old Grace spoke of — like learning to drive a car or watching a Clark Gable film. She talked about women voting, and I didn't know what that meant and why it mattered. I craved bologna, even though Grace told me it was gross. It was from out there, so I wanted it.

Angel had been my way out of self-pity for most of my life. But it wasn't working anymore. Knowing Angel loved his work and didn't have to sleep in a patient building made him feel different from me now. He was happier than I'd ever known him to be. One day when Dr. Woburn was on the ward, Angel watched and studied his doctor uncle's face as intently as his eyesight allowed. I knew he was looking for resemblances. I refused to see any.

"Brighton." Grace's voice was behind me. "Why weren't you at breakfast?"

I didn't answer.

I stared at the wall. And every brick I placed over my soul, the better I felt. The vacant stare was a balm. I let my mind wander between imagining what my life might've been if I'd had a different mother to pure blankness. My imaginations were as fleeting as Lorna's sensibilities. The barren canvas of my mind was easier to control.

Was this what had happened to so many others who came to Riverside with their wits intact but eventually lost the battle and spent their days staring at walls? Was this what it was like for my mother? Could it be this easy to stop being Brighton and start being a patient? A real patient? To let go of all my hopes?

"Brighton," Grace repeated several more times, shaking my shoulders. "Are you sick?"

I couldn't speak. My mouth was an empty space, and the only words I had left were soundless and littered upon the floor for nurses, carts, and shuffling patients to walk over. I was locked inside myself with the images in the camera box.

"What's wrong with her?" Grace asked whoever had entered the room.

"Brighton?" It was Joann. She came to me, and the cot slumped from her weight. She put her hand on my cool forehead. She whispered to Grace to go.

Grace didn't leave right away. I felt her hand on me for several long moments before she rubbed my leg and then stood up. I heard her feet pad across the floor, and the room felt emptier without her. I hadn't been alone with Joann for weeks. Of course Mother was there, but that was the same as being alone.

In these weeks I'd longed to move a step closer toward Joann. I missed her. But every time I touched my half-inch-long hair, the hurt surfaced, rushing over me like steam rushed out of the hydro room when the door was opened. Then I would let the pain cover me, and I'd dream of the outside world and wake up even further from her.

"Bright, it's me, Nursey." The edges were gone from her voice. So different from the day she'd had my hair cut. It was also no longer the voice that pleaded for my forgiveness. Instead, it was the voice that had grown around me like a vine since my birth. The voice of the person who had always been a mother to me. And she wasn't the eighteen-year-old nurse who had cared for me as a baby anymore. She was a grown-up woman who had set aside her own life for me.

"Where are you?" she asked.

Did I even know? Patients often left their minds and souls lying around while their bodies moved and walked. What far-off places did their minds travel to? I wanted to go there.

I hadn't gone far. My soul was still tucked inside of me. But I was afraid it might fly away at any moment.

Knowing that what I'd seen through that camera box would never matter had changed something within me. The innocent years of growing up alongside Angel with the doting attention of Joann had passed. And now I thought about what Joann's real life was like. Her life outside of this place. With all that she'd given up for me, she'd also kept some things from Angel and me. And then there were all the things she'd done to me.

I began to blame her instead of love her.

I felt as trapped as the images inside the film cartridges.

Joann was not responsible for my being in the hospital, but I saw her as the reason I was still here. My soul hadn't fully captured my reality until Joann had rearranged my whole world with what she'd done.

"Who am I?" My voice had returned.

"Oh, my darling, you're Brighton. The person I love the most." She smoothed her hand over my short hair like she was moving phantom tresses away from my face. My hand gripped the edge of my bed so that I wouldn't push her hand away.

"If you love me so much, then why?" I squeezed my eyes shut.

She cleared her throat, but her hand didn't stop her smoothing caress against my head.

"I was scared. I was so scared of losing you. If you tell anyone what you know and they investigate, we'll be fired. And if we're fired, then Angel will certainly go to the men's ward because there will be no one here to advocate for him. You'd be stuck here without him. You'd be here without *me.* This would be your life."

I turned over like a tornado had rushed over me and my gaze met hers.

"This already is my life." These words flared up like a windstorm of energy. "And you didn't answer my question. Why am I still here? Couldn't there have been another way for me?"

Each syllable held the weight of grief.

"At least we could be together."

"That's not enough." The words were truer than anything I'd ever spoken. I felt a layer of myself peel away like scraped-away skin. What about a future? A real one where I had the chance to be a wife and mother or the sort of woman who lived as vivaciously as I expected Grace had. Or at least have choices. Did I have any hope for that life anymore?

I'd spoken what neither of us wanted to believe. This was my life, yes. But she'd made it sound like it was worth it because she and I could be together. But it wasn't. If I had a choice I'd live anywhere else, even if I'd never see her again. I hadn't known this about myself until now. The kindness and effort given to me from my childhood had anesthetized me to what was real. It had numbed me from the life that was laid out before me. It was as if I was waking from a lifelong coma. I couldn't be enough for Joann, and she couldn't be enough for me.

Joann clenched and unclenched her jaw and diverted her eyes.

"Would you want to live here?" I asked.

"I almost do." She chuckled a little as a tear dripped down her cheek.

I sat up in bed, anger propelling me upright. "No, you don't. You get to go home every day. You get to choose where you live. You get to choose everything you do. You're free." My throat felt full of every patient's voice. "I'm not free. I'm as captured as my snapped photographs. I don't even feel alive."

"There are laws. You're —" Joann paused and stood and turned toward my mother. She sniffed back tears. Or maybe anger. "Legally you're both stuck here until he takes you out."

"My father?" She never brought him up. "Tell me his name."

She shook her head. "It wouldn't matter if I did tell you."

"But he could take me out if you told him about me? My father could come and take me out of here, and I could be his daughter out in the real world? I know how to care for Mother. I could take care of her." This was all I wanted in the whole world of desires. I imagined the moments before Sara Crewe learned her father still lived — would I live in those moments of anticipation for the rest of my life?

She didn't say a word. Instead, she got up and went to my mother, who hadn't had breakfast because I hadn't taken her.

"What was he like? What did he look like? Was he tall?" I sat at the edge of my bed now.

"Brighton, we've been through this." She straightened my mother's gown and held her hands so that she would stop scratching her fuzzy head. "Your mother — your mother was found alone in a condemned apartment. Neighbors heard her fits. Someone finally thought to call the authorities."

This story wasn't familiar.

"So her husband didn't bring her in? Where had he gone?" We looked at one another as if we were both afraid of the answer.

"She had no husband."

"No husband?" I repeated in a whisper. "But I heard you tell Dr. Woburn about him."

My mother had conceived me without having a husband. What sort of woman did that make her? I'd heard the ladies on the ward speak dark, black words of women with loose morals. Had my mom been one of those types?

"Brighton, breathe." Joann came to my side and pushed my head down toward my knees.

I slapped her away. I hadn't even realized I was gasping for air. That night on the balcony they'd called him a convict; they had known something about him.

"But that night on the balcony," I reminded her again, angry now.

"Fine, Brighton. Yes, your father is a convict and was in jail when he should've been taking care of your mother. He could have at least married her and made her an honest woman." The air was peppered with her bitterness. "Is that what you want to know?"

But the practical truth was that I had lost my freedom the moment I was conceived. My mother had been loose and volatile. My father was a criminal. None of that mattered because I was trapped here either way. There was no one to come to my rescue.

But then the thread of an old tune caught my attention. It was one Mother used to hum when I was a child, but hadn't now for many years. My mother, who was sitting on her bed with chasm-deep eyes, was humming. Her voice was more gravelly than in years past, but it was the same tune.

I closed my eyes, and my breaths began to slow and lengthen. In a few minutes I stood and walked over to my mother. I sat next to her and put my head in her lap. Her humming remained calm and strangely steady. A few minutes passed, and then she did something she hadn't done in a long time. She rested her hands on my body, and we were warm together.

Her wordless tune and my life had no voice — we weren't as different as I'd always thought we were.

1940
Where I Come From

I threaded the new film through the camera. We'd been without film for many months. But finally I convinced Joann to give us one more. The other six canisters were neatly tucked into a slit in my mattress. Grace and I made a pact that as soon as one of us was released or we escaped we would develop them and take them to a newspaper.

I imagined a day of escape. When and how we would get away, I wasn't sure.

Though I feared I would never see the photographs, I still imagined the final products. Would Angel's face be entirely washed out because of his paleness, or would you see that he had high cheekbones and a strong jawline? Would it show that he had full lips and not straight lines like Dr. Woburn, his uncle? Would my photos show the clarity of every curl that Grace had as her hair grew back, or would it simply look like a dark mass?

To have the answers to these questions would mean I was free.

A lot had changed since Grace had arrived nearly a year ago. Patients were being added to our ward almost daily, and every room was crowded now. More patients always meant more sickness, and Mother was not doing well. Any illness that came through the ward, she got. She'd had pneumonia several times. She'd gotten shingles. Some type of stomach influenza stuck with her longer than anyone else. She often needed cleaning up and a tender touch. She needed me.

She was like a chain linking me to Riverside, giving me pause whenever I considered a plan of escape. Of course, it was possible that Grace's parents would come for her before we could run away. They were visiting soon. My insides twisted into knots at the possibility. How I wrestled with the sweetness and bitterness of that.

Those thoughts plagued me as I walked my tiny, skin-and-bone mother to another meal. She scooted slowly down the hall, and when she was served her food, she would barely eat. But somehow she was still stronger than seemed possible. It took both Joann and me together to handle her when she became especially agitated.

I tried to take photographs of her when she was still and her version of happy. Those images would be just for me. Of course, she wouldn't pose for me, so often half of her was washed out by the sun's rays from the window in our room, leaving her in the gray. I prayed to Rosina's God that someday these images would come to light. Maybe Grace could sneak them out and take them home. Maybe someday someone would know about our lives here and tell others. Maybe then it wouldn't happen to more people.

A few days later I found myself on the hall floor outside of the stairwell. Grace was on the first floor meeting with her parents. It was all she'd spoken about for weeks. Her father had come to see her six months after she was admitted, and all of our hopes had been dashed when he had walked out unfettered. Grace had pleaded with him to let her go home. She'd even told him about me and how we were treated. But he had been unmoved. Her father did promise he would return in a few months with her mother. Grace was sure the second visit would work.

She wrote to them every week but hadn't received anything except a Christmas card from her younger sister, Hannah, whom she spoke of often. Hannah was my age and had true-blue Scottish red hair. Grace said it was redder than any hair I'd probably ever seen. Grace said Hannah was the only person who loved her.

"But I love you," I told her that day as she gently slid the Christmas card under her pillow. She lay her head down, and I noticed how thin her jaw and neck were. When had she gotten so small? It was like pieces of her had slowly gone missing.

But maybe today would be different. I hated myself for not wanting her to leave. What would I do without her? I still had Angel, but things were different between us. Angel had grown tall and handsome and strong, and he'd begun to watch over me like I'd always done with him. Asking me if I was okay, if I needed more food, if I needed another blanket. What I really needed was a way out.

I heard yelling. It was Grace's voice. There was crying, and the deep voice of a man I didn't recognize was bookended with one I did: Dr. Woburn. They were in the stairwell. I stood and put my ear to the door.

"Please, Gracie," a woman's voice said thickly, layered with emotion. "Your father only wants you to agree."

"I won't," Grace yelled.

"Grace," a calm Dr. Woburn said, "please,

come back downstairs. We can talk about this."

I peeked through the long, narrow window on the door. Grace's eyes were as wild as her hair. Her mother was perfect and beautiful. Her eyes and wide, full mouth matched Grace's, but that was the only resemblance. Grace's olive skin and curly hair were so different from her mother's straight black hair and porcelain skin. Her father stood stiffly in a suit. His red and pointy mustache and wavy red hair gave him a fiery appearance that matched the anger in his eyes. His fists were clenched.

"I won't have you disgrace our family with your behavior with that boy and your insistence on what you think you know." He pointed at Grace like his finger could poke a hole through her.

"But I love him and he loves me," Grace yelled. "I don't want to hide who I am anymore."

"Gracie, please, listen to your father," her mother cried. "We just want you home. You'd give up your life for him?"

"I'm not giving up my life for him. I'm trying to live my life being the person God made me, and I can't keep pretending."

Her father scoffed. "Look at you. Your hair is untamed and unkempt. You don't even look like my daughter anymore." Then he turned to his wife. "She's gone completely mad."

"Father, if anyone could understand why I fell in love with a Negro, you could."

Grace had told me that the world of people beyond our doors was as separate as water and dry land. Everyone was segregated by color.

Of course Negroes were treated differently here in the hospital, but the reasons why had never been explained to me. When possible, Negro patients were kept separated from the white patients. They were the last to receive their medicines, food, and treatments. I'd seen this my whole life. The only explanation I ever got from Joann was that the administration preferred the groups to be separated.

"Grace Douglass," Grace's mother scolded. "You will be silent."

The polished older woman's tears were replaced with a stern expression.

"And what will you do to me if I don't *stay silent,* Mother?" Grace yelled back, her wet face shining in the electric lights. "What will you do?"

"Do not speak to your mother like that." Mr. Douglass again pointed a long, refined finger.

"There's nothing more you can do to me." Grace's voice deflated and her arms flopped to her sides. She stood and wept, and when neither parent comforted her, Dr. Woburn pushed past Mr. Douglass and went to her.

"Let's find Nurse Derry and get you calmed down." His sincerity gave me a small measure of affection for him.

"Dr. Woburn," Grace cried into his chest, and his arms slowly went around her shoulders. "I don't want to feel this way anymore."

"That's why you're here, Grace," he said. "We can help you."

She shook her head and pulled away. Slowly she wiped her face with the short sleeves of her hospital gown and shook her head again. "No, you can't help me. You can't make me all white, Dr. Woburn. If you could, then maybe Mother would stay and you could *fix* her too." Her mother gasped, and her father yelled for her to stop. "She doesn't look it, does she? But I do. Don't I? You can see it, can't you?"

She looked up into Dr. Woburn's eyes, and he gently touched her curls. I'd never seen him so gentle.

"I fell in love with a Negro boy, and my parents hate me for it."

Dr. Woburn released a long-buried sigh.

"I think we're done here, Doctor. Grace will remain. She's talking madness." Mr. Douglass's voice shook when he spoke. Then he looked at Grace, like every word was gripped in the vise of his jaws. "I'm sorry for you, Grace. But your outbursts and choice of suitor will ruin us. Completely ruin us. I will not have it. You're acting as mad as your grandmother."

"My *Negro* grandmother?" she yelled at him. "You're race prejudiced, Father, and that means you're against Mother and me. Your wife and your daughter."

Mr. Douglass cleared his throat. He was like a filled syringe waiting to be plunged. He didn't linger and didn't look at Grace again but turned to his wife and with a snap of his head gestured for her to come.

Mrs. Douglass's eyes dripped with longing. She loved her daughter — I could see it. She reached for her from the several steps below Grace.

"Goodbye, Grace," Mrs. Douglass said, then spoke something so quietly I didn't catch it. She carefully walked backward a few steps but kept her eyes trained on her daughter. Then, when she got to the landing, she turned and walked away. She didn't look back.

"My father brought me here before Jonah

and I could run away," I heard Grace's muffled voice tell Dr. Woburn. "Everything would be different if he and I had run away a week earlier."

When I looked at Dr. Woburn, I saw, for the first time, the resemblance between him and Angel. The worry that teased between his brows and caring eyes.

"I don't know what to say." His typical deep and direct voice was lush and velvety.

Then Grace turned and saw me through the window. She looked aged and raw. "At least I have Brighton."

She and I looked at each other. The circumstances that had brought us to the hospital were different, but why we were kept here was the same. We weren't mad or feeble-minded. We didn't belong here. But no one would listen. No one wanted us. No one claimed us. There was nowhere else for us to belong. Any hope of Grace getting out and then her being able to help Angel and me had faded to nothing.

1990
Find the Light

"Cat got your tongue?" Lorna's voice parrots. "Cat got your tongue?" She won't stop. She echoes herself incessantly from down the hall, so I go to find her. She's in the dayroom. It's been so long since I've seen her, and the familiar ache in my soul journeys to my heart, mind, and hand. I wave at her. She waves back and then says it again. "Cat got your tongue?"

"Lorna?" I say. My body feels old, my back is aching, but my laugh and voice are young. I turn to see my reflection in the window, and I'm sixteen-year-old Brighton again. It's been so long since I've seen me too. Lorna suddenly stops repeating her refrain, and I turn back to see that the dayroom has changed into a graveyard. And on the other side of it I see that bright, white light that I wish I could get to but can't. The buzz of an electroconvulsive machine makes me sit up in bed. I'm a mass of sweat and I'm Nell again. And old. My face is wet from sleepy tears, and my heart tries to race and beat itself.

"Calm down, kid," I say aloud. "Doc isn't home to call 911, so you can't have a heart attack."

I stopped feeling silly about talking to myself decades ago. It started when my kids went to school and I was alone in the house again. My kids had been good company, and I made sure they never knew how much I needed their chattering and giggles. The house was so quiet then that it drove me to get a college education to become a teacher.

I never wanted to be like Joann and keep my children hostage from their own lives to make my life better. I wanted to be a good mom and let them grow and have their own unique lives. And they did. They come home for visits, but they live far enough away that it isn't as often as I'd like. They bring home with them those little souls called grandchildren too. It's like all the good in the world was pulled together to make them. Being a grandparent strips away one more layer of pain in my life because I don't want all that burden around them. But I miss them and wish I could see them more.

The only time I was alone when my kids were little was when I was in the bathroom

— and sometimes not even then — and I would often think of Mother. She and I were rarely apart. It was hard for me to mother any other way.

Speaking of bathrooms — I have to go. My old bladder is about as small and thin as a tea bag.

Once I'm done I can see that I left the kitchen light on. I hesitate because I know that's where I left those new, old photographs. I can't blame the dreams on them, though. I've had those ever since I left all those gray walls and souls.

I walk into the kitchen and stare at the photos scattered over the kitchen table.

Joann washing Mother on the bed.

Angel in front of Willow Knob.

The hydrotherapy room with women in tubs. Who knows how long they'd been in there.

A few photos are duds — my finger covering up the subject in the shot or poor lighting.

But when I see these faces and the pain in their eyes, or the nothing in their eyes — the swirl and cramp in my stomach won't let me look away.

There is Lorna. The day she'd been put into a camisole and sat on the hall bench all day looking at the floor. A dribble of saliva on her lips had dripped on her lap, creating a wet circle. My young self would've seen this image casted in dark and light and wanted to tell the world of the sadness and mistreatment. But my old self knows if I did that, I would not just be sharing a picture; I'd be putting pieces of myself on display.

And Rosina. Her hand extended out from the solitary room. I knew she was praying behind the door.

Dear Carmen. Cuffed in restraints on her bed. She'd had an outburst that no one wanted to deal with. The restraints remained for several days.

So many women naked in the dayroom. They soiled themselves too often for clothing.

Grace. Looking over her shoulder. Full of life.

Oh Grace.

There she is — my surrogate sister — but where is the grace in these captured moments? And where is the grace for me, watching all of this happen and incapable of changing the outcome? And now they are gone. They'd been held captive in their lives and now again in the film cartridges.

I can still hear them speak in my head. Not just Lorna. All the antics and the praying and the asking for food. And the screaming. The yelling through the solitary-room door. The moaning at night. The shrieks that came when someone was dragged down the hall for electroconvulsive therapy. And, almost worse, the silence when they returned.

Before I know it my arms run against the table and all the photographs go flying. They lie like dead leaves on my laminate floor. But many of them are faceup, and the faces continue to stare at me. Especially Joann's.

To reconcile the good and the bad that is folded up into one person is hard. Who had she been anyway? My nurse? Or a liar and deceiver? Or was she really the one who loved me most like she always told me? Had she been my real mother and Helen my captor?

I move to the floor near the pictures and assume a sitting position I haven't used since those years long ago when my body could bend and turn better. I grunt a little as I settle. I pick up the pictures one at a time. I have to crawl on all fours to gather several. The stack in my hand is heavy and the voices are loud. Almost all of them lie in that old graveyard in that back quarter of those thousand acres. They'd never be known all the way out there, and someday it'll be forgotten that there was a graveyard there at all. The stones will become dust and the weeds their markers.

1941
Every Key Has a Lock

I pointed the viewfinder at Joann as she handed out medications. Each patient took their small cup of water with the dissolved powdered medicines in one quick swallow. Joann had never made me take anything for what was supposed to help depression or melancholia, but Grace had had to ever since her meeting with her parents the previous year. That awful row in the stairwell. After that she was no longer the easygoing, companionable patient. She'd begun to yell and even hit the staff, especially upon threat of sterilization. Her refusal to eat enough to stay healthy worried me. She was told her parents were considering sending her to a doctor who did a special brain surgery that could cure her. It was called a lobotomy, but I knew almost nothing about it.

Grace had made a poor and unplanned attempt to rush past an aide who was escorting her near the first-floor door. She'd done this knowing that if she was successful she'd be leaving me in this prison. I knew this was evidence that I was losing Grace. She was losing the battle of her mind. Because of her attempt, now her every action was scrutinized even more and the possibility of sterilization and brain surgery was real.

More than half on our ward had been sterilized — my mother had years ago. Grace and I had not been. Joann told us that Dr. Woburn made sure I was not on the list for sterilization. But Grace was a more difficult patient because she had parents who would demand that she follow a more traditional plan of treatment.

I continued to watch Joann through the camera. We hadn't had film for a few months and Joann refused to buy more. My antics and blackmail opportunities were long wasted. The staff knew I had no film, but I kept watching the life around me through the camera lens. There was a sense of separation it gave me in order to survive.

Joann smiled at me. Things had improved between us. But the life I'd had before Grace was a distant dream. Those years before my hair was shorn and before Joann had broken my trust were not my life anymore.

I tightened the camera's focus on Joann. She had sweat marks beneath her arms and her hands shook as she handed out each little cup. At thirty-six, the aging process had raced ahead in the last few years, but she and Dr. Woburn were still sweet on each other. The doctor had become kinder with age and more present, but Joann was slipping away into somewhere I couldn't reach. An ashen mood and exterior replaced the grit, self-assurance, and beauty she used to have.

The barred windows were behind me and the day was bright. There was enough light not just to see well but to capture the scene. I clicked the shutter. If I had film, would this photograph have shown how the deep creases on her forehead had formed a permanent grimace — much like the old scar of Dr. Woburn's?

Grace walked into the dayroom. She didn't even look over to where I sat on the couch. The shuffle of her feet along the floor was just like the other patients. When had she become a patient instead of Grace?

Grace had been in solitary for three days, and her time in isolation was happening frequently now. In her two years here, she'd become only bones wrapped in skin that was now more ashen than olive. When she got to the head of the medicine line, she put her hand out for the cup from Joann.

I lifted the camera and snapped the pretend photo. I documented this moment in my mind. Perhaps it was the submissiveness that rested alongside such sadness that I was drawn to, proving how there were snatches of time when she'd been broken into obedience. Though she would fight against it other times.

After the first click I kept the camera up to my eye. I watched closely as Grace took her medicine cup and dumped its contents on the tray in front of her. I snapped again. Oh, how I longed to have these moments captured.

Joann looked over at me, and I pulled the camera from my eye. What was Joann asking of me in her gaze? Did she think I could bend Grace back into compliance? While we were as close as sisters could be, she had become angry and distant even with me. She'd ruined an entire cartridge of film because of her temper, intentionally opening the camera box and exposing everything inside. She slammed doors shut. Slammed Joann against walls. She cried a lot.

I let the camera hang on my neck and

stood from the putrid couch and went to my friend.

"Can we go for a walk? It'll make her feel better." Of course, nothing but release would make her feel better.

"Brighton," Joann started. "You know the rules. You're not children anymore."

"Send Angel with us," I said. "He's practically an aide now. Besides, where would we even run to? We'll just go to the garden. We could pull some weeds."

This was my best argument because garden work would be starting as soon as it warmed up a bit.

Joann handed out a few more medicine cups before she looked back at me. "All right," she finally said. "But if she gets in trouble, you'll be responsible. I'll ring for Angel to meet you outside."

Once outside, we were shivering, but breathing outside air and sitting in the sun, filled the empty in my corners and spaces. As we sat near the garden, I saw Angel coming toward us. I hadn't seen him in a week. I ran to him and hugged him. His hold on me lingered longer than normal, and I sank into his chest and he buried his face between my neck and shoulder. We sat close together and I felt warmer. Grace just gazed into the distance.

In awkward silence, Angel opened up his coat — with Mason's name on the chest — and pulled out a brown paper package. He unfolded it and handed each of us a bread roll. They were golden brown, and while they weren't very soft, they were better than anything we'd eaten in months. With over-crowding, shortages were at their worst, and I couldn't remember the last time my stomach had been full.

"They're old, but Joyful gave them to me — she baked them for the staff a week ago. She's taking the rest home to her children."

Angel and I ate quickly, but Grace only nibbled. I let the dry, buttery texture linger on my tongue before chewing it. I thought about Joyful taking leftovers home to her family, and I couldn't help but imagine how her children would run to her and tell her how much they missed her. She would hug them and smile at them and give them each a bread roll.

"Brighton." Angel's voice was soft and warm near my ear. "Where are you?"

I smiled and shrugged. I'd been far away for a moment but fought the urge to stay there, fearful that one day I would remain in that distant world.

When I had eaten half of my roll, Grace stood and looked far off, away from the buildings, past the gardens and orchard and everything contained in our world.

"I'm leaving," Grace said and took off. Her bare feet couldn't have felt good against the dried, yellowed grass; but despite her weakness, she ran fast.

Without a word between us, Angel and I stood and chased after her. We wove in and out of the gravestones in the graveyard before we reached the furrows of an ancient garden and then flung ourselves through the trees. We'd never been this far before. I stopped and looked ahead. Angel was only a step behind me, and he too stopped and stood at my side. Grace continued to run through the tall, dead grass, then the trees that grew thicker with weeds and brush and bushes — tangled, unkempt, and dark. This was part of the thousand acres of land that was my whole world, and yet I'd never seen it. I'd never been with Grace when she attempted an escape — if they could be called that. She'd only made it past a few aides and into the stairwell. The audacity of this moment was frightening and thrilling — but it was impossible.

Grace slowed as she pushed her way through the underbrush — and then I couldn't see her anymore. I held my breath and grabbed Angel's arm, pulling him. What if we couldn't find her? What if she actually escaped?

What if that meant that I could too?

But what about my mother? Would she feel my abandonment?

My speed picked up despite the bushes cutting my legs. Angel grunted behind me. None of us were wearing shoes. Grace was in sight again, ahead of me, fighting with thistles that gripped at her hospital gown. She used words Joann had outlawed from my mouth when I tried them out when I was eight.

"I need to get out," she yelled between deep breaths as she pulled her gown free, tearing it. She pushed farther through the thickness and started banging her hands against a metal fence that had appeared almost like a weed. It was tall and impossible to overcome and covered in overgrown weeds and vines. "I need to get out." Her anguish wilted the leaves around her.

She turned to us, her face streaked with tears. With gasping breaths she leaned against the fence. "We need to escape." Her shaky voice was quiet and serious now.

Angel and I looked at each other. In all our years at Riverside we'd never even seen this fence. Was it possible to get through?

Grace hadn't heard from her family since

that terrible day in the stairwell. She'd never been the same. But now there was a fire in her eyes, and even though her body sagged like our dingy gowns, there was a renewal in her. She leaned forward and reached for our hands. Angel and I took hers, making a circle.

"Let's escape, please. I can't go on like this. This place is killing me." She looked back and forth between Angel and me. Her arms and legs were scratched and smeared with blood. Her grip was so tight I wouldn't have been able to pull free if I'd wanted to. I knew after thinking about it for too long what we needed to do.

"Let's escape." My voice floated dangerously around in the woods and cut the trees down right in front of me. I put my gaze on Angel to tether me.

"I'm not sure," Angel said.

"We can climb it," Grace suggested.

"There's razor wire on top," he protested.

"Find wire clippers in that shed," Grace threw back.

The back and forth of their words made me dizzy. Then they both looked at me for answers. As if I had them.

"Where would we go?" Angel finally said to Grace. "Besides, I have a job. Responsibilities."

"A job?" Grace spat out. "A job?" Then she got mad. "You're a patient who wears a different uniform, Angel. Do you get paid?"

Angel hesitated, then shook his head no.

"It's not a job. It's slave labor," she yelled.

Angel pulled his hand from hers, and Grace's and mine dropped.

"Where would we go?" Angel asked again, this time more sober. "We don't know anyone out there, unless you think your family is going to take all of us in."

Grace laughed an awful maniacal laugh while she shook her head. "I have friends. They're a little ways away, but it wouldn't be more than a day's walk."

"A day's walk?" Angel repeated, and it was his turn to laugh at her.

"You think that's worse than staying here? Maybe you do belong here, because you're crazy if you think that walking a day would be worse than living out your life here in this loony bin." Her words came out harsh and littered with curse words.

Angel pulled his stare from her, let it land on me for weighty moments, then turned to leave. "I just don't see how it's possible."

Grace yelled so loudly the trees swayed against her force. I turned to look at her. She grabbed a thornbush and yanked at it until her palms were ripped and bleeding.

"Why, why, why is this my life? I can't live like this anymore." The rawness in her throat could be heard in every syllable.

I took a few steps toward Angel. I would never let him get too far away from me. I took his hand. "Wait."

"We need more information before we can escape," I said.

I saw my oldest and dearest friend in denial about his life and my stand-in sister falling apart into a pile of ashes where once a fire had been thriving and growing. And what about me? My mother surely wouldn't want me to live out the rest of my life in this place. Maybe, if I could get out, I could find someone who could help Mother. I knew how to care for her. Maybe I could get a house, find a place for her with me. I would be her next of kin and could take her away from here.

"Information?" Grace asked, breathing heavily.

"We need to get our files." I looked between the eyes of one hopeful friend and one suspicious one. "Angel and I have family out there somewhere and our history is in there. We deserve to know more about ourselves before we run."

"Maybe I could find Jonah."

"I could find my mother."

I didn't know who I had out there, but maybe my files would reveal something. Maybe then we could break through the fence and start a new life.

"They're in there." A windstorm of voices and strong arms of several aides broke our plans and thoughts.

They didn't hurt us on purpose, but expecting a fight they still handled us roughly. Angel pulled his arm away and explained he was needed in the grounds-keeping shed. The aides didn't know how to respond, knowing his duties, so they let him go. Grace and I let them take us back because we knew what our next step was now. Finally we knew.

Grace and I were immediately put in solitary. We were across from each other, but Grace didn't stay up and talk with me this time. She retreated to some cavern of the room and left me alone. I slept for much of the time and dreamt of a dad I'd never met. In my wakefulness I prayed to a God I was sure was out there somewhere to help me find something in my files.

The night of the second day my door was opened quietly. I sat up, surprised. Nurses and aides left solitary patients alone at night unless there was a problem, but it wasn't an aide. It was Angel.

He smiled and held up a ring of keys.

1941
Pandora's Call

At first Grace fought us in her disillusionment. It was like she didn't know who we were. But when her eyes sharpened, she stopped her struggling. We had her out a few moments later. With both the solitary doors shut it appeared we were inside and quiet. We tiptoed down the hall toward the back stairwell door. Angel had already made sure the hall was empty. The one benefit of understaffing — no one was around.

We continued to scan the dimly lit hall. We saw no one, and all we could hear were several snoring patients and Carmen's moaning. Her stomach had been hurting for days and she wasn't eating. But Joann didn't know when Dr. Woburn would get to her. There were so many patients, and it could take days.

Angel produced another key and opened the records' office door. We slipped inside and the door clicked behind us. Angel led us between shelves filled with files. We sat together, and Grace began twisting her hands like they were wet cloths being wrung out.

"I came in earlier and found our files. They were alphabetical, so it was easy." Angel was the picture of confidence. His brow unwrinkled and mouth turned up in a smile, his pure white skin a beautiful reminder of the purity I'd always seen in him. He pulled four folders out from the bottom shelf and brought them close to his eyes, reading the name in the corner, then handed us each our files and an extra one for me — Mother's.

I sat for well over a minute looking at the file folder with my name on it. I was afraid. Nervous. Uncertain. Angel and Grace didn't seem to have any hesitations.

"Let's take turns," Grace suggested. "Angel, you go first since you already started."

"Look at this," Angel said and took out a photograph from his file, and as he pulled it close to his face, he leaned toward the small cascade of light. I looked with him. It was of a toddler of maybe three who was purely white. "It's me, right?"

I just nodded, my throat choked to the brim with hope and fear.

His voice was nostalgic and almost wistful. Like he was mining the memory of the photograph. I looked closer and saw a young boy of white sitting — no — nestled in the lap of a beautiful, youthful blond woman.

"I bet that's my mother. Cynthia, right?"

I nodded again. That night two years earlier, when I heard so much on that balcony, now seemed like an eternity ago.

"There's not much here." Still leaning toward the light and squinting, he finally handed me an official-looking document.

"Your mother's name is Cynthia. But her last name and your father's name are blacked out of this paper. See? Looks like your first name was marked over too, except I can see an *L*. Your name starts with an *L*."

He grabbed the document from my hands and desperately tried to see it for himself. He held it up to the light, but after a few moments he sighed and carefully folded it and put it down. He riffled through a few pages of medical records — his checkups and documentation of his poor eyesight. But there wasn't anything else. His smile faltered like a passing breeze, and his gaze returned to the photograph before he put it into his chest pocket.

"It was worth a shot." He sighed and

looked over at Grace. "Your turn."

Grace bit her lower lip and slowly opened up her folder. Numerous letters fell out, and Grace pored over them first. Her hospital records fell out of the file toward me. The files listed every outburst, escape attempt, refusal to eat or be medicated, confinement, and more. The words *anorexia nervosa* were listed. I knew this diagnosis well.

"Anything on there about sterilization? I've been threatened, you know." She said the words without emotion as she looked through the letters.

"Yes," I admitted. "It's mentioned that you've been evaluated for it as a possibility."

"More than a dozen here." Grace's whisper rose in pitch as she splayed the letters in her hands. I wasn't sure she'd even heard me.

"From your parents?" I asked.

She shook her head, and a tear dripped down from her face to the papers.

"Mostly my sister. And one from my father. They're all open."

Her hands shook as she carefully pulled out a letter. Her father's name was on the return address. Her eyes scanned the lines, and after a minute she folded it back up. Her face remained blank as she spoke.

"He said that if they deliver any letters to

me from my sister or Jonah, he will pull his generous monthly funding." She pinched her lips together. "There are nearly a dozen from my sister. Only one from Jonah."

She looked at the postmark dates and put them in order.

"Go ahead," Angel said to me. "It's your turn to find out who you are."

"Angel, I know who I am." A surge of defensiveness rushed through me. Maybe it was because I was afraid I would learn that there was nothing to know.

Angel tilted his head toward me. "This is what we've been wanting to do ever since Nursey gave you that photograph of your mother on your fourteenth birthday, Bright. Only we never had the guts to do it. And we trusted Joann too much. Go ahead. See what's inside."

I slowly inhaled and opened Mother's folder first. It was thinner than I expected and there was nothing inside except medical findings. No correspondence. No photographs. No old documents with maybe the name of my father on them. There was nothing.

I held my breath as I pushed it aside and opened my own. Several photos slid out. One was of my mother and an older man who appeared to be her father. My grandpa.

I analyzed him head to toe, and nothing about him seemed familiar. The next photograph was also of my mother, a little older this time, though with a young man at her side. He had to be my father. He was handsome and had a mustache. He had dark hair. His skin looked smooth, and his eyes were sharp. Like he knew something. They were handsome together, and I guessed Mother to be about my age.

The rest of the photos were ones Joann must have taken of me. One of me getting a bath in a washbasin. One of my mother holding me. I couldn't have been more than a few months old, and my mother was nursing me. She was looking at me. I couldn't see her face; it was curtained by her hair. But the baby — me — in the photo was looking up with a hand raised to my mother's face. So I knew there had been a time when our souls had connected.

I flipped through the annual birthday photos, and when I found the one of Angel and me together I took it, along with the baby photo. No one would ever know.

"Jonah still loves me," Grace whispered. "But he went west to San Francisco to build ships for some war in Europe."

Her voice faded as her eyes continued to scan the letter in her hands. "He wanted a fresh start." She finally released a sigh, then went back to reading her other letters.

I returned to my file and pulled out the medical section. It was small, but I wanted to comb through everything possible while I had the chance. It was Joann's writing, so small it was difficult to read. I glanced through most of it. Nothing more than weights and heights and occasional fevers. Not much of any importance.

"Wait," Angel whispered, putting his hand over mine and Grace's. "I heard something."

I held my breath. Footsteps came down the stairwell at the end of the hall. Angel's hand tightened on mine and our gazes held fast. We were tucked away enough that if someone looked in the office window, they would not see us. A minute later we saw the shadow of an aide dragging a patient toward the therapy room. I couldn't tell who it was.

We waited and listened. We didn't breathe. We heard a few doors open and close and the heavy door to electroconvulsive therapy click shut. Why it was important to administer shock therapy this late at night instead of during their normal day hours, I did not know. But our first concern right now was to get back to our rooms undetected.

"We should go," Angel said and closed his file and carefully put it away. He reached for mine next.

I hesitated.

"I'm not putting mine back," Grace said a little too loudly. Her cut and bandaged hands held her file to her chest.

"Take the letters out of their envelopes and return everything else to the file. We don't need anyone getting suspicious," Angel said. We all knew the nurses were in and out of her file often these days.

She stuffed the folded letters into the back of her underwear.

"If we're caught, we're dead." She eyed us both. "Come on, Bright."

I was still holding my file. I flipped through it and pulled out a sealed yellow envelope before I handed the rest to Angel. I too stuffed the envelope and a few photos I'd grabbed in the back of my underwear.

Angel quickly escorted us with his ring of stolen keys back to solitary. He let Grace back into her room first and then, before closing me inside mine, he held me close.

"We're doing this, right?" he asked.

"Yes. We need to make a plan. Maybe steal those keys again. Maybe find a way through that fence in the back." I shook my head because I really didn't know.

"We'll figure it out."

After Angel left me I got into the dingy

cot and pulled out the yellow envelope. It was sealed and blank on the front. I looked over at the high window. The golden moon shone through the bars, and for a brief moment I reveled in its beauty. It didn't matter that I was looking at it through a cracked and ugly window — it didn't keep the moonlight from glowing or keep it from being lovely.

I ran my hands over the envelope. Was this a Pandora's box? If opened would it bring chaos to my world — more than I already had? Pandora had never been able to close it again, and because of that her life was never the same.

1941
Till Death Do Us Part

I didn't open the envelope that night. There wasn't enough light to see what was inside anyway. But even when the sunlight poured into the room the next morning, I still didn't open it. And when Grace and I were both released before breakfast I kept the envelope closely tucked into my thin, worn-out underwear.

We were ushered to the breakfast table, and I watched as Grace tried not to walk stilted because of the letters she'd stuck in her underwear. We sat at the table with Lorna and Rosina and a few ladies I wasn't familiar with. Carmen was in her room, still wailing over her stomach. And Angel was suddenly a few tables over, holding trays of plates to be served by the kitchen staff. It wasn't uncommon for us to see him a few times a week. He peeked over and smiled. I smiled back, and Grace hit my thigh under the table.

"I stole a candle and match from the office last night," she whispered.

"What? I didn't even notice."

"That was not the first time I've stolen something." She winked at me. It was a comfort to see her more like herself this morning. Like the Grace I'd known for the last two years.

"And?"

Her eyes became small pools, and her smile began to shake from emotion. "I used it to read some letters last night. My sister." She sipped the coffee in front of her before making a face. "She is trying to get me out."

Out.

The small word rattled around in my mind like a wild patient in the solitary room. I squeezed my eyes shut for a moment. Would we go from talking about escaping and stealing files to complaining about our rheumatism and growing soft in our middles? If that was the case, my mother would probably be long dead. What if Grace got out and I was left here? Would she even be able to find a way to get me out? And what about Angel? But she'd been here long enough now that being released became less and less expected.

"Is your sister changing your dad's mind?"

"No." She paused and groaned when the

bowl of porridge was placed in front of her. "She's trying to trick him into signing papers that he doesn't realize will release me."

Hearing that was a letdown. Tricking and playing games? That was how Hannah thought she could get Grace out? I had only seen her father for a few minutes and knew he wasn't a man who was easily manipulated.

I let her talk until she had no more words. And then I saw Joann down the hall through the open dining room doors.

"We need to talk about — you know." Grace leaned toward me.

Grace talked about hitchhiking, how to earn money on the road by washing dishes, and how we could save enough money to take the train west to California. She went on and on about how we could go to the beach out there and work in the factories that were popping up that her sister wrote her about — something about a war — and how we'd eat steak and drink real coffee every day and on the weekends we'd eat cheesecake and drink lemonade.

There was so much of what she said that made little sense, but what did make sense was that I was losing Grace. Her hold on reality was wrinkling up like an old newspaper that couldn't be ironed out again.

"Lorna" — Grace's eyes were crazed — "did you ever try to escape this hellhole?"

Lorna was in a mood this morning. Quiet and brooding. Her words were few and not entirely in clichés. She whispered under her breath and looked around like she was afraid or suspicious. Oh Lorna. She'd had spells like this for as long as I could remember, but the good stretches had been so good. She looked at Grace and tilted her head, her effort to understand visible all over her face. Her thin, wispy lips came together.

"Dance with the devil." Her whisper back came from both parts of her mind, I was certain. The tilted and the lucid one. "Dance with the devil."

She repeated her phrase and looked around like she was looking for this very devil.

"Don't think about it." Rosina looked up from her bowl of picked-at porridge. But she wasn't looking at Grace; she was looking at me. "There are many ways in, but without someone from the outside, there's only one way out."

I knew she was right.

"Maybe we have to dance with the devil to get out. We're already in hell. He should be easy to find." My words braver than my heart.

Later that day there was a great thunderstorm after lunch. Everything on the property had lost power and we would not be served dinner. The main problem was that the lack of lights made patients difficult to control. It was so dark, I could barely see my hand in front of my face.

Hours into the blackness the emergency lights from the generators finally bloomed. They were dim, and only a smattering of soft light was thrown into the halls. Before Joann had left I had stolen her flashlight when she set it down briefly. It made the rest of her shift incredibly difficult but I didn't care. I wanted the light. I touched my back where the yellow envelope protruded out of my underwear.

Patients were slowly but surely directed or escorted to their rooms. I made sure to help Mother. When I tucked her in, the sharpness of her shoulders pressed against my hands like daggers. She was so thin I was surprised she could still hold herself up in any way. The electroconvulsive therapy had made her sleep deeper, and she seemed to be further away than normal. She didn't even moan much during the night anymore, and there was part of me that actually missed the sound.

I was standing over Mother when a shrill sound from down the hall made me jump. Mother gasped and awoke with wide eyes. It was Carmen. No doctor had made it out to her today as promised.

The shrieking didn't stop. Nurse Wilma yelled from another part of the hall that she was coming. She had her hands full as the only nurse on the ward that night.

I poked my head into the hall, then walked out. My eyes had fully adjusted to the dim lighting, and I could see I wasn't the only one in the hallway. I went across the hall and peeked inside Carmen's room.

Wilma rushed over from another hall, her breathing rapid. When she passed me she left behind a layer of her sweat on my arm.

"She's dying, she's dying," Rosina said as the frantic nurse entered, then she returned to kneel at her sister's bed. She crossed herself. "Jesus, Mary, and Joseph. *Dios te salve, Maria.*" She began to recite what I knew she called the "Hail Mary" prayer. I understood the first few words, but the further she went on in Spanish, the more I lost their meaning. I didn't, however, miss the comfort in her words. Her desperate pleas needed no translation. I became a companion in her prayer.

I hadn't often prayed, but deep within myself I knew exactly what she said. Pleading and begging were a well-understood language. I'd done plenty of that myself, so perhaps I'd prayed more than I realized. Maybe even my first squalling cry as a baby was a type of prayer. Were my words still considered prayers when I wasn't sure anyone was listening? Maybe Rosina's God heard me too.

Rosina's weeping words whispered throughout the darkness. Wilma checked Carmen's vitals, and the dampness in the room crept around me like a second skin. The emergency lights shuddered at a crack of thunder, and another onslaught of rain began pelting the roof. My skin felt clammy, and my toes curled on the cool, moist floor. The layer of stickiness made my stomach churn.

Wilma got a syringe of insulin ready to calm Carmen, and when she tapped the air bubbles, her narrowed eyes almost crossed. As a child, I used to laugh when she did this.

"Wilma, is she going to die?" In the dense air of the room a whisper sounded like a yell and every breath like a gasp for life.

"Go to bed, Brighton," she snarled. "It's probably gas."

"No, no, no." Carmen groaned louder than Rosina's strung-together holy words.

Wilma threatened me again, holding up the insulin syringe as if she'd use it on me. I retreated and returned to my room. Many of the patients had become agitated at the disruption, and the noise all around the hall sounded like the buzzing of bees. Those of us who were well enough were forced to help restrain the difficult ones while Nurse Wilma gave Carmen her attention.

The insulin didn't help Carmen quickly; she didn't settle for a few hours, which was odd. Then the sudden stillness crawled along the halls like spiders. I was covered in sweat — not all my own — and breathing heavily. So were those around me. But the silence was cavernous and growing.

We gathered in the hall near Carmen's room. I leaned against the wall a step away from her door. The beams of light from the few flashlights caught on our shining skin and eyes.

But then came Rosina's cry. Louder than Carmen's had been.

My heart stopped. The tension was tighter than any camisole anyone had ever worn. No one breathed a breath.

Wilma appeared at the doorway of Carmen's room, and Rosina's crying stirred the very molecules in the air.

"I think her appendix burst," Wilma said, her words falling from her mouth between gasps of panic.

Beside me Grace whispered a *no.* I sank to the floor. Memories of Mickey's heart attack years ago resurfaced. Another one lost in this cruel world. And there had been so many others I hadn't known. Bodies in white shrouds carried out so often they were forgotten before they could even become the ghosts that haunted our peeling-plaster-walled rooms.

We were all ordered back to our rooms, and Wilma's own grief made us obey. We left Carmen to her eternal sleep, her dingy gray blanket covering her face. Rosina was at her side, her words trapped by her grief. The entire floor felt like death and shock and sorrow. A death like this happened in the infirmary — not on the ward floor for everyone to witness.

I kept the flashlight with me as I walked to my room. Mother had fallen asleep in her camisole and seemed calm enough now. Given how thin she was, I was amazed at the effort it had taken Grace and me to fit her into the straightjacket a few hours ago. But it was for her safety — though I didn't know when I had come to this conclusion.

Why did safety have to come with pain and fear?

Even behind my door I could still hear Rosina crying. How could I possibly sleep with the sorrowful serenade?

I lay corpse-flat on my bed like Carmen would in her casket, but instead of clutching a bunch of flowers in my cold hands, I held a small piece of light. The flashlight moved up and down with my breathing. I flicked it on and then off. On and off. I liked the control, even though the light temporarily blinded me every time it was on.

The ward now was filled with cries, wails, and groans. And the envelope called my name.

I distracted myself for a little while, almost convincing myself to wait another day to read it. I was so tired — but mostly I was afraid.

I turned over and pulled the envelope out from where I'd finally stowed it between the bed frame and the thin mattress. I sat up. I touched every part of the envelope. Then, finally, I carefully peeled back the flap, realizing it had been opened at least once before but so long ago that it had resealed.

There was one sheet of paper inside. I tucked the flashlight under my chin and pulled the paper out. It was folded in two places and appeared to be an official document.

I unfolded it.

Across the top read *Death Certificate.*

Death?

I looked at the name of the person listed as dead.

Female Baby Friedrich.

With the date of my birth.

This was my death certificate.

I, nameless me, was dead.

1941
Waking Up Dead

When I woke the next morning the sun looked different. Mother looked different. The stench down the hall smelled different. Nothing was the same anymore. Knowing that my life had been blotted out of existence broke the small sliver of hope for survival that I'd hidden away in my heart. Every breath I'd breathed was a lie according to that certificate. The greatest of all realities I now lived in was that because of my death, there really was no hope for anyone to come for me.

It made my desire to escape greater and my motivation to plan it impossible. I wanted to hide away and took up my old habit of retreating nightly to the Juliet balcony. Grace's poor behavior kept getting her sent back to solitary, and every time she came out, she looked less like herself. She wasn't lucid long enough to talk about anything significant. I was afraid for her —

afraid for us both. Our only reprieve from the ward was peeling potatoes in the damp basement and scrubbing sheets in the laundry room.

I didn't see Joann often anymore either, but I'd seen Dr. Woburn more in the last few weeks than I had in months. Things in the ward were changing. New therapies I'd never heard of were being tried. Convulsive therapy using injections was now almost entirely replaced with the ever-growing electroconvulsive therapy. Almost every patient had been administered this new treatment.

Mother continued her sessions, but it did not improve her lucidity. It only made her more compliant. I did not believe anything would bring her back to herself. I didn't believe anyone thought there was a therapy that would. But it was clear she'd become an experiment. The shock therapy did seem to make her physically stronger after days of sleeping it off, which made her desire to wander greater. So instead of sitting or lying around for many hours in the day, now she would walk laps in the dayroom in agitation. Like she was trying to find a way out. Like she wanted to climb the walls and seep through the cracks.

In this we were the same.

The rate of sterilizing patients had increased. One of Grace's roommates, Geraldine, cried through her recovery. Her husband had given permission for the surgery, making the twenty-five-year-old woman unable to ever bear children. She was told that the melancholy she'd experienced because of pregnancy and delivery was reason enough to never give birth again. But the forced sterilization had made her little more than a shell of a woman, and her previous melancholy was only a glimpse of what she experienced now. She said she'd never be well again. But no one listened to women like her, and she was forced into shock therapy for the mental wound the hospital itself had inflicted.

I squatted low in my small balcony. The constant rain we'd been receiving had let up, but the cool air around me was still damp. The fresh scent wooed me. With my head back and my eyes closed, I let the call of a cardinal and the high-pitched squeal of a warbler serenade me from a nearby tree. What freedom birds enjoyed.

I held tightly the local paper I'd swiped from Joann's bag earlier and hidden my death certificate inside. Having a newspaper would not get me into trouble. Most of the newspapers around the ward were decades old. A patient from my childhood, Ethel

Block, used to read the same several newspapers from 1914 every day because it kept her calm. Was she still alive?

I wasn't.

We had begun to hear of the possibility of war, and we were losing staff at a speed no one anticipated. Aunt Eddie and Nurse Wilma were transferred to other wards. The entire hospital was over capacity — the highest number of patients in the hospital's history with only half the staff. A nurse or aide was charged with the care of over a hundred patients now. Joann was working harder than I'd thought possible. All available camisoles were being used, and some women were restrained for days until a nurse had time to come around again. And while I was busy on the floor helping the staff, I was only allowed to take direction, even if I saw a patient left unattended.

After a distant roll of thunder and a tear of lightning, the rain started again. The bright light reminded me of how with multiple lightning strikes there was sometimes a circle of safety in the center. I'd read once about how a man and his horses were all struck, but the wagon's passenger was not.

Was I that passenger in these moments? Was I being spared?

Louder than the thunder was Rosina's screaming, which squeezed through the cracked open window of the balcony. I ran in from the balcony and rushed toward the yelling. Lorna was pulling Rosina out of her room by her hair. I looked around, and there was no aide or nurse to be seen.

"Grace," I yelled. "I need help."

Then I remembered she was in solitary. I cursed under my breath.

I grabbed Lorna around the back to trap her arms tightly to her body. She wasn't very strong, nor was Rosina, and she let go quickly. Lorna continued to scream and fight, but she wouldn't be able to best me.

"Lorna," I said, "calm down or I'll have to put you in a camisole."

The voice was mine, but the words felt like Joann's or any other nurse's.

"Calm before the storm. Calm before the storm," she repeated a few times and then tried to bite me, but she couldn't get close at her angle.

"Rosina, please, just go to your room and close your door. Push a bed against it. I don't know why she's after you."

"She said I was the devil." Rosina looked confused. "I don't know what happened."

"Speak of the devil. Calm before the storm." Lorna tried to wrench from my grasp and kept repeating the two phrases.

Joann came in and exchanged Lorna for Grace in the solitary room. For the first time in my life I wished for a dozen more solitary rooms. Or maybe just one for me. The dayroom echoed with the groaning of restrained patients. Lorna was still screaming. Rosina's crying could be heard through her door. Grace's dead expression, however, was the loudest in my ears. She stood statue still where Joann had left her. I put her to bed.

Joann and I worked together for the next hour to get everyone else to bed. Then I went with her to the first floor and worked with patients I didn't know. The new night nurse arrived and was more drill sergeant than caregiver. Hours later Joann and I were in the stairwell. We slid down to the floor and leaned against the second-floor stairwell door. The coolness went through my thin gown, and it felt good. Rain cascaded down the outside of a nearby window and gave me a chill. But I was next to Joann, and for a few minutes it felt like old times.

But then I thought about my death certificate. I didn't know who was responsible for it, but because of the conversation I'd heard when I was sixteen about the secrets she had, I guessed she would at least know about it. Why was I considered dead?

"I shouldn't be sitting here. I have well over a hundred patients, and I haven't seen half of them today." She shook her head, and tears began to trace down her cheeks. "Which means that a dozen of them are still in hydrotherapy and have been since yesterday. And my shift ended hours ago. Oh, Brighton, I'm doing nothing more than the custodial care aides provide because there's little time to do anything else."

She wiped the ready tears from her eyes with her sleeve. Sweat lined her hairline. She looked over at me.

"This isn't what I ever wanted for my patients. This isn't what I wanted in being a nurse. The neglect isn't intentional. This neglect —"

She paused and then went on to talk about the war on the horizon. I couldn't follow so much of what she said, but knew the places she mentioned: England, Germany, Poland, Russia. I knew those countries from the globe she had taught me with. What had happened to that globe?

She broke down then, weeping so deeply she had a hard time catching her breath.

I took her hand like I used to when I was a child. It used to make us both feel better. Would it now? The questions about my death certificate sat impatiently on the other side of my tongue. I needed to know more. I opened my mouth.

"Can I tell you something?" Joann said before I could speak. She let go of my hand and put her arm around me and pulled me close to her soft chest.

In a moment I became my ten-year-old self again. She still smelled the same — of some perfume mixed with the sweat of work. It was the scent of the woman who had acted as mother to me.

"Hm?"

"Sid — Dr. Woburn and I —" She paused. "We're married."

I turned in her hold and looked into her eyes. Married? Had I heard her correctly? "Truly?"

She licked her finger and made a cross sign over her heart. "Till death do us part."

She looked down at her left hand and rubbed her fourth finger. She held it up and wiggled her fingers.

"I never wear my wedding band here." She released what I could only interpret as a happy sigh. But her nervousness surfaced when she chewed on her lower lip.

"How long?"

"Last year. A bright, sunny Sunday afternoon — April 14."

"A year now."

She nodded. I knew why she hadn't told me. She knew it would scare me to think she'd quit working. But she was still here.

Silence settled as I wrestled with this confession.

"I'm going to have a baby, Brighton," she said and put a hand on her abdomen. She smiled, and her eyes again filled with tears. These tears looked clear and crystalline instead of like thunderclouds. "I'm going to have a baby."

I didn't know what to think or say. I looked down at her belly. I'd never known anyone who was pregnant. I'd only heard about how babies grew inside a woman's belly and how her stomach got larger every month until the baby was born. I'd seen diagrams in our science books, but I'd never seen it in a real person. I couldn't stop from putting my hand on her abdomen too. It just seemed like a regular belly.

"A baby is really in there?" I asked, feeling something inside myself that I'd never felt before. What was it? In the almost eighteen years I'd lived in the asylum, I'd seen a lot of people die, but I'd never seen anyone born. Would I ever even see this baby?

What this really meant was that I would

not see Joann anymore. She would quit at the hospital, ceasing our relationship, or our escape would be successful. Either way, our days together were numbered. For us, it was not like a marriage with the sacred words of *till death do us part.*

She would be leaving me, even though she said she never would. Or maybe I would be leaving her.

I pulled myself from her warm hold, suddenly feeling alone and cold.

She didn't let me get far, though, and put her hand over mine, and our hands were warm for a while. "It's early still. We haven't even told our parents."

I'd never considered Joann having parents. But of course she did. This child would have grandparents and maybe aunts and uncles. Maybe sisters and brothers or both someday. Joann would be the real mother to this baby, not just a stand-in. I was losing her.

Suddenly I realized this baby was Angel's cousin.

I pulled away from her hold. She didn't seem to notice, and her hands laced on her abdomen.

"What are your parents like?"

Her eyes shone like the springtime dew. She already loved this unborn baby. And she loved the baby more than she loved me, and while I knew that was a good thing, it hurt deeply.

"They're going to be dizzy with excitement that I'm finally giving them a grandchild. It has been a constant argument for years — first to get married and then to have a baby." She inhaled deeply, and her sigh came out in words. "They don't know — well, why it's taken me so long."

She went on to talk about her nieces and nephews and why this baby would be the star of them all. She talked about how she hoped for a girl and liked names like Rebecca or Suzannah but that Dr. Woburn wanted to name a daughter after a famous woman of science like Marie Curie or Elizabeth Blackwell.

But my mind remained on what Joann had said earlier — that her life choices had been an argument with her parents for years. That was because of me. They didn't know why she'd said no to that boyfriend long ago or Dr. Woburn for years, because they didn't know about me. I was her secret — the girl who died on her birthday but was still alive eighteen years later.

"You'll be leaving, then," I interrupted her.

Should I tell her I was leaving too? With Angel and Grace? Of course I wouldn't. I wouldn't let myself wonder if it would ever happen. Joann's mouth froze, open midword. She held her breath. A few long moments later she looked at me and pressed her lips together. "Yes."

"When?"

"Soon. Nursing colleges have graduation in May. We are hoping to hire some then."

"That's next month."

Silence like dust floated in the air.

"One more thing," she whispered. "I saw Grace's name on the list."

I looked over at her. Did I even have to ask?

"She's going to be sterilized soon. Her father has already approved it."

Later this conversation rolled and spun in my mind as I lay sleepless in my bed. I thought about how Joann was having a baby and she'd be leaving the hospital. About Grace's fate. And would we ever leave here? The little protection I had would be stripped away, and I might even be subjected to the therapies and treatments that other patients went through. A new nurse would come in, and I would be considered just another patient claiming to be sane. None of the secrets I thought mattered would matter anymore; I would just sound like another lunatic.

Grace was already suffering, and the worst

was yet to come. Angel was being worked worse than an employee, because he was just a patient, after all.

An idea had come to me on how to get out. Maybe it was crazy to try, but I believed now that it was crazier not to.

If we couldn't find a way out, this life would be my second death. It was time to at least try.

1941
Lightning

I woke to learning that Grace was in solitary again. So I would have to wait until she was released. I tried to act normal during our sparse meals and hid a slice of bread and a few boiled potatoes — we'd need to take any food we could pull together. I didn't know how or where we'd get food once we were out. Angel wasn't anywhere to be seen, and I had no way of getting a message to him. He slept in the tool shed now, and I believed if Grace and I could get out there, we could quickly find the tools to free us.

When Grace was released the following morning, I said nothing to her about my plans, but I did tell her she had to behave. I was her shadow until bedtime so she wouldn't lose her temper and get thrown back into solitary. With so little supervision now, I was able to hang around the stairwell door. The new aide with his strange shaven upper lip and dark beard framing his jaw was too new to notice me catch the door behind him when he rushed away from the floor. He didn't see me stuff a piece of newspaper into the doorjamb space so that the latch could not catch. Things were changing in the ward and supervision was low. If we could get through this locked door, we had a chance.

I knew I wouldn't be able to sleep in the hours before we'd make our escape. Not just because of the plan with the door, requiring me to be alert — but because these might be the last hours I'd ever have with Mother.

I sat cross-legged a foot from her bed through the night and watched her. I didn't have to memorize her face. I'd already done that every day for as long as I could remember. The spray of lines at the edges of her blue eyes. Her thin, dried lips. The patchy, dusky, gray-blond hair that curtained her ashen skin. This was my mother.

But I knew that someday when someone asked me, "What was your mother like?" I would tell them that my mother had golden-blond hair, and I would describe how it would flow behind her when we ran through our huge flower garden, chasing butterflies. I'd say that she loved hide-and-seek and liked to eat cake more than anything else, even though she wasn't much for kitchen work. Mother's laugh was the sound of silver dewdrops, and she cried in the beautiful way that made other women envious. That was really who Mother was. I knew that was what she would've been like if she'd had the chance.

I believed she loved me. Because I believed this, I knew our escape was what she would want for me. I knew I needed to do this. I needed to leave Mother behind.

It seemed odd to me that in a few hours — the quietest time of the night — I would walk away from this place in the hope that I'd never see it again. I was so ready to leave. Leave the old Brighton, the unknown girl, dead at birth — for the bright unknown.

Mother's camisole lay over her bed rail. After a few days of wearing it, I was glad an aide I'd never seen before had come around frantically removing camisoles and relieving women in the hydrotherapy.

Now her breathing was even, and her arms and legs had lost their stiffness. She seemed peaceful.

Long gone was the safe and secure existence of the hall I'd been raised in. Joann had made my room and hall into some type of counterfeit world — a wonderland in comparison to the way the other patients lived. Isolated just enough but with lawns, friends, and a doting nurse-mother.

Everything was different now. It wasn't surprising to go more than a day without food. Patients were left in wet packs with drying sheets tightening around them or in hydrotherapy baths or restraints for days. I couldn't do this for the rest of my life, and I wouldn't subject Grace to it either. But what did it mean that I would leave these people for the outside world instead of staying and trying to help? Who would hear their cries? Wasn't I bound to remain and help since I knew there would be no rescue?

And how would I survive in the real world? I could sew. I could peel potatoes. I could garden. I could read. Were those ways I could take care of myself? I didn't even know my father's name. Grace knew about the world and had said we could become our own family and maybe make it out to San Francisco and find Jonah. I was sure Angel would want to find his mother, and I felt the same way about my father. These were three different directions — all our needs could separate us more than we already were.

I got out of bed, and before I did anything I checked the hall. It was empty and dark. I ran across and down a little to see if the door was still unlocked. If someone had caught on to my scheme, my entire plan would be foiled. I checked, and the door hadn't latched. This plan never would've worked in the days when we had someone on the ward every hour, so the understaffing was to our benefit. Now I could only hope that the door on the first floor would be abandoned. Thankfully, with the coming war, only a few night guards remained.

I returned to the room I shared with my mother and stripped off my pillowcase to use as a bag. I put the few photographs I had, my death certificate, the bread I'd wrapped in a piece of cloth I'd torn from the corner of my sheet, the camera, and the hidden half-dozen film cartridges inside. I pulled my blanket into a sling around my back and shoulder. It had been rainy and cold this spring, and we might need it.

I wished I had socks or shoes, but what I was wearing would have to do. It didn't take long to gather everything I could take. My breath was held hostage in my lungs when I looked at Mother. It was time to say goodbye. I wanted to touch her. To give her one more hug. I put my hand on her arm — it was the best I could do. It was so thin and bony. Her skin was rough. She seemed entirely hollow, but I knew better — she was trapped inside herself. She wasn't just a shell; she was still somewhere inside.

I'd touched her for too long, making her stir. She turned over with fire in her eyes. The slap she sent across my face was so unexpected I gasped loudly. The second one came even harder. I put a palm to my face, and my eyes stung from the pain that came from every space inside of me. I wasn't prepared to feel such rejection. All the words I'd wanted to say to her would have to be left unspoken. I had meant to tell her how I would miss her humming and that I loved her — but especially that I was going to find someone to help her and the other women on the ward. Someone to be a rescuer and savior.

And then she turned away and faced the wall and curled up with her knees to her chest and quietly hummed. Her sudden calmness after such an outburst was unsettling. Maybe Grace was right and she really didn't know me. But I knew her, didn't I? I knew how to calm her and how to feed her.

I took a step toward the door. I needed to wake Grace. When I looked back at my mother, one last look, her humming turned into groaning.

I should stay. I can't stay.

I exhaled all of my doubt and ran quickly to Grace's room. She woke with confusion and turbulence, but after a minute I calmed her and put her beloved letters in my pillowcase and pulled her blanket into a similar sling and fitted it around my friend. She just watched me do everything without a word. She had four roommates; two were dead asleep and two were away, either in some drawn-out therapy or solitary, I didn't know. The room was crowded but quiet for these precious minutes.

We scurried back down the abandoned hall toward the door I had rigged. I wouldn't say goodbye to Lorna or Rosina or anyone else. I didn't have the dark courage it took to rest my eyes on the incomprehensible misery and still walk away. I knew them in ways I'd never known Mother, and in the morning they'd recognize my absence in a way Mother could never express.

They would understand — of course — but would they feel I'd abandoned them? What would they think about how I'd taken Grace with me but asked none of them to come too? When I lightly shut the stairwell door behind me and led Grace down the stairs, I let my second-floor thoughts go. Let them wander away with the women I'd loved enough to call family. I wanted to rescue them all, but I couldn't begin to do that if I didn't rescue myself first.

I carefully unlatched the back door's internal locking mechanisms, knowing that once we let it latch behind us, we would not be able to return inside. We would be entirely shut out. But as soon as I knew we were safe in the cover of darkness and I saw no security, I let it click shut and then we ran to the groundskeeper's shed where Angel slept in Mason's old space. The old groundskeeper Angel had assisted had passed half a year ago. Angel now did the job of two.

I tried the door, but it was locked. I knocked lightly but heard no rustle inside. After a few slightly louder knocks, Angel opened the door. He stood with bleary eyes, but without explanation he pulled me inside the shed and into his arms. I wrapped my arms around him and recognized how bony and sharp he had become. My own thinness against his magnified our desperate situation and hunger. Grace stood outside the door until we together pulled her in and closed the door behind her. She was only half aware of what was happening and cried off and on and said almost nothing intelligible. I knew I'd waited too long to do this and that she might never regain herself.

Without a word, like he read my mind, Angel understood it was time. And as though he'd been preparing for our escape, he was already wearing a coat and grabbed two more near the entrance.

"I found these two in the trash barrels over the last few weeks. I think they were from incoming patients." He gave one to each of us.

I spoke quietly to Angel about needing something to cut the fence. Something strong. He showed us through to the back of the small shed and into a room filled with tools. They littered shelves, every wall space, and a large portion of the floor.

"Mason wasn't much for cleanliness. I've been weeding through these when I can — but time just . . . Well, we mainly just use grass mowers and shovels, you know." Of course, for the dead. "I did put these aside after we found the fence, thinking they might work. They're hedge clippers."

He produced a tool that looked like a large pair of shears only a giant could use. He looked so tired, and I grew angry at how hard he was worked. Why hadn't I noticed before now how frail he'd become and that he was even more colorless than normal?

"You're dying, Angel." I choked on my words.

His hollow-eyed gaze lingered over my face, and such sadness was sewn into his skin.

"We're all dying," he finally responded. "Come on, help me find an ax."

It took us at least twenty minutes to find an ax, and while Grace turned circles in the corner, I also found a hammer, another pair of hedge clippers, and wire cutters that didn't look like they'd be able to cut through the fence but seemed worth bringing just in case. We'd each found old boots crusted with ancient mud. Almost too stiff to be wearable, but we decided it would be better than going barefoot.

Then it was time to go. Angel moved close, so close, and our eyes locked. He snapped up my coat like he was my protector. His arms held mine longer than they needed to in our hurried state. And before he let go completely, his hand went to my face and his touch was so soft. He looked at me with such despair and care all at once that I never wanted to look away.

"If I can't keep up," he said, cupping my cheek, "because of my sight —"

"I'm not leaving you." I gritted my teeth.

"If I can't keep up," he repeated more sternly, "you have to keep going. I'll find another way, another time."

"I'd rather die here with you." I meant it.

His eyes turned to glass but didn't break open.

"Come on," he whispered.

My entire body began to shake, even with the warmth of the stolen coat. Adrenaline. I'd learned that from Joann. My eyes scanned the edge of the hospital lawn and road. On the other side of the road were the large doctors' houses and the nurses' apartments. Joann was in there somewhere. With her husband. With a baby growing under her heart. She wasn't thinking about me right now, so why was I thinking about her? That part of my life was over.

We carefully stepped out of the shed. Storm clouds had moved in. Only an occasional star could be seen and I imagined the little Crux — that cross constellation. Why did crosses carry the weight of promise and hope? Rosina would have crossed herself if she'd been with us. I nearly did myself, but Angel gently taking my hand brought me back to what we were doing.

We were standing in the darkness outside the circle of the electric light that cascaded from the lamp on the side of the little shed. Our eyes connected. As long as I could be with him, I knew I could leave this place. We were two pieces of a whole, he and I, and we had been ever since we'd met.

"Here we go," he said, and suddenly I was afraid those would be the last words I'd ever hear him speak to me.

I pushed that thought away and nodded my head. We'd already wasted a lot of time. The sky lit up, and a loud crack ran across the sky. A moment later another bolt of lightning ricocheted, and the surge of energy startled the ground around us. The long, outstretched fingers of the trees in the horizon flashed, then disappeared.

Suddenly awakened, Grace began running toward the back fence. Angel's grip tightened on my hand and we followed.

1990
The Memory of Wind and Birds

How many years has it been since I was in the town of Milton? Since that fateful day when I escaped? And even then, I hadn't gone through the city or ever knew the town my hospital-home had been in. As I come into town, I don't take time to take it in but drive straight to the old hospital grounds.

When I was a girl I'd heard that the town was twenty minutes away, but the community has grown, so the town is closer now. A lot has changed, and Riverside Home for the Insane became known as Milton State Hospital before its doors closed. Of course we don't say words like *insane* or *mad* in the progressive 1990s. We say *mentally ill. Mad* means something different now too. Words are veils and masks, and there's always something more on the other side of them than we want to believe.

Some tried to rectify the messed-up laws and inhumane treatment of people in those bygone asylums days. Some people think it's just a myth that fathers and husbands put women away for not being happy and content enough. But I know the truth. Why anyone would think something akin to a prison sentence would bring back happiness and sanity, I will never understand. It is strange to think that people felt better turning those deemed flawed invisible. That putting them out of sight was what was important. I'm sure there were those who had good intentions and believed the doctors were only trying to help, with a copy of the Hippocratic oath on the wall in every office. No, many families weren't to blame. Naivety and ignorance aren't sins, after all. But I'm not sure the hurt they caused is entirely forgivable.

From my infancy to now, an irritable sixty-something, much has changed with mental-health treatments. But it didn't change my experience or the lives of all those women. Just because society finally realized some of the wrongs that had been done doesn't mean that our stories have been told. The wrongs can't be righted, but remembering and knowing are important. Without remembrance, there is often repetition.

As I drive out of town, I notice a small

subdivision and a strip mall with a gas station, a sandwich shop, and one of those new coffee places where people spend three dollars for a cup of something they can make at home. That's what I find crazy — and I don't use that word lightly.

A ball's throw away stands the main asylum building. My lungs and soul gather together like a straightjacket has been tightened around me. I can't breathe. I pull over and get out of the car. I put my hands on my knees. Lines from an old mantra travel through my mind, but I push them away. It has been well over a decade since my last attack and I'm ashamed of myself. Shouldn't I be strong enough now? I'm not even going inside today, but Kelly Keene has promised she'd make it happen another day.

When I'm breathing normally again, I stare at the administration building. I didn't spend any time inside that place, but it is the iconic face of Riverside. It's Willow Knob's placid facade that was my reality for eighteen years and invaded my nightmares for the rest.

I return to my car and drive the remaining distance. Many of the buildings have been torn down or have collapsed over the years. I wonder if the graveyard is still out there. I hope it is. The gravestones are probably all sunk and swallowed into the earth and planted like seeds. Lonesome seeds made of sand, rock, water, but mostly loss.

I lose my very balance the moment I set eyes on Willow Knob. It takes my breath away, but not the way a new baby or a sunset does. My heartbeat changes to the pulse of courage. Am I really here? On the outside of the walls and fences? I almost turn around and return home.

I haven't seen these buildings since I left when I was just a girl. I park along the side of the road and take my camera from the bag on my passenger seat. It hangs around my neck, and as I walk, it taps against my middle in a rhythm that comforts me. The camera itself has become a veil of detachment for me. Giving me space. I am, after all, Nell Friedrich, photographer. Most of that identity has been as a teacher at a local art center, but I've also had the chance to travel with Doc and I have looked into the souls of many, holding this black box between us so that they can't get a glimpse into mine.

I stand where the main drive used to be. The pavement is broken up, and what's left has grayed in the sun. The iron fences left are imposing and ugly. One side of the front gate is connected at the bottom hinge but is otherwise lying on the ground at an awkward angle. The other I can't see anywhere. Long yellow-green grasses are blowing in the constant June breeze, reminding me of a warm, romantic westerly wind from some pioneer romance film. But this isn't a romance.

I don't walk up yet but glare at the Willow Knob building. It doesn't flinch at my presence. It's close enough to be gawked at from the road, but far away enough for the guts and souls inside to be invisible.

Broken. Busted up. Burned. But there stands the building of my childhood. During my years here I thought about all the places outside the walls. And when I was free, I thought about the one place that was tattooed on my heart. This place was a force. A living being in my memories — and to think that my nightmarish childhood was littered with giggles, friendships, and a settling in of dreams. The modern woman might find these dreams of marriage and family too commonplace. They're wrong. Especially when such dreams require a freedom that is out of reach.

The willow tree is still in the front, swaying in the wind like nothing else matters. I pull my camera up to my eye, and I take a picture from the distance and capture its stance against the sun's glow. The idea of capturing the building that captured me puts a smile on my face.

After a dozen frames I walk hesitantly toward it. Even though I told Ms. Keene I want to go inside, right now I don't even want to go near it. There are so many ghosts calling for my attention. But after a few deep breaths, I greet them — they aren't nightmares; they are memories and people I knew. I take pictures and I remember them. My heart softens, and I get the sense they are welcoming me. They know I want to honor them and not forget them.

What will happen to these forgotten souls when the buildings are gone and in their places are recreational fields and office buildings? Will the pain of all the people who lived and died here be lost? Changing landscape doesn't change memories or pain. That isn't the way human souls work. The passing away of buildings doesn't change the past. Memories are immortal and unchangeable.

My finger is snapping so fast that I run through my first roll of twenty-four in minutes. Every frame is filled with exhumed recollections. I reload and go around the back and find the door that we'd always run in and out of in those early days. Our giggles — Angel's and mine — are spread thick through the air. I hear them. And Joann yelling for us not to run to the graveyard. The very same door we'd snuck out of one stormy night. The night everything changed for us.

My gaze roams to that back corner where the graveyard should be. I almost think I will find my former self there.

But I can't go there today.

I take pictures of the brick exterior and the bars on the windows. The word *haunted* is graffiti-painted on one of the walls alongside a scary face that reminds me of a mask from a tasteless horror flick. I walk around to my second-floor bedroom window and take more photographs. I was born and raised on the other side of those broken panes.

I turn to see the children's ward. Only half remains.

The wind and birds sing in chorus together, their voices welcoming me home. They know me. They recognize me. They remember me. They know why I am here, and there's some comfort in that.

I look back up to my old window. Is someone still there? Is it a ghost or the scrap pieces of the soul of the lost girl I used to be? Everyone who used to be here was lost in one way or another. If they didn't start out lost when they got here, they became lost before they left — alive or dead. I sometimes still feel that way. It takes gumption to live, you know, and all the grit you can muster, though there were times in the earlier days I nearly gave up.

The hush of the wind over the grasses lulls me back to myself. I make a loop around to the front of the home — the building. The asylum. It never should have the word *home* attached to it, but it does.

I walk slowly now, knowing that the Juliet balcony is up to my left. I can only see it in my periphery. Can I look at it? I had avoided looking directly at it when I walked up. Like a shield, I put my viewfinder to my eye and turn toward it, but I can't snap the photo. My soul aches. My chest is tight, and every heartbeat hurts. I can't pull my hands down, and through my lens I see things. Things I don't want to see. I see a girl up there. Sitting. Hiding. Wishing. Hurting. And then other faces — skin around souls — stand behind her. They all look at me.

I need to get out of here.

I have snapped four rolls of film. I am doing all I can. I am facing it, and there is good in that.

But when I finally pull the camera from my eye, I can't catch my breath. My feet work better than my lungs, and I turn and run.

I want to be okay with this. I want to feel that if I never gaze on these buildings again I will be all right. Oh, the lies we tell ourselves.

My car is close. I run, feeling the shapes of many behind me pressing against me. When I climb into the car, I don't even take my camera from around my neck or put on my seat belt. I turn the key, make a U-turn with a spray of gravel behind me, and leave. I am crying and shaking, and I put as much distance between me and that building as fast as I can.

I don't look back.

Not this time.

1941
Gone

Before we arrived at the tree line, the rain started, making it hard to see what was ahead of us. When I tripped in the blackness over M. Porter's grave and cut my leg, a cussword wrestled itself out of my mouth and I nearly hurt myself worse with the ax I was holding.

Angel caught himself before he fell, then helped me up, and we continued to run. Angel and I were two parts of one whole. He needed my eyes, and I needed his presence. We were no good without the other.

Our running slowed down because of my cut leg, but every time the lightning flashed we could see the way a little better. The more we ran, the more my fear swelled. We hadn't even left the property yet and my courage was already failing.

I stopped running and Angel bumped into me from behind.

"Brighton," he yelled. "What's wrong?"

I looked back and could see lights on in several buildings. I couldn't tell which was which anymore. There were so many now on the nearly one thousand acres. So many more than when I was a little girl. Did that mean there were so many more mad people now? It was rare that anyone left, but people kept coming. They wouldn't miss the three of us, would they? Why would anyone care that we'd left? There would be three fewer mouths to feed, three fewer to care for, three fewer to burden the State.

And what about Mother? I dropped Angel's hand from my own.

Suddenly I was spun around to face away from the buildings. Grace's grip was tight on my arm even through the bulk of the coat. Her face was rain-drenched like mine, her hair soaked and flopping down around her ears and forehead. She had the expression of a wild animal, and her chest heaved up and down as she breathed rapidly.

"Come on," she yelled over the storm. "We have to go now."

"I'm scared," I finally admitted as the pelting drops slowed some and the black sky turned to navy. We were already soaked, but if we escaped now, by midmorning these captured raindrops would have evaporated into the air of freedom. I played that possibility over and over in my head. What would it be like to be on the other side of those fences? To not be a patient. To be free. Could we even survive? How long would my mother survive? Long enough for me to rescue her or find someone who could? Or would she be just another body unclaimed and buried? *H. Friedrich.*

"She'd want you to run — to leave," Grace said like she knew my thoughts.

I looked at her, still catching my breath. My hand went to my chest, and I doubled over, releasing what I didn't know I carried in my stomach, the burden of this decision now on the drenched grass.

Mother would want me to leave. I straightened my back and my breathing slowed and I met the eyes of my two best friends and nodded.

I grabbed Angel's hand and again we ran. It was hard to get through the brush and thornbushes but thankfully we had the oversize boots to keep our feet unscathed and we reached the fence faster than the first time.

"Come on, come on," Grace said, hurrying Angel to get out the tools. Angel tried the hedge clippers first, but the wire wouldn't cut. Grace tried. I tried. But we weren't getting anywhere.

"It's not working," Grace said and threw the broken tool into the grass. She pushed Angel's shoulder. "It's not going to get us through this fence."

"Stop it," I yelled. "It's not his fault."

I grabbed the ax and raised it high to swing. The first wallop I gave the fence vibrated my entire body and stung me through. The ax bounded back toward me, and the wooden handle banged against my shoulder with such force I cried out. I took a few deep breaths then tried again, but nothing we were doing even damaged the fence. The ax hitting metal rattled my bones, and my shoulder ached. Because Angel kept hitting it, so did I. But after minutes of this, we still had not done any damage to the fence.

Grace bent over and leaned her hands against her knees, crying. Her crying was raw and deep. I wanted to cry like that, but instead I felt numb. Maybe from the vibration of the ax; maybe because our escape was failing.

We moved down the fence in both directions to see if there were any breaks, but none could be found. We also tried to dig beneath the fence, but with all the roots it was impossible.

Exhausted from effort and breathing heavily, I leaned against the fence. A faint glow had grown and the neighborhood of madhouses almost looked pretty. The misty air hung like cobwebs around us. The beauty in this spring dawn was an insult.

Spring.

"What's the date?" A new panic rose in me.

It was only a beat before it dawned on Angel where my mind had just landed.

"Your birthday," he said, his voice rough and exhausted.

He grabbed me and we ran, leaving Grace alone. I lost a boot before I got out of the wooded and brushy land. I didn't know if Grace was behind me or not, but I had to go. My mother would be in the middle of her fit, and if I wasn't there, no one knew what to do. Who knew if a nurse would even be around? Joann wouldn't be there yet — unless her memory had served her where mine hadn't.

We ran until we had to stop and catch our breath, but when my eyes caught sight again of Willow Knob, I started again. I let the other shoe fall off and ran faster in my bare feet. The ground was soft and didn't hurt. Angel was still right behind me.

"What time is it?"

"Maybe around five?"

Cars pulled into the parking lot far off on the right with arriving employees while the nurses and aides, who lived on the property, walked toward the buildings. They were going to see us, and then we would be in trouble. I ran faster.

Of course the back door was locked. I couldn't get in.

"Open up," I yelled and pounded my fists on the door. "Open the door."

The door flew open, and Joann stood there looking like a used piece of fabric.

"Where have you been? Do you have any idea the trouble you're in?" Her hair was pinned in curls, and her face was pale and unmade. She was wearing a regular dress and a cardigan sweater. Why was she here? Like that? Her eyes were puffy and red rimmed. "And you, Angel, how could you let this happen?"

"I was — We —" I couldn't tell her that I'd been running away.

"You were running away." Joann grabbed my arm and gave Angel a side glance as she let us both in.

"But what about Grace?" I asked.

"You have other things to worry about." Joann shut the door behind us.

"I won't leave her to take the blame for this. It was my plan."

"Neither will I." Angel's voice broke. Was he upset because our escape hadn't worked or because he knew what it meant that I wasn't with my mother? Had she started her phantom labor pains as she did every birthday? I looked up the stairs waiting to hear her wild screams and shrieks.

Angel gripped my hand, and when I looked up at him we both heard Grace's screams. She was being dragged by a security guard and an aide. Grace's stolen coat was nowhere to be seen and her legs were soiled and bloody. Were mine too? I didn't look to see.

"You both know better." Joann was frantic. "This will change everything."

"Just let me go to my room," I said, trying to push past her. "I need to get to Mother."

She blocked me, but I kept pushing.

"Stop, Brighton," she said and then repeated herself two more times, so firmly that I finally stopped.

"What?"

I watched her as she lowered her eyes and shook her head. "By the time I got here it was too late. It was too late."

"Too late for what?"

"For me to help her." She took the pillowcase bag from me.

I looked at her and then at Angel. His eyes

grew wide. Mine mirrored his.

"What are you saying?" Angel spoke what I thought.

"Your mother." She looked at me. "She's gone."

"Gone?"

"A nurse found her at the bottom of the stairs. Somehow she'd gotten into the stairwell. The door wasn't latched and —"

"Gone?" My hand went to my neck.

"I'm so sorry, Brighton." Joann pulled me into a hug.

It had been my fault. I'd rigged the latch to escape all the heartache and pain and melancholy. She'd gotten her own escape now. I was still here.

I had killed my mother.

I pulled away from Joann, and somehow she let me and I ran up the murderous stairs and barreled through the second-floor hall.

"Mother," I called over and over. I ran into our room and stopped at the door-frame.

Joann had followed me. "The aide put her here until the morgue could come."

She was so small lying there. Joann had covered her with a white sheet. So still. She didn't need the camisole that was draped over her bedpost. She didn't need an insulin injection that was always at the ready in every nurse's apron. She didn't need anything anymore. She didn't need me anymore. My mother was dead, and it was all my fault.

1941
Metamorphosis

My breath was held captive in my lungs as I stood in front of my mother, my dead mother, when I heard Grace screaming in the stairwell. Joann went down to calm her. Shouldn't I be the one screaming? Wasn't I the one who had just lost my mother and was responsible for it? Grace began calling my name over and over. I heard her being dragged away somewhere downstairs and toward what I knew to be the shock therapy room. Also my fault now.

A minute later a few men in white uniforms came to my room. They pushed past me without giving me a second glance and one started to wrap the white sheet tightly around my mother. The other placed a stretcher next to her bed.

They were going to carry her to the morgue.

They were going to take Mother away.

Without warning, I flew at them. I yelled

at them to stop and pulled their jackets, their hair, scratched them with my jagged, ragged fingernails.

"You can't take her. She's my mother." The grief-filled words were like the scrape of a dayroom chair against the old linoleum, and my throat grew raw.

"Hold her while I get the body." His voice was in a shade of panic I understood. But I didn't stop fighting and kicked him between the legs, and he bent over in pain. Then the other grabbed me and pulled my arms back, leaving me vulnerable to a solid punch in my middle.

"You will unhand her." Joann marched in. The man took his arms off of me. I doubled over and fell to the floor, but from the corner of my eye a flash of white crossed the room and tackled the aide who had hit me. Angel.

The blur of chaos continued until Joann whistled and everyone stopped what they were doing. Except for me. I was still on the floor holding my stomach and coughing. The two aides righted themselves. One had a bloody nose from the tussle and both were staring at Angel with clenched fists. Angel's hair was mussed and his shirt had been yanked out of shape, but he was fine otherwise. His gaze was on me, and it was like nothing else was in the room.

He saw what I saw.

He knew what I was thinking.

He knew it was my fault. His face broke into a thousand pieces.

I was ashamed for him to look at me. So I looked away.

He moved toward me and wrapped his body around mine, like a cocoon, like we used to when we pretended to play butterfly the year we learned about metamorphosis. How I longed to change from my caterpillar state and be a butterfly that could fly away. But every time I left Angel's cocoon, I was still the same Brighton.

Our tears mixed, and we watched as Mother was wrapped in a white sheet. Her rest had begun from this life, and I knew now I would never rest.

Before the men could leave with her body, patients began to come. Our friends. Our family. They all entered with such sacred quietness but for a few *hmms* and sniffs. Then Joyful came in. She was crying big, round tears that trailed down her dark cheeks. Her thick hands rested on my back and head, and they felt like heavy blankets that covered me. Her full voice sang a song about a river and prayer. I loved the comfort in the heavy melody.

Rosina left her room for the first time in weeks and walked in, quietly saying the Lord's Prayer. My mouth moved with hers. She cried between her holy Spanish words.

Patients I'd known my whole life and some who were new came. They walked the path as one. In through the door, up to Mother's bed — some of them lightly touching her sheathed body — then turning toward my bed and walking a circle around Angel and me as we sat in the middle of the floor. They were paying respects. They were mourning and grieving with me. With sad eyes they traced from Mother's body to my face. Some of them said they were sorry and some just looked at me as blankly as Mother used to, their sympathies blocked inside themselves. The sheer number of them and their concern brought me comfort.

And the two aides who were supposed to take my mother just stood staring. They did nothing to stop this funeral march and the sorrowful, moaning dirge. The only one my mother would ever have.

My back grew straighter and Angel's wrap around me loosened, but he remained close.

"Everyone's been dreading this day," Aunt Eddie said to Joann. When had she arrived? "We all knew it would happen eventually. How much longer could that poor woman

— and our sweet girl —"

Joann sniffed and nodded.

"What's going to happen to her now?" Aunt Eddie wrapped her arms around her ample frame.

Joann flinched at the question, and her eyes flickered to me and then back to the bed.

"She's in trouble, Eddie. She tried to make a run for it. Angel and Grace too."

"It ain't right and you know it." Aunt Eddie's tears rushed as her voice grew passionate. "That she's here. All three of them."

Joann clenched her jaw, but her eyes remained trained on Mother's body.

"She doesn't belong here. She never did. Poor dear hasn't got a soul to care for her."

"I don't know what to do." Joann spoke with thick, pasty words. "Sid will watch out for her, but —"

"That's all you have to say? The little girl you raised could be sterilized before the year's out, and that's all you have to say — that your husband will watch out for her?" She guffawed. "Maybe I should've been her stand-in mother instead. Criminal or not, her father would take better care of her than you."

"Don't." The word squeezed between gridlocked teeth.

"You don't scare me no more, Jo," Eddie said. "Besides, you have a foot out the door. You ain't my boss neither. I've kept quiet for all these years so I could get the safe jobs and good shifts — for my family's sake — but not no more."

Then she looked down at me, her nostrils flared.

"Attempted escape will guarantee you'll be given treatments. Angel too. Anyone who attempts something that crazy — well, they should expect that." Then she turned back to Joann. "You should've let her father take her."

I stood.

"Take me?" I asked Eddie.

"He was nothing but a convict," Joann snorted. "It wasn't possible."

"I looked in my file and Mother's," I said, accusingly. "I found my death certificate."

"What? How long have —" Joann put her face in her hands. "I never wanted you to know —"

"That was wrong and I didn't agree." Eddie eyed Joann. "Joann has his address in a secret file in the records office."

"Don't even try to find it, Brighton," Joann scolded, raising her head. "You're in enough trouble already."

Eddie took a step toward me with a quivering mouth and eyes drowning in their small pools of tears. "I'm so sorry, dear."

She hugged me, then gave Joann one last stern look before she left the room.

"This wasn't the way things were supposed to go," Joann whimpered.

Then she was gone. Eddie was gone. Mother was gone.

1941
A Long, Dreamless Moment

Without warning, two more white-coated men I'd never seen before came in. One grabbed Angel with rough hands. He struggled in their grasp, but it was useless.

"Stop," I yelled.

I beat the man on the back until the second man's arms clamped around me. The aide's fingers interlaced together like a concrete statue.

Joann rushed back. "You will be gentle as you put them in solitary."

"But I have a job," Angel growled at Joann. The anger he had toward her was remarkable considering how he'd always been so forgiving.

"This one is going to Orchard Row, not solitary, Nurse," the larger aide said.

"On whose orders?" Joann choked.

"Dr. Wolff, by way of Dr. Woburn."

Joann turned pure white. Whiter than Angel. Whiter than their uniforms. She stepped back, filling the doorway with her small frame.

"Bright — Angel — I'm so sorry. I can't — I don't," she stuttered and shook her head back and forth.

"Don't let them." A feral surge rushed through me.

Joann opened her mouth, but the words inside were never spoken as the aide pushed past her with Angel.

"The girl is scheduled for treatment downstairs before solitary," the aide said.

With an animalistic yell Angel pulled out of the aide's arms and lunged for me. Before he reached me the aide beat his back and he was on the floor in the next moment. Blood poured from his face.

I screamed. Joann was mute. And all we could do was watch as Angel was pulled through the stairwell door without much effort. His blood smeared on his clothes and the floor. I kept yelling for him. I kept struggling. I wouldn't quit.

"Joann, you have to get him out," I urged. I pulled and ratcheted my body to try to break free, but I couldn't get away.

Joann swallowed and then came to herself.

"You will put her in solitary. I'm the managing nurse here so you will listen to me. If a doctor asks you, tell him to come to me."

"Dr. Wolff said that if she gives me any trouble, she goes straight to ECT."

Joann pulled out a shot from her dress pocket and after a sting on my thigh I heard, "There, now she won't give you trouble."

The insulin rushed through me. I could feel it. My legs began to weaken and it was harder and harder to keep my hands fisted.

"Don't fight it, dear girl," Joann whispered closely. "Forgive me."

Then she turned and went down the steps where Mother had just fallen to her death.

My head was so heavy and my mouth felt damp and I couldn't wipe the wetness away. My eyes lost their focus, and even though I could feel my body moving, I could only see blurred images flying in front of me — doors along the hallway and wandering patients. The scent was even more acrid than usual, and I began to vomit.

I couldn't keep up, so I was dragged. Once inside, I was put on the cot and strapped down with all four limbs splayed out. And then everything went dark.

I didn't know how long I'd been out, but it seemed like only a moment. A weighty, dreamless moment. Like several pages of a book were turned at once. It seemed like a new me woke. Like the one who'd fallen asleep wasn't real anymore. Like she had died.

Someone had loosened my restraints, but I'd worn them long enough to have a steady ache in my wrists and ankles. I looked up to see only blackness pour through the broken window. The room spun and my head was pounding and my whole body felt snapped like a rubber band. Dried vomit covered my gown and the rancid scent filled me.

Someone was humming loudly. Mother?

No.

A wave of reality reminded me that she was gone. Was she buried already as *H. Friedrich* — forgotten before she was known?

The humming was coming from across the hall. It would stop for minutes at a time and then resume. I recognized the tune as one Grace used to sing in the early weeks of her arrival. It was a simple melody with words about dreams coming true, and I remember she said it was sung by someone named Ella. That was all I knew. I squeezed my eyes together, wishing she would share the words. Maybe they'd be of some comfort.

Could anything comfort us right now?

My whole body hurt when I pushed myself up to stand. The wound on my leg from our escape had been dressed. My shoulder ached from the ax. I limped to the door and looked through the square hole. I put my mouth to it and whispered her name. The humming stopped briefly, then began again. I called to her a few more times, a little louder.

She quieted again, and there was a shuffling.

"Hannah, is that you?" she returned.

She thought I was her sister.

"Grace, it's me, Brighton."

Grace rushed to the door and put her mouth against the small square hole.

"Be quiet, Hannah." The whisper came like her throat was filled with gravel and fear. "Jonah is coming soon. I left the back door unlocked for him. Don't tell Daddy." She disappeared from sight, and I heard the rattle of her doorknob.

"Grace, I'm not —"

"Hannah." She was angry now. "Why did you lock the door? Did Daddy put you up to this?"

She rattled and pounded on the door and yelled for Hannah to unlock it.

"Grace, quiet," I whispered loudly. "You're going to get into trouble again. Listen to me."

She couldn't hear me. Through the window I could see her bouncing around in wild, erratic movements. It went on for several minutes, then stopped and she was quiet.

"Grace," I said in a loud whisper.

"Brighton?" She looked through the little window.

"Yes." I was relieved. "It's me, Brighton. You have to stop fighting everyone. I think Eddie might —"

"Brighton, guess what?" she said. "Hannah was just here and Jonah is on his way. I left the back door unlocked so he can get in."

"Grace, no," I said, but she didn't hear me. She went through the cycle again with the confusion of the locked door. And when she couldn't unlock it, she went back to scolding her sister.

Grace was lost.

I put my back against the door and slid down to the floor. I didn't remember falling asleep there, but the next thing I knew the door was creaking and pushing me. The person on the other side grunted and I scurried out of the way. My vision was like looking through gauze, but I could see a soft orange light coming through the window high in the wall. I turned to see the blurry figure and round shape of Aunt Eddie.

"Eddie?"

"Oh, Brighty, you're awake." Eddie leaned forward and with little effort pulled me to my feet and walked me to the cot.

"How long have I been in here?" I sat down.

"About eighteen hours, dear." She sat on the cot next to me. "Joann told me what she done. With the injection."

I looked away. It wasn't that I'd forgotten, but the details were only hanging around in the corners, making it easier to ignore. But now the facts had gained traction in my mind. Our failed escape. Mother's death. Angel taken to Orchard Row. Any reserve hope I'd stored for so many years had vanished.

"She done it because they were going to take you to shock therapy if you didn't calm down."

What was I supposed to say to that?

"She been here for hours with you, when her shift finished," Eddie continued. "She was hoping you'd wake. Dr. Woburn made her go home finally." The older nurse shrugged. "You know, ain't good for the baby."

Yes. The baby. Being here wasn't good for her baby.

"Is Angel —" I started.

"Orchard Row."

Grief struck me and I moaned, my body falling slack, crying. I'd lost everyone.

1941
There Is No Grace

I was alone for the rest of the day. The grief over Mother was like the dust and dirt on the walls. It covered everything. There was no way to get away from it. The realization that the hope of escape was nearly gone was in everything else. It was heaviness in the iron cot frame. The way I couldn't see the moon. The way the cot smelled of urine and vomit that weren't mine.

And then there was Angel. The purest soul I knew. Would I see him again in this life? How much longer could we survive? And what about Grace?

Rosina's prayers came to mind. I repeated some of those words as I sat in the corner. I'd cried all my tears. I was too tired to sleep. And the cliff of hopelessness was so close. But for the light that cascaded in from the broken window, all seemed lost. In that small ribbon of warmth and light there was something I couldn't place. I couldn't see how it might all happen — but in film light banished darkness. Could that happen in life? Was my sliver of hope enough?

Approaching steps caught my attention, and I got up from the floor and peeked through the door window. The backs of men entered my view.

"Hey, what are you doing?" I yelled. They ignored me.

They proceeded to open Grace's door, and as though she'd anticipated it, she flew at them. My square window only gave me flashes of aides battling her barred teeth and claw-like hands. She was so small and so out of her mind it didn't take much to best her. I yelled her name. I didn't know if I should tell her to keep fighting or to stop. Both seemed right. The aide kicked my door and told me to shut up, but I didn't.

"Just you wait," he said to me.

Grace's cries as she was dragged away could have peeled paint from the walls. Her door was left open and the emptiness that stood before me filled my soul.

Where was Joann? She said she'd never leave me. She said she wouldn't forget me. Eddie said she'd been here while I slept, but I hadn't seen her. I'd been given food once, dried bread and water. Whoever dropped it off didn't even show their face but slid in the tray and rushed off. The racket in the ward was louder than I thought was common and I heard talk of a stomach influenza. That always caused deaths. Who would we lose this time? I kept my ears out for Lorna's clichés and Rosina's prayers, but heard neither.

I went between watching out my door window for signs of Grace to looking out the window in the wall. At the close of the second day I was greeted by fog and dampness and eventually fell into a fitful sleep, believing my fate was sealed to spend another night in the smallness of these four walls.

The solitary door opened and slammed against the wall behind it. The same aides from before had come for me. One walked in with his arms out toward me as if bracing for an attack. I jumped up from the floor and backed into a corner and analyzed whether it was possible to get past them. Could I grab the keys that jingled on the waist of the smaller one? At the first grip on my arm something arose out of me that brought such understanding of all the women I'd loved over the years; my resisting was savage and natural.

A desperation to fight for my life took over. My muscles contracted painfully against their greater weight and strength. One finally grabbed me around the back, pinning my arms down, and the other held me around my ankles and lifted me.

I bucked and reared and bloodied the nose of the man at my feet. The dayroom was empty as I passed through in their grasp, and they had to reposition me when we got to the stairwell door. We were so close now to the room of my birth, my childhood, my memories, my mother — my whole life.

"Mother." My neck muscles strained, and all the lumps and sighs and stones of guilt I'd swallowed down for the last eighteen years rose up out of me. I was bathed in tears.

The aides' hold on me was unrelenting, and once we were on the first floor and I recognized which room they were taking me to, I started weeping. Not the gnashing I'd just done in a whirlwind and fit of grief, but the kind of sadness that made me only as strong as the bread dough Joyful let me touch once. I was soft and could be molded and separated into a thousand pieces. I now understood the giving-up so many had done who had gone before me.

1941
I Never Knew You

A familiar and once-despised voice told the aides to put me on the table. All I could see was the floor and the feet walking on it.

"She's going to fight," one said. "She's a tough one too."

"Leave her on the table," he demanded.

They did as they were asked, roughly laying me on my stomach on the table before complaining about their pay.

As soon as their hands were off of me, I flipped over and saw the door slam and the back of Dr. Woburn standing near a table with medical instruments on it I'd never seen before. I guessed this was the electroconvulsive therapy room.

He turned around, and the scar across his forehead had never looked so prominent. He held a clipboard in front of him, but his gaze fell upon me only briefly and then went past me. A click sounded from behind me. A door. My sight snapped over, and Joann frantically moved in beside me. Her eyes were round, and her hair was not pulled back behind her nurse's cap but instead fell around her shoulders. I didn't know that it was so long. She wasn't wearing her white uniform, and I could feel her nubby sweater against my arm. She was wiping my face with delicate hands and saying over and again to forgive her. The despair in her voice scared me.

"What's happening?" Was she going to help her husband shock my brain? Was that why she was pleading for forgiveness?

"Joann — time." Dr. Woburn raised an eyebrow.

"Right." She looked at him, then back at me, and forced me up to a sitting position and started to unsnap my gown.

"What's going on?" I asked, looking back and forth between the two while trying to keep my gown on. Was this how electroshock was done?

"Go, Sid." He was gone in a moment, furthering my confusion.

Joann won the battle of my gown, and it was off me. She had a bag on the floor next to her, and she frantically stuffed the gown inside and pulled out a tan-colored blouse and a navy-blue skirt. "I didn't have an extra brassiere, but put this camisole on first and see if that will help."

"Help what?" I said, and in my own fear I became frightened enough to put on what she called a camisole quickly. This one wasn't a straightjacket.

"Your breasts, Brighton. You have them, as small as they are, and it's vulgar not to wear a brassiere." She gestured for me to move quickly, and when I was ready she threw the blouse around my shoulders and pushed my arms through the sleeves. It was a fine shirt. Nicer than anything I'd ever worn, and for a moment I smoothed my hands down from my chest to my waist. "Promise me you'll get one as soon as you're able."

"Get what?"

"Get a brassiere."

I was like a doll in her arms and was pulled to standing. She had me change my underpants, then she put the skirt down by my feet and gestured for me to step in. When I did, she pulled the skirt up to my waist in a blink. I had a waist. It was shocking to see. And it was small.

"What's happening?" I nearly slapped Joann to get her attention.

Her hands stopped buttoning at my waist and moved to my face. Gently she held my cheeks and looked into my eyes. I was her little girl again.

"You are leaving tonight, my love." A tear streaked down her face, and she didn't move to wipe it away, so I did it for her. "I should have done this years ago."

She was helping me escape? Tears I didn't know I had left poured and wetted my cheeks. There was hope in that sliver of light.

"It's not going to be easy, Brighton, but you'll have to trust us." She was so firm that I expected her tears to dry, but instead more came. She took off her sweater and put it around me.

"We'll be fired if they figure it out," she said without looking at me. "But it doesn't matter because we're leaving — Sid and me."

"Leaving?"

She nodded. "Florida. Can you believe it?"

While I shook my head in disbelief, tears streamed down her cheeks. She grabbed her bag and pulled me to the door.

"To start fresh." She peeked into the hallway before leading me out.

"What about Angel — and Grace?" I grabbed roughly at Joann's arm and she winced.

"I'll explain everything once we get out."

"No." The passion to exert that small word

made me feel woozy and my knees buckled. She caught me and held me up for a long moment, looking around us. When I nodded I was okay, she kept us moving toward the door — the very same one I'd snuck out of with Grace only a few days ago. "Please, tell me."

"Sid is working on getting Angel." She slowly turned the knob to keep it quiet. I knew the trick too.

"And Grace?"

"We can't help her now."

"What does that mean? I promised her." I pulled away from her. I didn't want to leave the building without Grace.

"Promises are minions of love, aren't they? Grace is in the infirmary. Her father was very upset over hearing about her attempted escape and wanted her treatment accelerated. She might be transferred."

I was the reason for all of this. What would they do to her?

"Take me to her," I begged too loudly.

Joann pushed me against the wall and put her hand over my mouth.

"Quiet, you." She spoke so quietly I barely heard her.

I nodded, and she let go of my mouth. "Listen to me. You cannot help Grace. You're going to leave this place and settle somewhere. Then you can write to Eddie — but use a different name on the envelope. She will get it to Grace. Do you hear me?"

I nodded without a word. This was really happening. My heart began to beat too quickly and my eyes blurred with tears. We were so close now, for the second time, but what if it didn't work again?

"Come on." She pulled me outside and quietly closed the door behind us.

"How long have you planned this?"

"Listen, you need to walk normally. Like we're just off-duty nurses." She handed me her purse and she held the bag with my gown.

I nodded but still looked up toward the second floor. The windows were dark, but I could almost see the forms of the ghosts that reached out their arms to hold me close. I looked away and walked on. It was harder than I'd expected. Harder than I wanted it to be.

"My things." My steps stuttered. "My pillowcase."

Joann shook her head and kept me moving forward. "Sorry, love, it's in the attic."

I looked back, and Joann whipped me around to face forward. My things. I'd never see my things again. I wouldn't fulfill the promise I'd made to show the world what was being done to us. All the care I'd taken to hide the film cartridges, and now they were gone.

"But my mother's photo. My film."

"Forget about them. I have a bag in the car. There are other photos of your mother inside, ones you've never seen. Some of her things. They'll have to do."

As we rushed down the sidewalk, Mother's ghost seemed close, pushing me. Telling me to go.

The purple in the sky silhouetted several buildings, and I knew which one was Orchard Row. Joann directed me to look ahead. We stopped next to a car. Joann opened the door and told me to get in the back. She climbed into the front seat — but not behind the wheel. Would Dr. Woburn and Angel come soon? Would they come at all?

Joann and I didn't speak — maybe we didn't even breathe. Until Joann scooted toward the wheel. She gripped it.

"Sid said to only give him twenty minutes." Her grasp was so strong her knuckles whitened.

"Give them longer." My throat was tight with words. I leaned forward on the edge of the cold seat and pressed my hand against the window.

Then I saw movement from the other end of the parking lot. Two men with white coats. They were moving fast in our direction, but they were not close enough yet for me to see their faces.

"It's them," Joann said and moved away from the wheel. I got out and ran to Angel. Holding him was like holding my own heart, so heavy in my arms. Real and beating. He winced.

"Are you okay?" I checked him over as he moved us both toward the car.

We were back inside, and Dr. Woburn started the engine. Angel and I looked at one another and held each other's hands, but as we pulled out of the parking space I looked back. Was this finally happening?

I exhaled a long breath — had I been holding it for years? That exhale pushed out all the sorrow and disappointment and death that were locked away in those walls. It was rotten and dingy air that I thought I'd never be rid of. Though I didn't know who I was without it.

Angel squeezed my hands, and I searched his steady and strong eyes.

"Grace?" he asked.

I shook my head.

The row of houses that I'd learned long ago were for the staff didn't have even one window lit. The dark and sleepy houses were my first glimpse of real homes. Real families lived in them. There were lamps on long poles along the side of the street, but the lights looked more like ghosts. I couldn't put into words how these moments felt. There was such a mixture of grief and anticipation that I couldn't parse. Angel and I ducked as we passed through the iron gates with a night guard. With a wave of Dr. Woburn's hand, we were permitted to exit.

"Where are we going?" Angel finally asked, sitting up.

"The train station," Joann said after several long moments of silence.

"Are you coming with us?" I asked.

Dr. Woburn shook his head. Joann whispered, "No."

"But we don't know how to live out there — out here." I sat on the edge of the seat. "You're sending us away so quickly?"

"It's the best we can do," Dr. Woburn said.

"It wouldn't be safe, love," she said to me. "Sid purchased tickets. You'll leave in a few hours, so you'll have to stay on the platform until you hear the conductor call your train number."

"That doesn't mean anything to us," Angel shot back. "None of that makes sense. What's a platform, and what do we do if someone speaks to us? What if we're hungry? We might have been the more capable ones in the hospital, but out here we aren't. We'll need help."

Instead of answering, she handed us both sandwiches wrapped in wax paper. We grabbed them quickly. Joann told us to take care to eat only a little because neither of us had eaten much in days. My stomach roiled after half a dozen bites so I stopped. Angel didn't. He ate the whole thing like a wild animal consuming downed prey.

"I know, Angel," Joann finally answered. "And I'm sorry that we won't be able to help more. We'll try to explain everything. I've packed more food in a bag. And there's money in there too. There should be enough."

"Enough for what?" I asked. What did that mean?

Joann began to talk in detail about train stations, platforms, how to use money, and what to expect once we got to a city called Pittsburgh. It sounded like another language to me. All I could focus on was the sound of the tires against the road and the whistle of wind coming from the car somewhere. I closed my eyes to it.

"There's an address in your bag." She bobbed her head toward me. "You'll be going to see a man named Ezra Raab."

"Ezra Raab?" Angel repeated.

There was a full beat of silence before she answered. "Ezra Raab is Brighton's father."

I looked at her with eyes that seemed to stretch my skin.

"But how — You said —"

"I know I should've told you more." She shook her head. "He came once."

"For me? When?"

"Listen, he's a convicted criminal. I was not going to hand a one-year-old over to him."

"I was one? What did you tell him?" I asked, but as soon as I did, I knew. "The death certificate."

"I couldn't —" Joann shook her head and bit her lower lip.

"What did he do?"

"He's not dangerous, but — what would he have done with a baby?"

I opened my mouth to respond, but she spoke before I could. "It doesn't much matter if you're angry about it. I did what I thought was best, and we can't go back."

The rough-hewn silence in the car was like a leather strap that tightened around me.

"He wrote," Joann finally said. "Every few years — asking after your mother."

"And?" I looked from her and Dr. Woburn, who was clenching his jaw, to Angel.

"I wrote him back, telling him of her poor condition." She looked straight ahead. "He wanted to know about her."

"But he thinks I'm dead."

"She did what she could." Dr. Woburn's voice burst forth. "She went around to more than a handful of homes for children — orphans, foundlings — and spent weeks looking for a safe place for you."

"What?" I asked.

"Sid, it doesn't matter now." Joann patted her husband.

"Yes, it does, Jo. I won't have her thinking that you didn't try. That you didn't do everything you could for her." Dr. Woburn went on. "Every place she found was dirty or dangerous. The children were always sickly and malnourished. She knew she could do better than those places. And she also put me off for most of that same time."

I scooted back and took my hand from Angel's and put it in my lap.

"No one wanted to adopt a child from a lunatic mother," he added. "Don't think she didn't try that too."

"That's enough, Sid," Joann scolded. "Brighton, it doesn't matter now. I know you've suffered greatly."

"And why now?" I finally asked. "Why couldn't I have gone to my father years ago?"

"After he was released from jail he worked far away. Somewhere out west. And only recently, in the last few years, moved to Pittsburgh. Everything's in your bag. There may also be an aunt."

The car felt like it was moving so fast now. Like we were heading far too quickly into the future.

"An aunt? My mother had a sister?"

She nodded.

"The picture. The hand on Mother's shoulder?"

She nodded again.

"Why didn't you say anything to me?"

"I didn't know much. Just that your father once mentioned her and said she was very ill. I never heard anything more."

An *ill* aunt. Ill like Mother?

"Can I find my mother?" Angel asked, breaking the silence.

"Your father won't ever allow that," Dr. Woburn said, wringing his grip on the wheel. "Take my word for it — walk away from all of this and start fresh."

"Oh, Angel, please listen to Sid about not contacting your family."

Dr. Woburn eyed Joann and cleared his

I couldn't keep them connected, and I looked away, off into the glare of the electric lights. I realized the conversation I was overhearing was one they'd likely had for years. The contradiction of everything we were in the midst of was alive and growing. Freedom was right. But I didn't know how to be free and I had no one to teach me.

"I won't let anything happen to her, Joann." Angel spoke. He took my hand. "I love her, you know. And I'll never let anyone hurt her."

He loved me? Did he mean like a sister?

"I'll never leave you," he told me. "I do love you. You know that, don't you?"

I took him in. His eyes shone more blue right now than red. I nodded. I guess I'd always known we loved each other. His grip on my hand tightened, and I suddenly felt we were going on some grand adventure that I didn't have to be afraid of as long as we were together.

"Come now." Dr. Woburn's voice drew me away from Angel. He leaned in and whispered to Joann. I wondered if it was about their baby or that he was grateful this whole mess was soon over or about Florida. I didn't know what he said, but she nodded her head and he helped her up and out of the car.

Angel reached back into the car and got out the two bags Joann had packed for us. I took mine from him, then we followed Joann and Dr. Woburn into the train station. It wasn't an overly large building, but it was so unfamiliar. Picture books and newspapers really didn't prepare me. It was a red-orange brick color, and there were electric lights guiding us in. Dr. Woburn pointed at a sign and showed us a map and where we were going. A city called Pittsburgh.

The place where we would start our new life. With a man whose only memory of me was my death certificate.

Dr. Woburn cleared his throat and took charge.

"Your train leaves in the morning at nine twenty-seven. A man will call for you to board for Pittsburgh, and he'll stamp your ticket when you're on the train and —" He paused and continued after a deep breath. "You'll have to watch what the others do around you. That's how many of us learn anyway. Do what they do. Understand?"

Angel nodded. I didn't.

"Suppose Ezra Raab wants nothing to do with me — with us?"

Joann inhaled deeply and eyed her husband before looking back at me. "I believe he will at least be willing to help you," she said. "But whatever you do — don't come back here. Milton isn't a large city — Angel is too recognizable."

"And you'll be gone?" How could it be possible that these were our last minutes together? That we would say goodbye for our whole lives?

"We —" She couldn't finish her thought and broke down. Dr. Woburn took a step forward, but she held a hand out to stop him. She sniffed and wiped her eyes before wrapping her arms around herself. This tightened her blouse, and the smallest of roundness boasted evidence of the baby growing within her.

"Maybe I'll be lucky enough to have a little girl like you," she said when she saw me looking.

Dr. Woburn showed us where to sit and where the toilets were and reminded us to keep to ourselves. We had food and money in Angel's bag. He explained about cars called taxicabs and how one could take us right to Ezra Raab's home if we showed the driver the address. He showed Angel how to count money.

Then Dr. Woburn extended his hand to Angel, and after a few beats Angel offered his in return. It struck me that I'd never seen this gesture offered to Angel — and I knew it was the beginning of our goodbye. After the lengthy handshake Dr. Woburn nodded at me, eyed Joann, then stepped toward the parking lot and waited for his wife.

Standing in the train station, its tall roof above us, on a sidewalk open to the tracks, nothing felt familiar except for the hovering sky. At least that didn't change.

After years of so much noise, the silence around the three of us was jarring. None of us knew what to do. Then Joann took a step toward Angel. He put down his suitcase, and they embraced. Angel was more than a head taller than her now. He was wearing denim pants and a button-up shirt and a coat. He had a gray cap on his head. Nicer than the stocking cap he wore sometimes when it was cold. This one had a bill that buttoned in the front in a wooly fabric.

They released one another but held each other's gaze. Angel wiped a tear away and cleared his throat.

"Goodbye, Joann," he said, and it sounded so final.

"Goodbye, my boy," she said as a tear escaped down her pale cheek. Then she turned to me. Angel instinctively took the bag from my hand and stepped back toward the bench where Dr. Woburn had told us to wait.

"I can't say goodbye to you." Until I said those words, I didn't know what I would say. But the words fell from my mouth like they'd been sitting there for all time. Perhaps the truest words I'd spoken, but a truth I had to let go of.

We were near each other's height now, though she was still a mite taller than me. She closed in the space between us and smoothed my hair and tucked the strands behind my ears. She took a handkerchief from her skirt pocket and wiped my tears. She smiled through her own.

"You were a perfect baby — *my* perfect baby. You looked right into my eyes the morning you were born."

I nodded and untangled the words in my throat. "I'm so sorry I've been so angry with you." All the anger I'd been carrying had fallen away somewhere; I didn't know where or when, but it was gone. I loved her.

"Don't." She put a finger to my lips like a mother would, then smiled as she tapped my nose. "Know that you're my first daughter, and I will tell this baby all about their big sister, Brighton."

Then she released a heavy sigh.

"Remember when you were a little girl

and we read *Pollyanna,* and you asked me a question? Do you remember?"

My throat was camisoled, and words were fixed tightly in the small crevices inside. I only nodded, but Joann waited until I could answer.

"I asked if I had an aunt like Polly or a grandmother like in *The Princess and the Goblin.*" Was I still that eight-year-old and this was just a dream within a dream?

Joann nodded.

"Maybe you do have an Aunt Polly, Brighton-girl."

My brow wrinkled up and my toes wiggled in my shoes.

"But you said you don't know if she's alive. Or anything about her."

"I don't. But I believe there's an Aunt Polly out there waiting for you. It might be your father or maybe this long-lost sister of your mother. But it might be someone neither of us knows but that God has already put in place for you — and Angel. Look for her. Look for the ones with the kind faces like Pollyanna, Wendy, Sarah, Anne, and so many more."

"But those are just children — just little girls. What could they do to help?"

"Little girls grow up and become women." Joann's eyes glassed over and she gripped my hands. "Find them, Brighton, and they will help you. You still have a chance. All this heartache. All these poor decisions. Blame me for all of it. But don't let any of that anger keep you from living a full life."

Her voice got fierce and ragged and old. "You are strong. The strongest person I know. You need to be brave. You need to want this new life."

We held one another and cried. My throat was swollen with hurt and thankfulness. I'd loved the mother who had given birth to me — I always would — but Joann had mothered me. She'd kept me safe and in many ways thought of my life ahead of her own. She'd made some poor choices, but had also given up so much of her life for me. That was what a mother did. She was my mother in so many ways that mattered.

"Will we really never see one another again?" I asked.

She held me close and my head rested against her chest, so near to her heart.

"I don't think so, love."

"What will you say if they ask you — about me?" I wondered aloud.

"I'll say I never knew you." Her ghostlike words created cobwebs in the corners of the train station. "Besides, you're registered as dead."

I pulled away from her and looked at her deeply in her eyes. We lost ourselves in one another's gazes, and I thought maybe we'd stand like this forever.

"I love you." She held me so tightly my heart slowed down. I felt calmer in her arms.

"I love you, Mother." I'd never called her that before, but nothing had ever felt more right than saying that now. Her gasping cry echoed in my ears. Was she in physical pain like I was? My heart hurt.

Then without warning she pulled back and looked me in the eyes.

"You're free now, my bright girl," were the last words she spoke to me before she turned and walked away. She didn't look back.

1990
Questions Without Answers

I need to wash myself. Wash the dirt and sweat that are clinging to me from that place. The place that has too quickly become familiar again. All the ghosts. The voices. The fear.

I don't want to remember it.

I don't want to do this project with this woman. I don't want to be the person I am. I don't want to be Nell or Brighton or Doc's wife.

I want to be a plain, old regular human walking on planet Earth who doesn't have anything special about me.

The phone is ringing when I rush into my hotel room. Doc and Kelly Keene are the only ones who know where I am. But I can't talk to anyone right now. If it's Doc, I'll call him back later. When I am ready to talk about it. Will I ever be? The ringing phone starts to sound like those birds again — the birds from the asylum property calling me by name. The sound reminds me of who I am and how they heard my first cry, my first giggle, my first fit of anger, all of my firsts. And how I am responsible for Mother's death. Did they hear her falling? Would they answer the questions I'd had my whole life? Did she cry for help? Did she hum her song? Did she say my name?

I press my eyelids tightly together upon my twisted wonderings.

I am cold. I am shivering. I rush to the bathroom and pull off all my clothes, and like my son when he was young I let them fall on the floor. I turn on the shower and sit on the floor of the bath. The water comes out so cold it takes me back, so far back that it feels like yesterday. I reach up and turn the knob. After another ten or fifteen seconds the warmth coats me. I lean against the back wall and let it run over me. The pressured water feels like needles, anesthetizing me. My eyes are still closed, which means I can see everything from those years. If I can only open them I will return to this hotel room — this life, *Nell,* the person I am now — and let go of that other hurting girl I used to be.

Breathe. Breathe. Slowly. Deeply. All things bright.

I do what the voice from deep within me

tells me to do. But gasp when I realize the voice isn't my own. It isn't Doc's either. It is Nursey.

When was the last time I'd called her that?

I cry and I sit there for a long time. In short intervals the phone rings again — a dozen rings and then silence. After five or ten minutes it rings again.

I get ahold of myself, but it might've been thirty minutes or two hours. I don't know. I haven't felt this sort of attack in a long time. But it has brought something out of me that couldn't wash down the drain, so it still covers me like an invisible shroud.

I dry myself, get dressed, and comb my soaked hair.

I startle when a series of knocks sounds at my door. Then someone saying "hello" a few times. Impatient people do that sort of thing.

"I'm coming, I'm coming," I say.

I open the door to find a small, dark-haired young woman with busy curls. She has big eyes and a round face, like she hasn't lost her baby fat yet. And maybe she hasn't — she is young — younger than my own children.

"Let me guess — Kelly Keene?" I meant to hide the irritation in my voice, but the day has been long and my reserves are low.

"I called a few times," she says gently with a shrug and a nervous giggle that I can't hate her for. "But no one picked up."

"Yes." I cleared my throat. "I was in the shower."

Then we share an awkward pause, and every coherent word has flown from my mind.

"Do you want to go downstairs to the restaurant to talk, or do you want to stay in here?"

I am glad she broke the silence.

I turn around and look. There's really nowhere to sit, so downstairs it is. But it is the last thing I want to do now that the cloak of exhaustion has settled in. All my contracted muscles and nerves have released now and taken all my energy. But we only have a few days together, so it must be done.

Or I can leave and pretend Kelly Keene doesn't exist.

But I know what it's like not to exist. I wouldn't wish that on anybody.

The girl — she doesn't seem to be much more than that — is polite enough to wait downstairs at a table for me while I dry my hair. It's pin straight and quick to dry. In less than twenty minutes we are sitting in a corner booth at the hotel restaurant. The shadow of my panic attack hovers near me.

"About my film." The practice of formalities never caught on. This always perturbs Doc's colleagues.

Kelly doesn't look surprised and hands me a bag like she's proud to have fulfilled a promise. She will never know that the weight of the bag is heavier than just an old camera and a handful of cartridges. I can't look in the bag now or I fear I will have another attack. There's not a whole lot left inside of myself today. I rub my fingertips against the dirty pillowcase. This had been mine. I can't get used to the idea but keep my hands on it.

"Are you going to look inside?" She sounds hopeful.

"Not now." I force a smile. "How did you find me?" I ask without warning. Another question I'm not going to pretend isn't important.

Kelly finishes her sip of coffee and gives a sheepish smile.

"There were letters along with the film in that pillowcase," she says. "Finding this felt like treasure among all the old files. Our job was to look through every item."

"And you connected Nell Friedrich and Brighton Friedrich?" I knew I should've changed my last name, but it was all I had left of my mother, so Doc, as a psychologist, never pushed me.

There's that cute little shrug again.

"Grace's sister's letters mentioned you. And your letters to Grace after your release were put inside also."

That would've been Aunt Eddie's doing.

"I didn't have to make the connection when it was all there." She pauses, then in double speed she says, "I read the letters."

"You read my letters?" Should I be insulted or grateful?

"I did. All of this was before I really understood what I was dealing with. Not just old dusty files but people — real people." Then she touches my hand. "I could tell you really loved your friend Grace."

I move my hand away.

Grace. After I'd escaped I had written those letters with such hope and hadn't known anywhere to send them but Riverside. But I never heard from her again.

"So when you understood that patients were actually human, you stopped being a snoop?" I wish I could raise an eyebrow, but I've never mastered that — but I do smile a little. I can't help but like the girl.

"Not at all." She smiles in return. "I felt it was my duty to find any owners of these items or who they should go to all these decades later."

She is right about that. And just like that we talk like old friends or maybe a niece and aunt.

"So tell me about all the cataloging," I say.

"Two other graduate students and I were assigned for a summer to catalog everything that was left behind because the community center project was in the works. All the archived files, suitcases, clothing, so many personal items — most of which was unlabeled, so we don't know who to contact. They'll either stay in a labeled storage box or get tossed. But there were a few things — personal things — that I couldn't overlook."

There is an unexpected pause, and I can see there is something she needs to say.

"What's that you've got on the other side of your tongue, Miss Keene?" There I go again, not being graceful. Graceful? I am Grace-less.

"Grace's file." She breathes in deeply.

"Have you found her too?" I lean toward her.

Then her face does that thing people do when they don't want to talk about something. Her lips purse. Her head tilts. Her eyebrows have that wavy, knit-up look to them. It's bad. I know it. She just shakes her head.

I never learned anything more about Grace since my last glimpse of her. There were several possible scenarios. Sterilization. Transfer. Even a lobotomy. Of course, at the time I didn't understand what a lobotomy really was. I didn't know, along with so many, that it ruins the person. Shatters them. Traps them.

"Her file showed a transfer — but the place she was taken to shut down decades ago. I'm not sure how to find out more." Kelly shakes her head. "I'm sorry. I really wish I had more news for you."

"Did you contact her family? I'm sure they'd want some of these photographs." I rush my words. "She had a sister who loved her."

She shakes her head. "I'm trying. Her parents have passed. I looked there first. It wasn't like finding you. You were easy. Between your letters to her with your new name and the newspaper's ways of finding people who don't want to be found, I had everything I needed."

Without knowing it, I'd led her right to me. Things I'd done so many decades ago out of survival were giving me a chance to bring pieces of my friends back to life. But excavating all of this is doing something to me that I haven't prepared for.

My face feels red. Warm. Full of tears. I shake my head. I will have to digest all of this later, not now. I inhale deeply and wipe a hand down my face.

She pulls an old envelope from the bag at her side. She slides it across the table.

I look at it. I know the handwriting.

"It's from your nurse," she says. "This was also inside the bag of film. She wrote that she hoped all of this would make it back to you someday. And the photographs of you — as a baby." She shakes her head as if in disbelief of what she's seen with her own eyes.

My breath is caught in my throat. I never saw Joann again. Not because I hated her — I loved her — but because there were too many memories. Too many hurts.

"Did you read it too?" My tough voice cuts up my anguish for a moment, giving me a chance to breathe.

"Wouldn't you have?" She smiles sweetly.

I nod and swallow hard.

"You loved this nurse — Joann — very much."

"Yes, we were close." I want to say more. I want to use the word *mother,* but that word is buried so deep inside of me. My own children were never allowed to call me that;

they called me *mom* or *mama* but never *mother.* I brush my hand against the old paper and begin building the courage I'll need to read it later.

"The old photographs of you as a baby have your name, dates, your age, and sometimes even your weight and height. I was hoping it wasn't true or that I was misunderstanding something. All of it seems so crazy."

I can't contain my laughter over her use of the word *crazy,* and it breaks the stunned nature of our conversation and makes a few people turn to look at us. Kelly puts a hand over her mouth.

"Don't." I wave off her embarrassment. "There was a lot of *crazy* that happened." But even in the laughter, nostalgia takes over. "There was also a lot of not crazy in those walls — sadness, loneliness, and misunderstandings."

The pause we share has an almost holiness to it. It reminds me of the moments before you take communion bread in your mouth and chew — the joining of remembrance and thankfulness.

"I'm kind of surprised you're normal, you know? You hear of children who weren't given a normal upbringing and how it ruins their chance at a typical adulthood." She rambles and I stifle a chuckle. "I'm a psychology minor."

"Believe me, Kelly, I'm not normal — and neither are you, for that matter. What's really normal, anyhow?"

She tucks her lips, looking embarrassed. "I'm so sorry. I didn't mean — I keep putting my foot in my mouth."

"It's all right." Then I pat her hand, because that does feel entirely *normal.* It's odd how fluidly we all use that word, and it's equally as odd how indefinable it is.

"So, it's true then? You were born there?"

I carefully open the old envelope and slip out the few photographs inside. In the first I'm sitting, smiling, in a washbasin for a bath and the young, thin arms of Joann hold me steady. Her face isn't in the picture, but I know she's on the other side of the yellowed edge. I also know that my mother was probably somewhere in the room. Oh, how I long to move the frame one way or another to see them. To see their faces. I'm taken so far back. But instead of the terror, what I see is love and hope. What is more hopeful than a baby?

"Photographs only capture a small square of a scene and there's so much a photograph can't contain. My mother and I both had dirty-blond hair. She had blue eyes and long, elegant fingers — like she might've played the piano if she'd had a different life. I will never forget those details. A photograph cannot serenade me with the voice of my mother saying 'Brighton' over and over after she delivered me."

I turn over the image to show her, even though I know she's seen it before. I feel my own eyes twinkle. The memory of Nursey telling me this story as a little girl has always brought me joy. I know now that children love to hear the story of their birth.

I speak slow and steady and share myself in a way I never have before. "It's almost like I remember my birth — though I know it's not possible. But there are people who say that babies have a way of remembering things that happen to them. My husband is a doctor and he's told me as much." My eyes linger over the photograph. "I was at Riverside from birth until I was eighteen, and I rarely repeat or revisit the memories from those years."

"Was leaving what you expected? Freedom how you expected it to be?"

Oh, that word. "Expectations can be dangerous things, and freedom isn't easily defined."

"It's like a fairy tale. It doesn't seem real," Kelly says.

I smile at her. "More like a Grimms' fairy tale. I've looked for answers my whole life. Why I was born to a mother the doctors called mad and why most of my friends were what the good old days called feeble-minded or imbeciles." That sentence is peppered with those fancy air quotes and laughter. Laughter hurts less than anger that might otherwise build up. But it doesn't reduce how I feel about all of the lines we draw between one another.

"So you don't think the patients needed treatments? They were misdiagnosed?" she questions sincerely.

"True mental illness should be treated — but the treatments were barbaric and degrading and often unhelpful. Mishandling of the human mind breaks the spirit in anyone."

"Do you still keep searching for understanding?"

"No, I've just been trying to forget."

"What will happen if you decide to remember?" And she pushes the pillowcase bag filled with images of dark and light closer to me.

1941
Stranger, Stranger

When I was about six years old I found a caterpillar outside. It was dark brown with a little orange stripe along its back. When I first picked it up it curled into a fuzzy circle in my hand. I thought it was dead, and since death wasn't foreign to me but something to be understood, I watched it so closely I nearly went cross-eyed. But it wasn't dead; it was just getting used to me. I petted it gently and eventually it woke up and started to crawl around my hand and up my arm.

I named her Sister, and when it was time to go inside I tucked her in my little curled-up palm and didn't tell anyone. Joyful had once given me a jelly jar for my little found treasures — mostly pretty rocks — so I put Sister inside and hid her in the corner of the room under my bed. After two days Joann found Sister and made me put her back outside.

That afternoon during our outside courtyard time I cried when I pulled Sister out of her jar and set her on the edge of the sidewalk — close to where I'd found her so her family might find her again. As soon as Sister touched the concrete she curled into a circle like she had that first day in my hand. Maybe she was nervous again. Maybe she knew that people walked on the sidewalk and she could easily be stepped on. I didn't know.

Sister never unwound. The next day she was still on the sidewalk like a small fuzzy circle. The day after that she was there. I called to her — "Sister, Sister," I said. But she didn't move. The third day she was uncurled like the letter *C.* I picked her up, but Joann slapped her out of my hand, saying it was gross because it was dead. Until then I didn't know that dead was gross or that staying in the same place without moving meant death. Sister was so afraid to crawl across the sidewalk that she died where I left her. And I cried about her dying because I knew I had caused it by holding her captive.

I thought I'd done the right thing by putting Sister back in the world where she belonged, but all of my keeping and touching had ruined her. She'd been gone from her world for too long.

That morning as we boarded the train with a few other people, I felt like Sister being returned to my rightful world. All I wanted to do was curl up on the sidewalk because I was so afraid. But knowing I had a father and maybe an aunt out there — could this strange new world actually have inside of it a Pollyanna life saved just for me? I tried to consider this and reminded myself of my new freedom even when everything was strange.

Angel took my hand, and we walked on board the train with our small bags. His eyes were wide and open, and he didn't seem to notice that the man with the funny hat stared at him. No one stared at him at the hospital because we'd all grown used to him and the way he looked — his bright, white self. Out here, however, was different.

But Angel moved us forward and I kept breathing. When I had to let go of Angel's hand and follow him down a narrow aisle, I grabbed the back of his coat instead. I was afraid he would disappear if I let him out of my sight or let him get out of reach.

"Here?" He turned and pointed at two seats.

I looked around before nodding my head. I sat next to the window, then Angel sat too and we held our bags on our laps. Then we just had to sit and wait. Under Angel's vigilant gaze and with him holding my hand, I finally let myself fall asleep. I dreamed I was playing with Angel at the graveyard. I was young and innocent. My young self stopped in front of the gravestone marked *H. Friedrich* and it startled me awake.

When I opened my eyes, the recurring wave of grief cascaded over me.

"I want to go back," I said to Angel, and my breathing sped up.

"Don't, Brighton." He was firm but not mean.

I shook my head. "No, not to stay there. But I want to see Mother's gravestone."

Angel squeezed my hand and gave me a small, understanding smile. His smile was always filled with hope. I memorized it, fearing that one day he would also be gone like everyone else I loved. But he did say he loved me and promised not to leave me.

Promises are the minions of love. I heard Joann's words in my mind. I shook them away. Angel would not leave me.

When I wasn't asleep I was taking in everything around me.

There weren't many in the train with us. The smiling train man with the funny hat and striped shirt said a cheerful good morning to us when he took our tickets and stamped them. There was a mother with a young son. An older couple a few rows in front of us, both had canes and spoke too loudly. We learned they were visiting their daughter who had just had a baby.

The landscape flashed by us so fast my stomach turned. I'd never gone so fast before. But eventually I got used to the steady, rocking pace. I took in the fields and farms. Would I ever be known in this big world? Grace had told me so much about its wonders . . .

Oh, Grace.

Guilt rose in my throat like vomit. This city — Pittsburgh — might as well be another planet. I would never be of any help to Grace so far away. I would write to her once I got to my father's home. I didn't know how to mail a letter, but maybe my father could show me. And would Grace even get it? I would have to try.

"Cows and horses." I pulled at Angel's arm so that he would look through my window. I'd only ever seen pictures of these animals. They were smaller than I'd imagined. The old red barns were nearby with what looked like goats or sheep — I couldn't tell the difference. Would I ever learn what I needed to know about this world? Even farm animals were new to me.

A boy rode his bike on some small dirt road that ran alongside the train. He waved and pumped his arm and the train *choo-choo*ed.

The sky was a white-blue behind the trees and fields, above the roofs of houses, and in the great horizon that we moved so quickly toward. For years there was no movement at all, then suddenly everything moved at once.

1941
Chase Yourself

Just as the green landscape and rolling hills of the farmlands calmed me, the rush of buildings and concrete spurred my heart rate to a gallop. The entire world went from green to gray, and it wasn't only because of the weather. The buildings were gray, the sky had turned gray, and the haze in the air was gray. Was this Pittsburgh? Nothing looked as pretty as the willow tree outside my small balcony, especially when it bloomed and the petals fell like raindrops. Nothing looked as bright as the row of tomatoes that could woo anyone to bite into one like an apple. Nothing was as familiar as the tiled floor that I'd learned to walk on and Joann's bright, red-lipped smile.

The rhythm of the train changed, and I sat straighter. We were slowing down. I reached out a hand to touch the window. The chill from the glass spread through my body. My other hand gripped Angel's. I looked out the window and could feel Angel's breath on the side of my neck. He was looking out too. But was he afraid like me? He didn't grip me as I gripped him. But at least we were looking in the same direction — taking the same road.

Before I knew it we had stopped underneath a domed roof in what I could only assume was Pittsburgh. I rolled the name around in my mouth without saying it, trying to make the rough, concrete sounds familiar and real. The few folks around us began to stand and stretch. It was time to get off the train. But I couldn't get up. Suddenly I longed for the weight of the familiar and the security of knowing who cared for me.

Angel let go of my hand when he picked up his bag and stood. But I still sat and kept watching the flow of people through the window. On the sidewalk were a man and woman looking toward the train expectantly. They were both dressed in tailored clothes, looking the very opposite of the billowing asylum gown I was accustomed to wearing. My palms smoothed my waistline as I suddenly remembered that I wore clothes like that now too. The suited man had a firm jaw that clenched and unclenched, and the woman's eyes were filled with anticipation.

Suddenly they both broke out in bright smiles and a young man joined them. He wore what looked like a uniform from head to toe in dull green. He greeted the woman first, and her porcelain face broke in half and tears fell through the cracks as they hugged. The man patted the younger one's back as his own face twitched and stuttered.

The shared hug aged the woman. Or maybe the tears had. Tears had a way of doing that.

"Brighton, it's time." Angel sounded so sure of himself.

I inhaled deeply as I grabbed my bag from the floor. I followed Angel down the narrow aisle and carefully down the steep steps. I was afraid to leave the train and walk on the concrete of this city that didn't know me.

When we stepped off the train, no one noticed us. Didn't we have the story of our escape written on our foreheads? I looked down at myself again and was reminded that I looked more like the woman I'd just seen than Mother. My face twitched at the thought of her. I was fake. I was supposed to be wearing a sack-like hospital gown and look like myself instead of like a lady.

Angel squeezed my hand and brought me back.

I looked up at him. The hat made him look older and so handsome and like he knew how to handle himself. His shirt had a collar — I'd never seen him wear something like that before. It didn't seem to bother Angel that we were walking, talking liars.

But after a few minutes, some people did gawk at Angel. We pretended not to notice and kept walking.

"I'm not going to let anything happen to you." He said it like he'd read my mind. "You told me the first time we met that you'd be my guardian; now it's my turn."

I searched his violet eyes. I knew them better than my own. These were the eyes that had looked at me with such fear that first time in the graveyard, but now there was strength in them. He didn't need me like I needed him, and that scared me. A weak smile crossed over his lips. I nodded my head and together we walked into a building unlike anything I ever could have imagined.

My mouth opened, and both Angel and I said, "Wow." We dropped our hold on each other and took in our surroundings. I looked up and my eyes filled with the sight of a bright dome. It was ornamented with decorative squares and made the most beautiful ceiling I'd ever seen in my life. Sunlight descended through the skylights and lit my face. The lights that hung from chains were so large that I didn't stand underneath them. What would happen if one fell? And there were tree-trunk-size pillars that went floor to ceiling of what I could only figure was marble. And there were benches built in a circle where one could sit and enjoy the beauty for as long as desired.

"This is a train station? It doesn't look like the one in Milton," Angel said.

I shook my head. No, it didn't.

My shoulder got bumped as I turned in place, still looking up. Then I got bumped a second and a third time. The large space was filling up fast. I spun around to find Angel but couldn't see him in the sudden crowd.

"Angel?" I whispered it at first but after only a few seconds I said it louder and then louder yet. A man gave me a dirty look and then a woman too. Then another woman said to me, "Oh, chase yourself."

Because of Grace I knew it meant *get lost.* Well, I was lost. Why a strange woman would tell me that didn't make sense. Grace hadn't really explained that part. But I was chasing myself. I was always chasing after my real self and never catching up.

Before I could panic further a hand took mine and plucked me from the crowd. We sat on a bench catching our breath until the crowd thinned out. Then without a word of warning, Angel pulled me up and began walking toward the large section of doors. I could see that familiar gray through them. I wanted to resist, but this was the only direction we could go. Into the daylight and our new lives. Toward Ezra Raab, my father.

1941
Father

The brightness outside the train station hurt my eyes. I squinted at the dull white, and my nose found the scent of smoke and sewer all at once. I wanted to pinch my nose like I used to do as a child, but my hands were full.

This world was so large. So colorless. So tall with buildings reaching high into the foggy sky. The road ahead of us was filled with vehicles moving too fast, but like magic they didn't run into each other. It was so loud and I couldn't look anywhere without seeing too many people and too many things. I saw all of them but they didn't seem to see each other. They didn't look up from their newspapers. They walked fast around corners without care.

There were yellow cars mixed with the more quiet colors, cream, black, tan, dark green. Joann had mentioned something about the yellow cars, right? Green-uniformed men and women walked around in groups. Their strides were firm and sure, and they looked so smart. So different from me.

It started to drizzle, and the drops dotted everything around me. Black umbrellas popped up everywhere. We scooted beneath the awning of the building.

Angel rummaged through his pocket and pulled out money.

"Dr. Woburn said that we should ask one of the yellow taxis to take us to your father's address."

"How do we do that?"

Neither of us spoke, but we did what Joann told us to do — we watched and learned.

"You'll have to be my eyes, Brighton. The rain is making things a little harder to see."

A woman in a raincoat and heeled shoes ran toward the street, waving a hand over her head and yelling, "Taxi." A few moments later a yellow car with the word *taxi* on it stopped. She opened the door quickly and hopped inside.

Before another few minutes had passed it happened again. This time it was a man, and instead of the word *taxi* he gave a loud whistle.

I led Angel toward the corner where I'd

seen the first taxi. I waved and, like a miracle, one slowed to a stop in front of us. Angel turned to me and smiled.

"Wow. That wasn't hard," he said.

I smiled back. We stepped toward the yellow car when a man barreled past us and hopped into the cab ahead of us. This happened once more before we finally were able to get into a taxi. By then we were covered in a fine layer of drizzle. I couldn't control my shivering. At least this chilled-to-the-bone sensation felt natural enough.

Angel scooted in first and then me. The taxi smelled like the hospital basement. Like it had been almost dry for a long time. It was dirty enough that I kept my bag and hands on my lap.

"Where you —" the driver started, with a thick accent, then stopped and stared at Angel. "Something wrong with you? You sick?" He tucked his chin.

"There's nothing wrong —" I began, then Angel patted my knee.

"I'm not sick, I just have light skin." He said it like he'd rehearsed it, though I'd never heard him say anything of the sort.

Angel pulled out my father's address and showed him. "Here? Can you take us here?"

The driver's eyes lingered on Angel for several long moments before he finally took the piece of paper. He looked at it, then handed it back to Angel. "All right, I'll take you. You could've just said to take you to J & L."

We didn't know what that meant.

The ride in this car was nothing like when we were with Joann and Dr. Woburn. We braced ourselves against each other and our arms against the doors. The driver didn't seem to notice how we were being thrown around. A moment later a question surfaced. What would happen if my father didn't live there anymore?

And what if he did but didn't want Angel to stay? That idea was like a needle traveling through my brain.

I didn't stop thinking about those prospects as the driver passed us under a drooping clothesline attached between buildings and swaying power lines. People walking along near the road didn't seem to notice our speed. Weren't they afraid to walk so close to the fast-moving cars? The buildings grew drearier and shorter and became more run-down. They reminded me of a few of the older buildings that sat in the back of the hospital grounds that weren't in use.

Then we stopped. The driver turned.

"J & L factory is just up ahead." He put the flat of his hand out. "Two dollar."

Angel pulled out a bill. He looked at it closely; it had a five in the corner. The cabdriver grabbed the bill from Angel and told us to get out. We did as we were told, and a moment later we were standing on the edge of the road. I looked in the direction the driver pointed and heard the taxi speed off.

There was an odor in the air, different from the hospital stench. It was acrid, metallic, and rotten. Angel's face twitched, and I covered my nose.

"Where are we?" I asked, as if Angel knew.

I turned in a circle and took in my surroundings. The buildings in the distance were shadowed in the light gray sky. We were on a poorly paved road that was worn down and broken along the edges. There was a set of rickety-looking wooden stairs that went down the steep hill, reaching to the ground level of what the driver called a factory and all the surrounding buildings. How many worlds would we cross into? This one was dirty and muddy. At the bottom of the stairs were small, two-story buildings stacked next to each other. On their laundry lines dingy, gray clothing hung. People must live there. Smoke poured out of the long tubes that reached into the sky. What were they called? Images from newspapers, magazines, and books came back to me — smokestacks maybe? There was a *J* on one tall tube, a symbol for *and,* and a third with an *L* on it. A nearby sign said Jones and Laughlin Steel Company. Now I understood the J & L.

"How do we know where he lives?" I asked Angel, as if he would know any more than I would.

He took out the address and looked at it again.

"We're going to need to ask someone." He stuffed the address back in his pocket, then I helped him down the stairs. They were tall and rugged, but we reached the bottom safely. There were people milling around on the sidewalks. Some carried bags or walked with children dirtier than those in the children's ward. As soon as we reached the bottom, several scurried away with strange expressions on their faces.

"Ignore them," I told Angel, knowing they'd run because of him.

We followed the flow of people walking toward the buildings with the laundry lines.

"Let's follow them. Maybe we'll see street signs. Or something," Angel said. "I wish we had a map. Remember the maps we made of the hospital as kids?"

Of course I remembered. Suddenly everything good that had littered our childhood came to mind, making me miss Joann even more.

"You'll have to ask," Angel said. "People are afraid of me. Ask that woman where this address is."

He handed me the paper with my father's address on it. The woman he pointed at was sweeping her small porch. She looked tired, and her apron was a dreary gray, as was the color of her skin, though both had been white at one point. I didn't know what to say. Out here everything felt so hard. Angel gestured for me to take a step toward the woman.

I cleared my throat and she looked at me.

"I said I can't pay today," the woman said. Her accent made her words move up and down like a kite. She started to go for the door.

Angel jabbed me in the back.

"I'm not looking for money. Just a question," I said quickly. "We're looking for this address."

I walked up and showed her the paper. She leaned her head back and eyed me from the bottoms of her lids. Slowly she set her broom against the tired wood siding of the house, leaned over the rail, and put her hand out. I stepped toward her and handed the paper to her. The lines of her calloused hands were black and inky, but her face was young; she was not much older than me. She looked at the paper, then looked toward the other two-story buildings.

"It's just there," she said, pointing off to the left. "On the corner. The number will be above the door."

My eyes went above her head to her door-frame and to the number 278 in faded paint.

"Thank you," Angel said and gestured for me to come.

"He hasn't got any money either," she called after us.

I turned. "What?"

"He hasn't got money — Ez hasn't — if that's what you're seeking."

Ez. My father. Ezra Raab. She knew him. My heart tipped and spilled all over my insides. I paused, and my gaze and the woman's locked. I wanted to ask her so many questions. What was he like? Was he handsome? Did I look like him? Was he married? Did I have any brothers or sisters?

I shook my head. "I don't want his money either," I said. That seemed to be what she was most concerned about. "He's my father."

I shouldn't have said that. The woman's face told me more than I wanted to know. She began laughing.

"Father?" she said, then with a smirk she continued. "Well then, I'll wish you luck. He's apartment B."

As Angel and I walked in the direction that the woman pointed, all I kept repeating was one word. *Father. Father.*

1941
I'm Not Dead

There was so much to take in while I looked for my father's house number. The world down here was strewed with broken windows and dingy porches and doors. There weren't many people about. I assumed most were working. But there were children sitting on the porch next to Ezra's.

They were dirty from head to toe. The oldest of the three couldn't have been more than six. There was darkness under their eyes and in the windows behind them and maybe in their whole world. Had they been left alone? They were sharing a slice of bread — the soft white showing grimy smudges from their fingers. In their faces I saw my own — being left in a world unfairly — but the pain of hunger in that season of life was not part of my history. These children didn't appear to have a Nursey in their lives as I had. My throat went tight.

I looked over at Angel. His forehead was

creased and leaden. Could he see that the little one had tears streaked through the dirt on his face? They looked sickly and were covered in a red rash and bug bites. The oldest had one entirely white eye. They blended in with the gray and dismal so much it was almost as if they'd grown out of the cracks in the concrete. What world had we walked into?

"Is this it?" Angel squinted at the door.

I pulled my gaze away and matched the written address with the painted numbers. 743. The lady with the broom said apartment B.

There were three steps up to the front door. There were two windows on either side of the door and two windows above those on the second floor. A few curtains raggedly hung across a few windows. Several others had broken panes.

"Should we go in?" Angel asked, but I think he really meant *we should go in.*

I took the first step that would usher in the next part of my life.

Inside there was an A door and a B door and steps to the second floor. I knocked on the B door, but no one answered. We slouched down all the way to sitting against the wall next to the door. And we waited.

At some point during our waiting we fell

asleep, and when I opened my eyes again the sky through the window was dusky. The next thing I saw was a lanky, dirty man looking at me. He was wearing a newsy cap — that's what the fashion magazines called them. It was filthy and creased. His face was bony and smudged. He smelled like the factory smoke. He looked at me with a furrow cut so deeply into his brow it was like he'd never be able to undo it.

I elbowed Angel. He was startled but stood with me. I knew I must be wrinkled and dirty after having slept for hours on the floor. My neck was kinked and every joint hurt.

"Homeless aren't allowed in here," the man said with an accent I couldn't place. He pushed his hand into his pocket and pulled out a few keys on a ring. He moved toward the door. His hand shook as he tried to find the right one. His other hand was bandaged in what used to be a white cloth. It was covered with traces of blood and grime. Small sweat trails traveled down his temples. The factory must have been hot. He wore overalls, and his shirt underneath looked so thin, I could almost see through it. "I said run off, beggars."

"What's wrong with him?" The man gestured at Angel, as if suddenly noticing him.

"Some kind of disease? Get him out of here. You too."

"Ezra? Ezra Raab?" I asked. My voice barely sounded familiar.

"I don't have any money," he said and cursed when the keys dropped from his hand. He picked them up and tried again. If he got inside and closed the door, I'd never get the chance to speak to him. I needed to hurry.

"I'm not here for money. My name is Brighton Friedrich." Then I shook my head. "I mean, my mother was Helen Friedrich."

The jingling keys paused, then he found the right key and the door popped open. He was about to go inside.

"I'm your daughter," I said.

"That's not possible." He didn't look at me. "My daughter's dead."

So this really was Ezra Raab. This was my father. It had to be.

"I know that's what you were told, but it wasn't true. It's not true. I'm not dead."

Ezra continued to stare straight ahead, like a statue.

"Can we come inside?" I asked.

Ezra sighed. "I don't have much food."

"We don't need much. And we brought some." I gestured toward Angel's pack.

He opened the door farther and walked

in, leaving it open for us. I wasn't sure what I expected to see inside, but what I did see was far worse than any possible expectations. This dismal place was painted in various shades of gray. If there had once been color, it had not survived. If I stayed here, would I turn into some shade of gray and grime too?

"You can have a seat," Ezra said and gestured to the couch. It was worse than the one that had been in the dayroom at the hospital. The one I'd sat on so many times with Grace. The one I would never sit on again. My heart went flat with that memory yet inflated with hope in the shape of Ezra Raab.

Ezra left Angel and me in what seemed to be a living room. He went into a small bathroom. In the same area there was a few feet of counter space in the corner that had a sink and two burners. There was a miniature, smudged refrigerator against the wall. The window had droopy curtains, and there was a bed in one corner and a small table and two chairs in another. Angel sat on the couch and I followed.

"I can't live here. We can't live here. It's worse than the hospital. Well, it's dirtier anyway," I said, knowing my quick judgment was unfair.

"Let's talk to him first." He patted my knee.

Ten minutes later an unrecognizable man returned. His hair was nearly blond, like mine — only shaded with gray. His skin was bland and his whiskers freshly removed. His blue shirt and denim pants were a few sizes too big and reminded me of oversize hospital gowns.

"I can make coffee." He paused. "Do you drink coffee?"

Angel and I nodded. He did everything in silence before he handed us both mugs. He brought over a chair from the small table. He sat and looked at his hands for a while before he spoke. I sipped the hot drink, finding that it tasted nothing like the hospital's coffee. After a few more tastes I decided I preferred the darker and earthier taste of my father's coffee.

"Your mother, she is —" he asked.

"Gone." The reluctant words clung to my tongue before I let them out. "She died — recently."

The days had blurred together. Had it only been less than a week ago?

He bounced his head up and down and leaned forward with his elbows on his knees. There was silence again for a few minutes.

"How was she?"

"Do you mean, the psychosis?" I hovered strangely between neutralizing everything with a more medical view or falling into my father's arms in a fit of tears.

"Is that what it was called?" His *th* sounded like a *z* and every *w* like a *v.* "I have always worried about Helene."

"She wasn't well. She never was."

His eyes grew glassy and, like a mirror, mine did the same.

"I'm sorry to hear that. She was a good woman. A very good woman."

"Did you know her well?" Had he loved her or only used her? Why hadn't they married?

"We are from the same village in Germany. We were children together. She was a happy girl, and we fell in love when we were younger than both of you." He stopped and looked out the window. "Her mother — she had a hard time and she was very unwell. She —"

"How did she die?" The unplanned words fumbled out.

He looked at his hands. "She didn't always know what she was doing. Didn't understand it would kill her."

She'd killed herself. I didn't know if I wanted to know more so I moved on.

"How did my mother come to America?"

"After Nell's death, Otto, your grandfather, brought Helene and Margareta to America." He spoke in a halting and disruptive way, requiring patience on my part. "To start again."

He stood and walked to a cabinet and after a few moments returned and handed me a photograph. I looked at Angel and then back at the photo. It was the same photo Joann had given me, only mine had been cut. The hand belonged to a sister, I knew now. My grandmother sat stiffly in a larger chair with her hands gripping its arms. A stout man with a strong jaw stood behind her with his hands on her shoulders. And my aunt looked so much like my mother, only quite younger. Really, she was only a girl. The girl would now be an adult.

"This is your mother when she was a little younger than you. That is her mother and father, your grandparents, and her sister."

"I have seen this photograph," I told him but still took in the photo like the first time. "You came with them to America?"

"Otto didn't want Helene and me to get married — he said she was going to be like her mother and that he was sure she could get help in America. But Helene and I loved one another very much, so I followed her here." His voice broke, and I could see the loss was still fresh.

He shook his head. "You must know that she was a very kind and loving woman and I would never hurt her — I loved her. I still believe I could've kept her from that depth of madness that you say she succumbed to — my poor Helene. Otto did not believe this, though."

I looked again at the photo, at my grandmother's eyes that were like my mother's. Blank and lost. Her wrists were tied to the chair arms with black strips to blend in with her dress. Restraints. Why hadn't I noticed that before now?

On the back was written *Otto and Nell Friedrich* and beneath was *Helene and Margareta.*

"There's so much I don't understand." I stood and walked to the window and stared out into the dirty dusk. "When she found herself pregnant, why didn't you marry her?"

There was a long pause.

"I am not proud to tell you, but I was in jail when she was taken to the hospital." He cleared his throat. "We, her father and I, didn't know she was expecting. Helene may not have known herself. By the time I got out, Otto had died. After questioning neighbors, the police, and the local hospital, I found where she was taken. By then she'd been in there for nearly five months and was not herself. She did not know me. She was near her time, but I had no right to her. I was not her husband."

He straightened his back in his chair, and I could see he was uncomfortable with all of this. The lines on his forehead wrote the story of those years, but it was muddled up and I couldn't read it.

"I visited to ask after you. A nurse told me you had died."

"But I'm not dead."

"I see that now." His voice was quiet, like a dandelion puff in the wind.

"But you would have taken me if you had been able to?" I asked.

He nodded. "It would've been difficult. But it could've worked."

No one spoke for several minutes. My worlds were colliding. My father had wanted me.

"She used to hum a song," I said.

"A song?"

"Just a little tune." I hummed a short part of the melody and was met with his tenor voice joining in, but he was using real words — German words.

"Shlaf, Kindlein, shlaf." He sang several lines, then eventually faded into humming

as if he'd forgotten the rest.

"What does it mean?" I asked.

"Sleep, baby, sleep. Your father tends the sheep. Your mother shakes the little trees, there falls down one little dream. Sleep, baby, sleep," he recited softly and looked right at me when he spoke.

He stopped and cleared his throat.

"Where have you been all these years? How did you find me?" My ears heard his questions, but I was sure my face responded in confusion.

"Where have I been?" My breath choked in my throat. Angel took my hand. "Where else? I've been there. At Riverside until yesterday. My nurse — Joann — the nurse who raised me — us — helped us escape and gave me your address." Every word fumbled out of my mouth.

"You were there? At that hospital all of these years?" His voice broke, along with his face.

I nodded.

"You were raised with *those* people?"

I nodded. "Those people were my friends — my family. I saw the good in them the way you did in my mother."

"Of course. I understand."

I believed him because he loved Mother when she wasn't perfect.

"Can you tell me anything about my aunt?" I asked.

"Margareta?"

"Is she alive?"

"Yes. And she is well now after many years of sickness." Then, like he knew I needed to know what sort of illness, he spoke again. "Polio."

Angel and I looked at each other and smiled. This was good news.

"Wait, now, what did you say your name was?" he asked.

"Brighton." I sat up straighter. "My mother said it over and over again to the nurses when I was born. Does it mean something?"

His head bounced up and down, and he pulled in his lips. After a minute he leaned forward on his elbows again.

"That's not your name," he said.

"What do you mean? Of course it is." I wanted to laugh but instead felt panicked and my hand found Angel's.

"I knew your name sounded familiar." He stood and pulled an envelope out from his desk and handed it to me. "Look at the return address. Brighton is the name of the town where your aunt lives. She wasn't choosing your name; she was telling your nurses where to send you. To Brighton,

Michigan, to Margareta — your aunt."

I looked in the corner of the envelope and saw for myself that the city was Brighton. He was right, Brighton was not my name. It was the name of a town.

I had no name. I was registered as dead and I was nameless.

1990
Love, Nursey

I am not sure how prepared I am to hear from Joann. It's been decades since I hugged her goodbye. Called her Mother. And watched her walk away. I am back in my hotel room with the letter in my hands. One letter after all these years.

I know that if she were alive, she would be eighty-five. Our years have grown closer; we wouldn't be like child and mother anymore.

The front of the envelope has two Return to Sender stamps from a postman years ago. One is scribbled out. My father's Philadelphia address was written in Joann's curled script. I turn the envelope over in my hands and read what has been written on the outside flap.

My darling Brighton, I don't know when or if you'll ever get this letter. I sent it to your dear Aunt Eddie to put with your precious belongings in the hopes that maybe someday it will all be returned to you.

I lift the flap and remove the photographs again. I don't look at them this time, not wanting to travel that journey twice in one night. But this diverging road I am on will be much harder to bear. When I inhale, the pungent stench of the dayroom and the feel of a razor running along my scalp return to me. My hand grazes my bobbed hair — still there. Just a memory, I remind myself.

September 15, 1941

My dearest Brighton,

You've been gone for four months now, and there have been days where I've stayed in bed missing you. If it wasn't for Sid and for our baby, perhaps I would still be there. The realization of all that I did that hurt you is overwhelming. I must ask your forgiveness again. Though that grace may be a deeper scar yet.

I have walked the halls of our ward in my mind looking for your smile, but I know I won't find you there. And that is as it should be. The guilt and regret I carry is also as it should be. But they play tricks on my mind, and I have fought to hold on to reality.

I never returned to Riverside after your escape. And while there was some investigating, everyone covered for us. In the end, your escape just became more skeletons in the closet. I do know that Angel's father was furious after learning of his disappearance.

I need to tell you something. In one of your father's letters when you were around ten, he mentioned an aunt. He said she was recovering from polio in Brighton, Michigan, and asked if Helen would ever be able to live with her when she was well. Of course Helen was too ill to do that, but this was when I realized that your poor mother meant for you to be sent to your aunt in Brighton — not to name you. But, my darling girl, you are still Brighton. You've never been anyone else in the world but Brighton. Please don't question who you are.

I regret I never learned anything more about your aunt. But since you'd been documented as deceased for so many years, Sid and I both would've lost our licenses to undo the mess I'd made — and I would've lost you, which I wasn't prepared to do at the time. I don't suppose I'll ever really forgive myself for all of this.

I wish I could tell you that I did everything out of my love for you. But there was more to it. All around me were women who were hurting and unable to bear the burden of their pain. That was and still is my greatest fear for myself. My fear that I would become one of them if I lost you, since losing you would be like losing a part of me.

I don't suspect we will meet again in this life, but I pray you can forgive me, though undeserved. So I ask God to give me peace. Know I love you and always will.

Love,
Nursey

P.S. I have a baby son. His name is Jason, because it means "healer."

Have I forgiven Joann? Yes. Every day. That's how often I take it back and then spit the venom of bitterness from my mouth. Perhaps I will go to the grave still learning how to forgive the woman who both loved and hurt me most.

1941
UNBRIGHT

It would not have mattered if Lorna had walked into the apartment yelling one of her clichés. Or if Carmen was complaining loudly from the other side of the room that there hadn't been enough food on her plate to feed a mosquito. I would not have heard anything. My ears were filled with cotton. Filled with water. Filled with lies and the bitterness of truth.

I looked at Angel. My eyes must have covered most of my face and my mouth was open, but nothing was coming out. I looked then at Ezra. My father. His mouth was moving, but I still couldn't hear anything. He looked sad and worried. What was he saying?

I was shaking, but it seemed like it wasn't me. Angel was shaking me. Trying to wake me up from being awoken.

"Brighton, Brighton," I finally heard.

"That's not my name," I whispered back.

My ears were ringing.

"But it is. It became your name, regardless of what your mother intended. My name was never really Angel. I don't know what my name is." His voice was like the peeled wallpaper from my asylum room — brittle and broken.

I squeezed my eyes closed until they almost sank inside my head. I needed to get away from this new pain. I needed for it not to fill my mind and taunt me. Surely Joann knew what my father had just explained to me. The anger I'd let go of last night came back to me like the years I'd spent at Riverside were stacked upon my heart, pressing down.

The burden of truth had exhausted me. My eyes were heavy. My arms were like rods of iron. My very heart seemed to question if it had the strength to beat once more — and once more.

And what would happen next? Would my father ask me to stay? The tenderness we had shared in those moments speaking of Mother had to mean something. But he had said nothing of helping or of us staying or of how we could start a life together.

Did he wish I'd stayed dead?

My father's face was pained and waning, but he didn't look away from me.

"I'm sorry," I said, not knowing what to say.

"For what?"

For coming. For intruding. For not being dead.

"For" — I wasn't sure which one to say — "coming."

His eyes burst with blueness, and I could see where there were fragments of a handsome face.

"Do you see this way that I live?" He gestured around the room, his gaze landing out the window briefly before returning to me.

Was I supposed to nod? Then he went on.

"This isn't the life I wanted to live. Helene and I wanted so much more. We talked about children and family."

Why had he never married another?

"I made many promises to your mother and couldn't keep any of them. Your grandfather was a harsh man, but he did his best — life was hard."

"Because of my grandmother?"

He nodded. "When he saw Helene fighting the same demons, he thought America the beautiful would hold all the answers." He paused. "Do not be sorry, for I am not sorry that you came. You are like a star in the night sky. Now I know Helene will live on."

"But?" I asked.

"But you cannot stay. This is no place for you."

"I could get a job. I wouldn't be any bother to you. And Angel is a hard worker too."

"It will not work, *meine schatzi.*"

Hearing him call me *meine schatzi* was like a gentle restraint around my heart. Was I really his dear one? Was he avoiding the use of the name that wasn't mine as a kindness or manipulating me with a false endearment, or did he really see me as dear? Pretty words were soft like cotton. But when a patient was wrapped in cotton for therapy, when dampened and allowed to dry, it squeezed the breath from their lungs, forcing some to faint from lack of oxygen. That's what his words did to my soul. "There's no room here for three."

"But we have nowhere to go."

"I have family." Angel spoke like the rush of a breeze coming through the enclosed room. He looked at me. "I went through my bag when you slept on the train. I found part of an address."

"But Joann —" I started until I saw Angel pull out a folded paper. Lines of black marker crossed out large sections. Angel showed Ezra the address.

"These are admission papers and an address is here. I think they just missed crossing it out," he said.

"This address is not so far," Ezra said. "It's on the outskirts of the city." Then he paused. "And this is your family?"

"Joann said not to go to them," I inserted and had to fight the urge to grab the paper from his hand and tear it up.

"I have to try." Angel looked at Ezra. "Maybe you could help me find this address?"

While this exchange had lasted only a few minutes, Ezra's rejection would linger with me much longer. He didn't want me.

In slow and unhampered movements he pulled out a map from his cabinet. With quiet steadiness he showed Angel the area the address was in. I didn't look at the map but heard soft words about a cab drive and asking if we had enough money.

Ezra didn't want me, but he had wanted my mother — even with her fits. And soon we would leave and I would probably never see him again.

I got up. I needed air. I needed the expanse of the inky sky. I needed out.

"Where are you going?" Angel asked.

"I need — I'm just going to take a walk."

My step out of the house did not lift the weight I bore. The stench in the air was insulting and severe. I'd withstood horrible smells my whole life, but the outside air had always been a salvation and rescue from that. But here, I was trapped.

My toes wiggled in my shoes as I stood on a burdened sidewalk that had known more lives than I could wonder over. Across from where I stood was another row of wearied, dull houses and farther in the distance were the initialed stacks that poured putrid smoke into the night air. My eyes traveled up. The sky was a mere charcoal canvas. No blue night, no splash of stars, no tiny Crux to be seen.

"In Germany the sky bursts with stars over castles and forests." My father's voice came from behind me. I hadn't heard him come outside.

"It does at the hospital too," I offered.

Ezra stepped up to stand at my side.

"The factory and city lights have stolen away all that beauty from us." He said it so dearly and affectionately I turned to look at him.

"You deserve better, *meine schatzi.*" He'd said *dear one* again. He squared his shoulders to look at me. Was he going to hug me?

His arms went up a little, then he lowered them. "I have nothing to give you. But your aunt and I write sometimes," he said with a shrug. "I have her address. It is different from the one you have."

"Why didn't she come and get my mother out?" I asked. "Even if she thought I was dead?"

"She was very ill for a time — polio — and had to care for herself. She has had a hard life. When she was well enough, she asked me about Helene, but the asylum doctors had already told me that your poor mother was too unwell to be released to anyone." He tilted his head as he looked at me. "You remind me a little of Helene's mother."

But hadn't she been mad and hadn't she committed herself to eternity?

"Don't worry — not the way you are thinking. You do not have their eyes, where the madness shows. You have mine. But your build and porcelain skin, the way you are. Mannerisms, I think they are called, are your grandmother's before she was afflicted." He smiled and stepped forward, touched my shoulder-length hair. "I knew her before her mind deceived her. You would've liked her. A woman of light and — well, nervous energy, Otto used to say."

He dropped his hand.

"Please, let me stay."

"Brighton, go to your aunt. Maybe someday you will let me know that you are settled. I will write back. After everything you've been through, you deserve a real home. I cannot give that to you here." His eyes lingered over mine for only brief moments. I knew what shame looked like because of my own reflection. His shame would force him to give me up a second time. The first time because I was dead and the second time because I was alive. Then he cleared his throat and looked back off into the night.

"There's a war coming, you know."

I shook my head. We'd heard very little about it in the hospital.

"I will tell you that Germans are not loved here in America because of this war." He niggled the sidewalk pieces with his toe. "They will let me go from this job soon, I know this."

"Because you're German? But you're not in a war." This was all very confusing.

He didn't answer right away.

"We are always in some war." His gaze returned to me. "When you make it to your aunt's home, let me know — perhaps if I am let go from this job, as I suspect, I will travel to you. Come now. You and Angel stay for the night. Everything will look better in the morning."

But it didn't. The next morning I said goodbye to a man I'd only just said hello to. I agreed to write him, and he promised to write back. This was all I could hold on to.

Ezra hugged me gently when we parted and gave me some photographs and my aunt's address. He was going to work, and we were setting off into another unknown.

1941
Welcome Home

When we walked out of the apartment, the same three little children were on their steps again. I went over and gave them the rest of our bread. I was sure they needed it more than we did. The oldest took it fast and distributed a slice to each.

"Thank you, lady," the oldest said, and the others followed after a few elbow jabs.

I stood there and watched them. What did their future look like?

Angel came up from behind me and wrapped an arm around me. His other held his bag. This way of holding me was new. There had been so many new things.

"I don't know if I can leave." I was glad I didn't have to look at him when I spoke. My tears were at the ready, and I didn't want them to spill over.

"Your father said he'd write back." Angel turned me around, put down his bag, then wrapped both of his arms around me. I nodded but didn't trust my voice. The way he looked at me made me think about what he'd told Joann in the train station parking lot. That he loved me. "We will find our place, Brighton."

"Don't." I looked away and closed my eyes. "Not that name anymore."

He leaned into me and whispered, "Brighton."

Then he did something I wasn't expecting. He lowered his lips and pressed them gently against mine. For several long, perfect moments my worries were gone and my heart glowed like his skin. This was a kiss. I'd only ever seen Dr. Woburn do this to Joann but never imagined I'd ever get the chance to be kissed myself. What else I hadn't expected was how our lips touching would bring to the surface every bit of love I'd ever felt for Angel. His hold on me tightened and my arms mimicked his and brought an added headiness to the kiss.

When he pulled away I looked at him in confusion. Why now, and why did he stop?

"You can call yourself whatever you want. But you'll always be Brighton to me, and you will always be the person I love most in the world."

I sank into his chest and loved him back with all my warmth and my hold, even though I had no words to put to it except for one question.

"Why now?"

As he held me he rubbed my back through the thin satin of my shirt, sending warm sensations from my abdomen to my head. I didn't know what that feeling meant or what it was, but I'd never felt so whole. It gave me such hope and expectation. He pulled me away and looked into my eyes.

"I've wanted to do that for a long time. But now we get to start a real life together." His voice was husky and serious. He kissed me again with a surge of passion I didn't know existed in him. I didn't want him to stop.

"For the first time in our lives, we get to make choices for ourselves. And I choose you."

I caressed his face and couldn't believe how long I'd loved him this way without knowing it. "And I choose you."

Then we picked up our bags and, with fingers entwined, I led him back up the steps we'd traveled the day before.

When we reached the top, we began walking toward the city. There was a strange feeling where my heart, mind, and stomach were three tangled strands because the skyline ahead of us bore a familiar engraving in my memory. How quickly memories could master the soul and make natural things that were unnatural only a short time ago.

This alien familiarity happened again when out of a reflex I didn't know I had, I raised my hand and called out, "Taxi." The driver waved an arm out his window that he'd heard me. I turned and grabbed Angel's arm and pulled him with me. The instinctual moment made me smile. I had learned something in such a short time in my new world.

This cabdriver was not like the last one. He had black hair that waved over his forehead. He had tan skin and friendly, dark eyes.

He winked at me when I got in, but Angel's entry put the driver in a different mood quickly.

"Whoa, there, fella." He looked over at me. "This weirdo with you, sweetheart?"

My face twitched. I didn't like that he called Angel a *weirdo* and me *sweetheart.*

"We'd like to go here." Angel ignored the driver's words and handed him his parents' address. The driver cautiously took the paper. But before he looked at it, he glanced over at me again.

"You're too beautiful to be with this jack."

I opened my mouth to speak but said nothing. Joann was the only person to ever call me beautiful.

"Aren't albinos witches or something?"

Why wouldn't he stop talking and drive?

"He's my friend," I finally said. He eyed us both and mumbled something as he turned around. He looked at the address once more, then threw the paper back at us and started driving.

This time as we drove everything became more green; the yards grew longer and wider. The houses became more ornate and oversize. Families lived there. The word *family* was such a strange and fickle word.

"Here you go," the cabdriver said and put his hand out. "That's a two-fifty, pay up."

Angel quietly counted out the money and handed the change to the driver.

This neighborhood was different from Ezra's, but we didn't belong here either. A woman pushed a baby carriage down the sidewalk — something I'd only ever seen in picture books. When the baby cried she stopped and patted it and the baby stopped crying. Another child ran in circles around her. Like she could feel me watching her, she looked up and our eyes met. She moved quickly away from us, yanking the little boy by the arm to stay close to her.

"This is it. This is my family's house." Angel nodded his head toward a huge house as he stuffed his hands in his pockets. "I can't believe it."

Joann had used the word *dangerous.* She'd warned us of his father. But I understood the primitive and innate need to know where you come from. My mother was mad and a German immigrant and my father was a convict, but it was my history, so therefore it was important. The imprint Ezra made on me had changed me — I'd lost my very name — and yet, he wanted to write me. The paradox of what it had cost me to gain a sliver of a father, I would never understand. Would these people change Angel? I would defy anyone who would want to change him.

Angel didn't wait for me as he opened a white gate and walked down a long, straight sidewalk with a flower garden on both sides toward a large brick home. It boasted white pillars in the front, and a woman was sweeping the patio. As we got closer we could hear her humming a tune. She had dark skin like Joyful. She was wearing a black dress and a white apron. She didn't look much older than me.

"Hello?" Angel's voice broke through the girl's tune.

She was startled and jumped and pushed her back against the house. The broom dropped, slapping loudly. She spoke some words that sounded like a different language and then she switched to English.

"You are money," she said with slow pronunciation and slid toward the front door. "You should run."

"What?" I asked Angel.

Angel kept looking at the uniformed woman. "I need to speak with Cynthia Sherwood."

Angel didn't seem bothered by how afraid of him the woman seemed to be. Or that she called him *money.* What did she mean? He stepped closer to the front porch. The girl carefully walked toward us and looked so hard at Angel it was as if she wasn't sure he was there. She raised her hand up and touched his face and checked her fingertips. I stood with them but felt invisible.

"Be careful," she whispered.

"Careful?" he asked.

"Where I come from, you are money." Her English was broken and her accent unlike anything I'd ever heard. People sold albinos for money? She looked over at me and then back at Angel. "Why are you here?"

"I'm here to see Cynthia Sherwood."

"What's going on out here?" A woman's

soft, lilting voice came from the front door. "Reni, who's here? What have I said about talking to —"

"This stranger come to see you, Mrs. Sherwood," she interrupted.

The woman's eyes followed the girl. Reni kept her head down and picked up her dropped broom. The woman's eyes were sharp and lips tight as she waited for an answer.

"They be turning bewitch. Be careful of the light one, ma'am." The whites of Reni's eyes shone brightly.

"I've told you not to use those island phrases anymore. Dr. Sherwood doesn't . . . ," the woman started but then turned toward us and her voice faded away, as did her natural rosy complexion.

The woman's gaze only grazed over me but stopped on Angel. It didn't take long for her eyes to go from confusion to something like recognition.

I wondered at how much they looked alike. The shape of their eyes and mouths. His mother was a beautiful woman with light-blond hair, though nothing like Angel's. Her skin was creamy, but she was turning paler by the moment.

Suddenly she ran down the steps and threw her arms around Angel. And he hugged her back, like they'd done this before. Like he remembered her. Maybe he did but never told me. How opposite it was to my father's reaction when we met.

She wasn't as tall as Angel, and she pressed her head against his chest and he bowed his head into the crevice of her neck and shoulder. She began to cry, and I'd never seen Angel cry the way he did now. He'd cried once when he'd broken his leg and another time when Joann had to give him stitches on his arm. There were other times, but never tears like this.

Why couldn't Ezra have greeted me this way? But he did what he could. I knew that much.

His mother pulled away and looked at him in his eyes. Her gaze roamed his entire face. She took off his hat and handed it to me without a glance. She ran her hand through his hair, almost rustling it like a mother would a small boy, and then her palm cupped his cheek. They both giggled in the way you do when you share a memory.

"Is it really you, Luke?" Her tears were like a row of diamonds that trailed her face. She looked even more beautiful when she cried.

"Is that my name? Luke?" he asked. He looked at me, smiling. "My name is Luke."

I raised my eyebrows and smiled back. Angel had just been given his name; mine had been taken away.

"You didn't know your name?" she asked, her voice hiccupping in her throat. "Then what were you called all these years? How are you here?"

"Angel," he said and then pointed toward me. "She named me Angel, so everyone called me that."

"Angel," his mother said in a whisper, like she was contemplating the name. "Well, now you'll be Luke."

"I like Luke," Angel said. *Luke* said. Which one was he now?

The two looked at one another for several long moments. Then her countenance shifted, and she peered around the sidewalks like she was wondering if anyone was watching. Her expression went from shock and joy to concern.

"Let's put your hat back on, Luke," she said and put her hand out toward me. I handed the hat to her and she returned it to his head. "Come inside with me." She took his hand and began leading him inside, then she stopped and took me in. I had not moved from my spot. Was I to go with them? "Are you two — married?"

Angel turned to look at me and took a

deep breath before he spoke. "No, we're not married. This is my best friend, Br—"

"Nell," I interrupted. "I'm Nell."

"Nell." Angel's flossy voice felt approving even though I knew what he preferred.

"Nell." The polished beautiful woman nodded as she said it. "Please, come inside with us and we'll get acquainted."

I followed behind the two. My father said I resembled my grandmother, but I still wondered why I had chosen her name to use as my own. She had died unhappy and not in her right mind. She'd been like my mother. Had I just sealed my fate? But I wouldn't take it back, because as soon as I'd spoken the name, I knew it was what I would use for the rest of my life. It was small, simple, and almost invisible.

Once we got inside, the woman dropped Angel's hand and went to the girl, Reni, who had snuck in behind us. She spoke quietly to her as I looked at our surroundings.

"Can you believe this?" Angel's smile was bursting from his face.

I shook my head but didn't look at him. If I had, I would've cried. Because his mother loved him. Because his real name was Luke. Because he had a name. Because his family didn't live in a gray world but in one full of color. I wasn't sure how to be happy for Angel — Luke — in my sadness. I had lost so much, and I was afraid of losing him.

This morning we'd stood in my father's one-room home with decades-old furniture, scampering mice, the scent of sewage and something rotten in the air, and everything had a fresh layer of coal soot. And now here we were, in a redbrick home that stood statuesque against the expansive yard framed by a bright blue sky — no smoke-stacks in sight.

I had no idea people lived in such luxury. Of course, I'd never been inside a real house, a real home, for a real family. My father's place wasn't really a home; even he said so.

A curious-eyed girl walked down from the curved staircase to my right. She was beautiful. She was also fair, like her mother, but not like Angel. Her blond hair and pink shiny blouse both beamed in the sunlight that flooded the staircase window. She stopped halfway down and looked at Angel, her gaze passing over me unconsciously.

Maybe I was dreaming all this.

Angel was looking back at the girl on the stairs. Neither said anything for the length of about twenty or more ticks from a large clock in the corner. The ticking was so loud

I couldn't help but count it. It calmed me and gave weight to my legs so I wouldn't float away.

Finally she spoke. "I found a photo of you about two years ago." She came down a few more steps. "You were a year old and you were smiling."

I looked at Angel and he swallowed hard but remained silent.

"I was only thirteen, and I wasn't sure why Mother would have a faded photo of a boy I could see was — different. I knew it wasn't Howard Junior." She walked the rest of the way down the stairs and stood a few feet away from Angel, looking at him so intently. The way she clasped her hands and tilted her head — it was like she was part water, her movements were so fluid. "I asked Mother about it and she told me. I couldn't believe she'd kept you a secret for so long, but she said she couldn't do it anymore. Daddy was angry and threatened to take away my trust fund and cut Mother's allowance if we told anyone. But here you are. What would Daddy say now?" She shook her head, and her wood-thrush laugh filled my ears.

What was a trust fund?

"My school library had a book about albinos. Besides the obvious facts, there was folklore and myths about magic and sorcery. I didn't believe it, though. I was sure that you weren't much different from me."

Angel nodded and chuckled. He was smiling now. She stepped closer.

"Hi, Luke. I'm your sister, Bonnie," she said and put her hand out. "We resemble one another, don't we?"

He awkwardly shook her hand.

"Bonnie, there you are." Angel's mother returned from wherever she'd been. She inhaled deeply and shook her head. "Oh my, to see the two of you together."

Her eyes were glassy, and the newly introduced sister and brother looked at each other and smiled. This was a family.

Angel — Luke — was home.

1990
From Dark to Light

That girl Kelly had the dark room at the local high school secured for us by morning. A fact that causes so many contradictory emotions inside myself. I feel pulled in two. The night before, Kelly and I talked until the restaurant closed. I was surprised how talking about my stories and life at Riverside to a perfect stranger loosened the straightjacket I'd worn around my soul for so long. And brought the kind of healing I'd never given myself over to. Talking things over with my husband and throwing occasional prayers up to the Big Guy were the extent of my raw openness. Nobody needed to walk all over the brittle fallen leaves of my life.

But I am thinking a bit differently about it now.

"What happened to your arms, Ms. Friedrich? How did you get so scratched?" Kelly gently touches my skin. I bristle and pull back. “Does it hurt?”

Yes. It hurts. That is the truth of it. But the scratches are not what I mean. The reason why they are there is what hurts. It happens sometimes. Often enough that I don’t always notice in the mornings.

I shrug. “I’ll be fine. And please, call me Nell. Ms. Friedrich feels so formal.”

“Why didn’t you take your husband’s last name?”

The question surprises me.

“It’s just so modern and unexpected.”

I smile. “My husband understood it was important to me.” I clear my throat, not expecting the emotions it brings up. “To feel closer to Mother.”

She smiles and doesn’t ask again about the scratches.

She also is trying to convince me to attend the town hall event promoting a positive vote for the demolition of the old asylum so a community center can be built. I started considering going when she told me that the town council was planning to name it Wolff Community Center after a hospital administrator who was documented as handling the overcrowding and understaffing during wartime and was considered a hero. A man they didn’t know. But I did. I hadn’t thought of Dr. Wolff by name in years. I didn't have many dealings with him, but I could picture his face. I knew him to be a heartless and cruel human being. The idea that he might be honored for the torture he put Mother, my friends, and me through brought back the reason I took the pictures to start with — so that someday I could expose what was happening inside the walls.

Once we get to the dark room my mind shifts gears. I force myself to wear the hat of professional photographer and teacher instead of former asylum patient. I thread two filmstrips at a time, one for each of us. I teach Kelly along the way — this is what I do. Once we develop the five cartridges, I start exposing the negatives. I use the enlarger, and after I teach Kelly how to rock the developer trays, she handles that part.

There are many duds — my amateur photography skills are obvious — but when the photographs begin to appear correctly, I have to fight the urge to run away. The faces of my past appear, and with them the sounds and smells that photos should never be able to convey so distinctly. But these do.

These photos — memories — had been captive inside these small cartridges for almost fifty years, and I was afraid bringing them freedom would make me captive a second time. But as each photo comes into focus, I am also freer. I am recognizing that my version of moving on looked a lot like hiding. These pictures will finally be seen and the truth revealed and my friends from long ago will be heard. Will this mean telling the world all of my secrets? I'm not sure I can do that.

My eyes glance over the images, but I fight allowing my soul to take them in. I only view the images with the eyes of a technician and nothing else. Not yet.

"How could you have —" Kelly searches for the right word, her eyes surveying the many photographs. "Survived all of this?"

"Someone told me a long time ago that 'all the darkness in the world cannot extinguish the light of a single candle.' " This wisdom of Saint Francis is like a long exhale. "As long as I kept my eyes open there was always a sliver of light to follow."

The five empty canisters line up like valiant soldiers having done their jobs. Within those slim pieces of plastic so much has lived. I release a long-held breath and finally let myself walk around and look at the images hanging on the wire. The faces are everywhere. They are all around me, and it doesn't feel bad. I smile at them until my eyes settle on Grace.

My Grace. I remember the day I took the picture. It is from those early days with her on the ward. Her hair had been shorn, like mine. Her beauty was still profound and brightness beamed from her eyes. She didn't think the stay would be longer than a few weeks — a month at the most. She thought it was just one more ploy by her parents to control her.

"She's bald." Kelly stands next to me. "She'd seem like a revolutionary now for doing that."

"Not her decision." I smile. "It was lice."

I take the photo from its place on the wire and press it to my chest.

I'd never even told my husband that I always look for her — for Grace. I don't just mean in every building I go in or every sidewalk I travel on — though that is true. But it is bigger than that. When there had been a choice to move to dull, factory-filled Pittsburgh or warm and faraway Texas, I still picked Pittsburgh. I had a feeling Grace wouldn't have gone that far. She might be somewhere in Pittsburgh.

A few times I made phone calls to people I found with the name Grace Douglass or Hannah Douglass, hoping I'd recognize the voice or be able to probe enough to know if

I'd found the right person. Once, when the kids were in school and Doc was out of town, I drove all the way to the address I'd found for Grace's parents. It was a two-hour drive. I was in my midthirties by then, and I was sure I'd used up a lifetime of shocks and surprises. That was not true. The opulence and luxury of the home Grace had come from was startling. She'd told me they were wealthy and influential, but the iron gate with the name *Douglass* scrolled at the top was far more than my imaginings. I never got closer than fifty yards from the front door and was still on the other side of the grand gate. I never caught a glimpse of anyone but the gardener. That day I learned that the Douglass family owned the newspaper and the banks in town. Had donated wings of hospitals, libraries, and schools.

Just last week I heard someone say the name Grace at the grocery store, and when my head snapped over I found a toddler, not my dear friend. I'm not sure I'll ever stop looking for her.

I place her picture on top of the stack. I need Grace to see what I am trying to do for her — for all of us.

1941
Rose-Colored Glasses

With angelic movement Angel's mother gestured for us to follow her. "Come. Let's sit down together. Reni poured some iced tea and set out some cake."

Angel turned around and looked at me. His expression was shock, awe, and fear all mixed together. Where disbelief and guilt had veiled my father, I saw joy and confidence in Cynthia Sherwood. But shouldn't she have some guilt too? Ezra had been told I was dead, but he had had good intentions. From what I knew, Mrs. Sherwood had given up Angel. I didn't trust her.

I touched Angel's arm and pulled him a few steps away. "Don't you think we should —"

"She can come too," his mother said, interrupting me.

"Come on." Angel walked away from my hold and nodded for me to come with him. I followed behind him, and his mother linked her arm through his with a fluidity that tightened my rib cage and squeezed my heart. His sister led the way for all of us and opened doors that led to the outside patio; she even pulled a chair out for him. Her smile reminded me of Joann's when I was a little girl. Cheerful and happy and loving — and like there was something to cover up.

Angel was between his mother and sister, and I sat opposite him. All of us were looking at him while he sipped his tea from a sparkling, rose-colored glass. Angel's chair scraped against the patio floor as he moved to keep his eyes in the shade of the awning. It was bright today, and nothing like the gray day from yesterday.

"It's too bright for you, isn't it? I read about this. Mother, maybe we should go inside. His eyes are very sensitive. Do you want to go inside?" Bonnie was already protective of him. I'd watched over him my whole life, and suddenly she had taken my place. My jaw tightened.

"It's okay." He waved off her words. "As long as I'm in the shade and . . ."

His voice faded away. Explaining his vision issues, why his eyes looked the way they did, why his skin was so light — clearly made him uncomfortable. He inhaled deeply, and through the glass patio table I could see his knee nervously bouncing.

His stuttering and the sweat beads at his temples made me sit up straighter, considering how I might need to come to his defense.

"So, Luke —" his mother started.

"That sounds so strange to me." He chuckled and rubbed the tops of his legs.

"Well, it's your name, Son." Cynthia reached and patted his forearm then rested her hand on his.

He nodded with that innocent smile I knew so well and sipped his tea, his eyes diverted away from all of us.

No one spoke. This was wrong. Even though my father hadn't welcomed me with open arms. Even though he hadn't been able to give me a life then or now. Even though he had pulled the veil of my identity away — he still gave me answers.

Images of Angel at the graveyard all those years ago flashed through my mind. With no name. No mother.

This perfect woman with her perfect daughter couldn't get away with all of this without answers — I wouldn't let that happen.

"Why did you leave Angel — Luke — at the asylum? Do you know the life that he lived?" I hoped my nerves weren't as transparent as my hopes had been with Ezra.

"Bri— I mean, Nell — I mean," Angel stammered, then looked at his mother. "I — um —"

His mother cleared her throat, and his sister raised an eyebrow high off of her forehead.

"It was because of your father." The words rattled out of Angel's mother like she'd been shaken. Her eyes buzzed around. "And my parents. They forced me to give you up. They told me you couldn't learn and that you were better off in the asylum, where people could take care of you."

He pulled his hand free of her touch — gently, but intentionally.

"But you didn't visit?" Angel's voice cracked when he spoke. "I didn't even know my name."

Angel paused and rocked back and forth a bit — his hands back on his legs, rubbing up and down. I tilted my head, watching him. He'd never done this before. The rocking was something the patients did when they were agitated.

"Your father said you weren't normal." Her voice was firm and her breathing was fast and erratic. "They all convinced me. Howard told me it would be better if you were with other people like you. Mother agreed. They said you would get a suitable education for a boy like you and that you would never even remember me because of your condition." Her words came so fast it was hard to keep up. Her elegant perfection had fallen away, and she was nothing more than a ragged woman with poor excuses. Ezra had been more prepared to handle my questions.

"I understand. It's okay," Angel said quietly. So quietly his words could've been missed. His eyes rested on the cake in front of him.

"No, it's not." I blurted out my words before I could arrest them. "Have you ever visited Riverside?"

"Riverside?"

"The hospital where Angel and I lived."

"Yes, Riverside. That's the place." She turned away from me. "After you were born I moved to Pittsburgh and Mother hired round-the-clock care for you for almost three years, until that nurse couldn't be trusted any longer. Mother said Howard had found a special school for children like you. She wouldn't let me see you anymore. It was 1923 when they took you. I had no rights to anything. If I left Howard for you, I would have lost everything. My husband, my parents, Howard Junior, who was a baby then, everything. I would've had to give up everything."

"But what about me?" Angel whispered.

"Riverside doesn't have a school," I prodded.

Everyone was as silent as snow.

"But Howard said — I didn't think you'd know any better, Luke. You can't blame me for that."

Angel just stared at his hands gripping his iced tea in the prettiest glass I'd ever seen.

"I was told my brother would watch out for you." She plastered a smile on her face.

"Watch out for him? Did you know that when Angel broke his leg if I hadn't found him he might've died waiting for help? And that for years of his life he was bathed with a cold water hose?" I paused briefly, looking between his mother and sister, who were both stoic and motionless. "They made sure to do it on the side of the building so that no one else would see what was happening. Did you know he was in a crib until he was ten and had terribly achy joints because of it? He ate like an animal and didn't even know how to use a spoon. He didn't even know what *mother* meant when I met him."

"Stop," Cynthia said. "Why are you telling me this?"

"You don't get to not know anymore. It was nothing like you could ever imagine in your worst nightmares. That's the *school* you sent him to."

"Luke, you don't blame me, do you? Mother visited, and she never told me any of this. It couldn't have been as bad as what your friend says."

"No, it wasn't as bad as she says." His voice was a low rumble, and he looked directly at his mother. "It was worse, Mother. If it wasn't for Brighton, I wouldn't have survived. But I still don't know why. Why didn't you —"

"I couldn't raise you as our son." She twitched and gasped between each word. Then suddenly she gathered her composure. "It would've been so hard for you, Luke, so different from everyone else. We didn't want that for you. There you could at least be with others like you."

"I've never met anyone *like me.*" He remained sober and contained. "I was the only one."

"That can't be true."

I hated her. I hated her so much that I couldn't even bear to look at her. I stood, and the scrape of the chair vibrated my brain. I didn't want to leave Angel, but I couldn't stay.

"Wait," Angel said to me and took my hand. Then returned his gaze to his mother. "I think we should go."

My surprise at this couldn't be measured. The shock of the other two was just as palpable.

"You'll be back, won't you? Do you live nearby?"

"Live nearby?" Angel almost laughed aloud. "Your brother, Dr. Woburn, helped us escape the hospital only two days ago. We don't have any place to stay. We've lived our lives in the halls of an asylum, and we need help." He was passionate now. "That's why we're here."

"Oh?" She blinked and put a hand to her chest. "You thought you could stay here?"

"Did you think this was just a casual social visit?" I yelled.

Angel twitched and stood so quickly his chair fell backward.

"Oh, Luke — Well, your father, he'd never —" Her eyes bounced everywhere except at Angel. "How could we — There would be so much to explain." She shook her head. "I could make some arrangements — maybe?"

Angel and I looked at one another.

"Arrangements?" Angel asked.

Cynthia Sherwood bit her lip, but a moment later her polished demeanor returned.

"Your father would never allow you to stay here — and we could never tell him. It would be very confusing for our friends, not to mention Howard Junior. I'd have to find a way to pay for it, but as long as your father never finds out, I might be able to help you."

"We could use my trust. Daddy never checks how it's spent," Bonnie piped up.

"You mean you might be able to help *us*?" Angel said, nodding his head to me.

His mother turned toward me. "Nell, right?"

I nodded. Angel's hand gripped tighter.

"Surely you have family — or someone — to go to who could be responsible for you. You wouldn't want to hold Angel back, would you?"

My panic heightened, but I couldn't find the heart to recite my mantra. There was nothing bright or beautiful about this. She was asking me to leave Angel. And Angel wanted his family so much. Enough to stay by himself? My breathing was more shallow with each passing moment.

"What's happening to her? Is she having some type of fit?" Mrs. Sherwood said.

"Brighton." Angel gripped my shoulders. "Breathe."

Then he pulled me close and whispered to me, "I'm not going to let her separate us.

We're staying together. I won't leave you. I love you."

"Didn't you say her name was Nell? Who are you, really?"

Her voice was like a crystal bell in my ears, even though I felt like I was breathing underwater. But Angel was here, his warmth and presence and words reminding me that we were doing this together. He was bright and beautiful. My breathing started to even out — quicker than usual. But even though my breath was returning, the lingering sense of dread didn't go away.

"She needs doctors and help," Angel's mother said. "She never should have left the hospital if she has fits like that. She needs to be with others like her, not in civilized society."

"I'll never let her go back," Angel growled. The strength in his voice that had seemingly been lost all day was back. "We won't be separated."

"She'll hold you back, Son. We could get her the help she needs — we know doctors. Think about what I could give you. There might be some medicine now that could fix your complexion."

"Fix him?" I said between breaths.

"I would have to be kept hidden?"

"Father will have you readmitted if he

catches wind of you," Bonnie blurted out.

"Never." Angel held my hand tightly, tethering me to him.

His eyes, caught by the sun's rays, reddened. He squinted, then moved his free hand to block the glare. "We won't be separated, and we're *not* going back there."

"Not your hospital. He would take you to his." Bonnie started crying. "You won't survive, Luke. Neither of you will. Mother, you won't let that happen, will you?"

"Bonnie, get ahold of yourself."

"Why do you live with such a man?" Angel looked at his mother, yelling now.

"You really don't know anything about the world, do you? What choice do I have?" His mother's voice filled the space around us. She stood and turned away, weeping. "I'd be ruined. Everything would be ruined. The children would have no future. I'd be cast out. I'd lose everything."

She'd chosen to send her son away to salvage a reputation, which made her a prisoner worse than Angel and I had been.

"Go, Luke," Bonnie breathed quickly. "She will call if she feels threatened."

"Bonnie," she yelled. "You will —"

"Call who?" Angel asked.

"Father — or his hospital. Go, now."

His welcome had been so deceiving — her

joy mixed with deception. There was such heartbreak in rejection, and if my heart wasn't already shattered it would have broken for him.

"We have to go, Brighton," he said in a deep, guttural voice. "We just need to go."

He took my hand and we walked back inside, through the opulent rooms, and into the large entry where our small tattered bags still sat on the shiny floors. When we turned around, Bonnie rushed up behind us. She was crying.

Bonnie threw her arms around Angel, and when they finally let go of one another, we left through the large, heavy wooden door. We turned before it closed, and once again his mother was nowhere to be seen.

1941
Not an Angel

I was certain we would never see Cynthia Sherwood again. Not her light-blond hair. Not her bright blue eyes. Not her perfect house or her daughter, who had tried to save us.

When we left the house, the afternoon sun was bright and Angel put his hat back on low, down to his eyebrows. He stood his coat collar up and tucked his chin down. Going unnoticed was the best plan. Though we had no idea where we were going.

As we walked we didn't speak. We didn't look at each other. Leaving the Sherwood home felt like a second escape, but I knew for Angel it was like losing his mother a second time.

After walking for a few hours I found a bench and sat down. I didn't want to go one step farther. I didn't know where we were or where we were going. I didn't know anything. All I wanted was to be somewhere safe and to sleep so I could get away from all the hurt and confusion. How I wished Grace was with us. She knew the world. She would know how to get around in it. I wondered if we should go back to Ezra and ask him for help — but I didn't want to walk away from my father again.

Angel plopped down on the bench next to me but didn't say a word. He sat next to the armrest on the other side. He rarely did that. He was the one who would sit so closely that we breathed each other's air. But since we had run out of his mother's home, he hadn't touched me or spoken a word. His grieving was in the aging day and all around in the balmy May air. It reached me like the long fingers of the ghosts we'd left behind, making me nervous.

His chest looked empty. Her tarnished and broken response to him wasn't what I'd expected — but I couldn't help but remember the warning. I wondered if Mrs. Sherwood would tell Angel's father about our visit or if she'd keep that a secret.

"I'm sorry, Angel," I whispered. He turned his face away from me. He'd never hidden his tears from me. This hurt wasn't something he had made room for — he hadn't expected her response. What had been before him for years was behind him within an hour. I kept thinking that Joann would know what to say. She would have some words that would help that I didn't know.

We sat on the bench as people came and went, through the lunch time. He didn't say anything. Maybe he couldn't. Maybe if he did try to speak, everything inside of him would come out and leave him as a shell of skin. As my death certificate and the death of my mother had done to me. By the time Ezra Raab stripped me of my name, I was completely numb and nameless. Now we were both like husks without seeds. How would we survive this world?

The bench was near a park, and like the asylum dayroom we'd sat all day. The sunset was in full bloom, and most people were indoors. We were alone. But in our aloneness I was burdened with the noise. Everywhere. Car engines. Car horns. Sirens. Sometimes yelling. The noise at the hospital had always been steady, but this was so different.

I scooted close to him and rested my head against his shoulder. He didn't stiffen at my touch, but he didn't warm either. I wasn't sure when I fell asleep. When I woke his arm was around me and we took up the whole bench now. At some point I'd pulled my legs up and Angel also slept.

There was a layer of dark clouds overhead, and the world around us was quiet. The tree branches around the park bobbed up and down, throwing leaves into the breeze. I sat up and hugged my arms around myself. It had cooled considerably.

"You're not supposed to sleep here." An abrasive voice barreled through the cool, calm night air. A man was coming toward us. He was wearing dark clothes and rode a horse. The animal was much larger up close than in the fields or a storybook. I leaned back. I shook Angel's arm to wake him. Then the horse made a terrible sound, and I hid my face in Angel's shoulder and a shrill scream escaped my lips. This woke Angel. He sat up, and the man spoke to us again. "I'll be back around in about an hour. You'll need to move on by then."

He made a clicking sound with his mouth and his body began to jostle forward. The horse's hooves sounded sharp against the pavement. I squeezed my eyes shut until the sound grew quieter.

Angel was groggy and rubbed his face and stretched.

"Who was that? He said we had to move on." My voice shook. I was cold. I was scared. I was confused. I couldn't stop shaking.

"I think he was some type of police officer."

"Police?"

"I've seen them before bringing criminals into Riverside." Angel stood, and I felt colder on the side where he'd been sitting. I shook harder. "We have to go."

I stood. My teeth chattered. "Where?" I never imagined how empty such a small question could sound.

He turned and put his bag on the bench and began rummaging through it.

"What are you looking for?"

"A map." He said it so quietly I wasn't sure he'd spoken.

We stood under the lamp and shared the glow with a swarm of bugs. On the top of the map was printed the words *State of Pennsylvania.* Angel put his finger near Pittsburgh. He moved it left until it went off the page. He put his face as close as he could. We were in the circle of light together, but I felt disconnected from him. His weight of grief was heavier than he had experienced in his life. I wanted him back.

"We'll go west, to your aunt." The emptiness in his voice hollowed my heart.

There was such finality in his words. He didn't look at me when he spoke them either. He was lost somewhere inside of himself, and I couldn't blame him. At least we were together in our grief. A loss like this was like veins of sadness flowing through your entire body. "Ezra showed me how to read a map."

"Can we take a train?"

He shook his head. "We don't have enough money."

"What about a —"

"It's way too far for a taxi. That's for short distances." His tone was irritated, and when he abruptly folded the map, he turned away from me.

"Ezra did say she was nice," I added and put a shivering hand on his arm. I didn't know how to give to Angel the comfort I also needed. I knew my words were thin and shapeless. "Ezra thinks she'll take us."

"Sure." He nodded. I'd have to be okay with the pieces of Angel that were left. What else could I do? He was the reason I hadn't curled up somewhere and died alone.

"We'll do this together, Angel. Me and you." The kiss and his profession of love always hovered over us. I wondered if he regretted it.

He swallowed hard — I could see it in his throat. But he didn't look at me.

"Would you have stayed with me and my family if —" He finally looked at me, and his stare wandered around my face for a moment before finding my eyes. "Would you have given up on your aunt?"

While there was a slight edge to his tone, his voice was like a single thread that could snap in two at any moment.

I opened my mouth to speak but stopped. I hadn't belonged there as much as he hadn't belonged to Ezra. I only would have stayed for Angel's sake. His mother's embrace had made him happy for those precious few minutes. The happiest I'd ever seen him in all of our years together. Happier than I'd ever been. Happier than when he'd kissed me? I didn't know. Maybe. This evolution of our hearts was painful and left many unanswered questions.

"What matters now is that we'll figure this out together, right?" I didn't answer his question, and my soul winced at my cowardice. He looked away and walked around me. "Angel?"

"I think I'd like to be Luke." He stopped and looked just above my head — as if he could see all the way back to that big brick house where his dreams had died.

"But your mother. The things she said. I don't —"

"You don't understand," he yelled suddenly. He'd never yelled at me before. "I wanted to be that Luke. I wanted to be the kind of son she would love. I wanted that life. Not this one."

The words themselves made me step back and out of the lit sidewalk and into the soft grass. He didn't want me was what I heard.

"Your father at least wants you to write him."

That was what he saw? What I saw was a shocked man who only offered to write because he felt beholden. I saw a man who had stripped me of my name but not given me another. Angel and I were not so different, I thought. But from the beginning his expectations were too high for truth to match them. If only we'd heeded Joann's warning.

"Please — Nell." My new name sounded strange in the tenor of his voice, and I nearly regretted my request. I searched his face. His eyes were bloodshot and his skin ashen. And he was so thin. Getting him well was what mattered.

I nodded in agreement, that I would call him Luke. Then we walked into the unknown darkness of the night. Toward Margareta. Toward Brighton.

1941
Behold the Crux

We walked in the dark, cool evening for hours. We were alone, and I didn't know how Angel knew where we were going. Did he sense west?

The few cars on the road slowed as they passed by but didn't stop. I looked the other way so they wouldn't see me. Angel did the same. My stomach growled in my hollow insides — except for my mind. It was full. We had nothing left to eat. We'd gone hungry so often; maybe it had been preparing us for this.

With every hour we walked the houses grew farther apart. The starry sky took me back to the little Juliet balcony and to the conversation I'd had with my father. After a long stretch of road there was a subtle glow that marked the navy sky.

"I can't see what that is, can you?" Angel called back to me and I ran up ahead to him. I was glad to hear his voice. He hadn't spoken in hours. The only voice I'd been hearing was the one in my head.

The small bloom of light came from some type of building.

"I don't know. Some small building, only one story. I can see cars and trucks in front of it. There're a lot of windows. The sign says 'Diner,' but I don't know what that means."

When we got into the parking lot, we could see people inside. It was some type of dining hall. Everyone was eating or drinking at tables. Only a few cars were parked in front, and there was a truck with a large white rectangular box on the back. It sat up high and intimidating.

I'd longed for the cake that had been set before me at the Sherwood house — I hadn't even taken a bite. I could almost feel the spongy texture in my mouth. Why hadn't I eaten it before I opened my mouth to defend Angel? Watching the people eat now only made me hungrier. Hungrier than I'd been at the hospital. I fought feeling weak from hunger and fear.

Angel sighed, and his shoulders sagged under the parking lot light. He looked through the windows and then at me and then back again. He had to be as hungry as I was, and he hadn't eaten that lovely cake either. He was close enough to the window that I could see his faint reflection in the glass. The person on the other side of the diner window was startled by Angel standing so close. Angel didn't notice, but the man's brow furrowed and he slid away. I pulled at Angel's sleeve and brought him closer.

"I'm so hungry," he finally said.

"Me too." But would food fill us?

"We'll watch what other people do, like Joann said." He sighed. "Maybe it won't be hard."

As nervous as I was about going to this place called Diner, I wanted to eat. I took Angel's hand and he clung to mine.

When we walked inside, everyone turned toward us. Their gazes lingered for several beats of my held breath, then they turned away. A few people looked over their shoulders at us a second time. Whispers floated around and brushed against my ears, but I was glad I couldn't make out the exact words. The only other sounds came from behind a large opening in the wall where a man in a white apron worked in the kitchen. He must have been the one making the food. I didn't know that men cooked in kitchens. Only women cooked at the hospital.

The sizzling and slapping of kitchen implements came in bursts. There was a haze of smoke and bright lights, making me squint. Angel pulled his hat down even farther. His eyes squinted painfully, having gotten used to the dark. The scent of food surrounded us and my emptiness craved even the unfamiliar smells.

"Just the two of you?" The tired voice of a woman came from my right. Her head was down, and she was counting paper money in front of some type of gray machine with a drawer. Her yellow dress and white apron went to her knees, and her little hat reminded me of a nurse's cap. Her brightly made-up face didn't keep her from looking tired and bored. She pushed a pad of paper and pencil into her apron pocket, then her eyes raised to meet us — to meet Angel.

"Another albino? Good Lord, I thought you freaks had left already." She looked at Angel and then at me as if we'd already squandered all of her patience, even though we'd just arrived. "What're you, doll, some kind of handler? You're not beefy enough to be his bodyguard."

A handler? I couldn't fathom what she meant.

"It ain't natural, with those red eyes and all. That lady albino was the first I'd seen, ya know, just about scared me solid."

"A lady albino?" Angel stepped toward her. "Here?"

She scoffed. "Don't pretend you don't know about that side show that's been moving through here." She raised an eyebrow.

"Side show?"

"You know, the strong man, dwarves, bearded ladies." She made a gesture like she was pulling something down from her chin. "The lady albino with the see-through skin like you. You ain't part of the troupe?"

Angel and I shook our heads.

"Well, it don't matter to me as long as you don't give me no trouble." She walked down the aisle of tables and gestured for us to follow her. "The name's Sandy. I'll be taking care of you tonight."

Taking care of us. With little understanding of what that meant, I walked with Angel to the table where Sandy pointed for us to sit. We slid into the bench-like seats facing one another. They were cushioned and not uncomfortable, considering we'd slept on a park bench not so many hours earlier.

The lady put two papers down in front of us and turned to leave.

"What is this?" Angel asked me but loud enough that Sandy turned back toward us.

"Your menu." Her expression was loaded

with confusion.

"A menu?" When Angel spoke I wanted to hide under the table. Why was he so open about his ignorance?

"Just lay off the act, rube," the woman said. "I've got my eye on you two. Don't yous leave without paying neither."

Rube?

Paying for the food hadn't even crossed my mind. What else would we have to pay for that we were used to being given?

"You ask too many questions," I whispered harshly at Angel. "We don't need more attention."

"How are we going to learn if we don't?" He glared. "At least we know what this is called now." He tapped the menu.

The menu had rows of what I knew were foods, but I'd never heard of some of them. Omelets, eggs Benedict, French toast. I didn't know what any of those things were. Angel was looking at his menu wearing an expression that mirrored my thoughts: confusion.

"We get to choose one?" Angel said finally.

"There are dollar signs next to each meal. Do we have enough money?" The writing was quite small. I leaned forward and whispered, "Can you read it well enough?"

Angel looked a little closer at the menu.

His eyes were only a few inches away.

"Let's share something just in case."

I nodded.

"The foods sound so strange. Listen to this —" I turned my menu and pointed at the word *omelet* again. It didn't make sense to me. I read, " 'Plain omelet with ham or bacon.' What is an omelet?"

"Anything we get will taste good."

Angel actually smiled, then he squinted and moved closer to the menu. A moment later he reminded me of the pancake Joyful had brought us a short time ago. We'd split it, only getting a few bites. We'd also eaten eggs before. So we ordered what they called the Classic Breakfast. Just one, though. We each got a pancake, a fried egg, and a slice of bacon. It was my first time eating the salty, crunchy meat, and I savored it from the moment it touched my tongue. It was also my first taste of syrup. It all tasted so good, but the food was gone before my stomach was half full.

Half full was better than nearly starving. At the hospital we'd been starved for food, love, and a family. Would finding Margareta Friedrich change that reality? Would it be days or weeks or more until we found my aunt, and would she even want to be an aunt to me? I'd seen maps as a child and generally knew the geography of our country. Michigan was so far away. And what seemed further away was the idea that a family member cared enough. What if she'd also grown to be more like my grandmother and Mother? What if she wasn't able to help? Then what?

It seemed like years since my mother died, but it had only been about a week. It seemed like years since Joann put us on the train, but it had only been days. It felt like an eternity since Grace knew herself and we'd made plans.

When Sandy kept the three dollars that Angel handed her and said, "Thanks for the tip," I was reminded that I had so much more to learn. Who would I ask?

"You been looking at that map an awful long time." Sandy looked over Angel's shoulder. "You trying to get somewhere?"

"Brighton, Michigan."

"You got a way to get there? I didn't see no car with yous."

Angel shook his head.

"Herb," Sandy called over her shoulder. "You want some company again?"

1941
When It Rains

Once we got outside, I looked up. My little Crux constellation — full of hope — was long gone, having passed through our northern sky only briefly. But the rest of the sky was still unlike anything I'd seen before. I wasn't looking through a dirty, broken, barred window. This was like sitting in the center of the universe and I could look up and see it all happening at once. The dark part of the sky directly above me had small pinholes of light, and then as my eyes cascaded down toward the horizon, the colors went from pink to yellow to a deep blood-orange.

I let myself get lost in the painting of light and hope when a voice called and reminded me that we'd just accepted a ride with a stranger driving a big truck with a white rectangular box on the back.

"So you ready to go, cowboy?" The man, Herb, wore a wide-brimmed hat, baggy denim jeans, and a shirt that was well-fitted around his belly. He had a smile on his rough-red face. He clapped Angel on the back, hard, and it pushed him forward a step.

Cowboy?

"We're ready." Angel righted himself and looked nervously between Herb and me.

"Well, aren't you as cute as a button, little lady," he said, looking at me as he opened the door that was several steps up.

I nodded and walked toward the open truck door.

"So an albino and a mute — got it," he said and nodded a little and then kept talking.

Angel and I got settled in the truck, and it was different being so high up. It reminded me a little of riding in the train. But when we got on the road it didn't have the smooth, rocking rhythm of the train; instead, the buzz from the engine was loud but strangely relaxing.

"Gets awful lonesome driving as much as I do. Nice to have the company for a few hours here."

"We don't have any money." Angel tossed his words toward the man.

The man sighed. "Sandy said that was probably the case. But that's okay. I get paid to drive anyway."

After having walked for hours and eaten a meal, sleep was all I could think of. In my sleep I could see familiar faces and step away from my fear for a time.

"I can get you into Ohio, but once I unload there, I'll be going back to Pittsburgh," Herb said. "Maybe you can find another trucker who can take you a little farther."

Herb paused for a few long moments.

"But be careful, not everyone is as nice as I am." He winked, and when we didn't have anything to say, he began fiddling with a knob that turned on music.

That was the last thing I heard before I fell asleep. It was a calm, dreamless sleep. I wished it had lasted longer than a few hours. My body must have sensed when the truck stopped and I opened my eyes. It was gray, and I knew what that meant. We would have a day of rain.

The driver door opened, and Herb's wide smile and loud voice infiltrated the small space.

"Good morning, travelers," he said. "You were terrible company, I have to say."

I didn't know how to respond. I jabbed Angel, and he roused.

"What?"

"We're stopped," I said.

"Oh, you ain't a mute after all." He laughed a little.

Herb helped me out of the tall truck and shook Angel's hand. He pulled Angel aside, and they looked on a map and talked some things over for a spell. Angel nodded more than he spoke. Then Herb pointed us to a diner across the street. Another one?

The diner looked so much like the one we'd been at only a few hours ago, except it was bigger and looked older. There were large windows in the front, like the other one, but these windows had curtains on the inside that could be pulled. This time Sandy was named Bobbi Jean, and she was wearing blue instead of yellow. She looked at Angel with wide eyes but didn't say anything about another albino. We didn't have to ask what a menu was. Even though I'd never seen or eaten an omelet, the word was familiar now, and it felt strange that it was. We split the same meal but ordered an extra pancake for us both. We also ordered a few muffins for the road.

Not much later we were on the road. But this time our legs were all we had. For the next several hours there was a constant drizzle. I was soaked. My feet ached. My shoes weren't meant for this much walking.

Angel looked as miserable as I did, but we didn't talk much.

Angel had started a cough the day we fled, but it was much worse today and his lips were almost the same color as his skin. His eyes drooped. Was it melancholia or was it the influenza that had been going around the wards when we left? But he kept walking. When one of us stopped we'd eat some of the food we'd purchased at the diner that morning.

The long stretches of road and stretches of sunset were ahead of us now. I was up in front, but when I looked back I could only see the shadowed figure of Angel. He was so far behind and coughing more. I started looking for shelter. A few flashes of lightning peeled open the sky and forced the drizzle into a steady rain. When the rain began piercing through us like liquid needles, I went back and began pulling Angel. He was shivering uncontrollably, and his teeth chattered loudly.

"There," I yelled and pointed. The rain was so loud my voice drowned in the roar. "I think it's a barn."

I had never been inside a barn. I'd only seen pictures of them in books and encyclopedias. The prospect of encountering animals made me hesitate, but I had to get us out of the cold rain. It took me a few minutes to figure out how to open the door — it slid. Why didn't it open like a normal door?

I stepped inside to find that it was mostly empty, and this relieved me. It was also cleaner than I had anticipated. The dirt floors even appeared swept. Was that common? There were stacks of hay or straw — I didn't know the difference — up the side wall. I pulled Angel through the doorframe in the midst of another coughing fit, and his hacking filled up the high rooftop space. The only thing louder than Angel was a large animal in the corner. Once I drew closer I recognized it as a horse. It was the only animal in the barn, and it was disturbed by our racket, neighing and stomping. On the other side of the barn was some type of black carriage.

"Come on," I said and pulled off Angel's coat. "I need to warm you up."

"So cold," he said through chattering teeth.

I pushed him down to sit on one of the bales and scurried around the barn looking for something to keep us warm. I focused hard on Angel's needs through the creaking of the barn in the wind, the horse's occasional racket, and a constant skittering from something unknown. I grabbed a large, thick pad that I put in the empty area on the other side of the horse's space — a pen or something? The horse was starting to quiet, so it was okay to be near it, I supposed. Then I went to the carriage.

"Blankets," I yelled, excited. Then I clapped my hand over my mouth. A house sat only a stone's throw away, and I hoped no one had heard me. It was dark, but we couldn't risk getting caught.

I pulled out the blankets and took them back to the pen where the pad was. I used a rake and gathered some loose hay into a pile and put the blankets over it. I helped Angel over in the dark. My eyes had adjusted well enough, but he stumbled the whole way and I wasn't sure if it was his eyesight or sickness. I stripped him down to his undershirt and long underwear. I took my soaking coat off too but didn't feel right about taking off more. Though Angel and I had been best friends since we were children and Joann had on more than one occasion stripped us down to give us a quick washing together after an outdoor escapade, this was different. Things had changed between the two of us, and I knew enough to try to maintain some modesties. I used a wet handkerchief in his suit coat on his forehead, but it was hot in minutes.

The night fell, and we only had one diner muffin left. I broke it in half, but Angel waved off eating and fell into a restless sleep. I ate my share, hoping he would eat a little in the morning. Between Angel's coughing, his rattled breathing, and the heavy rainfall, I wasn't sure I could sleep. My eyes roamed around the room until they landed on our shoes. Worn and falling apart. But they were walking us to freedom. I wrapped the last blanket around me and held him as tightly as I could until he stopped shivering. Then I relaxed my own body and followed him into a deep sleep.

I didn't wake until I felt that strange awareness that someone was watching me. Angel's breathing was even; he was still asleep. I was afraid to open my eyes, but the stare was too heavy. I opened my eyes and saw a child watching us. A little boy. Maybe five or six. He was wearing a black wide-brimmed hat and a black suit. He had hair cut straight across his brow, and his brown eyes were big and round.

"Hi." I pulled my bag near me. I quietly shook Angel awake and whispered for him to sit up. He didn't move much, and I jabbed him again. I wished I'd kept his clothes closer. Angel roused. He was still feverish but had cooled some. When Angel noticed the little boy, he tried to get up, but fell into a coughing fit instead.

The little boy just stared. He spoke a few words, but I didn't understand him. I carefully stepped away, and the boy watched every move I made as I grabbed the stiff, dry clothes off the wheels.

The little boy's face was clean and looked freshly pink and washed. He had round and full cheeks, and his mostly black clothes didn't fit him perfectly but looked to be clean and crisp. I'd never seen a well-cared-for child, but I knew he was one. The only children I'd seen were ward children — though mostly at a distance. Joann refused to let me go over there, afraid they would keep me. The children at the factory houses looked about as bad off as asylum children. But this boy, I enjoyed looking at him. Looking at his wholesomeness and the appearance of being cared for.

"Don't you worry about us," I said in a sweet voice like Joann used to speak to me. "We'll be gone in a few minutes and you don't need to tell anyone we're here."

"Freemie?" A woman's high voice cut through the quiet in the barn. "Freemie?"

He took a few steps toward the voice and spoke, then pointed at us. I rushed to help

Angel put his clothes on, then grabbed his bag.

"We have to go," I said and yanked him toward the barn door.

There stood a plump and strangely dressed woman. Even I knew she was strangely dressed, in a black dress and white bonnet. Her face was clean and plain looking — it wasn't made up like I usually saw. I knew there was a tradition in the real world to wear black when someone died. Or was this the way she always dressed?

"Hello. Are you in need?" She spoke simply and stepped back as if afraid, even though her face didn't reflect that. I felt bad. We knew what it meant to be afraid, and I hated for anyone to feel that about us.

"We're leaving. We were caught in the storm," I said. Angel was hunched over with one of the blankets balled up in his arms. I held both bags and my damp coat. "Can we keep a blanket?"

She nodded. "You can take whatever you need."

I looked at Angel, then back at the woman. She had a nice face. "We're awfully hungry. Do you have any food?"

The woman nodded with an unalarmed expression and walked toward the house. She said a few words to the boy, and he ran inside ahead of her. What was the strange language they spoke?

I helped Angel tuck the blanket around himself tighter. Where we stood waiting I could see the woman moving around in the house. She moved with a steady grace and not the rush fear brought. She seemed undeterred by our presence.

After ten or fifteen minutes she came back and handed me a bag — it was a rough weave with threading loosened on top. It was full and heavy.

"May God be with you," she said plainly and with such softness in her eyes and face.

I reached for it and said thank you. She turned to leave and I asked for her name.

"Lydia," she said. "And this is my son, Freeman Junior."

Freeman. Free man. I liked that and nodded to her.

Then we were off again. I looked back twice, and the two kindly strangers stood at the end of their driveway and watched us.

The day was damp but more like the leftover rain than fresh. But Angel continued to cough. I had to find somewhere for him to lie down. We started to enter a town, but I veered us off in another direction. Too many people. Eventually we were on a gravel road that was lined with woods on both sides. There were a few smaller barns, like our previous shelter.

It was late afternoon, and the gray and dampness were heavy. The road we traveled ran through a dense forest. It would give us good cover and get us out of the drizzle.

"Over here," I said and took Angel's sleeve. We walked deeper into the wooded area, and I was sure I could find a space for us to at least rest.

I made sure the ground was dry before I helped Angel down, then tucked the blanket around his curled-up body. I took off my coat and put it under his head. He was asleep in minutes. I leaned against a tree trunk and tucked next to Angel to keep myself warm. I ate a little of the bread and cheese Lydia in the black dress had put in the bag, but Angel didn't want to wake to eat.

I looked up through the clearing above the treetops. A collection of gray clouds raced over us. Somewhere in the midst of the whistle of a wood thrush and the skittering of a small animal, I fell asleep and woke to the night when the stars outweighed the dark.

Night sounds choired alongside the rattle in Angel's chest. His head was hotter than ever. I tried to wake him up to give him some of the water out of a jar Lydia had put in the sack. But he wouldn't rouse. I rocked him back and forth, but he didn't even so much as groan. I tried to be like Joann and take his pulse, but I was shaking too much. I started shoving him hard and yelling for him to wake up. What was I supposed to do? I yelled for Joann. I stood in the forest yelling over and over for help. But who would come? We were alone.

1941
Fancies and Fears

I yelled for Angel. I yelled for Joann. I yelled for my mother. I yelled for anyone to help me. My gaze landed on every part of my surroundings until I finally saw lights. I frantically ran while still yelling for help. Running toward the lights between the gaps of tree trunks.

I ended up at the road. There was a long line of vehicles. Trucks and some that reminded me of a train car and others looked like a small house on wheels. I couldn't see how many there were, but it reminded me of a train without rails. Could I trust strangers? They were all I had, and all I could think of was Angel. Losing him would be a wound that would never heal. Life without Angel would be the kind of alone that might make me want to die or, worse, return to the hospital and be forgotten and forget myself. No, I couldn't do that. I could never let that happen.

I turned to look back to where I'd run from. Angel was out there, out of sight. Feverish and sweaty on the ground in a dark forest. So I kept following the voices and the light because Angel needed me. I started yelling again and stepped so close to the road I nearly got run over. I heard horns blaring and shouting to stop. They'd heard me — seen me. I stopped my yelling and running. I watched as the vehicles pulled over. In the starlight and beams I saw some faces looking out through the windows. Mostly women. My head told me this was a bad idea, but my legs betrayed me and wouldn't run away.

After another minute no one had approached me.

"My friend needs help," I yelled. "I need help." My voice was so ragged it could've scared the bark off the trees.

A door opened in a truck from the back, then I heard fast footsteps against the road coming toward me. I held my breath.

A few moments later, someone stood in front of me — the tallest, largest person I'd ever seen. Broad shoulders. A thick neck. I took a step back. Then my fear pushed me a few more steps back.

"What's going on?" This voice came from the shadows. A man with dark hair and ready eyes. I caught his gaze instantly and his face softened. "Hello. I'm Conrad. Who are you?"

When I didn't answer Conrad spoke again. "Are you in need of help?"

He took several strides toward me and I turned toward him and my hands posed like claws — like an afraid asylum patient. Conrad raised his hands in surrender, but before he could speak I was squeezed from behind. It was the giant, and the hold was tighter than a straight-jacket. My lungs constricted and I couldn't breathe. All I could think of was Angel. He would die without help, I was certain. It would be my fault. Another death. But no amount of struggling freed me.

"Let go, let go, let go," Conrad repeated rapidly to the giant. I saw concern in his eyes. "It's all right. She's just afraid."

The grip around me loosened, and the giant stepped away. People were everywhere now, one of them a masked man, and I regretted my decision to come this way.

"It's okay. We aren't going to hurt you." Conrad reached out toward me, and just as I realized my balance was failing, he steadied me. A heavy wooziness hung over me, and I began to see things that didn't seem real. Three identical women. The giant holding a woman who was as small as a doll. A woman who was as white as light. Like Angel. Was I hallucinating? They were all standing around the vehicles, some in blaring headlights, some in the shadows. Who were these people?

It didn't matter. I needed to help Angel, and they said they wouldn't hurt us. I pulled my arm free and pointed toward the trees.

"Do you need help?" Conrad repeated and our gazes connected, and I was sure he knew everything I was thinking.

"Is there someone with you? Out there?" He pointed over his shoulder toward the woods.

I nodded. "My friend. He's sick. He needs help."

He looked past me and nodded, and several rough-looking men and the giant ran off to where I'd come from. I wanted to go with them, but when I tried to follow lightheadedness overtook me. A gentle arm came around me and kept me upright.

"We found him," I heard voices saying from the woods. Then a few minutes later one of the men ran back with a furrowed expression. He whispered to Conrad.

"An albino?" Conrad said breathlessly, dropping his arm from me.

"Yes, but that's not what's wrong with

him. He's sick. But please don't take him to a hospital."

Would they think he was feebleminded like his mother had believed? I couldn't — wouldn't — let them hurt him.

"Get Gabrielle," Conrad said. Then he turned to look at me. "We won't hurt your friend. How long have you been out here?"

I was afraid to say too much. "We've been walking for a few days."

"Just the two of you? Alone?" His voice was soft and kind. He had a shadow of whiskers that matched the dark hair that fell naturally over his forehead and eyes. He swiped it away every so often.

"Just us."

The giant with arms as round as tree trunks came out of the woods carrying Angel. I tried to walk toward him, but Conrad regained a grip on my arm. I was feeling so physically weak all I could do was watch. Hadn't I left the hospital to avoid this overt control over our lives? But I also needed help.

Then a woman appeared. But not just any woman. It was the woman of pure white light that I thought was an illusion. She was beautiful and glowed like Angel. She wore a long pale dress that wrapped and tied at her small waist. She was tall, and with elegant steps she moved toward Angel. Even in my fear, the serenity in her movements brought some measure of peace. The giant stood there on the side of the road holding Angel steady for her.

"Oh, my sweet boy," she said, touching his face and mothering him like she knew him. She looked around until she found me, her eyes doing what Angel's always did. When she found me she came close; her gaze pierced through me. "What is his name?"

"Angel, I call him Angel." I winced, wishing I'd called him Luke.

"Angel." The way she said it sounded like a magic spell, then she returned to Angel.

"I need to go too." I pulled my arm roughly away from Conrad, a surge of strength returning. Flashes of my history with Angel burst into my mind — playing, crying, dreaming. He was all I had, and I wouldn't lose him.

"We will not hurt him or take him away from you. We have a doctor who will give him attention." Conrad's voice was a braiding together of sincerity and mystery. But Angel. I stepped toward Angel when my eyes caught sight of three men walking out of the woods with our things. Each nodded a hello to me as they passed me. One man came and wrapped my blanket around me, and it was heavy and warm and weighted with care and relief. I didn't know that I was shivering.

Angel was carried away from me with the bright woman at his side. I decided to trust — for now — the kindness of strangers. Yet there was something odd about the group that made me question why they were so willing to help us. Especially when there was sickness involved. Conrad held the heavy blanket around my shoulders and kept an arm around me.

"We are friends," he said and walked me in the same direction as Angel.

Angel was taken to a truck with a room built on the back. A door was opened and a yellow, inviting glow poured out. Angel was placed inside, and Gabrielle slinked in after him. Then the door was shut.

"I need to go inside with him."

"It's okay. Your Angel will get some medicine, and you both need to rest. We'll talk in the morning. You won't be apart from him for long."

"But where are you traveling to?"

"West. Toward Chicago. But we will be setting up camp in the morning here in Ohio."

I thought for a moment and pictured

where Chicago was on a map, thankful for being taught geography. We would at least be heading in the right direction.

"Come." He nudged me forward, but I resisted. I looked him in the face and tightened my jaw, hoping he wouldn't see my fear.

"First, who are you?"

He paused and seemed to consider my question. "Well, you know my name. What's yours?" He stepped back and smiled, waiting.

I began forming the sound of a *B.* But then I stopped.

"Nell," I said.

"Nell. All right." He smiled and nodded. There was something so honest in the way he looked at me that it made me hope I could trust him. "Come. We must be off."

He led me to another truck, similar to the one Angel was in. He opened the door and gestured grandly for me to enter.

Inside were several women, and it looked as comfortable as I'd ever seen a bedroom look. I turned back to Conrad.

"You haven't answered my question." I gestured to the line of vehicles. "Who are you?"

"Who are we? We are the Fancies and Fears, my dear." He bowed and rose with a flourish. "The show that will thrill your dreams and confirm your nightmares."

He looked at me as if he was waiting for some response. But I stood there ignorant of what he was talking about. I'd already had enough nightmares in my life. He must have understood something in my expression.

"We're a troupe of performers," he explained further.

"Performers?" I repeated.

He squinted at me like he saw something in me that shouted my stupidity. "Where are you from?"

I would never tell him the truth.

"Pennsylvania." Then without warning I lost all my breath in that single word. My chest tightened.

Conrad put his hand on my blanketed shoulder, and I looked up at him. His mouth was moving, but I could not hear him. His eyebrows and forehead wrinkled up in concern. My hand went to my chest, the blanket fell, and I was heaving for air. Why now? My eyes remained on Conrad. He helped me stumble, step over step, into the truck room. I fumbled my way through the doorway, half resisting, half relenting.

A woman spoke. I could hear her words but didn't understand them. I looked at her, but everything was moving in slow motion as I tried to catch my breath. The woman had dark hair, tanned skin, and Rosina's smile. Oh, I missed Rosina. Her hair was slicked in a knot at the back of her neck, but Rosina's was often short because of the lice. But the slack jaw was also the same.

The woman who was not Rosina sat me down next to her on a soft mattress and rubbed my back and spoke in a soft, unknown tongue that soothed me. Her words were laced with a thick accent I didn't recognize, and even though she wasn't singing, it reminded me of a lilting tune. After another few minutes my breathing began to slow down. But every part of me was afraid, and I wished I'd never found these people who had just managed to separate Angel and me.

"You okay now, my dear?" were the woman's first words in English. It was a voice of age and weight and wisdom all folded together as one.

I shook my head. I wasn't okay. I was scared. And then the pressure in my chest came again and I gasped for air.

"Now, now," she said and patted my back. "What you afraid of, *kotik*?"

Even though I didn't know what that last word meant, the affection and tenderness in her voice weren't lost on me. She shushed me, and her hand against my back was the kind of touch I needed.

Across from me were three identical girls who appeared around my age. The three tilted their heads to the left exactly the same way and smiled.

They sat so closely to each other, like they were one. They were beautiful. Dark eyes, dark hair, dark skin. Their faces were all eyes and smiles. Their straight black hair hung like thick curtains down the sides of their faces. I was mesmerized.

"We cannot pronounce their real Hindi names, so we call them Persephone, Penelope, and Thalia. They are the Sirens. Say hello, *kotiks.*" One year I'd read a little of the *Odyssey* and knew Sirens could lure the hardest of hearts.

"Hello," they said together.

"I am Alima, *kotik.*"

"What does that mean?" My question was breathless and quiet.

"Mean?" Her accent separated her from my memory of my asylum friend. She was different.

"It's not English," I said, still gathering my breath.

"Kotik?" Her eyebrows lifted into her hairline. "Oy, it means 'little kitten.' "

She'd called me kitten. I liked it.

There was silence for a few long moments, and then I had to ask another question. "They won't take Angel away from me, will they?" *Breathe,* I told myself. *Breathe.*

"Your friend? The sick one?" Alima's thick voice rested in my ears.

I nodded my head.

"He will be okay," she said and patted my knee. "Doctor will take good care of the albino boy."

His name is Angel, I wanted to yell. *He isn't just an albino boy.*

"So it's true?" one of the Sirens asked. I didn't know which one had spoken, even though I was looking right at them.

"True?" My breath was still thin, and I had to concentrate so it wouldn't thin further.

"An albino came with you?" one of them asked.

"*Tishe,* quiet about that," Alima admonished. She smoothed my hair from my face, then returned her attention to the three across from us. "Sing for her. Soothe our new friend."

And without consulting one another in any way that I could see, they began. And everything in my body was heavy and tired and moved slowly. A small thread of smoke from a corner began dancing as the truck moved and rocked me to sleep. It was warm, and suddenly I couldn't keep my eyes open.

The Sirens sang me to sleep.

1990
Evolution

Kelly wants an explanation of every photograph, but when we get to Angel I pause. She wants to know, but I've always held him tightly to me and can't tell her. She doesn't push.

The photo of Angel, however, makes me laugh a little. His trademark innocent smile is so wide, like it had always been. But I can see now, as an experienced photographer, that I'd gotten the exposure entirely wrong. It made for a decent photo for our purposes, but I wish that I'd done better. The photo is washed out and brighter even than his albinism. The boy I knew. The boy who had saved my life so many times and in so many ways. He'd also broken my heart more than maybe anyone else ever had, but that was well after this picture had been taken.

When we get to Rosina and Carmen, I tell Kelly about the prayers and the food and how much they loved each other. And

Lorna. The room full of women in tightened camisoles. I will never be able to remember every name. Then the picture of hydrotherapy surfaces.

"I can't believe I got it right," I whisper, that day returning to me.

"What?" Kelly asks.

"See the light in that window?" I point. "The beam didn't take over the photo but made the steam more visible, and for a photo older than the hills — it's good. We broke the rules taking this shot, and I've wondered since I was sixteen if I got it right."

Then there is me.

A river of hot tears washes my face. Oh, the girl I was. The girl in the photograph didn't know what life she was about to live and all she would have to endure for the freedom she needed. I grieve for her. How lost I was without Brighton. That girl believed she would never see anything but the four walls around her, even though she had hopes and dreams. But being forgotten in the asylum was her truth at the time of this photo. I know better now.

The next set of photos brings such dark clouds. My hair had grown, but Grace's had begun to fall out. She was so thin. Her skin, even in the black-and-white photos, looked ashen and aged. The twinkle in her eyes couldn't be caught in a photo any longer. Her smile had been lost long before.

"Tell me about her?" Kelly asks quietly.

I nearly forget she's with me.

"This is what the asylum did to her — what it did to most patients." I tap the photo and hold it up so she can really see. "I was spared some of this — *evolution* — because I'd been, well, as Dickens would've put it, I was raised by hand there. I'd been cared for and loved and, for a time, kept away from so much. I was played with and educated. It was all I knew. But Grace had lived in the real world with a real life. Then she had to give it all up." I pause and look. "I wish I could've saved her."

1941
A Family

When I woke, I was alone. I was curled up among heaps of blankets with remnants of the earthy scent from the night before still circling in the air. Light came through the thinly curtained windows. Voices snuck in from outside, though indiscernible and so mixed together that it reminded me of the asylum dayroom. But I wasn't there. I was somewhere in Ohio in some type of house truck with people who called themselves the Fancies and Fears. Performers, the man had said.

I sat up with a gasping inhale.

Angel.

Where was he? It took me several nerve-wracking moments to remember everything from the previous night. He'd been carried off under the watchful eye of an elegant albino woman. She made me feel far away from Angel. Like he would never see me the same way again.

I had to find him. My bare feet chilled on the truck floor. Where were my shoes? I pictured Alima taking them off and tucking me in like I imagined a grandmother would do. But she didn't seem real anymore. Had there really been a woman who had spoken sweet, oddly comforting words to me? Had I really seen three identical girls? The visions from the night before were blurry.

I found my shoes and slipped them on, breaking the shoelace of the left one. I cussed and then slapped my hand over my mouth. Joann would have threatened to wash my mouth out with soap if she'd heard me. But she was far away. I closed my eyes and breathed in and out, in and out. I rubbed my hands over my face and smoothed my hair into a small ponytail, then opened the door.

I welcomed the cool breeze that caressed my cheeks. We had moved from the road to an expansive field, and all the vehicles were parked along the edges. Numerous trucks with those rooms on the back and some larger vehicles that looked like something between a bus and a train car. I'd never seen anything like it. Some had curtained windows and a porch on the back, like a caboose on a train. A few tents had been built, and the smell of food found my nose.

Farther ahead a small platform and walls were being constructed. A dozen people carrying crates passed me without even noticing me. Children helped with smaller items and their wiggly bodies zoomed around with spills of laughter every few moments.

Beyond the movement of workers and the vehicles I saw a small town. With a lineup of storefronts. Another diner. A building with a cross on the top of a white point — a church? My eyes lingered on the cross, and I could see Rosina making the sign of the cross over her body. I almost did the gesture myself. Beyond the town and all around us there were houses and other buildings and a large lake off into the horizon. The scent of a farm was in the air.

But where was I? And more important, where was Angel?

I looked back at the truck where I'd slept and noted that the door was yellow, chipped and crooked too. I didn't want to forget where my bag was. I would leave it for now. I needed to find Angel. Besides my apprehension about this unusual group of people, my main concern was helping Angel get well and finding out if we could trust the doctor.

I went to the truck house next to me and nervously stood in front of the door and knocked. The door opened and the smallest woman I'd ever laid eyes on opened it. I could've held her on my hip like a child. I stepped back. Was this the woman I'd seen in the arms of the giant last night? She was dressed in a multicolored red and purple skirt threaded with gold. Her hair was wrapped in a scarf. Her shy smile revealed gaps between her few teeth.

"Oh, it's you," she said in a hundred-year-old voice. An untucked strand of silver hair contrasted with her dark skin.

My brow knit up. None of this made sense to me. The vision of the giant from last night and then this tiny woman in front of me. The other albino. Conrad had called them Fancies and Fears and said they were performers. What did they perform?

In shock I shut the door in the woman's face and ran to the next truck, but before I knocked I would try to see through the window. This one had no curtains. The words from the first diner lady, Sandy, came to mind. Something about a troupe and an albino woman, and she'd used the word *freaks.* Were these the freaks she was talking about?

Then through a hazy side window of the truck, I saw him. I saw my friend. My only friend. The one who said he loved me. He was sitting up and looked better than the night before. What sort of doctor had been able to do that? No doctor at Riverside could have. When patients were as sick as Angel, they often died. He had that healthy subtle pink in his lips again. He was wearing different clothes. A white shirt that was cut low in the chest, cuffs unbuttoned. His pants were white also. There was no harsh crease down the middle, and both the shirt and pants were loose on his body. The clothes reminded me of his hospital uniform and were nothing like what Dr. Woburn had given him.

And she was there too.

Gabrielle. Hadn't that been the name Conrad had called her?

I could see that she was older than him. Nearly his mother's age, I guessed. Her white hair trailed down to her waist, and her white lacey dress was also cut deeply down her chest. She was holding his hands. Was he holding hers back? Every now and again she would take one of her white, graceful fingers and stroke his face or smooth his hair. He tilted his head and looked so intently at her. Like he was studying her face.

Had he ever looked at me like that? Then she put her arm around him, and he nestled against her chest like a small child would with his mother. His real mother had held him also — but then rejected him. He closed his eyes and seemed to be more relaxed and content than I'd ever seen him. The kind of contentment his mother had never offered.

Then Gabrielle turned and looked right at me. It startled me, and I turned away from the window, only to find that Conrad had come up behind me. He stood so close that his smoky and musky scent encircled me. He was handsomer than I'd remembered. He wore denim pants and a loose shirt that was similar to Angel's. A blue bandanna was tied around his thick neck. Under other circumstances I would have said that his dark hair and light eyes were memorable, but in the presence of this group with such unusual appearances, he was entirely commonplace. The giant, the tiny woman, the three Sirens, Gabrielle, and even something about Alima seemed almost mystical — though I couldn't reason it out. But Conrad wasn't like any of them. He was like me. Ordinary.

"You have questions?" He lifted his eyebrows.

I nodded.

"Where are we?" I needed this simple

question answered first.

"We're somewhere in Ohio still. A few hours from where we found you — or you found us. Come, let me show you around."

"What about Angel?" I didn't want to leave him again.

"You can see he's made a remarkable recovery — our doctor is gifted — and is in good hands with Gabrielle." He gestured toward the truck.

"If he's well, then we need to be on our way. We —"

"All in good time, Nell." He offered his hand. "Come."

I studied his confident expression. It reminded me of Dr. Woburn's arrogance — but diffused with such charisma it warmed instead of cooled me. So I took his hand.

I'd never held any man's hand but Angel's. It didn't feel the same. Angel's had always been soft next to my own, warm and familiar and protective. But Conrad's hand was thicker, and his skin was tough. He held my hand a little tighter, but not protectively; it felt controlling. My guard was up, but I wasn't frightened.

He led me back toward the trucks. He waved at some people, and they all looked from him to me and then back to him with different expressions. Some winked. Some raised an eyebrow. Conrad's arm stretched back holding on to my hand, and I had to work hard to keep up because of my broken-laced shoe, and my insecurities.

"Who are all these people?" There really were so many more than I'd realized the night before and so many of them were ordinary like Conrad and me, confusing me further.

"The common ones are our workers and builders, and the gifted ones are our performers. You might use the words *normal* and, well, *abnormal.*" He turned around and smirked.

The way he said *normal* was something I understood — the inflection, the insinuation. I knew what he was trying to say, and it made me feel itchy as if I wanted to slip out of my skin. It took me too far back to where I didn't want to go. But I couldn't resist the memory of Joann calling me normal, saying that I wasn't like a real asylum patient. I wasn't what they called feebleminded or mad. I wasn't mentally disturbed and had never starved myself like Grace — though I had been starved. I didn't hear voices or see people who weren't there — though now I often heard the voices of my patient friends in my head and recognized them everywhere in the people I was meeting. And here I was being called normal again, because I wasn't too tall or too small or too light.

On the other side of the erected tent, there was a wooden fence. It separated our field of tents and trucks from the sidewalk and town. Boys ran over from the neighborhood and stood on the bottom rail.

"Freak show, freak show, freak show," they chanted over and over, reminding me again of Sandy's words.

A small group of children on our side of the fence who were playing with marbles stopped and looked over, listening. The largest two boys stood. Their fists balled and their mouths grew straight and solid. Conrad called to them and nodded a stern *no.* Discontent dripped from their faces, but they retreated back to their game playing. The taunting, however, did not cease.

Unflinching, Conrad kept our conversation moving. "These men here build the stage and the walls and the corridors for patrons to come and look."

"Look?"

"At their fancies." He let go of my hand and turned to walk backward to face me and gestured with grandeur. "And fears." His eyes sparkled.

I was starting to understand, though what

they performed was still a mystery to me. I just looked at my surroundings, taking in as much as I could. Conrad lowered his arms and stopped walking. His gaze locked on me.

"You have a question."

"What do the gifted perform?"

He smiled and put his hand out to me again. "You'll see tonight." I took it and he comfortably tucked my arm close to his side and led me on. "But now you must meet someone very important."

Conrad walked me toward the colorful tent behind the stage. The only thing I could think about was a picture I'd seen once of a circus. It was from a brightly illustrated children's book Joann had read to me when I was a child. Was that what this was? A circus? But didn't circuses have animals? Lions, horses, tigers, monkeys. Was there such a thing as a circus without animals?

When we got to the curtains, I wasn't sure how Conrad could find his way through, but he held open the curtain for me, revealing a dimly lit hall. I hesitated and looked back at the truck that held Angel and Gabrielle.

"He'll be okay," Conrad said with a convincing smile. "Don't worry about him."

I let him lead me through several curtained hallways. I didn't see anyone else but I could hear voices. I recognized Alima's voice and the Sirens singing quietly, but Conrad kept me moving and led me to a curtained wall, then stopped.

"Lazarus?" he called loudly.

"Yes?" the voice said.

"I brought the girl," Conrad responded.

It was strange to be referred to as *the girl.* It was like nothing had changed except the people around me. I was still just *the girl* who didn't belong.

"Come on in," the curtained voice said.

With Conrad's hold still firm on my arm, together we ducked through the lighter-curtained doorway and entered a fabric-lined room. The room inside was darker than even the hallway. There was a table, dark wood and heavy looking. A man stood behind it with his back to us. He wore a soft-looking jacket that I wanted to touch. It was a shade of deep red like almost everything else around me. The man was fitting something over his head, and we stood there for a few stretched seconds before he turned.

I gasped. It was the masked man from the night before.

He was just average height. His red jacket was longer in the back than the front, and it made his belly protrude. What made him remarkable was that his face was half covered with a black mask. There was an almond-shaped hole where his left eye could see out. It traced around his nose and across his cheek, near his mouth, with straps that tightened like a belt around the back of his head. Everything else about him was of no significance.

"Lazarus Hale, at your service." He put his hand out to me. Conrad let go of me, and I slowly reached out and took the man's meaty hand. "Don't be afraid of me. Or of this." He pointed to his mask. "It's just a piece of leather to cover up some ugly scars from the war. Mustard gas and — Well, you understand."

No, I didn't. I didn't understand at all. I didn't know what mustard gas was, even though I knew what leather was and it always made me think of restraints. But that leather had caused wounds, not hidden them.

"Your name is —" He looked at Conrad.

"Nell," Conrad reminded him.

"Ah, yes, Nell," Lazarus Hale said. "Such an unusual name. Where does it come from?"

"My grandmother," I answered too quickly.

He nodded and kept his eyes trained on me. "And you came with the albino. Angel." He widened his arms out like he had wings. He cast his face to the ceiling as if catching some glow from heaven that wasn't there. My skin tingled in a funny way. I didn't like this man.

After a moment he lowered his arms and his eyes connected with mine — despite the mask. "It's perfect — really, quite perfect."

"Perfect?" I asked.

"The albino boy with that name." Lazarus chuckled a little. "That's perfect. That's all I mean. Where did you find him? How are you — together?" Lazarus sat and leaned back in his chair. "Are you married?"

I would never tell him the whole truth, but I did say, "We grew up together. We're not married."

"And why are you two alone on the road?" This man was asking too many questions. What was he after?

He leaned forward and laced his fingers together, and his thumbs twirled around themselves. I thought for a long moment about how I should answer this. But when I didn't he spoke again. "Did Conrad here tell you who we are?"

I cleared my throat, hoping to make my

voice strong and full. "Fancies and Fears, right?"

"You know what else we are?" His uncovered eyebrow rose.

I shook my head.

"We're a family. And I'm the father." He pushed the chair back and stood. "And I don't trust outsiders."

His words hung out around us and became like the tent poles, holding up the heavy curtains.

"He wants to make sure you're not running from the law or something," Conrad leaned in and clarified.

I shook my head. We weren't running from the law. We were running from the men in the white coats, though.

"No. We're traveling to see my aunt," I said without a stutter, taking on the strength and boldness I'd witnessed in Grace. I made eye contact with both men. "She lives in Michigan. A town called Brighton." I paused again. They didn't say anything. "We don't have any money so we're walking. We got a ride with a truck driver a few days ago."

"I see." Lazarus nodded with several bobs of his head. "Well then, you can stay — for now. But everyone pulls their weight around here."

I hadn't asked to stay, but I kept my face

stoic and sure. Angel needed help, but the moment he was well enough, we would leave. I had never asked to stay at Riverside either, and I was there for eighteen years. I wouldn't let that happen again.

"Can you sing?"

I shook my head.

"Acrobat?"

"No."

"Can you talk to the dead?"

"What?" I said louder. I didn't know anyone could and I was sure my face displayed my ignorance.

He sighed. He looked at Conrad, then at me. He came from around the desk toward me, lifted my chin, extended my arm out straight, and looked my body up and down.

"Conrad will figure out what you're good for. Alima will help." He walked toward the curtain opening.

Then with a wink he walked out.

"What does he mean? What will Alima help with?" I asked, having too many words in my mouth at once. "We aren't staying. We're going to my aunt's as soon as Angel is strong enough." I hesitated for a moment. "We don't belong here."

Conrad turned and looked me right in the eyes.

"Where do you belong, *Nell*?" And the

way he said my name gave me gooseflesh. What had Angel told these strangers?

1941
The Sirens' Call

I wasn't taken to Angel; I was told that he was still weak and needed to rest. But I had been fed, and since I'd slept through breakfast I was ravenous. But serving me a meal didn't eradicate my distrustful suspicions.

Conrad left me with the cook since he had things to do for tonight. Before he left, he reminded me that everyone had to do their part — including me. I was certain I was being kept away from Angel intentionally and that it had something to do with their show. But I also was sure he was safe, so I was going to bide my time and maybe slip away during the night.

Until then, I peeled and cut potatoes — just like I'd helped Joyful. After hours of it, my hands ached. And the sun was setting. A few electric lights on long wooden poles were turned on and the half a dozen colorful tents illuminated.

"Hmm, maybe I did find what you're

good at." Conrad jogged up and pointed at the potatoes and flashed a smile at me.

"It's just peeling," I said. "I'd like to see Angel now."

"Soon. I have something for you and then you can see your Angel." He put a hand out to me — this was becoming a habit. I was glad to put down the peeling knife and take his hand.

He led me past the truck house where I'd seen Angel earlier. I tried to look through the window as we walked by, but it appeared empty. He took me to a tent on the fringes of their circled area. He bowed in a grand gesture, directing me inside.

Alima was there, with a smile on her face and a makeshift bath and shower next to her. She looked different from the previous night. Her face was made up, and her lips and cheeks were bright. She was draped with beautiful scarves and jewelry.

"Come inside, *Nell.*" She said my name the same way Conrad had.

I looked back at Conrad, who encouraged me with a smile to go ahead.

"I don't understand."

"Since you are not planning to stay, we want you to look your best tonight and show you a good time."

I inhaled and looked back at the shower

and bath. How nice it would feel. One night here. Just one.

"A shower would be nice," I admitted. "And then I can see Angel?"

With a nod Conrad left me with Alima.

Over the next hour several little girls came in with pitchers of hot steaming bathwater. When I was finished, Alima dressed me in the most beautiful dress I'd ever seen — pale pink, nearly the color of my skin. She styled my disarrayed hair that was just past my chin and put makeup on my face for the first time in my life. It felt strange sliding across my skin and lips.

"Krasavitsa," Alima said. "Such a beauty."

"I'm not," I said, feeling shy at her compliment. I knew what I'd seen in the mirror my entire life was nothing but a girl with ashen skin and stringy, dirty-blond hair. Joann was beautiful, with porcelain skin and bright lips and shiny blond hair. I had always been plain.

"Oh, you know this, huh?" Alima's eyebrows lifted high. "Let's go to mirror."

She walked me out of the tent bathroom and my dress whisked around my ankles in the breeze.

"Shoes and mirror — come," Alima said and flicked her hand for me to follow.

She took me into another tent, and inside

was a woman in a pink dress. It was like the one I was wearing, only she was elegant and her face sparkled.

"You like?" Alima pointed.

"What?"

"That's you, *kotik.*"

That wasn't another woman; it was *me.* I walked toward the mirror, within inches of the glass. I'd never seen myself like this before. The dress was sheer across my shoulders and heart-shaped over my chest, and there was a wide, shiny belt at the waist. The sheer skirt went down to my ankles, and the underskirt slipped softly against my bare legs. I was mesmerized by my reflection. I gently touched my hair that was rolled in beautiful waves similar to Joann's. My face was smooth and creamy like a doll. And my eyes looked wide and large.

Alima placed a pair of shoes in front of me and told me to fit them onto my feet. They were a little tight, but it didn't matter. It was one night. But the fact I'd never had so much personal attention since my childhood wasn't lost on me — and by strangers, no less. And they were helping Angel get well. Maybe my distrust of Lazarus was unfounded.

"Why?" I asked Alima.

"He wants you to be beautiful tonight."

She winked at me.

"Conrad?" I felt heat come to my face and under my arms.

"No." She leaned in toward me. "The Mentalist."

"The Mentalist?"

"Father Lazarus, of course. Our keeper, our deliverer."

Why would that man want me to be beautiful tonight? My spine prickled. Was Angel feeling the same concern and suspicions that I was? I took in my appearance again. This wasn't me, and I wanted to get my other clothes back on. But I had the feeling I had to play a part right now in order to get to Angel. Lazarus might want me to look beautiful, but what he really wanted was Angel. I could see it clearly now. Why did it take me so long to see that?

"Why does Lazarus want me to be dolled up for his circus tonight?" I tried not to sound suspicious.

"Circus? *Nyet, nyet.*" Alima made a face. "Don't let Laz ever hear you say that word. We are not circus. We are performers. The circus is for simpleminded beasts."

Alima took me outside and told me to wait for Conrad. The scent of roasted chicken danced in the air, and my stomach growled loudly. Beyond the tent was a line of people, like the entire town was here to see these performers. The Fancies and Fears.

There was a booth and an archway where a line formed and a few men were taking money from the townspeople. The people began making their way toward the seating area and followed signs directing them into another tent with a sign that said *Oddities Inside.* People exited with hands over their mouths, wide eyes, tears. I even heard a few screams from inside.

"You are beautiful, Nell." Conrad was suddenly at my side, though I hadn't seen him walk up. "Alima did well."

I didn't know what to say. He wore a suit, and his black hair was greased back. When he smiled at me, I felt my heart drip like wax into my stomach. That was also new to me. He took my arm and curled it around his own.

"Do I get to see Angel?" I was hopeful but feared he had other plans.

"Of course. But first I want you to meet a few others." His voice was as smooth as cream, and his smile lit our way toward the oddities tent.

When we stood in front of the first curtained door, my heart began to pound harder.

"Don't be afraid," he whispered closely into my ear and caressed my arm. I had tightened my hold on him without realizing it. "I won't leave you."

I didn't like to hear him say that. Joann had said that. Angel had said that.

When we stepped into the first room of the tent, a gasp escaped my mouth. The room was lit enough for me to see a small boy. He couldn't have been much older than ten. He stood there with only pants on and made muscles and did poses. But what was I seeing? He had two extra arms. They hung limply at his sides. They did not move with the rest of his body. There was a sign near him that said "Rollie, the Four-Armed Boy."

"Good job, Rollie," Conrad said and squeezed one of his muscled arms and feigned being impressed.

"Four arms?" I asked when we turned around.

"He was born that way. Nobody wanted him — so Laz took him in and is his father now."

In the next room the tiny woman from earlier sat on a small chair on top of a table. She was smaller than a two-year-old child. She nodded and smiled, and her eyes glinted with tenderness. Next to her was the sign saying that her name was Bitsie and that she was the smallest adult in the world and that she came from South America.

I stared at the display in the next room for several long moments until Conrad explained that it was the remains of a mermaid. Laz had acquired her from some Romanian gypsy. The skeleton was exceptionally small and inside a glass case.

"Mermaids don't live long outside of the sea." Conrad spoke gently and closely. "They don't belong here, but imagine how beautiful she would've been if she'd never left the ocean."

In the next room was a caged man covered in scales. His hands were webbed, and the skin between his shoulders and his ears had a webbed appearance. He didn't frighten me, though he seemed to try. I let go of Conrad's arm and drew closer. I put my hands on the bars that kept this man contained. When he hissed at me, I didn't falter. I was used to this sort of behavior, but my throat thickened. Conrad warmed me from behind.

"The cage," I stuttered. The sight brought memories of the cries and banging of many patients inside solitary. "Get him out." I hit the cage, and the man stopped hissing. His gaze softened.

"He's okay," Conrad whispered, his breath

filling my ears and senses. "This is just his job."

I looked from the caged man to Conrad.

"This isn't right." I banged on the cage again.

"Get her outta here," the webbed man said, baring his teeth.

Conrad escorted me quickly past the next rooms of more cages and people ready to shock their onlookers. I didn't like this.

"No." I pushed Conrad's touch away. "This isn't right. They are people, not —"

"Not what?"

I didn't know what.

"They are making a living, Nell," Conrad explained.

"But why?" I yelled loud enough to cause others to look over. Conrad pulled me farther away. "Why put them on display like this?"

"What else can people like this do but shock people? And look at this crowd. Everyone loves oddities. Like your Angel." His hands held my waist and he pressed his body close to mine. My hands rested on his forearms.

My entire body heated at both his words and his touch.

"How do people really see him?" he asked. "As an angel?"

Several words came to mind, none of them nice. I shook my head.

"Feebleminded. Incurable." My voice was all breath and realized fear and almost no sound. "Like he should be ashamed of himself."

"Right. But here he's different. He's worshipped and adored and is perfect, the way God made him."

When he said *God* it didn't have the sacred ring to it like it did when Rosina said it.

Then he leaned in to my ear. "What's odd about you, Nell?" Then he kissed my cheek and without a response from me he led me through the crowd toward the rows of chairs in front of the stage.

We passed by a tent with a sign of a large hand with circles drawn on the palm. I could see Alima inside with a woman opposite her. Her hooped earrings and bracelets jingled as she reached for the woman's hand. We walked around men on stilts, juggling knives and fire, and another man swallowing the length of a sword in front of a small gasping and impressed crowd.

Conrad took me to a seat, but I wasn't sure I could sit. My nerves had tightened like a noose. I never should have let them take Angel anywhere the previous night, but he had been so ill.

"I'll be back shortly. Just wait here and enjoy the show until I return." He said all of this while stroking the outside of my arm, sending a tingle up my back. Then, with a smirk, he was off.

"Ladies and Gentlemen," a man announced, and a crowd of townspeople flooded into the chairs, making it impossible for me to do anything but sit.

Then the lights and the music began. Voices like magic started to sing. Voices I recognized from the night before.

Then a beaming light shone on the stage — and the red curtains slowly opened. The three Sirens, Persephone, Penelope, and Thalia, floated to the middle of the stage, their feet not visible beneath the one large skirt they wore together. They moved like one person. And they sang. Oh, their voices. I'd never heard anything like it. The sign on the stage said that the Sirens were conjoined triplets. I'd heard of this before from medical books I'd read of Joann's. As shocked as I knew I should be seeing all of these oddities, all I could think about was that there was still something I was missing. And it had something to do with Lazarus, and maybe Conrad also.

Everyone around me was spellbound by

the Sirens' voices, and by the time their song was done, there was not a sound to be heard.

Not even a whisper.

1941
The Mentalist's Call

As the Sirens retreated back behind the curtain, Lazarus bounded up onstage. The cane in his hand had a golden handle, and he raised it high as he welcomed the crowd from the town of Springville, Ohio. He introduced Octavia, the armless woman, and a curtain opened off to the right. She was sitting on a table, and between her toes she had paintbrushes. On the floor in front of her was a canvas. Lazarus announced that she would be painting the most beautiful woman in the crowd. Ladies began batting their eyes, and I heard a few men telling the woman at their side that surely it would be her. A few scoffed at the possibility of an armless woman painting at all.

"We are the Fancies and Fears — the show that will thrill your dreams and confirm your nightmares. And now —" With a grand flourish Lazarus regained the crowd's attention, and there was a loud rolling, booming sound offstage that stopped when he called out, "Golithia, the strongest woman in the world."

The giant who had carried Angel away the night before was a woman and not a man, as I had assumed. She walked onstage and performed feats of strength. There were aahs and oohs from the crowd. But I could only see the face of a sad woman. I'd seen that face so many times in the hospital and recognized it well.

After Golithia's act she marched her sweaty body offstage and Lazarus returned. The spotlight narrowed so that only Lazarus was lit. Out beyond the stage the sky was black, and the moon was covered by inky clouds, leaving only a small patch of gray in the sky. The poor moon was held as captive behind the haze as I was in the confusion of this new world around me. Another world I didn't belong in or understand.

"For those of you who have never seen one of our shows, you may not know my story." Lazarus walked the stage, and the tap of his cane on the wooden stage echoed in the quiet of the crowd. "You might know Lazarus from the Bible, though."

He stopped walking back and forth and turned to face us. He didn't say anything for several long moments. Not a breath could be heard around me.

Rosina had told me some Bible stories, and the name Lazarus was vaguely familiar.

"The Bible says that Lazarus was one of the most beloved friends of our Savior, Jesus Christ." He looked up into the sky with a dramatic pause. "So loved, in fact, that Jesus brought him back from the grave."

Lazarus continued, "As some of you know, I died in the Battle of the Lys. I was nineteen years old and was blown off of my feet." The crowd murmured. He held his hand out to the crowd. "You don't have to believe me. It's all right. Not everyone believed that the Lazarus of the Bible walked out of his tomb either or even that Jesus himself did the same after three days dead."

The crowd silenced.

"I lay on the battlefield for three days, so I'm told. My company and my commander had already listed me as dead. Until I wasn't — anymore. I wasn't without wounds and scars across my face, but I had been returned to the living."

The crowd whispered loudly this time, and a few men called out that he was a liar and a fraud.

"Oh, it's all there in the war records." He

lifted his chin and resumed his pacing. "My own return to life after death opened a door of sorts. I became a mentalist. And can now speak to them — those lost souls beyond the grave where I once was. And tonight I'll prove it to you all."

The murmuring crowd became louder, and a family near me left. A few others went as well. The buzz of voices heightened until Lazarus put his hand in the air. Everyone went silent.

With that raised hand he removed his hat and tossed it offstage, then put his hand on his head. He closed his eyes. The crowd was completely still. Lazarus hummed. For almost a whole minute we watched Lazarus hum and sway.

"I see a woman," he said. "A mother. She's sick and frail and is mostly kept to bed. A small room. There's a window — a broken window — in the room. When she was alive she would scratch at the walls, like she was trying to get out."

I inhaled and pressed my back against my chair.

"Woman, what is your name?" he asked out into the air, and I was certain that all of us held our breaths as we waited for an answer. Would we hear it along with him? "She's not telling me her name yet, but she says she knows one of you."

He opened his eyes finally and pointed at the crowd, and my heart thrummed deeply in my chest.

"She says that one of you here knew her in her life and that one of you was her daughter."

There was more than hushed conversation now.

"Is it my mother?" A woman on the other side of the aisle stood. Her voice quivered. "Her name was Alice. She died last week. She was sick with pneumonia."

Lazarus held a hand out to her as if to have her wait and after a few moments answered. "She says her name is not Alice."

The woman sat down in a fit of tears, and the man next to her began to comfort her. My gaze snapped back to Lazarus.

"I see something bright. But it isn't the sun. It's a person. She was also in the room. She was the daughter. But she is not dead. She is here" — he paused — "in the audience. Today. This bright daughter is one of you. Woman, what is your name?"

My eyes began to burn. But I didn't want anyone to notice me so I didn't leave. I was like a rock buried in sand with a current of water rushing over me, sinking me deeper. My body was heavy and stiff and unmovable. Was he speaking to my mother? How much of this could I believe?

"She wants to say something to her daughter. She says that the world is a scary place. That she must find a family to *protect* her. She is reminding her that there was a nurse who protected her when she was a child — and other women, Mickey, Rosina, Grace — and she still needs protection from the world. To walk alone out in the world will be her destruction — like a mermaid out of the sea."

I fought the urge to buy into this, knowing he could've learned all this from Angel, but the way he was describing my life strangled my senses, making it hard to parse out what was real and what wasn't. I pinched my mouth shut, hoping to hold back my racing heartbeat and shallow breathing.

"There's another bright one in the room. A bright soul who is alive. She says that he will not be enough to protect her daughter — this daughter who sits among you now."

"Who is it?" a man yelled from the audience.

A woman in the front stood up and turned to face everyone. "Yes, stand up, woman, and show us who you are."

"Brighton," Lazarus yelled. "Your mother

is speaking to you."

I gasped for air I couldn't find and ran down the center aisle toward the back. I needed to find Angel. We needed to leave. These were not our people. There was something wrong with a man who would choose to do this to someone else.

Lazarus was calling out for me to return. "Brighton. Brighton," he shouted several times.

Before I got far, Conrad grabbed me from behind. He shushed in my ear that it was okay, that he understood how hard this was. He began walking me back up the aisle, and no matter how I fought him, I couldn't break free from his grasp. I craned my neck to look at him and he didn't look the same. His jaw was tight. His eyes had sharpened and even seemed to have grown darker.

"Brighton," Lazarus, the Mentalist, called out, "is that you?"

I looked at the man onstage. His face was red with heat and passion. I could see a forehead vein pulsing.

He pointed at me. "Are you Brighton?"

"Tell him the truth," Conrad hissed in my ear as he held his arms around me. To others it might've looked like he was comforting me, but in reality he was my straightjacket. "Then all of this will be over."

The shroud between my past and present was so thin that for a long moment I wondered if Lazarus really was speaking with Mother, who was locked away in eternity.

"Answer him." Conrad broke me from my doubt.

"My name is Nell." I didn't yell, but I was loud enough to be heard by a few rows around me.

"Just play along," Conrad said in my ear. "Let this be your gifting."

"No, I will not." I didn't yell, but I did break free from his hold.

Then I ran. I saw the truck where Angel had been and ran to it as fast as I could, throwing off my heeled shoes, but when I yanked open the door to the truck I was sure was his, remembering it had a long scrape along one side, he was not inside. I went to the next one with a red door and it was not his either. I ran farther and opened another with a green door. Angel was not there, but there was a girl about my age in the bed. A small man sat next to the bed. He was not as small as Bitsie; he was a different kind of small. A dwarf, I remembered. We'd had one as a patient long ago. A woman sat on the other side of the bed. She was beautiful with glowing red hair.

I was out of breath and just stood there

not knowing what to do. The younger girl's arms, neck, and shoulders were covered in black drawings. I knew they were called tattoos from magazines and books, but I'd never seen one, let alone the many this girl had. The red-haired woman looked at me, and her eyes were filled with pain and maybe an entire sea of sparkling water.

"You're the new girl?"

I nodded, still breathing heavily.

"Find your angel and run away as fast as you can." Her voice warbled. "Get away from Lazarus."

I looked back at the girl in bed who was perfectly still and then back at the woman.

"Hurry," she said. "He's probably backstage."

I slammed the door and ran toward the tent. I could hear Lazarus talking again of another spirit that he was conjuring with his powers. The audience was silent again.

I raced into the tent, and the dark hallways closed in on me. I followed the corridors farther, deeper, until I got to the center opening of the tent. From where I stood I could see the back of the stage. The light seeped through the edges and center of the red curtain. On a wooden platform was a young boy ready to pull the curtains open at the appointed time.

I took a step closer, and then I saw him. And her.

Angel and Gabrielle were inside a large cage.

They were wearing white and faced each other with their palms pressed together. And on their backs were the largest, most beautiful feathered wings I ever could have imagined.

Gabrielle's winged back was to me. I moved closer, and Angel's eyes found me. I was just far enough away that I could see he didn't know who I was. I had forgotten how Alima had dressed me like a doll and made up my face. I walked closer. I was angry with him for telling Lazarus about us, even though I would do whatever it took to free him. He was caged in a new way now.

As I drew nearer I could see recognition dawn over his eyes. And as I walked closer still, he shook his head ever so slightly, prompting Gabrielle to turn and see me. Her eyes were on fire, red and passionate.

"Leave us," she rasped, then turned back to Angel.

From the other side of the curtain came Lazarus's voice. "Not even Mr. Barnum has anything close to my next and last act. My grand finale. He might have the tattooed man and a grand menagerie, but he doesn't have what you're about to witness with your very own eyes." He paused. "Are you ready?" he yelled, and the crowd went wild.

"I give you . . . the Fallen Angels."

The Sirens began humming a wordless, haunting tune as the curtains opened and Angel and Gabrielle's cage was rolled onto the stage. The audience gasped in wonder.

1990
Shifting Light

The keys are cold in my hands and shouldn't feel so heavy. It is late afternoon, and the town hall meeting is the next day. Yesterday, when we developed the film, I told Kelly I wouldn't attend unless I could get inside my building. She'd handed me a set of keys within hours.

"And what did the mayor say?" I asked, pretending to hold the keys casually even though they burned the palms of my hands.

"Well, he really wants to create some excitement about the fund-raising and wants the bill to pass for the new community center, and he thinks your —" She cleared her throat with a smile. "*Stories* will help donators, supporters, and voters to really turn out for the meeting."

"He's agreed to my entry and me sharing the photos?" My heart skipped a beat.

She nodded. "He'll introduce you and then you have the floor." She bit her lip and paused. I wondered what she was about to add. "He doesn't know you're going into the building — but because I've been in there recently, I know it's safe."

Safe. It's not safe. It's never been safe.

This conversation rolls over in my mind as I park my car near the old iron gates. My camera is heavy against my soft chest, and my heart hammers beneath it, though it feels tinny and empty.

Seeing the photographs yesterday heightened the bidding from the building. I couldn't quell it, even in my sleep, seeing visions of everyone I once knew walking the halls. A younger and older Joann bustled around me. And Grace with hair and without. All of them with cloud-like bodies. And I kept wandering the halls, trying to find Angel, saying I wouldn't leave without him. Even Doc was there, walking the halls. He told me I shouldn't be there and reminded me to walk right on out.

As I walk around to the back now, I imagine the grad students cataloging the left items. The spirits of women who had been pulled apart and broken here can never be cataloged. But I can do something for them.

I stand and stare at the door for so long I almost grow roots. This is the door I escaped out of almost fifty years earlier. Impossible, surely. How can it be that long ago? How am I that old? All of these moments feel so fresh. Time is such a thin and frail thing, I know.

I pick one of the keys to try, but then I drop the ring. The dull *clink* on the rough concrete slab spins my nerves. Careful not to let my camera swing out, I pick up the keys and try the first key my hands touch. It doesn't work. The fourth key on the ring is the one that slips in, and before I turn it I look around, making sure I am alone, even though I know better, before I open the door.

The knob takes some convincing to turn. But finally it does, and I pull hard to open it.

I instinctively reach for the light switch and know right where it is — but of course it doesn't work. Before I completely return to the familiar darkness, I pull out the flashlight from my back pocket and click it on. As strange as it is, I am not afraid. Nothing I will encounter today could compare to what I have already endured in this same space in my past.

But when I stand there, I hesitate and consider leaving. Not just the building, but leaving Milton completely. But Kelly has all of my negatives, and I will not lose those again.

I need to do this; there's no other choice. I need to see my room. My mother's room. Where she'd lived and where she'd died is all so close now. I push into place a rock big enough to keep the door ajar, then I go inside.

The light from my flashlight catches the metal rails of several stretchers strewn about in the hall. A few are intact; others are not. One even has a sheet lying on it. But for the dirt and dust, it's almost as if someone had been on it only moments ago.

A breeze pushes at the door, throwing slivers of light into the space. I exhale, then bear up my courage and walk past the stretchers and toward the stairs that are to my right. My breathing heightens, and by the time I force myself up a few steps, I am reciting Rosina's prayer that over the decades has also become mine.

When I get to the top, the quiet and gloom creep through the broken windows and cracked walls. And the deeper I get, the more unnerved I am to be there alone. I wish I'd agreed to let Kelly come along. But I told her I needed to do this by myself.

The door at the top of the stairwell is off its hinges and lies sideways. There are marks up and down the inside of the door. Deep, like something metal had been used.

I step over the door and walk off to the left down a hall, toward the double doors. One is ajar and hangs crookedly, and the other one is closed. I gently pull one open, and the squeal sounds like a greeting. Like it has been waiting for me. I go through the doorway and I am standing in the dining hall.

Only a handful of tables and chairs remain. Everything is in disarray. I'd eaten so many meals in this room. I don't go in far or touch anything — afraid memories will swallow me up. But I stand at the edge of the room and close my eyes and I can see it all as it had been and hear the mumbling of voices that stirred through every meal. I can hear the scrape of spoons and the shuffling of cups and plates. And I am reminded of how hungry we were.

"Are you going to finish that?" I can almost hear Carmen ask.

"No. You can have it," I almost answer aloud.

I didn't expect to feel any sense of warmth inside this decrepit building, but here I am smiling in the dining hall. Smiling. Because there really had been such love woven through the despair and fear.

I walk back to the hallway. Words in graffiti about rejection and loss and needing help litter the walls.

I'm facing the little Juliet balcony that had been my favorite place in the entire building. I walk up to it, and when I try to open the window, the glass rattles and the hinges creak. When my hand rests against the glass window that is covered in a thick film of dirt, I see that I'm trembling.

I step back from it and watch as the window moves in the thread of wind that courses through the opening, cooling me in the warm stickiness of these walls. I follow the rest of the hall and dodge a stretcher, mattress springs, and a rolling doctor's chair — all rodent-chewed. I don't touch anything but walk past the ruins like I might any historical sacred space.

Straps of memories begin to wrap around me, and I am eight again.

Aunt Eddie brought in roller skates that tied to your feet or shoes. All day I skated — back and forth — and then she took them home. They were her son's. Strangely, I still remember that his name was Wayne. Did he know that for one whole day an asylum patient had used his beloved roller skates? I giggle at the thought, and the sound that echoes weakens the rafters and framework of this house of horrors.

The small bathroom and some closets are off to my left. To my right is the hall leading to the dormitory rooms. My heart is heavy and light all at once. Like it doesn't know if it will drop through the floor or float high above me. Maybe I shouldn't be here at all. Maybe Doc is right — that this gateway of remembering is too much. These stirred-up ghosts, camisoled to the very air inside, might never leave me now that I've awoken them. Considering the intensity of my panic attack only a few days ago, I should've listened to him. But I didn't, and instead I keep moving in deeper.

The dormitory door on this end of the hall is shut. Fear wraps around my courage like a leather restraint. What if after all of this I won't get inside my room? I decide that if the door is locked and no key on the ring unlocks it, it's a sign I should leave.

My hand shakes when I reach for the metal knob. It's locked. And I tremble as I try all seven keys. None of them work. The disappointment is greater than I expect. I lean my forehead against the door and breathe in this old familiar air. What I've seen so far is enough, right? Maybe this is all the closure I need. Maybe this is all I can handle.

I don't waste time but walk back the way I came. Now I'm on the other side of the dormitory. The side with the smaller infirmary. I peer inside the infirmary window. There's a stretcher inside and a corner metal medication cabinet lies facedown, the glass shattered around it.

But there are no memories for me to exhume here, so I force myself to move on. I come to the solitary rooms. I won't look at them, having spent some of the worst hours of my life inside. I don't need to revisit those rooms — where I last saw Grace. Was she still inside?

I turn away and toward the second dormitory door at this end of the hall. It's open.

I am supposed to go inside, I conclude.

I am supposed to see the room where I'd been born and where my mother had lain in her death. The room that had for a short time looked like a real bedroom because Joann had tried so hard to make a home for me. Books lining the walls. Curtains on the windows. Even wallpaper when I was very young. A cozy rug on the floor. But Dr. Wolff didn't allow that for long, so then the books were pushed under beds and in closets. The curtains and the rug were taken away, and eventually the wallpaper peeled off.

"You're going to learn if it's the last thing I do," I can hear Nursey say. Her voice echoes against these ancient walls, and instead of strangling me as they would have a few days ago, they warm me. The dorm rooms line both sides of the hall. Every room welcomes me to peek inside and promises to show me what they remember. I only sneak a glance at most of them, afraid their memories will take me captive. I'd walked too many corridors and peeked through too many doorways in my life and seen things no one wanted to see — but those things will remain in my memory, unstirred. What I need to see is my room.

I step slowly past the rooms and their broken-down doors. Bed frames leaning against the walls. Broken windows. Several medical books, some equipment, and even a stethoscope are tossed about. Then I get to it. I turn toward my room and stand in the doorway.

It is nearing sunset now, and light is streaming through the broken and busted window. The tumbling of light comes through like a small rainbow against the floor. There is only one bed frame in the room. The paint is entirely chipped and one of the legs is broken, putting it at an awkward angle.

All I can think to do is sit and be here. I lean my back against one side of the wall that faces the window and slide down to the dirty floor. I sit cross-legged and watch as the light shifts across the room and just let time pass. The orange glow eventually falls toward the bedroom door. I stare at the side of the room where Mother had been and remember that last day when she'd died while we tried to cut through the fence. The desperation is painful to remember, and I choke on my breath and tears.

The series of events plays out — the realization of my birthday, the race back with Angel at my side. The way Joann met me at the door and told me that while I was busy running away Mother had fallen to her death. Angel cocooning me to let me grieve. Oh, the pair that Angel and I had been in those clashing years and how things had changed so much after that day. In the days to follow and in the weeks as we journeyed. That sacred path that bonded us so tightly to the other also divided us.

1941
Stay

What was I supposed to do? Angel was caged like a prisoner. How would we leave? And worse yet, would he want to leave now that he had Gabrielle? Considering this and considering what Lazarus had done onstage, how he knew so much about me, I knew we needed to leave before Angel was too deeply entangled in this life.

We did not belong here. But it wasn't because of the oddities of the members of this troupe. It was Lazarus's malicious strength over them that frightened me. It was more like he owned them than fathered them. It reminded me of the power the doctors had over the patients at the hospital.

I would not stay. But I could not leave without Angel.

Would I have to convince him to leave with me? I swallowed down the force of panic that wanted to fill me up.

A breeze pulled through me and the sheer

dress I wore, and I shivered. My arms wrapped around myself, and all I could think of was the time I'd been restrained and my hair had been shaved. My fingertips moved to touch the ends of my short hair and my wrists ached remembering. Standing in the open air, with no walls and with no restraints, the invisible boundaries tightened.

"Why did you run off?" Conrad's voice sounded from behind, and his presence gave me a greater chill than the evening breeze. My mind carried a mixture of fear, anger, and curiosity toward him. A man treating me like a beautiful thing was new — but he knew what Lazarus was going to do onstage and had forced me to endure it. "We wanted you to see how welcome you are. How much we want you here. How much good you could bring to our show. Everyone needs a job. Remember?"

His breath smelled like something strong and ripe — I couldn't place it. Part of me enjoyed his presence — I had to admit it. But I despised myself for it. His betrayal toward me didn't keep my body from responding to his closeness as he drew nearer. And while he had angered me with how he had held me in place as we stood before the stage, there was also something about him that stirred me.

He ran the back of a finger down my arm a few times. His eyes drilled into me in a way that no man's ever had. I opened my mouth to tell him I didn't need a job, because we were leaving, but he interrupted me.

"I know you don't want to cause problems — especially for Angel."

"What?" I questioned.

"We owe the audience a good show." His hand continued to graze my forearm, shooting a sensation through my stomach. The expression on his face wasn't alarming or frightening, but it was soft and reminded me of how Dr. Woburn looked at Joann when they were alone. "You lied to us about who you are and now you owe us, right? We didn't call that wretched place, and we have kept you safe from being sent back."

"Owe you?" Was he threatening me? I swallowed in sudden nervousness. He was so close, and it made it hard for me to think clearly. The air stirred around us and tightened and tightened as he got closer and closer.

"Don't worry, we won't call that asylum." He rubbed his hands down my arms. "Listen, we healed your Angel, fed you both, gave you shelter. Those things aren't free.

He told us everything because he trusts us. You should too."

His finger grazed my jawline.

"I'm not the girl you think I am." Could he see through my lie? "Why do you think I belong here?"

"Because you're like all of us. None of us belong anywhere. I wanted you to see tonight how much we want you to stay." Then Conrad leaned in and whispered in my ear, "With me."

My body warmed and I felt embarrassed. Had anyone heard the desire in Conrad's voice as I had? I held my breath.

Then Conrad pulled me toward the painting the armless woman had created using her feet. I saw at once that it was a painting of me standing among the crowd of people. Everyone else was a shadow but me — I was the bright spot in the painting, with my pink dress and glowing face.

Conrad squeezed my arm and left me to stand alone. He walked toward a long table that had been set up where the troupe and workers were eating, the show now over. The townspeople had returned to their homes.

The boy with extra arms walked around with a chicken leg in his hand and the sauce all over his face. He was smiling, and even though he wore a coat that covered his extra arms, I knew they were there. The giant woman, whose name was not really Golithia but Norma, carried Bitsie around and they ate off the same plate. All of the people who had been in those dimly lit curtained rooms were suddenly around me. They didn't seem strange or unusual, just like people who could be my friends — maybe even my family. But I thought of my aunt. That was where I wanted to go.

"Why do you let him touch you like that?" Angel asked, moving close to me.

"You saw?" was all I could say as he turned me toward him, putting his hands gently on my shoulders.

I wanted to ask him why he did it. Why did he tell them about us and why did he agree to go in that cage? But all I wanted in that moment was to be in his arms and to feel safe and to be away from here. Like he knew, he pulled me close and nestled his head in the crux of my neck.

"I've missed you, Brighton," he said, and I could feel him breathing me in.

It felt good to hear his voice say my name, and I wanted to cocoon inside his arms and stay there.

"I've been looking for you all day." We parted to look at each other. "How did you get well so quickly?"

"Their doctor had Gabrielle give me a tonic over and over through the night, and it didn't take long before I started feeling better." He was smiling and the worry lines across his forehead were gone. "I still feel a bit weak, so Gabrielle said I still need a lot of rest."

He moved closer to me and whispered, "Isn't she incredible?"

I didn't answer his question. "Why did you do it, Angel — the cage and wings?"

"After all their help, I couldn't say no. And it felt nice not to hide myself."

I could only imagine the relief he had in that, especially after what happened with his mother. But still, I couldn't shake the feeling of betrayal.

"Why did you tell them everything about us? Did you see what they did to me? That man, Lazarus, pretended to talk to Mother's spirit."

"I didn't know Lazarus would do that. I was just so glad to be feeling better, and they kept asking me questions and I got caught up in my excitement over Gabrielle." Angel tucked my hair behind my ear, then rested his hand back on my shoulder. "I'm sorry."

I would forgive him, of course.

"They really do want to help us. They aren't bad people." Then he smiled and drew a little closer. "I hardly recognized you at first."

"Don't say that. I'm just a made-up doll."

"You're beautiful, Brighton." His eyes roamed my face in a new way, and when I opened my mouth to tell him we needed to make a plan to leave, he caressed the curve of my jawline. His touch against my skin radiated through my whole body. "We *could* stay, you know. Start a life together with them. It really does seem like a family. They don't care that I'm albino. And they don't care where we come from."

I looked around, then pulled him farther from the crowd. I told him about the girl in a bed and how the woman said we needed to leave. "She said we should get away from Lazarus right away. They've lied to us and to the audience. We don't belong here. And what about my aunt?"

Angel scoffed and shook his head, then stepped back.

"But I'm free for the first time. I can be albino without hiding. Out there —" He pointed toward the town. "That's not free. That's me hiding and pretending to fit into a world that will never see past my skin."

"So we give up on my aunt and a life out

there?" I said a little too loudly.

"Think about it. I can be myself here. Out there is where I'm caged." He paused for a moment. "Give it a chance — for me. Gabrielle is like a mother to me."

"Hey, Nell." Conrad strode up. "Is he upsetting you?" He put his hand on my arm, and before I could pull away Angel grabbed Conrad by the coat and threw him to the ground, away from me.

"Keep your hands off of her." Rage burned from his tightened muscles and bared teeth. The last time he'd done this he was defending me from asylum aides.

Conrad didn't appear rumpled over his fall. He smiled up at Angel.

"Sure, pal," he said and got up and walked right back to me. "Remember what I said." Then he walked away.

"What does he mean?" Angel said, breathing hard.

"He wants me to stay too." I looked up at Angel. "To be with him."

"What?" Angel scoffed, his jaw and fists still tightened. "But you barely know him."

"No less than you know Gabrielle." I hated that we were arguing in the few minutes we had together. I wanted to take his hand and run as fast as we could, not caring if we left everything behind. I wanted to leave with him and not look back. Conrad meant nothing to me in the ways that mattered, in the way Angel did.

"Angel." A woman's stern voice spoke. It was Gabrielle. "Come."

At first he didn't move. He swallowed hard and moved toward me and put his hand on the back of my neck and gently pulled me close. He lowered his gaze and our eyes met. "Please, Brighton, don't let him —"

"Angel." Gabrielle's voice cut through.

"I have to go," he whispered in my ear before delivering a quick and unseen kiss to my cheek.

Then he jogged over to Gabrielle and she linked her arm through his and led him away from me.

1941
Invisible Cages

The troupe was on the road again by morning. I felt trapped. I didn't want to be there, but I didn't know what to do about Angel. Part of me understood how he felt. In our short time outside of the hospital he'd been stared at, called a freak, and rejected by his mother. Then last night he was considered beautiful.

But this wasn't just about him being accepted. It was about being under the thumb of the deceitful man and what he expected of the people he seemed to have a strange power over.

I was comforted that at least we were still going toward Michigan. The second night I was put in the same house truck as before, with the Sirens and Alima. The next morning, however, I was determined to find the girl with the tattoos. I wanted to know why the other woman had warned me. And who was the girl in the bed?

Were we actually in danger?

We were in a new town in Ohio before noon the next day. And as we settled into an open space, everything was built again like it was before. Conrad was directing the assembly. He caught my eye briefly and winked.

"You look a little different," he said when he approached me.

I looked down at my clothes. My pink dress had been taken away from me sometime during the night and a pair of slacks, a shirt, and shoes had been left in its place. Men's clothes. Alima said the clothes I came in weren't suitable or practical for me since I needed to work. These new clothes were for workers.

I was consigned to more kitchen duty, but as soon as I wasn't being watched, I went to see if I could find the tattooed girl.

When I found the truck with the green door, I put my ear to it. I couldn't hear anything, so I knocked quietly. The door cracked open. It was the small doctor. His face and large nose protruded from the door.

"What do you want?" he asked in an abrasive whisper.

I stepped back for a moment and asked myself the same question. What was I after?

"I have questions for the woman in there," I said with a strange sense that I was breathing for the first time in my life — making the next move on my terms.

The doctor's eyes darted around.

"Quick, before anyone sees you." He widened the door.

I scurried inside.

The scene looked the same as it had the day before. The sleeping girl and the red-haired woman sitting by her side with tired eyes. She didn't even look at me when I entered.

"Why did you tell me to run?" I said, knowing I was asking too much for her to focus on anything but the girl.

She waited so long to look at me I wondered if she'd heard me.

"This is my daughter." She offered a weak smile as she gently moved a strand of hair off her daughter's forehead. "Lazarus's daughter. I am his wife."

"And she's unwell?"

"Why do you think she's lying there like that?" the small man said, rolling his eyes. He looked at the woman. "I'll be back in a little while to check on her." And then he left.

"I'm sorry to bother you," I said when we were alone. "I am trying to find a way to make my friend leave with me."

"The angel?"

I nodded.

"What's your name?"

This was a hard question for me, but I knew how I needed to answer it.

"Nell. What's yours — and hers?"

"I'm Cara. This is Becky."

"What happened to her?" I asked quietly and sat next to Cara.

"One of Barnum's biggest crowd-pleasers is his tattooed man — George Costentenus. Laz said that he was going to outdo him and have a tattooed woman. He picked Becky — his own daughter — to fill that role. It became an obsession. To be the best at any cost."

She paused and I decided to wait until she was ready to speak again.

"The doctor says she has a blood infection from the tattoos. He's never seen that happen before."

Cara uncovered Becky's arm from under the sheet. The underside was a bright red, swollen tattoo surrounded by cracked skin.

"This is just one of the infections." She retucked the girl's arm before speaking again.

"She didn't want to do this, but I convinced her. She wanted to leave and have a normal life. She's never been a greedy girl — she just wanted the life she saw the townsfolk living, not what we have here." She brushed her daughter's hair away from her face. "He knew if she was tattooed, she would almost certainly have to stay. And I didn't want her to leave me, so I didn't stop him."

She choked on tears before speaking again. "She hasn't woken up in over two days."

We watched Becky's chest rise and fall in the sacred stillness of the small space.

"You're next." Cara broke the quiet.

"Next?"

"He has a plan for you — to be his tattooed woman."

"But I can tell him no."

Cara shook her head. "He won't accept that. You owe him because he's fed you and cared for your Angel. Leave while you can. Even if you have to leave Angel behind, you need to go," Cara said, her eyes darting from the window to the door behind me. She kept her voice no greater than a whisper.

"I won't leave Angel."

Her gaze lingered over me and then went back to her daughter, who was so still it was like she was already dead. Then she looked back at me.

"Becky wouldn't leave without me either, and now she's going to die because of it. I would rather be here alone and have her out there somewhere alive, even if it meant I'd never see her again, than this. Leave, Nell. Before he owns you like he does everyone else."

"Owns?"

"He adopts the children. And tricks the adults into servitude. It doesn't matter. He makes sure they can never leave without great risk or consequence."

"But they seem so happy. Like a family."

"What other choice do they have? Where will they go after what they've become here? After what he's forced them to become." She paused. "They're good people, with a taskmaster who will use them until they're in the grave."

The more I watched this mother sit vigil at the bedside, the more I felt like a caged beast. With quick words I told Cara how sorry I was and thanked her. She never even looked up from Becky when I left.

"What are you doing?" Conrad came up behind me as I slipped from Becky's truck.

"I-I —" I didn't know what to say. "I thought this was my truck. They all look the same." I tried to giggle my lie away.

He was studying my face. He knew I was lying.

"Careful — my sister's sick. It might be catchy." It sounded more like a threat than concern.

His sister?

So Lazarus was his father. How trapped was he?

"Is she going to get better?" I said, pretending not to know the truth.

"The doctor, well —" He didn't finish, then looked away.

"Have you always wanted to live this life?" I asked before I could pull the words back.

"What do you mean?"

"All of this. Is this what you want for the rest of your life?"

"I was born into this." He lit a cigarette and took a long drag as he looked far off into the distance and then back at me. "It's all I've known."

"But — why this life? Why not live out there?"

He shrugged. The cigarette smoke masked the air between us.

"I need to go to my aunt," I said slowly and quietly. "Angel and I can't stay. My aunt is my only family."

He came so close I could smell soap underneath the scent of the cigarette. "I don't think your Angel wants to leave."

I inhaled deeply, taking in a lungful of his smoke. How did he know that about Angel? I exhaled the smoky air, not letting him see my worry.

He leaned back and handed me the cigarette. I'd never smoked before, but the scent alone dulled my senses and I took it. I put it to my lips and inhaled just a little. Then turned my face away from his and blew out the smoke.

"Ah, you're a natural," he said, and his smile congratulated me. He let me have the rest of it, and I smoked it until there was nothing to hold on to.

1941
Unmasked

The rest of the night was almost the same as the night before. Except I didn't wear the pretty pink dress. Conrad pretended not to care. But I knew he did. And it meant Octavia had to paint someone else and the Mentalist had to dig for someone else's secrets.

When Angel came out in his cage, the gasps were even louder. I'd lost Angel a little more with this show. Gabrielle was winning him over.

And then Becky died.

It happened near the end of the show when Lazarus — the Mentalist — was doing one more mind trick on the crowd. I hung out on the fringes. I was still in men's working clothes, and I'd pilfered a hat. I wore it tightly on my head and tucked my hair inside it. I was so thin I looked like a young boy.

As the audience sat in awe, Cara came

running into the tent screaming. Her arms flailing. Her face streaked with tears.

"It's all your fault," she yelled, pointing at Lazarus. "She's dead because of you."

The portion of Lazarus's face that was unmasked lost all color. He stepped back, like he'd been pushed by the unseen force of her grief. I wondered if he had been. Maybe there was some power in Cara's sorrow that could do that. If there was, I understood it.

"Conrad," Lazarus called, his chest heaving and his voice like a sail without wind. "Get her."

Conrad seemed to materialize, and he had his mother by the back of the arms. He was coaxing her gently, but she pulled away from his grip. She turned around and looked at Conrad. She took his face in her hands and spoke so gently but loud enough for all to hear.

"Oh, Son. She's dead. Your baby sister is dead." Ragged words fell like heaps of rubbish, mounding between mother and son.

She sounded like the ladies at Riverside. Grief-stricken to the point of losing herself. Her eyes buzzed and her breathing was erratic. *My own eyes filled for her loss and for the life that had been taken.*

"Mother," Conrad said, sweetly and almost reverently, "come with me."

Hearing his voice break broke another piece of my own heart.

Her wailing quaked into a growl. I sensed what was coming next, but Conrad wasn't prepared. She pulled away roughly, then slapped him across his face. Then she flew onto the stage with a leap and clawed at Lazarus. He tried to get away, but anguish was a strong monster and she took him down and ripped off his mask. There was yelling and crying. Some of the audience stood and leaned in to see better, and some covered the eyes of their children.

Lazarus stood, clutching his face. My gaze instantly went to find his distinctive scars from the Great War, but instead I saw that there was nothing wrong with his face. The crowd saw it too and gasped. It was unblemished and without a single mark. His story had all been a ruse. He was a liar. What else was he lying about? Everything?

"He's not scarred," a woman said from the front row. Words like *fraud* and *liar* came next, and a few men stormed the stage as Lazarus ran through the back curtains.

As Conrad pulled his mother from the stage floor, our gazes locked. For several long moments it was just the two of us — like no one else was there, and he knew that

I knew all of this was a farce.

And that Lazarus wasn't the only liar. He was a liar too.

Many of the townsfolk streamed out faster than they'd come in, leaving behind overturned chairs and tent walls pulled down. The few who stayed were either angry or nosy. The building crew ran them off quickly. Then Conrad finally had his fainted mother in his arms, like a child, and moved toward the trucks.

"Quick. Follow me," he said, and without questioning, I did.

He opened up the truck where I had been sleeping and put his mother inside on my bed, and when he caught sight of the small doctor, he waved him over. He closed the door behind them both, then he grabbed my arm and pulled me behind the truck.

"Let's go," he said.

"Go?"

"You and me," he said, his eyes wide. "Let's get out of here and start a life somewhere and forget all of this."

"I —" I stepped away from him when he pulled me close, and before I could consider what was happening, he was kissing me.

Not the way Angel had kissed me. The hard edges of Conrad were gone and he was soft against my body and his lips were soft against mine, but he was kissing me with an urgency I couldn't keep up with. Panic took over. I tried to push him away, but he was so strong and his hand held my head in place.

I began struggling and hitting him, trying to make him stop. This wasn't what I wanted.

"What's wrong?" He stopped kissing me but kept his hold on me. "Don't you feel it between us?"

"Feel what?" I wanted to hate him, but I couldn't. "Your sister is dead and you're kissing me?"

He didn't say anything. He just looked at me.

"Conrad. Son." Lazarus's voice was unhinged and riotous, so much like the voices I'd been raised with. Nothing like the controlled and cunning way he'd been since my arrival.

Conrad let go of me and walked to his father. Lazarus looked entirely different. He was still in his performance suit, but his mask was stuffed into his pocket and his whole, unscarred face was white with grief, shock — reality. He suddenly appeared entirely common and small.

"Where is she? Where's my little girl?" His movements were twitchy and erratic. He was crying through his words. "Where's my Becky-girl?"

"Pop, over here." Conrad put an arm around his father and guided him away. "Come."

Lazarus continued to speak, but his words didn't make sense. The powerful man I'd met only a few days ago was reduced to a raving man grieving over something he himself had caused. I couldn't divert my eyes from them. Conrad loved his father, despite the deceit. Lazarus was as responsible for Becky's death as I was my mother's. I was no better than this man.

Conrad stopped for a moment and turned to me. He mouthed the word *wait.* He wanted me to wait for him? And run off together?

He was in front of me a moment later, digging through his pockets, then handed me money. My hands were full of bills, and several coins slipped through my fingers. Next to Conrad, Lazarus collapsed on the ground like a puddle.

"If you walk through these woods, you're going north. There's a town on the other side of it. This little town here doesn't have a bus or train station. Find one in the next town and get as far away as you can with the money." He spoke fast and rushed. "If you don't have enough, wash dishes at a diner or find a boardinghouse where you can work until you make enough. Be tough. Be smart. Now go."

"I'm not leaving without Angel." I shoved the money into my pants pocket before he could take it back.

"Listen, once my father comes to his senses, he'll be worse than ever. He'll find a way to own you, Nell — Brighton — whoever you are, whatever your name is. I don't want that to happen. Do you know how hard it is to come across a girl like you? No ties to the world. No one to come looking for you. He'll send out his men to find you if you don't go now. These people aren't free. He owns them. And he plans to own you too." His arm gestured to all the people who stood nearby. Some of them looked at me, and the sorrow in their eyes was more than just because of Becky.

Then I watched as the rest of the troupe walked toward Becky's truck. The Sirens were weeping, each in her own skirt, walking on her own legs. Alima gathered them close. The child with the extra arms had his working arms around the woman without any. The reptile-looking man and the acrobatic man stood there, eyes cast down. The crew who built the tents stood with hats in hand, chins quivering. Their weeping filled the night air.

Gabrielle stood in the very back with Angel. Holding his hand.

The few townspeople who were left were taking photographs, but no one seemed to care.

This was our chance.

While Conrad pulled his father from the ground and led him away, I ran to Angel.

"Angel?"

Gabrielle let go of his hand and didn't look at us when I pulled Angel away from the crowd. He was still wearing his white costume, except for the wings, and every part of him glowed.

"Conrad said we need to go," I told him. "He gave me money and told me what to do."

Gabrielle twitched. She was listening.

"We have to." I told him about Conrad's warning.

Angel's stoic expression from yesterday softened. His hands found my arms and his touch reminded me that we were doing this together. He turned and looked at Gabrielle, then back at me. I knew this was hard for him.

"Okay," he whispered.

"Will she stop you?" I asked. "I think she

heard me."

He shook his head. "No, she wouldn't do that. She's a good person."

We made a plan to meet after he changed his clothes and grabbed his bag while the crew dismantled the tents. There would be so many people around it wouldn't be hard for us to slip away.

Then the Sirens sang their melancholy tune as desperate as the song of mythological Orpheus. And like his song, theirs could bring no one back from the grave. It was a song of farewell.

It was time to go.

1941
Disturbed Places

The Sirens' song ended and slowly everyone retreated to their trucks in small groups. Including Angel. The tents went down in record time, and none of the townsfolk lingered further. I tried not to look suspicious. I hadn't seen Lazarus since he'd melted like butter before Conrad took him away. And I'd only seen Conrad at a distance. He'd caught my eye once and nodded his head for me to leave. I looked away, not wanting him to see the secret behind my eyes that I was waiting for Angel.

Another hour passed, and the performers were all tucked into their trucks. Where was Angel? Conrad had taken his mother back to her own truck, but Alima and the Sirens were asleep with sorrow-dampened faces. But I sat and waited until a quiet knock came to the door.

"Nell." The whisper pushed through the cracks. Angel would've said Brighton. This had to be Conrad. "Nell."

I peeked around to see if the whisper had disturbed anyone else in the truck, but it hadn't. I leaned over and opened the door.

It was Conrad. I tiptoed outside and into the cold air. "What are you doing?"

"Why didn't you leave when I told you to?"

"Angel went to get his things but hasn't come back yet. As soon as he comes we're leaving."

The work crew began calling out instructions and the men headed to their designated trucks. Headlights and motors were turning on, covering the song of the crickets. I looked around, sure Angel would appear soon.

"Do you have the money I gave you?" Conrad asked.

"In my bag," I said and pointed to the truck.

He stepped toward the truck, opened the door, and in a moment tossed my bag at me.

"What?"

"You're not coming with us." Conrad started to walk backward, away from me. "Remember what I said about how to get to your aunt's."

"Conrad? I'm not leaving without Angel.

He'll be here any minute." I craned my neck to see if I could catch sight of him. I started walking toward his truck.

In a few big steps Conrad rushed toward me and had his hands tightly around my forearms. His face was so close to mine I could almost feel his whiskers against my skin. His breath smelled like cigarettes. He pushed me away from the line of trucks. When I fell backward the wind was knocked out of me. But I rushed to stand, sputtering to breathe.

"You aren't hearing me, Nell. Lazarus knows you're trying to take Angel and that you know everything about Becky. You have to go. Now." His eyes were wilder than they usually were.

A few of the trucks started moving slowly through the field toward the dirt road we'd come through. I frantically looked around for Angel's shadow coming toward me.

"Where is he? Gabrielle's behind this, isn't she?" I yelled, making my throat raw.

"She doesn't have that kind of power. Lazarus already owns him. He has to pay us back for all our help. It's too late for him."

He looked me up and down. "Things could've been so different." He shielded his eyes from the glare of headlights and moved closer to me. "I would've taken care of you,

you know." Then, without warning, he ran over and jumped into his truck and was gone.

I started running alongside the moving trucks, yelling for Angel. Lights inside the truck houses started turning on, and I kept yelling. I knew his was the one with the long scrape on the side. It was rolling forward, but not quickly.

"Angel," I called after him without pausing.

"Brighton," he yelled back over and over.

His truck was moving faster, and I couldn't keep up. I heard him calling my name, but I couldn't see his face. I might never see his face again. I kept running, but then the last truck in line was passing me.

"It's over, Nell. Just go," Conrad yelled from the passenger side of a passing truck.

The caravan was completely out of sight before I finally stopped running. My lungs had never burned so much. My broken heart was scattered around me on the edge of the empty field. The crickets were my Sirens, singing my funeral dirge. I turned and looked at the empty field. It was dark. The only visible signs of the troupe were the deep ruts from the trailers and a few tent pegs that had been left behind. Like me. But otherwise it was like no one had been there.

The Fancies and Fears were gone.

Angel was gone.

And I was lost.

My grieving cast an iron-strong echo into the night. I had no cocoon to mourn within. I had no restraints to hold me down. I only had my skin to keep everything inside from exploding into a thousand pieces.

I wasn't sure if I fainted or if I'd actually fallen asleep crying, but at some point the brightness of the dawn assaulted me. I was lying in the tall dried grass on the edge of the field where the caravan had been, my bag on top of me.

I ached. My body felt too solid for the emptiness inside. Through swollen eyes, my blurred vision fell upon the cascading sunrise. I didn't want to see the beauty. I didn't want a new day to start. But maybe it was a sign that the east held my future. East was the direction of Riverside. East toward Joann. East toward an expected life instead of unpredictability and loss. East.

My tears fell onto the fragile, brittle grass and wetted the ground. As the grass continued to grow, would I still be here? Even if my body moved on, some part of me would be left behind. The shape of me. The sprawling and curl of my body like an imprint of the wrong that had been done.

I didn't move for hours. I hummed Mother's tune. I wrapped long handfuls of long and dry blades of grass around my wrists. My skin became raw and chafed in the nature-made restraints. By the time night came, I had grown to be part of the husks around me. Empty and done — growing dead. Dead in the ways that mattered. I still lay there when evening fell, and when the first star shot across the sky, I heard it.

I heard Joann's voice in my head. *You are strong. You need to be brave. You need to want a new life.*

Hot tears burned as my mind told me to listen to her voice while my heart ached at the idea of moving on.

I pushed up, then stood. The shape I'd made in the bed of crinkled-up grass didn't look like a girl had stayed there for a whole day. It didn't look like anything but a disturbed place on the ground. And that's what I was becoming. Disturbed. And invisible.

It took all my energy and grit to grab my bag and begin walking.

I winced when I flung my bag around my shoulder. There were scratch marks up and down my arms. When had I done that to myself? I started walking. My feet shuffled against the dead earthen field, then scraped against the paved sidewalk. Away from the empty field. Away from the broken-up pieces of myself, knowing I'd never have them back. Away from the lake in the east, where the sun would rise. Away from the kind woman in black and her little son. Away from Riverside, where the fragments of my soul could float away into memories.

I heard Rosina's voice in the wind. *Our Father, who art in heaven.* All the disturbed places in my mind rose to the surface, filling in the spaces and gaps inside. *Hallowed be thy name.*

I stopped walking. In a world where only the sky and stars were familiar, hearing these words reminded me of home. Was it a sign pulling and wooing me back to a home that had almost killed me? But then I realized the words were not coming from my mind.

"Thy kingdom come."

The voices were nearby.

"Thy will be done."

I followed the words. It wasn't Rosina's voice but many voices — speaking together. I came back to myself, and the voices took me up the steps of a tall white-steepled church.

"On earth as it is in heaven."

I stood in the open and ready door.

"Give us this day our daily bread."

These voices spoke in unison and my breath escaped my lips in a whisper as I recited with them.

"And forgive us our trespasses, as we forgive those who trespass against us."

How could I forgive what had been done to me? Hot tears rushed my eyes.

"And lead us not into temptation —" I spoke and faces turned toward me.

"But deliver us from evil," I yelled and I yelled. So loud my ears rang. Over and over again until finally I couldn't speak another word.

All the other voices had stopped. Every head had turned toward me. Every eye saw my rough, dirty clothing and the marks on my arms.

But my eyes drew past them and to the Crux in front of me. But this time it wasn't a star in the sky, sparkling at a distance, only to disappear shortly after, but a wooden one, hung high in front of me, with a man on it. He had restraints in the shape of nails, and his face was so sad.

I couldn't help him from his captivity, but I wondered if he could help me from mine.

Then I fell. The wooden floor was softer than my heart, and all my pieces filled in the spaces between the nailed boards. I couldn't hold myself together anymore.

1941
Pieces of Myself

But there were hands and voices that held me together, and the image of that man wouldn't leave me. I was picked up, or maybe I was floating. Being helped to live or allowed to die, I wasn't sure.

I could do nothing but dream. I dreamt of Conrad and Gabrielle and Becky and everything that had happened the last few days. But mostly I dreamed of Angel. How was it possible that days felt like years? I'd only been away from the hospital for a week, though it felt like months.

I heard words like *poor dear* and *where did she come from?* and *was she part of that carnival troupe?* There were also many whispered prayers.

The darkness behind my eyes fought against these gentle, velvety words. Evil was inside the dark, and I could find no delivery from it. So I let my mind roam into all the safe places and maybe I could find my way home. Maybe I could wake again.

But before I did, I walked back — far back in my dreams — and found her. And the others who had loved me so well. Grace's shadow was far away, though. How I wanted to see these dear ones, to hear them talk, to feel their nearness.

"Where have you been, young lady?" Joann said, pushing a cart of medications down the hall.

"I got lost," I said and picked up behind her. "I couldn't find my way."

I had to walk fast to keep up with her and passed by so many open doors.

"You're a fish out of water," Lorna parroted and ran across the hall into Rosina and Carmen's room. They called out my name and waved.

But when I tried to wave back, my arms wouldn't move. They were wrapped in dried grass and strips of leather. I could hear Mother hum softly. She was close. I walked into my old bedroom. The restraints were gone and Mother was sitting there with a nursing baby nestled in her arms. Her hair was a golden brown, softly cascading down her shoulders. Her face was rosy and full, and her smile was so real.

She looked up and found my eyes. She found my eyes.

"Come, look at my baby. I call her —"

"Brighton," a voice called to me, and I turned. Grace. She had her hair back and her rich olive coloring had returned. She smiled and without any effort pulled the restraints away from her arms, and suddenly her hands were outstretched and our film canisters dripped through her fingers.

"Don't forget. Don't forget," she said.

"Where's Angel?" she asked as I tried to catch the falling canisters, missing every one of them, then she faded away.

"I lost him," was all I could say.

Then everyone vanished, and the image of my aunt was all that was left in my mind.

1990
Safe and Free from Violence

Kelly Keene is right. More people are at the meeting than I'd expected. There are several hundred in the high school gymnasium, and the palms of my hands get sweatier by the moment. When I walk in I'm sure I'll faint from heat and nerves. My stomach roils, and I have to find a bathroom before I can even think of talking to Kelly.

When I've calmed myself, I see her. She's talking to an oversize man with huge eyes, red cheeks, and a smile a little too big for his face. I have a feeling this is the mayor.

She walks him over to me and I put on a calm, confident face — which almost breaks it in half.

"I'm Mayor Vince Keene and you must be Nell Friedrich. Kelly has told me so much about you." Hm, Vince Keene? I smell a rat. I eye Kelly *Keene.*

I shake his offered hand.

"Is that right? What have you heard?" I

probe. I want to make this young woman feel a little on the nervous side for not having told me that she's related to the mayor.

"Well, Kelly here tells me you have some pictures to share and some stories that will help my constituents see the need to remove those run-down buildings. I'm counting on you to help."

"And how do you think I'll be helpful with a few pictures and stories?"

He leans forward then and becomes the world's best close-talker.

"Any attention that this proposal can get is good attention. Those buildings are an eyesore for a pretty town like ours, and something's got to be done. Doesn't really matter what you're going to say, as long as you're not planning to lobby against me." He looks at Kelly with a raised eyebrow. "She's not, is she?"

Kelly shakes her head and smiles. "No, she's not lobbying against you."

He winks at me, then moves on to the next person waiting to greet him.

"So, you're related?" I ask Kelly, looking at her from the corner of my eye.

She tilts her head in that sweet way she does.

"Yes, he's my father," she says. "But my motives are pure, I promise. When he asked me to be part of the cataloging for a summer job, I had no idea what I'd find. The attention helps his cause, but regardless of all that, it's time people know what you and those women went through. I think your story brings hope."

"Hope." While I have gone through a lot in the last week in reliving and reconsidering my life as a patient at Riverside and my escape, I don't know how that will affect anyone else. I'm not even certain what I'll really share tonight — how deep I'll go. They need to see that there were people mistreated in that building, that my fellow patients along with those before and after deserve to be remembered. That people are people — regardless of diagnoses. They need to see so that it will never happen again. I move in close to Kelly, whom I've grown to care about in the past few days. "I'm so nervous. I'm not sure what to say now."

"After everything you've shared with me about your friends, they'd be so proud of you. Just be yourself, *Brighton,*" Kelly says quietly before skipping away. She turns around and calls back to me. "Everything is set up. Just tell me when to change the slides. Oh, and your reserved seat is up in the front row."

I nod. But my mind is stuck on hearing her call me Brighton.

The crowds are congregated in rows of chairs on the floor and in the stands. A local TV crew is set up. Not all of the crew look excited to be there, but they all have their cameras aimed at the microphone and the reporter standing in front of it is speaking.

Why are so many people and a TV station here for a simple town hall meeting? Milton is a well-known tourist town with a downtown that boasts of the best food in Central Pennsylvania. Sure, the hospital is old and ugly and doesn't fit in here, but even with all of that, it doesn't seem newsworthy enough for such a crowd.

I walk up toward the right side and find my reserved seat on the far end of a row. Then I wait. A woman wearing a red pantsuit taps at the mic on stage, startling us. She gives a sheepish grin and scans her eyes from left to right, taking in the crowd. She clears her throat, and the mic picks it up; it sounds like thunder across the domed ceiling. People around me chuckle, but my nerves just tighten.

"I'd like to bring this town hall meeting to order," she says with an official-sounding voice.

The mayor takes a moment to greet everyone. They go through some of the administrative items. A few people shuffle on and offstage, and then he gets started on a few small community issues. Waste management. A library reading program for the summer season. And then a little excitement over high school football. Of course.

"The main reason we're all here today is because of Milton State Hospital. The hospital has not been used since 1965, and I don't have to tell anyone what an eyesore it is now twenty-five years later." He goes on to explain that for the last ten years there have been efforts to tear down the buildings, but the proposals were always voted down. He explains that the proposal this time comes with more than just a teardown, but a building-up as well.

Maybe this is why so many people are here. They don't want their taxes to rise because of this project.

Then red-pantsuit woman, who is the community director for Milton, is introduced as Mari Silva. She flips through slides that show animated images of the current buildings disappearing and new ones being erected, bright and shining. She mentions that the main building is projected to be called the Wolff Community Center to commemorate a well-known hospital administrator and town councilman. She reminds everyone that he donated an unseemly amount of money to the town. When she finishes everyone claps. I do not.

Mayor Keene shakes Mari Silva's hand with gumption.

"Now I have a special guest for you all," he says with a smile. "As many of you know, these buildings were used as a hospital from 1845 to 1965. That's a long time. As many of you also know, last summer we had a team of graduate students go through the buildings to catalog everything that was left behind. Listen, we don't want these buildings around no more, but we still want to be respectful of what was left inside over all these years. My daughter, Kelly, was one of those graduate students, and as you saw in the paper, this special guest has some interesting things to share with you about this hospital that will give you some insights on how the buildings were used. Everyone likes *vintage* everything these days, so I expect it'll be quite a treat to see these exclusive, never-before-seen vintage photographs."

I'd been mentioned in the paper? Kelly hadn't said anything about that.

A rumble moves across the audience like

a physical wave. Whispers and smiles and people sitting a little taller. I hear someone saying they are hoping for pictures of crazy people and for the photos to prove that the buildings are haunted. Another woman cranes her neck to see the projection screen better, as if she's ready to watch a movie.

"Show us the freaks," a loud voice shouts from the back of the stands, and there's laughter throughout the gym. A few others hoot and holler in agreement.

Is this why so many people came to this meeting? Because Kelly said something about me putting on some type of freak show? My mind returns to my days with the Fancies and Fears. Is that all I'd turned out to be, a freak onstage for everyone to gawk at?

I get up and walk through the aisles. I won't do it. I won't be that person. Not again.

"I'd like to invite my new friend Nell Friedrich up to the stage," I hear Kelly say.

I turn to see her behind the mic, searching the audience for me where I'd been sitting. Even at my distance I can see her eyebrows knit together. The crowd murmurs, and I imagine Kelly sharing my photos without me or not at all. It will be as if my photos are still stuck inside those black canisters. Our stories still hidden away.

And what will the point have been for me to have taken the pictures if after all these years I continue to hide them? My mind goes back inside that building, inside the room I'd shared with my mother. Inside the halls where I'd wandered for so many years. Inside the solitary room where I'd been so isolated. *Cat got your tongue?* I can hear Lorna's voice in my mind like she's standing right next to me.

"No, it doesn't," I respond to her in a whisper, and it gives me the courage to walk up the center aisle.

Kelly smiles nervously at me, and I hope my knees won't give out. When I stand in front of the microphone, I look out, and the crowd of faces looks so eager.

"Thank you, Kelly, and hello, everyone," I say first and get used to how I sound in a microphone. There is utter silence. In my nerves I clear my throat, take a breath, and then begin. "Milton State Hospital wasn't always the name of these buildings. It used to be Riverside Home for the Insane. Some people call these hospitals names like *loony-bin* or a *lunatic asylum.*" A few laugh, and that same boy from the back screeches the word *freaks* again. I ignore him. "*Asylum* comes from the Latin word *asylos,* and it means 'safe' and 'free from violence.' "

I look at Kelly, and the lights dim and the first image is projected.

A collective gasp sounds as they view a picture of Lorna. She's standing tightly camisoled. Her mouth is wide in a scream and naked patients stand around her but aren't paying her any mind. I can hear her scream in my mind still.

"This is Lorna and this picture was taken in 1939. She was elderly by this point and diagnosed as schizophrenic. In her later years she only spoke in clichés. She was admitted to the hospital in 1900 when her husband decided she didn't seem happy enough. This was a typical scene during the day in the Willow Knob building for non-dangerous female patients. To get put in a straightjacket like that she might've attacked a nurse or simply been a nuisance or yelled about being hungry."

I gesture for Kelly to click to the next picture.

I go on to show images of Carmen in bed restraints, Rosina's arm reaching out of the solitary door window, and many patients in hydrotherapy. I explain hydrotherapy and how it could last for days, even though it was never meant to. The crowd is captivated;

I see open mouths, wide eyes, all completely still and silent.

"Riverside also had a children's ward. Being bathed with the spray of a cold-water hose outside the building was normal for these youngsters. Generally, many of them were diagnosed with Down's syndrome, mental retardation, basic erratic behavior, blindness, deafness, and a number of the children were simply unwanted or were orphans. There was even an albino there for almost twenty years — though he is not in this picture. We know now that albinism is not a mental illness, just as blindness and deafness aren't, but there were many years when people believed otherwise."

I go through more. A dayroom full of naked patients. A plate of the food the patients were served that we wouldn't give our dogs. A memory of getting this image in the kitchen with Joyful runs through my mind.

Then someone finally stands. "How do we know these awful images are real?"

"It's creepy," someone yells loudly.

"Humor me for a few minutes and I will explain more," I say.

The woman is exasperated but sits back in her seat.

The slide advances. I swallow hard.

"This is Brighton. This picture was taken after she was in solitary confinement, where her basic needs were barely met. Most of the patients' heads were shorn because lice were pervasive in the dormitories. But she didn't have lice. She was dragged to a chair and strapped in leather restraints. Her head was held still by her nurse while another nurse shaved her head. She was angry and sad, and when the nurse put her hand over her mouth, she didn't think she would ever tell her story to anyone." Warm tears are running down my face, and my fingernails dig into my soft palms.

"You didn't answer my question," the same woman demands.

"To answer your question, how do I know if these images are real and why do I know these stories?"

The woman's shoulders slump as if in response.

"Because I am Brighton. I am that girl in the picture. My friend Grace and I took all of the photographs that I'm sharing with you today."

The crowd isn't simply murmuring now. They are all talking at once, and when I think I need to run off the stage, I find that my spine and heart have strengthened and my throat is open and my voice is strong. I raise my hand to quell the voices, and the simple gesture works.

"I was born at Riverside. This is my mother, Helen Friedrich." Kelly moves to the next slide. "She was emaciated and sick. But even weeks before her death she would hum to me. She knew me and she loved me, and she deserved a better life and a better death. She gave birth to me in that room, and that's where we lived together for eighteen years. She was a German immigrant and was put into the asylum when she was found alone in an apartment unable to care for herself."

Kelly goes to the next shot.

"When Grace was admitted into Riverside she brought her camera, not knowing where her parents were leaving her. We had a nurse who looked out for us —" I pause, my throat turning to knots. I clear it because I need to tell this story. "She tried, anyway. We blackmailed her into allowing us to take pictures. She agreed because she knew we'd never get the chance to develop the film. In the time we had the camera, we took these photographs, but they've been sitting in a pillowcase in the attic since 1941, when I escaped with my friend Angel — an albino boy I met when I was five. I got the film back last week." I pause and nod to Kelly.

"This is Grace when she arrived at age eighteen. She was vivacious and full of life. She was unlike anyone I'd ever met. She taught me a lot about the world — your world — the one I'd never lived in. She was institutionalized because, according to her parents, she loved the wrong man."

Kelly moved on.

"This slide shows Grace after she was hospitalized for about a year. You can see that she's just a skeleton. Her hair was falling out by then. She couldn't eat much without vomiting. Her skin was dusky and flaky because of dehydration." I have to pause as I look back and stare at the large image of her on the screen. I loved her so much. "And I escaped without her." I choke, and everyone gives me a moment. "I still don't know what happened to her. But she was my friend, and I loved her. I believe many of you would've also, and I hope she found a way out. And she's why I'm here today. We made a promise to one another, and today I'm able to fulfill it by sharing with you how we lived and how so many died. We knew if someone didn't speak up, our stories would be lost and our voices muted. I wish she could be up here with me today."

I have to catch my breath with a long,

shuddering inhale. I don't know if I can keep talking. But Kelly continues with the slides. It is hard for me to speak when I see the next image. He was so beautiful and lovely. He was so bright. He was my Angel. Can I even speak about him?

"I met this boy in the graveyard in the back acreage of the hospital property. He didn't know his name. He didn't know what a mother was or what a bath was or what a book was. He didn't know anything. I taught him to eat properly. A kindhearted nurse taught us both to read — though he required a magnifying glass. He was given up by an affluent Pennsylvanian family when he was a toddler because they were ashamed of him being albino. He was at Riverside until he was twenty-one. He was an intellectual young man and my best friend. I called him Angel."

My entire face is now wet with tears as I relive these friendships that meant so much to me. The friends I lost so many years ago. Who would they have become if they'd been given a chance?

I turn back to the crowd, and everyone is in stunned silence.

"These patients weren't just patients to me. They were my friends. My family." Kelly continues to click through the other photos.

"This is one of my friends, Rosina. She taught me the Lord's Prayer in Spanish and some basic Bible stories. B.J. read me her favorite story no less than half a dozen times, so if any of you high schoolers need help with Robin Hood and his Merry Men, I can help." I smile as I see some of the good and humorous in all of this hurt. "There were aides taking care of us, and fewer nurses and even fewer doctors. The nurse who raised me, Joann Derry, at one point had over a hundred and fifty patients to take care of with the help of only one attendant. We were at almost double capacity when I finally escaped just before we entered the Second World War. This was a trend nationwide in asylums, not just at Riverside."

I look at all these faces. What do I want them to know? They'll have these images with them forever, I know that. But what do I want them to think about when the images come back to their minds? Because they will.

"Build your new buildings, if that's what you want. Build them and make them a great place to connect as a community and to enjoy each other. But don't forget the sacred ground that they will be built upon. Don't forget that thousands of souls lived and died there and were ostracized by society. Many are buried in the back corner because no one claimed their bodies. Don't forget the history of what has happened at Riverside and other facilities like it, and don't let history repeat itself. And when you meet someone who might struggle with mental illness, see the person behind the frightened eyes. Not just the diagnosis."

I pause, reluctant to say what I feel I must. It was not my agenda to besmirch a person's reputation, but I can't turn away from this. "The hospital administrator, Dr. Wolff, did not keep his Hippocratic oath, and if I had a vote, I wouldn't want anything named after a doctor like him. Name it for your community and let it be a place where hope exists instead of the darkness I and so many others experienced."

The place is more silent than it has been throughout the entire talk. I pause and know that I am done, but I'm not sure how to finish. So I say something I haven't said in decades. "My name is Brighton Friedrich. Thank you for hearing my story."

It's hard to leave the gymnasium. People are trying to talk to me and even surrounding me. They want to know more. They want more pictures, more stories, more of everything. All I want is to leave and clear my mind.

Kelly helps me, and finally I'm in the gym parking lot with her. My body feels fuller than it has in a long time. The stories I told today I am now ready to tell the important people in my life.

"You were amazing in there," Kelly finally says when we are at my car and she's helping load all the photos and slides into my trunk. "You held them captive."

I smile, and it doesn't feel fake. Her choice of word makes us laugh together.

"What's all this about a newspaper ad?" I ask. "And did you call the TV station?"

"I wanted as many people as possible to hear your story." Her voice carries a sigh in it. "I may have called the station and the newspaper saying that a special guest would be sharing stories that would 'thrill your dreams and confirm your nightmares.' "

I purse my lips and raise my eyebrows at her.

"You mentioned them in your letter to Grace."

Then I exhale and smile at her. "I can't believe I'm saying this, but thank you, Kelly. For all of this. I didn't know that this was what I needed for so long."

When we hug, she hugs me back like a daughter would, and I like that.

"I don't think you're finished, though."

Her excitement is bubbling over and she can barely keep up with herself.

"What do you mean?"

She throws a thumb over her shoulder. "The local TV station is sending your talk to the national networks. They want your story to be heard by more than just our audience."

"I don't know what to say." My hand goes to my chest, holding my heart in place.

"I also heard my father say something about changing a part of the proposal."

"Really? What change?"

"The name." She pauses. "He said that Grace Place has a nice ring to it."

I nod in agreement. It does, and Grace would be so pleased.

"And I have this for you." Kelly hands me several envelopes. I put on my reading glasses. I file through them, not recognizing any of the names. I stop at one that lists *Hannah James* as the sender.

"I don't know who this is. Or any of them."

"These are the families of the asylum patients I've been contacting about belongings. I told them about you and they have written you."

She pauses and puts her hand over mine.

"That top one is Grace's sister," Kelly

says, and like a healing balm she adds, "I found her."

I gasp and don't hold back fresh yet long-held tears.

"Just tell me —" I pull off my glasses and wipe my eyes. "Is she alive?"

Kelly inhales deeply. "No, she's not, but she did not die at Riverside. Hannah fought for her and got her out, but not, unfortunately, before she was sterilized and lobotomized."

"No," I gasp and wonder why she is ruining this special day with such awful news. My hand shakes as it covers my mouth.

"But Hannah says that she lived a happy life despite her terrible years in the asylum. She only passed a few years ago because of health complications. Hannah called her the best, most fun-loving aunt her children could've had because she was so childlike. There were challenges, but she was happy and they were together. It's all in the letter."

I press the letter to my chest. How I long to have one more conversation with my Grace.

"I didn't want to give this to you before the meeting." She shrugs. "I didn't think that would be fair."

I nod. My words are stuck in my throat. I

hug and thank her again. I can't ever repay her for how she's helped me. For all she's done for my Riverside friends.

But I have one more stop to make.

1941
Something Pretty like Hope

The first week under the care of the church in a town I didn't know was a quiet one. A woman named Natty, who had a round belly and was expecting her first child, took care of me in the softest bed I'd ever been in. The blankets were warm and feathery. I sank into the mattress that felt like a large pillow. No one made me talk, and they hadn't even pushed to know my name; they cared so well for me. I'd slept and dreamed most of those hours.

"Where are you from?" Natty finally did ask a few days after my arrival. She brought me a mug of hot chicken broth.

I sipped it carefully, and the salt in the broth made my tongue come alive. I took another two sips before I answered her. I didn't want to stop drinking in the broth, and I had to think about what I would tell her. Where was I from?

"Milton," I said quietly. That was true. I

couldn't possibly tell her that I was from an asylum.

"Milton?"

"In Pennsylvania." I sipped again. I tried not to look too hard at her rounded belly that was carrying a baby. I'd never seen someone so pregnant, or a baby for that matter. It made me think of Joann.

Her brows pulled together, and her lined forehead looked like stairsteps up to her brown hairline. She just kept bringing me food; she put salve and bandages on my arms for days. The sun threw its light and warmth through the lacy curtain, and next to the window was a cross on the wall — only this one was plain wood without the man on it. Like he'd been rescued. Like the restraints had been taken from his hands. I believed that.

"Where are you going?" Natty asked on the fourth day when she brought me a hot drink that afternoon. I'd never tasted anything like what she gave me. She called it hot cocoa.

"To my aunt," I said before I could swallow back the words. "She lives in Brighton, Michigan."

"Would you like me to write her? To tell her you're safe?"

"No," I said too quickly and without explanation.

"Why didn't you just take a train or a bus there from Milton?"

I was afraid to answer questions, especially because of what happened with the Fancies and Fears. But I knew she deserved some answers, given all that she was doing for me. I looked at the cross, and I could almost feel the smooth wood on my fingertips.

"I don't have much money," I said.

"We found money."

The chocolaty drink burned my tongue and I didn't mind. My tongue needed to be restrained or I would let everything inside of me out.

"Someone gave me the money to buy a train or bus ticket, but I don't know where a station is."

Someone. Conrad. The one who stole Angel.

I was given everything I needed and left alone as much as I wanted for the first two weeks I was with them. I just kept staring at the small wooden cross on the wall opposite. Natty was always so kind and quiet and loving. She looked tired some days, and her belly grew larger than I thought possible.

I slept so much during the day that at night I felt wide awake and I would look out the window for my bright little Crux. I'd look for Angel. But found neither. I did discover that Joann had packed in my bag all my birthday photographs. I'd stare at the one with Angel, willing him to come back. Then I'd return to sleep.

On the second Sunday in this little Ohio town, I didn't stay in bed. I sat in Natty's parlor when her church friends came over, and I listened to them talk. They talked about a local woman who had been awarded with a Teacher of the Year designation and a diner owner who was doing a pancake breakfast to raise funds for the high school. They ate cake and drank tea and spoke so kindly to one another. And they just let me listen.

I started to sit at Natty's kitchen table for meals. She served me food but never made me feel bad for being quiet. Her husband, she said, was in the army and not home right now. She told me all about him and he sounded like a nice man. She said I could stay as long as I needed to and that she liked my company.

One night I got out of bed quietly. The wood floor was warm under my naked feet, and a thin breeze rustled my hair and the nightgown I'd been given. I stepped through the bedroom door, down the steps, out to the front porch, then stood on the sidewalk. My toes curled from the touch of the rough concrete.

I looked up. It was an entirely dark night. A black canvas hovered above me and felt heavy on my heart, pushing me to sit on the bottom step.

"The Ladies Aid raised enough money for you to take the train all the way to Brighton." Natty's voice pulled me from my melancholy. "We want to help you get to your aunt."

I turned and watched as another angel in my life sat next to me on the porch step. She leaned back and sighed. She smelled of sweet things that I didn't know well enough to place. Her hair was rolled and covered with some type of net. She wore a robe even though it was warm.

We sat in silence, and I looked off into the field across the road and down the hill. Where so much had happened. Where I'd lost the last person I had loved. It was empty, and the tracks from the trucks weren't visible anymore. It was as if they'd never been there.

"I don't know what to say," I finally said. I'd spoken so little, it was odd to hear my voice. It was so different from the voice I spoke in my head telling me how to feel, what to do, and where to go. That one sounded like the sixteen-year-old girl yelling at Joann.

Then she put her hand on mine, and for a moment I thought it would feel as if she were holding me down, keeping me there, confining me. But it didn't and she wasn't. She was lifting me up. She was letting me go. Then she jumped and laughed.

"This baby is busy tonight."

"What?" I asked, sitting up straighter.

"The baby is kicking." She put her hand on her swollen abdomen.

"You mean you can feel it moving?" I turned toward her, shocked.

She nodded. "You don't know these sorts of things, do you?"

"I've never —" I didn't know how to finish my sentence. I've never seen such a pregnant woman. I've never felt a baby move. I've never seen a baby except in a storybook.

Natty took my hand and pressed it against a bulging spot on the right side of her belly. A few breathless moments later I felt it. This little person inside Natty had just kicked my hand.

"Wow," I said, and a surge of something I couldn't name surfaced. "Is it a boy or a girl?" I asked, keeping my hand in place.

"You're silly — I don't know yet — not till it's born." She sighed and looked up. "Look, the first star."

She pointed and I looked up. The pinprick of light was brighter than any star I'd ever seen.

" 'All the darkness in the world cannot extinguish the light of a single candle.' "

If I could've weighed the truth of that statement, this one would've toppled the entire earth.

"Is that in the Bible?" I asked.

"No, but close," Natty said with a giggle. "Saint Francis said it."

"It's true, though, isn't it? Even though it's not in the Bible," I asked, hopeful.

"It is."

We watched in silence as the little star was met by one more, then another, and then hundreds burst out of hiding.

"I want a girl." Natty patted her belly.

"What will you name her?" I asked almost thoughtlessly, but as soon as I'd spoken the words I wished to take them away. Names were too important to throw around on porch steps.

"Something pretty, like Hope." She looked at me.

"Hope." I repeated the name, and for the first time I realized that sometimes the very best things in our lives are those things that take time to unfold.

Then I told Natty everything, and she cared for me anyway.

1941
One Bright Window

Five days later Natty delivered her baby. And just like she wished — it was a little girl, and she named her Hope. She was pink-skinned with a burst of red hair and rosebud lips. Her cry sounded like a song, and her eyes shined like a mirror into the future.

"Here." Natty put her in my arms before I could say no. I was so afraid of hurting her.

And there she was, innocence wrapped in the softest skin I'd ever touched. For the first few minutes she was awake, her glassy blue eyes looked right at my face. But as her eyes drooped in slumber, she gripped my pinky finger in her whole hand and I was sure I could never give her back to Natty. But of course I did when she bawled to be fed. Natty took her, gently rocking and nursing her.

"It's time for me to go," I said as we sat together.

It was finally time for me to make my way to my aunt and into the unknown that was hidden with expanding and growing hopes. In the weeks since I'd lost Angel, I began to realize that my next steps would be alone. Hope and sorrow braided together into one path. But standing still was not an option.

But oh, how I missed him. Where was he?

When I'd been with Natty for nearly two months and Hope was a few weeks old, I accepted the money from the church ladies. They gave me new clothes to wear and many hugs and prayers and requested a visit back someday. And they told me that if it didn't work out with my aunt, I had a permanent home there, with them.

I arrived at the Brighton Depot with a shadowy black sky overhead. My fingernails were nubs. My jaw ached. My mind raced. My ears rang. More so than when I left Riverside and when I was about to meet Ezra. Maybe it was because this was my last hope, or maybe it was because an aunt was the closest thing to my own mother I would ever get. And maybe she would know how to find Angel.

But what if she didn't want me? What if she didn't even live there, even though Ezra said she did? What if she was dead? What if by tonight I was still alone? Natty said I could come back. That she would take me in as long as I needed.

But I had to take this chance. I'd given up everything for this — even chasing after Angel for now. My breath caught in my throat when my loss surfaced in my soul, and I swallowed to push it back into place. He was always on my mind. Every thought I had was hemmed in with wondering about him. Every sleepless night was filled with memories and tears like the scattered stars. Was he trying to escape? Or had he just accepted his new life? When I knocked on Margareta's door and knew if she'd accept me in or not, maybe then I would know if it had all been worth it.

I went to the ticket clerk and slid my aunt's address to him.

"Is this nearby?"

He picked it up and looked through his small round glasses that sat at the end of his nose. He nodded.

"Ithaca Drive. Well, it's a bit of a walk, maybe ten blocks away." He pointed past the depot. "For a nickel I'll give you a map."

I pulled out a few coins and ran through my mind which one was the nickel. I found one — proud of the lessons I'd learned with Natty. He took it and slid a town map toward me. In a few minutes I found the depot on the map and then under the light of the train platform my finger traced the line of streets until my aunt's road was at my fingertip. Ten blocks was nothing compared to how far I'd come. I wasn't going to stop now.

So I started walking. As I walked through the neighborhoods I could see shadows and outlines of people behind curtains of a few dimly lit windows. When I finally turned onto Ithaca Drive, I stopped and caught my breath. I was in what appeared to be a simple and quaint neighborhood. The tall ash trees hung over the road like a magical pathway.

I inhaled and caught the scent of rich, damp soil, evidence of an earlier rain. Then I took a step off of the curb and crossed the street toward the house number Ezra had given me. A yellow light cascaded out onto the front yard. This house stood out from the rest of the gray shadowy houses.

I didn't have to look at the envelope with Margareta's address because I knew the house number was 102 and the lit window was the place I had walked this long journey to find.

In the dim light of the moon, with old wispy clouds passing over, I just stood there. I closed my eyes and imagined that when I opened them I'd find Angel ambling along and that he'd tell me that he had only been a step behind all along. A naïve dream, I knew. When I opened my eyes, I was still alone and my eyes burned brightly with tears that I blinked away.

My eager toes wiggled in the shoes Natty had found in something called a missionary barrel. I was clean and looked unlike myself in the white blouse with lace at the cuffs and a blue skirt. I even wore stockings. Natty had cut my hair into a real style, and I had been taught how to fix it. I'd learned what Nell looked like. Perhaps I should've journeyed wearing the hospital gown with my hair hanging around my face — maybe that was the way my long-ago aunt should have met me because that was the me I knew. But I wasn't that girl anymore. She was gone now. Lost and far away.

I looked back at the house. The bright window. Then up to the moon, my only companion but for the little cross that was shining up there somewhere, reminding me to endure.

Halfway up the sidewalk path, leading to the front door, I still didn't know what I would say. How would I tell her who I was and where I'd come from? How would I even know that it was, in fact, my aunt? As

I got closer, the strains of a piano came through the golden window. A ragged voice sang, and I waited at the front door until the song was done. It seemed rude to interrupt, and I liked hearing her sing. Then I took my chance to knock.

At first I was afraid it was too quiet. But then I heard movement, shuffling, a creaky floor, something inside that had stirred at the sound of my knuckles against the door.

When the rattle on the other side of the door sounded, I inhaled and almost ran away. The porch light turned on, then the door opened and there she was — a small woman, shorter than me, leaning on two canes. She had white hair that was cut to her chin and round, soft features. She didn't look like my mother at all except in the shape of her eyes, but hers were brimming with life.

"Hello," she said musically and with a smile.

My mouth was open, but nothing came out for a few beats.

"Are you Margareta Friedrich?" I finally said softly.

"I am." She twinkled and smiled.

"I'm —" I stopped. Who was I? "I'm Helen Friedrich's daughter."

Her hand shook and went to her mouth

with a gasp, and one of her canes hit the floor with a slap. She fell against the door-frame. Her other cane also fell. Her face twitched. And her tears were like stars as she opened her arms to me, and I bent close to her and rested there with my head on her shoulder. She was soft and warm, and she was my home.

Then there was a shadow of a man behind her. I straightened and looked more closely.

When he stepped out of the dim light, everything became bright.

"I got away. I told you I'd never let you go."

He'd found his way back to me.

Angel and I were finally home.

1990
All Because of Grace

I'm not afraid to make my final stop anymore. The sun is half set by the time I get there, and the broken old buildings don't scare me this time. I don't need to creep around, but instead I walk freely onto the property that used to hold my soul. That used to hold me captive. But doesn't any longer. Not me or anyone. The long grass brushes against my legs, and I enjoy the gentleness of it and I don't rush the walk back to my haunts, back to the graveyard.

From a distance I can see that many of the gravestones have fallen and it is in great disrepair. But as I get closer I realize that it isn't the same place it used to be for another reason.

Where once only dried grass and death had persisted now a meadow grows, bursting with color, not unlike the sunset that washes over me. Wildflowers now grow where nothing else could. The old ground has found a renewed purpose. The breeze rushes over the tips of the tall flowers and grasses, and they dance for me. There is new life. Uncultivated and rogue and unfettered. Free.

Then I see him.

He's walking around to the front of the angel statue that he is repositioning back on the pedestal. The angel figure looks so small now — it is so much bigger in my memory. With his hands he brushes away old dust and dirt. He has a smile on his face.

His ever-pure white hair moves in the breath of the evening air. He's as handsome as he ever was.

Angel.

"You're here?" I walk up to my husband, and he takes my hands in his. "But how?"

"From the Pittsburgh airport I took a train and two cabs to get here." He can't drive because of his vision, so he's always finagling ways to get around. Nothing slows him down. "I knew you'd come here."

He takes in everything around us. I'm not the only one who needs to heal from those hard days.

"You were amazing up there." He looks back at me. "I'm so proud of you."

"How could I have missed you?"

"There were a lot of people and I've

learned ways of going unnoticed." He winks, and it's almost too innocent for a man of his age but so believable. "This was *your* promise to keep, not mine. I didn't want to be a distraction."

He gestures with his head for me to follow. The dried-up grass against our feet is so familiar that I wonder if the blades remember us. The sun is setting off to our right, casting bright rays upward across the sky.

"I found your mother," Angel says, and we stop in front of a marker. "H. Friedrich."

We both bend over. In my mind the stone should be brand new because I've never seen it before, but it's decades old, sun worn and chipped. I trace her name with my finger.

"H. Friedrich," I repeat, thinking of our old game. "Dirty blonde. Hums. And loves her daughter."

We sit together and I rest my head against his shoulder.

"I'd like to move her. She should be buried next to Dad, Aunt Marg, and Rebekah Joy." Angel and I had so many years with my aunt and my dad once he moved to Michigan. The four of us made quite a family before our own children came along.

"Do you sometimes wish you'd kept in

touch with Joann?"

I don't need time to think about this because this choice has been part of me for so long. "Knowing she was okay through Bonnie's news was enough for me. I'm sad that she's gone, though."

Cancer took her five years ago.

The silence bears aged voices that say my name in that abiding and surviving way that reminds me that souls are eternal and our stories don't cease to exist after death.

"Kelly found Grace." I tell him everything I learned about our friend as I gather a handful of wildflowers around me and put them by Mother's grave.

His sigh is so heavy it makes a hole in the ground. "She had joy." He pulls me closer. "I'm so glad Kelly found her sister. Though I'm mortified that she had to experience those barbaric surgeries."

"I know." We're quiet for a while. "We've had such a good life, haven't we? Mostly as Dr. Angel Sherwood and Nell Friedrich." We both laugh a little, having had such angst about our names and making independent choices that worked the best for us.

"We had to fight for everything," he adds. "There was so much pain then, but there was always a light on our path to keep us from giving up."

I nestle closer to him, knowing all about slivers of light and the courage hope gives. But the losses have been great.

"Oh, what a life Grace could've had if she'd never been admitted in the first place," I say.

"But if it wasn't for Grace," Angel suggests.

"I never would've had all those photos and no one would've ever known them. Known you. Known me."

"If it wasn't for Joann putting you in solitary, you might never have forged the relationship with Grace that you did." He kisses the side of my head. "A lot of bad had to happen for us to have all the good in our lives. For the truth to be told. For people to know."

I nod. "Yeah." My little word is featherlight in the air and travels around the graves, greeting them. My throat is filled with knots and tears and a bittersweet joy I can't explain. For several long minutes we sit there. We don't speak but let the voices from our past rise up to meet us, to welcome us, and to be grateful that we've shared so much life and love.

Angel stands, but I don't know if I'm ready. We could sit together on the dry earth and reminisce forever. I know we won't be back. I know when I leave I'm done here.

"Come on, Nell." He puts his hand out to me and helps me up.

I inhale and shake my head and speak the words I've longed to say since I was eighteen.

"It's okay now, Angel. You can call me Brighton."

ACKNOWLEDGMENTS

With the completion of each book I'm always at a loss for how to really thank and acknowledge all the people who made it come together. It's never a solo effort. Without so many this book would never have come to be. And more than with any other book I've written, I needed every bit of the light these people shared.

To God, the Father of lights: Every reference to light in these pages is a reference to You and Your goodness.

To my grandma-in-love, Joann: It was the true story you shared with me at my kitchen table that was the seed of this story. I honor you with this book.

To my husband, Davis: You are my Angel, and you are the brightest person I know.

To my daughters, Felicity and Mercy: You are both hope wrapped in skin, and the future is in your eyes.

To my family: Your constant encouragement and persistent belief have been a buoy to me.

To my agent, Natasha: You are Natty, delivering wisdom and love with great conviction.

To my friend Kelly: You know what this book has meant to us. The path is bright and filled with grace.

To my editor, Jocelyn: Your faith and confidence in this book carried me when I lacked the faith and confidence in it myself.

To marketing and sales and Kristen for her cover design: You've all put so much of your wisdom, knowledge, and understanding into this book. I am humbled and grateful.

To Julie Breihan: I am in awe of your editing ninja skills. Know that you were a bright spot in this book journey. Thank you so much for your hard work.

To my friends: So many have gone out of your way to pray for me, encourage me, and help me spread the word: Alicia Vaca, Pam Weber, Carolyn Baddorf, Carla Laureano, Jennifer Naylor, Susie Finkbeiner, Carrie Fancett Pagels, Becky Cherry-Hrivnack, Jolina Petersheim, Rachel Linden, Amanda Dykes, and Cathy West and my launch team. Even if you didn't realize it at the time, your kind words or simple messages have meant a lot to me.

To the Community Evangelical Free Church Book Club, for your sweet encouragement and support. It was so unexpected, and I'm so grateful to call you my home church.

And finally, to my readers. May each of you find the brightness and hope you need in your life. May it come from the Father of lights, and may you find peace within the lines of this story. Thank you, thank you, thank you for reading.

DISCUSSION QUESTIONS

1. *The Bright Unknown* begins with an epigraph from Emily Dickinson: "I am out with lanterns, looking for myself." How does this quotation foreshadow the story?
2. Describe the relationship between Brighton and Nursey as compared to Brighton and her mother. How do both women fulfill the role of mother for Brighton?
3. Why is Brighton reluctant to escape? What holds her back, and what is she afraid of confronting and leaving behind?
4. When Brighton and Angel meet, they form a unique friendship. How would you describe the type of bond they have? Why is it different from her friendship with Grace and Nursey?
5. Grace comes from an affluent family and is punished because she doesn't want to keep their family secrets. How have you seen secrets dividing people and families?
6. At one point in the novel Brighton wants

to give up. She believes that letting her mind roam will be less painful than engaging with her reality. How do you understand Brighton in these moments? Where do you see yourself gaining strength when in the midst of sorrow and pain?

7. Angel talks about feeling free among the Fancies and Fears because his differences are celebrated instead of demeaned. How does this ring true? If it is true, why would staying with the troupe have been dangerous for Angel and Brighton?
8. Nell challenges the definition of *normal.* In what ways do you see society defining what's normal or abnormal? Do these views help or hurt individuals?
9. Mental illness and its treatment play an important role in *The Bright Unknown.* In what ways have views changed since the 1930s and 1940s? What stigmas exist that still need to be overcome?
10. Do you believe that the novel ends with hope? Why or why not? What do you think happens next in the story?

ABOUT THE AUTHOR

Elizabeth Byler Younts gained a worldwide audience through her first book, *Seasons: A Real Story of an Amish Girl.* She is also the author of the critically acclaimed novel *The Solace of Water* and the Promise of Sunrise series. Elizabeth lives in central Pennsylvania with her husband, two daughters, and a small menagerie of well-loved pets.

Visit her online at
ElizabethBylerYounts.com
Twitter: @ElizabethYounts
Facebook: AuthorElizabethBylerYounts
Instagram: @ElizabethBylerYounts

The employees of Thorndike Press hope you have enjoyed this Large Print book. All our Thorndike, Wheeler, and Kennebec Large Print titles are designed for easy reading, and all our books are made to last. Other Thorndike Press Large Print books are available at your library, through selected bookstores, or directly from us.

For information about titles, please call:
(800) 223-1244

or visit our website at:
gale.com/thorndike

To share your comments, please write:

Publisher
Thorndike Press
10 Water St., Suite 310
Waterville, ME 04901

CISTERCIAN STUDIES SERIES: NUMBER ONE-HUNDRED EIGHTEEN

THE HERMIT MONKS OF GRANDMONT

by

Carole Hutchison

Illustrations by Kate Douglas

Cistercian Publications
Kalamazoo, Michigan
1989

Cistercian Publications Inc. Editorial Offices
Institute of Cistercian Studies
Western Michigan University
Kalamazoo, MI 49008
Cistercian Publications are available in Britain and Europe
from Cassells plc
Artillery House Artillery Road
London SW1 P1RT
Elsewhere, including Canada, orders should be sent to
Cistercian Publications
St Joseph's Abbey
Spencer, MA 01562
The work of Cistercian Publications is made possible in part
through support from Western Michigan University
to the Institute of Cistercian Studies.

Library of Congress Cataloguing-in-Publication

Hutchison, Carole, 1938–
The hermit monks of Grandmont / by Carole Hutchison ;
illustrations by Kate Douglas.
p. cm. — (Cistercian studies series ; no. 118)
Includes bibliographical references.
ISBN 0-87907-618-6
1. Order of Grandmont. 2. Hermits—France. 3. France—Church
history. I. Title. II. Series.
BX3672.H88 1989 89-22108
271'.79—dc20 CIP

Printed in the United States of America.

IN MEMORY OF MY MOTHER

TABLE OF CONTENTS

ACKNOWLEDGEMENTS

The purpose of this outline history of the Order of Grandmont is to draw attention to a sadly neglected area of monastic history. Much of the spadework has been carried out by scholars of this and previous generations but their work is not readily available. In particular I wish to express my gratitude to Dom Jean Becquet, OSB and Dr J-R Gaborit for allowing me access to their published and unpublished works. The conclusions drawn and resulting errors are my own. I also wish to thank Mr Pierre Campagne for his help in locating relevant source material: Dr Paul Betts whose mastery of Latin eliminated many errors in the quotations from the first Custumal of Grandmont: Messrs Robin Newman and Joseph Manighetti for correcting the draft manuscript and Sr Deborah Doll, O.D.C., who painstakingly edited the final draft and drew my attention to several unhappy errors concerning the religious life. I also owe a great deal to Frère Philippe-Etienne for his encouragement and for his helpful explanations of Grandmontine life and custom. Mr Cecil F. Wright, M.S. & Dipl. Arch. kindly read the architectural section and I am most grateful for his comments especially regarding the design of the Grandmontine apse. A special word of appreciation to Miss Sandra Clayton for so carefully typing the manuscript.

I would have been unable to study Grandmontine architecture at first hand were it not for the kindness of many of the present owners of the priories. Not only did they permit us to examine and photograph every nook and cranny of their homes, they also regaled us with the most warm and generous hospitality. In particular I wish to thank: Pierre and Christine Bastide of *Comberoumal* where we spent weeks researching. Also: Mr Bec, Saint-Michel de Lodève: Mr & Mme de Beauvais, *Puy Chevrier*: Mr & Mme Gerson, *Bois d'Allonne*: Mr & Mme Gromard, *Clairefontaine*: Mr & Mme Huet, *Fontblanche*: Mr & Mrs Richards, *Craswall*: Mr & Mrs Wilde, *Alberbury*: La Fraternité Saint-Dominique, *la Haye d'Angers* and la Communauté Ursuline, *Louye*.

I also wish to thank the following colleagues and friends: the Rev'd Christopher Armstrong for his help and encouragement: Ron Shoesmith, Director, City of Hereford Archaeological Committee and Ruth Shoesmith who have always made us so welcome in Hereford: Gilles and Jeanette Bresson, Société pour la sauvegarde et l'amemagement de Grammont, for their hospitality at Chassay: José and Thérèse Falco and Pierre and Charlette Boutes who, for three seasons invited us to join their archaeological team at Pinel and accommodated us in their homes: Jean-François Mougnaud, President de la Société des Amis de Saint-Sylvestre et de l'Abbaye de Grandmont and Françoise Mougnaud for their hospitality at Saint-Sylvestre. Messrs Georges Frugier and Jean-Gabriel Gabiron cultivated my interest in the Grandmontine's, a subject which they have been studying for many years.

Finally I wish to thank Kate Douglas who has accompanied me on thousands of miles of journeying through Grandmontine France and who is also responsible for most of the photographs and all the drawings which grace these pages. Without her unfailing support and friendship this book would not have been realised.

Carole Hutchison

Buckhurst Hill
1988

ABBREVIATIONS USED IN THE NOTES

Bec	Dom Jean Becquet
Bec SOG	Jean Becquet, *Scriptores Ordinis Grandimontensis*, Corpus Christianorum Continuatio Medievalis 8 (Turnhout, 1968).
BSAHL	*Bulletin de la Société Archéologique et Historique de du Limousin*, Limoges: 1845–
Gui	Louis Guibert, *Une page de l'histoire du clergé français au dix-huitième siècle, destruction de l'Ordre et de l'Abbaye de Grandmont, BSAHL*, 23–25 (Limoges 1875) Republished in one volume of the same name: (Paris and Limoges: 1877)
Lev	Dom Jean Levesque, *Annales Ordinis Grandimontis* (Troyes 1662)
PL	J.-P. Migne, *Patrologiae cursus completus, series latina*, 221 volumes. Paris, 1844–64
RG	Rule of Grandmont, PL 204: cols. 1135 - 1162 Also: Bec, *Scriptores Ordinis Grandimontensis*, Corpus Christianorum series, Continuatio Mediaevalis 8. (Turnhout, Belgium: 1968)
RMab	*Revue Mabillon*, Liguge, 1905–
RS	Rolls Series: *Rerum Britannicarum Medii Aevi Scriptores* or: *Chronicles and Memorials of Great Britain and Ireland during the Middle Ages*, published under the authority of the Master of the Rolls (London 1858-97)
VCH	Victoria History of the Counties of England, London: University of London Institute of Historical Research.

INTRODUCTION

TOWARDS THE CLOSE of the eleventh century, Stephen, son of the Viscount of Thiers in the Auvergne, established a little group of hermits at Muret some twelve miles from the city of Limoges. Following his death in 1124, the company moved a few miles away to Grandmont and there built a monastery. This remained the mother house of their Order until its suppression in 1772, ostensibly for lack of numbers but in reality to satisfy the greed of certain secular-minded bishops.

Few people today have heard of these hermit monks of Grandmont although they constituted the most austere monastic order to emerge from the Middle Ages. In the twelfth century the 'Bonshommes', as they were popularly known, enjoyed a reputation for zeal and piety similar to the Cistercians. Their diffusion was equally remarkable. By 1163, just thirty-nine years after the death of the founder, thirty-nine houses had been established in France.

The roots of what proved to be a very unusual religious order were embedded in the monastic reform movement which originated in Italy in the last quarter of the tenth century and which subsequently swept through France, causing that great churchman and reformer, Peter Damien, to observe: 'It seemed as if the whole world would be turned into a hermitage'. The essential cause of the turmoil which shook the monastic world to its foundations was the desire to return to the ideals of the primitive church, the *vita apostolica* as it is briefly outlined in the Acts of the Apostles: ''All things were in common unto them and distribution was made to everyone according as he had need.'' Such notions of poverty, simplicity and detachment were not wholly original. They are implicit in the sixth-century Rule of St Benedict which still remained the standard, authoritative legal code for western monks. However, in the intervening centuries and certainly in their Cluniac interpretation, its prescriptions had been stretched to the limit. Austerity was abandoned in favour of elaborate ceremonial which occupied the major part of the monastic day, leaving hardly any time for private prayer and contemplation. Manual work, one of the essential requirements of the Rule, was relinquished to hired servants whilst the monks became increasingly involved in worldly affairs and administration. The opulent splendour of many of the traditional monasteries, the sheer scale and extent of the properties owned by the abbeys, held little attraction for those seeking to dedicate themselves completely to the service of Christ. It is significant that the lifetime of St Stephen of Muret, founder of the Grandmontines, coincided with the apogée of the cluniac experience under the long abbacy of St Hugh (1049–1109). During this period the empire of Cluny attained gigantic proportions. Its church, the largest in Christendom, must have seemed as much a monument to human achievement as the glory of God.

Since its fourth century origins in the deserts of Lower Egypt and Syria, christian monasticism continued to incorporate two distinct traditions. The eremitic, the solitary life led by anchorites, and the coenobitic, the way of the monk living in an organised community ruled by an abbot. These were never intended as diametrically opposed alternatives but as distinctive stages along the path of spiritual perfection. St Benedict himself, whilst legislating for life in community, nevertheless observes that this is for certain individuals but the primary stage of a monastic career. He regarded the monastery as 'the school of the Lord's service', and the eremitical vocation a form of postgraduate monasticism suitable for 'those men who have learnt to fight against the devil, well taught by the companionship of many brethren; and now well trained, they are competent to leave the ranks of their brethren for the single combat'.[1]

The benedictine tradition never entirely lost sight of the eremitical ideal and even the Cluniacs sometimes made provision for a hermit dwelling within the monastic enclosure. Thus it seems reasonable that at a time when worldliness and decadence were everywhere apparent, when monasteries were distinguished more for the splendour of their architecture than for their piety, certain reactionaries should consider the hermitage as their only possible alternative. The widespread opting-out of monks from the traditional monasteries in the eleventh century gave rise to a strange paradox which was repeated time and again. The monks who left regular communities to become solitaries invariably attracted followers and ended up by founding new monasteries which were merely stricter versions of those they had left in the first place. Hence, the eleventh century hermits are often indistinguishable from reformed religious. The experience of the monk turned hermit reverting to monk can be seen initially in the case of St Romuald of Ravenna (*c.* 950–1027). When he left the cluniac monastery of St Apollinare in Classe, it was with the avowed intention of reviving the solitude and asceticism of the 'desert fathers'. In fact, he spent the remainder of his life travelling and reforming existing monasteries, as well as founding his own monastery of Val di Castro where the Rule of St Benedict was strictly observed. After years of training, suitable candidates were permitted to retire to an individual hermitage on the slopes of nearby Mount Camaldoli. Thus, Romuald also became the founder of the hermit order of Camaldolese although his own experience of the hermit's cell was somewhat limited. A similar pattern is discernible in many subsequent monastic careers. Robert of Arbrissel, Stephen of Obazine, Robert of la Chaise Dieu, Vitalis of Savigny, Bernard of Tiron, all began by rejecting the coenobitic life, but their years in the 'desert' were curtailed when their followers became so numerous that they were forced to organise regular communities to contain them.

In this context, Stephen of Muret, founder of the Grandmontines, emerges as a notable exception, for he never lived a regular life in community, and after becoming a hermit at the age of thirty he never again left his retreat at Muret. Moreover, Stephen never envisaged founding a regular monastery for his disciples. It was not until thirty-two years after his death that they themselves finally submitted a Rule for a properly constituted Order of Grandmont to Pope Adrian IV for his approval. Even when the Grandmontines began living what was to all intents and purposes a regular life in community, they retained something of their unique character and continued to regard themselves as hermits. It is therefore necessary to consider to what extent such a claim can be justified. It is possible, in fact, to draw a clear distinction between, on the one hand, the traditional hermits who imitated the 'desert fathers' and lived in total seclusion and, on the other, this novel brand of medieval hermits who organised themselves into communities. While the former group shunned all human contacts, their medieval counterparts accepted, even welcomed, like-minded companions. Solitude for them did not exclude fellow religious, nor did it implicitly exclude all secular contacts. As their patron the Grandmontines adopted St John the Baptist rather than St Antony of Egypt. Even though they were explicitly forbidden to practise any form of active ministry they were nonetheless exhorted to preach by example. As the Rule of Grandmont points out, John the Baptist did not leave the desert even to seek out Christ but waited patiently for Christ to come and find him. One of the more appealing and humane chapters in this otherwise uncompromising Rule concerns the welcome and hospitality to be afforded to guests. Furthermore, the Grandmontine churches were never as strictly enclosed as those of the Carthusians and Camaldolese; anyone wishing to join the brethren in their prayer was welcome to do so, at least in the early days of the order.

Of the numerous hermit groups which blossomed in the Middle Ages, only three managed to survive the centuries as independent religious orders. The Camaldolese in Italy, the Carthusians and Grandmontines in France. The latter French hermit groups were close contemporaries. Stephen of Muret commenced his life of solitude around 1076 and Bruno of Cologne, Founder of the Carthusians in 1084. A comparison between the two reveals the essential difference between the Carthusians, hermits in the more traditional sense, and the Grandmontines, religious hybrids who pursued their eremitical ideal within the framework of a regular life in community. For, if there was one requirement which the Grandmontines rated more highly than solitude, it was their need to live in conditions of extreme evangelical poverty and this explains why they adopted a widely differing life style from their contemporaries of the Chartreuse.

A Carthusian monastery or charterhouse is an exceedingly expensive establishment both to build and maintain. Each monk occupies his own 'cell' which is, in fact, a completely individual house, often two storied and having its own private garden. All the usual conventual buildings: church, chapter house,and refectory, also have to be provided both for the formation of novices and for the professed hermits who on Sundays and feastdays customarily meet together for a meal and recreation. Additionally, a fairly large number of lay brothers who are required to attend the monks have to be housed in a separate establishment, the so-called 'lower house'. The Carthusian hermit therefore enjoys the most perfect conditions for a life of reflection and prayer. He passes the major part of each day alone in his 'cell' and is left totally free both for prayer and intellectual pursuits. Manual work such as tending his garden or engaging in some craft is by way of relaxation, because all necessary domestic chores and heavy work are performed by the lay brothers.

By contrast, the Grandmontine hermit could expect little solitude apart from the community with whom, for reasons of economy, he was expected to share his cell. Thus, a Grandmontine house came to be something of a cross between a large hermitage and a monastery in miniature and was referred to simply as a 'cell'. It was intended to house a maximum of thirteen; four or five contemplatives, the choir monks, and the remainder, lay brothers. Unlike the Carthusians, however, there was no juridical distinction between the contemplative choir monks known as the 'clercs' and the lay brother 'convers'. Further expenditure was eliminated inasmuch as both groups worked and prayed together, shared the one choir, chapter house, refectory, and dorter. This communal dorter was actually divided by wainscotting into separate cubicles which critics of the Order were to condemn as a luxury. If a space approximately seven feet by five can be considered in any way luxurious, it is, however, worth noting that this was all that remained of the original hermits' huts at Muret.

Charterhouses generally consist of fine buildings surrounded by a considerable acreage of land, efficiently exploited by the monks to gain produce both for their own domestic requirements and to augment their income by selling on the open market. The Grandmontines were absolutely forbidden to own lands outside the immediate enclosure of the cell which was simply a small forest clearing. 'Woods are suitable places for monks to build their homes' states the Rule, and throughout their history they remained faithful to this tradition. They were thus dependent for their livelihood on what amounted to no more than a smallholding together with what they might or might not receive by way of alms. They were denied any form of fixed income. Whenever extra assistance was needed with building, maintenance, or agricultural tasks, the choir monks were expected to labour alongside the lay brethren and they were also expected to fulfil their share of the everyday chores. Hence, the hermit monk of Grandmont, unlike his Carthusian counterpart, had little time for study, and any recruits might expect plenty of hard toil but little compensation in the way of reading matter. Certainly, no great tradition of learning ever developed within the Order.

All the other groups of reformed religious of the period, even the Carthusians, retained the Rule of St Benedict as their chief source of reference and their own customs were derived from it. Only the Grandmontines deviated in their insistence that St Benedict's Rule along with those of St Augustine and St Basil represented simply cuttings from a single plant. The Gospel, maintained Stephen of Muret, is:

> The one primary and fundamental Rule of Rules for our salvation and all others derive from it like springs from the one source. This is the Holy Gospel which was given by the Saviour to his apostles to be by them faithfully proclaimed to the whole world.[2]

It may well have been this steadfast, almost stubborn determination to adhere to the evangelical precepts of their founder which spared the Grandmontines the fate which in due course overtook other groups of contemporary religious. By the mid-twelfth century, the others had all been assimilated either by the Cistercians (Obazine, Dalon) or various of the congregations of regular canons (Esterps, Chalard, Artige, Benevent, and Aureil).

Just why monks turned hermits in the eleventh century and reverted to their cenobitic state in the twelfth is not easy to determine. One possible explanation lies in the personal appeal of the founders themselves; Robert of Arbrissel, Stephen of Obazine, and Robert of la Chaise

Dieu are illustrative of the many outstanding and charismatic religious leaders who arose at this time. Yet once the direct influence they exercised over their followers was removed, the only means of holding the group together lay in firm and competent legislation. Organisers of the calibre of Stephen Harding whose *Carta Caritatis* ensured the smooth and efficient government of the Cistercian Order, are few and far between and many deficient and inadequate attempts at organisation were doomed from the start.

A further and equally plausible explanation for the early demise of so many hermit groups lies in the realisation that success can in itself be a prelude to failure. Fifty or so years after their foundation, many of these communities had grown out of all proportion. The resultant problem was voiced by Hugues de Fouilloy, prior of the canons regular of St-Laurent-au-Bois: 'Our troubles increase in proportion with the numbers of religious. So large a number require many goods, and many goods not only cause strife between religious and seculars, but also among the religious themselves. . . . What used to be freely given now has to be bought, and property that was once peacefully owned can now be held only by means of a law suit'.[3] A limited number of hermits settling in a neighbourhood might be welcome—even considered an asset—but a large community seeking a livelihood in a country area of limited means and resources might represent a major problem. In times of hardship, as when the harvest failed, such communities could inflict a heavy additional burden on the local inhabitants.

The Rule of Grandmont expressly forbade ownership of lands and properties outside the immediate limits of the enclosure. Although the brothers were permitted to accept the gift of a piece of land on which to build, if the donor or his heir subsequently refuted such a gift they were instructed to relinquish it peacefully and without argument. Recourse to law was absolutely denied them, as was the holding of title deeds which might help them to plead their case.[4] Deprived of any stable and permanent means of livelihood, the monks of Grandmont were often dependent on alms and thus led a very insecure existence. In the early days of the Order when the brothers were few in number, the problems outlined above by the prior of St-Laurent-au-Bois could not have affected them. The first hint of any parallel weakness can be identified in the far-sighted judgement of Hugues Lacerta. Hugues had spent his youth as a soldier fighting in the first crusade. He joined Stephen at Muret in 1111, choosing to serve as a lay brother, and it is therefore possible that he was primarily responsible for material administration at Muret during the lifetime of the founder. On his death bed in 1157, thirty-three years after the death of the founder, whose friend and confidant he had been, he expressed his concern at both the increase in monks and in establishments and implored the brothers to impose a restriction on the reception of novices.[5] Obviously, the expansion of the Order beyond the limits of the Limousin and the immediate jurisdiction of the prior of Grandmont seemed to Hugues incompatible with the primitive spirit of the hermits who had shared the solitude of Stephen at Muret. Unfortunately, his advice went unheeded and the Grandmontines only avoided the fate which overtook similar religious groups by mitigating and altering their constitutions time and time again. By the fourteenth century, these changes had rendered their communities almost indistinguishable from those of benedictine monks or even canons regular. Sadly, much of the original and distinctive grandmontine character was sacrificed in the process.

At least during the first century of their existence, the hermit monks of Grandmont held fast to the fundamental ideals of evangelical poverty and simplicity which distinguished their Order. John of Salisbury writing at the time tells us that they had nothing whatsoever in common with the mainstream religious orders which followed the Rules of either St Benedict or St Augustine. Instead they acknowledged just one master, Our Lord Jesus Christ, and followed one Rule, the Gospel.[6] If in the years that followed, their customs and practices began to resemble those of the Benedictines and Augustinians, at least something of their primitive spirit continued to be reflected in their architecture. The very considerable visible evidence which survives demonstrates clearly that in the course of nearly seven centuries only very limited attempts were made to extend, remodel, or embellish their churches. Not far from the grandmontine cell of Craswall in Herefordshire is the cisterican church of Dore Abbey. One has only to glance at its magnificent ambulatory to be aware how far and in what a comparatively short space of time the Cistercians had departed from the aesthetic ideals of St Bernard. By contrast, all of the grandmontine churches which have survived have retained their basic, simple ground plan. Even the later, thirteenth-century examples were built in accordance with the romanesque blueprint which was never superseded. A seventeenth-century plan of the priory of Boulogne, in the departement of Loir and Cher, reveals a rather splendid formal garden laid out behind a remodelled west range which was redesigned to house the commendatory prior. When compared, however, with the palatial and sumptuous refurbishing of the west ranges of various french cistercian abbeys for the same purpose, Boulogne appears remarkably unostentatious.

The Order of Grandmont has been styled: 'that ill fated order' but it is debatable to what extent its fortunes proved more unfortunate than some of the better-recorded religious Orders. The major internal crisis involved the notorious lay brother revolt; yet others, including the Cistercians, suffered similar uprisings on the part of their lay brethren; the one which disrupted the Gilbertines was equally bitter albeit of shorter duration. Another form of schism occurred early in the Order's history and was provoked by the struggle for supremacy between the mother house at Grandmont, within Plantagenet territory, and Bois de Vincennes, in the Ile de France, ruled by the Capetian monarchy. The division of the Order into *Fratres Gallici* and *Fratres Anglici,* and the scandal their squabbling for domination provoked, was equally not peculiar to the Grandmontines. Few religious orders have avoided some measure of internal strife and partitioning in the course of their histories. The Cistercians became involved in a particularly dramatic thirteenth-century scandal when feuding broke out between Cîteaux and Clairvaux, two of the proto-abbeys of the Order.

Problems external to the Order included the sufferings inflicted by the Hundred Years' War and later, the Wars of Religion, but again these particular troubles were by no means unique to the Grandmontines. Most of the monasteries of France suffered to a greater or lesser degree in times of war. Under the commendatory system, that other great scourge of monasticism, the Grandmontines fared somewhat better than most. No doubt partially because of the smallness of their houses, they were spared much of the misery which unscrupulous holders of commendatory titles inflicted on the greater abbeys of France. In fact, the mother house itself actually prospered under its third commendatory abbot, Cardinal William Briçonnet who contributed a great deal towards the restoration of the abbey and its church.

For as long as the Order of Grandmont retained its initial fervour and remained true to the ideals of its saintly Founder, it prospered. By the mid-twelfth century it numbered 1,200 monks, excluding the even more numerous lay brethren. It may be counted as unfortunate that this boom period was so short lived. The lay brother crisis which broke out in 1185 was without doubt responsible for an ensuing decline in numbers. The unfortunate outcome of the dispute itself was the reconstitution of the Order by Pope John XXII in 1317, and a consequent loss of identity.

An initially successful attempt by Dom Charles Frémon in the seventeenth century to reform the Order and re-establish the primitive observance of the Rule had an exceedingly unfortunate outcome in that it split the Order into two branches, the traditional and the observant. Such a division cannot in itself be termed unfortunate, and numerous other Orders of religious have split into separate branches in the course of their histories without any lasting ill effects. Within the Franciscan Order in particular, the Friars Conventual became independent of the mainstream group as early as the thirteenth century and a second reforming group, the Observants, emerged in the fifteenth. These and many subsequent franciscan congregations flourished and remain much in evidence throughout the world today. The unfortunate aspect of the grandmontine division was that it occurred at a time when numbers within the Order were declining and recruitment was low. Neither group had sufficient strength of numbers to satisfy the commission for religious reform in the following century, so Dom Frémon's well-intentioned efforts unwittingly hastened the demise of the Order. In 1772 the mother house of Grandmont was suppressed.

INTRODUCTION - NOTES

1. Rule of St Benedict for Monasteries, tr. Dom B.B. Bolton (London: Ealing Abbey, 1969) ch. 1, p. 7

2. RG Prologue, ed. Bec: SOG p. 66

3. H. Peltier, 'Hugues de Fouilloy chanoine régulier, prieur de Saint-Laurent-au-Bois', *Revue du moyen âge latin* 11 (1946) 32.

4. RG, ed. Bec SOG. For ownership of lands see ch. IV, p. 71; on returning gifts and properties to the heirs of donors, see ch. XXIII p. 80, on prohibitions against holding title deeds to properties and against having recourse to law, chs. XXIV and XXXI, pp. 82,94.

5. PL 204: 1216: 'Nova nemora, fratresque novitios super omnia plus necere. Posse timeo et sentio.'

6. *Policraticus: Johannis Sarisberiensis*, ed. C.C.J. Webb (Oxford: 1909) 2: 204– 06. 'Alii Basilium, alii Benedictum, alii Augustinum, isti singularem magistrum habent Dominum Jesum Christum.'

I

SAINT STEPHEN OF MURET

A VOICE IN THE WILDERNESS

The life of St Stephen of Muret is clouded with uncertainties. It is difficult to unravel the facts from the various accounts which are mainly dependent on hearsay or derive from pious biographies. Even the *Life of St Stephen of Muret* attributed by its first editor, Dom Martène, to Gérard Ithier, seventh prior of Grandmont (1188–1196), is regarded as highly suspect by current historians.[1] In fact, it has recently been shown that Gérard merely added a few details to a preexisting Life distinguished from his own work by the title *Vita A*.[2] The additional details take the form of edifying anecdotes together with some accounts of posthumous miracles attributed to Stephen. It is worth noting that Gérard was the prior responsible for submitting the cause for Stephen's canonisation to Pope Clement III in 1188, shortly after his election to the priorate. A priest and accompanying lay brother were dispatched to Rome with letters from the General Chapter supported by testimonials from King Henry II of England as well as several high ranking ecclesiastics.[3] Meanwhile, it is recorded in the Annals of the order that the brethren prayed unceasingly to invoke Stephen's aid and numerous miracles were reported and attributed to his intercession. They include: recoveries from various crippling ailments, restoration of sight, a couple of resuscitations and the cure of a young boy suffering from possession.[4] The following year, 1189, the pope granted the request and sent a delegate to represent him at the ceremony held on 30 August at Grandmont.[5]

Vita A itself dates in all likelihood from the time of Stephen Liciac, fourth prior of Grandmont (1139–1163) under whose direction the *Liber Sententiarum*,[6] the *Thoughts* of Stephen, were compiled and the Rule deriving from them was formulated. The writings which emerged at this time were wholly dependent upon the testimony of the early brethren who had known Stephen personally, notably the chevalier Hugues Lacerta, who joined the little community at Muret as a lay brother and became Stephen's closest disciple and friend.

The traditional date for the birth of Stephen is 1045, although some authors give 1044. His father was Stephen, Viscount of Thiers, his mother is known to us simply as Candide. Various of the biographies contain lengthy details of the exceptional piety of his parents, culminating in an anecdote which recalls the circumstances surrounding the birth of St John the Baptist. This prophet, recognised as the patron saint of hermits, was held in particular veneration by the hermit monks of Grandmont, so it is not surprising that the Grandmontine biographers had recourse to a legitimate technique employed by hagiographers of the period and provided a suitable parallel between their saintly founder and his scriptural inspiration. In company with the parents of the Baptist, Stephen and Candide were elderly and still unblessed by children despite a lifetime of prayer. In desperation they vowed that if God would heed their supplications they would dedicate the child to his service. Their prayers were at last rewarded and Candide lived to bear three sons. Stephen was the first born, the second was destined to continue the line of the viscounts of Thiers, while the youngest became, in due course, Lord of Montpensier, founder of the family of counts of Chalon which much later became interrelated with the Bourbon dynasty.

That the child of elderly parents noted for their exceptional piety should have received an extremely religious upbringing is only to be expected. The highly coloured accounts of the young Stephen's precocity for prayer, contemplation.and mortification while written, no doubt,with the best of intentions, fail utterly however, to build a convincing portrait of a man of outstanding character, whose spirituality and humility were coupled with an immense ability for spiritual influence and leadership. Stephen's pious boyhood, combined with the harshness of the Rule which he inspired, do little to endear him to the world at large. Small wonder he has never received much attention as a cult figure outside the Order of Grandmont and the limits of the Limousin.

It is in the *Liber Sententiarum* rather than in the early and unsubstantiated biographies, that something of the real nature of this very striking character begins hazily to emerge. The work is an anthology of the ideas and teachings of the saint recalled by those disciples who shared his solitude at Muret. Most notable among them was the favoured disciple, Hugues Lacerta, whose name is the only one recorded in the prologue to the Rule. The work comprises one hundred and twenty-two chapters of varying length. Its format was almost certainly determined in the course of a general chapter held at Grandmont around 1156 under the direction of the fourth prior, Stephen Liciac. The essential message [summarised in the statement: 'There is no rule but the Gospel'] was basically an insistence on the fundamental christian message coupled with Stephen's personal conviction that the simple teachings of Christ should not be cluttered with complicated legislation and elaborate liturgical practices. In the twelfth century at least, this rendered the hermits of Grandmont celebrated and admired throughout Christendom. That Stephen himself represented the true driving force behind this distinctive religious enterprise is borne out by the numerous tributes paid to him by contemporary writers no less than the later annalists of the Order.

The first verifiable error to emerge from the various accounts of Stephen's early years concerns a pilgrimage he made with his father to the shrine of St Nicholas at Bari. Throughout the twelfth century, as the authors of the account must have been aware, this shrine flourished as a popular centre of pilgrimage. Nevertheless, it cannot have constituted the spiritual goal for the Viscount of Thiers and his young son midway in the previous century, for the relics of the saint of Myra, in Lycia, were not translated to the Adriatic seaport of Bari until 1087. By that time Stephen was over thirty years of age and already well established as a hermit in the wilderness of Muret. The destination of the pilgrims was in all probability the sanctuary of San Michele on Monte Gargano, a shrine which from the mid-tenth century ranked almost as highly as Santiago de Compostella as a popular centre for pilgrimage. The main route from the north to Monte Gargano would have permitted the pilgrims to include excursions to both Rome and the monastery of St Benedict at Monte Cassino in their itinerary.

Unfortunately, none of the accounts of the journey given in *Vita A* and elaborated upon by later writers, stands up to close scrutiny. Not only does the author appear altogether vague concerning the chronology of Stephen's youth; the only precise date he gives is 1076, the year Stephen embraced the religious life at Muret at the age of thirty. And yet, he is supposed to have undertaken a pilgrimage to Italy at the age of twelve (approximately between the years 1056–59) to a shrine which was not established until over thirty years later. Then, it appears that he fell ill in the city of Benevento and was left by his father in the care of Archbishop Milon who, it transpires, was not appointed to this city until 1074.

Happily Archbishop Milon of Benevento, about whose career the author of *Vita-A* appears singularly uninformed, is a fairly well-documented eleventh-century cleric. This is mainly attributable to his close association with the great reforming pope, Gregory VII, who was responsible for his appointment to the diocese of Benevento. However, his term of office there proved remarkably short; it is known from a chronicle that he was consecrated in 1074 and died the following year. One of his acts dated 1074–5 remains and his successor makes mention of it as early as 1076.[7] The previous history of Milon is also known to us through a piece inserted in the cartulary of the monastery of St Florent de Saumur. This refers to his appointment as a dean in Paris, when he mediated with Gregory VII to honour his promise and confirm the foundation charter of the priory of St Florent of Dol in Brittany.[8]

Following his recovery from the severe illness which detained him in Benevento, Stephen did not, it seems, return directly to France. The *Lives* tell us that he remained an incredible twelve years in the care of Archbishop Milon, attended the schools of the city and was carefully prepared for the priesthood. As we have seen, whoever was responsible for Stephen's welfare and education at this time, it certainly was not Milon. When, where and by whom he was in due course ordained deacon cannot be ascertained, though once again the early chroniclers are adamant that Milon was the prelate responsible. The tradition that Stephen was in deacon's orders is very strong, as is the belief that he refused the priesthood itself for reasons of humility. This, together with the account of the circumstances surrounding Stephen's birth is something of an hagiographical cliché. The same has been said of other saints, notably Francis of Assisi. While there is no concrete evidence to support Stephen's very lengthy sojourn in Italy, it seems unlikely that his close companions would have been mistaken in their accounts of such a major episode in the life of their founder. These disciples, we are told in the prologue to the Rule, conversed frequently with the Master and it would seem only natural that in the course of such conversations Stephen told them something of his youth, his travels,and people he had known, particularly those who had impressed or edified him. When, following the passage of years, these witnesses, now elderly men, attempted to recall the details of such conversations, it is equally likely that they became confused and at variance over specific details. It is always possible that Stephen met Archbishop Milon, who was a well-travelled churchman, in either France or Italy, or in both. Certainly, the fervour with which Milon implemented the reforming policies of Gregory VII, his insistence on clerical celibacy and his encouragement of dedicated religious communities, would have appealed to Stephen and may well have provided subjects for his own spiritual discourses. It is just possible that Milon was also responsible for ordaining Stephen a deacon, although he is unlikely to have served as archdeacon of the diocese of Benevento as the biographers would have us believe.

An interesting local tradition has emerged concerning Stephen's diaconate. In the parish church of the little town of Ambazac near Grandmont, a dalmatic of reddish gold silk is carefully preserved. According to a fifteenth-century inventory of the Abbey of Grandmont, this vestment was presented to Stephen by the Empress Matilda. The fourth prior, Stephen Liciac was the more likely recipient of this gift, for Matilda remained the wife of the Emperor Henry V until well after Stephen's death in 1124 and arrived in France to wed Geoffrey, Count of Anjou, only in 1128.

At some stage in his career, Stephen became acquainted with a group of Calabrian hermits whose austerity and customs were to constitute his main source of inspiration. Although we are once again dependent on the verbal testimony of the brethren for this particular encounter, it seems plausible enough and the early sources refer to it constantly. The Annals record Stephen, almost at death's door, outlining his way of life for the benefit of two visiting cardinals and lauding the poverty and detachment of the *fratres in Calabria* who, he says influenced his own ideas on the religious life.[9] That the brethren were so impressed by

the Holy City, maintaining that Stephen held a responsible clerical position. Once again they omit to give any conclusive details and concentrate instead on his ever increasing determination to substitute the splendours of high ranking ecclesiastical living for the hermit's cell. One motive for asserting that Stephen was employed for a time within papal circles may have been to lend respectability to a bull which authorised him to found a religious order. This bull, purported to have been given by Pope Gregory VII, is dated 1074. It was, in fact, forged late in the history of the Order.[13] *Vita A* mentions the papal authorisation but not the name of the actual pope involved and only much later accounts stipulate that it was Gregory VII, adding that Stephen had petitioned to found an Order in accordance with the Rule of St Benedict.

A serious and very damaging controversy arising from the spurious evidence of this bull developed as late as the seventeenth century and was centred around whether the Grandmontines formed a branch of the Benedictines, the Augustinians, or the Carthusians.[14] More essentially, were the religious of Grandmont intended to live as monks, canons regular, or hermits? The result was that the Grandmontines suffered a crisis of identity which can only have been aggravated by the opinions expressed by outsiders. Dom Lévesque recalls in the Annals of the Order how in various documents issued by the roman Curia, Grandmont was at times referred to as an offshoot of the Benedictines and at others, a branch of the Augustinians.[15] The great benedictine historian, Dom Jean Mabillon (1632–1700), was among those who took up the dispute and drew attention to the differences between his own Order and that of Grandmont. He concluded that in accordance with the teaching of their founder, the Grandmontines recognised no other rule but that of Our Lord Jesus Christ.[16] The evidence for classing the Grandmontines as canons regular of St Augustine was especially tenuous and based itself on the trivial factor that the religious of the 'common observance' wore surplices and birettas, the customary choir dress of regular canons. Although the reformed group had reverted to wearing the habit in choir, the tradition of the surplice was very ancient indeed. Gérard Ithier, seventh prior of Grandmont (1189–1198), states distinctly in his work, *The Mirror of Grandmont*: 'in choir all wear surplices'.[17] After a great deal of turmoil, the matter was resolved and an entry in the Annals states decisively that the Order of Grandmont is to be regarded as a distinctive order which, while originally intended to be eremitical, in the course of time adapted to coenobitism. Hence for the future, the Order should be regarded as a combination of both forms.[18]

Whatever the arguments about identity which disturbed the Order in later times, one thing is certain: Stephen's own vocation led him straight to the hermitage. The various sources have it that this vocation developed and matured during his stay in the Holy City and that from there he returned to France to settle his affairs and bid farewell to his parents prior to embarking on the life of a solitary. From Thiers in the Auvergne he travelled to the Limousin and is supposed to have stayed for a while at Aureil, just a few miles to the south–east of Limoges. To this spot St Gaucher, another famous hermit, had attracted a fair sized contingent of followers who lived according to the Rule of St Augustine in the monastery of St Jean d'Aureil. Unfortunately, Gaucher built another monastery just a few leagues away and intended to receive the women who, no less than the men, were moved by his example and instruction to a life of prayer and penitence. This development reputedly proved too much for Stephen who, if we are to believe his biographers, suffered from a particularly virulent form of misogyny and so he took leave of Gaucher. In fact, the entire story is pure invention because Gaucher, who hailed from Normandy, arrived at Aureil only in 1078, when he would still have been a mere youth of eighteen.[19] The truth would appear to have been far more simple.

Stephen knew a great deal about the various forms of religious life prevalent at the time; this much is explicit in his 'Thoughts'. Such knowledge can only have been gained by personal observation; if not at Aureil, then certainly in other monasteries where he would have stayed in the course of his travels. In a period which experienced more than its fair share of monastic turmoil and upheaval, Stephen was not exceptional in his conclusion that a thirst for solitude, silence, and austerity could only be satiated outside the traditional monastic structure, alone in a hermitage.

As regards the suggestion that Stephen fostered a particular antipathy towards the female sex, there is no evidence in his own 'Thoughts' to support such an assertion. Antifeminist sentiments bordering on the fanatic can, however, be traced to the fourth prior, Stephen Liciac. He was in all likelihood responsible for the hysterical tirade which constitutes chapter thirty-nine of the Rule and which sets forth the reasons why women were excluded from the Order.

> We forbid you absolutely to receive women into this religious life. If a woman succeeded in tempting the first man from the delights of paradise, who else could be capable of resisting her wiles? If gentle David, wise Solomon,and strong Samson were all captivated by the snares of women, who could fail to surrender to her caresses? In the devil's absence, is it not she who tempts men?

The date for Stephen's entry into the 'desert' at Muret varies somewhat, but it was almost certainly sometime between 1076–1078. Dom Jean Becquet considers it to be closer to the latter[20] and, this being correct, it would have afforded him time to visit Archbishop Milon in Italy immediately beforehand. Once they have him established at Muret, a site on a wooded hillside not far from the town of Ambazac, the biographies became dependent upon Stephen's original followers for information on his lifestyle and practices, and allowing for the odd exaggeration, there seems little reason to doubt their accuracy. In fact, his way of life was in essence very similar to that of numerous other hermits of the time. He built himself a simple wattle dwelling and wore the same clothes in winter and in summer. The celebrated and bizarre costume illustrated by Père Helyot, and subsequently by J.C. Bar, has done little for Stephen's image and, in any case cannot be regarded as truly illustrative of his attire. The chain mail is probably authentic. It is referred to in all the *Lives* and according to Frère Philippe-Étienne the wearing of chain mail against the body in lieu of a hair shirt was an accepted form of austerity and customary among the Camaldolese.[21] What is exceptional is the excess of zeal which moved the eighteenth-century illustrator to deny his subject the coarse woollen tunic which would have covered the penitential garment.

Traditional costume ascribed to St Stephen by the eighteenth century illustrator Jacques Charles Bar.

A similar enthusiasm for self-denial bordering on the eccentric pervades the early account of the diet. Frugal it may have been, but it seems unlikely that Stephen attained the age of eighty living exclusively off nuts, berries and the odd 'floury dumplings'. He slept on bare boards and his days were passed in meditation and in reciting the traditional monastic hours to which he added the three separate offices of the Blessed Virgin and the Holy Trinity and the Dead. The reference in the *Life* to these offices *ex devotio* is somewhat strange, however, for there is no mention of them either in the Rule or in the 'Thoughts' of the saint. Moreover, the Blessed Virgin is nowhere singled out for any particular honour or devotion. Stephen, we are told, was wont to recite all these prayers bent forward on his knees so that his forehead constantly touched the ground, a practice which resulted in his nose becoming permanently twisted while his forehead became severely calloused! For the first year or so he was left to himself but gradually, as his reputation for holiness spread abroad, he was joined by others who desired to dedicate their lives to God in solitude and poverty. Many years later these early disciples would testify that they received from Stephen 'all the loving care of a true father.'[22] In their accounts of Stephen's relationship with his spiritual sons, the style of the biographies softens and we begin to glean some understanding of the true character of this very exceptional man. There is always a tendency among the writers of saintly lives to ascribe to their subjects a kind of misplaced heroism. This is manifested in vivid descriptions of their capacity to endure physical hardships and their constant and merciless chastisement of the flesh with flails, thorns, and hairshirts. To whatever extent Stephen may have adopted the accepted practices and penances common to the religious of his time, his conversations with his disciples reveal a man of integrity and moderation, understanding and tolerant of human weakness who, we are told, never imposed tasks which were too demanding or taxing of human endurance. Certain of the instructions which eventually formed the basis of the Rule of Grandmont are, in a modern sense, undeniably harsh; but no more so than the Gospel Rule of Christ on which they are based. Stephen demanded of his followers no more and no less than Christ himself asked of the 'rich young man'. The conditions of acceptance into the brotherhood of Christ are clear, precise,and allow for no half measures.

One of the major fascinations of the Order of Grandmont lies in its retaining its particular identity for so long after its foundation, an achievement which can only be attributed to the enduring charismatic attraction of the founder himself. Even following the mitigations of the fourteenth century, when the Order became to all intents and purposes indistinguishable from any of the religious congregations living according to the benedictine or, augustinian Rule, something of the founding spirit of Stephen prevailed. Desmond Seward has written:

> Devotion to the founder plays a large part in the life of all orders, but the cult of St. Stephen was the driving force throughout Grandmontine history.[23]

Certainly, the example and inspiration which the first Fathers of Grandmont derived from Stephen in the wilderness of Muret proved sufficient to perpetuate the life of the Order so that it avoided the fate of other hermit groups which evolved in the eleventh century only to vanish without trace in the twelfth.

While the 'Thoughts' attributed to Stephen reveal the depth of his spiritual insight, they are not sufficient to account for his outstanding spiritual attraction for others, although they do provide evidence of the paternal care which he afforded his spiritual sons. It is the Prologue to the Rule which immortalises his caring nature:

> It was as a father of a family that he dedicated his time to counselling others . . . he drew daily from his treasury of riches those jewels whose worth he had himself proved by means of long and pious perseverance, so that by his own example his disciples should become not hearers alone, but doers.

Of course the holding of religious conferences as a method of training aspiring hermits was by no means exclusive to Stephen. He must have been aware that he was pursuing a tradition originated by the Desert Fathers. John Cassian was just one of the young hermits who, in the late fourth century, made the rounds of the venerable elders in order to learn from their wisdom and experience. Whilst this practice was ordered by the Rule of St Pachomius (286–346), it was Cassian who introduced it into Southern Gaul when, at the request of Castor, Bishop of Apt, he wrote the series of twenty four *Conferences* which, together with his *Institutes* provided the basic spirituality for western monks. Throughout the Middle Ages monasteries retained copies of the *Conferences* from which sections were read aloud at appointed times and both Stephen and the actual compilers of his 'Thoughts' and Rule must have been familiar with the work. Certainly the two basic grandmontine texts reveal some striking similarities to it. Probably the most remarkable resemblance can be identified in Stephen's division of the brethren into contemplatives and workers, two separate but interdependent vocations which are exemplified by the sisters in the Gospel. When Martha, overburdened with work scolded Mary for her laziness, Christ rebuked her for not accepting that Mary had chosen the better part. Cassian comments 'The Lord, you see, placed the chief good in divine contemplation.'[24] The Rule of Grandmont states: 'The better part which the Lord praised so highly in Mary, we impose upon the clercs alone.' But the first Fathers of Grandmont went on to ratify this same gospel precedent by reference to Acts 6:44, as follows:

> It is not reasonable that they should leave the word of God to serve at tables. Besides, vowed as they are exclusively to prayer and contemplation, they will become the dispensers of spiritual realities.[25]

If an attempt to isolate some element of the outstanding spiritual example and leadership which must have distinguished Stephen's career at Muret proves decidedly unfruitful, the additional effort to uncover some evidence of basic practical organisation among the primitive hermit group is even less rewarding. When, following a period of total isolation, Stephen began to be joined by others, the sum of his administrative effort appears to have consisted in allocating them huts grouped around a simple oratory. Presumably, the strange grandmontine custom of leaving all practical management and, significantly, all financial responsibility in the hands of the lay brethren had its origins at Muret, for we do know that Hugues Lacerta, Stephen's closest disciple, chose this status for himself. The peculiarity of this custom, which is without parallel in any other religious order, lies in the fact that the position of the lay brothers or *convers* as they came to be known, was in every respect equal to that of the choir brothers or *clercs*. Not only did they share the same quarters, but when their duties permitted, they joined in the daily celebration of the offices in choir. Perhaps the most significant aspect of what can only be described as a rare, if not entirely unique, manifestation of medieval democracy lies in the fact that the grandmontine lay brethren enjoyed the same juridical status as their contemplative confrères. At chapter meetings their opinions carried equal weight and they exercised the right to vote. They might even be called upon to represent their respective houses at the annual general chapters held at the mother house. In Stephen's own lifetime, of course, chapters would have been little more than family discussions and the original settlement at Muret would hardly have boasted a choir proper. The oratory, a word which was retained to describe the exceedingly austere grandmontine churches for several generations, consisted in the very simplest of stone structures modelled, according to Adrien Grezillier, on the primitive rural churches prevalent in the region at that time.[26] The daily round at Muret would seem to have been conducted in accordance with the usual monastic horarium with the brethren coming together at set hours of the day and night for the celebration of the Divine Office. When the original community began to outgrow the rustic accommodation available, Stephen solved the problem by swarming. Groups of trained hermits were dispatched to found new settlements, but all within the immediate vicinity. Such settlements were known as 'cells', a distinctly eremitical part of the grandmontine nomenclature which was retained until many of the houses were upgraded to priories as part of the reconstitution of the Order in 1317.

Judging from the lack of archaeological evidence on the sites of cells which tradition states were founded within Stephen's lifetime they must have represented the most primitive and basic of settlements. They were in all probability modelled on the primitive 'laurae' of the Desert Fathers and Stephen may have personally encountered similar arrangements in Calabria. 'Our Calabrian brethren', he said, 'serve God without either property or possessions.'[27] The Franciscan historian, Father Gratien, has likened his intransigence on this point to St Francis of Assisi, whose repudiation of worldly goods and property afforded no compromise.[28] For Stephen, however, poverty was coupled with solitude. The fundamental notion expressed in his 'Thoughts', and later made explicit in the Rule, was that the hermits were to embrace poverty in solitude and become as though dead to the world. Where better to find a suitably lonely site than in the densely forested hillsides of the Limousin?

What we know of the hermitage at Muret is dependent on the annalists and it is not therefore possible to separate its appearance in the lifetime of Stephen from subsequent developments. Shortly after Stephen's death in 1124, the Benedictines of Ambazac laid claim to the land on which it stood and the brethren were forced to relinquish it. They were, however, able to return and build anew at a later date, almost certainly during the term of office of Stephen Liciac. The site itself would certainly appear to have accorded completely with Stephen's ideal of the 'desert'. It remains quite isolated even to this day; in the eleventh century it would have been exceedingly wild and remote. The Annals describe the oratory as having incorporated the typical semicircular grandmontine apse but unusually sited to the north-west rather than the east and with the living quarters located to the south. This does not, however, describe the 'cell' in which Stephen actually lived and died, and which has been identified to the south of the later monastic buildings. It stood on a sort of rocky terrace at the far end of a little valley surrounded by trees. A few markings in the form of small holes and depressions in the rocky surface can be discerned and these constitute the only trace of the buildings of the original cell. The foundations of the later oratory show it to have been approximately five by three metres. While these foundations date only from the thirteenth century, their extreme smallness at this late date in the architectural history of the Order indicate that they do correspond to the original building.

If little is known concerning the precise location and appearance of the original cell at Muret, even less is known of the others which were contemporary with it and which by tradition owe their foundation to Stephen himself. The fact that these earliest cells have proved difficult both to locate and to date can be attributed to the very nature of the life pursued within them, which dictated that they should be both small and insignificant. One thing which it is possible to determine is the uniform appearance of the sites which they occupied. Traditionally, the Grandmontines have always regarded three cells as contemporary with Stephen and all three are located fairly close to Muret itself. Boisverd, which has retained just a few identifying stones, was constructed on a plateau overlooking the river Vienne. Châtenet, which is somewhat less characteristic as regards siting, has a late south range which includes a fine twin compartmented servery together with some earlier vestiges of what may or may not be the original cell. At Cluseau, the third example, sections of the foundations of the cloister are evident together with an artificial mound which almost certainly conceals the foundations of the apse. Additionally we may include Plaine which, if not founded within the actual lifetime of Stephen certainly emerged a very short while after his death. Situated within the commune of Savigniac in the Dordogne, its location is similar to that of Boisverd. This particular cell was ruled by the lay brother Hugues Lacerta and so takes on a very special significance in the early history of the Order. Sadly, the form of the original buildings is almost impossible to determine as they have been completely obscured by seventeenth-century buildings.

Towards the close of a long life, Stephen appears to have acquired a certain notoriety. Within the immediate vicinity of Muret he and his followers were already known by the familiar title of 'Bonshommes', a name which was to distinguish them throughout their long history. This was attributable to their reputation for sharing everything they had with the local poor whom they encouraged to visit and whom they treated with exceptional solicitude and generosity.[29] The Grandmontines have always been recognised for their courteous and kind treatment of visitors. While it is extremely unlikely that Stephen's holiness and wisdom became, within his lifetime at any rate, as celebrated among the various courts of Europe as his biographers would have us believe, yet his fame did reach beyond the limits of the Limousin and eventually attracted two very important visitors to his retreat at Muret.

It was during the last days of his life that Stephen received the two apostolic delegates, Cardinals Gregorio Papareschi and Pietro Leone. These two primates, who were on their way from Rome to attend the Council of Chartres (1124), are well known from contemporary sources and they became Pope Innocent II and the antipope, Anacletus II. In the course of the quarrel and fighting over the papacy, Innocent was forced to flee to France and it is said that he took refuge for a while with the brethren who, by this time, had transferred from Muret to Grandmont. Unfortunately, we have too little information about this remarkable encounter; the biographies provide only superficial details except for Stephen's own reference to his acquaintance with 'the learned and holy doctor Archbishop Milon'. The cardinals, for their part, seem to have been eager to learn something of the religious life embraced by Stephen and his associates and especially whether they considered themselves to be canons, monks, or hermits. According to the Annals, Stephen informed them that this group belonged in none of these categories. Having drawn their attention to the fact that the brethren were clad neither in the manner of monks nor of canons, he pointed out that canons, in accordance both with their customs and the tradition of the apostles, exercise the power to bind and loose. Monks are concerned with nobody's spiritual welfare save their own, while hermits are required to remain in their cells and dedicate the whole of their time to God in silent worship and contemplation.[30]

The two dignitaries, who must have been suffering agonies of cold and deprivation in so remote and comfortless an establishment, appear, nonetheless, to have been impressed by this somewhat negative response. Possibly they discerned in it something of a genuine Christlike humility which was not always so apparent in the religious houses they normally frequented. At any rate they gave Stephen their blessing and observed: 'Man of God, if you persevere in this way your reward will be equal to that of the saints, apostles and martyrs for you are surely following in their footsteps'.[31] Hugues Lacerta is reputed to have been present at this interview and if he was he can no doubt be relied upon to have reported it as accurately as his memory would allow. While it could be argued that the entire interchange was invented by later annalists intent on gaining respectability for the Order of Grandmont as a unique religious institute, *Ordo peculiaris*, the sentiments are very much in tune with Stephen's essential and oft-repeated message, 'There is no rule save the Commandments of Almighty God. Whoever observes these is a religious in the true sense but whoever ignores these Commandments has no part in any order or rule. All that we attempt to do without God is worthless.'[32]

It is not easy to comprehend the tremendous attraction which Stephen exercised over these two sophisticated clerics, and equally over the generations of imitators who were inspired by his example to dedicate themselves to a life of poverty and extreme physical hardship. Stephen's biographers have unfortunately never really succeeded in gaining any kind of universal appeal for their subject. He demonstrates none of the dynamic quality which characterises his close contemporary, St Bernard of Clairvaux, nor the attractiveness of personality and broadness of vision which distinguish his later counterparts, St Dominic and St Francis. Alongside these towering figures, Stephen appears decidedly nondescript. One of his most appealing qualities, and the one which is strongly apparent in his 'Thoughts', is the intense humility which prevented him from ever indulging in any overt criticism. His references to other religious orders are always respectful and tactful. Bernard of Clairvaux went to Rome and castigated the abuses of the roman curia; Stephen must have found these abuses equally abhorrent but instead of overturning the tables of the moneylenders, he quietly followed his Christ into the desert. Once there, he proceeded to demonstrate that reformation can be achieved more effectively by good example and gentleness than by thundering abuse. His achievement, the full uncompromising application of the plain Gospel of Jesus to a regular life of shared solitude, has never received the acclamation it warrants. Stephen of Muret, patron saint of the unrecognised, has thus remained throughout the centuries one of the unsung heroes of the christian Church.

On the 4 February 1124, just eight days after the celebrated visit of the cardinals, Stephen's health began to fail and he knew that death was near. His last days were spent consoling and inspiring confidence in his brothers. A part of these final conversations was faithfully recorded in Chapter Fourteen of the Rule and consists of a very beautiful exhortation to trust in Divine Providence:

> I leave you in the care of God alone upon whom all life depends. For his love you have renounced both the world and your own free wills. If you remain constant in your love of poverty and if you trust God alone, his

> Providence will provide for you always. For fifty years I have dwelt in this wilderness, in times of hardship I have never lacked for anything any more than in times of plenty have I ever had more than I required. God has always watched over me like a good Father. For you he will be the same always providing that you cling fast to the principles which I have given you and which are drawn from the Gospel itself.

On the morning of 8 February, Stephen became very ill and the brethren carried him from his cell to the oratory where, after hearing Mass, he received the last rites. Shortly after noon he murmured, 'lord into your hands I commend my spirit' and breathed his last. The brothers buried him secretly in the little cloister against the wall of the church in order to prevent prospective venerators from disturbing the peace of the cell. Yet Muret was not destined to be Stephen's final resting place.

The life and death of Stephen of Muret enfolds a striking double paradox: he tried to lead the life of an absolute solitary and died surrounded by disciples; he would be hailed as the founder of the Order of Grandmont yet he never intended founding a religious order and never set eyes on Grandmont.

For a different view of the *Vita Stephani Muretensis*, see Maire M. Wilkinson, 'The *Vita Stephani Muretensis* and the Early Life of Stephen of Muret' in Judith Loades, ed., *Hallmark Studies in Ecclesiastical History*, to be published in May 1990. The author regards the account of the saint's early life in the *Vita Stephani* as essentially fictional in form and actually fictitious.

NOTES

1. *Vita Venerabiles Viri Stephani Muretensis,* PL 204: 1065– 72. Also, Bec, *Scriptores Ordinis Grandimontensis* 111 in CC *Continuatio Mediaevalis* 8 (Turnhout, 1968) pp, 101– 137

2. Bec,'Les premiers écrivains de l'Ordre de Grandmont', RMab 43 (1963) 121– 37.

3. PL 204: 1048– 49.

4. Lev, pp. 168– 72.

5. Ibid., pp 166–67.

6. PL 204: 1085– 1136. Also, Bec; see above note 1.

7. Dom Becquet gives a full account of Stephen's association with Archbishop Milon in BSAHL 86 (1957) 403–09. The dates of Milon's archiepiscopacy are given in Chalander: *Histoire de la domination normande en Italie et en Sicilie* 2 (Paris: 1907). The chronicle referred to is in the *Annales Beneventani* in *Monumenta Germaniae Historica* 3, ed. G.H. Pertz (Hanover, 1839) p. 181.

8. Bec (see above, note 7)p. 406.

9. Lev, pp,79– 80.

10. J. Mabillon, *Acta Sanctorum Ordinis S Benedicti* 9; pp. 34– 5.

11. On the graeco–calabrian monks, see J. Gay, *L'Italie Meridionale et L'Empire Byzantin* (Paris: 1904) pp, 254– 86 and 376– 86.

12. RG Prologue:' . . . dicatis christianae primae ac principalis regulae evangelii scilicet, quod omnium regularum fons est atque principium qualescumque vos observatores confiteri non erubescatis.'

13. L. Delisle, 'Examen de treize chartes de l'Ordre de Grandmont', *Mémoires de la Societe' d'Antiquaires de Normandie'* 20 (1854) 172–73 and 88.

14. There is an interesting discussion of the problem in J-B. Hauréau, 'Sur quelques écrivains de l'Ordre de Grandmont', *Notices et extraits des manuscripts de la Bibliotheque Nationale* 24 (1876) pp. 251– 52.

15. Lev, p. 55.

16. J. Mabillon, *AA SS OSB* 9: p.50; also *Annales Ordinis S Benedicti* 5 (Paris: 1713) pp 65,79.

17. J-B. Hauréau, *Notices et extraits,* 24, p. 260

18. Lev, p. 57: 'Ordo Grandimontis est Ordo peculiaris, qui olim fuit Eremiticus postea Coenobiticus, nunc mixtus.'

19. Père J. Fouquet OMI and Frère Philippe-Etienne, *Histoire de L'Ordre de Grandmont* (Chambray: 1985)

20. Bec, 'Grandmont, Ordre et Abbaye de', *Dictionnaire d'histoire et géographie ecclëiastique* (Paris 1986) col 1129.

21. Fouquet Philippe-Etienne (note 19), p. 121.

22. *Vita Stephani*, XXIV; and RG Prologue; ed. Bec, CC Continuatio Mediaevalis 8:pp 117 and 65.

23. D. Seward, 'The Grandmontines – A Forgotten Order', *Downside Review* 83 (1965) 257– 64.

24. John Cassian. *Conferences* 1.8; tr. 0. Chadwick, *Western Asceticism* (Philadelphia-London: 1958) p. 200.

25. RG ch. LIV ed. Bec (note 22) p.92

26. A. Grezillier, 'Vestiges Grandmontains' *BSAHL* 86 (1957) 421.

27. Lev p. 80.

28. R. Gratien, *Histoire de la Fondation et de L'Evolution de L'Ordre de Frères Mineurs au XIII Siècle* (Paris: 1928) p. 55.

29. RG chs. XXXVII and XXXVIII ed. Bec (note 22) p.86.

30. Lev p. 80.

31. Ibid p. 81.

32. *Liber Sententiarum*, Epilogue ed. Bec (note 22) p. 62.

II

THE GROWTH OF GRANDMONT

1124 – 1171

Of Stephen of Muret's immediate successor, Pierre de Limoges (1124–37), we know only that he effected the transfer of the disciples from Muret to a similar wooded solitude at Grandmont as the direct result of the illnatured interference of the Benedictines of Ambazac. Professional jealousy seems the only possible reason why these monks should have asserted their rights to a few hectares of inferior land which can have afforded them very little return. For the hermits to plead their own claim to the land on which the Seigneur de Rancon, Amélius de Montcocu, had permitted them to settle was out of the question. The teaching of the Master about litigation was precise and prevented them from putting forward any plea whatever. The injunction: 'We firmly forbid you to dare to plead your case against anyone or to enter into judgement in any way', which in due course found its way into Chapter xxiv of the Rule, establishes the grandmontine position. Thus, the brothers prepared for their departure, and a Mass of the Holy Spirit was celebrated to obtain guidance in deciding their destination. The Annals record that just as the *Agnus Dei* was intoned, a voice audible to all who were present proclaimed 'To Grandmont'.

The stoney hillside of Grandmont is a beautiful spot about fifteen miles to the north of Limoges and only three miles from Muret. Today a well-posted tourist route passes straight through the tiny village and winds upwards through breathtaking hill and lakeside scenery. Tourists, attracted to the region in summer by the excellent sporting and camping facilities, drive straight through the little hamlet which is apparently without interest. Few can be aware that the little square chapel which stands all alone in an open space beside the narrow roadway marks the site of a once great and famous abbey. When the church and conventual buildings were dismantled following the suppression of the Order of Grandmont in 1772, the major part of the fabric was carted away to Limoges to be used in building a house of correction. The devout villagers managed, however, to obtain sufficient blocks of ashlar for the construction of the little memorial chapel of St John the Baptist, patron of hermits. Dedicated in 1825 by Dom Vergniaud, the last surviving grandmontine monk, it is cared for to this day by the Société des Amis de St Sylvestre et de l'Abbaye de Grandmont, and remains an enduring monument to St Stephen and his Order of hermit monks.

The hillsides below the village are green and fertile, but higher up little flourishes apart from heather and sturdy conifers. In the Middle Ages it must have seemed a savage and desolate spot indeed. While it is quite far to the south, the altitude, combined with the prevailing north winds, render it glacial in winter, and in summer the constant build-up of clouds over the surrounding summits subject the area to a greater than average rainfall. Around the year 1184, Gérard Ithier, seventh prior of Grandmont, wrote the following description:

> Grandmont is stern and cold, infertile and rocky, misty and exposed to the winds. The water is colder and worse than in other places, for it produces sickness instead of health. The mountain abounds in great stones for building, in streams and sand, but there is scarcely any timber for building. The land around the monastery scarcely ever suffices to provide necessi-

> ties, for the soil is so infertile, sterile and barren. At the foot of the mountain there are vines and fruit trees which bear well when they are not spoiled by cold and lack of sunshine; and also meadows, gardens and arable fields. The place which was chosen by God is a solitude for penitence and religion, and those who dwell there lead a hard life.[1]

Such was the destination of the advance group of brothers who set off from Muret. Having satisfied themselves that the rocky terrain was a suitable site for their new foundation, they applied to the Seigneur Amélius de Montcocu who, ever generous, granted them as much land as they required for their purpose. As soon as a small oratory, together with some simple huts for dwellings, had been constructed, the remainder of the brethren removed from Muret, bearing the mortal remains of their saintly founder to be reinterred beneath the altar step in their new oratory.

We can only conjecture that life in those early years at Grandmont followed the customs initiated by Stephen himself. The regulation governing enclosure was strictly enforced, and permitted the brethren only minimal contact with outsiders when unavoidable. The horarium included the specified psalmody of the Church; in addition the Annals mention a particular devotion to the Blessed Virgin which these hermits practised with the daily recitation of the Little Office of the Virgin.[2] The evidence for such a tradition having emerged within the Order of Grandmont at this early date is however, somewhat tenuous, for no particular marian devotion can be attributed to the founder himself. Only once is the Blessed Virgin even mentioned in the *Liber Sententiarum* and then she is only given as the supreme example of a sinner saved and graced by God.[3] A peculiarly grandmontine cult of the faithful departed almost certainly dates from this time, and took the form of thrice daily processions to the cemetery where the Office of the Dead was recited. Meals were taken in common, accompanied by reading, and there were also regular chapter sessions. The general regulations for life in community which eventually became incorporated into the Rule must have been based on the customs of these early years. In particular, this document places great emphasis on the obedience and respect due, not just to the pastor, but mutually between brothers. This injunction which is also included in the Rule of St Benedict,[4] is considerably expanded upon in the Rule of Grandmont. This has no less than three chapters which treat of obedience in general and a fourth specifically concerned with mutual obedience. Such similarities between early grandmontine customs and those of the Benedictines indicate that, while the disciples of Stephen continued to regard themselves as hermits, and their living arrangements still resembled a simple hermit colony, they represented, in fact the embryo of an organisation, which was coenobitic in character and would develop in the second quarter of the twelfth century to reach full maturity in the third. While it is not possible to be absolutely precise as to the chronology of these stages of growth, the principle milestone is the actual appearance of a written Rule under the fourth prior, Étienne de Liciac (1139–63). A second landmark is the Custumal, which supplemented the Rule, and was formulated under the fifth prior, Bernard Boschiac (1163–70).

Early in their history, the community at Grandmont encountered a problem familiar to monastic communities throughout the ages: a constant and distracting influx of visitors. It is remarkable how solitaries have always attracted crowds, the genuinely pious along with the merely curious; no desert is so remote but they will seek it out, and Grandmont proved to be no exception. According to the Annals, the disturbances commenced with a local gentleman, Raymond de Plantadis, who was suffering what appears to have been the typical paralysis consistent with a stroke. He was carried to Grandmont and into the oratory, where 'he happened to touch the altar step', whereupon he made an instant and complete recovery. 'Assuredly,' he said, 'the body of a saint lies buried here.'[5] Once news of this miracle was noised abroad, the public descended on Grandmont with a vengeance and reports of cures began to multiply. Eventually the brethren, driven almost to distraction by the constant and unrelenting invasion of their privacy, threatened to cast the body of their saintly founder into the river. So drastic and irrevocable an action was happily averted when Prior Pierre led the community in prayers, beseeching Stephen to call a halt to these miracles. Their prayers were granted and, for a while at any rate, peace was restored to Grandmont.

Stephen of Muret himself has always been regarded as first prior of the Order of Grandmont so when Prior Pierre died in 1137, his nephew, Pierre de Saint-Christophe, became the third prior. His term of office proved remarkably short as he died the following year. With the election of the fourth prior, Étienne de Liciac, in 1139, the Order of Grandmont passes from the realms of legend into history. De Liciac proved to be a man of great authority and feverish activity. His first major act upon election was to call the General Chapter which formulated the Rule of Grandmont. That the communities at Grandmont and elsewhere had survived so long without any attempt at coherent regulation says a great deal for the inspiring leadership of the first Fathers. Nevertheless, the haphazard arrangements for daily living which would have sufficed for the original little band of hermits at Muret must have proved strikingly inadequate for the rapidly increasing community at Grandmont. Furthermore, fifteen years after his death, the charisma exerted by Stephen himself must have been declining as those disciples who had known him personally became increasingly few while newly-arrived brothers would not have experienced anything of his influence and leadership except at second-hand.

The Rule, when it did emerge, proved to be a masterpiece of spiritual aims and objectives centered around the fundamental principles of poverty and solitude, but it contains little in the way of practical legislation. Thus it was ultimately successful in perpetuating the spiritual ideals of the Founder which would continue to inspire the Order for generations, but it did not provide anything like the far-sighted guidance which distinguishes the Rule of St Benedict and which, from the very start, ensured the efficient management of his Order. While St Benedict's Rule combines firmness with sufficient flexibility to deal with developments and altered circumstances, that of Grandmont is both rigid and uncompromising. In fact, it constitutes little more than a formal embodiment of the *Liber Sententiarum*, the thoughts and teaching of Stephen.

Prior Liciac was not the only religious superior faced with the problem of legislating for a group of hermit monks whose numbers were growing rapidly. Several leaders of eleventh-century groups of reformed religious had proved as near-sighted as Stephen in their failure to provide practical directions, so that the responsibility fell heavily on the second generation. The communities of Artige, Dalon, Aureil,and Obazine provide just a few of the numerous examples occurring at this time. The task of reconciling primitive eremitical ideals with a life evolving more and more along coenobitic lines must have placed an intolerable burden on these superiors. Their inadequacy is apparent in the numerous communities which were forced to abandon their autonomy and become daughter houses of Cîteaux or, alternatively, canons regular. That the Grandmontines succeeded where others failed is all the more remarkable, given the singular intransigence which would not permit them to depart from their primitive ideals however impracticable they might be. A clear illustration of this can be found in their unswerving resolution to retain the unusual authority vested in the lay brethren. Before the century was out, this resulted in a crisis which almost brought an end to the entire institution. As long as Prior Liciac was in command, however, his own authority, determination, and strength of character proved sufficient to balance the deficiencies in the Rule, which received the approval of Pope Adrian IV on 25 March 1156.

At the same time as the General Chapter convened by Prior Liciac was deliberating the nature and content of the Rule, the building of the priory church of Grandmont was going forward. Little information exists concerning this second church which replaced the original simple oratory and eventually gave place to Grandmont III in the eighteenth century. The description in the Annals, by a sixteenth-century monk, Pardoux de la Garde, has been shown to be inaccurate on several counts.[6] Written in 1591, it postdates the considerable rebuilding and modifications rendered necessary by damage sustained in the course of the Hundred Years' War and the Wars of Religion, when, on several occasions, the entire locality was devastated and Grandmont subjected to bombardment.

It was during Prior Liciac's term of office that the Order began to benefit from the patronage of King Henry II of England. His mother, Matilda, had already shown considerable interest in the Grandmontines when she arrived in France in 1128 to marry Geoffrey, Count of Anjou, but Henry's own interest probably dates from the time of his marriage to Eleanor of Aquitaine. Henry's admiration for the brothers of Grandmont is revealed in a story in the Annals for the year 1127, which describes his miraculous escape from disaster at sea. On one of his frequent Channel crossings a terrible storm raged and all aboard feared greatly for their lives. Henry calmly asked the captain the time and on hearing that it was midnight precisely, replied:

> Let us proceed courageously, for the Grandmontine brothers in whose prayers we trust have risen at midnight and are praying for us at Matins. It is impossible for us to perish while the brethren are watching and praying for us.[7]

The tempest instantly abated. Unfortunately, this delightful little tale proves to be something of a monastic chestnut, for Professor Margaret Deanesly recounts an identical incident with a Carthusian bias:

> Then the King himself at length broke forth with these words, 'O', he said, 'if that little Carthusian of mine, Hugo, were now pouring forth his private prayers, or if he were standing with his brethren, newly risen from their beds, and saying the night office, surely God would not have forgotten me for so long'. Then he called upon God to have pity on him through Hugo's prayers and merits: and without delay the clash of the tempest and the whirling of the wind subsided, the floods fell, a gentle breeze returned, all thanked the divine mercy, and the King in future held Hugo in the greatest veneration.[8]

Thanks to the generous gifts of Henry II and other benefactors, by 1166 the church was sufficiently advanced to permit consecration. It was dedicated, as were almost all subsequent grandmontine churches, to the Blessed Virgin. This custom of the Grandmontines eliminated the need for additional Lady chapels in their churches, but it was not confined to them; the Cistercians have always maintained the same tradition of dedicating their churches to the Virgin. St Michel de Lodève represents one of the few grandmontine exceptions to this rule. There are two splendid prehistoric dolmens near the site and legend has it that because the monastery was built on land once associated with pagan rites, a more forceful guardian was needed to repel any lingering forces of evil. Who better than the warrior archangel who vanquished Satan himself?

Pierre, Archbishop of Bourges, presided at the ceremony of consecration, assisted by the bishops of Limoges, Angoulême, Cahors,and Séez. Numerous other dignitaries, both ecclesiastical and lay, were also present, but regrettably two of the most outstanding characters in the early history of the Order were unable to witness this momentous event. Prior Étienne de Liciac had died in 1163, preceded by the capable lay brother Hugues Lacerta in 1157.

Under the direction of Pierre Bernard Boschiac (1163–1170) and Guillaume de Treignac (1170–1189), the fifth and sixth priors, work on the church continued. In 1170, Henry II became seriously ill at his castle of Motte de Ger in Normandy. Benedict of Peterborough records that he gave instructions that his body should be conveyed to Grandmont for burial at the feet of the holy Father Stephen. His counsellors protested vehemently that his entombment in the church of a minor religious order, whose mother house was not even classed as an abbey, was beneath the dignity of his kingdom.[9] Henry recovered and was eventually laid to rest at Fontevrault, a house of aristocratic nuns of impeccable reputation. That he was not, after all, interred at Grandmont was most probably attributable to the fact that, by the time of his death in 1189, the reputation of the order of Grandmont had suffered considerably as the result of a violent internal dispute. Yet in deciding to be buried at Grandmont, Henry conferred a great mark of favour on the Order. Nevertheless, as E.M. Hallam has pointed out, the Grandmontines in their turn were honouring the king. Gerald of Wales reveals that they would bury no one in their houses except their patrons, which indicates that Henry had been especially generous towards them.[10]

Henry II's attitude towards monks in general and the Grandmontines in particular is discussed by W.L. Warren who says:

> Though he joked with Walter Map about the Cistercians there is little sign that he shared the genuine hostility that lay behind much of the secular clergy's ridicule of their righteousness . . . Henry II had a deep regard for holy men, and his personal attachment to the austere Grandmontians seems to confirm it.[11]

That the king demonstrated exceptional generosity towards the brethren of Grandmont, supplying both money and materials for the completion of the church, is substantiated by the events of 1170, the year of Archbishop Thomas Becket's murder. When news of the crime reached

Grandmont, work on the church was suspended and the king's workmen dismissed. Prior Pierre Boschiac reputedly wrote the king a stinging reprimand containing the comment: 'the gold of your crown is tarnished and the roses which adorned it have fallen'. The disillusioned prior retired from office soon after addressing this letter, but his successor Guillaume de Treignac is supposed to have supplemented his rebukes with others equally caustic, concluding with the words: 'we cannot be a party to your evil deeds'.[12]

In 1172, Henry II was publicly absolved at Avranches for his part in the murder, having declared on oath that he neither ordered nor desired the Archbishop's death although he admitted that his rash words might have been responsible for it. He was duly restored to full communion with the Church and work was resumed at Grandmont. In 1176, Henry had two shiploads of lead mined near Carlisle dispatched from Newcastle to France. On arrival at La Rochelle, the cargo was loaded into eight hundred carts, each harnessed to eight english horses who drew the loads to Grandmont. This seemingly exaggerated account has been verified by Rose Graham who traced two entries in the Great Roll of the Pipe for the years 1175–76. Henry paid £40 for the lead and a further £12 9s 4d for the hire of the ships.[13] The following year, the king was at Grandmont in person for a business meeting with the Count of La Marche. He returned in June 1182 with his son Geoffrey while a General Chapter of the Order was in progress. The chronicler Geoffrey de Vigeois tells us that on this occasion both father and son ate in the refectory with the brethren who had assembled from the various cells for the meeting.[14] This would have constituted a singular honour, for Walter Map records that the Grandmontines only permitted entry to their houses to 'religious and occasionally such exalted persons whose approach cannot be properly denied by reason of the reverence due to them'.[15]

A short while after this event, the brethren of Grandmont became far less happily involved in the affairs of the

Plantagenets. In the summer of 1183, Henry's eldest son, the young King Henry, led an uprising against his father and to help pay his mercenaries, he plundered the church of Grandmont, removing all valuables including a sacramental pyx in the form of a golden dove which his father had presented to the monks. Having also robbed the shrine of St Martial at Limoges, he managed to flee the city which his father was besieging. His progress southwards was an orgy of sacking and pillage; churches and sacred shrines were mercilessly laid waste. These crimes did not go unpunished for long, for while the king was still besieging Limoges, young Henry fell ill with dysentery and died on the 11 June at Martel in the Perigord. It was a monk from Grandmont who actually broke the news to the king, who was sheltering in a peasant's house outside the city. Prior Guillaume de Treignac prepared to receive the prince's body for burial, but was opposed by Bishop Sebrand-Chabot of Limoges on the grounds that the deceased was an excommunicate, guilty of numerous acts of sacrilege. When eventually the king personally undertook to restore the items stolen by his son, the bishop relented and a requiem for the prince was sanctioned. His brain, eyes, and entrails were removed and interred in the part of the grandmontine cemetery which was always referred to as 'Angleterre', while the corpse was removed first to Le Mans and subsequently to Rouen where it was interred in the cathedral choir. When Henry II himself died in 1189, the Grandmontines received the sum of £2000 stipulated in his will, drawn up in 1182 at Waltham.[16]

The extent of the interest taken by Henry II and later his son Richard I in the Order of Grandmont cannot be established with any degree of certitude, owing to the stringent ruling of the Order which prohibited the brethren from holding title deeds to property. The relaxation of this decree in the thirteenth century only served to add to the confusion, when numerous charters began to appear, many of which have been found to be forgeries. Some cells claimed royal foundation in order to acquire additional privileges, while others invented Plantagenet foundation or connections in order to gain protection from the French crown.[17]

By the time of Prior Pierre Bernard Boschiac's retirement in 1171, the Order was reaching its point of maximum expansion and the 'Bonshommes' had become celebrated far beyond the limits of Aquitaine for their spirit of austerity and detachment. The duchy of Aquitaine occupied the large southern region of France which, following Henry II's marriage to Eleanor of Aquitaine in 1152, had become part of the vast assemblage of Plantagenet lands. It incorporated the counties of Poitou and Angoulême as well as the province of the Limousin where the initial grandmontine expansion had been concentrated. In the 1170s, the territory ruled by the Capetian King Louis VII was contrastingly small, confined to the Ile de France, the area immediately around Paris. It was bordered by the duchy of Normandy to the west, Flanders, to the north, the county of Champagne and duchy of Burgundy to the east and Aquitaine to the south. Thus, the twelfth-century cells fell into two distinct categories, those sited within the domains of the Plantagenet kings and the others within the territory of the Capetians. The brethren themselves were hence divided into two national groups, 'Fratres Anglici' and 'Fratres Gallici'.

King Louis VII (1137–1180) and his son Philip II Augustus (1165–1223) both patronised the Grandmontines, and at the time of the latter's death, around thirty cells had been founded within his kingdom. By far the most important was Bois de Vincennes near Paris which owed its foundation in 1158 or 59 directly to Louis VII. It did not, however, receive a charter until 1164, the year following Prior Étienne de Liciac's death when the strict ruling against the possession of charters may have been slightly relaxed. Capetian foundations were quick to follow: Notre Dame de Louye near Dourdan (Essonne) and La Coudre (Loiret), both owed their foundation in the early 1160s directly to Louis VII. Among the neighbouring foundations known to have been made at more or less the same time are: Meynel (Seine & Oise) founded in 1169 by Bouchard de Montmorency; and Raroi (Seine & Marne) by Simon, Vicomte de Meaux, in 1170.

Henry II was somewhat less influential than Louis VII, for although the mother house itself gained significantly as the result of his marriage to his rival's ex-wife Eleanor of Aquitaine, when the lordship of la Marche came under his control, the daughter cells with which he is associated appear to have been for the most part seigneurial rather than royal foundations. That is to say they owed their foundation to the generosity of local lords and other high ranking personages like the Lord Amelius de Montcocu who granted the monks land on which to build the mother house. Just three cells can possibly claim to have been founded directly by Henry II: Notre Dame du Parc lès Rouen, 1156 or 1157; Bercey, (Sarthe) circa 1168; Bois Rahier, (Indre & Loire), which cannot be dated more precisely than between 1157 and 1172. Villiers, (Indre & Loire), 1172, and La Haye d'Angers (Maine & Loire) have also been attributed to Henry II but the evidence in these last two cases is exceedingly tenuous.[18]

Hugues Lacerta, the knight turned lay brother, may have been indirectly responsible for the patronage bestowed on the Grandmontines by both the Capetian and Plantagenet monarchies. From time to time, Hugues was visited at the cell of la Plaine, in the Dordogne, by Geoffrey de Loroux, a former scholar of Angers who was Archbishop of Bordeaux from 1136 until his death in 1158. Throughout his term of office, he proved to be a friend to individual hermits as well as a supporter of the new orders and of ecclesiastical reform in general. He is said to have received his archbishopric as a reward for helping St Bernard of Clairvaux preach against the schism of the antipope Anacletus, and he is mentioned in the Annals as having vouched for the loyalty of the Grandmontines to the lawfully-elected pope Innocent II.[19] The admiration which Geoffrey professed for the Order of Grandmont may well have influenced his former pupil Eleanor of Aquitaine. Following her marriage to Louis VII in 1137, Geoffrey received considerable favours from the french crown for his houses of canons in Poitou. Eleanor's subsequent marriage to Henry II in 1152 was followed, as we have seen, by the king's not inconsiderable interest in the Order and his assistance with the building of the church at Grandmont. His connection with the mother house continued intermittently until his death in 1189. Indeed, one of his final actions was to petition Clement III to declare Stephen a saint.

Regrettably, the final years of the reign of King Henry II also ended the golden age of Grandmont. Following the priorate of Pierre Bernard Boschiac, the Order began to sink into a decline from which it never fully recovered. This was occasioned by a series of unfortunate incidents which not only provoked disharmony and discord among the brethren of Grandmont but impeded the welfare of the Order in general for several decades.

NOTES

1. Gérard Ithier, *Speculum Grandimontis*; J-B. Hauréau, 'Sur quelques écrivains de l'Ordre de Grandmont'. *Notices et Extraits des Manuscripts de la Bibliothèque Nationale* vol. 24 (1876) p. 255.

2. Lev, p. 64.

3. *Liber Sententiarum* 97:2; Bec SOG, p. 47.

4. RB 71. Chapters I–III of the RG treat of obedience in general, while chapter 59 exhorts mutual obedience between brethren.

5. Lev, p. 100

6. J-R Gaborit, *L'Architecture de L'Ordre de Grandmont* vol 1 (Unpublished thesis, École de Chartes: Paris: 1963).

7. Lev, p. 112: 'Eamus audacter quia fratres Grandimontenses in quorum orationibus confidimus, media nocte ad orandum pro nobis surrexerunt ad matinas, et nullomodo possumos perire, ipsis fratribus vigilantibus et pro nobis orantibus.'

8. Margaret Deanesly, *History of the Medieval Church* (London: Methuen, 1925) p. 126. Unfortunately Deanesly does not tell us from what source she is quoting.

9. *Gesta Henrici Secundi* 1, 7; ed.W. Stubbs (London: Rolls Series, 1867).

10. Elizabeth M. Hallam, 'Henry II, Richard I and the Order of Grandmont', *Journal of Medieval History* (1975) 168–69.

10. W.L. Warren, *Henry II* (London: Eyre Methuen, 1973) p. 12.

12. PL 204: 1168–69.

13. Pipe Rolls 22 Henry II, (London: Pipe Roll Society, 1904) pp. 137, 141, cited by Rose Graham, *English Ecclesiastical Studies* (London: SPCK, 1929) p. 217. For the extent of Henry II's involvement in lead mining in the north of England and details of shipments sent to France, see A.L. Poole, *Oxford History of England*, 3 (Oxford: 1951) pp. 82–3.

14. 'Chronica Gaufredi Coenobitae Monasterii S Martialis Lemovicensis ac Prioris Vosciensis coenobii'; P. Labbe, *Nova Bibliotheca Manuscriptorum* 2 (Paris: 1657).

15. Walter Map, *De nugis curialium* 1: xxvi; M.R. James, Anecdota Oxoniensia, Medieval and Modern Series part 14 (Oxford: 1914) pp. 54–55.

16. *Receuil des Actes de Henri II, Roi d'Angleterre et duc de Normandie concernant les provinces françaises et les affaires de France*; L. Delisle and E. Berger 2 (Paris: 1920) p. 220.

17. Elizabeth M. Hallam, pp. 165–86, has made a thorough study of this question; see above note 10.

18. Ibid., p. 175.

19. Lev, pp. 101–2.

III

THE YEARS OF CRISIS

1171 – 1228

GUILLAUME DE TREIGNAC was elected in 1171, the sixth prior of a flourishing and highly respected religious order. On 18 October 1188, he died in Italy, deposed and driven from Grandmont by a usurper. Echoes of the dispute which broke out at Grandmont in 1185 reverberated well into the thirteenth century and shook the Christian world to the core. The cause lay in a fundamental malaise; the inadequate legislation provided by the Rule especially with regard to the functions of the *clercs* and *convers*: Other factors may have contributed. Hugues Lacerta, for example, may have discerned an initial sign of weakness as early as 1157, when he expressed his disquiet about the too rapid growth in numbers. Again, prosperity can in itself herald disaster, a consideration which receives some treatment in contemporary sources. Walter Map, for example, that vociferous twelfth-century critic of monks in general and the Cistercians in particular, is normally somewhat uncharacteristically appreciative of the Grandmontines but he did give a clear indication of the troubles that lay ahead. In the course of his travels with the entourage of King Henry II, Map visited various cells and made several favourable comments, but following a stay in Limoges in 1173 he wrote:

> Our King is so greatly generous towards them that they lack nothing. They give alms to all comers but admit no one save it be a bishop or a prince. I am rather afraid of what may come, for now they are present at councils and handle the business of kings.[1]

The crisis when it broke had two distinct aspects, disciplinary and political, to which may be added the economic consequences of so much disruption. The costs incurred by constant appeals to the roman curia were alone sufficient to bring the Order close to the verge of ruin.

The political nature of the dispute became obvious when King Philip II Augustus involved himself in an attempt to settle the alarming state of affairs which was apparent in cells within his domain. Bois de Vincennes near Paris rivalled Grandmont itself and was the chief cell of the *Fratres Gallici*, so when the king took the initiative and called a general council of the Order there in 1187, he was effectively overriding the authority of the mother house and asserting his influence within Angevin territory.

While the crisis eventually developed something of an international character, fundamentally it amounted to little more than a domestic squabble over what the choir monks considered to be the excessive authority wielded by their colleagues, the lay brothers. As such, it was a mere disciplinary dispute. It is always a temptation to equate the disturbances that disrupted the Order of Grandmont with the series of similar incidents which affected other religious orders, especially the notorious revolt of the gilbertine lay brethren in 1166. Thus the behaviour of the grandmontine lay brothers is mistakenly assumed to be part and parcel of a tendency towards lay brotherhood uprisings which troubled monasteries in general at this period. The series of revolts suffered by the Cistercian Order in the thirteenth century were provoked, however, by circumstances which were in striking contrast to those which prevailed in the

Order of Grandmont. At Grandmont the lay brothers had evolved as the masters and consequently the choir monks resented them; with the Gilbertines and Cistercians, it was the lay brothers who rose against their masters, the choir monks. The resentment, which expressed itself in the violent uprisings of groups of cistercian lay brothers, can be attributed to the social transformation taking place in Europe in the course of the thirteenth century. Within most religious orders, the lay brethren were quite simply the monastic equivalent of ordinary labourers or serfs who were beginning to demand new freedoms in the thirteenth century, as serfdom was gradually disappearing from western Europe and peasants were becoming free rent paying tenants. Thus poverty and uncertainty no longer served as major incentives to join lay brotherhoods. Dom Louis Lekai has attributed the decline of lay brother vocations within the Cistercian Order to the improvement in social conditions generally. The consequent problem of recruitment led in turn to a lowering of admission standards, while the necessity of providing material benefits in order to entice recruits led to increased worldliness within the cistercian granges and consequently insubordination and breakdown of discipline.[2]

The status afforded the grandmontine lay brethren was, however, without precedent in the Cistercian or any other religious Order. Before proceeding to the unfortunate consequences of that policy we need to consider it in some detail. When the Grandmontines were founded, both the orders of Vallombrosa and Camaldoli had already introduced lay brothers to perform domestic tasks as well as to deal with minor aspects of external administration which involved contact with lay persons. Thus the choir monks were left completely free to devote themselves to their spiritual duties. This practice was in due course adopted by the later eleventh century groups of reformed religious, notably the Cistercians, Prémonstratensians, and English Gilbertines. Within these orders, however, the supreme administration of the monastery remained firmly and conclusively in the hands of officials elected from the ranks of the choir monks. The notion of instituting a class of worker monk to be loosely responsible for temporalities was not, therefore, peculiar to the Grandmontines. That, having adopted the system, they carried it to extremes by entrusting total responsibility for all administrative and financial matters to the lay brethren was exceptional to say the least. As we have seen, Stephen's original followers resembled numerous other hermit groups which arose in the eleventh century. There was no distinction between these religious other than their occupations; the more capable being entrusted with the more responsible tasks. That the recitation of the offices required a degree of literacy was the only factor which originally distinguished *clercs* from *convers*. This was certainly the case among the early hermits who were led by Robert d'Arbrissel at Fontevrault.[3] Eventually, when several of these groups were forced to surrender their independence and to amalgamate with the 'established' monastic and canonical organisations, the *clercs* became monks or canons whilst the *convers* joined the ranks of the lay brothers or associates and became, quite clearly, subordinate religious entrusted with domestic or agricultural duties under the supervision of a choir monk official. At the Grande Chartreuse shortly after its foundation, the Carthusians provided for the accommodation of their lay brothers in the 'lower house' where, in the charge of a choir monk 'procurator', they catered for the needs of the 'upper house' as well as discharging the obligation of dispensing hospitality to guests. The Premontstratensians instituted a similar establishment known as the *domus conversorum* or, familiarly, the *cour*.

At Grandmont, such denigration of the lay brethren was never even considered. It was as though the compilers of the Rule desired to safeguard the legal equality of the two categories of religious, and at the same time afford the *clercs* total seclusion and freedom from worldly cares. They therefore awarded the *convers* exclusive authority over everything which concerned administration, work, and dealings with outsiders. Outlining the sphere of responsibility of the *clercs*, the Rule of Grandmont states:

> The better part which the Lord praised so highly in Mary, we impose upon the clercs alone, so that freed from all temporal cares they may be able to say in all truthfulness: 'The Lord is the portion of my inheritance' (Ps 118: 57) and again: 'It is not reasonable we should leave the work of God and serve tables.' (Acts 6:2). Besides, vowed exclusively to divine praises and contemplation, they will be the servers of spiritual realities both to themselves as well as to the other brethren who confess their sins to them.[4]

This instruction is not dissimilar from those found in other texts governing the religious life; it is the following injunction allocating the *convers* a truly exceptional degree of authority, that represents the striking departure from the norm:

> In order that conversations with outsiders and care for exterior things shall not hinder the Divine Office, in order that their souls should not forget the sweetness of interior satisfaction (which St Gregory deplored should happen to him) for these reasons we entrust the temporal care of the monastery to the convers alone; in matters worldly and all other business, they are to command the other brethren, both clercs and convers, not in a domineering way but in all charity, conserving intact that humility which is the guardian of all virtues. Was not the Creator of all things himself obedient to his creatures Mary and Joseph, as it says in the Gospel:'and he was subject to them'. (Lk 2:51.)[5]

Needless to say, the success of this idealistic piece of legislation was almost entirely dependent on the goodwill of the *convers* who were merely exhorted to wield their authority in a spirit of humility. For their part, the *clercs* presumably regarded a certain subjection in matters temporal small price to pay for the spiritual advantages. It left them at liberty to follow the contemplative life of Mary in the same way as the Carthusians, while the *convers* took upon themselves the role and consequent cares of Martha.

As regards superiors, both the Rule and the Custumal make it clear that the Prior of Grandmont was overall general superior. Referred to as the 'Pastor', he it was to whom all major problems and serious disciplinary questions were to be referred. This, incidentally, must have involved a great deal of to-ing and fro-ing between the mother house and the dependent cells. It accounts for the lengthy discussion in the Rule which treats of the undesirability of brothers leaving the solitude of their cells to travel around the countryside, but at the same time, accepting the necessity for such absences. It probably also explains the brothers' reluctance to take on foundations at too great a distance from the mother house, and certainly not for a long time to cross the English Channel; the three english houses came into being comparatively late in the history of the Order. The prior himself was required to make a vow of stability upon election to office, which meant that he was bound to reside permanently at Grandmont.

Both the Rule and the Custumal, when it appeared in 1171 or 72, make incidental mention of officials who became known as *curiosi* and who had charge of the separate cells (*curae cellae*). They were responsible for the distribution of clothing and necessities. They were charged with determining the common diet and were also responsible for the care of the sick. It was the *curiosus* who occupied the senior place in each of the cells and from the nature of the duties entrusted to him, we may conclude that the position was held by a *conver*. It was not until 1216, following the first crisis, that we hear of a spiritual director, a *corrector* being appointed in each cell. The lengthy exhortation to practise mutual obedience which occupies chapter fifty-nine of the

Rule seems to suggest that apart from the *curiosus*, grandmontine cells before this date had no superiors in the conventional sense at all. Novices were trained at the mother house, and only following profession would each brother be assigned to a daughter cell in accordance with the wishes of the *pastor*. Thus the early grandmontine cells appear to have taken the form of communities of mutually obedient religious, with the *convers* outnumbering the *clercs* at a ratio of three to one,[6] under the management of a *curiosus* but directly responsible to the *pastor* at Grandmont.

What could have been the reasons which led Prior Étienne de Liciac and his colleagues to the unprecedented legislation which subjected the *clercs* to the *convers* and which in due course caused the latter group so to abuse the authority vested in them? In the first instance, we have the example set by the founder himself when he entrusted the day to day management of affairs to his close disciple, Hugues Lacerta. Dom Becquet has found a further motive in the systematic way in which the authors of the Rule sought to resolve the problem of the two classes of religious. They could not, for practical reasons, attain the absolute ideal of permitting all the religious without exception to follow the contemplative life, but neither did they wish to institute the rigid division between choir and lay brothers which existed in other orders. Their resolution had, therefore, the practical effect of subordinating the *clercs* to the *convers*, a decision which they justified by reference to the scriptural precedent of Christ subjecting himself to his parents and which is alluded to in the Rule of Grandmont.[7] Thus the notion of 'Martha and Mary', which first finds utterance in the promulgations of St Augustine, and is developed more fully by John Cassian in his conferences, became a firm institution under the Grandmontines. It is interesting to note that St Dominic in the regularisation of his Order of Preachers in 1216, was to entertain a similar idea. He was dissuaded because at that precise moment troubles manifesting themselves at Grandmont as the direct result of the arrangement were giving Pope Honorius III and his curia considerable problems.[8]

The Initial Crisis

The unmitigated quarrelling which broke out during the priorate of Guillaume de Treignac was the end-product of pent-up resentments which had been smouldering for some time within the ranks of *clercs* and *convers* alike. Jacques de Vitry, Bishop of Acre (d. 1240) summed up both sides of the argument: The *clercs,* he comments, think that they ought to be over the *convers* in all things as in other Orders where the capitals are put on top of the columns and not on the bases. The *convers,* for their part, insist that church services should be arranged to fit in with their occupations, while the *clercs* should be content to take their ease in the cloister whilst they toil in the heat of the day. They read nowhere that Mary complained about Martha.[9] These observations were written in the early part of the thirteenth century, by which time the troubles had entered a secondary phase. Guiot de Provins gives a somewhat earlier eyewitness account. As an ex-troubadour he had been in the Holy Land for the third crusade. When he returned to France, ageing and penniless, he decided to end his days as a monk. He toured various monasteries sizing up the advantages and disadvantages of each, before finally opting for Cluny. His wanderings and experiences supplied the material for his 'Bible Guiot', a satirical poem criticising the various classes of society. Completed around 1206, the section on the monks provides a curiously lucid insight into the problems occurring at Grandmont. He began by praising the performance of the liturgy and the charity of the brethren who are exceptionally generous in affording food and alms to all comers. He was highly appreciative of the standard of the food served in the refectory which is greatly improved by the addition of garlic and spicy sauces, a welcome change from the monotonous fare served up at Cluny! What deterred him from making his home permanently with the Grandmontines was, however, the behaviour of the *convers*. The *clercs*, he wrote, dared not commence any service in church before the *convers* gave the word and, if they did, they could expect severe beatings by way of reprisal:

> The convers are lords and masters there, I should be frightened if they were my lords. I am frightened when I see them. Rome permits this, and why? Because the convers possess gold and silver. Clercs and priest are subject to them. . . . There the carts go before the oxen.[10]

Despite any undercurrent of unrest, the priorate of Guillaume de Treignac began peaceably enough. He has been described by various authors as pious, orderly, and efficient. Between the years 1174–1185, he worked arduously to consolidate the fame and reputation of the Order. He was an avid collector of relics and the monastery became, as a result, an attractive secondary destination and halt for pilgrims on their way to Compostella, Rocamadour, and other celebrated shrines. The site of Grandmont itself was lonely and isolated, but the main pilgrim route from the east passed through the little hamlet of St Leonard, just a few miles away. Prior Guillaume's most outstanding success occurred when he managed to obtain the approval of the Custumal from Pope Alexander III in 1171 or 1172, as well as an official approbation of the Order from Pope Lucius III in 1182. Unfortunately his positive achievements were all too soon outweighed by his failure to govern with the tact and firmness which might have averted the impending conflict.

Hostilities were initially concerned with trivialities–the *convers* refusing to supply the *clercs* with such necessities as items of clothing. Some of the incidents which were reported are not without humour, as when the *clercs* complained because the *convers* had apparently taken it upon themselves to organise church services. The *convers* responded by hiding vestments and altar utensils so that services were constantly being delayed or disrupted. The report that they deliberately supplied the officiating priest with vestments of the wrong liturgical colour so that he would be obliged to celebrate a Mass of the Virgin in black or a requiem in white,[11] is, however, exceedingly unlikely. In the first place, it was an odd but usual custom in the twelfth century to celebrate festivals of the Blessed Virgin in black vestments anyway. It was not until the pontificate of Innocent III (1198–1216) that even an outline of a roman rule governing liturgical colours was defined and a general rule was not formally imposed before the reformed missal of Pius V appeared in 1570.[12] If the *convers* were working in the fields, they would delay ringing the bell for Compline until nightfall. In vain did the poor *clercs* vainly invoke the dignity of their priestly office and the importance of keeping regular hours. A more serious complaint asserted that the *convers* were keeping their business transactions secret and refusing to render accounts in chapter in the customary way.

At Grandmont events took a violent turn when the *convers* barricaded Prior Guillaume in his room, declared him deposed and elected Étienne, a *clerc* from the cell of Bois de Vincennes, in his place. When news of this insubordination reached Rome, Pope Urban III responded with the first of a long series of papal bulls attempting to put matters to rights. Dated 15 July 1186, it confirmed the overall authority of the prior of Grandmont in both spiritual and temporal affairs. It confided responsibility for all practical management to the most able of the *convers* in each cell, but at the same time made it clear that decisions regarding spiritual matters were to be made by the *clercs* alone. In addition, it ruled that no *conver* had the right to preside over the daily chapter of faults and mete out punishments and that the management of the church and the conduct of divine worship should be the responsibility of the *clercs*. In conclusion, the pope re-approved the Rule and Constitutions and granted the Order exemption from episcopal control.[13] The bull had little effect, and shortly after its arrival the *convers* invoked the final chapter of the Rule, which gives the brethren the right to depose a prior if he is considered by the majority to be unfit for office. Guillaume de Treignac was once again replaced by Étienne de Vincennes, despite the fact that the majority of the *clercs* regarded this election as scandalous. Two hundred of them, together with thirteen faithful *convers*, are said to have accompanied the prior into exile and sought refuge in the houses of other religious orders, mainly the Cistercians. The most celebrated refugee from Grandmont was a certain William who was received into the cistercian abbey of Pontigny, where he was in due course elected prior. He concluded his career as Archbishop of Bourges and was eventually canonised St William of Bourges.

There followed the secular intervention of Philip Augustus, who summoned both *clercs* and *convers* representatives to a convention at Bois de Vincennes. Chief among the delegates who sought reconciliation was Brother Bernard de la Coudre, a wise and saintly monk who had made a name for himself outside the Order as an advisor to popes and kings. In 1166, Pope Alexander III had deputed him along with a Carthusian, Simon du Mont Dieu, to attempt a reconciliation between Henry II and the ill-fated Archbishop Thomas Becket. This particular mission proved a failure. Philip Augustus, for his part, evidently placed great trust in Brother Bernard and, before departing for the crusade in 1190, appointed him advisor to his joint regents, the queen and the archbishop of Rheims for all ecclesiastical appointments.

It was most likely in December of the year 1187 that the meeting at Vincennes took place. Eighteen resolutions were in due course approved and submitted to the General Chapter at Grandmont as well as to the roman curia. The resolutions do little more than clarify the vague directives given in the Rule but as they summarise the main abuses and disagreements which were provoking the discord, it is worth giving them in full:

1. If a king, an archbishop, a bishop, or a prince wishes to enter any of the cells of the Order of Grandmont, he is to be accompanied by only four men.
2. *Clercs* and *convers* are to receive equal treatment, they will partake of the same food and drink in the refectory and sleep in the one dorter. Their habits are to be made from cloth of the same quality.
3. All alms received, together with the names of the donors, are to be made known at the morning chapter held in each house of the Order.
4. All goods belonging to or received by the cells of the Order of Grandmont are to be accounted for at the morning chapter as well as anything distributed in alms.
5. The prior is to delegate two brothers, a *clerc* and a *conver*,to visit each and every cell annually and they are to have full authority to investigate and correct abuses.
6. Unless he is sick, the prior is to sleep in the common dorter with the brethren.
7. Everything distributed within the cells is to be accounted for to the prior.
8. When a new prior is to be elected, both *clercs* and *convers* will nominate six from among their number and these twelve shall proceed to elect the prior.
9. *Convers* have no right to effect the transference of the *clercs*. It goes without saying that any such transference is the sole right of the prior.
10. The prior is to regulate spiritual matters with the *clercs* and temporal business with the *convers*; however, as regards the latter he will consult with two *clercs* of his choice.

11. Altar vessels, vestments, and liturgical books are to be in the charge of the *clercs*.
12. The prior and the *clercs* are to be responsible for the regulation of the offices and all other spiritual concerns.
13. The daily recitation of faults will be made to the hebdomadarian priest at the morning chapter. A simple reprimand will suffice.
14. If a brother commits any sins, he is to confess them to one of the priests within the cell, who will administer a penance. It will never be deemed necessary for him to leave the cell to confess his sins.
15. The *clercs* are to be responsible for calling the brothers to the collation [the spiritual reading which precedes compline] and it will take place even if the *curiosus* is called away to attend to visitors or to welcome guests. In addition, this official has the right to employ one or two brothers of the house to assist him in such business.
16. Besides what has already been stated, it is taken for granted that the newly elected prior shall promise truthfully and upon his soul that he shall in no way wrong the *clercs* who opposed the *convers* in the course of these discords. Similarly the *clercs* will promise in their turn not to plot against the *convers* by reason of these discords.
17. In addition, Brother Bernard and his colleagues will undertake that should the prior and the other brothers refuse to accept or observe the articles of this peace, they will place themselves firmly on the side of the *clercs* and assist them to enforce these articles. The *clercs*, for their part will promise to obey the prior.

The final article reinforces the authority of the Rule which is to be obeyed to the letter and not adapted or altered in any way.[14]

The compilers of the Articles of Vincennes attempted to eliminate the basic causes of dissent by redefining the official spheres of responsibility of the two contending groups. There is little in the document which is not already implicit in the Rule or the Constitution approved by Alexander III. That a prestigious royal council should have been required to deliberate over such seemingly obvious matters as priests being the proper persons to be entrusted with the regulation of divine worship and the care of church vessels and vestments appears utterly ludicrous. That such rulings as those contained in Articles 12 and 15 proved necessary, must indicate that the *convers* had actually been depriving the *clercs* of the right to run their own department. Article 9 has much more serious implications. From it, it appears that the *convers* had taken it upon themselves to transfer *clercs* from one cell to another. As the prior of Grandmont alone had the right to order transfers this was a very serious offence indeed. Article 14 points to another major contravention of the Rule. In the first place, the brethren were not permitted to leave their cells without permission, but that a brother should seek to make his confession to a priest outside his own congregation was totally at variance with accepted religious practice. The fact that some of the *convers* were finding it necessary to seek absolution for their sins outside their own Order is in itself an indication of the degree of mistrust and hostility which existed between *clercs* and *convers*. Article 18 has an unpleasant implication. Although corporal punishment with rods or cords was a generally accepted practice in the monasteries of the Middle Ages, it was administered at a properly appointed time in chapter; yet we know from Guiot de Provins, that the grandmontine *convers* were beating the *clercs*, at times excessively.[15] As the grandmontine cells had no superiors in the conventional sense, the daily chapter sessions were conducted by the hebdomadary, an official appointed on a weekly basis. The need for the Council to stipulate that the hebdomadary should always be a priest suggests that this was another function which the *convers* had assumed and were abusing.

At Vincennes the egalitarian notions contained in the Rule received reinforcement specifically in Articles 2, 6, 7, and 8 and these rulings can have provoked little opposition, although which group stood to gain from the parity of diet and clothing is a matter for conjecture! By contrast, Articles 3,5,and 7, while they appear reasonable enough, are nevertheless the thin edge of the wedge leading away from grandmontine equality. The formal requirement that the *convers* make their business public and render up accounts represents an initial wary move to relieve them of their temporal powers and subject them firmly to the authority of the *clercs*.

When the decisions reached by the Council of Vincennes were received at Grandmont they were dismissed out of hand, the majority of the *convers* considering them to be far too favourable towards the *clercs*. Whilst the 'loyalists' took refuge elsewhere and occupied themselves by addressing indignant letters to Rome, the *convers* at Grandmont proceeded to rebel in an increasingly violent manner. By this time the appalling scandal affecting the Order of Grandmont was common knowledge and the Holy See was forced to take a more active role. The pope dispatched a five member commission to the mother house, as the result of which the anti-prior Étienne de Vincennes was excommunicated and Guillaume de Treignac restored to office. In a noble attempt to keep the peace, however, he resigned voluntarily and departed for Rome where, old and infirm, he died one year later. Amid all this confusion the new pope, Clement III, who replaced the short lived Gregory VIII in December 1187, cannot have heard of Guillaume's resignation because he proceeded to order his removal along with the usurper Étienne. Thus, the way was officially clear for a General Chapter to proceed to a fresh election. The result was an inspired choice. The eloquent and scholarly Gérard Ithier became seventh prior of Grandmont, and with his election the first serious crisis within the Order was brought to a close. The pope reapproved the Rule and confirmed all the privileges of the Order granted by his predecessors including exemption from episcopal control.

The Cold War

The priorate of Gérard Ithier proceeded in conditions which Frère Philippe-Étienne has described as 'La Guerre Froide'.[16] For while the grievances of the *clercs* had been temporarily appeased, there can be no doubt that the *curiosi* elected from the ranks of the *convers*, remained the real masters of the grandmontine cells. For his part, Gérard made no secret of the fact that he considered equality between *clercs* and *convers* the fundamental principle of life in a grandmontine cell:

> How good and righteous it is for brothers to exist together in one spirit with *clercs* and *convers* living harmoniously together in community.[17]

Within the small enclosed world of the monastery, it has frequently been said, small matters get blown up out of all proportion. In this way it was the seemingly trivial subject of 'The Bells' which came to be writ large in the history of the grandmontine troubles. The bells seem to have constituted one of the principle grounds for disagreement between *clercs* and *convers*. The task of sounding the call to the collation which preceded Compline had always devolved on the *convers*. In summer, when they wanted to benefit from the daylight and continue working in the fields, they often delayed ringing the bell until nightfall when they were free to attend this office. The *clercs* complained bitterly at this unconventional arrangement which not only threw their timetable out of gear, but must have deprived them of some of their rest as well. In 1191, the *convers* still reserved this right to themselves despite the efforts of the *clercs* to relieve them of it at the convention of 1187.

When Gérard Ithier resigned in 1198, he was replaced by the eighth prior, Adémar de Friac. The morale of the *clercs* reached an all time low and they addressed a letter to Pope Innocent III outlining their grievances. This proved to be the first of a whole series of interventions which the long-suffering Innocent and his successor, Honorius III, were forced to undertake. On this occasion, the pope hoped, rather too optimistically, that a simple reply addressed to Prior Adémar would set matters to rights. When this failed, he was forced to a more active intervention, and so he deputed Archbishop William of Bourges, the grandmontine monk who became a Cistercian at Pontigny, together with the bishops of Paris and Limoges to visit Grandmont, deal with any abuses, and institute some measure of reform. Nothing was achieved by this mission. The central issue was still the collations bell, the *clercs* complaining about its lateness and the *convers* persisting in their refusal to sound it any earlier. The failure of the papal emissaries meant that settlement of the question devolved upon the pope himself. Thus, the supreme pontiff was obliged to postpone any weightier matters whilst he solemnly deliberated over the problem of who should ring a bell! Should the responsibility remain with the *convers*, given that it sounded the conclusion of work, or alternatively, should it pass to the *clercs* because equally it was the call to prayer. Following discussion with the Sacred College, Innocent III pronounced *ex cathedra* that the bell should be sounded at a stated hour and that if the *conver* responsible failed to carry out his duty then a *clerc* appointed by the prior should step in and do it for him.

Another major cause for grievance among the *clercs* involved the persistent refusal of the *convers* to submit their accounts. Innocent III thought to settle the matter by formally sanctioning the Article of Vincennes which had instituted an annual visitation of each cell by a *clerc* and *conver* acting as direct representatives of the prior. The *clercs* expressed the somewhat novel grievance that they were being outnumbered by the *convers* who consequently had a physical advantage over them. The pope dictated that in future the ratio of *convers* to *clercs* should be two to one. It was further ordained that when the *clercs* were required to work in the fields, they should be accompanied by the *convers* and not return without them. The only exception being the duty-clerc for the week who was not allowed to leave the cell under any pretext. Any *clerc* leaving the cell without permission was to be 'proclaimed' at chapter. Both *clercs* and *convers* had an equal right to 'proclaim' their fellows but the officiating priest alone might administer a reprimand. It appears that *clercs* were still being surreptitiously transferred to other cells by interfering *convers*, and when this particular complaint reached the pope's ears he again added the weight of his authority to the Article of Vincennes which stated that such a decision could only be made by the prior after due consultation with his counsellors.

In 1211, Innocent III again requested the archbishop of Bourges to visit Grandmont, this time accompanied by the bishop of Orleans, and deal with any abuses of the Rule. It seems that the *clercs* were once again accusing the *convers* of violating certain statutes. The following January, he was again forced to return to what must have seemed the eternal question of the bells. This time he decided firmly in the *clercs'* favour and the duty of ringing the bell for collation was delegated to a *conver*, then to a *clerc* designate and, finally, to any *clerc* as necessity might dictate. The difference was that this time anyone contravening the order was to be punished not by the Prior of Grandmont but by direct order of the pope.

The Climax of the Disputes

Prior Adémar de Friac was inclined, like his predecessor to favour the *convers*. But when he died unexpectedly in Viterbo on his return journey from the Lateran Council of 1215, his successor, Caturcin, tended towards the opposite view and the days of *convers* dominance were numbered. A renewed outbreak of violence on their part served only to hasten the final and decisive victory of the *clercs*.

1 May 1216, marked the turning point in the whole ugly affair. Pope Innocent III pronounced decisively in favour of the *clercs*. His ruling determined that in the future an official with the title of *corrector* be appointed by the prior to each cell. These officials were to be regarded as overall superiors responsible for all administrative concerns; they were to be chosen only from among the *clercs* and they were further required to be ordained priests. Not only was the *corrector* to take the place of the *curiosus*, the sole administrative post legislated for in the Rule and traditionally held by a *conver*, but he also obviated the need for a weekly rota of priest functionaries by presiding permanently over church and chapter assemblies.

The changes set in motion by Innocent III continued under his successor, Honorius III (1216–1227). In 1217, Honorius went a stage further when he suppressed the article of the Rule which bound the prior to reside permanently at Grandmont and gave him the right to visit and inspect the various cells in person. He also settled once and for all that persistent, trivial and yet abrasive issue, the collation bell, by ordering that it be rung only by a *clerc*. Finally, he made it legally binding that the *curiosus* in each cell render monthly statements of accounts to the *corrector* in the presence of the entire community assembled in chapter.

This was too much for the *convers* of Grandmont to swallow and they rallied their outside supporters for a last desperate stand. Then, aided by a contingent of men at arms they broke into open and violent revolt and imprisoned the prior and his supporters. When the representatives sent by the pope to deal with the situation arrived, the *convers* responded by pillaging the priory, throwing Prior Caturcin and the forty *clercs* who supported him off the premises and electing in his place a *clerc* who was sympathetic to their cause. At this juncture the pope had no alternative but to appeal to ecclesiastical and french lay authorities to recruit the forces necessary to combat the *convers* and restore order.

Reprisals were terrible; all those guilty of aiding and abetting the rebellion were excommunicated. Prior Caturcin, who had taken refuge in the cluniac abbey of St Martial at Limoges, was restored and the *convers* forced to beg his pardon. The leaders of the revolt were permanently deprived of their charges, sentenced to be whipped each Sunday in chapter, ordered to fast on bread and water every Friday at the prior's pleasure, and deprived of the sacrament for a year unless they were in danger of death. The usurping prior and the guilty *clercs* were banned from celebrating Mass for as long as the prior saw fit to impose the measure.

A state of somewhat uneasy calm prevailed until Prior Caturcin resigned his office in 1228 or 29 but the intervention of further papal commissions proved necessary on several occasions. Later in the thirteenth century, the frustrated delegates of one such commission concluded despairingly that nothing short of a total reform of the Rule would guarantee a lasting peace.

A consideration of the terrible crisis which crippled the Order of Grandmont within a century of its foundation reveals a number of key factors amid the morass of disagreement and petty squabbling. All of them can, in part at least, be attributed to the near-sightedness of the compilers of the Rule in failing to take account of the eventuality of priests becoming numerous within the Order. True, this document takes the presence of priests for granted when it forbids the ownership of churches or any form of active ministry. However, it contains no specific directives concerning the admission of priests nor has it anything to say about the status to be accorded them once accepted. This omission is in striking contrast to the Rule of St Benedict which devotes an entire chapter to the subject. The benedictine Rule states clearly that priests wishing to enter the Order must not be accepted too readily. Moreover, it is to be made plain to priest candidates that no allowances will be made or privileges afforded them on account of their office. They can celebrate Mass and administer the blessings only at the abbot's bidding. They must not take liberties and they are to be subject to regular discipline.[18] The benedictine priest's subjection to his abbot underlines a further deficiency in the Rule of Grandmont, the idealistic notion which rendered superiors, at least in the conventional sense, superfluous. The result was that when the Rule's exhortation to practise mutual obedience ceased to be observed, there was no one to enforce any kind of discipline.

By the 1180s, a significant proportion of *clercs* were ordained and this begs the question to what extent was their status and priestly dignity compatible with their subordination to lay religious? Admittedly the mother house was ruled by a prior who was always a priest, but within the daughter cells the situation was altogether different. Here there dwelt small combined communities of *clercs* and *convers* subject to no authority other than that of a prior who lived far away from them and a *curiosus* who was himself nominated by this inaccessible prior. Given such circumstances, it is not altogether surprising if certain priests became discontented and resentful. Far from receiving the respect which they felt the dignity of their state warranted, they found themselves reduced to the status of mere chaplains at the beck and call of a group of lay religious who had taken to arranging the monastic horarium to suit themselves and their work schedule.

A situation in which ordained monks were purposely instituted to serve lay religious as chaplains was not of course without precedent. Both Gilbert of Sempringham and Robert d'Arbrissel founded monasteries in which contemplative nuns were central to an organisation which incorporated lay sisters and brothers together with canons to serve as chaplains. In both instances, however, it was understood from the start that the overall superior would be the abbess. Furthermore, both the Gilbertines and the Fontevristes lived in clearly defined enclosures which kept the various classes of religious segregated. There can have been no question of misunderstandings and arguments arising over simple domestic issues. The vast, efficiently organised and compartmented abbey of Fontevrault bears no comparison with a typical grandmontine cell situated in remote rural surroundings and where the occupants dwelt in close and confined quarters. Such conditions must have provided ideal breeding grounds for germs of discontent.

Within these vulnerable enclosures the grandmontine *clercs* nursed three outstanding grievances which they aired at various times during the lengthy dispute. All three can be attributed to feelings of inferiority which resulted from their ill-acknowledged status. In the first place they were made to feel inferior simply because they were outnumbered by the *convers* at a ratio of at least two to one. A fragment of an *obit*, which can be dated between the years 1140–1150, testifies to a much higher ratio, one *clerc* to seven or eight *convers*, but this has to be exceptional.[19]

While it can be argued that the proportion of lay brothers to choir monks was notably higher in, say, the Order of Cîteaux, here the lay brethren lived outside the cloister, completely isolated from the choir monks. The fact cannot be over-emphasised that the grandmontine *convers* were not just auxiliary religious as were the cistercian *conversi* — but were fully professed monks with the same rights and privileges as the *clercs*. It is most unlikely that the words *clerc* and *conver* were included in the vocabulary of St Stephen, who cannot himself be properly assigned to either class of religious. Although he was ordained a deacon, and therefore technically a clerk in holy orders, yet he never aspired to the priesthood itself and as a simple hermit in the tradition of the Desert Fathers he was dependent upon others for his spiritual needs. Neither did it occur to him to draw any distinction between himself and his disciple Hugues Lacerta whose own vocation was active rather than contemplative. That the fraternal and harmonious living conditions which prevailed at Muret were destined to be disrupted, that the sons of St Stephen would become so divisive that the smaller group would feel physically threatened by the others, this was a situation which neither St Stephen nor the compilers of the Rule could possibly have envisaged.

Apart from status, two other types of inferiority gave rise to resentment among the *clercs*. These had to do with finance and with their actual living conditions. In both these areas it would appear that they were being deprived by the *convers*. While the Rule entrusts the *convers* with all practical administration of the revenues of the Order, this was intended to spare the *clercs* the distractions which active dealings with outsiders would occasion. It cannot have intended them to be utterly deprived of any say in the management of their households, or to be silenced when corporate decisions were called for. In the course of events, it became clear that the information about sources of income and expenditure was being completely withheld from them. It had always been customary in the Order of Grandmont as, indeed, in other religious orders, for the procurator to render accounts at chapter meetings. The fact that the *convers* were keeping their financial transactions to themselves must have been responsible for some unhealthy feelings of suspicion and distrust not conducive to a life of peaceful contemplation. With regard to institutional matters, the *clercs* were again made to feel inferior by not being permitted a voice in the planning of the horarium or management of the household. In certain cases they had been forced to move from one house to another by interfering *convers* acting without the knowledge or consent of the prior. That *convers*, through sheer weight of numbers, were able to impose their will upon the *clercs*, must have had a profoundly demoralising effect upon the clergy.

The mother house of Grandmont never really managed to revert to the state of calm and spiritual serenity which prevailed before the commencement of the unfortunate and oft-violent disputes. Over half a century, quarrels, fighting, and legal processes had caused the religious life to break down almost completely. In 1247, Pope Innocent IV gave the Grandmontines the text of a new constitution which firmly and indisputably placed the *convers* under the authority of the *clercs*. This action had a limiting effect upon the disturbances but minor troubles persisted until the total reorganisation of the Order by Pope John XXII in 1317.

NOTES

1. Walter Map, *De nugis curialium* 1: xxvi; M.R. James, *Anecdota Oxoniensia*, Medieval and Modern Series, part 14 (Oxford: 1914) pp. 54–55.

2. L.J. Lekai, *The Cistercians, Ideals and Reality* (Ohio: Kent State University Press, 1977) pp. 334–46.

3. PL 204:1052: 'Laici et clerici mistim ambulabant, excepto quod clerici psallebant et missas celebrabant, laici laborem spontanei subibant'.

4. RG, ch. LIV; Bec SOG p. 92.

5. *Ibid.*

6. Bec, 'La première crise de l'Ordre de Grandmont', *BSAHL* 87 (troisième livraison 1960) p. 295.

7. Bec, 'La Règle de Grandmont' *BSAHL* 87 (première livraison 1958) 25.

8. M.H. Vicaire, *Histoire de Saint-Dominique*, 2 (Paris: Cerf, 1982) pp 215–19.

9. Jacques de Vitry, *Histoire Occidentale*, eh. XIX; cit. Lev, pp. 150–53.

10. Guiot de Provins, 'La Bible'; J. Orr, *Les oeuvres de Guiot de Provins* (Manchester: University Press, 1915) pp xi–xvi.

11. Rev. Père J. Fouquet OMI and Frère Philippe-Étienne, *Histoire de L'Ordre de Grandmont* (Chambray: 1985) p. 39.

12. G. Cope, 'Colours Liturgical', *A Dictionary of Liturgy and Worship* ed. J.G. Davies (London: SCM, 1972) pp.139–40

13. Bull no. 13; PL 202: 1416.

14. Bec (note 6) pp. 306–07. A copy of the original text of these articles was made at Grandmont circa 1300 and is contained in the Charleville MS No. 54., f. 32, cap. LII.

15. Orr (note 10) p. xv.

16. Fouquet (note 11) p. 42.

17. Gérard Ithier, *De revelatione*; PL 204: 1050.

18. RB 62: 2–4.

19. M.C. Dereine, 'L'obituaire primitif de l'Ordre de Grandmont', *BSAHL* (troisième livraison 1960) 325–32.

IV

THE 'MIRROR OF GRANDMONT'

Grandmontine Life and Custom in the Late Twelfth Century

EXPANSION AND RECRUITMENT

DESPITE THE CRISIS WHICH DISRUPTED life at Grandmont, the two decades which marked the close of the twelfth century were years of outstanding achievement especially as regards the continuing growth and expansion of the Order. Numerous new cells were founded within the period normally associated with unmitigated strife. The troubles which were responsible for a considerable exodus of novices from the mother house must also have discouraged recruits, so that the founding of new cells at such a time can only have been possible because they did not require large communities to people them.

Each cell would have housed an average of thirteen, but this number was at times surpassed and at others considerably reduced. An ideally sized community consisted of a *curiosus* and twelve additional brothers, symbolic of Christ and the apostles. Dieudonné Rey has estimated the size of the communities by the number of dorter windows.[1] Whilst this varies from cell to cell, the actual areas assigned to sleeping quarters differ little and in general would accommodate thirteen. Quite early in the history of the Order these dorters were partitioned by wainscotting or some other means into separate cubicles each measuring approximately 3.3 by 2.7 metres. This was all that remained of the hermit's individual hut within a laura and was not, as has been suggested, a luxury. The separate stone vaulted rooms, which are always found at the far end of the dorter against the wall of the church, remain a subject for controversy. They may have served as night oratories or infirmaries, even a combination of both. The suggestion by some authors that they represented the superior's quarters is most unlikely as superiors in any conventional sense did not exist before Pope Innocent III instituted the office of *corrector* in 1216, while these rooms formed part of the standard architectural plan long before this date.

Unfortunately we can obtain little idea of actual cell populations simply from looking at the space available, and figures, even where they are available, are widely dispersed both as regards time and area. The confirmation charter given to the monks of Craswall in Herefordshire by the founder, Walter de Lacy,[2] is helpful in this respect. It informs us that the cell was founded for 'tribus fratribus clericis et decem fratribus capellanis'. The latter adjective is confusing for it would seem to indicate 'choir monks'. We can safely assume, however, that the 'tribus clericis' designates choir monks while the 'fratribus capellanis' are *convers*. It is inconceivable that the *clercs* should have outnumbered the *convers* by more than three to one. The description 'capellanis' can be explained by the Grandmontine Constitution, which unlike that of the Cistercians, expected the *convers* to attend and to the best of their ability participate in the Divine Office. Should their work prevent them taking part, they were instructed to recite a number of Pater Nosters by way of dispensation.[3]

The first known grandmontine census was taken in 1295, a hundred years after the priorate of Gérard Ithier and the year when numbers inhabiting the cells were reduced for the first time. Even then, the total figure, 886, quoted in the Annals, takes no account of the *convers* who, we are told, were still numerous.[4] At this time the average number of *clercs* per cell was around five. Towards the close of the twelfth century and well into the thirteenth, the *convers* still far outnumbered the *clercs*. In the matter of their recruitment it is difficult to ascertain to what extent humility, on the one hand, and illiteracy and ignorance of Latin, on the other, played a part. The main attraction of the grandmontine lay-brotherhood was that it permitted the individual to perform the tasks best suited to his capabilities, and yet afforded him an active role in the religious life of the community. The freedom to participate to whatever extent he was able in the recitation of the offices was a privilege denied to this class of monk in other Orders. We can see the equality which amazed various contemporaries in the appealing image of grandmontine life reflected in Prior Ithier's 'Mirror of Grandmont':

> Behold how good and pleasant it is that the brethren live together. That their way of life is such that both clercs and convers always share the same oratory, cloister, chapter house, refectory and dorter. Thus a conver is equal to a clerc and there is never any distinction between them except, as has been stated elsewhere, regarding the tonsure and the style of beards.'[5]

Prior Gérard Ithier

This mild, unassuming man proved to be one of the few outstanding scholars in an Order which as a general rule did not promote or encourage learning. His *De Institutione novitorium* is a treatise on obedience which found its way into a large number of medieval libraries and was long thought to be cistercian in origin.[6] It is, however, his *Speculum Grandimontis* which stands out as one of the few clear, first-hand, and unbiased accounts of twelfth-century monastic life and conditions. It represents the chief primary source for any study of the Order of Grandmont. Rose Graham has suggested that Gerald of Wales may well have seen this work before describing the Grandmontines in his own *Speculum ecclesiae*.[7] The 'Mirror' of Gérard Ithier consists of a vast two-volumned manuscript containing the *Vita A* of St Stephen in forty-six chapters together with the additional sixteen chapters of *Vita B*. There follows a ninety-two stanza poem honouring the saint, a compendium of his miracles, an account of his canonisaton, two treatises of sixteen and ninety seven chapters respectively, and finally, the *Liber Sententiarum, vel Liber de Doctrina*, the 'Book of Thoughts' of St Stephen.

Down-to-earth, humble, tactful,and eloquent, these are just a few of the qualities which distinguished the man who in 1188 shouldered the unenviable task of leading the Order back to some semblance of normality. That Gérard Ithier had a keen awareness of human frailty is apparent from the manner in which he succeeded, albeit temporarily, in reconciling both parties within the dispute. He showed himself capable of combining the intellect of the educated priest with the genuine humility which the Rule required of the lay brethren. Attitudes to authority in the heavily class-orientated system of his day recognised only a clear-cut master/servant relationship and this had proved largely responsible for the abuse of power by the *convers*. By contrast, Gérard wielded his authority with the skill and gentle understanding which makes for enlightened and tolerant leadership. He was inspired by the ideal of equality so dear to Stephen of Muret, and in attempting to implement such radical teaching within a fully fledged religious order he was centuries ahead of his time. It was most likely his concern to restore the mother house to normality and its occupants to a state of peaceful coexistence which lay behind his decision to promote the cause for canonisation of the founder. This project would have had two major aims: distracting the brethren from their personal animosities; and at the same time encouraging them to renew their pride in the Order and emulate its saintly founder. After all, the raison d'ętre of the mother house was to create a favourable environment for the aspiring hermit to turn his back on the world and, in the words of Stephen, *Soli Deo adhaerere*.

Shortly after assuming office, Prior Gérard put his plan into action and was rewarded in March 1189, when Pope Clement III ordered the name of St Stephen of Muret to be inscribed in the Roman Calendar. The following August, a splendid ceremony was held at Grandmont in the presence of the papal legate, Cardinal Jean de St Marc, and numerous high-ranking churchmen and nobles. Following a solemn high Mass, the relics of the saint were carried in procession around the cloister and reinterred in a magnificent shrine above the high altar itself. Following the suppression of the Order in 1772, the bishop of Limoges was granted the mother house along with all its possessions and he caused the church treasures to be distributed among the parishes of his diocese. The shrine of St Stephen was given to the church at Razès, but was destroyed during the Revolution which broke out a few years later. The sixteenth-century annalist, Pardoux de la Garde, tells us that it was of copper gilt, enamelled, and ornamented with semi-precious stones and crystals.[8] Six further relic chests were arranged on either side of St Stephen. Of these only one has survived, but it is of particular interest because its form is said to represent the second church of Grandmont, which was replaced by Grandmont III in the eighteenth century. It is preserved in the parish church of the town of Ambazac just a few miles from Grandmont.

The Cluny Panel

In addition to the relic chests, the high altar at Grandmont was ornamented with a series of panels of Limoges enamel depicting scenes from the life of St Stephen together with companion scenes from the life of Christ. Only two survived the Revolution: 'St Stephen conversing with Hugues Lacerta' and an 'Adoration of the Magi'. They are both in the Cluny Museum at Paris. The panel portraying St Stephen is the most outstanding relic of the Order of

Grandmont as well as providing valuable historical evidence. In fact, it illustrates three distinct aspects of this very unusual order of hermit monks: their spirituality, organisation, and unique style of architecture.

The setting of the panel is distinctly architectural: St Stephen and Hugues Lacerta are framed in a romanesque doorway, the rounded arch of which rests on the decorated capitals of a pair of columns. It is typical of the entry into any grandmontine church. Over the arch are five domes, four of which cap an equal number of rounded structures which in turn are balanced, somewhat precariously, on the slated roofs of four corresponding structures. The centre dome is larger than the others and surmounts a rectangular building of which a side elevation with its range of five windows is alone visible. The remaining structures are rounded and six of them each have three apertures. There can be little doubt that they are intended to represent the typical rounded apses which enclosed the sanctuaries of grandmontine churches and always had three windows. The rectangular building in the centre stands out as the church of the mother house, the only one which did not conform to the rigid architectural rules which applied to the building of the daughter houses. We know that the church of Grandmont was uncharacteristic because instead of having just four windows—three in the apse and the fourth in the centre of the west wall—it had windows ranged along the side walls. The failure of the church of Grandmont to conform to general grandmontine custom is attributable to its having been originally intended to house the tomb of King Henry II. The way in which the apses encircling the mother house seem to be piled one on top of the other could be part and parcel of a discreet grandmontine attempt to publicise their Order. Madame Geneviève Souchal has dated these panels to the last quarter of the twelfth century, and there can be little doubt that they were actually placed in position in time for the grand ceremony which marked the canonisation of St Stephen in 1189.[9] By this date approximately one hundred fifty grandmontine cells had been founded, quite a remarkable achievement for a religious Order which had been in existence for less than a century. Given that Gérard Ithier was just at this time intent on restoring the image of the Order, what better way was there of distracting attention from the recent failures than by highlighting successes? Hence, the Founder is framed in the architecture of his Order, while the daughter cells mushrooming around Grandmont symbolise the wide and successful diffusion of his ideals between his death in 1124 and canonisation in 1189.

St Stephen of Muret used to be identified as the figure on the left wearing the tunic and short-hooded cloak of a hermit. The companion figure in the chasuble was said to be St Nicholas, although there is no good reason why Stephen should be portrayed conversing with the saint of Lycia save for the spurious account of the pilgrimage to his shrine at Bari in the *Vita A*.[10] The false identification of the figures was the result of an erroneous interpretation of the inscription engraved on the panel just beneath the arch and which can be read as:

+NIGOLASERT: PARLAAMNE TEVEDEMVRET

In modern French, 'Nicholas était parlant au seigneur Eteve de Muret'. This was the interpretation of E. Rupin, who noted that in the patois of the Limousin EN indicates *dominus*.[11] It was also accepted by the english historian Rose Graham who gives it in her article 'The Order of Grandmont and its Houses in England'.[12] Since the publication of this work in 1926, Madame Souchal has provided both linguistic and grammatical evidence to show that the inscription actually reads:

N'IGO LASERT : PARLA AM N'ETEVE DE MURET

'le seigneur Hugo Lasert parle avec le seigneur Etienne de Muret'.(The Seigneur Hugo Lasert speaks with the Seigneur Stephen of Muret) In the first instance Madame Souchal points out that ERT in the Langue d'Oc has never been used to express *est* or *était*—forms of the verb *être*—and that it is even less likely that the Latin *erat* would figure in a sentence in the vernacular. Even if it did, it is inconceivable for it to be followed by a second verb PARLA, and in the present indicative. While it could be argued that PARLA was intended as an alternative of the french verbal form, *est parlant*, this is a comparatively recent linguistic development and never employed in the Limousin dialect. Finally, Madame Souchal notes that it is not possible to read the name 'Nicholas' in the inscription at all because the third letter is not a 'C' but a 'G'. A secondary problem concerns the name Hugues or UGO commencing with an *I* rather than a *U*, but this Madame Souchal attributes to an orthographical error of the sort which she has found to be common enough among the illiterate twelfth-century enamellers of the Limousin. LASERT is without doubt the vernacular form of a name normally expressed in its Latin form Lacerta, simply because its bearer is known to us only through Latin texts.[13]

A further factor which contributed to the false identification of the characters in the Cluny panel has to do with costume. Whilst Hugues wears what must represent the original humble habit of the Order, a tunic and lightly indicated belted scapular beneath the short, hooded cloak, Stephen is resplendent in a chasuble, a vestment worn only by officiating priests. As Stephen, according to tradition, was only in deacon's orders, he has no right whatsoever to this attire. Once again Madame Souchal has been able to cast light on the problem. She recalls an anecdote found in the early biographies of Stephen. The night following his death he appeared in a vision to a friend of his, a certain canon, who seems to have expressed less surprise at the ghostly apparition of his friend than at the uncharacteristically splendid garment in which he was clad. 'This is the symbol of the roman pontiff which Christ himself has conferred on me', replied Stephen by way of explanation.[14] Gérard Ithier immortalised this anecdote in his own writings and it seems reasonable to suppose that the artist entrusted with the execution of the panel derived from it his inspiration for a stylised Stephen in glory.

Somewhat more appropriate than the simple title, St Stephen conversing with Hugues Lacerta might be St Stephen entrusting the Rule to his disciple Hugues. That the panel is illustrating a posthumous event is clear from Stephen's halo, and what else might the book clasped in his right hand contain but the Rule of the Order based on his own 'Thoughts'. We know that these were recalled and committed to writing by the first fathers, notably Hugues himself. Something of the fundamentalist spirituality of the Grandmontines can be associated with this magnificent volume. The vivid scarlet binding and golden clasps would seem more appropriate for a Bible than for the text of a rule for simple hermit monks who placed so great an emphasis on their vow of poverty that even church vessels were required to be of non-precious metal. But then, as has already been noted, the Rule of Grandmont is not a practical manual of directives for life in common. It is rather a series of spiritual guidelines based on the apostolic life of Christ, and nearly a third of it is direct quotation from the Gospel. The luxurious binding is appropriate therefore, for it encloses Holy Writ.

Something of the organisational pattern of the Order of Grandmont also becomes apparent through the manner in which the figures on the panel are portrayed. This defies the medieval artistic convention which expected the relative size of a figure to indicate his status within a complicated hierarchical class structure of ecclesiastics, nobles, and commoners. St Benedict and St Bernard, for example, are invariably drawn to a larger scale than the monks to whom they are preaching. But here, we have Hugues Lacerta, a lay brother, a lowly creature in clerical eyes, drawn to the same scale and shoulder to shoulder with a choir monk. Not just any choir monk either but the founding father and, as is clear from the nimbus, a canonised saint.

Could Gérard Ithier have exercised any personal influence over the artist's treatment of his subject? The gentle prior's main ambition that *clercs* and *convers* should live harmoniously together is well known from the *Speculum*. What better way of exhorting the brethren to be more understanding and tolerant than by placing before them this poignant reminder of the perfect unity and harmony which existed between their founder and the lay brother Hugues? As part of the general high altar ensemble, the panel would be permanently before the eyes of the community, and hopefully encourage them to contemplate its message.

Grandmont as a Centre for Pilgrimage

By the close of the twelfth century, it was not only the relics of the sainted Stephen which were attracting pilgrims by the score to Grandmont. The priory church was also renowned for a portion of the True Cross brought to the monks by Bernard, Bishop of Lydda, in 1174. This priceless relic was an offering from King Amaury I of Jerusalem, uncle to Henry II of England.

There is an interesting account in the Annals which concerns another important acquisition by the Grandmontines of some particularly highly prized relics from the city of Cologne.[15] In 1106, workmen digging near the city walls uncovered an extraordinarily large number of female skeletons. They were said to be those of St Ursula and her eleven thousand companions who, according to legend, were massacred by the Huns on their return from a pilgrimage to Rome. The earliest reference to St Ursula accords her just eleven companions, so just how and when this was multiplied by a thousand is a matter for speculation. The bare facts reveal only that at some early date a number of young women were massacred at Cologne, and the twelfth-century excavation gave rise to pious beliefs that the bodies were those of the ursuline martyrs.

The Grandmontines became directly involved in this history in 1181 when the abbot of Siegburg and Canon

Guoderan of Bonn called at Grandmont on their return from a pilgrimage to Rocamadour. They were warmly welcomed by the prior who then asked the abbot if he would use his influence with the archbishop of Cologne to obtain the body of one of the martyrs. The abbot willingly agreed and shortly after his departure two priests with two attendant *convers*, guided by the canon, followed him to Cologne. Their journey is vividly described in a contemporary source.[16] The weather was absolutely foul and they had to contend with snow, hail,and torrential rain. Arriving at Cologne on Palm Sunday, 28 March, they were welcomed at the abbot's house where they marvelled at the comforts and the quality and abundance of food. The following morning they received the body of St Albina as well as that of a second unnamed virgin. Just how the monks had ascertained the name of one of the women is not known. The brothers were invited by the abbot to remain throughout Holy Week but accepted instead Canon Gouderan's invitation to accompany him to Bonn. They spent a night in the canon's house and visited a monastery of nuns, after which they returned to Cologne. This time they called on Phillip, the archbishop, and he gave them an introduction to the abbey of St Martin. Their stay was extended to include visits to other monasteries and churches including St Maria in Gradibus and St Gereon. Everywhere they went they accumulated further relics, until on the Tuesday after Easter they started for home with the bodies of no less than seven ursuline martyrs, plus some male bones said to belong to soldiers of the Theban Legion. This was the legendary third-century legion of roman christian soldiers who mutinied at Agaunum (St Maurice en Valais) in Switzerland, because they were required to participate in pagan sacrifices. When the grandmontine travellers eventually arrived back at Limoges bearing their sacred cargo, they were met by the bishop and prior who headed a solemn procession to the church, where the relics were installed in the magnificent chests which formed the superstructure of the high altar.

We cannot be certain whether portions of these relics were distributed among the daughter houses, though it does seem to have been a distinct possibility. The Roman Catholic Church has always required relics to be inserted into altars when they are consecrated. It may be significant that in the course of excavations carried out in the early years of this century at Craswell Priory in Herefordshire, a lead casket containing a female forearm and hand was uncovered close to the altar.[17] It is now in the Hereford City Museum.

News of these exceptionally dramatic relics soon spread abroad, with the result that the priory of Grandmont developed into a celebrated centre for pilgrims travelling to and from the more famous shrines of Rocamadour and Santiago de Compostella. The splendid church, with magnificent gilt and gem-encrusted chests and reliquaries illuminated by myriad lamps and candles cannot, therefore, be regarded as being in any way typical of the Order of Grandmont. Both architecturally and aesthetically, it had nothing in common with the plain, single-aisled churches which served the daughter houses. It is to these widely dispersed little cells that we must turn in order to view the true image of the grandmontine way of life reflected in the 'Mirror' of Gérard Ithier.

Life in the Grandmontine Cells

The daughter houses of the Order of Grandmont can by no means have been equally affected by the troubles which shook the mother house. Indeed, it is reasonable to assume that the inspiration of St Stephen lingered within many of them throughout the twelfth and well into the thirteenth century. Architectural evidence reveals that no major building or embellishment work was effected at this time, and the almost total lack of period documentation for the daughter houses is indicative of their obscurity and unimportance, very much in keeping with the spirit of the Order. Grandmontine cells were little more than small holdings whose occupants were expected to lead a life of extreme asceticism. The Rule anticipates franciscan teaching in its exhortation to the brethren: 'Let poverty itself be your wealth and your treasure'.[18] Indeed, the brethren were often in such dire straits that they did not know where their next meal was coming from.

The Grandmontines were only permitted to maintain lands sufficient for their own needs, and even if they managed to produce a surplus there was no question of their disposing of it on the open market. Originally they were not permitted to keep any animals, certainly not to maintain herds: 'Dedicate to the service of God alone the solicitude you would employ in buying, breeding and selling', enjoins the Rule.[19] This ultra-severe ruling must have been waived comparatively soon, however, for Gerald of Wales noted in his 'Mirror of the Church':

> No beast of the female sex is allowed within the bounds of Grandmont but on account of their poverty the brethren have a dispensation to keep cattle and sheep and animals in their other houses.[20]

Gerald may have had the grange of Coudier, just a few miles from Grandmont, in mind. This establishment was built on lands donated to the mother house in 1178 by the abbey of Solignac. From the living quarters, which included a small eastern facing oratory with the standard 'triplet', we may deduce that it was intended to house a permanent group of *convers* engaged in farming for the benefit of the mother house. Two similar but more distant establishments also existed: Balezis in the Limousin: and Montmorillon in Poitou. Sections of the latter remain incorporated in what is today a large town house. There is evidence that it was originally surrounded by vineyards and specialised in the production of wines for the mother house.

While in the course of the thirteenth century the severe dictates of the Rule were gradually relaxed, still the Grandmontines never came to be associated with large scale farming ventures and certainly not on any commercial basis. They never made the wilderness bloom in the manner of their cistercian contemporaries. By the 1220s, we find them the recipients of gifts of land often widely dispersed but they showed little managerial capability and on the whole derived negligible benefits from such possessions. This is clearly shown in the case of the cell of Alberbury in Shropshire. In the 1220s the founder, Fulk FitzWarine, granted the brethren considerable gifts of land and other endowments, including his Leicestershire manor of Whadborough. Other gifts followed, but nevertheless the entire history of the cell reveals continual mismanagement and a total inability to make ends meet. In 1344, when Edward III ordered the seizure of the house as an 'alien' priory, it was reported that lands and rents together were worth only £2 ls 2d yearly. The parish church which represented the main source of income brought in 20 marks annually and stock, £9 6s 'which altogether did not suffice for the maintenance of the prior and six brethren'.[21] The other two English houses, Craswell in Herefordshire, and Grosmont, Yorkshire, fared little better.

Deprived as they were initially of the usual revenues relied on by monks for their support, the Grandmontines were forced to depend entirely upon the resources present within the enclosure. Forbidden by their Rule to improve the soil in any way other than to provide for the bare necessities of the penitential life, they were reduced to an implicit reliance on divine providence, which meant that they were in fact almost totally dependent on the alms they received from visitors. When all else failed they were instructed to make their needs known to the bishop in whose diocese the cell was situated. If he would not agree to help them, then, and only after two entire days of fasting, two of the brothers, the most advanced in the religious life, were sent out from the monastery to beg from door to door like any other beggars.[22]

The extent to which the brothers built or participated in the building of the cells has not been satisfactorily determined. Although the Rule itself forbids the employment of secular workers, the Custumal which supplemented it sometime between the years 1170–5, takes lay assistance for granted when it permits the brethren to allow outside workers to live in their hospice until such a time as the building is complete. It also outlines a procedure for brothers compelled to absent themselves from office for reasons of work:

> When the bell sounds . . . If it should happen that they are working in the company of lay persons, then they are to remove themselves to a discreet distance and disregarding the genuflexions, they should recite the said prayers.

A further instruction concerning dress is of particular interest:

> When the brothers find it necessary to work in company with lay persons, they are on no account to remove their scapulars and they are to keep themselves apart save when the work in hand be concerned with carpentry or stone masonry.[23]

The Grandmontines did not observe a strict rule of silence; in fact their Rule appears somewhat uncharacteristically lenient in dealing with this matter, confining itself mainly to a homily on the evils of idle chatter. It insists however, that silence be maintained at prescribed times and in appointed places: church, cloister, refectory, and dormitory. Further than this, it avoids any hard and fast ruling and accepts that even during the so called 'great silence' (after Compline until close of morning chapter) there will be occasions when it may be absolutely necessary to speak. Outside witnesses, including Nigel Wireker, Guiot de Provins, and Jacques de Vitry, are unanimous that the Grandmontines were relatively liberal in their attitude to silence. Additionally, they did not at the outset make use of a sign language as did the Cluniacs and Cistercians although such a system was developed in the thirteenth century. Guarded speech when necessary for purposes of work was allowed by Article 8 of the Custumal.[24]

Both the 'Book of Thoughts' and the Rule speak continually of the Grandmontines' vocation as life in the 'desert'. Clearly the ideal was that once a brother had made his religious profession within the 'desert', there should be no further prospect of returning to the world. Ideals are never easily reconciled with reality and so both the Rule and Custumal make provision for the occasions when brothers were forced by necessity to travel and mix with lay persons, insisting nevertheless, that such expeditions be kept to an absolute minimum. Brothers might be required to leave their cells for several reasons. (1) They might attend the annual General Chapter held at the mother house on the feast of St John the Baptist. (2) Additionally, brothers might of their own free will travel in order to seek the direct advice of their spiritual father, the pastor at Grandmont, although the Custumal makes it quite clear that any such visits were not to be treated as opportunities for roaming round the countryside and they were to come and go by the most direct route. (3) The *convers* were obviously permitted to leave their cells to attend to business matters such as the buying or selling of provisions but any such assignments were to be carried out as privately and discreetly as possible and under no circumstances might they involve the brethren in attending public auctions or fairs. Wherever possible, the patrons of Grandmontine houses appointed a trusted man to transact business on behalf of the community. (4) Again, brothers might be sent out to make representation to the bishop of the diocese, and in extreme cases of hardship onto the local highways and byways to beg. Pilgrimages were specifically banned by the Rule so that the Cologne expedition referred to earlier was a very unusual occurrence indeed.

Priests were accepted into the Order from the start, but it was late in the twelfth century before the Grandmontines began submitting their own candidates for ordination as a matter of routine. The priests were not allowed to minister to outsiders even if they were dying relatives. 'Let the dead bury the dead' is the Rule's pronouncement on this subject, harsh, but it nevertheless echoes the Gospel. However, it softens a little to allow a grandmontine priest to attend a dying person within the locality if, and only if, there be no secular priest available. Neither were the brothers permitted to attend the poor and infirm within the neighbourhood, because, as the Rule points out, in the Gospel Mary made no attempt to help Martha. There was absolutely no question of brothers leaving their cells to preach. They were expected to live in accordance with the teaching of Pope Gregory the Great who said that 'a good life is preaching by example'. Again, it was not considered to be in any way advantageous to go out in order to hear others preaching, however celebrated and edifying they might be. Once again the Rule invokes a gospel precedent: John the Baptist did not leave the desert even to listen to Christ himself.

The Grandmontines did not, however, sever all connection with outsiders. The most beautiful and appealing chapter in the Rule concerns itself with the welcome and hospitality which was to be afforded to guests. The brothers were expected always to show a pleasant countenance to visitors who might seek them out in the 'desert' and treat them as generously as they would God himself.

Extra courtesy and respect was always to be shown towards religious callers, priests and brothers from other Orders. The poor in particular were to be made very welcome and if any among them should wish to make a modest offering, the brethren were instructed to accept it graciously and give their full attention to the conversation of such people by way of thanking them. Their familiar title of 'Bonshommes' seems to have been wholly justified, for their kindly welcome and exceptional generosity towards the poor is praised in several contemporary accounts.[25]

Priests and Liturgy

Until 1216 each cell was managed by an official widely referred to as the *curiosus*. Although the duties of these officials were essentially of a temporal and domestic nature, the articles which emerged from the Council of Vincennes make it clear that they had assumed a certain degree of religious authority, and were apparently discharging duties which in the houses of other religious orders would have been reserved to the abbot or prior. The fact that the grandmontine lay brothers actually had a voice in daily chapter meetings would have astonished any Cluniac or Cistercian contemporary, but it seems that certain *curiosi* had gone even further and made themselves responsible for the actual conduct of meetings. The Articles further indicate that laybrothers were also assuming responsibility for liturgical matters. Although Innocent III declared as early as 1216, that each cell was to be managed by a priest with the title of *corrector*, it was not until 1317 that superiors in the normal sense were introduced into the Order. At this juncture many of the correctors were upgraded to priors, while the prior of Grandmont was elevated to the rank of abbot.

The Rule implies that the prior of Grandmont, whom it terms *pastor* was invariably a priest, but not before the emergence of the Custumal is any definite provision made for *clercs* in holy orders, and this tells us only that when a brother has received the order of the priesthood he must sing his first mass at Grandmont unless the prior for some reason instructed otherwise.[26]

It is possible that in the twelfth century many of the cells were not staffed with priests, for the Custumal includes an odd rider: to the instruction that the brethren are not to permit outsiders to be present at their offices:

> Secular clerks, provided they be of mature years and suitably dressed, may be introduced for the purpose of celebrating the Divine Office, if there are no brothers present who are capable of performing it.[27]

This really is an extraordinary direction. Not only does it provoke thoughts as to what may have constituted the medieval equivalent of priests exercising a preference for jeans rather than clerical grey, it also suggests that some of the cells lacked not just priests but enough sufficiently literate brothers to recite the offices. Given that the average size of a twelfth-century community was thirteen, of whom only about a third were *clercs*, the annual General Chapter held each year at Grandmont would have necessitated a fairly lengthy period of absence for at least one of the *clercs*. If he also happened to be the only priest there could be no eucharistic worship in the cell pending his return.

The term *clercs* applied to the grandmontine choir monks has led to some confusion in that scholars have automatically assumed that they were, without exception, priests. It is necessary to take into account, therefore, that throughout the Middle Ages a clerk was quite simply any administrator capable of wielding a pen. *Clerici* were instituted during the pontificate of Gregory the Great (590–604) to act as secretarial and administrative assistants to the bishops, and very few of them rose above the status conferred by minor orders. Margaret Deanesly has pointed out that the parish 'clerk' of the Middle Ages was no more nor less than this seventh-century *familia* of episcopal clergy reduced to a minimum.[28]

The incidence of grandmontine ordinations rose considerably in the course of the thirteenth century, and during the fourteenth some of the cells which had been upgraded to priories annexed small exterior chapels to their churches. Seemingly, they were needed for the extra household priests requiring to celebrate Masses. Unlike the Cistercians and Cluniacs, whose churches were invariably constructed to a cruciform plan with transepts which could be divided into several Mass chapels, single-aisled grandmontine churches could not accommodate altars in this way. A further and somewhat simpler solution to the problem was the provision of a secondary altar at the base of the nave. In several of the surviving churches there is a piscina fashioned in the side of the wall of the nave which indicates that an altar once stood in this position.

The division of the monastic day into periods allocated to the recitation of the offices, private prayer, and work was similar to other religious houses of the period although there were two essential differences. In the first place the lay brothers were able to take part in the celebration of the offices in choir whenever their schedule of work permitted. The second difference concerns the actual performance of the liturgy within the cells. The directives given in the Rule are meagre in this respect, observing only that the brothers should conduct the various rituals in accordance with normal monastic customs and usages. Of one thing we can be certain, the celebration of the liturgy within a grandmontine cell would have occupied far less of the brothers' waking hours than it did in other religious orders notably, among the Cluniacs who were notorious for their long, elaborate rites. A solemn High Mass with all its attendant ceremonial did not constitute the climax of the grandmontine day as it did elsewhere and all non-essential ritual was omitted from the offices. the Grandmontines did substitute a certain amount of extra community worship, such as the thrice daily visit to the cemetery for the recitation of the Office of the Dead, still there must have been plenty of time remaining for private devotions and meditation by the *clercs* and work for the *convers*.

According to Dom Lévesque, the seventeenth-century compiler of the Annals, the medieval office for the feast of St Stephen was composed before 1200 by an english monk Arnold of Goth. The Proper of the Mass of St Stephen is traditionally said to have been inserted in the *Ordo* of Limoges by Bishop Aymerie de Serres, following its adoption on 30 August 1189, at the first ceremony performed at Grandmont to honour the newly canonised saint. This was never eliminated from the rites of the diocese, although the medieval office was abandoned in 1621 in accordance with the new liturgical directives agreed at the Council of Trent. The General Chapter of the Order devised a new office of St Stephen when it met in 1643. A very beautiful 'Litany of St Stephen' which has been attributed to the reforming priest Dom Charles Frémon also dates from this time.

By the close of the twelfth century, three separate days of the year had been declared feasts in honour of St Stephen: the 'Transitus or passing of the Saint on 8 February, the Translation commemorating the transfer of his body on 23 June 1167; and the Revelation which marked his canonisation on 30 August. Other major grandmontine feast-days included the Virgins of Cologne, and the feasts of St John the Baptist and St Martial, the third century bishop and patron of the city of Limoges.

Clothing

The Rule of Grandmont makes no mention of attire, confining itself to the method of distributing all necessities by the *curiosus*. The Custumal remedies this deficiency by outlining the regulation habit. Something in the tone of this document suggests that when it emerged some of the brothers were not conforming to the regulation habit and, additionally, were adopting superior quality materials which were not in keeping with the ideal of poverty expressed by the Order. Why else should the opening paragraphs warn against all form of luxury in regard to dress and recall the camel hair worn by the patron of hermits, John the Baptist? Apparently the brothers sometimes received presents of cloth because they were told to exchange for more common stuff any material which was too rich for the clothing of those dedicated to a life of poverty and penitence. Some brothers appear to have gone to the other extreme, for the Custumal warns against wearing torn clothing, and in the same paragraph, garments made of ox-hide, except as night attire. There is no particular instruction given about style, although several references to the scapular indicate that the typical grandmontine habit consisted of a plain tunic and broad scapular. Round hoods were permitted so long as they were of the same cheap cloth as the remainder of the clothing and were worn only in cases of necessity. Belts were worn, but a brother was to possess only one, which had to be plain; buckles were expressly forbidden. Woollen mittens were allowed by the Custumal but not gloves except for work purposes. The 'Mirror' of Gérard Ithier describes the clothing thus:

> They wear sackcloth next to the skin, that is clothing made of very coarse flax or hemp, and over that a brown tunic, a scapular or short cloak with a round hood, woollen gaiters and leather shoes.[29]

The 'brown' tunic would not have been brown in any modern sense. Before the advent of synthetic dyes, there was no product that produced brown by itself, and the common way of manufacturing it was to blend the juice of the madder plant with varying proportions of yellow shaded with reddish pigments obtained from peach and other similar woods.[30] The submission of cloth to such a complicated dyeing process is firmly ruled out by the instruction in the Custumal that cloth be: *sine tinctura*. Grandmontine brown was in all probability akin to what later became known as 'Franciscan grey', which the French termed 'couleur de bure', the natural greyish brown sackcloth colour of rough homespun.

That the original cheap garments eventually yielded place to a more comfortable and costly variety is revealed in an ordinance of Pope Clement V (d. 1316). Here the brothers are not only forbidden to use dye to achieve a more becoming dark-shaded attire, but are also warned against the adoption of amply cut hoods to make the habit appear more graceful. From the same ordinance we also learn that some of the brothers had taken to wearing linen undergarments!

The Grandmontines' rejection of the cowl provides singular proof of the degree of austerity they originally practised. The cowl, the standard monastic garb worn in choir, has often been confused with a simple monk's hood. In fact, it is a long flowing choir robe which envelops the wearer like an individual tent and helps retain body heat. The practical Benedictines tempered austerity with common sense, realising that it provided an effective way of keeping tolerably warm in cold stone churches in winter. Even their stricter colleagues the Cistercians retained this garment which they must have considered not so much a luxury as a reasonable precaution against an untimely death from pneumonia. The Grandmontines stand out therefore as being the only group of medieval monastics to discard this effective way of keeping themselves warm in winter. Presumably it was their extreme notions of poverty; the cowl requires a great deal of cloth so cannot have been a cheap garment to produce. They therefore decided to wear linen surplices instead. In the seventeenth century these surplices formed part of the argument that the Grandmontines were canons regular rather than monks. Some later authors alternatively considered the surplice to be a late innovation synonymous with the decline in strict monastic standards. But Gérard Ithier wrote as early as the 1180s: 'in choir all wear surplices'. In fact, the adoption of this canonical style of choir dress by an order of hermit monks so early in their history, far from being illustrative of decadence, could be regarded as an additional penance, and a cheap way of covering work-soiled habits so as to be presentable in church.

Diet

Unlike the Cistercians, who permitted meat to be served to the sick within the confines of the infirmary, the Grandmontines had no dispensation. Perpetual abstinence was expected of the healthy and infirm alike. During Lent and from the feast of All Saints until Christmas, all were required to fast and the diet was wholly vegetarian. During the summer season, a second meal was permitted in the evening. The Custumal is specific regarding the choice and preparation of meals. Of the three foods—fish, eggs and cheese—which were permitted along with vegetables, only two could be offered at a time and were not allowed to be presented in different ways at one and the same meal. Until well into the thirteenth century, when at least one eyewitness account asserted that the food was rendered pleasantly palatable by the addition of spices, it must have been decidedly bland, for the Custumal expressly directs that: 'the manner and preparation of food shall not be spoiled by the addition of sauces'. As regards drink, the Custumal permits wine but only in diluted form and warns the brothers diligently to observe the Gospel precept which says: 'make sure that your hearts are not weighed down in inebriation and drunkeness'.[31] The use of additives in the form of colouring and spices, a common practice in the Middle Ages to improve the flavour and appearance of the drink, was only permissible for the Grandmontines as a way of supplementing the wine when shortage required.

In company with other religious orders, the, Grandmontines gradually modified the rigid dietary laws as the years passed until eventually restrictions disappeared altogether. In 1642, Dom Charles Frémon instituted an experimental primitive observance of the Rule at the priory of Epoisses near Dijon, and here the brethren returned to the practices which were current before the mitigations permitted by Pope Innocent IV in 1247. Severe fasting together with perpetual abstinence became once again the rule rather than the exception.

The Sick and Infirm

> The brother who is struck down by a sudden and severe illness will not be able to follow the community life and so he is to be placed in the infirmary. The *curiosus* of the monastery will then select one brother or more, if it be necessary, who are to attend upon the

> sick brother both day and night and they are to be the only ones who enter the sick room.[32]

There is no apartment in a grandmontine cell which can definitely be identified as the infirmary or sick room, though it is possible that the small room at the end of the dorter alongside the church was assigned for the purpose. The care of the sick as it is outlined in the Rule is geared more to preparing the poor unfortunate for death than to achieving a cure. Hence a room alongside the church and directly over the cemetery passage seems appropriate.

The harsh ruling that a sick brother is to be totally isolated from the remainder of the community the better to prepare himself for the approaching encounter with his Maker is explained thus:

> When, in effect, a brother has dwelt for a long while under religious discipline and throughout all this time has shunned the world with all his strength, when he finally becomes ill and is close to his end, it is then at the moment when his soul goes forth to receive its recompense that he has the need of greatest vigilance. They who are at the end of their earthly course must be like competitors in a race who redouble their efforts towards the finishing line, for to rest when they are close to the finish would mean that all their previous work had been in vain. It is also desirable that a sick disciple should not listen to worldly conversation which will encumber his spirit with futilities. And the more that intruders are reduced, the less the sick man will be subjected to listening to them.[33]

As we previously noted, the dietary regulations were not relaxed for the benefit of a sick brother but there is a strong element of compassion in the Rule when it states:

> If it should be that the monastery cannot provide something which is necessary to a sick brother, you are ordered to sell the church ornaments which are destined for the service of God rather than permit the

> sick to lack what is theirs by right. Is not the sick brother himself the tabernacle wherein God dwells? [34]

Dom Becquet has pointed out that this ruling surpasses even the benedictine Rule which is exceptionally solicitous in its provisions for the care of the sick.[35]

No specific instructions governing the death of a sick brother are laid down in the Rule. The community do not appear to have been summoned to witness his removal from bed to a layer of ashes on the floor as was customary among the Cistercians. The brethren were buried without exception in unmarked graves in a cemetery which was invariably located close to the east range and alongside the church apse.

With regard to the chronically sick, the aged, and the infirm, the Rule states simply that they are to be accorded all necessary services in a spirit of humility and solicitude. Periodic blood letting—phlebotomy, which was customary in medieval monasteries—does not appear to have been practised by the Grandmontines. The Rule expressly forbids the acceptance of lepers into the Order, but should a brother become infected after making his profession he could not be expelled. The cell of La Haye near Angers was provided with a leper hospital soon after its foundation in the 1180s and a further such establishment was provided at Bois Rahier near Tours. According to Robert S. Gottfried, one of the theories proposed by modern medical authorities to explain the decline in the numbers of victims of leprosy in the fourteenth century is an advancement in medical techniques at the time. The manifestation of the disease is akin to many common skin ailments and it is possible that many so-called lepers had been previously misdiagnosed.[36] The incidence of the disease among the twelfth-century Grandmontines must have been comparatively high if it warranted two lazar hospitals within the same region. One wonders therefore just how many of the unfortunate 'unclean' brothers banished to one or other of these houses were in reality afflicted by acne, scabies, or impetigo.

The Patrimony of St Stephen of Muret

The rules which ordered the lives of medieval religious were written mainly for coenobites and their lengthy and detailed directions were considered necessary for very large communities living in vast monastic complexes such as Cluny and Cîteaux. St Stephen, however, was the father and spiritual director of a limited family of contemplatives. His immediate successors, particularly Hugues Lacerta, continued restricting the numbers inhabiting any one cell and it was only when the mother house began increasing its community and extending its activities that problems ensued. Nevertheless, many of the widely dispersed communities which represented the extended family of St Stephen in the late twelfth century must have remained relatively unaffected by the disgraceful occurrences at Grandmont and continued cultivating the virtues of poverty, humility, and mutual obedience so dear to their founder. Why else should the Order have remained popular with such patrons as the Yorkshire heiress Joan Fossard who was responsible for the first english foundation in 1204?

It seems reasonable to suggest that communities conforming to the tradition of the Order were inspired less by the rigid formality of their Rule than by the spiritual teachings of the founder. These teachings were compiled by the first Fathers into the *Liber Sententiarum* and it would be inappropriate to conclude a discussion of grandmontine life and custom without at least a passing reference to this outstanding spiritual work which articulates the very essence of the grandmontine vocation.

The text provides the aspiring religious with the means for attaining their spiritual goal; total union with God. The Prologue makes it clear that the only way to God is through his divine Son. 'There is no rule but the Gospel.' It is Christ himself who is at the centre of all the discourses; his ideas, his actions and reactions but above all else, his sublime love for humankind permeates Stephen's own thoughts. The novice who is about to follow the Rule of the Gospel is told that he is entering into a partnership with Christ himself and he is warned that such a partnership has no hope of succeeding if it is all one sided:

> Here is the reason—more important than any other—why the upright person holds to the belief that God will make him a partner for eternity in his heavenly kingdom: because now, in this world, God has so humbled himself as to deign to dwell in his human creatures who are but earthen vessels. (VII. 2)

and again:

> Shall God give himself wholly to you? If that is what you want, then he is ready to do so, but only if you for your part, give yourself wholly to him. (XCIV)

Although Stephen was immediately concerned with the spiritual direction of a dedicated group of hermits, in treating of the divine Rule he never loses sight of the fact that its Author intended it not only for religious but for all humankind. Thus Stephen speaks of 'the monasticism of all believers' and is at pains to point out that Christ treats all his faithful people as religious, regardless of their state. In chapter 68, he even speaks of the 'breastplated monk' who sets out on a campaign with all the right intentions and manifests his desire to be first and foremost a soldier of Christ seeking only good and scorning evil. So long as he is prepared to 'render to Caesar that which is Caesar's and to God the things that are God's,' so long as his intention is to serve God wholeheartedly in all that he does, then he is truly a monk.

To those of God's people who are called to turn their backs on the world and follow the Rule of Christ to the letter within the confines of a monastery, Stephen issues a serious warning. While the greatest distinction is to be found in knowing God, yet the religious who dedicates his entire life to the achievement of this end is in graver danger than the average, sincere lay person. The sinner who is close to God sins more gravely than the offender who remains at a distance. A single, evil thought caused the metamorphosis of the brightest angel into the foulest fiend. The sin of Adam was all the greater because of his closeness to his Maker. In the first chapter of the 'Thoughts', where Stephen instructs his successors in what they are to say to would-be novices, he utters the chilling words: 'It is a hundred times more preferable to be damned in the world than in the monastery because the greater the fall, the greater the injury. If you fall into hell from here, you will be among the lowest of the damned.'

Neither was the intending novice left in any doubt as to the severity of the life awaiting him within the hermits' enclosure. The words of greeting which the *pastor* is to employ are lifted directly from Matthew 16:24 and must be the most disconcerting words Christ ever spoke: 'If any man will come after me, let him deny himself and take up his cross and follow me.' And, just in case the intending hermit should fail to grasp the full significance of Christ's invitation, the pastor is instructed to make it almost brutally graphic as follows:

> Brothers, gaze upon the cross; if you choose to dwell here you will be nailed to it. You will have to abandon your own self-will entirely and you will be deprived of every liberty; even the right to eat or fast, sleep or wake, will be taken from you. You will never see your family home again and if your parents visit you here, you must conceal your poverty from them. Are you capable of turning yourself into a lowly peasant and bearing loads of wood and dung? Are you prepared to become a humble servant and wait on all your brethren without distinction? You will be a prisoner in a stronghold from which there is no escape. You are free now to knock on the door of any other monastery where you will find fine buildings, delicate food according to the season, extensive lands, herds and

> possessions; here you will discover the cross alone, and poverty.

The key to the religious life of Grandmont is summed up by Stephen in the words: *soli Deo adhaerere*. Fundamentally, the aspiring religious must divest himself of every burden, free himself from every possible worldly interest and involvement the better 'to cling to God alone'. The extent of grandmontine poverty, which has been equalled only by that of the Franciscans, has already received considerable treatment in these pages. The justification for this life of poverty is expressed however, in some of the most beautiful of the 'Thoughts':

> If the Son of God, when he came down upon this earth, would have known of a better way to reach heaven than by a life of poverty, would he not have chosen that? Love your own poverty then, since Jesus himself chose the better part. (Epilogue).
>
> In his grace, God willed to share in the poverty and weakness of humanity—are we so proud that we will not share in God's wealth and glory? (XVII)

Those who would 'find joy in God alone' must be clear that this will involve the banishment of all worldly distractions and interests the better to achieve the state of perfect contemplation necessary for achieving this goal. There is some beautiful imagery to be found in Stephen's exhortation to his novices to practise the virtue of detachment:

> As wood which is retrieved from water will not burn brightly unless it be dried out, man cannot be warmed by the fire of the love of God so long as he is full of the humours of imperfection. Like waterlogged wood, he must first be dried out. (IX. 6)

Worldly detachment is the loosening of the bonds which bind the individual to the base path of human endeavour. Once freed from their restraint, he can begin to direct his steps towards the ultimate, blissful union with God.

It is indeed fortunate that the 'Book of Thoughts' of St Stephen survived the destruction of the Order of Grandmont, for they contain a wealth of spiritual riches which are as fresh today as when they were first committed to writing by the Fathers of Grandmont. Adrian Baillet, an eighteenth-century translator, said of them: 'They are the effusions of a heart overflowing with God' and certainly it is in these 'Thoughts' that we find the reflection of that spiritual countenance which inspired generations of Grandmontines.

NOTES

1. D. Rey,' Le Prieuré de Comberoumal en Lévézou' *Études d'archaeologie grandmontaise* (Rodez: 1925).

2. Muniments of Christ's College, Cambridge, God's House Drawer C.

3. 'L'Institution: premier coutumier de l'Ordre de Grandmont', article 7; ed. Bec, *RevM* 46 (1956) 18.

4. Lev, p. 242: 'non computatio forte conversis quorum adhucingens erat numerus'.

5. Gérard Ithier, *De revelatione*; PL 204:1050.

6. J-B. Hauréau, 'Sur quelques écrivains de l'Ordre de Grandmont', *Notices et extraits des manuscripts de la Bibliothéque Nationale*, 24, part 2 (1876) 247–67

7. Rose Graham, *English Ecclesiastical Studies* (London: SPCK, 1929) p. 214.

8. Pardoux de la Garde, 'Les Antiquités de Grandmont', cited in L. Guibert, 'Destruction de L'Ordre et de L'Abbaye de Grandmont', BSAHL 25 (1877) Appendix J, pp. 273–80.

9. Geneviéve Francois-Souchal, 'Les Emaux de Grandmont au XII Siéle', *Bulletin Monumental* 121 (1963–64) 41–64.

10. 'Vita Venerabilis Viri Stephani Muretensis', Cap. III; Bec SOG, p. 106.

11. M. E. Rupin, *L'Oeuvre de Limoges* (Paris: 1890) p. 97 note 1.

12. See above, note 7, pp. 218–19.

13. See above, note 9, pp 352–53.

14. Lev, pp. 85–86.

15. Lev, pp. 143–47.

16. *Itinerarium a Guillelmo et Imberto fratribus Grandimontis conscriptum*; Bec SOG, pp. 251–264.

17. There is an article on this subject by G. Marshall: 'Craswall Priory and Bones of one of St Ursula's 11,000 Virgins of Cologne', *Transactions of the Woolhope Naturalists' Field Club*, volume for 1942–1944, pp. 18–19.

18. RG ch XII; Bec SOG p. 77.

19. RG ch VI; p. 55.

20. Gerald of Wales, *Speculum Ecclesiae*; ed. J.S. Brewer, *Giraldus Cambrensis, Opera* 4 (London: Rolls Series, 1873) pp. 257–58.

21. *Calendar of Letters Close* for the years 1343–46, p. 76 (London: Public Record Office).

22. RG ch XIII, Bec SOG pp. 77–78.

23. 'L'Institution' Articles 8, 11 and 14; see above, note 3, pp. 18–19.

24. According to Louis J. Lekai, sign language was introduced at Cluny under Abbot Odo (942–962) and spread among the reformed congregations of the eleventh and twelfth centuries: *The Cistercians, Ideals and Reality*, pp. 372–73.

25. Giraldus Cambrensis, *Speculum Ecclesiae*; J. Brewer, *Opera* 4, p. 259. Guiot de Provins, 'La Bible'; J. Orr, *Les oeuvres de Guiot de Provins* (Manchester, 1915) verses 1498–1501. Walter Map, *De nugis curialium*; ed. M.R. James (Oxford: 1914) p. 54.

26. 'L'Institution', Article 56 (d); (see note 3) p. 10.

27. *Ibid*, Article 48; p. 23.

28. M. Deanesly, *History of the Medieval Church*, p. 34.

29. Gérard Ithier, *Speculum Grandimontis* (see note 6) p. 256.

30. K.G. Ponting, *A Dictionary of Dyes and Dying* (London: Bell & Hyman, 1980).

31. 'L'Institution' Article 21; (see note 3) p. 20.

32. RG LVI; Bec SOG, p. 93.

33. *Ibid*, p. 94.

34. *Ibid*.

35. Bec 'La Règle de Grandmont', *BSAHL* 87 (1958) 19.

36. R.S. Gottfried, *The Black Death—Natural and Human Disaster in Medieval Europe* (London: Robert Hale, 1984) pp. 13–15.

V

RELAXATION OF THE RULE

1219 — 1317

In 1217, Pope Honorius III had accorded the *clercs* additional privileges which provoked such a violent reaction from the *convers* that armed intervention of the king and bishops of France was necessary to subdue it. Then, on 1 March 1219, the pope issued a major bull which afforded the Order a Privilege intended to compliment the Rule and which constituted the fundamental legislative text for the Order of Grandmont throughout the ensuing century. It is significant that throughout its length, the religious of Grandmont are referred to as 'hermits' as though the pope were anxious to retain something of the unique character of the Order, despite the forceful counter-arguments he had been subjected to, some of which proposed its amalgamation with the Cistercians or canons regular.

The pope had already suggested to the prior that he visit the daughter cells and regulate their affairs personally. Now, the Privilege formally released him from the obligation of residing permanently at the mother house. It also confirmed his indisputable authority over *clercs* and *convers* alike. He was further afforded the exceptional sacerdotal prerogatives of conferring the tonsure and blessing the altar linen, but at the same time, he was exhorted to practise poverty and humility according to the Rule and to sleep in the common dorter.

The authority of the correctors was reinforced by the Privilege and the *curiosi* were charged to render them account at regular intervals. The *corrector* and *curiosus* of each cell were required to attend the annual General Chapter at Grandmont. Three correctors elected at the General Chapter were empowered to act as visitors to inspect the mother house itself. The said visitors were also to exercise triumveral authority in cases of *sede vacante*. Correctors alone were given the authority to preside at the daily chapter of faults and impose penances. On Sundays, they were required to give a spiritual conference which all were obliged to attend. Despite the fact that correctors were beginning to seem more like regular superiors, the cells themselves were in no way autonomous; on the contrary, they remained wholly dependent on the mother house as before. None of them possessed novitiates and they were not even permitted to recruit novices on their own behalf. Communities were not established on any permanent basis, moreover, and any brother could be transferred to another house at the prior's pleasure.

The Privilege reaffirmed the responsibilities of the *clercs* over the care of altar vessels, linen and vestments as well as sounding church bells. The ratio of two *convers* to one *clerc* was upheld and *clercs* were left free to do manual labour or not as they chose. A notable piece of minor legislation required the brethren to maintain a continual silence and a sign language was evolved to assist its enforcement. One cannot help wondering just how many troubles might have been avoided if this regulation had been included in the first Custumal!

In conclusion, the document conferred certain general rights upon the Order of Grandmont including exemption from episcopal jurisdiction, the right to present candidates for ordination, and that highly valued medieval privilege, freedom to toll bells in times of interdict. A copy of both the Rule and the Privilege was ordered to be kept in every cell.

The primary goal of the General Chapter which met in 1221 was to adapt and modify the Constitution of the Order to bring it into line with the terms of the Privilege. The result combined with some additional and important internal legislation further to undermine the primitive asceticism and fervour of the Grandmontines. Although the strict laws governing fasting were retained, the dietary prohibitions were considerably relaxed. Presumably, this was the stage at which Grandmont acquired its culinary reputation, the 'garlic sauces' which so impressed Guiot de Provins.[1] Previous to this the brothers had been required to take it in turns to be responsible for cooking, but now it became permissible to appoint a permanent cook and no doubt standards improved accordingly.

The restrictions on buying and selling were lifted and the brothers permitted to transact business for themselves. The trusted laymen who had previously acted on their behalf were dispensed with. No longer were the brothers barred from entering private houses and, whenever it might be necessary for them to travel, they were free to visit their relatives and friends. They were also allowed to socialise with strangers they might meet on journeys. The article of the Rule forbidding the acceptance of ecclesiastical honours and titles was abrogated. The reputation for outstanding humility which had always distinguished the Grandmontines was lost forever when they were afforded this opportunity to rise in the ranks of the clergy. In fact, few Grandmontines ever did achieve high clerical status.

Honorius III, in his concern to retain something of the original spirit of poverty, had deliberately upheld the articles of the Rule forbidding fixed incomes and the holding of lands outside the immediate enclosure of the monastery. In fact, he went even further in ordering the sequestration of all irregularly acquired lands and possessions. This had the effect of placing the mother house in dire straits, for while a small group of brothers in a cell might be able to subsist entirely off alms, the large community at Grandmont could not be expected to live entirely from charity. Besides, the generosity of benefactors had been noticeably declining for some time, most likely as the result of the recent scandals. The bishop of Limoges and other high ranking ecclesiastical visitors to Grandmont expressed themselves appalled by the poverty and misery they encountered there. They obtained the agreement of the General Chapter to petition the pope to suppress the articles of the Rule which inhibited the Grandmontines from gaining a livelihood in the generally accepted monastic manner. They considered that even though the holding of lands and revenues was in direct contravention of the Rule, it was a lesser evil than the extreme deprivation which they had been forced to witness and were unable to alleviate permanently.

On 28 March 1223, the pope reluctantly agreed to the solution proposed by the General Chapter and supported by the bishops. The four most outstanding articles of the Rule, and the ones which lent the Order of Grandmont its unique mendicant character, were suppressed. For the future, the brethren were permitted to negotiate fixed incomes and own lands outside the enclosure. They were authorised to maintain the relevant charters and plead cases of land tenure in the civil courts where necessary. They were further permitted to raise herds and maintain beasts for work purposes.

The foundation of the three english houses coincided with the relaxation of the stricter observances of the Rule. Hence, with the possible exception of Grosmont in Yorkshire, which received its first confirmation charter from King John a few years earlier in 1213, they were never subjected to the full rigour of grandmontine discipline. The cell of St Mary at Craswall in Herefordshire has not been definitively dated, although the evidence suggests sometime between 1217 and 1222 and probably closer to the earlier date. According to the first charter of confirmation which was given by Henry III to the brethren in 1231, it was well endowed by its founder, Walter de Lacy. The third cell, Alberbury in Shropshire, proved to be the smallest of the three english dependencies of Grandmont and the last to be founded in the late 1220s. In company with Craswall, it was well endowed by its founder, Fulk Fitz Warine, and acquired further estates in the county of Shropshire in the course of the thirteenth century. As early as 1239, the corrector and brethren are found to be lending money as well as securing small parcels of land on mortgage.[2] Further small holdings appear to have been given to the brethren in return for spiritual favours, but the most substantial portion of the endowment of this house consisted of the parish church of Alberbury. The brethren had acquired the advowson and one of the portions by 1259 and they secured the appropriation of the church plus the remaining three portions in 1262. The Rule of Grandmont is adamant that its followers must not become either the owners of churches or the receivers of revenues appertaining to them. It further instructs that any offers of churches by way of gift be resolutely declined.[3] The infringement of this regulation by the english monks shows the extent to which they were distanced idealistically, no less than geographically, from Grandmont.

Following Prior Caturcin's resignation in 1228 or 29, Élie Arnaud was elected tenth prior of Grandmont. Unfortunately, his character possessed neither the wisdom nor the sanctity of his immediate predecessors. Shortly after assuming office he was accused of various faults and laxities. It was stated that under his charge the Rule all but ceased to be properly observed. The pope was once again forced to intervene in the affairs of the Order of Grandmont. While he did little more initially than forbid Élie Arnaud to undermine the decisions of the General Chapter, this at least had the effect of diminishing the somewhat excessive authority of the prior. Élie, however, continued arrogantly boasting his authority in such a way as to alienate many of the brethren and provoke them to acts of blatant disobedience. He rapidly became an object of ridicule for outsiders no less than for the brothers themselves. Following further and more forceful complaints about his behaviour, the pope resolved to depose him and sent three commissioners to Grandmont to implement his decision. Élie responded by confining the papal officers and making his own appeal to the Holy See. His deposal was nonetheless confirmed by two cistercian abbots along with two carthusian priors whom the pope nominated as visitors, and the General Chapter was ordered to nominate a successor. Élie proved a very difficult person to get rid of and he left for Rome in order to plead his case personally before the pope. He was still in Rome vociferously refusing to relinquish office when he died on 12 August 1239, and thus spared both the pope and the General Chapter any further trouble or unpleasantness.

The eleventh, twelfth and thirteenth priors of Grandmont each held office for a mere three years. The gentle and peace loving Jean de l'Aigle, elected in 1239, retired to the solitude of his beloved cell of Chêne-Galon in 1142 and was replaced by Adémar de la Vergne, corrector of the important cell of Bois de Vincennes near Paris. Adémar's brief priorate was marred by further unpleasantness in the form of a tussle with the four visitors elected by the General Chapter. In 1244, they began actively abusing the terms of their guardianship by personally decreeing statutes which the prior considered contrary to the Rule. It was left to Adémar's successor, Guillaume d'Ongres, to deal with the situation. In 1245, he resisted the visitors so energetically and successfully that at his request Pope Innocent IV quashed several of the disputed statutes. In order to clarify the legislation of the Order which a whole series of General Chapters had rendered inextricably complex, the pope issued the bull *Licet ad sapiendam* on 25 October 1247. This officially excised nine whole chapters of the Rule and afforded clear papal approval for the practices which Honorius III had reluctantly agreed to in 1223. Innocent IV issued a further bull *Licet in privilegio* in November of the same year. This Privilege somewhat modified that of Honorius III, but its most significant ruling concerned the prior, whose authority was considerably curtailed by the General Chapter which was empowered to check and balance any legislation he might introduce. A *definitor,* an executive officer after the cistercian model, was appointed to head the general chapter and his authority was to be independent of the four visitors responsible for the annual investigation of the condition and affairs of the mother house. The autonomy of the daughter cells was increased somewhat and the authority of the correctors over the lay brother *curiosi* was consolidated. Cells were no longer barred from recruiting novices on their own account and the establishment of novitiates was authorised in a few of them.

Hier Merle ruled as fourteenth prior of Grandmont from 1248 until he resigned in 1260. The singular lack of information concerning this fairly long priorate would seem to indicate that for a while, at least, Grandmont experienced a period of comparative calm. If this was indeed the case, it was the calm before a storm and was all too rapidly dissipated when Gui Archer became the fifteenth prior of Grandmont in 1260.

The notorious grandmontine lay brother dispute with its attendant histrionics has always received considerable attention from monastic historians. In consequence, another series of disturbances have tended to be overlooked. These were concerned with the international squabble which broke out at various times between the french brothers, the 'Fratres Gallici' dwelling in Capetian territory and the English, 'Fratres Anglici' who were in the majority within Angevin territories including La Marche where the mother house was situated. Back in the 1170s, King Philip Augustus had supported the french contingent in their effort to transfer the mother house from Grandmont to Bois de Vincennes in the Ile de France. The attempt failed and any further efforts in this direction were lost to sight amid the far greater internal struggle. Now, following a period of comparative calm in the mid-thirteenth century, this particular bone of contention was once again unearthed. This time it was the pious Louis IX who supported the French brothers in their attempt to transfer the seat of government of the Order. The ensuing schism heaped further disgrace on the Order of Grandmont, and it was the problem which the humble and gentle prior Gui Archer was forced to grapple with throughout his nine years of office. It quite probably constituted one of the main reasons for his submitting his resignation in 1269. His successor, Foucher Grimoard, continued the struggle against separatism with a greater measure of success, although his personal appeal to Rome, probably in 1269, resulted in considerable numbers leaving the Order rather than acquiesce with the papal decision and accept the penalties inflicted for their disobedience.

Somewhat paradoxically, it was in 1269, a year when the ranks of the Grandmontines were further reduced, that the fourth foundation on foreign soil was achieved. King Theobald IV of Navarre invited the Grandmontines to take over the former franciscan house of St Martial at Tudela in the diocese of Tarazona, now part of Spain. The king was also responsible for the foundation of a second cell within the same diocese at Estella.

The troubles which dogged the Order of Grandmont must have seemed interminable to the whole succession of popes forced to intervene in its affairs. In 1285 it was Honorius IV who was required to settle a somewhat novel disturbance involving the seventeenth prior. Pierre de Caussac was elected in 1281 or 82. A couple of years later he stood accused of both simony and perjury, charges which in actual fact were never proven. The four visitors proceeded to excommunicate him and put Bernard de Rissa in his place. Such a move without the assent of the General Chapter was a serious abuse of their powers. Caussac continued to attempt to rule the Order from Grandmont, while de Rissa established his headquarters at Bois Rahier in Tours. Sides were once more taken and the scene was set for a further battle.

The first papal commission empowered by Honorius IV to settle the issue quite simply failed in the attempt. The second took ruthless action in deposing both rival priors, and then used the opportunity to introduce further statutes of reform which were in due course confirmed by Nicholas IV and his successor, Clement V. The tenor of these is disciplinary and they give some idea of the degree of decadence which had pervaded the Order. Correctors were forbidden to maintain household servants and keep stables. They were also prevented from travelling with large retinues. The monks in general had to stop hunting, attending wedding feasts, and gambling. They were also forbidden to carry weapons which would seem to have been a wise precaution given the recent behaviour of some among their number!

In the course of the priorate of Pierre de Caussac a document emerged which treats of female religious. It is not known when exactly women began entering the Order of Grandmont but one thing is certain; it was in direct opposition of the Rule which insists: 'we forbid you absolutely to receive women into our observance'.[4] Even when the ruling against women was derogated and they were admitted into the Order, they were few in number compared with the men. Louis Guibert, the late nineteenth-century historian who set himself the task of identifying and mapping all the original grandmontine foundations, discovered only four houses which were indisputably nunneries. All four were in the immediate vicinity of the mother house[5] and of them Drouille Blanche at Bonnac-la-Cọte, Haute Vienne appears to have been the first to have been founded. A donation charter bestowed on this community is preserved in the archives of the Haute Vienne.[6] In the title designating the community the following words appear: *albarum monialium de Drulia*, from which it seems that these female religious wore white habits rather than the 'brown' of their male counterparts. The document was sealed in the church of Grandmont in the presence of the prior and ten religious, among them the chaplain of Drouille. This suggests that the cell had already become affiliated with the mother house although this is not specifically mentioned. A further document dating from 1223 given under the seal of the bishop of Limoges also refers to grandmontine nuns.[7] Drouille Blanche survived until 1756, when it was united with Châtenet, originally a house of male religious. When the Order was suppressed, Châtenet along with Grandmont itself passed into episcopal control. The last grandmontine nun was Marie Barny, who retired to her family when the Order was suppressed in 1772, but she was present at the inauguration of the memorial chapel on the site of Grandmont by Dom Vergniaud, the last monk, in 1825.

In 1291, Bernard de Gandelmar was selected to replace Pierre de Caussac who had been removed from office along with the rival prior. The appointment of the eighteenth prior was never confirmed, however, for he died the same year and Gui Foucher was elected in his stead. He proved to be an excellent choice, a born organiser and a capable financier who succeeded in alleviating the want and misery which was once again affecting Grandmont. He managed to achieve this mainly by imposing a levy on the daughter houses in the manner of the Cluniacs and Cistercians. In fact, this system of raising funds was not wholly new to the Grandmontines. It had been tried, not very efficiently, by Jean de l'Aigle back in 1240.

Prior Foucher was responsible for the first official census of the Order of Grandmont following the General Chapter of 1295. The figures which emerged as the result clearly illustrate the toll exacted by prolonged troubles and scandals. Several of the houses founded by the immediate successors of St Stephen had disappeared altogether by this time and the loss of houses had been particularly heavy within the diocese of Limoges, birthplace of the Order. The total number of *clercs* came to 886; *convers* were not counted. In compiling this exclusively clerical census, Prior Foucher may have had a number of considerations in mind: the selection of candidates for ordination; a reorganisation of the cells in order to achieve a more even distribution of existing priests, or to assist him in the appointment of *correctors* and other senior officials. Nevertheless, the omission of the *convers* is surprising at a time when documentary evidence reveals that other religious orders were recording the numbers of their lay brethren even if such records are sporadic and not altogether reliable. It certainly underlines the extent to which the Order of Grandmont had distanced itself from the democratic ideals of its Founder, so eloquently expressed by Prior Gérard Ithier only a century earlier.

Louis Guilbert has painstakingly located and listed the one hundred fifty cells which still existed at this date according to the seventeenth-century Annals of Dom Lévesque.[8] He points out, however, that Lévesque's list probably relies on an earlier one which was inserted in a bull of Lucius III in 1182, because some of the cells listed had verifiably ceased to be by 1295. There is valid proof that one hundred forty-four cells existed at this time. For visitation purposes Foucher also divided the Order into nine provinces as follows: France, Burgundy, Normandy, Anjou, Poitou, Saintonge, Gascony, Provence, and Auvergne. The map which Guibert included with his mammoth work illustrates these divisions or provinces which, with the exception of France and Normandy, emanate from Grandmont like the spokes of a wheel.

The year 1305 witnessed a momentous event. Clement V, the first of the Avignon popes, visited Grandmont in person. He had always been a great admirer of the Order, having been a pupil of the former Prior Pierre de Caussac at the cell of Deffech in Gascony, his birthplace. This was also the year when Gui Foucher handed in his resignation, according to some sources before the Pope's visit, although others state that it was immediately afterwards. According to Pardoux de le Garde, one of the sixteenth-century compilers of the history of the Order, Foucher's reason for resigning was his inability to defray the expenses incurred by the Pope's visit.[9] This seems an unlikely motive, however as the pope spent just five days at Grandmont and, according to Guibert, gave instructions to his intendant to reimburse the monastery for all expenses incurred during his visit.[10] An alternative explanation maintains that the prior resigned just before the Pope's arrival because he resented the measures taken by the papal commissioners appointed by Clement's predecessor, Honorius IV, particularly in deposing Pierre de Caussac along with the rival prior. It does not seem plausible that a level-headed and able administrator like Gui Foucher should have ceded office for either of these rather puerile motives. In fact, it would seem natural enough that he sought simply a few years of tranquil retirement after his fifteen hectic years of office culminating in a papal visitation.

Clement V, the pope who later became putty in the hands of King Philip IV of France by aiding and abetting him in the ruthless suppression of the Templars, descended on Grandmont like a whirlwind and went through the books with a fine comb. Having penalised the 'guardians' for their inefficiency, he proceeded to formulate a whole series of revised statutes for inclusion in the Constitution.

The prior was to retain overall authority and was bound to spend a minimum period of four months a year at Grandmont. When carrying out visitations at the daughter cells, he had to be accompanied by two brothers acting as counsellors, both of whom were required to be at least five years professed. The system of checks and balances was developed by the raising of the number of definitors to twelve according to the cistercian model. The said definitors were given the right to castigate the prior and if need be cause him to be removed from office.

The General Chapter was empowered to deal with all abuses against the Rule and Constitution. There was to be no right of appeal against any majority decision taken in Chapter. At the same time as the authority of the definitors was reinforced, that of the visitors was strictly limited to confirming the election of the prior. They had no right whatsoever to depose him. Presumably, the chaos resulting from the visitors' election of a rival prior in place of Pierre de Caussac influenced the pope to this particular decision. Visitors were further required to render full formal reports of their visitations at the annual General Chapter. A further move to balance the supreme authority previously wielded by the prior can be identified in the statute which required the General Chapter to elect two additional superiors, a sub-prior and a procurator general. The *curiosus* of Grandmont retained the right to represent the *convers* at the General Chapter, although his powers and responsibilities were severely curtailed.

The Prior still had the right to transfer brothers from one cell to another at his pleasure. Those cells which were more than two days' ride from Grandmont were given permission to receive and train their own novices, a decision which no doubt proved unpopular with those grandmontine *gyrovagi* who from all accounts welcomed any opportunity for a trip to the mother house. The benedictine practice of placing novices in the care of a suitably qualified master and keeping them reasonably apart from the professed monks for the duration of their training also became a statutory requirement. The cistercian method of training choir and lay monks in separate units was also applied to aspiring grandmontine *clercs* and *convers*. This must have had the effect of reinforcing the sort of monastic class distinction which St Stephen and the first Fathers would have found wholly unacceptable.

The remainder of the statutes concern the modification of customs which had the effect of bringing the Grandmontines even more into line with the Benedictines and canons regular. The disciplinary measures highlight the degree of decadence which was making itself apparent within the Order but which, it must be said, was by no means peculiar to the Grandmontines at the time. The fourteenth century has always been noted for a particularly high rate of abuse of monastic customs and privilege. There is always a tendency to read too much into documents which treat of monastic failings, and it must be remembered that legislation which, for example, forbade monks to gamble may have been necessitated by a very few who indulged this particular vice. Every lax monk was compensated for by several others endeavouring to lead dedicated and saintly lives. Money appears to have posed a particular temptation at this time, because the *curiosi* were instructed to provide the brothers with all clothing they needed and were forbidden to hand over the money which would enable individuals to buy their own. The brothers by turn were warned against adapting the style of their habits to suit their taste. As a precaution against the evils which accompany the accruing of debts, correctors were instructed on no account to borrow more than twenty five *livres* at a time. Among the luxuries which appear to have been finding their way into the cells were feather beds and fine quality linen. Brothers were ordered to return to the rough coverlets and course linen prescribed by their Rule. A further warning was given about the possession of weapons.

Abstinence from meat was maintained in principle but the Grandmontines, in common with other religious, were now permitted to indulge their appetite for meat twice a week, but with the proviso that they did so in a separate dining room. Meatless meals only were to be served in the refectory itself. Further, any brothers desirous of eating meat had to do so well out of the sight of laymen. Correctors were also ordered to see to it that a respectable number of the brethren partook of a meatless diet in the refectory each day. Mention is also made of invitations to eat at the corrector's table, a procedure which was a commonly accepted practice in benedictine and cistercian monasteries, but which could never have found acceptance with St Stephen of Muret. Correctors were also permitted to entertain laymen and talk with them at table.

The rule regarding silence was reinforced and the use of signs in lieu of speech approved. A further statute required that conversations, when absolutely necessary, be conducted in a special parlour assigned for the purpose. The brethren were still forbidden to travel alone; moreover, they were on no account to be permitted to choose for themselves the companion who should accompany them on a journey. Furthermore they were forbidden to eat or sleep outside the monastery if they were less than two miles distant from a grandmontine cell. The conditions under which a woman might enter a grandmontine church were very severely restricted, and the counselling or spiritual direction of women, including nuns and anchorites, was absolutely forbidden.

The corrector of each cell was obliged to see to it that both the Rule and the Custumal were read aloud to the brethren twice each year. Finally, an official formula was devised to be recited by brothers at their ceremony of profession. At the point when the Rule had been curtailed to such an extent that it had almost ceased to be, it is somewhat ironic that brothers were required for the first time to promise obedience and stability 'according to the Rule of the Blessed Confessor Stephen'.

Guillaume de Prémaurel replaced Gui Foucher to become twentieth prior of Grandmont and ruled until his death in 1312, when Jourdain de Rapistan was elected by direct papal mandate, and with his advent, troubles commenced anew. De Rapistan, who seems to have had a great deal of influence in high places, came from a noble family who held large estates close to Albi in the county of Toulouse. He set about ruling Grandmont as though it were a seigneurie rather than the chief house of a religious order vowed to poverty and humility. One of his first actions after election was to order the boundaries of the priory lands surveyed and marked. Then he assumed the right to administer justice within the little feudal lordship he had created for himself. He initiated a major building programme which included the re-roofing of all the conventual buildings with lead. The twenty-first prior also had the somewhat dubious distinction of effecting the last major bit of legislation within the *ancien régime* of the Order of Grandmont. Four years later, his spendthrift ways and haughty behaviour were directly responsible for the final blow to the spiritual ideal of St Stephen and the complete reconstitution of the Order.

At the General Chapter held in 1314, Prior de Rapistan completely revised the Custumal and gathered all the Statutes which had been enacted since the origin of the Order into one volume. The result came to be known as the 'Institutions of 1314'. It is predominantly a practical document and several of the Statutes, as we might expect from this prior, treat of financial matters. The disciplinary warnings range from the dramatic to the frivolous. For example, the brethren were not to wear their tunics casually open at the neck and certainly they were not to bare their chests, which were to be covered with the regulation course garments and not with fine shirts. In retrospect, an injunction to the brethren never to forget their hermit origins strikes a poignant chord so close to the time when all traces of the eremitical life were doomed to extinction.

The Institutions designated twenty-four houses to receive and train novices. A house of studies was established at Muret mainly for the training of novice masters. The size of the community at Grandmont was fixed at forty priests and twenty-six *convers*, but this figure took no account of additional unordained *clercs* or novices. Financial measures dealt with such matters as the extent of tree felling which daughter cells were permitted to undertake, and regularised the maximum amount of loans which an individual house might seek. Each corrector was ordered to keep a register of the possessions and revenues due his house and submit it annually to the visitor.

Having reaffirmed the rule of silence in refectory and dorter, the Institutions appended a considerable list of rather alarming behavioural sanctions. These were aimed at brothers found guilty of theft, slander, drunkenness, and associated misconduct, poachers, brothers leaving the enclosure at night without permission or indulging in any form of physical violence. Special mention is made of culprits who so far forgot themselves as to strike the corrector. Brothers who denied their vow of poverty were threatened. And a particularly harsh penalty devised for those who were discovered to have money about their persons at the time of their death; their corpses were to be interred in a dung heap. An intriguing little instruction had to do with the behaviour of brothers when in the prior's presence. Previously, they were required to prostrate themselves, an action which also had to be performed by any brother when he received or read a letter from the prior in his own cell. Now, a simple bow was substituted in the manner of the Cluniacs.

A year after these Institutions came into force, Prior de Rapistan was accused by the brethren of dissipating the possessions of the Order and leading a scandalous life. Summoned to appear before the Bishop of Limoges to answer the various charges brought against him, he refused and appealed instead to the pope. A further grandmontine war was declared. Confident that his separate appeals to the pope and King Louis IX would be successful, de Rapistan held sway at Grandmont while the rival faction led by the correctors of Bois de Vincennes and Bois Rahier, assembled for a general chapter in the franciscan friary at Limoges. De Rapistan was declared deposed and Elie Adémar was elected in his place as the twenty-second and last prior of Grandmont.

Repercussions of this affair were felt as far away as England. On 7 March 1315, Prior Elie Adémar wrote to

Arnold Rissa, corrector of Alberbury in Shropshire, commissioning him to receive the obedience of the english brothers on his behalf. He also made it known in this letter that he had heard that Prior de Rapistan had ordered Rissa to sell a manor and bring the proceeds personally to Grandmont. 'We forbid you,' wrote Adémar, 'to sell or alienate anything without our permission.'[11]

When, in 1316, Jacques Duèsne was elected to the papal throne as John XXII, this quarrel about the succession had manifested itself in appalling disorders and was threatening to continue indefinitely. According to Dom Lévesque, this pope was a former Grandmontine and corrector of the cell of Deffech.[12] While this claim was perpetuated by subsequent authors, notably Guibert,[13] there is little evidence to support it. According to Margaret Deanesly, he was trained in his youth by the Dominicans.[14] Certainly his tremendous ability as both canonist and theologian, which was demonstrated in his handling of the franciscan schism, points to a dominican rather than grandmontine background. Be this as it may, John XXII proved himself in many ways to be a man of great ability and he certainly tackled the grandmontine problems with tremendous energy.

The year 1317 makes the same impression upon students of the Order of Grandmont as 1066 does on english school children. It is one date invariably remembered. On the credit side, the bull *Exigente debito* which John XXII issued in the second year of his pontificate, spared the Order of Grandmont from suppression. However, it annihilated all that remained of individual grandmontine character and simply accelerated the evolution of its life along benedictine lines. As the result of *Exigente debito,* the Order of Grandmont survived — a mere shadow of its former self.

It seems likely that Pope John XXII's action was influenced, at least in part, by his compatriot, Guillaume Pellicier. Both men originated from Quercy, the region of southern France which is now divided between the départements of Lot and Tarn-et-Garonne. Pellicier attended the university of Toulouse while the future pope went to Montpellier. Both gained combined doctorates in canon and civil law. On 1 November 1317, when Grandmont was raised to the status of an abbey, Guillaume Pellicier became its first abbot. In compliance with the bull, thirty-nine of the cells were selected and upgraded to priories, while the remainder were united with various of these senior houses as dependencies. The mother house was given a cloistral prior who was to be responsible for domestic affairs under the overall authority of the abbot. The number of religious permitted to reside at Grandmont was raised to sixty *clercs* together with an unspecified number of *convers* and novices. The correctors of the thirty-nine priories were automatically created priors and each ruled over a community which numbered between sixteen and eighteen *clercs*.

Monasteries such as the english houses affiliated to the mother house, as well as the independent priories, were empowered within this system to elect their own superiors, although all such elections had to be confirmed by the abbot. Priories were also permitted to receive novices and profess them, but in company with the Benedictines, all candidates were required to promise *stabilitas,* that is to say, they were not permitted to transfer from the house where they made their profession without authorisation. Admissions to the various daughter houses were not, however, permitted if they raised the number of residents above the number allocated in the bull, unless it was by the direct consent of the General Chapter. The abbot had the right to visit any of the daughter houses at will, together with his four counsellors and a retinue suitable to his rank.

The General Chapter was to be composed of the thirty-nine priors and an additional *clerc* from each house. The number of definitors, previously set at twelve, was reduced to eight and they were not empowered to depose the abbot. The abbot for his part did reserve the right to remove a prior from office but only when acting in council with the definitors.

From early in the thirteenth century, the Cluniacs and Cistercians, no less than the hermit order of the Chartreuse, had been regularly sending a number of their members to study at the universities. The Grandmontines stood out as the only group of religious who did not actively encourage scholastic studies. With the election of the scholarly Guillaume as abbot, this prejudice against learning was finally overcome and Grandmontines began to attend universities. To defray the costs of administration of the Order in general, but particularly those of these students, the abbots were empowered to levy subsidies on the daughter houses, with the consent of the general chapter.

By the time all the directives of the bull of John XXII were complied with, very little of the old Order remained. Perpetual abstinence was retained in theory but seldom in practice. As had been the case among the Cistercians in the previous century, occasions when meat was eaten multiplied as the years passed. Perhaps the most striking and sad departure from the spirit of the Rule of Grandmont occurred in the new formula for profession. Whereas the earlier version inserted in Prior Jourdain de Rapistan's Institution required the candidate to make his promise of obedience according to the Rule of the Blessed Confessor Stephen, the 1317 version omits all mention of the founder and the Rule he inspired and the brother promises obedience simply before God. This version cannot have been definitive, however, because in the Archives of the Haute Vienne there is a formula of profession used by a certain Brother François Chautard during the term of office of Abbot François de Neufville (1561–1596) in which he vows stability and obedience, 'according to the rule of the blessed Confessor Stephen.[15]

The 'reform' instituted by John XXII and implemented by Guillaume Pellicier was as radical as it was efficient. For almost a century after its foundation the Order of Grandmont had striven valiantly to live like their saintly founder, and through their efforts they became recognised as the champions of the eremitical life. Even when they began leading the same sort of conventual existence as other groups of reformed religious, something of their originality was still discernible. In 1317, it took only one stroke of the papal pen to complete the final change of the Grandmontines into regular monks.

NOTES

1. See above pp. 78–79.

2. Muniments of All Souls' College, Oxford. Alberbury deeds: 71,82, 100.

3. RG Ch. V; Bec SOG, p. 73.

4. RG Ch. XXXIX.

5. Gui, 'Destruction de L'Ordre et de L'Abbaye de Grandmont', *BSAHL* 23 (1875) p. 69.

6. Article 341, cited by Gui (note 5) p. 70, footnote 3.

7. Archives de la Haute Vienne. The document cited by Guibert (note 5) p. 71, footnote 1, forms part of a collection of documents which has not yet been catalogued and is therefore not available for consultation.

8. Lev (pp. 5–10) lists 152 cells but one of them, Hentrua, has not been traced, while another, Berleria, is listed twice. See also Gui, pp. 60–65.

9. Pardoux de la Garde, 'Compilations des Antiquités de Grandmont', cited by Gui, p. 76.

10. Gui, 'Destruction' (note 5) p. 76, footnote 1.

11. Muniments of All Souls' College, Oxford, Alberbury collection No. 120. Cited by R. Graham, *English Ecclesiastical Studies* (London: SPCK, 1929) pp. 234–35

12. Lev, p. 294.

13. Gui, 'Destruction' (note 5) p. 80.

14. M. Deanesly, *A History of the Medieval Church* (London: Methuen, 1925) p. 183

15. Archives of the Haute Vienne, Séminaire de Limoges collection article 3931: Cited by Gui, 'Destruction' (above note 5) p. 58, footnote 1.

VI

GRANDMONT UNDER THE ABBOTS

THE ELECTED ABBOTS 1317–1379

GUILLAUME PELLICIER RECEIVED the abbatial blessing from the Cardinal Archbishop Nicolas of Ostia on 30 April 1318. The ceremony took place at Avignon, which since 1309 had been the recognised seat of the papacy. He was able to assume control of Grandmont secure in the knowledge that he had solid papal backing for all his actions. Apart from being a conscientious religious, the first abbot has been recognised both as a scholar and a man capable of wielding authority with firmness and flexibility. He certainly worked tirelessly to conserve the rights of the Order and strengthen its new structure of government. He made himself personally responsible for drafting the various decrees which in due course were submitted to the General Chapters for approbation. It is in large part due to these official texts that we are able to glean something of the institutional life of the Order during his years of office.

The most outstanding problem confronting Abbot Pellicier at the beginning of his rule was financial. The affairs of the mother house, let alone the daughter houses, had once again sunk into a lamentable state. This can in part be attributed to Prior de Rapistan's lavish expenditure, but years of general inefficiency and inept management had also to be taken into account. Pellicier had to devote considerable effort and skill to re-establishing the Order on a secure financial base. The subsidies which the 1317 bull had permitted to be levied on the daughter houses were strenuously resisted, and it required tremendous firmness and tact on his part to secure payment. This money was required to satisfy the Order's creditors. There were heavy additional expenses involved in running the abbey itself, but the new abbot was also obliged to satisfy the papal requirement that twelve students attend universities. The sum needed to make up the grants which would enable these students to complete the full seven-year course was considerable. Another and somewhat more delicate obligation involved the payment of costs incurred in legal processes relating to possessions acquired by communities outside their immediate enclosure. Involvement in secular court cases was not, however, a problem peculiar to the Grandmontines. Fourteenth-century monks in general were notorious for their frequent involvement in litigation.

A more fundamental difficulty arose when Pellicier turned to the task of establishing and safeguarding his authority over the priors of the Order. A related subject, and one which called for exceptionally delicate handling, concerned the exercise of his powers of visitation. At the General Chapter of 1329, the priors protested vehemently over what they considered the excessive authority the abbot wielded in investigating and regulating the affairs of their respective houses. Thirteen major questions were raised, and the disputations which followed became so involved in legal intricacies that the advice of secular lawyers had to be sought to help to unravel the issues at stake.

It says a great deal for Guillaume Pellicier's powers of leadership and persuasion that the Order emerged unscathed from the furor of protests aired at this particular meeting. In fact, the question regarding the spheres and limitations of abbatial authority once settled, the Chapter proceeded to introduce some clear-sighted and positive legislation. This was divided between the practical resolutions appertaining to the general management of the Order, and those decisions which affected religious observances and the rubrics governing the celebration of the liturgy.

Liturgical innovations are fully outlined in Guillaume Pellicier s work 'On the Celebration of the Divine Offices in the Order of Grandmont'.[1] They concern such matters as the inclusion of certain feasts and their octaves in the grandmontine *ordo* along with the requirement that the brothers confess and receive Holy Communion at least twice a month. Certain mitigations are also included, the most notable of which concerns the Office of the Dead. Up until this time, the monks were expected to assemble in the cemetery three times a day to recite it, presumably in all weathers. Now this undeniably harsh practice was dispensed with, although they were still required to assemble in the cemetery morning and evening except on feastdays and recite the *Miserere* (psalm 51). Two liturgical innovations which came about at this time are of particular interest and significance, revealing as they do the transformation of the religious life of the Grandmontines from the eremitic to the thoroughly conventual. The first ordains that Sunday and feastday masses be preceeded by a solemn procession in the cluniac manner. The second instructs that the daily conventual mass be sung with deacon and sub-deacon in attendance on the celebrant.

A considerable number of directives governing the acceptance and training of novices were introduced under Abbot Pellicier and compiled by him in another major text, *Liber de doctrina novitiorum*. Frère Philippe-Etienne, an authority on grandmontine life and observance, has observed that more than anything else this work illustrates the definitive transformation of the Order of Grandmont and its attendant loss of identity.[2] It is true that throughout its entire length St Stephen the Founder is only once mentioned while his 'Book of Thoughts', the fundamental inspiration of Grandmontine life, is totally ignored. By contrast, there are frequent allusions to and quotations from the writings of Bernard of Clairvaux, a saint whom Pellicier appears to have venerated rather more than his own founder. The length of the novitiate was set at one year and the acceptance of any religious wishing to transfer from other religious orders was forbidden. The latter prohibition had originally been stated in chapter 40 of the Rule. It is noteworthy that particular mention is here made of 'parasites coming from the mendicant orders' who are absolutely, under no circumstances whatsoever, to be admitted. This specific bias against the mendicants may well have been prompted by the franciscan struggle which was raging at the time and which had effectively divided that Order into two rival factions, the 'zealots' or 'spirituals' and the 'conventuals'. Quite a few of the friars sought to transfer to other groups of religious as the result of this schism. The grandmontine notion of poverty, although well watered down by this time, may still have appealed to some among the franciscan 'spirituals'. Their presence among the Grandmontines could have proved embarrassing if not downright dangerous, for their insistence on the poverty of Christ was closely akin to the teachings of St Stephen of Muret himself. As recently as 1323, Pope John XXII had condemned the teaching of the 'spirituals' and declared it heretical to assert that Christ and his apostles held no property whatsoever.

The disciplinary sanctions introduced in 1329 are a sad indication of increasing decadence, for it became necessary to remind the brethren that they might not leave their monasteries without having first sought permission, and never at night. A whole string of contraventions are listed: absenteeism, involvement in commercial deals, fraternisation with the wealthy and influential. It was even found necessary to forbid the sons of St Stephen to consult fortune tellers! A novel offence makes its appearance at this time; the direct result of the reconstitution of the Order. It would appear that some of the brothers were leaving the priories to which they had been officially assigned in 1317, preferring to dwell in one or other of the united cells, where presumably they could enjoy a fuller measure of independence and freedom out of sight of the prior and removed from his authority. The familiar warning that brothers must not alter their habits to suit their taste had also to be reiterated.

When Abbot Pellicier died in 1337, he left behind an efficient and stable institution. His successor, Pierre Aubert, belonged to a thoroughly ecclesiastical family. His brother would in due course become Pope Innocent VI and he himself was uncle to two future cardinals. In company with his predecessor, he had all the qualities which distinguish a good superior; he was pious, learned, calm, and detached in his judgments. Nothing serious occurred to disturb his peaceful years in office. The most notable change resulted from a bull issued by Pope Clement VI in 1346, which made some adjustment to the hierarchical relationship existing between abbot and priors, some of whom had never been happy at the extent to which the affairs of their houses were regulated by a distant superior. At their instigation, Clement VI restored some measure of the autonomy they had enjoyed before the reconstitution of 1317 had placed them firmly under the direction of the abbot. In time this slight slackening of the reins would lead to further relaxations.

Clement VI also decreed that the number of definitors be once again augmented, this time to a total of nine. It was required that four be chosen from among the monks attached to the mother house, while the remaining five were to be selected from the daughter houses. He also ordered that the superiors of the thirty-nine priories select capable administrators to govern the united cells in their charge. The abbot himself was required to see to it that these houses were subjected to visitation once every three years, but in order to avoid unnecessary expenditure he was not bound to undertake this task personally but could appoint a suitable delegate in his place. Both he and his representatives were instructed that their stay in any given house should never exceed three days. In the course of visitations, the visitors were required to assist the senior monks of the house in questioning and examining any novices. They were furthermore instructed to be ruthless in dismissing any among them who seemed incapable or who did not show a genuine vocation for the grandmontine life. On the death or demission of a prior, the abbot might select two of his valuables or horses for himself, and his entitlement to the annual payments from the daughter houses was confirmed. In 1295, the total amount of such payments had been fixed at 1,104 *livres*, but it was subsequently raised to 1,370.[3] All such contributions had to be submitted in the course of the General Chapter held each year at the mother house, and it was firmly laid down that under no circumstances could the abbot attempt to raise any further subsidies. A further privilege left the abbot free to choose which prelate he wanted to confirm and bless him in office. Another and somewhat more controversial right permitted him to appoint the priors of the first four houses which became vacant after his election.

Abbot Aubert died shortly after this papal intervention, and when his brother became Pope Innocent VI five years later, in December 1352, he granted all future abbots of Grandmont the right to the mitre in memory of his brother. He also gave them the authority to confer minor orders and administer a solemn pontifical blessing when visiting the houses of the Order.

For some obscure reason, Pierre Aubert's successor, Jean Chabrit, was not nominated by the General Chapter in the usual way but owed his election as abbot to the direct intervention of Pope Clement VI. Despite the conflict which might have resulted from this irregular appointment, not to mention the infringement of the right of each priory to nominate its own prior, the rule of the third abbot of Grandmont was without incident. Although the Constitution regulating grandmontine life at this time was clearly monastic in flavour, one of Abbot Chabrit's letters, sent from Tours in 1354, contains the information that the *clercs* were wearing both surplices and almuces to choir 'like canons'. This statement would in due course provide evidence for those wishing to assert that the grandmontines had always been intended as an order of regular canons rather than monks.

Abbot Chabrit died in 1356, to be succeeded by Adémar Crespi, and shortly after his election the interlude of calm came to an abrupt end. The years of turmoil which followed were attributable to external causes associated with the Hundred Years' War. The first phase, which broke out in 1337 and concluded with the Treaty of Calais in 1361, mainly affected the countryside to the north of the Loire. While the priories and cells situated in Anjou and Normandy reaped some ill effects, both Grandmont and the houses to the south did not suffer at all. When, however, hostilities were renewed in 1369, the Order of Grandmont did not escape so lightly. The advances through France led by John of Gaunt and Robert Knollys, while they achieved little in the way of military advantage, nevertheless devastated the countryside and left a trail of despoiled and plundered townships, castles, and monasteries in their wake. The French, having learned their lessons at Crécy and Poiters, ceased taking the offensive and successfully barricaded themselves in castles and walled towns which were beyond the powers of the English wholly to undermine and destroy. When Edward III made himself master of Aquitaine in 1363, he gave the Order of Grandmont a charter of protection and confirmed all its privileges. In 1370, however, the city of Limoges previously allotted to Charles V, fell to the Black Prince after a long and brutal siege. The english armies completely overran the Limousin, laying waste farms and villages and pillaging churches and religious houses. All the villages in the immediate vicinity of Grandmont were sacked and burned. Then the victorious soldiers turned their attentions to the mighty stronghold of St Léger la Montagne which they razed to the ground. Having made short work of the little local township of St Sylvestre, the marauding forces laid siege to the abbey of Grandmont. It comes as a somewhat poignant thought that, just two hundred years after a group of english workmen detailed by Henry II had helped to build up the great Abbey, another group of Englishmen were camped outside its walls intent on tearing them down. From all accounts they did not have as easy a task as they had anticipated. With the aid of the local inhabitants, the monks organised a strong defence which succeeded in prolonging the siege for some considerable time. But the English were led by two outstanding commanders, Sir Robert Knollys and Sir John Chandos. Eventually, the valiant efforts of the small army of locals who had rallied to the support of the monks proved of little avail against these thorough professionals with all the forces and equipment at their disposal. Grandmont was taken and when the English finally retired, the church and a major part of the conventual buildings were in ruins. Many daughter houses suffered in the same way.

When the Black Prince returned to England in 1371, broken in both health and reputation, he left the French in a position to take advantage of an english failure to consolidate their victories effectively by occupying most of the lands they had won. In 1373, Charles V once more made himself master in Aquitaine and thus was in a position to reaffirm the privileges of the Order. He further exempted both the mother house and those other priories situated within his territory from taxes, to enable them to make good the damages and losses they had incurred as the result of the fighting. Unfortunately, such concessions did little to alleviate the extremely miserable condition of the monks. The concluding years of Adémar Crespi's abbacy were singularly woeful and wearisome and whilst he laboured to restore the fortunes of the Order his efforts were of little avail. When death overtook him in 1379, he must have been a saddened and disillusioned man. Circumstances at this time were such that he was not even able to be buried at Grandmont alongside his predecessors at the entrance to the choir. At the priory of Bandouille in the département of Deux Sèvres, there is a tombstone with the figure of a mitred abbot carved upon it. This is said to have covered the tomb of Abbot Crespi interred at the priory.

The English Houses and the Hundred Years' War

The english houses had already been marginally affected by a wave of xenophobia directed against the 'alien' priories since the reign of Edward I. Between the years 1295 and 1303, the properties of various communities of french religious had been confiscated by the crown, and Edward II pursued the same policy as the result of the war of St Sardos in 1324. When Edward III came to the throne he in turn seized foreign monasteries after 1337. In practice, such confiscations involved no more than the appointment of a crown custodian to watch over the monks and make sure that they were not spying for the enemy. Custodians were expected to appropriate all rents and revenues due to the monks and having deducted sufficient to provide them with the bare necessities of life to forward the remainder to the Exchequer. Craswall Priory in Herefordshire was seized in 1341, but according to the Calendar of Letters Close for the years 1343–46, there were not sufficient funds available to pay a yearly rent to the Exchequer and at the same time to cater for the needs of the brethren. In 1342, Edward III gave the priory into the keeping of its guardian, Bartholomew de Burghersh, free of rent on condition that he provide for the needs of the brethren.[4] In these very reduced circumstances, Craswall managed to survive for a century until Henry VI, desiring to assist the universities to recover something of their former glory, seized all 'alien' priories still available. Craswall was among these and was given by the king to God's House, later united with Christ's College, Cambridge.[5] Alberbury, the sister priory of Craswall in Shropshire, was similarly disposed of to All Souls' College, Oxford.[6]

Grosmont, in Yorkshire, the third grandmontine priory, fared somewhat better and was able to survive a century longer than the other two english houses. Following an enquiry in 1344, the escheator for the county reported that all nine brothers in residence were of english nationality, but that they were bound to pay a yearly contribution to the mother house in France. The lands and livestock did not provide a reasonable living for these brothers who, despite the fact that they dispensed hospitality to all those in need, were forced themselves to depend on alms to supplement their meagre income.

Grosmont was released from custody as the result of this report. When war with France was again renewed during the reign of Richard II, Pierre Redondeau, abbot of Grandmont from 1388 until 1437, visited England; it has been suggested that he came in the dual capacity of religious superior and ambassador of the king of France. Realising the hopelessness of recovering anything from the impoverised daughter houses, he resolved to sell them if possible. In 1394, when this course of action failed to lead anywhere, he renounced all rights to Grosmont in favour of a certain John Hewett.[7] All connections between the mother house and the daughter houses in England appear to have terminated at this point. In 1360, Grosmont had suffered from a serious fire which destroyed the church and most of the priory buildings. In this sorry state it can have been of little interest to the Crown as a prospective source of revenue. Pope Innocent VI (1352–62) granted an indulgence to any who visited the church and gave alms on certain major feast days, and thus the house eked out a precarious existence until its dissolution along with the other lesser priories in the 1530s.

Although the english houses had ceased paying annual contributions to the mother house, the abbots of Grandmont continued to nominate the priors for a considerable while after the houses were subjected to partial custody. In 1317, they had not been included among the thirty-nine priories designated by Pope John XXII, but instead had been united with the mother house, which explains why the abbots continued to take a hand in their affairs. In 1359, Abbot Crespi intervened to depose John Cublington, a brother originally of Grosmont who had persuaded the abbot to nominate him prior of both Alberbury and Craswall. Cublington had been found guilty of several rather startling crimes which included seriously wounding one of the brothers and 'accidently' killing a woman named Alice Peckenhall.[8] Abbot Crespi appointed Robert Newton prior in his place at Alberbury and made him english superior with power to appoint the priors of Craswall and Grosmont. Newton was instructed to submit all three houses to an annual visitation, either personally or by means of a trusted representative. England then appears to have been infected by the hereditary grandmontine disease when, five years after being elected, Robert Newton died and two rival candidates vied with one another for his position. Abbot Crespi intervened once again and enlisted the help of the archdeacons of Coventry, Stafford, and Shrewsbury to hold an inquiry and restore the rightful prior of Alberbury.[9] This incident marked the last recorded contact between the english houses and the mother house before 1370, when hostilities broke out again and Grandmont itself became part of the theatre of war.

The Elected Abbots 1379–1471

Aimeric Fabri succeeded Adémar Crespi as fifth abbot of Grandmont and ruled through one of the most tragic decades in grandmontine history. During this time the trials and tribulations affecting the mother house knew no bounds. Eventually, things got so bad that it is recorded that the monks were forced to abandon their abbey to french soldiery whilst they themselves went out to seek a means of livelihood.[10]

Throughout the 1380s, the *routiers*, bands of partisan soldiers, roamed and terrorised the countryside. Whilst these wild undisciplined hordes purported to owe allegiance sometimes to the king of France, sometimes to the king of England, in reality they were concerned with little beside their own personal gain. It proved impossible to govern a religious order from a devasted mother house in such conditions, and when Ramnulphe Ithier was elected sixth abbot by common consent of the brethren, he was unable to take up residence at Grandmont and chose instead to remain at the priory of Bois Rahiers near Tours. This was where the General Chapter was held in 1386, the year following his election, and in the two years of his rule he never managed to enter Grandmont. When he died in Avignon in 1388, his body was buried in that city instead of being transported to Grandmont to be interred in its rightful place beside his predecessors. The previous abbot, Aimeric Fabri, had similarly been buried in front of the high altar at the priory of Bois d'Allonne.[11]

Following Abbot Ithier's death, Pope Clement VII personally nominated as his successor Jean Rallet, even though the General Chapter had put forward Pierre Redondeau as their candidate. Mercifully, Jean Rallet declined the office on his own account and so the Grandmontines were spared a further schism. Clement VII, the antipope and rival to Urban VI, agreed to uphold the General Chapter's decision and confirmed the election of Pierre Redondeau. The seventh abbot of Grandmont was destined to rule for almost half a century. A thoroughly exceptional character, Redondeau proved himself to he a very capable administrator while at the same time he acquired the reputation for being a pious and zealous monk, anxious to uphold the Rule to the best of his ability. Himself an ardent scholar, he became the Order of Grandmont's first great educator, encouraging the *clercs* whenever possible to proceed to higher studies. He himself had a doctorate *in utroque* and before his promotion had served both King Charles VI and his son Charles VII as chaplain and counsellor. Immediately after his election, he tackled the prodigious task of setting the affairs of the Order to rights, and shouldered the enormous financial burden associated with repairing the extensive damage inflicted by the war. Indeed, the abbacy of Redondeau would have proved a wholehearted success, a period associated with years of peace, renewal and prosperity, if the war had not taken so heavy a toll. The wounds inflicted had been deep and could not be healed quickly and easily. Money problems plagued Redondeau continually and hindered all his attempts at reconstruction.

Insufficient funding was the cause of an unpleasant incident which has always overshadowed any of Redondeau's positive achievements. His integrity was called into question at the time and he has been reproached by critics ever since. The root cause of the matter was the Council of Pisa which the Abbot was summoned to attend by the pope in 1409. Unable to raise sufficient funds to pay his expenses, he pawned the famous relic of the True Cross which had been given to the Order by King Amaury of Jerusalem. He was never able to redeem it and all his subsequent actions were coloured by this failure. The relic itself was to change hands several times and increase enormously in value before being returned to its rightful home seventy years later. It was King Louis XI who called a halt to any further traffickings by personally paying off the creditors and restoring the relic to Grandmont on condition that it should never be allowed to leave the church again.

The end result of this incident was that Abbot Redondeau has been rather unfairly blamed for all the laxities and lapses from the Rule which occurred during his long term of office. In fact, there were no major scandals or breaches of discipline during this time. The relaxations and general watering down of monastic usages which Redondeau had to contend with were no more than those which have come to be recognised as universal ills affecting many monasteries of the time. Redondeau would appear to have done all in his power to check the various concessions which were introduced before they went too far. For example, whilst abstinence from meat had become generally more common in the breach than the observance, Redondeau insisted that it be enforced on Wednesdays as well as Fridays. While he was forced to give way to the spirit of the times and allow the brethren to keep their own personal possessions, he nevertheless insisted that they be produced for the prior's inspection once a year. At a time associated with violence and unrest, journeys were not without their attendant dangers. Religious in general had taken to travelling armed with swords or daggers to protect themselves from the thieves and assassins they might encounter on the roads. Redondeau surely cannot be reproached for permitting Grandmontines to adopt this rather controversial practice. Despite the compromises to which he was obliged to agree, Redondeau took care that the essential constitutions were rigidly adhered to. He made sure that the General Chapters were held regularly and was responsible for a great deal of the sensible and efficient legislation which ensured the smooth running of the daughter houses. He it was who instituted the practice of appointing sub-priors in each priory to oversee the day to day running of the house and ensure that discipline was maintained in the absence of the prior himself. He found time to keep a watchful and fatherly eye on the twelve student brothers who, in accordance with the bull of John XXII, attended universities. He saw to it that all dues from the daughter houses were paid in time and he himself visited the houses of the Order regularly including, it would seem, the english houses.

A further accusation has been directed at Abbot Redondeau which has cast additional doubts on his character. The substance of this particular criticism proved to be a bitter foretaste of things to come. Not long after his election at Avignon in 1378, Pope Clement VII permitted him to hold *in commendam* Chavanon, the house which he had governed as prior. Thirty years later in 1409, the Council of Pisa deposed both the roman and avignese popes and elected the Franciscan Alexander v. The attempt to wind up the schism was a failure but the short-lived Alexander v, apart from conferring numerous privileges on his own Order, also awarded Abbot Redondeau a second priory *in commendam*. This time it was the important northerly house of Parc lès Rouen. It has been said that Redondeau actively persuaded both popes to confer these titles and their attendant benefits upon him.[12] If this was the case it still does not detract from the fact that in 1398 Abbot Redondeau inherited an institution sick in both mind and body, and that during the period of his rule both the fortunes and reputation of the Order were greatly revived and enhanced.

A very surprising election occurred as the result of Abbot Redondeau's death in 1437. Guillaume de Fumel, the eighth and last of the freely elected abbots before the imposition of the commendatory system, was not even a Grandmontine. He became a benedictine monk at the abbey of Tulle, and was appointed master of novices at the celebrated abbey of St Martial at Limoges before being sent to rule Rossac as prior. While the appointment of an outsider to the office of abbot was totally at variance with the grandmontine Constitution, the General Chapter appears to have been ready to make an exception in de Fumel's case, seemingly because he was so warmly recommended by both the king and other high ranking personages. Notable among these were two relatives of the abbot-elect, the Captain de Poton de Xaintrailles who fought alongside Joan of Arc and, de Tandonet de Fumel, captain of Chalucet. A further schism within the Order was mercifully avoided when the rival candidate, Pierre Brussac, prior of Bois de Vincennes died almost immediately after being nominated by the rival faction gathered at the priory of Petit-Bandouille in the diocese of Poitiers. Consequently, the election of the ex-Benedictine was immediately confirmed by Pope Engenius IV and peace, which had momentarily hung in the balance, was secured. In fact, Guillaume de Fumel confirmed his reputation for being a diligent and pious monk, although it has been said of his administration that he was inclined to be over-ambitious and somewhat authoritarian in his dealings with those under his command. This would seem natural enough in a man who was already experienced in diplomacy. Before becoming abbot, he had been entrusted with delicate state missions by popes and king alike. He certainly brought both his professional and diplomatic talents along with some downright benedictine practicality to bear on his government of the Order of Grandmont. The firmness and wisdom of his decision making proved very much to the advantage of the Order. Under his direction, the Grandmontines were able to enjoy an extended period of comparative peace and prosperity. He it was who undertook the outstanding major repair work necessary to restore the building of the abbey. His piety was such that following his death he was unofficially styled 'The Venerable'.

Abbot Guillaume de Fumel did not die in office but was 'persuaded' to tender his resignation in 1470, and with his untimely demission the Order of Grandmont fell prey to all the evils of the commendatory system.

Commendatory Abbots 1471–1596

Professor David Knowles has said of the *commendatory system* that it was 'a plague which blighted monastic life both in flower and fruit'.[13] Originally the term signified an official who was appointed as a caretaker to a monastery until such a time as a rightful ruler could be appointed or restored. It was subsequently developed by the popes as a convenient method of rewarding those who had served them well in some capacity or other. During the papal residence at Avignon (1309–77) and especially during the schism which ensued (1379–1417) both popes and antipopes used commendatory appointments widely to assure themselves of faithful supporters scattered throughout Europe. The system really started to degenerate when the pope awarded the power to grant abbeys and priories *in commendam* to secular rulers. No longer was a commendatory superior required to be a monk himself. Secular churchmen, cardinals, and bishops might be appointed, even lords and nobles who were not clerics at all. The system sank to its lowest ebb when children under twelve years of age began to be appointed to such offices. In theory, a commendatory abbot was expected to administer and protect his monastery and care for its monks. In reality, the conscientious among them provided for the basic needs of the brethren while retaining all additional revenues for their own personal profit; the worst were so motivated by greed that they totally impoverished the monasteries in their charge. The Grandmontines actually fared notably better under the commendatory system than did the other religious orders in France. None of their imposed rulers perpetrated any serious harm and one in particular, Guillaume Briçonnet, had a beneficial effect upon Grandmont, no less than the daughter houses which he assisted to recover their fortunes. Another commendatory appointment was that of Armand-Jean de Bouthillier de Rancé to the priory of Boulogne. He subsequently left to become a Cistercian at the abbey of la Trappe which he also held *in commendam* and eventually became the founder of the reformed, popularly titled 'Trappist', branch of that Order. It is interesting to speculate just how different the subsequent history of the Grandmontines might have been, had de Rancé chosen to remain at Boulogne and devote his inspiration and remarkable gift for organisation to the benefit of the Grandmontines rather than the Cistercians.

It was Jean de Bourbon, Duke of the Auvergne who, in 1471, employed threats in order to oust Guillaume de Fumel from office in favour of his brother, Cardinal Charles de Bourbon, Archbishop of Lyons. This particular prelate seems to have collected commends wholesale, for he held five other abbeys, including the vast mother house of Cluny along with four important priories one of which was the cluniac house of la Charité sur Loire. He further held several ecclesiastical appointments apart from his own archbishopric, and it is not surprising to discover that he never actually set foot in Grandmont. Nevertheless, the abbey did not fare badly under this first commendatory abbot. Charles de Bourbon made an inspired choice in his appointment of a vicar general in the person of Jean Cayrolis, ex-prior of Viaye in the Upper Loire region. Cayrolis was a holy and gentle monk under whose inspiration and guidance the Order of Grandmont prospered. General Chapters continued to be convened regularly and one in particular, held in 1473, is of interest in having been more than usually concerned with regularising the monks' dress.[14] The imposition of stringent laws governing clothing was an all too frequent concern of religious superiors in the fifteenth century, a time when more monks than usual appear to have been indulging their fancies as to what best constituted monastic attire. The Grandmontines had to be instructed that the main garment, the tunic or cassock, should always be stitched up to the neck. That is to say,it had to be donned by pulling it over the head. At least once before the Grandmontines had been admonished both for wearing fashionable shirts and for casually baring their chests. Although the earliest reference to dress, in the Custumal of the 1170s, mentions leather belts, by the fifteenth century these were replaced by woollen girdles which the statute of 1473 specifically states must be of wool and not silk. The brothers were further forbidden to wear what are termed 'little habits' except for work and when journeying on horseback. Presumably the garb referred to was a shortened, less ample and hence more comfortable, version of the habit which was itself required to be *longus, largus et honestus*. The General Chapter further found it necessary to rule out smartly polished shoes with fashionably pointed toes as well as the use of hats, except when riding. Hoods were ordered to be made of cheap material and never, under any circumstances, of silk. All the brethren were expected to retain the tonsure, the style of which was strictly regulated: the hair permitted to grow no longer than the space of three fingers over the forehead and just two around the crown.

In 1477, Cardinal Charles de Bourbon exchanged Grandmont for the bishopric of Clermont. Antoine Allemand, who received Grandmont, was a doctor of law and both bishop of Cahors and representative of the king of France to the court of Rome. Unlike his immediate predecessor, he did reside at Grandmont fairly often but, needless to say, his official business was such that he was quite content to leave all administrative concerns in the capable hands of the Vicar General, Jean Cayrolis.

The Grandmontines were exceptionally fortunate in their eleventh abbot, the third to hold Grandmont *in commendam,* for he turned out to be a truly remarkable and dutiful leader. Guillaume Briçonnet came from a well to do but simple bourgeois family in the city of Tours. He had risen as the result of his own efforts in the world of commerce to become eventually superintendent of finance to King Charles VII. He had been married but his wife died when he was still comparatively young and he then resolved to enter the Church. Once ordained, his career recommenced along new lines. He was nominated bishop of St Malo and the pope appointed him his legate in France and sent him a cardinal's hat.

On 22 October 1496, a dramatic event occurred at Grandmont when the Cardinal Abbot Briçonnet celebrated his first solemn high Mass assisted by his two sons, the bishops of Meaux and Lodève, acting as deacon and subdeacon respectively. Needless to say, the church was packed for the event and could not contain the whole of the vast crowd which had gathered to witness this family celebration. Guillaume, one of the sons, had been raised to episcopal rank when he was only eighteen years of age and in 1499, three years after this momentous event, he received the priory of Pinel near Toulouse *in commendam*. He proceeded to discharge this office as conscientiously and responsibly as his father did at Grandmont. All in all, the Briçonnets were a remarkable family.

The Cardinal Abbot worked tirelessly and unceasingly to renew some of the ancient splendour of his abbey while at the same time he saw to it that the monks kept up the regular observance of the Rule. He personally appointed the officials charged with the annual visitation of the daughter houses and he was present at and supervised the General Chapter's deliberations in 1497. On the practical side, he undertook an extensive programme of repairs throughout the houses of the Order and he furthered the work of restoration at Grandmont itself. The years during which he held office were crowned with success and he might well have led the Order to even greater achievements if he had not resigned his office after only eleven years.

There exists to this day a remarkable souvenir of Cardinal Briçonnet's years of office in the form of a silver reliquary, a hollowed head representing St Stephen of Muret whose cranium it was commissioned to contain. Amazingly, this important item from the treasury of the abbey survived the Revolution and is still preserved in the parish church of St Sylvestre. The head has an air of strength, nobility, and yet austerity and the eyes reflect serenity and compassion. Unfortunately, the bust which originally supported the head disappeared during the Revolution but from the description contained in the final inventory made at the abbey by agents of the clerical commission in 1771, it was covered with twelve silver panels. Four of these were emblazoned with the Cardinal's various coats of arms in enamel work, whilst the remainder depicted scenes from the life, death, and translation of St Stephen. This precious grandmontine relic is still brought out every year and borne in procession around the site of the abbey on the final Sunday in August.

In 1507, Cardinal Sigismond de Gonzague, of St Marie-la-Neuve, became the fourth commendatory abbot, but he was to resign just six years later and his term of office proved singularly uneventful. In 1509, his Vicar General, Nicholas de Grasset summoned the last General Chapter of the Order destined to be held for more than a century. No subsequent Chapter was held until 1643, an incredible gap of one hundred thirty-four years.

The next four abbacies proved even less remarkable. Charles Dominique de Carrest, archbishop of Sens and later of Tours, held Grandmont as a benefice for a mere two years and was replaced in August 1515 by Cardinal Nicolas de Flisc, bishop of Albe. He in turn resigned four years later in favour of Cardinal Sigismond de Gonzague who had already held the abbacy from 1507 until 1513. Thus, in somewhat bizarre fashion, the twelfth abbot of Grandmont was re-installed in 1519 and ruled as fifteenth abbot until 1525. It was just eight days before his death that, with the approval of Pope Celement V–, he relinquished his abbacy in favour of François de Neufville I.

On account of the religio-political circumstances prevailing at the time of his election, the sixteenth abbot was not able to assume control of Grandmont with the same facility as his immediate predecessors. The cessation of hostilities between the English and French in 1453 had opened the way for a period of monastic revival and renewal. Nevertheless, the process of recovery from so much devastation and dispersal had proved an arduous and lengthy affair. In addition, the mild attempts at a reform within the religious orders in general had barely taken effect when the commendatory system with all its attendant evils was unleashed upon the monasteries of France. Now, just prior to de Neufville's election, the Concordat between Francis I and Pope Leo X, signed in 1516, formalised the commendatory system and effectively gave the king the right to nominate candidates for all abbatial vacancies. Under the circumstances, it is small wonder that all attempts at disciplinary reform broke down completely and several of the ancient monasteries went so far as to seek and achieve secularisation. The Grandmontines, while they had not suffered as seriously as their religious counterparts in other Orders, had nonetheless been subjected to the unsettling effects of a rapid succession of rulers since 1507, and were no doubt feeling something of the bitter resentment which the Concordat of 1516 generally provoked. In November 1525, in defiance of the papal decision, they asserted their ancient right to elect their own abbot and nominated Claude de Laygue. Once again the scene was set for grandmontine schism and once again the situation was avoided by death, for de Laygue did not survive long enough to pursue his claim. The discontent which provoked this action must have been fermenting in the ranks of the brethren of Grandmont for some time, because de Neufville seems to have been well aware of its existence and was prepared to counteract any attempts to challenge his election. His contingency arrangements are all too apparent in the papal brief which was issued on 13 October 1525. This approved the resignation of Abbot Sigismond and confirmed de Neufville's appointment as abbot. The text then continued to warn the monks against attempting to elect an alternative candidate, because any nomination they might make would be automatically null and void and the perpetrators of the deed excommunicated. Thus the half-hearted attempts of the monks to assert their rights did no more than delay matters, and François de Neufville I was not able to commence his long abbacy until the September of the following year, 1526.

The Annals of the Order are ominously quiet throughout the abbacy of François de Neufville I. There is no entry at all between the year of his election and 1534, and a further silence throughout the years 1548 till 1561, when he resigned in favour of his nephew. During this time no General Chapters were held and the period represents a time of somewhat uneasy calm as a prelude to the storm of the Huguenot uprising, when sorrows were once again to be heaped upon the longsuffering Order of Grandmont.

The general disquiet which permeated religious life at this time finds dramatic utterance in a curious and strangely prophetic story which was recorded by the monk Pardoux de la Garde. This subsequently found a place in numerous accounts of the history of the Order. The anecdote foretells not only the destruction of the Order itself but predicts the Revolution which was to follow in its wake. In 1536 a certain brother named Charles Cadumpnat was seated in the cloister in company with the master of novices. Suddenly he voiced a fervent prayer to St Stephen whom he hailed:

Illustrious confessor of Jesus Christ, King of kings, the glory of the Auvergne: Woe and betide the day when the mighty tree shall be uprooted, ruin, tribulation and desolation will surely follow.[15]

Under the year 1534, the Annals record the dissolution of the english houses of Craswall, Alberbury, and Escaledale (Grosmont), adding that the homeless brethren sought refuge at Grandmont.[16] As we noted above,[17] Alberbury and Craswall had already been suppressed as 'alien' priories by King Henry VI and Grosmont alone survived by going 'denizen'. In fact, Grosmont was not finally disbanded until 1539, at which time the following five brothers are listed: James Egton (aged 68), Lawrence Bird (50), William Semer (36), Edmund Skelton (36) and Robert Holland (31). The last two on the list definitely remained in Yorkshire and turned up at an official inquiry into their pensions held in 1553. At this time, the commissioners noted that a certain 'James Ableson', whose pension was established at £4, did not put in an appearance. As this name does not appear on the original list, it is likely that he was confused with James Egton. Additionally, as his pension was considerably larger than that awarded to the other two brothers, who received just 66s 8d each, it seems possible that he was the prior. If this were in fact the case, at the time of the official inquiry he would have been over eighty years of age and his failure to appear can be attributed to death or debility.[18] It would be nice to think that the tradition which found its way into the Annals had some basis in fact, and that the two brothers whose nonappearance at the 1553 inquiry is not accounted for did find sanctuary at the mother house, but regrettably no evidence has come to light to support such a claim.

In 1561, François de Neufville II took over from his uncle and became the seventeenth abbot as well as the ninth and last of the abbots to hold office *in commendam*. He also became the first of the new line of regular abbots for, in May 1579, King Henri III gave his assent to the Ordinance of Blois which decreed that the abbots of the mother houses of orders such as Cluny, Citeaux, Prémontre, and Grandmont, should no longer be appointed by an outside authority, but chosen from the ranks of the religious in accordance with canonical constitutions.

As it transpired, the last of the commendatory abbots was himself a Grandmontine. François de Neufville II had entered the order in 1546 and made his profession at the abbey in 1553. Once installed as abbot, he did his best to protect the temporalities of the Order especially when he was forced to defend the abbey against Huguenot assaults. Like the seventh abbot, Pierre Redondeau, who pawned the relic of the True Cross, François II has been much reproached for his decision to sell off a considerable number of items from the treasury. This action became necessary in 1589 or 1590 when incessant fighting, associated with the Wars of Religion, laid waste much of the countryside and the sale was necessary in order to support the monks in his charge. Nevertheless, his decision was much criticised at the time by certain of the brethren and, in particular, the grandmontine chronicler, Pardoux de la Garde, who made careful notes on it in his writings. When

Pardoux died in 1591, Abbot de Neufville, who survived him by five years, ordered his manuscripts burned. A seventeenth-century monk has noted on one of the two manuscripts which escaped destruction: 'the books were burned by François de Neufville, Abbot of Grandmont, because their author committed falsehood.'[19] The anonymous monk's comment is not without some measure of irony, for in one of the two surviving manuscripts, 'Antiquités de Grandmont', can be found the spurious description of the church of Grandmont II which led Sir Alfred Clapham to the conclusion that all the daughter houses of the Order were modelled on that of the mother house.[20] Of the surviving works of Brother Pardoux de la Garde, the benedictine historian, Dom Jean Becquet has said: 'they cast more confusion than light on the origins of the Order'.[21]

It was during the abbacy of François de Neufville II that the Order acquired its own college in Paris as the result of a rather odd set of circumstances. King Henri III was on the look-out for a convenient monastery in the Paris area in which to install a community of Hieronymite brothers he had brought from Poland when his eye happened upon the formerly important priory of Bois de Vincennes. By this time there were very few Grandmontines living there and it was so suited to his purpose that he ordered the monks to relinquish it. By way of compensation, he gave them the Collège Mignon in the city, and ordered the abbot to see to it that it was kept constantly occupied with student monks attending the university.

Unfortunately, the attempt to revive some measure of learning within the Order met with little success. While the previous abbots, notably Allemand and Briçonnet had laboured to send the requisite proportion of young religious to the universities of Paris, Angers, and Poitiers, as the sixteenth century progressed numbers within the Order declined to such an extent that it eventually became impossible to satisfy the requirement. As a result, the Grandmontines were once again saddled with their former, rather dubious distinction of being the religious Order with the least educated monks. Considering that when Abbot de Neufville died in 1596, there were only eight monks in residence at Grandmont, the problem of finding twelve students to satisfy Pope John XXII's statutory requirement becomes understandable.

A further concern which occupied the seventeenth abbot during the troubled years of his tenure of office was the foundation of a new house of grandmontine nuns. In 1576, with the authorisation of Pope Gregory XIII, Abbot de Neufville II established a new community of nuns led by Anne de Neufville, a relative of his, at Châtenet. This was an ancient house of the Order situated to the south of Limoges but the religious life had long been extinguished there.

Throughout his time in office, Abbot de Neufville II was forced to contend with the unrest and frequent outbreaks of violence associated with the Wars of Religion (1562–1593). One of the greater sorrows which affected the monks at this time must surely have been when the Seigneur de Montcocu, descendant of the family which had granted the land for St Stephen's own little hermitage at Muret, as well as the land on which Grandmont itself stood, declared himself for the Protestant cause. They were forced on several occasions to fend off his assaults against the abbey, and when François de Neufville II died in 1596, he left the buildings once again in a sorry state, its walls caving in and the vaulting of the church threatening to tumble.

This was the scene of ruin and desolation which confronted François Marrand when he became the eighteenth abbot in the same year. At the very moment of his election, the protestant troops led by the Seigneur Saint-Germain Beaupré were preparing to overrun the abbey. Despite the support lent by the Marquis d'Urfe, nephew of the late abbot, the huguenot commander, was able to carry through his attack and the newly elected abbot had barely time to effect his escape with a small band of monks before the abbey fell. The ensuing destruction was appalling. The ancient treasures of the church along with all other valuables were plundered. The great relic chests, the most outstanding feature of the church, were stripped of their precious metal, gems, and enamel before being smashed and their contents scattered. All the other furnishings and ornaments were ruthlessly destroyed before the assailants turned their attentions to removing the lead covering the roofs.

The Huguenots occupied the abbey until 1604, during which time many of the daughter houses were abandoned and the monks dispersed throughout France. The Order of Grandmont limped into the seventeenth century, its leader an exile from the mother house. Few of the daughter houses escaped some measure of the ravages inflicted by this disastrous civil strife. As early as 1567, the priory of Louye, near Dourdan, had been devastated by the Huguenots, its church sacked and its relics profaned. The destruction of its valuable and extensive historical archives was just one of the many tragedies inflicted on the Order. Vieupou, near Auxerre, was subjected to the same treatment and partially burned. In the south near Toulouse, 1570 constituted the cruellest year in the history of the priory of Pinel. Not a village or church in the neighbourhood escaped the vindictive attentions of the Huguenots. Having carried off all the church valuables and ornaments they vandalised the fabric itself. Similar events were re-enacted time and again throughout the length and breadth of France and few monasteries escaped the scourge of the Huguenots.

On 5 November 1598, Abbot Marrand, whose efforts in directing a group of partisans to combat the armed intruders had proved singularly ineffectual, led his small band of monks along with the local villagers in a procession to Muret, 'to appease the wrath of God'. At the same time the brothers decided between themselves that the abbot was not sufficiently strong willed or capable of pursuing the warlike policy necessary to expel the Protestants and restore the fortunes of the Order. They therefore replaced him somewhat unceremoniously with Brother Rigaud de Lavaur. Marrand was, in all probability, not loathe to relinquish the cares of so demanding a leadership to a more energetic young man. Certainly the irregularly elected abbot proved himself to be more active and proceeded to organise those of the local seigneurie who remained loyal to the catholic cause into an army capable of combatting the Huguenots. There followed a series of campaigns which were at first unsuccessful. Charles de Pierre-Buffière, Viscount of Comborn and governor of the Limousin, attempted in vain to drive the enemy from their stronghold. Then, the catholic lords of Montignac and Basseneuve attacked and managed to occupy the abbey for a time before the Huguenots redoubled their efforts and they were again forced to retire.

This inconclusive state might have been prolonged indefinitely, had not the catholic leaders resorted to more desperate means of achieving their goal. In 1604, the decision was taken and the order given to bombard the abbey. The governors of la Marche and the Limousin brought up cannons and the walls of the abbey were eventually breached. A bloody battle followed which resulted in the total defeat of the huguenot forces who retreated in disarray and were eventually driven right from the area. The battle was won, but at what price.

Grandmont was retaken in a state of complete ruin. Numerous of the daughter houses were in similar plight, ruined and containing but a few monks. Several had been wholly abandoned, and in some of them the grandmontine Rule was never again revived. A few houses were in due course relinquished to other religious institutions: Bois de Verdelais in the diocese of Bordeaux, for example, was given to the Celestines by Cardinal de Sourdis in 1627. At Pinel, which as we have seen, suffered exceptionally, there was a half hearted attempt to reintroduce the grandmontine life, but this failed and the house eventually passed to the youthful Society of Jesus. Recent excavations at this priory have produced evidence of the violence perpetrated during these unfortunate wars. One of the tombs in the church has proved to have been used for several hasty inhumations. Four of the skulls which were unearthed bore traces of ashes testifying to the violence with which their owners had met their end. A further tomb revealed a skeleton with a severe cranial injury, typical of an armed combat wound. [22] The cell of Charnes near Bourges was ruined and abandoned at the time and in this case there appears to have been no attempt to revive the religious life. Aulnoy, near Sens, was eventually handed over to a congregation of franciscan Minims. Numerous other houses where the grandmontine life ceased can be found in the archaeological list of monasteries of the Order compiled by J.R. Gaborit.[23]

The election of Rigaud de Lavaur as abbot in place of the rightfully elected François Marrand was generally recognised as a necessary step given the circumstances prevailing at the time. It was nevertheless highly irregular and as such had been officially invalidated by the Parlement of Paris in 1599. The matter was amicably resolved in 1603, however, when Marrand formally resigned, leaving Rigaud de Lavaur to be unanimously elected in his place. In June 1604 he was finally and officially installed by the bishop of Limoges as the nineteenth abbot of Grandmont, and the almost superhuman task of reconstruction began.

Dom Lévesque, chief compiler of the Annals of the Order, concluded his sixteenth-century entries with the words:

> And so concluded the fifth century from the foundation of the Order of Grandmont, known from the harsh yoke of the commendators as an age when iron entered into our souls and the millstone was bound about our necks. I pray this has now come to such an end that it may never again be visited upon us.[24]

NOTES

1. For 'De ratione officii ecclesiae Grandimontis; see Bec, 'La liturgie de l'Ordre de Grandmont', *Ephemerides Liturgicae* 76 (1962) pp. 146–61. The 'Liber de Doctrina Novitiorum' was edited by E. Martène and U. Durand in 'Antiqua Statuta ordinis Grandimontensis', *Thesaurus Novus anecdotorum* 5 (Paris, 1717) cols. 1823–1844.

2. Père J. Fouquet OMI and Frère Philippe-Étienne *Histoire de L'Ordre de Grandmont* (Chambray, 1985) p. 67.

3. *Bullaire du Séminaire de Limoges*, cited Gui, 'Destruction', p. 85. A brief of Pope John XXII gives full details of these payments. Of them, by far the largest contribution came from N.D. du Parc lès Rouen and the smallest from Saint-Michel de Lodève. See Lev, p. 289, and Gui, p. 85.

4. *Calendar of Letters Patent 1343–1345*, p. 437, cited by Graham, *English Ecclesiastical Studies*, pp. 236–37.

5. Muniments of Christ's College, Cambridge, God's House Drawer H. See also *Calendar of Letters Patent* 1461–1467 (London: Public Record Office) p. 217.

6. *Calendar of Letters Patent*, 1431–1441, p. 565.

7. *Rolls Patent* 18, Richard II, pt. i, m. 11, cited Graham (note 4) p. 239

8. *Ibid.*, 31 Edward III pt. i, m. 24d, cited Graham pp. 237–38.

9. Archives of All Souls' College, Oxford, Alberbury Collection No. 122.

10. Lev, p. 318.

11. R. Garraud, 'Essai sur le Prieuré Grandmontain de Bandouille en Bressuirais', *Extraits du Bulletin des Amis du Vieux-Bressuire* 2 (1950–51) p. 29.

12. Gui, p. 89.

13. D. Knowles, *Christian Monasticism* (World University Library, 1969) p. 121.

14. Lev, pp. 345–46.

15. Cited D. Seward, 'The Grandmontines — A Forgotten Order' *Downside Review* 83 (1965) 264.

16. Lev, p. 376.

17. See above, p. 163.

18. The history and closure of Grosmont Priory has been treated in the following sources: J.C. Atkinson, *History of Cleveland*, part 2 (Barrow-in-Furness, 1874) pp. 200–202; VCH Yorkshire, vol 3 (London, 1913) p. 194; Noreen Vickers, 'Grosmont Priory', *The Yorkshire Archaeological Journal* 56 (1984) 45–49.

19. 'Libros quo combussit Franciscus de Vovilla, abbas Grandimontis, quia veritatem non celavit auctor.' Archives de la Haute Vienne, MSS 81, 82 of the Séminaire de Limoges Collection; cited in P. Bertrand de la Grassière, *Messieurs de Monneron, Mousquetaires du Roi et L'Abbaye de Grandmont* (Limoges 1974) p. 16.

20. A.W. Clapham, 'Architecture of the Order of Grandmont' *Archaeologia* 75 (1926) 192–93.

21. Bec, 'Les Institutions de l'ordre de Grandmont au Moyen Age', *RMab* 42 (1952) 33.

22. For details of the series of excavations which have been in progress at Pinel since 1979, see the annual reports, 1982 onwards, published by L'Association Sportive des Etablissements Aéronautiques de Toulouse, Section Archéologique.

23. J.-R. Gaborit, *L'Architecture de l'Ordre de Grandmont,* vol. 2 (Unpublished thesis of the Ecole des Chartes, 1963) *passim*.

24. Lev, p. 379.

VII

THE SEVENTEENTH CENTURY REFORMS

THE ORDER OF GRANDMONT has often been depicted as an especially ill-fated institution which was subjected to more than its fair share of misfortunes and troubles. Be this as it may, the particular form of tribulation which afflicted the Grandmontines in the second half of the sixteenth century was certainly not unique to them. Few, if any of the religious houses of France were spared the misery arising from the destruction and devastation inflicted by Huguenot forces in the 1580s. Scenes resembling those which occurred at Grandmont were enacted time and again as the religious houses of France were despoiled and laid waste. Of the sufferings of the Cistercians it has been vividly noted that:

> When the wars of religion finally had come to an end, the Cistercian annals closed the history of that tragic era with the necrology of 180 abbeys, helpless victims of greed and violence.[1]

In 1599, letters patent of King Henri IV evaluated the cost of the damage sustained at the mother house of Cîteaux alone at 200,000 lives, a vast sum for the time.[2]

Problems associated with fund raising and supervising building and repair works were by no means the only ones confronting religious superiors as the seventeenth century dawned. In spiritual terms there was also a great deal of reconstruction work to be done. While the charges of moral laxity levied by contemporary critics of the monks have always tended to be exaggerated, there can be little doubt that many communities were guilty of some measure of decadence and failure to observe their rule. Certain irregularities can be blamed on the commendatory system, which had subjected the monks to the government of secular clerics and laymen and often deprived them of conscientious religious superiors. In the absence of any effective spiritual guidance and example, it is not surprising that certain adverse criticisms were justified.

Once the religious wars had ceased, the parallel tasks of spiritual regeneration and material reconstruction began to be realised. Caught up in the tide of the Counter Reformation which was swirling through Christendom, religious superiors began implementing their own reforms. The decrees promulgated by the Council of Trent (1543–63) when, in its final session, it deliberated upon the religious life, had little effect because they depended too much on the good will of superiors. Nevertheless, the requirement that the monasteries of each region or province group themselves into congregations governed by general chapters effectively reduced the abuse of autocratic powers enjoyed by some superiors. In France this led to the formation of the benedictine congregations of St Vanne and St Maur. According to Professor David Knowles, the disciplined, scholarly Maurists were responsible for one of the 'golden epochs' of benedictine history.[3] In the Cistercian Order, the desire for reform gave rise to the branch of the Strict Observance which was eventually led by Armand de Rancé, former commendatory prior of the grandmontine priory of Boulogne.

The religious wars, inefficient government, and a general disenchantment with the religious life had emptied the novitiate at Grandmont. Hence it was a greatly reduced number of professed religious who faced the immense task of rebuilding both the mother house and the grandmontine image. Headed by their energetic abbot and no doubt encouraged by the notions of reform which were revitalising the monasteries of France, this noble little band applied themselves to their task.

From the very start, Abbot de Lavaur revealed his determination to effect a real and enduring return to the spirit of St Stephen and the Rule of Grandmont. While his efforts were ultimately doomed, he instigated an heroic and joyous revival of the primitive grandmontine ideals, prolonged under the guidance and leadership of a series of faithful and dedicated seventeenth-century superiors. Rigaud de Lavaur's contribution to the grandmontine recovery from ruin and demoralisation cannot be over emphasised. Desmond Seward's description of him as 'the saviour and restorer of the Order'[4] is no exaggeration; the part he personally played in fostering the indian summer of Grandmont was immense.

The first task which confronted the abbot after his election on 7 June 1604 involved ridding the abbey of the protestant troops still occupying part of the premises. The Huguenots were not entirely to blame for the financial ruin which menaced the mother house; catholic laymen no less than clerics had taken advantage of the confusion which reigned in the second half of the sixteenth century to feather their nests and in so doing had relieved the Order of various properties and possessions. The abbot enlisted the influential aid of the Jesuits in obtaining from Pope Paul v a formal brief which denounced the perpetrators of these trespasses and required the civil and ecclesiastical authorities of Limoges and Clermont to effect the restitution of the properties of the Order. This business successfully completed, de Lavaur set about rebuilding a part of the abbey in which to house his small community. Once he had reestablished the mother house as his seat of government, the energetic abbot turned his attention to righting the affairs of the daughter houses.

As a preliminary measure, Dom Jean Pasquier, sub-prior of the house of Boulogne, was deputed to visit all the houses and present a full report on the state of affairs prevailing in each. Dom Pasquier carried out his task efficiently and well. His report was painstaking and thorough but it made very sad reading indeed. The majority of the houses contained few religious and several had been totally abandoned to their respective fates. A few had been occupied by religious of other congregations, and the abbot was forced to negotiate their recovery. His attempt to repossess the parisian house of Bois de Vincennes which, in the Middle Ages, had rivalled the mother house in importance, was doomed to failure. It remained irretrievably under the ownership of the Minims.

Dom Pasquier's report on the moral and spiritual welfare of those houses still inhabited by grandmontine communities was equally thorough. In matters of discipline, his observations revealed a novel and startling abuse in some of the cells which in the 1317 re-organisation of the Order had been made dependencies of some of the thirty-nine priories. The day- to-day management of such cells was the responsibility of a senior monk delegated by the prior of the ruling house. It appears that some such officers had not only severed all connection with the ruling priory and waived their obedience to its prior but they were also assuming the title of prior in their own right. Abbot de Lavaur was unrelenting in his efforts to re-impose grandmontine discipline on these nonconformist groups, but to no avail. The secession of such houses was a *faît accompli;* the abuse had been going on for so long that the spurious priors were able to vindicate their claims by reference to papal briefs which, however inadvertently, had authorised and perpetrated the illegality. The full impact of the reforming abbot's failure to remedy this situation and to re-impose his authority on these rebellious houses would be felt only fifty years later, when it contributed to the state of almost complete anarchy to which the Order of Grandmont was reduced.

Abbot de Lavaur achieved a considerably greater success when he began to concern himself with matters of general discipline and custom. He ordered that the brethren without exception wear the traditional habit, comprising a tunic and broad scapular with attached hood. By this time black had officially replaced the nondescript grey-brown worn by the monks in the Middle Ages. An entry in the Annals under the year 1605, which treats of this ruling, makes it appear that the more fashion conscious among the monks had once again been considerably modifying their attire. While the Grandmontines traditionally wore surplices to choir, they were not supposed to substitute elegant lace rochets with stylish collars. The Annals also refer to the appearance of fashionable birettas.[5]

It was firmly laid down that all, without exception, should conform to a regular life in community and, in particular, that all meals be taken in the refectory. In an effort to ensure that the reforming spirit be disseminated throughout the houses of the Order, Abbot de Lavaur invited a number of brothers of the same inclination as himself to spend some time at the mother house. Under his personal supervision, this nucleus of reformed brethren was thoroughly trained in the observance of the Rule. Once the abbot was satisfied with their progress, they were returned to their respective houses where, true to the spirit of their founder, they taught by example.

In his efforts to re-impose and maintain discipline throughout the Order, the fatherly but determined abbot obtained the king's authority to remove persistent trouble makers from their houses. Nor did he shrink from employing forceful lay assistance when it proved necessary.

In 1623, Abbot de Lavaur obtained an ordinance from the Parlement of Paris which once again exempted the entire Order from episcopal control. An incident connected with this privilege is illustrative of de Lavaur's iron resolve. The bishop of Angers, for no other reason than the desire to assert his authority, had been meddling in the affairs of the priory of La Haye. When some of the brethren dared to remonstrate with him, he ordered them to be imprisoned. On hearing what had happened, the abbot did not rest until he had secured the release of the unfortunate monks, and the whole affair had been settled in the interests of their monastery.

Despite all Abbot de Lavaur's efforts, the ruined state of the mother house and the lamentable finances of the Order prevented him from convening a General Chapter throughout his years of office. Nevertheless, he gathered the Statutes of Pope John XXII with the legislation passed by the two successive fourteenth-century General Chapters, and submitted the result to several distinguished clerics, who had been recommended to him for their wisdom and piety. Among these advisors who assisted de Lavaur in the re-codification of the Grandmontine Constitution, was the celebrated and saintly cleric Vincent de Paul, the founder of a society of missionary priests, the Lazarists, and co-founder with Louise de Marillac of the famous Daughters (or Sisters) of Charity. Of this wise, compassionate and humble priest it has been said, 'there was no human suffering that he did not seek to relieve'.[6] Vincent de Paul was eventually canonised by Pope Benedict XIV in 1737. Until his death in 1660, the future saint took a continuing and lively interest in the affairs of the Order of Grandmont. In particular he was to encourage and advise the greatest of the grandmontine reformers, Dom Charles Frémon, whom we shall meet in a moment.

Although it did not receive confirmation before the General Chapter held in 1643, twelve years after its compiler's death, the revised Constitution was immediately implemented. While it was actually little more than a sensible updating of fourteenth-century customs, the enforcement of this resolute legislative code did much to curb the decadence which had taken root in the order.

Before the outbreak of internal strife which disrupted the Order in the 1180s, the hermit monks of Grandmont had been celebrated no less for their fervour and austerity than for the almost legendary charity they practised. The nineteenth abbot of Grandmont revived this fine tradition and became noted for his solicitude in caring for the poor and needy. Despite the cares associated with breathing new life into a spiritually weak institution and the practical problems involved in re-establishing it on a sound financial basis, he nevertheless made time to listen to and help all those who came to him in need. He is particularly remembered for the aid he afforded to victims of the plague which decimated the countryside around Limoges in the course of his abbacy. In the city alone, the pestilence claimed a large number of victims before spreading to the villages and hamlets around Grandmont.[7] This true son of St Stephen died unexpectedly of a stroke, which he suffered in 1631 while on a visit to his brother at the family home.

François de Tautal, the twentieth abbot, was elected on 15 April of the same year. He had served as novice master under Abbot de Lavaur whose aims and ideals he shared. Although his term in office proved to be remarkably short—only four years—he nevertheless made good use of this time in reinforcing and extending the reforms initiated by his predecessor. He travelled extensively in order to encourage the brethren in their efforts and he was generally liked for the tactful way in which he offered criticisms no less than for his gentleness in administering rebukes. It was in 1631, in the course of one of these visitations to the norman priory of Notre Dame du Parc near Rouen, that he made the acquaintance of a very remarkable monk whose actions were destined to have so great an impact upon the Order as a whole.

Charles Frémon was born in 1611 into a well-to-do family of Tours, one of thirteen children. His younger brother, Alexandre, was the first of the two to enter the Order of Grandmont and, in due course, ruled as its twenty-third abbot general.

As youngsters Charles and Alexandre are said to have played at being hermits in the woods of Saint-Cosme near their home. When Charles reached the age of twelve, his mother, in all probability sensing the inevitability of his vocation for the religious life, decided to send him to the prosperous benedictine abbey of Marmoutier, where one of her relatives was prior. Charles, aware that the discipline was lax and the Rule only casually observed in this celebrated abbey, refused to go. By this time, Charles' father, who was employed in the king's service, had been accused of some malpractice connected with his charge and was imprisoned in Paris. He was to die, still in captivity, in 1622. Following her husband's arrest, Madame Frémon no doubt felt the need to shift some of the heavy parental responsibility which had devolved on her alone. As Charles had turned down the opportunity of being educated for the benedictine life, she decided to pack him off to her brother's household at Nantes where, she hoped, he might learn something of the world of trade and commerce. Charles' religious vocation persisted, however, and when he heard that his brother had entered the grandmontine priory of Bois Rahier, he resolved to follow him, but not as a choir monk. He wanted to be a lay brother.

Madame Frémon was horrified and refused to countenance her son entering the religious life other than as an ordinand. There was stalemate until her confessor, a Capuchin, intervened and suggested by way of compromise, that Charles be permitted to join his own strict branch of the Franciscan Order. The famed poverty practised by the Capuchins appealed to Charles and he agreed to join their novitiate at Blois. Regrettably, the life there was not sufficiently austere for the young Charles who continued to be inspired by the example of St Stephen and yearned for a solitude as complete as his hero had experienced at Muret. Consequently, he left Blois and repaired to Orléans where he completed the secondary school studies he had abandoned when placed in the care of his uncle at Nantes. Two years later he again announced his intention of entering the grandmontine novitiate at Bois Rahier and this time his mother reluctantly gave her consent and her blessing.

Charles Frémon received the grandmontine habit on 27 October 1629, when he was just over eighteen years of age. At this time, although the spirit of renewal sparked off by Abbot de Lavaur was pervading the houses of the Order, recruitment was still at a very low ebb and there was a general lack of experienced, professed religious capable of filling responsible posts. Nothing emphasises this deficiency more vividly than the account of Brother Charles' novitiate in the 'Life' written by Dom Jean-Baptiste Rochias around 1690. Dom Rochias knew his subject well and was one of the first to follow him when he started a branch aiming at the Strict Observance.

'The person who was responsible for the care of the novices,' wrote Dom Rochias 'was little suited to his task. He lacked experience, was easy-going in his attitude and totally unfit to lead novices along a road which he had never travelled himself.' For the education of the young monks, Dom Rochias tells us, a lay schoolmaster had to be employed to instruct the novices.[8] Dom Rochias also recalls that after Charles had been in the novitiate for some months, and well before making his profession, the prior charged him with the care and instruction of the other novices. The prior of Bois Rahier at this time was Georges Barny, a wise and saintly monk; he later became one of the Order's great reforming abbots. He had obviously developed a high regard for the young novice, for he also entrusted him with the duties of porter. Traditionally this office was always allocated to a particularly experienced and discreet monk.

Charles Frémon was professed on 27 January 1631. He had already made a considerable reputation for himself on account of his piety and austerity. His keen devotion to St Stephen of Muret prompted him in his desire to live the Rule to the letter. His enthusiasm was by no means shared by all his contemporaries, some of whom regarded his behaviour as singular and began to resent him. At this point Dom Barny insisted that he pursue his studies for the priesthood, an obligation which weighed heavily on the young monk who thirsted only for solitude. Aware of the crisis of conscience which his decision had provoked, Dom Barny wisely determined to satisfy Charles' ambition, at least for a while, and so he transferred him to the nearby priory of Bercey. Isolated in the depths of a vast forest, this priory was wholly in keeping with the ideal of the hermitage. Although Charles spent only a few months there, it was sufficient to renew his spiritual well-being, although his thirst for total seclusion from the world was to remain with him for the rest of his life.

On 14 March 1635, Charles Frémon was ordained to the diaconate, and in obedience to his superiors prepared for the priesthood which was conferred on him on 22 September of the same year. Meanwhile, Abbot de Lavaur, who had become aware of his reforming inclination transferred him to the priory of Notre Dame du Parc near Rouen. It was here that in 1631, during the official visitation of Abbot de Tautal, that Charles Frémon articulated his burning ambition to live in accordance with the primitive Rule of Grandmont, which involved the observance of the strict monastic fasts and perpetual abstinence from meat. The abbot was sympathetic towards the young reformer, whose worth he fully appreciated. But aware, perhaps, that he had already provoked adverse criticism from certain of his confreres who regarded his behaviour as singular and his austerities as excessive, he sensibly advised caution. He refused Charles permission to live apart and follow the primitive observance but he made him privy to his own milder, less divisive notions of furthering reform within the Order as a whole. This in effect constituted an extension of his predecessor's school of reformers established at the mother house itself. At Grandmont, Abbot de Tautal intended to sow the seeds of penitence and fervour which he hoped might root and blossom throughout the daughter houses. Unfortunately, the abbot's untimely death prevented him from realising his dream of a comprehensive grandmontine reform. As for Charles Frémon, the time was not yet ripe for him to commence his personal mission of reform. He remained for a while at Notre Dame du Parc where he was afforded the opportunity to realise the worth of that other great grandmontine virtue, obedience.

An outstanding Abbot General, François de Tautal during his four years of office had governed with dignity and yet with that genuine humility which characterises a true monk. The Annals of the Order are eloquent in his praise and note especially that, whenever his duties permitted, he took his seat in choir and fervently joined in the recitation of the offices. He took his meals in the refectory with the brethren and, in accordance with one of the early customs, himself waited upon them on solemn feast-days. He was adamant that he should perform his share of manual work, especially when at the commencement of his abbacy it was 'all hands on deck' to repair and renovate the buildings damaged by the Huguenots.

Georges Barny, former prior of Bois Rahier, was elected the twenty-first abbot of Grandmont on 4 December 1635. His time in office turned out to be as long as his predecessor's had been short, and it was a success story from beginning to end. Under his clear and sensible guidance, the grandmontine dream of reform and renewal grew to fruition. One of his first actions following election was to bring Dom Frémon to Grandmont as novice master. In 1639 he also made him prior, but this did not prove to be as wise a decision. Dom Frémon had apparently been making good use of his spare time at the mother house searching through the archives to learn more about the original interpretations of the Rule and the primitive customs of the Order. His subsequent attempt to implement some of the more austere practices of the early fathers proved decidedly unpopular, and even provoked hostile reactions from those who preferred a milder, more comfortable brand of monasticism. Concerned that divisions, between the brethren who favoured what had come to be recognised as the 'traditional' or 'common' observance, and those aspiring to the 'strict' or 'reformed' observance, should be averted at any price, Abbot Barny sensibly revoked Dom Frémon's appointment. He was sent away for a time to be spiritual director to the grandmontine nuns at Châtenet. Once the controversy had died down, the abbot recalled him and sent him to Paris in the dual role of Superior of the Collège Mignon, the grandmontine house of studies, and Vicar General of the Order.

As Vicar General, Dom Frémon was required to visit and inspect all the daughter houses. The task afforded him ample opportunity both to circulate his own reforming notions, and to make contact with those religious who were similarly inclined, such as Dom Gaillard, his former superior at Rouen. Foremost among the reforming party was Dom Boboul, whom he had met at the mother house. When Abbot Barny finally gave his assent to a formal attempt by Dom Frémon to institute a grandmontine branch of the Strict Observance, he was the first to join. The priory of Beaumont in the diocese of Evreux was assigned to the two companions for what, initially at any rate, was no more than an experiment. The attempt of these two pioneers to live in accordance with the twelfth-century Rule approved by Innocent IV in 1156, was not, however, destined to succeed at Beaumont. Although the prior of that house had declared himself to be in favour of the venture, he subsequently changed his mind and the two reformers were obliged to leave. Ever patient and understanding, Abbot Barny then designated the priory of Epoisses near Dijon, as the house of Strict Observance. It was here that the reforming fathers encountered what was to be their greatest challenge. The property itself turned out to be an appalling ruin which the commendatory prior, more interested in the hunt than governing a monastery, categorically refused to repair. He was decidedly ill-disposed towards the two reforming priests, who were forced to tolerate many hardships, including near starvation. Their tenacity and courage eventually won the day however, and the Grandmontines of the Strict Observance became firmly established at Epoisses.

At the same time as Dom Frémon was pioneering the branch of the Strict Observance, Abbot Barny was seeking to cultivate the spirit of less radical reform sown by his two immediate predecessors. In this context, the Abbé Vincent de Paul became once again associated with the Order of Grandmont. He it was who actively encouraged and supported the abbot in his untiring efforts to foster discipline and maintain throughout the houses in his charge a regular monastic observance in conformity with the revised constitutions which had emerged under Abbot de Lavaur in 1625.

On 26 April 1643, Abbot Barny was at last able to convene a General Chapter, the first in a hundred and thirty-four years. The primary task facing this assembly involved the discussion, confirmation, and approval of the revised Constitutions. Sentiments of reform were certainly in the air at this meeting. The fathers not only applauded and encouraged the work of Charles Frémon, they also voiced the hope that the Order in its entirety would see fit to renew itself, albeit in a manner somewhat less extreme. Little did they realise that in encouraging the praiseworthy but separatist activities of Dom Frémon, they were effectively pronouncing the death sentence upon their Order. The Strict Observance would, in due course, attract and cream off the most fruitful and fervent of the brethren. By 1652, although this group numbered a mere thirty-nine members distributed among eight priories, it yet had an injurious effect upon the twenty-three houses which remained within the Common Observance, reducing their membership to just sixty-eight. In a letter addressed to Abbot Barny on 24 June of the same year, the Abbé Vincent de Paul expressed his dismay at the lack of religious within the Order.[9]

Frère Philippe-Étienne has expressed the effect of this division of the Order into Common and Strict observance as follows:

> The trunk of the Grandmontine tree which had been bending increasingly against the force of decadence, was too strained to withstand such a blow.[10]

In the Middle Ages, the spiritual and material fortunes of the Order of Grandmont had declined in proportion to its increase in numbers. Now, ironically, the Order became doomed for lack of numbers. In attracting to itself the most dedicated of the sons of St Stephen, the Strict Observance, founded to revive the primitive spirit of the Order, succeeded only in bringing its end closer.

In 1652, however, the unhappy conclusion of the history of the Grandmontines was still more than a century away. In practical no less than spiritual terms, the Order was benefitting greatly under Abbot Barny's control and passing through a period of peace and success. Of the abbot's leadership, Louis Guilbert has noted:

> In the entire history of the Order, few abbots left such enduring traces coupled with such moving memories. None demonstrated quite so much energy, nor applied himself to so many different projects.[11]

These projects included massive building and repair work and, in particular, the placement of enormous flying buttresses to reinforce the abbey church, the walls and foundations of which had been seriously weakened during the Wars of Religion. Abbot Barny relentlessly tracked down and re-assembled many valuable reliquaries and other church treasures pillaged during the protestant occupation. He also managed to recover much of the property which had been lost to the Order during the wars. He found time to travel extensively, and personally initiated rebuilding and repair work in many of the daughter houses. He took a keen and fatherly interest in the education of the young monks, and encouraged the pursuit of higher studies at the college of the Order in Paris. His most outstanding achievement however, and the one which survives today, as an enduring monument to his abbacy, is the *Annales Ordinis Grandimontis* which he instructed Dom Jean Lévesque to compile.

With the death of Georges Barny on 3 July 1654, the atmosphere of calm which had pervaded the Order of Grandmont for over half a century, was drastically interrupted by a further unpleasant division. The community at Grandmont elected Étienne Talin, prior of Raveaux near Angoulême. The action was illegal inasmuch as all the houses were not represented. Bitter squabbling resulted, and the absentees banded together to elect a rival candidate in the person of Antoine de Chavaroche, prior of Vieux Pou, one of the houses which had adopted the Strict Observance. Although the grandmontine family had split into two separate observances, both groups still acknowledged the abbot of Grandmont as their superior general and the eight cells of the Strict Observance sent representatives to the General Chapters of the Order as a whole. A year of quarrelling, unpleasantness, and litigation followed, and the affair was only settled when the King's Council intervened. In 1655 this august body promulgated two separate decrees, dated 8 and 10 April respectively. The first confirmed Dom de Chavaroche in office; while the second awarded his opponent, Dom Talin, a consolation prize in creating him second in command with the official title of Prior General. The case was decided, but unfortunately the decision failed to terminate the unpleasantness. Other issues combined to prolong the ill feelings and malice which existed between the supporters of the now legally appointed abbot and those of his former rival. A further royal writ had to be issued to bring the unruly objectors to heel and force their acquiescence and obedience but it failed to stifle the bad feeling which persisted.

Troubles of one kind and another continued to plague Abbot de Chavaroche throughout his term of office. Those cells which had severed all connection with their ruling priories had posed a major problem for Abbot de Lavaur which he had failed to resolve. Now, taking advantage of the conditions of unrest and resentment which were pervading the Order, the members of these cells began behaving in a manner which was little short of anarchical. Monks who had illegally assumed the headship of their respective houses were not only calling themselves priors, but refusing to recognise the authority of any other superior including the Abbot General himself. When the General Chapter attempted to submit these establishments to visitation by its officially appointed delegates, the spurious priors aided and abetted their followers in acts of open disobedience and defiance. Grandmontines in name alone, these unruly monks gave scandal to all by their persistent rebellion and neglect of the Rule. The Abbot was forced to appeal to the king and parlement and it was the secular arm of the law which ultimately restrained the rebels and forced the reunion of their cells with their appointed priories.

Abbot de Chavaroche's determination to re-impose and maintain discipline is evident from his dealings with the dissident cells. He did not shrink from suspending the prior of Notre Dame du Parc when it became apparent that his lax and ineffectual leadership was threatening to bring the house into disrepute. The twenty-second Abbot demonstrated all the qualities of a sincere and able administrator, and it is regrettable that a large proportion of his time in office had to be devoted to policing rather than in formulating constructive policies. Whether from discouragement or incompetence, he took no definitive action to further the reforms which his predecessors had fostered with so much drive and energy. He did, however, continue to support and encourage Dom Frémon in his work.

By this time, owing to a generous gift of land from the townspeople, the chief house of the Strict Observance had been fixed at Thiers; an appropriate decision, for this was the birthplace of St Stephen. Here the reform became firmly established and began to yield fruit. In 1665, the year of Abbot de Chavaroche's inauguration, a General Chapter was held which brought together representatives of the houses of the Strict Observance. Twenty articles—all of which recalled the early, austere customs of the followers of St Stephen—were formulated and in due course approved by the Abbot General. Prayer, silence, penitence, mutual obedience, and charity were practised as in the early days at Muret. The reformed brethren reverted to a diet which was wholly vegetarian for most of the year, eggs and dairy produce being permitted only on solemn feast-days. They existed once again in conditions of almost total poverty, sharing whatever they had with the poor and needy. The better to maintain the regular life and silence, the porticus alongside the main church doorway was once again used for the reception of visitors. The disciples of Charles Frémon echoed their first Father when they declared: 'There is no rule but the Gospel'.

By 1670, ten novices had raised the community at Thiers to fifteen and all of them, according to Dom Frémon's biographer, were worthy followers of St Stephen. Fifteen constituted a sizeable community by Grandmontine standards and the chapel in the little monastery donated by the town of Thiers proved too small to contain them. Dom Frémon was therefore constrained to build a new church which, Dom Rochias tells us, conformed absolutely to the traditional romanesque style of architecture which the Grandmontines never discarded. Unfortunately, nothing of this, the last grandmontine church to be built, has survived except the little porticus which remains appropriately enough as a monument to these hermit monks' ideals of silence, and hospitality.

The death of Abbot de Chavaroche would seem to have had few repercussions for the houses of the Strict Observance, but it was the signal for fresh disturbances among the remaining houses. For the second time in just twelve years, two rival candidates were nominated. The Council of State was again required to intervene and proceeded to quash both claims. At a subsequent election all the representatives, amazingly, voted unanimously in favour of Dom Alexandre Frémon, brother of the reformer. The abbatial blessing was conferred on him at Limoges on 25 March 1679, more than a year after the death of the previous abbot. Charles Frémon was present at the ceremony and immediately afterwards, much to his displeasure, was again required to be prior of Grandmont. He accepted humbly and obediently, but it was not long before he somehow managed to get himself dispensed from the office and his brother permitted him to return to his beloved priory at Thiers. At the same time Abbot Frémon gave his approval to all the statutes passed by the chapter of the Strict Observance except one. He positively refused to allow the reformed brethren to uphold one of the fundamental tenets of the early Rule and renounce possessions outside the immediate enclosure of the monastery. While it must have caused the idealistic reformers considerable disappointment, the decision showed common sense.

The past history of the Order had demonstrated only too clearly the impracticality of attempting to live without any stable means of support. To allow several houses to depend solely on alms, which might or might not be forthcoming, involved problems and responsibilities which a seventeenth-century abbot, quite understandably, was not prepared to shoulder. This was especially so in the light of past experiences, when popes themselves had been forced to intervene to mitigate this harsh and unworkable ruling. Before bidding farewell to his brother, Abbot Frémon made him Vicar General of the Strict Observants of the Order of Grandmont. Thus, two brothers ruled as respective heads of two branches of one religious family.

Considering the dramatic events which marked the outset, the ten years in which Alexandre Frémon ruled as twenty-third abbot of Grandmont passed uneventfully and peacefully enough. When he died in 1687, his brother was on a visit to the abbey and was asked to become acting prior. He refused on grounds of age, but remained at Grandmont just long enough to organise the electoral assembly and to remind the fathers of their duties and obligations. He issued a particular warning against permitting outsiders into the abbey during the period of *sede vacante*. All too often in the past, electors had allowed themselves to be influenced by well-intentioned and not so well-intentioned clerics and even laymen. Just before leaving for Thiers, he himself proposed two nominees; Prior Giraud of Beaumont and Prior Henri de la Marche de Parnac of Bercey.

On 9 September 1687, the Prior of Bercey was elected twenty-fourth abbot. Henri de la Marche had made his profession at Grandmont in 1661 and had been sent out to rule the priory of Bercey twenty years later. He was, without any doubt, an able administrator for, when he arrived at Bercey it was, by all accounts, still in a thoroughly dilapidated condition following the Wars of Religion. Not only were the buildings in ruins, scarcely habitable, but the handful of monks who were eking out a meagre existence were deeply in debt. In less than six years, de la Marche had succeeded in restoring the conventual buildings and discharging all debts, and had even managed to recover most of the priory's possessions. When he was summoned to the mother house in 1687, he left behind him a well-organised and flourishing community.

Apart from his administrative abilities, Henri de la Marche was something of a scholar and one of the few authors which the Order of Grandmont produced throughout its entire history. He was responsible for a short spiritual treatise on the religious life, as well as a biography of St Stephen, published in 1704. His intense devotion to the founder prompted him to petition to have the office of his feast included in the Roman Breviary. Regrettably his attempt failed, and to this day, the *Ordo* of

Limoges alone recognises the First Father of the Order of Grandmont. The contemporaries of the twenty-fourth abbot are unanimous in their praise for his fervent and reverent celebration of the liturgy.

Despite his obvious abilities, Abbot de la Marche actually did little to advance the fortunes of the Order but seems to have contented himself with preserving the status quo. He is best remembered for his grandmontine compassion, his generosity, and his warm hospitality. He was sympathetic in his dealings with the reformed religious and remained on excellent terms with the ageing Dom Charles Frémon. He permitted the Strict Observants to hold separate General Chapters without depriving them of their voice in the affairs of the Order as a whole. When Dom Charles Frémon died, it was the abbot who took it upon himself to nominate a successor in the person of Dom François Thomas. In 1692, Dom Thomas expressed his respect and admiration by dedicating the first printed edition of the Statutes of the Reformed Grandmontines to Abbot de la Marche who, in return, wrote a fine introductory preface of approbation.

At the time of Dom Charles Frémon's death, six houses had committed themselves to following the reformed version of the Rule. Apart from the chief house at Thiers, these included: Epoisses, near Dijon; the important house of Notre Dame de Louye, near Paris; Machenet, in Champagne; Chavanon, in the Auvergne; and finally, in 1679, St Michel de Lodève, one of the most southerly houses, in the département of Hérault. A further house, Bussey-en-Forez, was lost to the Strict Observants through a singular act of generosity on the part of Dom Frémon himself. When he returned to Thiers following the death of his brother, news reached him that the benefactor who had given the house to the monks was dying and in a state of extreme mental distress because he was heavily in debt. He could see no way out of his problems and was saddened at the thought of his financial responsibilities devolving on his family. Without hesitation and wholly in keeping with the spirit of St Stephen, Dom Frémon sought and obtained the abbot's permission to restore the house, lock stock and barrel, to its former owner.

Enhanced by actions such as this, Dom Frémon's reputation became almost a legend in his lifetime. When news of his death filtered into the town of Thiers on the third of November 1689, crowds flocked to the priory to pay their last respects and several were heard to exclaim: 'A saint is dead'. In the opinion of his contemporary biographer, Dom Rochias, Charles Frémon was the reincarnation of St Stephen. Certainly he was responsible for reviving that rare vocation which combined the hermit's ideal of solitude with true evangelical poverty. Throughout the sixteenth and well into the seventeenth century, recruitment had been at its lowest ebb. That Charles Frémon succeeded in attracting around sixty novices prepared to vow themselves not merely to the grandmontine vocation but to this singularly harsh version of it was an outstanding achievement.

The feeling of optimism which characterised the reform movement and revitalised the Order at the commencement of the seventeenth century was fast fading by the time of Abbot de la Marche's death in 1715. The election of his successor marked a further decline into decadence and the beginning of the end of the order of Grandmont. René-Pierre-François de la Gueriniѐre proved himself an ambitious, scheming, and extremely worldly person quite unfitted to be the father of the family of monks he ruled for close on thirty years. That he had any kind of religious vocation at all seems dubious, given his behaviour. He showed himself to be far more interested in the dignity of his office and the social position it afforded him than in the spiritual welfare of those in his charge. According to the Abbé Legros, he was raised and cared for by an uncle to whom, as a teenager, he announced his intention to be a priest. This guardian, somewhat doubtful as to his motives, questioned him further. Did he intend being a secular priest, entering a religious order, or what? After a few moments' thought, the precocious youngster declared himself resolved to become a Grandmontine. When asked to give his reasons, he stated quite simply that the Order of Grandmont had so few qualified monks that they were obliged to employ outside professors to teach higher studies. With his education and background he could thus look forward to very rapid promotion. He had also observed, quite correctly, that the abbot was an elderly man whose days were numbered. He intended to make himself so popular and respected that his fellow monks would elect him when the old man died. In fact, he achieved his ambition, and was elected abbot at the remarkably early age of thirty-four.

The Order of Grandmont had never been intended as a monastic haven for scholars and intellectuals. Certainly in the seventeenth century, any young man intent on combining a religious with an academic career would more likely have been attracted to one of the benedictine congregations recognised for its scholarship. But de Gueriniѐre was a mediocre scholar who opted to be top of the class at Grandmont rather than bottom in a benedictine college. As he had predicted, he did manage to gain the admiration and respect of his less able colleagues, and soon rose to be professor of philosophy at the Collѐge Mignon.

Abbot Georges Barny had made it his business to promote higher studies within the Order, but his motives were no more ambitious than training a few teachers capable of instructing the young monks in Scripture, theology, and moral philosophy. The fact that the Order of Grandmont was not prepared to encourage learning for its own sake is clearly apparent from a Chapter decision of 1643. Influenced in all probability by the notions of reform which emphasised detachment from worldly recognition no less than possessions, this forbade the students to receive degrees. As the direct and somewhat unfair consequence, the Order of Grandmont gained a reputation for being an order of ignoramuses. The Abbé Legros has an amusing anecdote based on the notorious lack of education among the Grandmontines. In the course of a conversation with a Recollect Father, Abbot de Guerinière teasingly observed that his superior was general in command of 'a hundred thousand beggars' which attracted the slick response, 'And you, of fifty asses!'[12]

Once he was installed as abbot, de Guerinière worked hard to maintain the ancient rights of the abbey, but appears to have shown scant regard for monastic observance. Neither did he demonstrate the least inclination towards furthering the reform of the principal branch of the Order. He refused to convene a General Chapter and, when the priors voiced their disapproval, plied them with such excuses as: 'the chapter house at Grandmont is in such disrepair as to be uninhabitable or, the mother house is afflicted with an epidemic of colic'. At last he came up with an altogether novel excuse. He did not consider it prudent to hold chapter meetings for so long as the 'troubles' affecting the church in general continued. He was, no doubt, referring to the Jansenist versus Jesuit dispute which was dividing the church in France at that particular time. In 1732, the frustrated priors addressed an appeal to the king imploring him to put pressure on the Abbot of Grandmont to call a General Chapter because he was ruining the Order. Their pleas were to no avail; de Guerinière still managed to evade the issue. Very few novices applied to enter the Order during these troubled years. It has been suggested as a reason that the abbot demanded a dowry of two hundred *livres* to be paid upon admission to the novitiate. While there is no confirmatory proof that this was the case, it is a fact that in just two and a half years de Guerinière's successor admitted thirty.

The accounts of Abbot de Guerinière's haughtiness and social snobbery are reminiscent of the twenty-first Prior, Jourdain de Rapistan. Both rulers brought the order to the brink of ruin as the result of lavish building programmes intended to make the abbey into the sort of palatial residence they deemed appropriate to their rank. To be fair, de Guerinière had inherited a complex of buildings which were, for the most part, centuries old, inconvenient, and uncomfortable. In view of the shaky state of the finances of the Order at the time, however, his ambitious plans were unwise, to say the least. He was prepared to settle for nothing less than a complete rebuilding of the abbey at the astronomical cost of 310,447 *livres*. The cost in terms of the spiritual welfare of the brethren was equally great. Oblivious to the inconvenience, even distress, he was inflicting on the monks by turning their monastery into an almost permanent building site, de Guerinière forged ahead with his plans. The community was actually housed in an isolated and wholly inadequate building, the former infirmary. The medieval church was demolished and the building of Grandmont III begun in 1732. It was not completed until 1768, under de Guerinière's successor, and just four years before Clement XIV issued the bull which approved the expulsion of the monks and the sequestration of their property by the diocese of Limoges. Twenty years' later, Grandmont III was in turn demolished. According to contemporary eye witnesses, this church was, 'one of the finest of its type and has no equal in the kingdom'. Basically, it appears to have been a cruciform structure with a cupola over the crossing, but no plans, drawings, or descriptions have survived. Grandmont III was a white elephant, an ill-fated building which should never have been built in the first place.

Grandmont was not the only building project undertaken by Abbot de Guerinière. He was also obliged substantially to rebuild the Collège Mignon at Paris. A large part of the premises proved to be beyond renovation after years of neglect when little or no repair work had been carried out. This second and very necessary building project placed a tremendous strain on the Order's depleted resources. In actual fact, it was only achieved because de

Guerinière devoted the entire revenue of the priory of Meynel to the purpose.

Once the college buildings were adequate, the Abbot began carrying out his plan to improve the somewhat dismal scholastic reputation of the Order. His intention was to handpick the brightest novices and young professed monks from every community to form an intellectual élite at Paris. At the time, there was actually only one grandmontine monk resident at the college as custodian. The establishment had become Grandmontine in name alone and for some years had been providing a small income for the Order from rooms which were let to student boarders attending the university.

Abbot de Gueriniére cast his eyes around for a capable and efficient superior to manage his brand new house of studies and decided that Dom Jean-Baptiste-François de Vitecoq was admirably suited to the task. On 30 September 1744, before he could put his plan into operation, the abbot died suddenly at the college itself. Raymond Garat who was elected the twenty-sixth abbot on the 10th December following, shared his predecessor's esteem for Dom Vitecoq. Aware that he had been intended for the post of superior with the task of supervising the remainder of the building works at Paris, he endorsed the plan. He went even further in that he also made Dom Vitecoq Financier General of the Order, in which capacity he was to be entrusted with large sums of money. In due course this would become a matter of grave concern for Abbot Garat's successor, the twenty-seventh and last abbot of Grandmont.

NOTES

1. L.J. Lekai, *The Cistercians, Ideals and Reality* (Kent, Ohio: Kent State University Press, 1977) pp. 334–46.

2. M. Lebeau, *Abrége chronologique de l'Histoire de Cîteaux* (Abbaye de Cîteaux: 1981) p.26.

3. D. Knowles, *Christian Monasticism* (World University Library, 1969) p. 154.

4. D. Seward, 'The Grandmontines — A Forgotten Order' *Downside Review* 83 (1965) 256.

5. Lev, p. 393.

6. Collet, *Vie de Saint Vincent de Paul,* Livre IV, p.398, cited Gui, 'Destruction', *BSAHL* 23 (1875) 98

7. Père J. Fouquet OMI and Frère Philippe-Étienne *Histoire de L'Ordre de Grandmont* (Chambray: 1985) p. 78

8. J.B. Rochias, *Vie du Révérend Père Charles Frémon* pb. A. Lecler (Limoges: Ducourtieux et Goût, 1910) p. 32.

9. Abbé P. Coste, *Correspondence de Saint Vincent de Paul* 55 (Paris 1921) p. 309

10. J. Fouquet, (note 7) p. 85.

11. Gui, p.99.

12. Abbé Legros, *Mémoire Manuscript,* p. 111, cited Gui, p. 117.

VIII

THE DESTRUCTION OF THE ORDER OF GRANDMONT

'THE DESTRUCTION OF THE ORDER of Grandmont' is the title of a major work by the nineteenth-century historian Louis Guibert published in the Bulletin de la Société Archéologique et Historique du Limousin, between the years 1875–77. It is a comprehensive, meticulous, and singularly unbiased account of the long drawn-out agony and death throes of this ancient monastic order. By contrast, the following pages attempt no more than a summary outline of these events and the borrowing of Guibert's title is in tribute to a great historian whose name is now as little known outside his native Limousin as is the religious order whose history he so painstakingly recorded. The title could not be more appropriate inasmuch as in its final years the order of Grandmont became the victim of a plot which was intended deliberately and systematically to achieve its destruction.

The Order of Grandmont began to develop symptoms of a terminal illness when Dom François-Xavier Mondain de la Maison Rouge was elected abbot in 1748. When he died on 11 April 1787, at the age of 81, the Order expired with him. He has been described as 'a good, loyal and pious man', 'a child of light' and, 'a worthy, holy and irreproachable priest and monk, a model of christian and religious virtue, a true Bon-homme.' Unfortunately such qualities were of little use to him in the worldly drama in which he was forced to play the leading rôle. His natural humility and gentleness rendered him incapable of competing against scheming bishops and wily lawyers and precluded the machiavellian tactics against which he was himself required to contend. Nevertheless, his failure to save the Order can in no way be attributed to weakness. On the contrary, he struggled ceaselessly and valiantly against the forces which sought to undermine his authority and annihilate the grandmontine institution.

The first unsavoury business which Abbot Mondain was required to settle has come to be known as the 'Vitecoq Affair'. Throughout Abbot Garat's short term in office (1744–8), Dom Vitecoq had been hard at work in Paris completing the elaborate Collège Mignon project instigated by Abbot de la Guerinière. The result was impressive. The Grandmontines were once again in possession of a fine, well-equipped house of studies. Regrettably, the costs of the project had multiplied over the years and the bills were presented for settlement at the same time as the building works at Grandmont itself began running into trouble. Badly executed work which had to be redone, the architect's demands for additional payments, rising costs, all these factors combined to raise the original estimates out of all proportion. The reserve fund held by the abbot was exhausted by the expenses incurred at the College and he found himself in a situation of acute financial embarrassment. He had little alternative but to terminate the expensive educational programme at Paris and disperse the students among the most important of the priories. In October 1749, he arrived at the college and personally reassigned all but four of its occupants. Dom Vitecoq protested loudly and vociferously against this decision which put an end both to his work and his ambitions. His insubordination and rudeness were such that at the General Chapter held the following summer, the abbot was forced to request his removal from office. Dom Vitecoq, however, had enough supporters among the assembled priors to oppose and defeat the motion. Encouraged by this minor triumph and determined that his ambitious plans for a prestigious college should not collapse, Dom Vitecoq perpetrated what is in religious terms an almost unforgivable deed. He defied his religious superior and appealed to the Parlement of Paris to overrule the decision. The abbot, understandably upset by this act of rebellion, was forced to take action. He applied directly to King Louis XV and obtained an order which forbade Dom Vitecoq to come within a hundred miles of Paris. Having discharged his duty as Superior General, Abbot Mondain reverted to being a patient, kindly father and did all in his power to effect a reconciliation. When his efforts failed, he ordered Dom Vitecoq to relinquish his dual office of Superior of the Collège Mignon and Procurator General of the Order.

Unfortunately the abbot was out of order with this decision because it did not have the formal consent of the General Chapter. In consequence, the Order of Grandmont found itself involved once again in a whole series of legal disputes which resulted in a major public scandal. Abbot Mondain again prevailed upon the King to intervene and the decrees were duly quashed. Dom Vitecoq then influenced the ruling body of the University of Paris to support his cause. The right of the University Board of Governors to intervene in the affairs of a constituent college had been recognised by a decree of Council dated 12 June 1752, and although the abbot opposed this intervention, it was legally valid and his protest was dismissed. Dom Vitecoq even received confirmation of his right to the title of Prior of Meynel, a priory united with the college under the same superior. Throughout the year 1753, lawyers' letters went to and fro and Dom Vitecoq clung tenaciously to his title of Procurator General although he had long ceased to perform any of the duties associated with that office.

The proportion and gravity of this scandal which involved the highest courts in the land in the defence of a monk who was defying his Abbot General, was eventually realised by the main body of grandmontine monks. Many of them eventually began to condemn Dom Vitecoq's audacity in waging a legal battle against his lawful superior. Several of his former supporters became alienated from him. On 3 September 1755, the Great Council returned the ball into Grandmont's court when they ordered a General Chapter to meet and deliberate the best way of settling the affairs of the college. When, on 23 November, the General Chapter went into session, it confirmed the constitutions and then voiced its approval of the abbot's handling of the affair. In order to discharge the debts incurred by Dom Vitecoq at the Collège Mignon, a tax proportionate to the means of every house was levied.

Dom Nicod, a religious of the 'Strict Observance' had been in temporary charge of finances at the College. Now, he was delegated by the fathers to attempt the difficult and delicate task of effecting a reconciliation between Dom Vitecoq and his Abbot General. In this he was greatly assisted by the sensitivity of the abbot who was only too willing to make peace with his fiery subject at whatever cost to himself. Dom Vitecoq was relieved of his former offices but was well compensated in being given the priory of Chênegallon, one of the most important houses of the 'Common Observance'. The abbot's generosity was severely censured by the numerous religious who considered that far from being rewarded, Dom Vitecoq should have been punished for his insubordination. The Collège Mignon reverted to being a simple hall of residence for both clerical and lay students attending the University of Paris.

In 1766, just ten years after the Vitecoq affair was concluded, King Louis XV was persuaded to appoint a 'commission of Regulars' charged with the investigation of all the religious orders and congregations of France and the institution of reforms where necessary. According to royal assurances, the fundamental purpose of the Commission was to bring about these reforms in line with royal decrees.

Some of them were undeniably sensible, treating of such matters as a minimum age for entry into the religious life. The most significant regulation the Commission imposed set a minimum number for the community of each house. The result was that four hundred fifty religious houses ceased to exist. The Commission was extraordinary for two reasons. In the first place, it included laymen as well as clerics, and several of its members shared, quite openly, the prejudice of the Voltairean age against the religious life in general. Secondly, a secular commission, responsible to the king of France rather than to the pope, had been invested with power so extensive that it enabled them to close down monasteries and in some cases suppress entire congregations.

The Commission of Regulars was officially presided over by Monseigneur de la Roche Aymon described by Louis Guibert as 'a prelate of little intelligence and feeble character'. The power behind the throne was, however, the archbishop of Toulouse, Etienne-Charles de Loménie de Brienne. Opinion continues to be divided over this unusual and ambitious character who was as much of a statesman as a churchman. To some he appears as a brilliant diplomat, to others he was a scheming rogue consumed by intrigue and stopping at nothing to further his own advancement. His cleverness and skill as an administrator were responsible for his elevation to the purple while still a comparatively young man and it was not long before he exchanged his first modest bishopric of Condom for the wealthy archdiocese of Toulouse. Whilst he ruled his diocese irreproachably and insisted on orthodoxy and discipline, he made no secret of his sympathies with the enlightenment and openly associated with the *philosophes*, some of whom he had known personally when he was a student at the Sorbonne. As a result of such open mindedness he was regarded as suspect both by his fellow clergy, who did not approve of his association with such anti-religionists as d'Alembert and Voltaire, and by the *philoso-*

phes who disapproved of his conservative ways. In his initial dealings with Grandmont he was undeniably fair and expressed the view that the 'Primitive Observance' in particular, 'merited the wholehearted protection of the King in the light of the edifying lives led by its adherents and the austerities which they practised'.[1] Unfortunately his attitude changed all too soon.

The Commission of Regulars had barely begun to invoke the powers vested in it by Louis XV before the superiors of the various religious orders began petitioning the pope to intervene and save them from this secular menace. Unfortunately, their pleas gained little response from Rome. Pope Clement XIII (1758–69) had already proved himself well intentioned but indecisive over the Jesuit question. In 1759, when the powerful portuguese minister, Pombal, had ordered the deportation of all members of the Society of Jesus, the pope's half-hearted protestations achieved the additional expulsion of the papal nuncio from Portugal. Hatred of the Jesuits was equally deep- rooted in France and it was not long before the French followed the portuguese example and in 1764 outlawed the Society by royal decree. The Bourbon powers subsequently united in pressuring the Pope to disband the Society for once and all, but influenced no doubt by pro-Jesuit voices at the court of Rome, he refused. Clement XIII died shortly afterwards and it was left to his successor, Clement XIV, both to suppress the Jesuits and to agree to the dispersal of the monks of Grandmont. Just as soon as Clement XIV found himself occupying the papal throne, he made the appeasement of the catholic powers of Europe a priority and his bull, *Dominus ac Redemptor noster,* suppressing the Jesuits, was regarded as a triumph for the enlightenment. Its citing of precedents of religious orders previously dissolved was fuel for the fire of the Commission of Regulars but bad news for the smaller french religious houses who were relying on papal intervention to save them from extinction. The pope himself was politically rewarded inasmuch as the papal enclaves of Avignon and Venaissin, which had been occupied by the French in protest against his predecessor, were returned to the Holy See.

If the Papacy itself was incapable or, for political motives, somewhat reticent about intervening in the affairs of the Church in France, what was the attitude of the french hierarchy? According to Guibert, while initially they were both resentful and suspicious regarding the activities of the Commission of Regulars, only a few went so far as to air their disapproval publicly. Christophe de Beaumont, the archbishop of Paris, was one prelate who made no secret of his views. The Church alone, he asserted, had the power to intervene in the affairs and conduct of regulars. He further maintained that a commission of five bishops and five councillors of state had no business whatever meddling with monasteries. The archbishop had already incurred the king's displeasure for opposing the decision to expel the Jesuits. The majority of the bishops, however, once they had got over their initial antipathy towards the Commission actually began to support it. One reason for their attitude was that they considered civil intervention would have more chance of succeeding and instituting a real and enduring reform within the monasteries than would a distant and all too often ineffectual roman curia.

A less worthy motive is also discernible. While certain of the seventeenth-century bishops had vast fortunes at their disposal, many of the smaller dioceses were verging on penury and their bishops were hard pressed to maintain themselves and their entourages. Any reservations they expressed about the work of the Commission were soon dissipated when they understood that the Crown had no intention of sequestrating religious establishments for its own benefit, that in every case the lands and possessions of a suppressed house would be transferred to the diocese in which it was located. The ruling bishop would be free to dispose of all such lands and possessions at his discretion. Of course, one of the more acceptable uses to which confiscated monasteries and their attendant wealth was devoted was diocesan seminaries. Several grandmontine houses ended up as training colleges for secular clergy. The attitude of bishops who were genuinely desirous of increasing the ranks of the clergy by providing free education and training for young men from poor families is expressed in a letter addressed to Loménie de Brienne by the archbishop of Tours on 18 November 1769:

> Nothing is more befitting the religion of the King than that the possessions of the Grandmontines should be utilised to provide free education for young men destined for the priesthood.[2]

In the case of the abbey of Grandmont, it was Monseigneur du Plessis d'Argentré, bishop of Limoges, who stood to benefit from its suppression. General opinion, not without reason, has always held this cleric to be the arch-villain who wantonly brought about the destruction of the Order of Grandmont. Guibert, however, did not blame the Bishop entirely and suggested that the ultimate fate of the Order had been decided by Loménie de Brienne even before the General Chapter of 1768 at which the religious were advised to adopt reforms in order to obtain the king's approval for the continuation of their Order.[3] Bishop d'Argentré's part in the initial stages of the procedure against the Grandmontines may have been exaggerated, for there is a complete lack of evidence implicating him. Nevertheless, his rôle increased infinitely in importance as time went on. Ultimately the manner in which he effected the expulsion of the monks and took possession of the abbey can only be described as ruthless and cruel.

On 3 April 1767, the Commission of Regulars secured a royal decree ordering all religious institutions to convene General Chapters at which they were to deliberate their constitutions and assess the extent to which they had departed from their fundamental ideals. They were also required to submit a report outlining their plans for reform and a return to the original observances laid down by their rules. The same decree banned all communities which counted less than ten religious, so that superiors were obliged to amalgamate certain houses within their charge before implementing a programme of reform.

One year later the political rupture between France and the Papacy in the person of Clement XIII had two significant consequences. In the first place it deprived superiors of their right of appeal to the court of Rome, and secondly, it prompted government to make itself solely responsible for promoting religious reform within the kingdom. The edict which appeared in March of this year placed all the religious houses in France—including those which had enjoyed episcopal exemption for centuries—firmly under diocesan control.

Unlike his contemporary religious colleagues, Abbot Mondain appears to have been blissfully and naively unaware of the peril which menaced the entire monastic Order in France when, in compliance with this decree he submitted his somewhat optimistic report of the state of the grandmontine institution. Conformity with certain of the new regulations, notably that which laid down the minimum age for profession as twenty-one years did not worry him. St Stephen himself had required this restriction and it was written into the Rule of Grandmont. When, however, he turned his attention to accounting for the precarious state of the Order's finances and compiling a census of the communities occupying each of the daughter houses, he encountered somewhat graver problems. His proposal to maintain nine houses in addition to the mother house still did not satisfy the statutory requirement of a minimum of eight religious to a community—novices and lay-monks could not be included in the overall figure. It was this ruling more than anything else which threatened the Grandmontines with extinction. Some of the more realistic among the senior religious were soon made aware of this possibility and certain of the less reputable characters among them decided to act independently of the abbot in order to safeguard their own personal interests.

Prominent among this group were Dom Razat, the Procurator General of the Order; and Dom Nicod, Vicar General of the branch of the Strict Observance. Dom Razat had already made something of a name for himself in a legal battle he had waged against Abbot Martial Sardine of the benedictine abbey of Nanteuil-en-Vallée. Dom Razat maintained that the Rule of St Stephen derived from that of St Benedict and in consequence entitled him, as a Grandmontine, to hold the benedictine priory of Saint-Vincent de la Faye *in commendam*. This case was not without precedent: grandmontine superiors had previously been permitted to hold benedictine benefices, as Benedictines had held grandmontine monasteries *in commendam*. Unfortunately for Dom Razat, times had changed radically. In September 1758, the Great Council ruled that the Grandmontines were bound to follow the Rule of St Stephen of Muret which neither derived from nor bore any resemblance to the Rule of St Benedict. Consequently, its members could have no right whatsoever to hold benedictine benefices. Dom Razat was obliged to relinquish his claim and console himself with the knowledge that, as Procurator General of the twin Observances, he held the highest and most prestigious office in the Order of Grandmont. This office moreover, entitled him to live in some style at the Collège Mignon in Paris. In this capacity, he was required by the Abbot General to prepare and submit various documents concerning the financial state of the Order to Loménie de Brienne. As the direct result of this he was able to form a close relationship with the secretaries of the Commission, which enabled him to find out which way the wind was blowing and harness it to serve his own interests.

In due course, a recommendation in Dom Razat's own handwriting was delivered to the Commission. Louis Guibert has described this document as 'The sentence of death pronounced against Grandmont by a Grandmontine'.[4] Dom Razat's conduct is rendered all the more distasteful by the fact that he delivered what amounted to a statement of capitulation on the Order's behalf without the knowledge of the Abbot General. Essentially the document maintains that the Order as a whole is unable to comply with the king's wishes and therefore the Commission should proceed to the speedy disbanding of the institute, without any further consultation of the religious. Disloyalty is rampant in Dom Razat's references to General Chapters which, he asserts, were simply occasions for 'reproaches, divisions, discussions about personal interests, intrigues, quarrels and generally speaking a great deal of hot air'. The real motive for this action is clear from the final paragraph in which Razat respectfully requests remuneration in the form of pensions for the religious. A note scrawled in the margin observes that the king would gain the right to dispose of the abbey of Grandmont following the death of its abbot, together with the right to dispose of four titular priories, the remainder of the priories having already been awarded to various owners *in commendam*.[5]

Given the dismal picture of the Order as drawn by one of its chief officials, it is not surprising that the subsequent judgments expressed by members of the Commission are equally derogatory. A summary report which emerged shortly after observes that 'the Grandmontines have always been a singularly ignorant body of religious who have never shown the least love of letters or tendency to produce works of the spirit. . . they are notoriously lax in their religious observances and have proved themselves as ignorant of the Rule of St Stephen as any other religious text. . . they have no sense of propriety, both as regards the celebration of the office and, general conduct. . . The men who make up their communities are, for the most part, coarse, uneducated and ill-mannered. . . Their most serious occupation is hunting and fishing.' The same report concludes with the opinion that the Grandmontines are not worth reforming and in fact, 'any such attempt would be doomed to failure given that to resuscitate a love of the Rule of the Founder would require a number of men themselves sufficiently inspired that they might pass on their inspiration to others. Such persons can nowhere be found among the superiors any more than the rank and file.'[6]

If Abbot Mondain was in total and blissful ignorance of the actions of his Procurator General, the beliefs and actions of another of his senior religious were only too apparent and their outcome must have wounded him deeply. Dom Nicod was the Vicar General of the branch of the Strict Observance which, in 1768, accounted for forty-two subjects including two novices. Like Dom Razat, Dom Nicod wrote secretly to the Commission agreeing that small numbers made the exact observance of the Rule almost impossible, and suggesting that the eight houses of the Strict Observance be reduced to four. The commissioners were only too willing to consent to this proposal. In consequence, the religious of the Strict Observance formed into four communities attached to the houses of Époisse, Macheret, Thiers and Louye.

In September 1768, Dom Nicod's act of separation from and defiance of his Abbot General was taken a stage further when he and his followers refused to attend the General Chapter convened at Grandmont. Abbot Mondain had been depending on the reformed brethren to assist him in implementing a general reform which he hoped would be the salvation of the Order as a whole. Their defection en masse must have been unnerving, to say the least. Just a few days before the Chapter opened on 25 September, Abbot Mondain's efforts to institute a reform received a further setback. This time it was the Commissioners who delivered a blow which struck both the Strict and Common Observants with equal force. An order was issued banning the reception or profession of novices. On 24 February of the following year the restriction was extended and the abbot ordered to send any remaining novices packing. The Commissioners could not have devised any surer means of bringing about the slow but certain end of the Order.

It was this ban on novices which, in all likelihood, was directly responsible for Dom Nicod's subsequent action.

All too aware that without recruits there can be no institution, he wrote once again to the Commissioners. This time he informed them that the arrangement which had restricted the reformed religious to four communities had failed. He requested therefore that the grandmontine branch of the Strict Observance be disbanded and its members left free to join other religious institutes of their choice. Once again, and without the Abbot General's knowledge, his request was granted, and as Louis Guibert wryly puts it: 'the Commission established for the reformation of the religious orders began its work by the destruction of a reform.'

Of the former Grandmontines of the Strict Observance, sixteen transferred to the strict Benedictine Congregation of St Vanne, twelve opted for Cluny and one became a Carthusian. Three were unable to make up their minds at the time and so their ultimate destination remains unknown. One of these appears to have been a lay brother who had been removed from the monastery by the military authorities and was being held in detention at Périgueux, accused of having deserted his regiment. It is significant that whilst five of the religious requested to be allowed to live out their lives in one of the otherwise deserted houses of the Strict Observance, not one expressed a wish to be transferred to the branch of the Common Observance. As the entire community at Macheret had joined the Benedictines of St Vanne, the house itself was handed over to that congregation. Louye, in its turn, was given to the Benedictines of Cluny, until the bishop of Chartres demanded that it be relinquished to his diocese. Epoisses also passed for a time to another religious congregation while Thiers, the mother house of Dom Frémon's reformed Grandmontines, was retained for the benefit of the five religious who had requested to live out their days in a former grandmontine priory. Their ultimate fate is unknown.

What of Dom Nicod himself? The man who must shoulder a large share of the responsibility for the loss of the order of Grandmont chose initially to join the Benedictines of St Vanne. There he discovered that the life of a reformed Benedictine was not to his liking and so he persuaded Loménie de Brienne to allow him to take up residence the former grandmontine house of Vieux-Pou near Auxerre.

An alternative and more seemly motive which may have moved Dom Nicod to provoke the suicide of the Grandmontines of the Strict Observance has been proposed by Desmond Seward:

> Nicod's dealing with the Commission may be interpreted as the actions of a man concerned for his vocation and for the vocations of those under his charge, with no confidence in Mondain leadership who when finally convinced that the cause of St Stephen was lost decided to seek refuge in a secure spiritual haven.[7]

Even if this were the case, it still does not excuse Nicod's lack of courtesy, to say nothing of his disloyalty and disobedience, in not making his intentions known to his lawful religious superior. Although Mr Seward maintains that Dom Mondain de la Maison Rouge was not the true spiritual superior of the Strict Observants, yet at no time did they make a formal break with the Order of Grandmont as a whole. While the reformed Cistercians under their leader Armand de Rancé fought tooth and nail with the cistercian proto-abbots in what had been termed 'the war of the Observances', Dom Frémon First Father of the grandmontine reform obtained the approval of the Abbot General of Grandmont for all his actions.

In September 1768, in accordance with the royal decree issued in 1767, the last General Chapter of the Order of Grandmont met in the presence of Loménie de Brienne and his colleague, François Tristan de Cambon, bishop of Mirepoix. This turned out to be the first round in a contest which was to extend over the next twenty years. Abbot Mondain has been accused of inaptitude and fecklessness for his failure to save his Order from extinction. The Abbé Legros considered till his lack of forthrightness and vigour ultimately responsible for the adverse decisions passed by the Commission of Regulars.[8] This is unjust. Abbot Mondain was untiring in his efforts to save the Order of Grandmont from extinction. His critics have always overlooked the fact that both his vocation and training fitted him to be a monk, not a lawyer, yet circumstances obliged him to engage in almost solitary conflict with the best and most devious legal minds in the land.

As soon as the General Chapter went into session, a list of all seventy-two members of the Common Observance was submitted. These religious were found among twenty-one houses which included the Collège Mignon, which had retained a staff of just two. On the average, individual communities numbered no more than three; the largest being Chênegallon where there were five. The mother house itself boasted a mere eleven religious, including the abbot.

Next, the Commissioners communicated the king's wishes to the assembled monks. The Rule of St Stephen, they insisted, had always been accepted as the fundamental legislation for the Order, despite successive mitigations which various popes had permitted in the course of centuries. Because of this, the king required them to fulfil two conditions in return for the right to continue as a religious order enjoying his protection. The first called upon them to undertake a voluntary and complete return to the practice of the primitive Rule and Constitution of the Order, and the second demanded the re-establishment at the abbey of a full conventual life and monastic horarium.

Although they had only a brief acquaintance with Abbot Mondain, the Commissioners must have been fully aware of the extent of his strong moral principles. Possibly Dom Razat and Dom Nicod had given them an idea of what to expect. At any rate they certainly seem to have been forewarned that the religious of the Common Observance were unlikely to play into their hands as had those of the Strict

Observance. This much is apparent from the unrealistic conditions which they sought to impose at the General Chapter and which were knowingly and cunningly contrived to produce the maximum consternation among the assembled fathers. Generations of superiors and popes had judged the imposition of the original Rule in all its purity, impracticable. It had been composed in an age of faith and fervour and its initial followers had been close to their Founder both in spiritual ideals and physical stamina. The austerities it required of its adherents had come to be regarded as excessive, even unhealthy, and it had been adjusted accordingly.

In vain did the religious protest to the Commissioners that their vows of profession had not bound them to practise a medieval interpretation of the monastic life. They pointed out quite reasonably that many of them were elderly and therefore incapable of adhering to the strict fasting and abstinence exacted by the primitive Rule. They besought the Commissioners to present their case to His Majesty and to ask him to dispense them from so grave an obligation. They professed their willingness to return to the practice of the Rule in accordance with the Statutes of 1625 and 1643. They declared themselves only too ready to obey the second requirement, and indeed they acknowledged the very real need that monks should lead an orderly and regular life in community. The Commissioners were adamant, however; the king required of them all or nothing and, for the first time, delivered the threat of closure. The assembled fathers protested vehemently but to no avail, and the Commissioners then proceeded to read the formal ban on the acceptance and profession of novices.

There can be little doubt that the Commissioners exceeded their authority at this fateful General Chapter. Just what should have occurred and what actually did occur is recorded in an appendix to a report entitled *Mémoire à Consulter et Consultation pour l'Abbé de Grandmont, Général de l'Ordre de ce Nom.*[9] Throughout the proceedings, Loménie de Brienne behaved in a thoroughly objectionable manner. He was by turn imperious, menacing, and downright rude in the way he silenced protestors. According to the Mémoire, the Commissioners' credentials, which were read aloud at the start of proceedings, only authorised them 'to assist at the Chapter in their capacity as Commissioners, to oversee and ensure that the proceedings were conducted in an orderly and decent manner'.[10] From all accounts, Loménie took over completely and conducted proceedings as though he were a judge in a court of law. According to another contemporary author:

> The prelate [Loménie de Brienne] forgetting that he was a bishop, behaved as though he were invested with royal powers. He was like a conqueror vanquishing a foe. The terror he inspired could not have been surpassed by a soldier. The terrified religious had neither the time nor the sangfroid necessary to defend themselves against his onslaughts. They had no means whatsoever of defending themselves. In the twinkling of an eye the order of Grandmont was judged, condemned, and sentenced to suppression.[11]

When Loménie returned to Paris at the conclusion of the shambles which passed for a general chapter, he carried with him a petition from the demoralised religious addressed to the king. This implored His Majesty to allow them to continue to live in their respective monasteries in accordance with their Constitution and to be permitted to elect a superior general to govern them when the present holder of that office should die. Should the king refuse to grant their request, they begged only that they be allowed to live out their lives in their monasteries, under the authority of the appropriate ordinary. Should even this pathetic plea be denied them, then they expressed their willingness to retire with pensions into the houses of other religious congregations provided the necessary papal authority were first obtained.

Abbot Mondain addressed a separate personal petition in which he requested the king to spare at least the abbey of Grandmont and in return, he would devote all his efforts to re-establishing a group of religious who would engage themselves under his direction to live the Rule of St Stephen to the letter.

Loménie de Brienne's own report on proceedings at the General Chapter, which he presented to the Commission on his return to Paris, was damnatory in the extreme.

> Of seventy-three religious distributed among twenty-two houses, there are twenty who, according to the evidence of their confrères, are wholly reprehensible. Either they are of bad moral character or given to drunkeness. A few among them have actually broken the law of the land. Forty or so are dissolute and slothful, leading totally secular lives. The remainder have conserved the spirit of their state to some degree and two or three would be capable of following the Rule in all its rigour.

The abbot, he reported, was a wise and virtuous man, distinguished for his love of good but too frail and gentle to be able to subdue troublemakers. 'He is divided between his desire to preserve the Order, and the hopelessness of the task of preserving it according to the Rule.' He further outlined the abbot's desire and willingness to assemble twenty-four monks who would agree to observe the Rule under his direction at Grandmont but expressed the opinion that this represented an impossible task.

A particularly blatant piece of falsehood is contained in Loménie's report where it states categorically:

> The Order of Grandmont has no wish to reform itself. While its preservation is dependent upon reform taking place, this does not exclude the religious from retaining the various authorised mitigations of their Rule.

This is in total contradiction of the terms which Loménie had dictated at the General Chapter in reply to the religious who asserted the impracticality of returning to the rigours of the fundamental Rule of St Stephen, but professed themselves willing to comply with the Statutes of 1625 and 1643. At the time, Loménie had absolutely refused to countenance any such half measures.[12]

The remainder of this document outlines a strategy so cleverly and cunningly contrived that the suppression of the Order will appear to be self-destruction. It interprets the petitions which the religious addressed to the king in the event of their institute ceasing to exist to mean that they were unanimously agreed that this should inevitably be the outcome. Their request for the award of pensions had been officially endorsed by the Chapter, and Loménie knew that it required only authorisation by letters patent to become effective. Thus, the agreement which the religious had signed in all innocence without realising its implications was twisted to imply that they wholeheartedly gave their assent to the dissolution of the Order. They had signed a document which they thought would afford them certain rights and securities if, and only if, all else failed; but effectively they had affixed their signatures to the death warrant of their Order. Loménie summarised his plan as follows:

> For as long as the Abbot remains alive, he shall continue to lead the religious. Upon his death, they will come under the jurisdiction of the ordinary. From this moment, the monasteries must be united [i.e. with their respective dioceses]. Thus the Order of Grandmont will cease to exist in France, without any heart-rending or suffering, without having to invoke the necessary authority. It will, of its own accord, simply cease to be and its possessions will be passed on for the benefit of worthwhile establishments within the various dioceses.[13]

Loménie's recommendations were received with wholehearted approval by the Commission and a month after the fateful General Chapter, Abbot Mondain received a letter from the king's minister, Saint-Florentin, Duc de la Vrillière, ordering him politely and kindly, but firmly, to send home any novices who remained under his jurisdiction. Despite the intense sorrow which the departure of his five novices must have occasioned him, Abbot Mondain did not despair and courageously began to work on a new set of reformed constitutions to be submitted for the king's approval. He still believed that he would be able to gather sufficient monks together at the abbey to make his proposed reform a reality.

While Abbot Mondain laboured to save his Order in blissful ignorance of the fact that its destruction was already a *fait accompli*, Loménie was equally hard at work implementing his devious plans, the outcome of which would enable him to say that the Order of Grandmont had destroyed itself. Acting on his instructions, a colleague on the Commission had already prepared the letters patent which would pave the way for the kill: 'without any great effort and without causing any unnecessary sensation.[14]

The tone of the letters patent is blatantly hypocritical, inasmuch as they express an excessive concern for the welfare of the religious about to be deprived of their spiritual home. Briefly it is stated that, the Common Observance of the Order of Grandmont having been reduced to a mere seventy-two religious including its Abbot General, many of the houses have found it impossible to re-establish a regular conventual life; that taking into account the advanced ages and infirmities of some of this limited number of religious as well as the wholly worldly lives led by others, there would seem to be no possibility of their ever being able to comply with the Rule of their Founder. Therefore, it dispenses the religious from the obligations set forth in the Royal Edict of 1768. It grants them the liberty to remain within their respective monasteries under the authority of their existing superiors, but forbids them absolutely to receive novices. In conclusion it authorises the bishops of the dioceses concerned to effect the suppression of grandmontine houses the instant they became vacant through the death or demission of their occupants. The bishops were further instructed to set aside sufficient funds from the revenues belonging to such houses in order to provide pensions for the former grandmontine religious. The residue of all monies and property were then to be transferred to the diocesan exchequer to be used for the benefit of ecclesiastical establishments such as seminaries. At no point in the entire proceedings was any account taken of the fact that the Order of Grandmont had been exempt from episcopal jurisdiction for centuries. Thus for the letters patent to invoke canon law to justify the manner of disposal of grandmontine properties was farcical. Even in the case of religious establishments which had not enjoyed such exemption, there had always been a general principle, upheld by canon law, that unions of this nature were to be effected only in cases of extreme necessity, when heresy or serious disorders left no other course open to church authorities. Where, on the other hand, a house was exempt, union with either another religious house or the diocese required the consent of the superior concerned. Far from giving his consent to these proposed unions, Abbot Mondain was actively opposing them. Furthermore, while the French canonists asserted that the general rule could be waived in cases where the bishop intended to award religious properties to seminaries, Rome still maintained its exclusive right to make the final determination.

In the light of this knowledge, Abbot Mondain considered formulating an appeal to the Holy See, but both time and political circumstances were against him. Pope Clement XIII had recently died and with him had also passed some of the antipathy which had existed between the papal court and France aroused by the Jesuit question. Clement XIV, did not maintain his predecessor's intransigent opposition to the Bourbon dynasty. In fact upon being elected, he made the appeasement of the Catholic powers a priority. Aware of these circumstances, and in order to avoid embarrassing papal relationships with France, Abbot Mondain tactfully addressed his petition to the king rather than the pope. His letter comprises several pages of pathetic hopes and illusions and begs the king in abject fashion to permit him to continue ruling Grandmont under a stricter régime in conformity with the bull of Clement V. He also implores the king to renew his right to admit novices as well as the right of the religious to proceed to the election of a succeeding superior general following his own death. The final paragraph is a particularly poignant and desperate plea for survival:

> Deign Sire, to give ear to my ardent and most humble prayers. Be pleased to grant your royal protection once again to this abbey which was the work of your ancestors. The re-establishment of the former regular life will shine with its ancient lustre, edification, and good example which others will emulate. All will inherit a new lease of life and this monastery will assuredly be transformed into an exemplary house, worthy both of your favours and of the early days of the Order; a holy retreat in which God will be served and invoked unceasingly for the preservation of a monarchy which bestows happiness upon its subjects.[15]

At the same time as he directed this appeal to the King, Abbot Mondain sent Loménie de Brienne a copy of his projected constitutions which closely resembled those formulated by Dom Charles Frémon a century before. Whether or not he took time to peruse them, Loménie certainly made no comment whatsoever. Then, in March 1769, the abbot journeyed to Paris where he was respectfully and graciously received by his adversaries who, notwithstanding, paid no attention to his pleas and remonstrations. Hardly had he returned to Grandmont when he received the king's answer to his request written in the hand of one of his chief councillors of state, the Duc de la Vrillière. Couched in honeyed terms, the letter congratulated him on all his good intentions but informed him that nevertheless: 'It is not sufficient for a reform to propose laws, however excellent they may be; it is also necessary to provide a certain number of religious who are prepared to execute them.' The letter then advises the Abbot that, if he can find twenty-four religious who, freely and voluntarily will agree to the project, then, and only then, will His Majesty be prepared to afford them his protection. Unless and until this condition were fulfilled, the prohibitions laid down in the letters patent of the previous February must stand.

The prohibitions were sufficient in themselves to bring about the slow but sure demise of the Order of Grandmont: all the Commissioners had to do was sit back and wait for it to happen. Several of the french bishops had already instigated the procedures necessary to secure the union of the grandmontine houses within their respective dioceses. Early in the year 1770, eleven priories of the Common Observance had been so transferred quietly and without fuss. Still the Mother House remained an unyielding stronghold of grandmontine opposition. Although Abbot Mondain lacked the ability and energy for an all-out combat, his tenacity did not fail him. The Commissioners had obviously been hoping that, once he realised his cause was irretrievably lost, he would surrender the abbey without further ado. Instead, he was holding out relentlessly and Loménie de Brienne' s patience was being taxed to the limit. Furthermore, the abbot must have become something of an embarrassment to him for two reasons. In the first place he had devised and submitted for the king's approval what amounted to a perfectly acceptable reformed constitution. A few religious, edified no doubt by their superior's example and determination, had elected to remain with him in his retreat. If news of this defiant yet praiseworthy stand should reach the ears of the pope, there could yet be serious and unpleasant repercussions from that quarter. Secondly, the finances of Loménie de Brienne's friend, Bishop d'Argentré of Limoges, were the cause of considerable concern. Monseigneur d'Argentré had obtained an enormous loan to enable him to finish building his new palace at Limoges, a palace which, as he expressed it himself in a letter, would permit him to live in a manner more in keeping with his rank. The bishop's creditors were beginning to press for payment and Loménie had assured him that he could count on the abbey and its revenues to discharge his debt.

There was only one course of action which would bring about the defeat of the Abbot and effect a speedier evacuation of Grandmont. The monks who continued to remain faithful to their Rule and loyal to their leader would have to be won over; and one monk in particular was to prove himself ideally suited to this devious purpose. Dom Daguerre had been at Grandmont for some time and enjoyed the confidence of the abbot, who had sent him on several missions to Paris as acting Procurator-General, Dom Razat having retired to the priory of Meynel. On one of these trips Loménie found the means of influencing him to perform the role of Rosencrantz Guildenstern in the drama which was beginning to unfold. He was sent on missions to various of the remaining grandmontine houses, ostensibly for the benefit of the religious, but in reality, to speed up the liquidation of these houses. At Faye Jumilhac, for example, the brethren were doing all in their power to prevent their house being taken over by the seminary of Périgueux. Daguerre was able to convince them that their procrastination could not and would not avert the inevitable. He persuaded them that they would be better employed rescuing what they could from the disaster by submitting their requests for pensions to the Commission. Once these requests were received by the Commission, they were interpreted as tacit agreement to the suppression of the house in question, which could then be efficiently and speedily carried out. Loménie also used Daguerre to pave the way for takeover, by sounding out the mood of the community in question. In this way he received advance notice of, and was prepared for, difficulties which might hinder the smooth transfer of a house to the diocese. For his espionage, Daguerre was well rewarded with the gift of the grandmontine house of Bandouille, one of the wealthier priories. Then Loménie entrusted him with an ultimate and decidedly more delicate task. He was instructed to persuade the abbot himself to end the stalemate and to relinquish Grandmont to the diocese of Limoges. A memorandum of instructions from Loménie to his agent, preserved in the Archives Nationales, contains a particularly reptilian set of instructions. The abbot, states Loménie, must be made aware of the futility of the task he is seeking to impose upon himself. He must be convinced of the king's interest, benevolence, and generosity, and he must be urged to submit a request for pension both for himself and for the good of those in his charge. If the abbot should refuse to accept the inevitable, Daguerre is required to influence the monks behind his back. They, in turn, are to be made aware of their own best interests and urged as a body to submit requests for pensions, as these will have to be deducted from the revenues of the abbey prior to their being transferred to the diocese. The monks must be made to realise that the king has their interests at heart and has no wish to deprive them of what is rightfully theirs. He will therefore appoint a crown administrator to take charge of the abbey's finances and compile an inventory of all lands and properties belonging to it. The long-suffering abbot had been obliged to dispatch his novices; now the few religious who had stood by him were to have their minds soured against him and be bought off by an official in whom he had placed his trust.

So confident was Loménie that Daguerre would succeed in his task that he included with his memorandum the following incredible letter of submission, addressed to himself and intended for the Abbot's signature:

> Monseigneur, the decision taken by the religious of Grandmont has reduced me to such a pitiable state that I am forced to throw myself upon the mercy of His Majesty; no other course remains open to me. I am resigned to witnessing the extinction of the house in which I have sought in vain to re-establish by example the regular life. Now I can do no more than consign it to the King who in his wisdom will determine its fate. I submit myself entirely to the views and wishes of the King, who is the best of fathers. From this moment, I place my abbey in his hands and I agree to its union with whatever benefice or establishment he shall see fit. I ask only that he be pleased to grant me, out of the revenues of this house, a pension of: (a space for the amount to be filled in is left blank) for the duration of my life, and which will enable me to live in whatever retirement I may choose. You will realise, Monseigneur, the enormity of a sacrifice which the piety of the King allowed me to consider as a much more distant prospect. However, the lack of subjects has rendered it necessary today. I beseech you to make my position known to His Majesty. At least I have the consolation that he will realise how much it is costing me to renounce the hopes that I had formed for the glory of religion and of my Order.[16]

Loménie also provided Daguerre with a letter for the abbot informing him of the inadvisability and futility of any further resistance. 'Further delays,' he warns him, 'are superfluous and against the best interests of those in your charge.' A copy of all three documents entrusted to Daguerre was sent to the Bishop of Limoges for his information.[17] A covering letter introduced Dom Daguerre to Monseigneur d'Argentré and observed that he might find it necessary to remain in the locality for six months or so in order to make all the necessary arrangements for the transferral of the abbey to the diocese. Monseigneur d'Argentré was absent from Limoges for reasons of health when the letter and its bearer arrived. It was some weeks, therefore, before he was made aware of the plot intending to oust the abbot. When he did get round to replying, he was able to inform Loménie that news of Dom Daguerre's mission had filtered round the diocese in his absence and given rise to a rumour which stated that 'A grandmontine monk sent from the royal court had arrived at Grandmont with orders to empty the house.'

No sooner had Daguerre arrived at Grandmont than it became clear to him that whatever results his devious methods might achieve with the monks, he was going to get nowhere with their superior. The abbot had been unable to save his daughter houses but he was certainly not going to relinquish the mother house. He still nourished hopes, based on a somewhat unrealistic picture of the goodness and mercy of King Louis XV, that he would after all be permitted to realise his ambition. In his naiveté, he could not accept that the Commission of Regulars was really seeking to annihilate the Order of St Stephen which had been in existence for over six centuries.

Daguerre performed his task well. He ignored the abbot and concentrated instead on worming his way into the confidence of the religious. He sounded them out and appealed to each in turn. He besought them, one after the other to be reasonable and to capitulate. He argued that they had no option but to safeguard their own interests. He played on their respective weaknesses, appealing to the simplicity of some and the better nature of others. He hammered them all unwearyingly, and to such an extent that he achieved his goal. On 23 August he was able to send Loménie a copy of a resolution passed at a chapter meeting held in the absence of the abbot and without his knowledge. This document bears the signatures of nine religious, all priests, who expressed their agreement with the Commission that the abbot could never succeed in the task he had set himself. In order to avoid any further unpleasantness and disagreement, they professed themselves ready to concur with the king's decision and to agree to the union with whatever ecclesiastical authority he would be pleased to consider. Their requests were twofold; they humbly begged His Majesty to grant them life pensions payable quarterly in advance, and they requested to be allowed to remain at the abbey with the abbot until his death.[18]

On 24 December 1770, the bishop of Limoges addressed a letter of just fifteen lines to Loménie wishing him a happy new year, followed by a postscript of considerable length. This describes a recent dinner conversation between himself and the abbot of Grandmont. The abbot had accused him outright of complicity with the Commission of Regulars and of attempting to accelerate the suppression of his abbey; and avowed that he had very reliable proof to support his statement. Having told Loménie that he had denied any involvement with the Commission, the Bishop appealed to him in the following, very surprising manner:

> As you see, Monseigneur, this is the first time that I have written you on the subject of the Abbey of Grandmont.[19]

Could Bishop d'Argentré's memory really have been so short-lived? The French Archives of State contain several letters which he addressed to Loménie de Brienne on the subject of Grandmont prior to this particular one. The promise to remain neutral which, in his letter, he says that he had made to the abbot, turned out to be utterly valueless.

Early in the year 1771, Loménie realised that his efforts to achieve any kind of amicable agreement with the abbot were getting him nowhere and that more drastic action was called for if he was ever to succeed in his ambition of gaining Grandmont for the diocese of Limoges. When the

Commission met on 27 February, he persuaded his colleagues to write officially to Cardinal de Bernis, the French Ambassador to the Holy See, and sound out the possibility of obtaining a papal bull of suppression. In the meantime, the Commission ordered an official inventory of the goods and possessions of the abbey to be compiled as soon as possible.

Loménie wasted no time in implementing the order of the Commission. By 2 March he had obtained a decree of council requiring the Intendant of Limoges or his delegate to proceed with the inventory. A few days later, he wrote again to Monseigneur d'Argentré telling him of his latest move and concluding with the following observation:

> The Abbot of Grandmont cannot complain because the time he requested has passed, and if it had been prolonged any further there would be a risk of his possessions being subject to mismanagement and falling into decay. It gives me great pleasure to find myself on the point of concluding a business which is so much in your interest.[20]

Monseigneur d'Argentré's reply to this letter reveals something of his true character. In the first instance, he informs Loménie that the abbot of Grandmont had dined with him on two separate occasions in the course of the previous winter and he had engaged himself to return the compliment and visit the abbot at Grandmont. However, he says:

> I confess to you that I have not been able to summon up the courage because they would think that I went there for the sole purpose of seeing the promised land and to take measures to assure its conquest. I have therefore written a very truthful letter to Monseigneur the Abbot, begging him to excuse me on account of the weather and poor state of the roads.

He then dwelt at some length upon the financial embarrassment his new buildings were causing him and asked

Loménie's advice as to how best he might acquit himself because, as he says:

> You are always well versed in finding such solutions, especially when friendship underlines your natural wisdom.[21]

Monseigneur d'Argentré did in fact meet the abbot shortly after this letter was written, but not at a convivial dinner party: the abbot was on a formal visit to Limoges. The bishop maintained that on this occasion he tried to convince the abbot of the futility of his putting up any further opposition to the royal commands. The abbot replied simply that he would do all in his power to obey His Majesty a fact which was duly reported to Loménie in a letter dated 19 April.

Meanwhile, the abbot had received word from Monsieur the Intendant of Limoges informing him that, in compliance with the writ of 9 March, he would be sending Monsieur de Lepine, his deputy, to carry out the required inventory on 17 April. The abbot responded with an assurance that Monsieur de Lepine would encounter no resistance on his part.

Anne Robert Jacques Turgot (1727–81) the celebrated economist, author, and associate of Adam Smith, has generally been regarded by historians as an enlightened and compassionate man. In the course of his intendancy at Limoges, he did a great deal to improve the conditions of the poor. He cannot have relished the distasteful charge which had fallen to him to perform and was no doubt relieved that the abbot intended to make it lighter by pledging his cooperation.

Had Turgot mistaken the exact implication of the abbot's words in his reply to him? Certainly when his delegate arrived at Grandmont on the day appointed, far from the passive acquiescence he had anticipated, he discovered the abbot and his handful of monks installed in the chapter house. When he made formal announcement as to the purpose of his visit, they adamantly refused to let him proceed. Monsieur de Lepine was obliged to retreat to the village and wait until he received further instructions from his superior.

Both Monsieur Turgot and Monseigneur d'Argentré may have expected the abbot to deliver a mild reproach or even air his objections to the injustice to which he was being submitted. They certainly did not consider him capable of such forceful opposition. When the deputy's messenger arrived to inform them that his master had encountered strong, formal, and unanimous opposition from the abbot and his monks, they were dumbfounded. Monsieur Turgot was obliged to authorise stronger methods. His second order instructed Monsieur de Lepine to proceed with his work in the presence of the religious and, if necessary, to send for locksmiths, blacksmiths, and whatever other assistants he might require to break down doors and open cupboards, coffers, and safes. Two days later Monsieur de Lepine returned to the abbey where he communicated his new instructions to the religious. They expressed their surprise that no account had been taken of their objections, but offered no further resistance. The abbot alone remained to witness the procedure; the remainder of the community retired still protesting. The report which Monsieur Turgot in due course submitted to Paris, attributed the initial resistance of the community to greed:

> I have been persuaded that they hoped to retard the compiling of the inventory in order to give themselves time to remove various effects for their personal profit. Various circumstances have led me to this suspicion and I am in consequence determined to order my delegate to apply seals to all the effects contained in the abbey with the exception of those necessities which are in daily use.[22]

The Bishop of Limoges expressed a similar opinion in the letter which he dispatched to Loménie de Brienne by the same courier:

> I am certain that several of them and, in particular the bursar, make money out of everything and that they are filling a goodly sized purse for themselves . . . at least they have been foiled by the seals which have been applied. They still have the means, however, of squandering the livestock on the estates.[23]

Although the inventory obviously marked the prelude to an official sequestration, the abbot and a few of the religious were still determined to continue the fight. Dom Pichon and Dom Muret began raising support for their cause among the local parishes, whose inhabitants stood to lose a great deal in terms both of employment and the charitable assistance provided by the monks. While the order of Grandmont could justifiably be accused of some measure of decadence at this time, the one great virtue which they had retained from their original Rule was the obligation to dispense charity to all who required it. Quite apart from the assistance which the monks of Grandmont afforded their immediate neighbours, when times were hard they also extended their help to the entire canton and beyond. The abbey served the locality as church, school, and hospital. Every possible form of assistance was afforded by the brethren: prayers, food, clothing, medicines, consolation, and advice. So, in unison with their respective clergy, various local worthies organised the inhabitants of the village of Grandmont and five other parishes in the vicinity in a series of protests against the closure of their beloved abbey. Several of the petitions addressed by these groups to the king are appended to the *Mémoire à Consulter et Consultation pour L'Abbé General de Grandmont*.[24] Apart from causing considerable local furore, these appeals were not without effect in certain high quarters. The outspoken Monseigneur Christophe Beaumont, Archbishop of Paris, for example, let his support for the monks of Grandmont be publicly known. The outcome was that the little community remaining at Grandmont was left in peace for a few short months while Monseigneur d'Argentré stewed over the possibility that his cherished prize might yet be wrested from his grasp.

The following June this dormant state of affairs was abruptly terminated when Loménie informed his colleagues on the Commission of the resistance being offered by the monks and the string of petitions they were addressing to various notables, including the king himself. On 12 June he wrote to Monseigneur d'Argentré telling him of the very latest petition which the monks had addressed to the sovereign and assuring him that it would avail them naught. 'We shall shut their mouths', he wrote; 'the Abbot is stubborn but we shall vanquish him with his own religious.'[25]

Loménie's next move was to secure a royal brief authorising the bishop of Limoges to approach the Holy See and request the suppression of the abbey of Grandmont and its annexation in perpetuity to the diocese of Limoges.[26] A blow to the monks was delivered on 22 June, when the King's Council issued a writ rejecting the abbot's petition and upholding all previous legislative measures taken against the abbey. It made a special point of approving the methods adopted by the Intendant of Limoges for compiling the inventory. The abbot had made a particularly strong protest against the affixing of seals to the abbey property. In the words of Loménie de Brienne, the Grandmontines had been well and truly 'shut up', for a while at least.

No one seems to have been in any doubt that the pope would do other than agree to the bishop of Limoges' request, supported as it was, by a royal brief. Now, as his financial commitments increased, the bishop's only concern was at the delay involved before he could get his hands on the abbey and its properties. 'We shall vanquish the abbot with his own religious', Loménie de Brienne had said and, in the interval while he awaited a papal bull of suppression, he occupied the time engineering this devious strategy. Thanks to the outstanding efficiency of his informant, Dom Daguerre, Loménie knew, somewhat better than the naive abbot, the true feelings of all nine religious remaining at his side. It appears that they fell into two distinct camps: Dom Chapellet de Fontrielle, the prior, in company with Doms Pichon, Muret, and Beaubreuil, were all four sincere in their fidelity to the Order and their devotion to the abbot. The remainder were decidedly more concerned with their own interests and the amount of their eventual pensions. Thus it was a simple matter for Loménie to write a letter to Dom Babinet, the most outspoken of this impressionable group, in order to win him over completely. The precise content of this letter is not known but Dom Babinet's reply has survived and from it we can assume that it sufficed to convince him that his abbot's cause was irretrievably lost. Almost certainly Loménie gave him fair warning that further resistance would jeopardise the future pension rights of all concerned. Whatever Loménie said, it had the desired effect, for Dom Babinet and four of his colleagues eventually scuttled out of Grandmont like rats from a sinking ship.[27]

The prolonged delay in obtaining a papal bull of suppression can be attributed to the super-efficiency of the Commission of Regulars itself. Cardinal de Bernis, the French Ambassador to the Court of Rome was a worldly and self-indulgent prelate who in his youth had fancied himself as a poet. His sentimental verse-mongering had earned him the nickname 'Babet la Bouquetière' (Betty Flowergirl). Nevertheless, he was an effective diplomat and the friendship which had developed between himself and Pope Clement XIV had made it possible for him to smooth the passage of many french appeals to the Sovereign Pontiff. Nevertheless, the cardinal had his hands full at this particular time, for apart from the Grandmontines, the Commission of Regulars was in the process of suppressing houses of Franciscan Observants and Celestines as well as amalgamating the Canons of St Ruff with those of Saint-Lazaire. The busy ambassador pointed out, quite reasonably, that he could not be expected to submit all these separate dossiers to His Holiness at one and the same time and expect him, with one stroke of the papal pen, to liquidate the lot. On the contrary, if His Holiness was faced with too many such requests at one time, he would be more likely to develop scruples and begin asking questions, some of which might be difficult to answer.

The statement which awaited presentation to the pope had been composed by a Monsieur Cressac, banker and legal advisor to Monseigneur d'Argentré. It constitutes the most important paper of all the vast dossier of documents concerned with the destruction of the abbey of Grandmont and its daughter houses, because the information contained in it was directly responsible for the eventual bull of suppression issued by the pope. In justification of his decision to issue the requisite bull, Clement XIV actually borrowed whole sentences from the overwhelming indictment which Monsieur Cressac committed to writing and which reads as follows:

> The Common Observance of the Order of Grandmont has been reduced to seventy-two religious distributed among twenty-three houses. These religious have abandoned—rather, they have never known the practice of a regular life in community. The Abbey of Grandmont itself is the only house in which the piety and good example of the Abbot General have been responsible for some semblance of regularity albeit lacking in fervour, study, and thorough application, among nine or ten of the religious. These same are still there, but if it were not for the abbot, the Order would have extinguished itself through lack of recruits and general bad management. The obligation imposed on all religious by the edict of March 1768 forced the houses to convene a General Chapter in the Septem-

ber of that same year and each was obliged to take a decisive part. For a long while previous to this, General Chapters were not held regularly, and when they did take place proved to be mere informal meetings between a few of the priors but with the religious themselves not properly represented. When it became necessary to establish in what the rule of life of the Common Observance should consist, His Majesty took measures to ensure that the Chapter deciding these factors be held in accordance with canon law and that each house be properly represented by its delegates. The two principle requirements contained in the Edict of March 1768 were proposed at the meeting: the re-establishment of a regular life in community, such a life to follow the monastic pattern. The first requirement was unanimously rejected as impracticable by these religious who, in the guise of the religious habit, had been leading entirely secular lives. The second requirement reduced the Order to just four or five houses. Moreover, with the exception of the Abbey of Grandmont itself, the houses were in no condition to receive a larger number of religious without first re-establishing regular monastic quarters [Presumably this refers to the re-establishment of such monastic features as a common refectory and dorter. Partitioning walls would have to be removed and the monasteries returned to their original plan]. It was agreed that this could not be effected without considerable expenditure which would have considerably diminished the resources of the Order. In consequence, the Chapter decided to implore the king to dispense the Order from his edict, and they resolved to submit themselves entirely to his will with prayers and supplications that, in case of the suppression and annexation of their houses, he would accord them the pensions necessary for their subsistence. Monseigneur the Abbot of Grandmont alone asked that he be permitted to work for the re-establishment of a regular community life at the Abbey of Grandmont.

The King received with equal kindness the requests of both the Chapter and the Abbot General. In letters patent dated the month of February 1769, and registered in the various parlements, His Majesty dispensed the religious of the Common Observance from obedience to his edict, and accorded them the right to live out their lives within the monasteries of the Order under the authority of the Abbot General and their immediate superiors but on the condition that they did not profess any further monks or admit any novices. Furthermore, he authorised the bishops of each diocese to take whatever action was necessary in accordance with both canon and civil law to suppress and annex the said monasteries subject to the consent of the religious. Also, in compliance with the requests and supplications of the Abbot General, he agreed to the re-establishment of religious observance within the Abbey of Grandmont until the death of the said Abbot if and when the Abbot should have furnished him with full details of what this would entail.

As the result of this arrangement, the Abbot of Grandmont addressed a petition to the King together with a proposed scheme for constitutions conforming with the primitive institution of the Order. The purpose of this was to obtain from His Majesty both his assent to the preservation of the house and the readmission of novices. This, on condition that the Abbot himself would follow a new régime in accordance with the above proposals and through his own example inspire the religious of the Order to follow these same reforms. The entire project was dependent upon whether or not it would be possible to reunite the religious of the Common Observance.

His Majesty deigned to reply to Monseigneur the Abbot of Grandmont that before reaching any decision as to the fate of that house, it would be necessary to find a sufficient number of religious willing to practise the Rule of St Stephen in accordance with the proposals that had been submitted to His Majesty.

More than two years have gone by and Monseigneur the Abbot of Grandmont has not found a single religious willing to support his own zeal. Even those of the Strict Observance have refused to join him, and the disorder is worsening because what has been destroyed by time cannot be repaired.

Those religious who fear that their monastic life will be extinguished without any consideration as to their plight have expressed their inquietude in this respect and asked that they might be allowed to benefit from the advantages afforded by the letters patent previously issued both at their request and that of the entire Order. Thus the King, convinced of the impossibility of Monseigneur the Abbot of Grandmont actually realising his plans, and at the same time informed of his willingness to comply with the King's will, has issued Monseigneur the Bishop of Limoges with a brief authorising him to seek the dissolution and suppression of the title of the Abbey of Grandmont through the Court of Rome. Moreover, to effect the annexation, in case of vacancy, death, or demission, of any possessions belonging to the Abbey which are situated within the episcopal see of Limoges; the endowment of the said see of Limoges being not proportionate to its needs and to the charges imposed upon so extensive a diocese. His Majesty has reason to believe that such an application of the Abbey's possessions constitutes an additional motive for His Holiness to authorise this annexation. The Abbot of Grandmont will place no obstacle in the way for he can no longer conceal the futility of his efforts. The majority of the other houses of the same Observance

> have been suppressed at the request of the bishops complying with the insistent wishes of the religious themselves. Those houses which still remain are urging the same treatment. No adherents to the Reform have been found even where one would most have hoped to find them. [In all probability this refers to the religious of the Strict Observance. In fact, several of these did come forward and supported their abbot to the last]. There is no longer any hope for Monseigneur the Abbot of Grandmont, and the best use that can be made of the possessions of a house which will be completely vacated when he dies, is to place it at the disposal of a poor diocese which comprises almost eight hundred parishes and receives less than 16,000 *livres* by way of revenue.[28]

Taken purely at face value, this document appears a true testimony of events. In fact, it is an almost total misrepresentation of the truth. In at least seven cases out of ten, the monks most decidedly did not give in freely and voluntarily to their houses passing into the possession of their local bishops. In just about every instance they were cajoled, bullied, and threatened with destitution if they dared offer any resistance. Furthermore, to state categorically that the abbot would place no obstacle in the way of the annexation of his abbey to the diocese of Limoges was a downright lie. To represent him as wholly incapable of promoting a reform was grossly unfair, given that every possible obstacle had been placed in his way especially by the ban on professions and the admission of novices. His authority had been systematically undermined by the turncoat monk, Daguerre, and his enthusiastic attempt to realise a reform had been sabotaged by enemies from within and without. In the whole of de Cressac's statement there is no single mention of the intense pressure to which the monks were subjected by the Commissioners Loménie de Brienne and de Cambon at the General Chapter of September 1767. The wishes expressed by the Chapter on that occasion are totally ignored and the annexation of their respective houses is represented in such a way that it appears they themselves were responsible. In conclusion, the actual request for permission to annex the abbey of Grandmont to the diocese of Limoges is made to appear as if it had the whole-hearted approval of the abbot. Many years later, the Emperor Napoleon passing near the town of Cluny is reputed to have refused to visit a place whose inhabitants had been responsible for the mindless vandalism of the great abbey which stood outside the town. The abbey of Cluny was torn apart by a wild, uneducated, unintelligent, and very irate mob of revolutionaries. Unfortunately the same cannot be said of the Abbey of Grandmont. In this case the iconoclasts who, in the words of a contemporary 'could not wait for demolition to commence', were well educated, highly intelligent, and sophisticated princes of the Church.

No sooner had de Cressac's statement been consigned to Cardinal de Bernis than the abbot resolved to register a protest at Rome. In doing so he drew down upon himself both the anger of the Commission and the intense displeasure of the king. In fact this 'protest' amounted to little more than a mild and humble supplication, in striking contrast to the scheming and cunning communication formulated by de Cressac at the behest of the Commissioners and Monseigneur d'Argentré. Abbot Mondain merely implored His Holiness to intervene and save the abbey or, at least, to allow it to continue for the duration of his life. He did not include a request that the pope should reverse any of the annexations already effected.

By November 1772, Cardinal de Bernis had acquired papal approval for the suppression of the ancient abbey of the Canons of St Ruff as well as Chancelade, another abbey of canons regular. He considered the time ripe for the presentation of the dossier on Grandmont. He began paving the way by disposing of the abbot's protest in a personal memorandum addressed to His Holiness which included the following observations:

> We have reason to believe that the Abbot of Grandmont has made his opposition to the King's brief known to Rome. He cannot and should not have done so without first having sought and obtained the King's permission. The laws of the kingdom prohibit any subject of the King from pleading his case abroad. Apart from this, Monseigneur the Bishop of Limoges as an interested party should have been informed . . . Besides which the matter is not of a kind which can be readily understood in Rome where all the background information is not available. It is the state of the abbey itself which must decide whether it be suppressed or conserved. This cannot be established except by evidence acquired by a commissioner nominated by the Pope. It is to such a commissioner that the Abbot of Grandmont should submit his opposition. Any alternative procedure is contrary to the law of France. It is only out of respect for the Holy See that the Abbot of Grandmont has not been indicted before a legal tribunal which would have punished him in accordance with the law.

Cardinal de Bernis continues to plead the case of the diocese of Limoges which he says:

> is located in mountainous countryside and is one of the largest in the kingdom. It comprises close on a thousand parishes in most of which the inhabitants are very poor. The Bishop has little by way of revenue and it is therefore impossible for him to provide his people with the help and care they so desperately need. It was this fact which influenced the King to transfer into his keeping a superfluous religious house where the Rule has ceased to be observed. Its suppression, and the annexation of its revenues by the diocesan exchequer of Limoges, could not be more

> in keeping with canon law nor more advantageous to the Church as a whole.[29]

It is significant that all the emphasis is on the poor and needy of the diocese. Not a word about the bishop's new palace and the debts which it led him to accrue.

Cardinal de Bernis committed a grave error of judgement when, in his memorandum, he mentioned the appointment of a papal commissioner to look into the affairs of Grandmont. In so doing he quite inadvertently made himself responsible for a long, tedious, and expensive delay. Loménie de Brienne had anticipated that Pope Clement XIV would be sufficiently influenced by Monsieur de Cressac's letter to grant an instant bull of suppression. Instead, he was swayed by Cardinal de Bernis' casual reference and ordered an official enquiry. This, he directed, should be implemented by Monseigneur d'Argentré in his capacity as bishop of the diocese. The Commission of Regulars however, judged that it was both unfitting and embarrassing for Monseigneur d'Argentré to carry out a task which required him to pass judgement in a case to which he himself was a party. They therefore proposed the substitution of Monseigneur Phélypeaux d'Herbault, Archbishop of Bourges. The decision served to reassure Monseigneur d'Argentré, inasmuch as Monseigneur d'Herbault had sat on the original Commission of Regulars and had plenty of experience in these matters; he had successfully stage-managed several similar annexations. The pope raised no objection to Monseigneur d'Argentré being replaced by the archbishop of Bourges, and issued the necessary authority to enable him to proceed with his task. The document itself contains a serious error in that the monastery of Grandmont is erroneously classed by the papal officials as belonging to the order of St Benedict.

The Archbishop of Bourges declared himself delighted to perform the task assigned to him by the pope and a letter of 26 March assured Monseigneur d'Argentré of his full cooperation:

> I will entrust to no-one, Monseigneur, the pleasure of carrying out an operation so agreeable to you and so beneficial for your diocese. I intend leaving Bourges on Easter Tuesday and will call on you to discharge the necessary formalities. As I shall have to go to Grandmont, I would ask you kindly to arrange for a horse litter as I am a bad horseman.[30]

To which Monseigneur the Bishop of Limoges replied: 'It will be the most wonderful day of my life when I have the honour of receiving you here.' Monseigneur d'Argentré was such a prolific and verbose letter writer that one is inclined to wonder how he found time to do anything else. This particular epistle rambles on for several pages which treat of petty details associated with Monseigneur d'Herbault's lodging and comforts. He refers to Grandmont as 'a frightful place' and the company there as 'not at all diverting'. He was therefore at pains to ensure that the Commissioner's stay be kept as short as is possible and reasonable.

While preparations for this visit were under way, Monsieur de Cressac was hard at work under Loménie's guidance to ensure the abbot's downfall. A communication which he addressed to Monseigneur d'Argentré in April 1772 contains several hints and ploys which he hopes will hasten the victory. Among other things, he had compiled a list of the religious who, in his own words

> will say more or less anything we wish them to say . . . there is nothing these gallants would like more than to get out of Grandmont. However, they still dare not admit to it . . . The others will do likewise and once the abbot finds himself on his own he will accept a pension.[31]

The archbishop of Bourges duly arrived in Limoges where he was royally received and entertained by Monseigneur d'Argentré. On 26 April, he left for the abbey, where he received a less enthusiastic but nonetheless respectful and courteous welcome from the abbot and his few religious. The following day, the first Sunday after Easter, he commenced his enquiry. The community assembled in the chapter house to be questioned, and their responses were duly noted by Monseigneur d'Herbault's secretaries. What they omitted to note, however, were the reasons which accompanied certain of these responses. For example, when the religious were asked if they had any novices, they replied no, because the King had obliged them to send them away. In the papal commissioner's final report it is simply stated: 'There is no course of studies and no novitiate.'[32] Furthermore, it is recorded in the *Mémoire à Consulter et Consultation pour l'Abbé General de Grandmont* that when the religious sought permission to summon a notary to record the proceedings on their own behalf, this was resolutely denied them. According to the abbot, Monseigneur d'Herbault also declined to read the full text of his papal brief to the assembled religious. Several other omissions and misrepresentations can also be identified in the report, which in due course was submitted to Rome. For example, Monseigneur d'Herbault contented himself with listing the number of religious still inhabiting each of the remaining daughter houses but omitted any mention of the devious circumstances which had led to the disappearance of twelve other houses in the space of four years. Once again it is implied that the monks had freely and knowingly abandoned their Rule and their communities. Finally, Monseigneur d'Herbault observed that:

> Despite the protection of His Majesty, the Abbot's attempt to re-establish a monastic life within the mother house of the Order has failed. He has not managed to obtain the support of even one religious.

The enquiry concluded, and the commissioner's report was read aloud to the religious who were then required to sign it. Only five out of the ten agreed to affix their signatures: the abbot and his prior, together with three other loyal religious, walked out after refusing to sign a document in which 'The truth was presented in such a strange way'.[33]

When Monseigneur d'Herbault arrived back in Limoges he was once again received with every possible honour. There remained only to note Monseigneur d'Argentré's official deposition of the state of his diocese which was appended to Monseigneur d'Herbault's own report. The diocese of Limoges, it stated, covered a very extensive area and included forty-seven towns, eight hundred sixty-eight parishes and forty-five succursal churches; the number of poor people dwelling within these parishes and succursals was considerable yet the resources at the disposal of the diocese were totally inadequate to lend them the aid that they required. This was all too true, the terrain in this very beautiful part of France is largely mountainous and agriculturally poor. The canton of Ambazac, where Grandmont itself is situated, remains very much as Gérard Ithier, the seventh prior of Grandmont, described it in the twelfth century: rocky and barren.[34] Even the major landowners had difficulty making ends meet while the peasants were almost totally and continually destitute. What the papal commissioner omitted to mention was that the annexation of the abbey of Grandmont was not intended for the benefit of the poor or to alleviate the misery prevailing in many local parishes: Grandmont was ear-marked to help meet the costs of construction of the fine new episcopal palace.

When Monseigneur d'Herbault's Report eventually arrived in Rome it was, not surprisingly, judged to be inadequate and Cardinal de Bernis was instructed to seek further information regarding five distinct points:

1. The exact amount of the revenues due to the Order.
2. A precise breakdown of all liabilities and expenditure.
3. Exactly what was intended to be done with the churches of both the abbey and the daughter houses.

4. Following the suppression of the mother house, who was intended to be superior in charge of the other houses of the Order?
5. Was the suppression intended to extend to these other houses?

The first two of these queries posed no problem whatsoever, for, as Monseigneur d'Argentré's financial advisor, de Cressac pointed out in a letter dated 20 June, the financial condition of the Order of Grandmont had already been ascertained by the Intendant of Limoges and was readily available. It was the fifth query which, as he put it:

> might cause a little bit more of embarrassment. The majority of [the daughter houses] have already been suppressed and their revenues disposed of. Rome must not hear of this.[35]

Monseigneur d'Herbault then set to work on a document, the contents of which had been dictated almost word for word by Loménie de Brienne, which it was hoped would serve to allay any remaining papal scruples. The information necessary to answer questions one and two was quite innocuous and, as Monsieur de Cressac had observed, readily available. Loménie de Brienne set it out in great detail so that it acted as an umbrella shading the questions which could not be answered so satisfactorily. No information whatsoever was included as to the fate of the churches attached to daughter houses; only that of the mother house. In Loménie's opinion, this church—which, it is worth recalling, had only recently been rebuilt— was not worth saving, situated as it was in a very remote and inaccessible locality. The district was already well served by the church of St Sylvestre, in the village adjacent to Grandmont. Here we have the first indication of the intention to demolish a brand new church which contemporary opinion rated as 'one of the finest in the land'.

The final query was dispensed with quite simply. Monseigneur d'Herbault officially informed His Holiness that although previous appeals had requested the suppression of the abbey of Grandmont only, that really they should be extended to encompass all the houses of the Order which would be placed under the jurisdiction of the local ordinary. They could then be put to good use as seminaries or houses of refuge for the aged and infirm. No mention was made of the fact that in numerous cases this had already occurred.

The calculated response to the papal enquiries had the desired effect, and on 22 July 1772, Cardinal de Bernis was joyously able to announce that Pope Clement XIV had granted the desired bull of union. The fate of the abbey of Grandmont and indeed the Grandmontines themselves was signed, sealed, and delivered. Numerous papal bulls had been directed to Grandmont in the course of the centuries, this, the last, incorporates two glaring inaccuracies. In the first instance, it makes reference to: 'the Order of Grandmont of the Common Observance according to the Rule of St Benedict'. Given that Loménie de Brienne and the Commission of Regulars had all along been seeking the suppression of the Order of Grandmont on the pretext that the religious were failing to conform to the Rule of their Founder, St Stephen, it is highly ironic that Clement XIV concluded by suppressing a non-existent off-shoot of the Order of St Benedict.

The second error involves a reference to the king's right to nominate the abbot of Grandmont. Although the right invested in the Order to elect its own abbot had been interrupted for over a century when the commendatory system was imposed, the Ordinance of Blois (1579) had once again restored the right of free election to the monks.

At the same time as Monseigneurs de Brienne and d'Herbault were formulating suitable responses to papal queries, the long suffering Abbot Mondain had, in his turn, been occupied with a last desperate petition to Rome. In this he begged His Holiness that,in the event of his agreeing to the annexation of his abbey to the diocese, it might at least be postponed until after his death. The pope had agreed and this single humane condition had been written into the bull, much to Monseigneur d'Argentré's discomfiture. This gave place to downright distress when the information was imparted to him that the expenses incurred in obtaining the bull, a total of 18,000 *livres*, were being charged to his diocese. It began to look as though Monseigneur d'Argentré's successor would be the only one who stood to gain from this unhappy union.

Loménie de Brienne was considerably more optimistic than Monseigneur d'Argentré and in a letter of consolation which he dispatched to him on 10 October he wrote:

> Do not permit yourself to be worried by the Bull of Union, Monseigneur, we can work out a means of getting rid of the article which permits the abbot and his religious to continue residing in their house.

In the following paragraph he observed:

> In order to spare you personally the expenses of the bull, we have been obliged to charge it up to your diocese, but even so I am counting on your not having to pay any interest, and sometime between now and Easter this matter will be put in order. M. de Cressac will be able to tell you how concerned I am to spare you any expense and to bring you joy as soon as possible.[36]

Once the inhabitants of the village of Grandmont realised that nothing could now save their beloved abbey from extinction, they delivered a further and somewhat different petition to the king. This asked that the Abbey church be designated parochial to be managed by four coadjutors. To provide for the charitable works which had always been discharged by the monks, they also requested the establishment of a school and six bed hospital. In addition they asked for the provision of an annual alms of three hundred setiers of wheat, previously supplied by the monks, for distribution to the poor of the local parishes.

Monseigneur d'Argentré had always maintained that the union of the abbey with his diocese would provide him the wherewithal to alleviate the misery and suffering so prevalent there. Now, however, he threw up his hands in horror at the enormity of the demands being submitted by the villagers. If the king decided to grant them, the burden of providing for them would devolve on him. He wrote, therefore, to the King's Minister to say that while he recognised the need for compensation to be made to the villagers, yet as the person directly involved in the payment of this he did not feel qualified to say what the amount should actually be. The delicacy of his position was recognised, and so the services of Loménie de Brienne, Monseigneur d'Herbault, and the banker agent de Cressac were requested to perform the task which Monseigneur d'Argentré found too delicate and embarrassing to carry out himself. The three official agents of the Crown went to work, and together they decided that the claims were exorbitant and unwarranted and scaled them down accordingly. They affirmed that when, and only when, the bishop of Limoges took possession of the abbey, the local inhabitants would be allowed a third priest to assist the curé and vicar of St Sylvestre with the additional parishioners from Grandmont who had previously worshipped at the abbey. There was no question of the abbey church becoming parochial. The stipends of both the junior priests or vicars would be provided and was set at three hundred *livres per annum*. An additional five hundred *livres* was budgeted for the employment of a schoolmaster to educate the boys of the parish and a further seven hundred *livres* to pay the expenses of two nuns who would undertake the instruction of the girls. These sisters would also be responsible for the care of the sick and they were to be provided with a further six hundred *livres per annum* which would enable them to provide both medicines and soup for the sick of those parishes which had always depended on the abbey to supply such needs. This sum was deemed sufficient for the sisters to provide help for the aged and orphans of the neighbourhood as well.

On the 21 February 1773, Leonard Barny, magistrate of the village of Grandmont, and Joseph de Latelise, physician, the most active campaigners for the preservation of the abbey, called a meeting in the priests' house alongside the church of St Sylvestre. Together they formulated a protest against the projected closure of the abbey which was taken down and attested by a notary. This document provides a very moving testimony to the services which the monks of Grandmont had provided to both themselves and their ancestors. It affirms that the infertile land of that mountainous region had always 'devoured the inhabitants' and its cultivators never reaped so much as the price of their labours. When times were especially hard, the abbey of Grandmont constituted the one single resource that heaven provided for the miserable inhabitants. It pointed out that the responsibilities which the monks had always been pleased to discharge would place an intolerable burden on the diocese. In fact, far from benefiting from the annexation of the abbey, the diocese stood to lose because the union involved only those revenues which were due to the abbey from properties contained within its boundaries. In the three years prior to 1773, the religious had dispensed over 60,000 *livres* in alms, much of which had been provided from revenues which the abbot had at his disposal elsewhere.[37]

On the same day and at about the same time another meeting was held by the inhabitants of the local market town of Ambazac and a similar document resulted. Other of the surrounding parishes also held meetings and compiled equally moving testimonies. The people who met together to formulate these statements came from all walks of life, representatives of the local nobility and landowners who, when harvests failed, were as dependent as their own labourers upon the monks' generosity. Local tradesmen, craftsmen, doctors, schoolmasters, all united to bear witness to the usefulness and charity of the religious of Grandmont. Their combined testimony is in striking contrast to the negative indictment compiled and submitted by Loménie de Brienne to Rome. Far from pursuing useless, worthless, and decadent lives, these monks would appear to have been not merely teaching but enacting the Gospel message throughout the region. If the Divine Offices were neglected and the choir stalls empty at Grandmont, it was because their occupants were caring for the neighbourhood as combined priests, schoolmasters, doctors, nurses, and social workers. The people of Ambazac make particular mention of the frequent ill-health suffered by their own pastor and his assistant curate and the number of times—thirty in one year— when a priest from Grandmont substituted for them. They speak of the willingness of the monks to come to their aid in all weathers and to negotiate roads which, even today, become almost impassable in winter.

Admittedly the Grandmontines had not been founded to perform a pastoral and social role, in fact their Rule specifically forbade it. However, other of the religious orders had been forced to adapt their lives and activities to suit the climate of the times, especially in the eighteenth century. Louis J. Lekai, writing of his own Order of Cîteaux, notes how such contemplative orders attempted to insure the survival of their organisations at a time when the monastic life was no less unpopular with a large proportion of the hierarchy than with the *philosophes*, 'by engaging their monks in activities of demonstrable social significance'.[38] Loménie de Brienne himself, in one of his letters to Monseigneur d'Argentré on the subject of compensation for the local people, was forced to admit: 'generally speaking monasteries give alms particularly within their own environs'.[39] However he considered the eighteen hundred *livres* demanded by the villagers to be exorbitant and proposed three hundred as more than sufficient.

The only local person who did not lend his support to the cause of the monks was the Abbé Bourdeaux, the vicar assisting the Curé of St Sylvestre. On 19 February, he wrote to the Bishop of Limoges to inform him of the meeting which was due to be held by the local residents in the presbytery and to offer his services as an informer. It is an ugly crawling letter through which the priest was quite obviously seeking preferment in return for his dubious services.[40] The behaviour of the vicar is in complete contrast to that of the parish priest himself. Monsieur le Curé Guérin was devoted to the abbot and singularly concerned regarding the detrimental effect that the disappearance of the abbey would have upon his already deprived flock. His own letter to the bishop, stating the need for his parish to be compensated, evoked a polite but curt response, through which Monseigneur d'Argentré made it quite clear that he regarded him as an adversary. His tone enflamed the worthy curé who immediately summoned a notary and in the presence of his vicar, Bourdeaux, and another witness, dictated a forceful protest against the expulsion of the monks and the closure of their abbey. He demanded, somewhat unrealistically, that half the annual tithes due to the abbey together with all endowments pledged to the church of Grandmont should be devoted to the welfare of his parishioners. He also demanded a second vicar to assist with the numerous duties which had previously been performed by the monks.

In the spring of 1773, Abbot Mondain decided to institute an appeal against the execution of the bull of suppression through the civil courts. Just four of the remaining religious were willing to lend their support to this move: Doms de Fontvielle, Pichon, Muret, and Beaubreuil. However, a further two supporters had turned up at the Abbey, both having been expelled from their own monasteries, Dom Salot de Tourniolles and Dom Vergniaud. The latter was destined to be the last of the Grandmontines.

On 26 February a canonical enquiry, the recognised preliminary to the execution of a bull of suppression, opened in Limoges. It was held in the great hall of the seminary and presided over by a delegate sent by the Apostolic Commissioner from Bourges, Monsieur de la Vauverte. Monseigneur d'Herbault was otherwise engaged seeking the closure of the great cluniac priory of St Benedict on the Loire. The canonical enquiry should have been a mere formality and hence neither Loménie de Brienne nor Monseigneur d'Argentré anticipated any problems. Their hopes of a speedy and smooth settlement were to be shattered, however, by Abbot Mondain's civil appeal. This had been formally noted by the Parlement of Paris with the result that, on the second day of the proceedings, there was a dramatic intervention by an official courier with orders to suspend the enquiry forthwith. Messengers were dispatched to Versailles to seek further instructions and both Monsieur de la Vauverte and Monseigneur d'Argentré were obliged to wait as patiently as they were able for their return. On 5 March, the King's Procurator arrived in Limoges and suspended the enquiry indefinitely.

Ever since its convocation in 1768, the Commission of Regulars had been becoming increasingly unpopular not only among humble country priests who deplored the closure of so many useful institutions, but also with certain high ranking clerics. Prominent among its critics was the archbishop of Paris and his friend Monseigneur Giraud, the papal nuncio to France. They shared the fairly general view that the expulsion of the Jesuits from France had constituted a disaster for the educational life of the nation. Their departure had in fact created a need which secular educators had been unable to fulfil satisfactorily. The projected suppression of the Grandmontines had also given rise to murmurings in high places, and a considerable correspondence on the subject had passed between the nuncio and the archbishop of Paris the previous year.[41] Unfortunately, this awareness came too late. The work of Cardinal de Bernis in Rome was already well advanced and the two eminent champions of the religious life decided that it was not worth while wasting their influence in the support of minor institutes or in defending causes which seemed irretrievably lost. Nevertheless, the suspension of the Limoges enquiry would seem to have been part and parcel of a general change of heart with regard to the religious orders and a corresponding diminuition of the influence wielded by the Commission of Regulars. Sadly, it came too late to save the Grandmontines from extinction.

The gloom and despondency which Monseigneur d'Argentré must have been suffering, as once again he was obliged to gaze upon his retreating prize, was temporarily alleviated by a Grandmontine who paid him a visit on the 2 March. Dom Babinet proved to be the representative of those of the religious who had been won over either by Loménie himself or, by de Cressac. Convinced that the Order of Grandmont had no possible future, they had turned against the abbot and were prepared as de Cressac had predicted to throw themselves upon the mercy of the king. Dom Babinet had a document of capitulation signed by four confrères who, by reason of their age and infirmities, were unable to make the journey to Limoges.

Monseigneur d'Argentré hastened to inform Loménie of this heartening betrayal, but also expressed his concern at the current obstacle which was barring his way to victory. In his reply, dated 7 March, Loménie wrote reassuringly:

> I am in receipt of the various papers you have sent me and I continue to be unafraid; even less since I have seen the Abbot's request which seems the most feeble defence that could possibly be proposed . . . I do not know yet which path we shall follow. The statement provided by the five religious is an excellent document.[42]

Loménie de Brienne had already warned Monseigneur d'Argentré that his presence in Paris might prove to be necessary, and as the Council of State was soon scheduled to concern itself with the business of Grandmont he suggested that the bishop should hasten his departure. Abbot

Mondain was also preparing to leave for Paris with the intention of enlisting the help of various protectors on whom he believed he could count. The bishop received word of this plan through one of his agents, a singularly distasteful informer who had managed to get himself accepted at Grandmont. This character was the brother of Dom Vergniaud, a former religious of the grandmontine priory at Rouen who, when this house was suppressed, joined the little community remaining at Grandmont, after spending some time with his family. He was one of the most devoted of the abbot's supporters. By coincidence, his brother was a parish priest attached to the diocese of Limoges and to all intents and purposes a staunch supporter of the monks with whom he spent much of his time. Little did Dom Vergniaud know that he was a spy for the bishop, to whom all his confidences were faithfully transmitted.

This priest-informer put most of his information in writing, and a lengthy note which he passed to the bishop shortly before the latter's departure for Paris, contains what must be an accurate account of the somewhat confused state of affairs prevailing within the abbey. Thus d'Argentré was able to learn, among other matters, just who were the supporters and protectors of the Order with whom the abbot was in touch both in the capital and elsewhere. Through Monsieur l'Abbé Vergniaud, Monseigneur d'Argentré also gleaned valuable information as to the state of the abbey's finances. He must have been particularly concerned to hear that the abbot had openly declared his intention to continue distributing considerable amounts of money in alms. Vergniaud also discovered and informed Monseigneur d'Argentré that the lawyer employed by the abbot was reputed to be somewhat inordinately fond of money and thus might be 'won over'. Having begged 'His Grandeur' the bishop not to compromise him in any way because the least suspicion on the part of the loyal religious would jeopardise his chances of securing any additional information, Vergniaud concludes his note with the words:

> I will keep the Grandmontine [his brother] here for as long as I am able in order to get from him all the information possible.[43]

The priest Vergniaud was also able to obtain from his unsuspecting brother a copy of the memorandum which Monsieur de la Balme, the abbot's lawyer, had addressed to the king. This was not only an attempt to justify the appeal; it was a carefully worded legal document which drew attention to all the irregularities and illegalities which had been perpetrated by those seeking the ruin of the Order of Grandmont. It represents a concise and lucid summary of the case for the defence and in the opening paragraph comes straight to the point:

> Sire, François-Xavier Mondain de la Maison Rouge, Abbot General of the Order of Grandmont, most humbly makes representation to Your Majesty inasmuch as he remains unconvinced that Your Majesty is properly informed as to all he has suffered as the result of the Edict of 1768. This did no more than command the reform of the religious orders, but it resulted in the emergence of a conspiracy to annihilate the Order of Grandmont and to suppress its Abbey.

The statement proceeds with an account of the origins of the Order and outlines the praiseworthy and austere life led by its founder, St Stephen. It recalls the family connection between the saint and the Bourbons. It notes the principle tenets of the Rule and the subsequent modifications. It refers to the vicissitudes which afflicted the Order in the course of the centuries, concluding with the unhappy events of the previous few years. It then protests against the successive measures which, in the four years since 1768, effectively reduced the Order from thirty houses and over a hundred religious, to a single house and fewer than ten religious. It maintains that the various letters patent and royal briefs authorising these measures were all obtained through devious and underhand means. Mention is made of the irregularity of the conduct of Dom Nicod, Vicar General of the Strict Observance. Reference is made to the misunderstanding which had arisen between the Commissioners and the religious as to the exact inference of the words 'return to the Rule'. It is clearly pointed out that the suppression of the branch of the Strict Observance represented an outstanding contradiction as they were already practising the reforms which the Commission was proposing. It calls the king's attention to the isolation and powerlessness of the abbot when his determined efforts to realise a reform were frustrated by the suppressions and annexations of monasteries without his consent. It continues:

> The Abbot of Grandmont is not the only one to complain about this suppression and the subsequent annexations which have taken place in the various dioceses where the possessions of the Order were situated. A considerable number of his religious of both Observances, faithful to their vows and mindful of their duties, motivated by the same spirit of piety and religion as the suppliant himself, have registered the most vehement opposition to these operations insofar as they have been aware of them. If others appear to have held their tongues, it was in fear of arousing displeasure or of being deprived of their only remaining means of livelihood. Moreover, a large number of novices remain at the ready to join their Abbot General and live in the Abbey of Grandmont in conformity with the new constitutions presented by the suppliant in conformity with the Edict of 1768. They await only for Your Majesty to grant them the necessary permission.
>
> The bull, together with the [royal] brief was obtained through the submission of false evidence. A regular community life is observed at the Abbey and

the Rule of St Stephen with certain mitigations authorised by the Holy See is observed. The Bishop of Limoges can count on 30,000 *livres* by way of revenue, his needs cannot be so pressing that in order to gain a supplementary income he is prepared to sacrifice such an illustrious Order, one which has been in existence for seven centuries, been enriched by sovereign monarchs and gained the respect of all. It is as valuable to the State as to the Church. Furthermore, the bull, which enfolds a number of reasons for the appeal, is completely contrary to the customs of the Gallican Church.

The presentation of this case has aroused a great deal of interest among the public generally and given rise to some inquietude regarding the activities of the Commission of Regulars. The initial clamour has died down and it is now the Council of State and the Parlement alone who will once again have to concern themselves with this case in a month's time. In order to combat the arrêt of 17 February, Loménie has prepared a paper which lists the main irregularities which are apparent in the bull which is currently being contested by the appellants with the assent of the Parlement. These irregularities having been presented for the observations and responses of the Commission. We hereby present a summary of this work which almost certainly has emerged from the pen of either de Pialle or de Thieriot. [Secretaries to the Commission of Regulars].

1. The Order of Grandmont was wrongfully designated inasmuch as it was said to observe the Rule of St Benedict.

2. It stated that the King held the right of nomination of the Abbot. This is a major falsehood.

ANSWER The Commission declares that it attaches no importance whatsoever to these two grievances.

3. The bull maintains that a regular monastic life no longer exists. This is false evidence; a regular community life has always been observed at the Abbey.

ANSWER The commentator has misunderstood the terminology. The bull employs the term *disciplina* not, *vita*

4. The bull contains certain unusual clauses which are contrary to the liberties enjoyed by the Gallican Church as well as the customs of the Kingdom. It dispenses with certain rules which have been prescribed by the Lateran and other Councils. According to the formal declaration of 1682 which is still upheld in France, the Pope has no authority over ecumenical councils.

ANSWER We maintain that the bull carries a special derogation not, a dispensation. Moreover, this derogation is formulated in the manner normally employed in bulls.

4. (Cont'd) Whilst the bull prohibits any recourse to law, it confers the right of judges to pronounce in conformity with its contents. The Sovereign Pontiff is therefore presuming to exercise the rights of sovereignty within this Kingdom.

ANSWER Mere formulas! If so strict a ruling were enforced it would no longer be possible to receive either bulls or brevets in France.

4. (Cont'd) It prohibits the lodging of any appeal whatsoever against its rulings before any court; it declares all judgments passed against it to be null and void.

ANSWER Formulas and more formulas!

5. The bull is the most irregular which has ever appeared in France inasmuch as it

dispenses with all the usual procedures which have been laid down for the conduct of such unions both by the councils of the Church and the laws of the Kingdom.

ANSWER It is a question of derogation not dispensation. Furthermore, this is mere quibbling over formalities.

6. In his report, the Archbishop of Bourges did not observe any of the required formalities.

ANSWER The information contained in this report is not merely sufficient, it is superabundant; moreover, it is all quite in order. The official concerned was acting within his powers when he checked the objectors.

6. (Cont'd) There are in this bull such manifest, such outstanding, abuses contrary to the Gallican Church and to the customs of the Kingdom that, if such a bull were to be enforced, it would set a very dangerous precedent. There would be no manner of claim which the Court of Rome could not authorise. The royal authority is being compromised, civil liberties dissipated and our most inviolable principles undermined. Parlement must consider it a duty to review the appeal against the irregularities contained in the bull. It is incredible that any of the King's subjects should even dare to take a stand against this arrêt.

ANSWER We reply that the claimants appear to be totally unfamiliar with the language of papal bulls. With regard to their last argument: It was the King who requested the bull in the first place.[44]

The abbot's main line of argument regarding the bull of suppression asserted that he was disputing the authority neither of the pope nor the king but the fact that they had both been erroneously advised; and the bull was irregular as the direct result of misinformation they had received from their advisors. This line of reasoning availed him naught as the Commission, advised by Loménie, continued to insist that the pope had issued the bull at the king's own request.

On 21 May 1773, the Royal Council issued a decree which effectively quashed the stay of execution which the Parlement of Paris issued the previous February and the procedure for the annexation of the abbey of Grandmont was able to go forward. The abbot, for his part, had succeeded in contacting some of the monks who had been dispersed from various of the daughter houses and was well on the way to assembling a sufficiently impressive number—around twenty-five—who desired nothing more than to live out their days peaceably observing the rule of St Stephen at Grandmont. He also made representation to several of the former grandmontine priors who still held their houses in *commendam*. These gentlemen knew on which side their bread was buttered, having been assured by Loménie that their rights and revenues would be respected. They were certainly not prepared to run the risk of losing these rights by lending their support to the abbot's cause.

Monsieur de la Vauverte, the deputy nominated by the archbishop of Bourges to conduct proceedings on his behalf, returned to Limoges in August 1773 to complete the task which had ben interrupted in February. By 25 August, he had managed to interview all the interested parties in Limoges and made a preliminary visit to the abbey itself for the purpose of assessing the state of the buildings. This business satisfactorily terminated, he returned to Bourges.

The same autumn, Dom Razat became directly responsible for a further attempt to sabotage the abbot's efforts to save his Order from extinction. Two of Abbot Mondain's main supporters, Dom Chapellet de Fontvielle and Dom Muret, had been dispatched to Paris to try to gain further support for their cause from various sympathetic notables including the archbishop and Madame Louise, the intelligent and pious daughter of Louis XV. While this royal lady, who ended her days in the seclusion of a carmelite convent, showed herself to be extremely sympathetic, her filial devotion to her spiritual father precluded her from querying a papal decision. The archbishop, for his part, frequently questioned and criticised the dubious activities of the Commission of Regulars, yet even he was not prepared to quarrel with a papal bull. The two unfortunate Grandmontines were very badly treated when, in desperation, they threw themselves upon the mercy of the Commission. It was in the course of this meeting that they encountered Dom Razat who had re-assumed the title of Procurator General of the Order but who, in reality, was aiding and abetting the Commission to succeed in its aims. He made a convincing show of consoling and assisting his brothers in religion, pleading for them and seeming to avert the Commissioners' anger. Later, at the Collège Mignon, this zealous convert of Loménie cunningly sounded them out and ascertained the extent to which their loyalties to the abbot could be undermined. Once he had wormed his way into their confidence, he managed to convince the completely demoralised brethren that they were fighting for a lost cause and should consider their own interests and accept the benefices which Loménie was prepared to offer them. The admirable pair stumbled and almost fell, but then, ashamed of their momentary weakness, they returned to Grandmont more determined than ever to support their abbot to the end. Dom Chapellet died before the abbot, while Dom Muret lived to experience the grief occasioned both by the death of his superior and the actual expulsion of the remaining monks from Grandmont.

At Grandmont, the five religious, the *cinq gaillards* as Monsieur de Cressac referred to them, who had signed their approval of the suppression in the presence of Monsieur de la Vauverte, now sought permission to leave the abbey and receive the pensions which they had been allocated. In all probability they had good reason for making this request, for their continued residence at the mother house must have been becoming increasingly uncomfortable with each day that passed. Their public approval of the union was known and they cannot have been exactly popular with the loyalists. Their formal request was drafted and submitted to the Commission by a lawyer, Monsieur Tanchon. It was heeded by the Commission which, on 18 September, issued a decree authorising the five of them to quit the abbey provided they transferred to a monastery designated by the bishop. Each of them was to be afforded a pension of 1,000 *livres per annum*.[45] As the abbey and its revenues had not yet been united with the diocese, the abbot was legally liable for the payment of these pensions to the ex-Grandmontines. Thus it was that a short while after their departure, he received letters from two of them requesting the payment of the first installment. Abbot Mondain accepted the justice of these claims, but instead of paying the money to them personally, he arranged for it to be sent to the superiors of the religious establishments to which they had been assigned. Brother Jabet responded bitterly saying that the decree had clearly awarded the pensions to each monk for his own personal use and that the abbot's action had forced him to purchase winter clothing on credit. He threatened to notify the authorities if this debt was not honoured. The following spring, Monseigneur d'Argentré was informed by his spy Vergniaud, parish priest of Magnac, that Jabet had asked to be received back into the community at Grandmont. The tolerant and patient abbot, it appears, was only too delighted to welcome him back despite the reservations of the religious. However, Jabet died shortly afterwards and the reconciliation was never realised.

In the October of the year 1773, Loménie de Brienne paid a personal visit to Limoges in a final bid to persuade the abbot to see reason, drop his appeal, and bow to the inevitable. Unfortunately there is no record of the encounter between the high-powered, cunning, and devious Archbishop Loménie and the humble but tenacious Abbot Mondain. Whatever tactics Loménie may have employed in his attempt to convince the abbot, they did not succeed. The archbishop went on his way and the deadlock continued.

Following the stay of Parlement which had been annulled by the King's Council, Abbot Mondain had managed to secure four additional parliamentary decrees which simply had the effect of delaying tactics. Each one called for further examination of the evidence submitted in the primary appeal against the bull. When, therefore, Monseigneur d'Argentré returned to Limoges following a prolonged absence of eight months, his delight in his almost completed palace surrounded by fine gardens which rivalled those of Versailles was marred only by the intolerable and wearisome delay which these appeals had provoked.

On 27 February 1774, Loménie secured a conciliar decree which declared all previous stays of execution ordered by the Parlement null and void. Once again the jubilation of Monseigneur d'Argentré was short-lived, for on 2 March the Parlement upheld the decree which it had issued the previous July and which stated that the Apostolic Delegate should not proceed with the union. Despite this fact, and in defiance of it, Loménie, backed by the Commission, pressed the Apostolic Delegate from Bourges to return to Limoges and resume his enquiries. Between the 22 and 25 August 1774, Monsieur de la Vauverte was once again installed in the great hall of the seminary at Limoges. All the parties concerned were given an opportunity to speak, but once again Monseigneur d'Argentré was conspicuous by his absence. Neither did his name appear on the list of notables who had assembled to witness proceedings. The protests aired by representatives of the parishes in the vicinity of Grandmont on this occasion bear a further heart-warming testimony to the useful and charitable activities of the last monks of Grandmont. Objections were also registered by the inhabitants of villages that lay further afield: Razés, Saint-Pierre, Saint-Léger-la-Montagne, Compreignac, Forges, Bessines, Bersac, Jabreilles, Saint-Michel-Laurière, and Saint-Sulpice-Laurière all sent representatives. In addition, numerous individual protests were heard.

The enquiry was a mere formality and once concluded it remained only for the Apostolic Delegate to proceed once again to Grandmont for an official survey. On 1 September, he arrived at the abbey accompanied by Messieurs Martial Chateau and Jacques Cajon, architects of Limoges. They were courteously greeted by the abbot and his monks who then retired as a body. Monsieur Barny, the local notary, then stepped forward and delivered a strong protest in the name of the community. He further informed Monsieur de la Vauverte that the religious would not cease in their efforts to obtain justice. He then demanded that Monsieur de la Vauverte should state whether he intended inserting his protest in the official record. The response was wholly negative with Monsieur de la Vauverte reserving the right to include it or not as he saw fit. Dom Pichon then returned and the inventory proceeded. Everything was found to be in more or less the same condition as it was when Monsieur de Lepine had compiled his inventory three years before. Monsieur de la Vauverte then left the abbey, but the two architects remained until 7 September surveying the building, lands, and properties.

The official enquiry and business once completed, there commenced the long wait for the decree ordering the actual enactment of the bull. Abbot Mondain continued to do everything possible to delay it even longer. He dug up every possible legal technicality which might prejudice the case of his adversaries. He had recourse to the most obscure laws and by-laws which might assist his cause and of which, as Guibert observes, there was a veritable arsenal in the France of that day. Groups of local protestors also busied themselves with claims and counter-claims having to do with the irregularities perpetrated during the formal enquiry. Far from reaching its logical conclusion, the business was becoming ever more complicated and Monseigneur d'Argentré must have despaired of ever being able to extricate himself from the sea of red tape threatening to submerge him utterly.

A memorandum submitted to the Council for Ecclesiastical Affairs by Monsieur Lalanne, the abbot's lawyer at this time, contains very little new evidence. It does, however, view the papal error which referred to the Grandmontine as Benedictines, in a significant new legal light. According to this lawyer, the incorrect appellation legally invalidated the entire bull. He further maintained that the pope had not only mistaken the facts, that he was also totally unaware of the magnitude of the act he had all unwittingly ordered. He thought he was uniting a single monastery and its few dependencies which together represented a dried up and degenerate branch of the Order of St Benedict. Instead, he had unintentionally given his consent to the extermination of a separate, independent religious order.[46]

This state of deadlock continued for five years. Then, on 27 April 1779, the religious were once again rudely shaken out of any false sense of security that this extended respite may have permitted them. The sudden renewal of activities detrimental to the cause of Grandmont was due entirely to Monseigneur d'Argentré. His patience finally exhausted, the prelate had, for the first time in the long history of litigation, stormed Paris and accosted the Commission of Regulars in person. He must have pleaded his case well, because the Commissioners instantly passed his dossier to the King's Council which quashed all previous stays of execution. The latest had been granted in September 1775 to permit the monks to pursue the appeals which had been little more than half-hearted legal sorties. The 1779 decree embraced and dispensed with all previous oppositions and declared that the king willed a single, firm judgement. A further year went by and in September 1780 the Commissioners ordered the canonical procedure to continue. In fact, there were only a few formalities to complete and on 27 June 1781, Monsieur de Maufoult, a senior official in the employment of the archbishop of Bourges, affixed his signature to the decree which ordered the union of the abbey of Grandmont with the diocese of Limoges.

By the year 1780, Louis XVI had been on the throne for six years, during which time religion had once again become fashionable at Versailles. The critics of the Commission of Regulars had met with a great deal more sympathy from the new king than they had from his grandfather. On 17 August 1780, Monseigneur de Lau, archbishop of Arles, addressed a strong and eloquent speech to the Assembly General of the Clergy, in which he lamented the wilful destruction of no less than nine separate religious congregations in France. The Grandmontines figured at the head of his list. The text of this speech was passed to the king himself and shortly afterwards, a petition was addressed to the pope in the name of the Assembly of the Clergy. This in turn speaks of the tears shed by the faithful throughout France over the ruin of so many houses of religion and the disappearance of so many religious congregations both of monks and canons regular.

Sadly this brief religious renaissance, no less than the piety of the ill-fated Louis XVI, came too late to reprieve the Order of Grandmont. Although the Commission of Regulars was disbanded by order of the king in March 1780, happily for Monseigneur d'Argentré, the death sentence had been formally and irreversibly pronounced. He was still to be subjected to some intensely irritating delays, however. In March 1782, the letters patent confirming the decree of union were submitted to the Parlement of Paris, which refused to endorse them. A report submitted the following month to the Commission for Unions made it known that the Parlement had once again noted certain irregularities in the manner in which the Apostolic Delegate had handled affairs. Further legal haggling ensued and the letters patent were modified. On 20 June they were re-registered without encountering any further parliamentary objections. In accordance with the letters patent, the pensions which had been allocated for the religious were raised from one thousand to twelve hundred *livres*. Permission was granted for the abbot and his religious to live the remainder of their lives at the abbey.

The number of Grandmontines who participated in the final stages of the history of their Order was rapidly diminishing. Dom Salot de Tourniolles and Dom Chapellet de Fontvielle had died, the latter while visiting Châtenet, the remaining house of grandmontine nuns just south of Limoges. Abbot Mondain himself was far from well; he had entered his eightieth year and twenty years of unmitigated struggle and litigation were taking their toll of the old man. Dom Muret and Dom Beaubreuil remained the only permanent residents at the abbey, where they were occasionally joined by Dom Pichon who was looking after the interests of the little daughter house at Muret, birthplace of the Order.

On 1 April 1787, François-Xavier Mondain de la Maison Rouge, twenty-seventh and last abbot of Grandmont, breathed his last. Apart from the three regular companions who had supported him through his last, painful years, two other Grandmontines attended him at his death: Dom Fabré, formerly of the Strict Observance, and Dom le Borlhe from the Rouen house of Notre Dame du Parc. The following day, these, the last five sons of the Family of St Stephen, buried their abbot in the cloister. The site of his grave and indeed those of his predecessors are now lost to view beneath the village of Grandmont.

The condition that the monks should also be permitted to end their days at Grandmont was totally disregarded.

As soon as Monseigneur d'Argentré received word of the abbot's decease, he contacted Loménie de Brienne and together they moved in for the kill. Just two of the monks remained in residence at the abbey; Doms Breaubreuil, le Borlhe, and Fabré, not wishing to undergo the process of eviction at the hands of the bishop, had returned to their respective families shortly after the abbot's death. This left Doms Muret and Pichon, together with a few aging domestics, as the only inhabitants. In July 1788, they received formal notice to quit. In vain did they plead that the terms of Article 7 of the decree of union be honoured. They were told that they themselves had requested at the General Chapter of 1768 that the community be allowed to remain in existence until after the abbot's death. Now the abbot was dead and that was that they must prepare to leave at once. The bishop backed up his decision by securing a decree of council dated 7 October ordering them to vacate the abbey. They were given one more fortnight in which to make their arrangements.

Dom Muret had been born and bred in the little village of Grandmont; he still had relatives in the neighbourhood and so he returned to live with them. Dom Pichon was from further afield in the Périgord and he was unable to reconcile himself to living so far away from the spiritual home in which he had vowed himself to pass the remainder of his days. He therefore begged the bishop to permit him to go and live in the little monastery of Muret. Monseigneur d'Argentré agreed to this and magnanimously gave him a small plot of adjoining land to cultivate. He also gave instructions that he be supplied from the sacristy at Grandmont with a chalice, paten, vestments of the various liturgical colours, and altar linen. Thus Dom Pichon was enabled to continue celebrating Mass in the little chapel close to the spot where St Stephen's own primitive oratory had stood and where, on 8 February 1124, he had died. For the next few years on this, the feastday of the founder, Dom Pichon was joined by his former brothers in religion until finally the Revolution caused him to abandon Muret.

According to an amusing anecdote still told by the local people of Grandmont, the last two monks had barely closed the door of the abbey behind them before the bishop rushed up to take possession of his prize. As he entered, he tripped and fell headlong at the foot of a statue of St Stephen. This prompted one of the villagers to cry out with glee, 'Look, Monseigneur is making his apologies to St Stephen.' Regrettably this tale has no foundation in fact and it seems most unlikely that 'Monseigneur' put in a personal appearance at the abbey at this time. Nevertheless, it was with somewhat unseemly haste that his officials set to work on the despoliation of the great abbey. Reliquaries and sacred vessels were distributed throughout the parishes of the diocese. The priceless Limoges enamelling and metals which coated altars and tombs was stripped off by the bishop's workmen who performed their task every bit as efficiently as the Protestants had done two centuries earlier. The precious manuscripts from the library were sold by weight to tradesmen for wrapping paper. The furniture and furnishings were auctioned off to the highest bidders. The lead which was stripped from the roofs of the almost new buildings alone fetched 30,000 *livres*.

In 1791, the curé of St Sylvestre was influenced by the revolutionary spirit which prevailed at the time to describe the scene of devastation thus:

> This fine, celebrated Abbey is nothing but a ruin which a whole horde of barbarians could not have reduced to a more deplorable and sadder state.

Shortly afterwards, the National Assembly ordered all the belongings of the clergy to be sold and the abbey itself was declared a *Bien national* and sold for the benefit of the State on 18 March 1791. The prize which Loménie de Brienne and Monseigneur d'Argentré had devoted almost twenty years to acquiring was lost almost as soon as it was gained.

It is to Monseigneur d'Argentré's credit that he refused to take the oath of allegiance which the revolutionary government required of the clergy. In consequence, he was obliged to flee from France as an émigré. He died, still in exile at Münster in Westphalia in 1808, aged eighty-five. In his will, he bequeathed the sum of 8,000 *livres* to his former diocese; 3,000 for repairs to the cathedral, 2,000 to the Sisters of Charity, 2,000 to the hospice at Limoges and 1,000 to help the poor of the city. It has been said of Monseigneur d'Argentré that he wanted to uphold the dignity of his ecclesiastical state and that it would have been more acceptable if he had maintained it with a martyr's crown a few years later.[47] It might be even more acceptable to consider that his long years of exile in Westphalia afforded him the time to consider and repent his part in this tragic history that the terms of his will represented a possible gesture of remorse and reparation for the vanity and greed which contributed to the wanton destruction of the Order of Grandmont.

NOTES

References to Louis Guibert, *Destruction de L'Ordre et de L'Abbaye de Grandmont* are to the single volume edition published 1887 (Paris: H. Champion; Limoges: Veuve H. Ducourtieux) and not to the original text which appeared in the *Bulletin de la Société Archéologique et Historique du Limousin* between the years 1885–87.

1. P. Chevalier, *Loménie de Brienne et L'Ordre Monastique* (Paris: 1959).

2. Archives Nationales, 0 567, no. 10, cited by Gui, p. 168

3. Gui, p. 169.

4. Gui, p. 195

5. Archives Nationales, 0 547, no. 1 dossier 2, cited Gui, p. 195.

6. The full text of this Report which, in all probability, was written by M. Thiériot, Secretary to the Commission, is preserved in the Archives Nationales, 0 547, cited Gui, p. 199.

7. D. Seward, 'The Grandmontines—A Forgotten Order' *Downside Review* 83 (1965) 262.

8. Gui, p. 216, cites L'Abbé Legros: 'On blâme le titulaire de cette abbaye de ne s'être pas opposé avec assez de vigeur a son extinction.' mss du grand-séminaire de Limoges. This collection of documents relevant to the disbanding of the Order of Grandmont is contained in the Archives de la Haute Vienne but is not available for consultation at present.

9. The full title of this work is *Mémoire à Consulter et Consultation Pour L'Abbé Général de Grandmont, au sujet de la Suppression de Son Abbaye, et de Son Union au Siège Episcopal de Limoges* (Paris: P.G. Simon, 1773).

10. Ibid., p. 34.

11. *Mémoire sur l'état religieux,* p. 405 ff, cited Gui,p. 227

12. The full text of Loménie de Brienne's Report for the Commission of Regulars is in the Archives Nationales 0 547, no. 1 dossier 2; cited Gui, pp 233–37.

13. *Ibid.*, cited Gui, p. 236.

14. Régistres de la Commission, Bibliothèque Nationale mss français, 13846; cited Gui, p. 240.

15. *Mémoire à Consulter* etc. *Pièces Justificatives,* No. 3 Représentations de L'Abbé de Grandmont au Sujet des Lettres Patentes du Février 1769, p. 7

16. The full text of the memorandum of instructions issued to Dom Daguerre by Loménie de Brienne is headed: 'Mémoire pour servir d'instruction à M. Daguerre pour less opérations à faire à l'abbaye de Grandmont en exécution des lettres-patentes du 24 février 1769' It is preserved in the Archives Nationales, 0 547 no. 1; cited Gui, pp. 285–89.

17. Monseigneur d'Argentré's copy of the memorandum sent by Loménie de Brienne to Dom Daguerre together with the drafted letter requiring the abbot's signature and his personal letter addressed to the abbot, are in the Archives de la Haute Vienne.

18. The document of submission signed by the monks is in the Archives Nationales, 0 547, no. 1; cited Gui, pp 294–96

19. Archives Nationales, 0 547; cited Gui p. 302.

20. Archives de la Haute Vienne; cited Gui, p. 309

21. *Ibid.*, cited Gui, pp 317–18.

22. Turgot's Report to the Minister, La Vrillière, dated 19 April 1771, is in the Archives Nationales, 0 547, no. 1, dossier 2; cited Gui, p. 317.

23. *Ibid*, cited Gui, pp 317–18.

24. *Mémoire à Consulter, Pièces Justificatives* 8–12, (see note 9) pp 15–25.

25. The letter from Loménie de Brienne to Monseigneur d'Argentré is in the Archives de la Haute Vienne no. 1200; cited Gui, p. 326.

26. The royal brief is in the Archives Nationales, 0 547, no 1, dossier 1; cited Gui, pp 347–48, footnote 1. The memorandum from Monseigneur d'Argentré which accompanied the brief is no. 1200 in the Archives de la Haute Vienne.

27. Dom Babinet's reply to Loménie de Brienne's letter co-signed by Jabet, Bresse and Lecomte is in the Archives Nationales, 0 547, no. 1 dossier 1.

28. See note 26.

29. Note attached to the dispatch sent to Rome by Cardinal de Bernis 16 November 1771. Archives des Affaires Etrangères: Correspondance de Rome; cited Gui pp 357–360.

30. The full text of this letter is in the Archives de la Haute Vienne, no. 1200; it is partially cited by Guibert p. 369.

31. *Ibid.*, cited Gui, pp 377.

32. Monseigneur d'Herbault's curt observation was actually 'Neque cursum studii, neque novitiatem existere pro paucitate religiosorum.' Procés verbal de L'Archévêque de Bourges, Archives Nationales, 0 570 no. 1 dossier 1.

33. For the full text of the Report of the Enquiry, see above, note 32. The observations and reactions of the religious themselves were reported in the *Mémoire* (note 9 above), pp. 12–24.

34. Description of Grandmont written by the seventh prior, Gérard Ithier, in *Speculum Grandimontensis* (see Ch. 2, pp. 56–57 above).

35. Archives de la Haute Vienne; cited Gui pp. 399–400.

36. *Ibid.*, cited Gui pp 427–28.

37. The text is included in the appendix of the *Mémoire Pièces Justificatives* No. 8 (see above note 9) p. 15.

38. L.J. Lekai, *The Cistercians, Ideals and Reality* (Kent State University Press, 1977) p. 168.

39. Guibert quotes from a letter written by Loménie de Brienne dated 6 December 1772 but does not reveal its whereabouts.

40. Letter of Vicaire Bourdeaux, 19 February 1773; Archives de la Haute Vienne; cited Gui pp. 443–44.

41. This correspondence is preserved in the Archives des Affaires Etrangères, Correspondance de Rome 1772.

42. Archives de la Haute Vienne; cited Gui, p. 465.

43. The Abbé Vergniaud's note is in the Archives de la Haute Vienne and cited in full by Gui, pp. 467–70.

44. Archives Nationales, O 570 no. 1 dossier 1; also Bibliothèque Nationale, ms français 13,854; cited Gui pp. 471–75.

45. Archives Nationales, O 570 no. 1 dossier 1; cited Gui p. 516.

46. This memorandum is among the personal papers of Dom Muret preserved in the Archives de la Haute Vienne; it is partially cited by Guibert, p. 554.

47. Père J. Fouquet OMI and Frère Philippe-Etienne, *Histoire de L'Ordre de Grandmont*, p. 109.

IX

THE ARCHITECTURE OF THE ORDER OF GRANDMONT

SITING

THE FOUNDING OF A GRANDMONTINE MONASTERY in the twelfth century would have been a relatively uncomplicated and inexpensive operation. It involved the construction of a simple church and living quarters, together with land sufficient to supply the needs of a small community. The fact that these monasteries proved so cheap to build helps explain both the exceptional popularity and rapid expansion of the Order in its early years.

By comparison with a cluniac or cistercian foundation, which required large, elaborate, and costly churches, as well as sufficient accommodation for a veritable army of monks, a grandmontine church was little more than an oratory. The exceptional austerity of the Grandmontines precluded even fireplaces. Thus for a comparatively modest capital outlay, a patron could expect every bit as good a return for his investment as the founder of a great abbey. The monks' prayers, which would assure the eternal salvation of himself and his family, must have proved a very satisfactory spiritual insurance policy.

Although the circumstances which caused the Grandmontines to establish themselves in one area rather than another varied considerably, the site itself had to conform to a set of very definite criteria. One major consideration resulted from the Rule's insistence that: 'woods are suitable places for monks to build their homes.'[1] The actual naming of various of the cells is often indicative of their

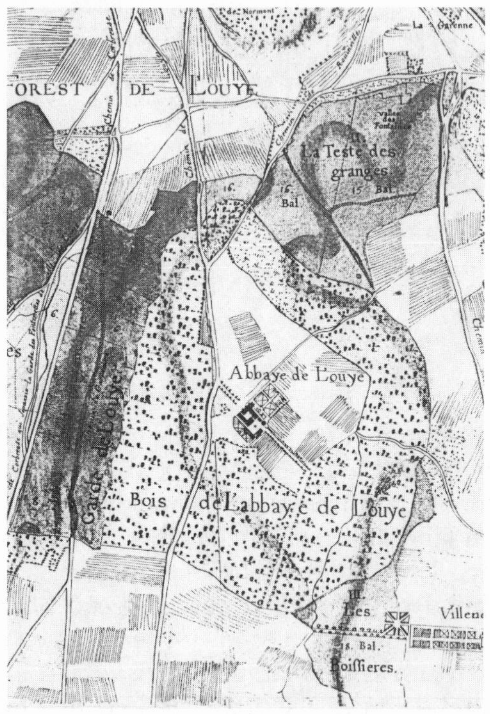

Eighteenth century plan of Notre Dame de Louye (Essonne) Archives de France.

surroundings: Bois d'Allonne, Bois de Vincennes, Bois-vert, to name but a few. Suitably wooded sites were often located in upland areas where the terrain was extremely poor. This did not deter the Grandmontines, who regarded such poor land as a challenge wholly in keeping with their Rule's promise: 'The worse the state of the land, the more will God manifest himself to you if you retain confidence in him.'[2]

The natural enclosure of trees proved insufficient for these contemplatives and they went to even greater lengths to distance themselves from the world at large.

Fences, rough stone walls, streams, and moats all contributed to the purpose. Where the enclosing fences and walls have disappeared, the original oval *circuitum* can often still be traced. Alberbury, in Shropshire, provides a particularly striking illustration. Here, the River Severn forms a natural boundary to the north of the original precinct, while a semi-circular moat completes the enclosure. The arrangements show up very clearly on a sixteenth-century plan preserved at All Souls College, Oxford.[3]

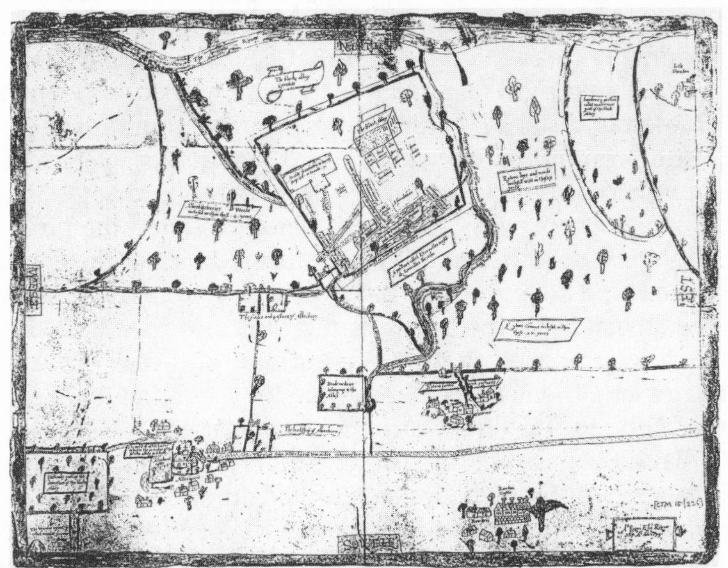

Plan of Alberbury Priory (Shropshire) 1579. Reproduced by kind permission of the Warden and Fellows of All Souls' College, Oxford.

While the cells are always located well away from other habitations, they are never too far distant from a main thoroughfare. The mother house itself was situated just a few kilometres from the main pilgrim route which ran from the north and east to Santiago de Compostella. Several daughter cells were built close to ancient roman roads which were still in use in the Middle Ages. There were two main reasons for this and both can be found in chapters of the Rule. In the first instance, the Grandmontines were bound to provide for all those in need:

> For the sake of charity you will show hospitality to our guests. If you store up and retain your goods you will be in need; but in giving and distributing you will have in abundance. Let it be a joy, therefore, to tend and give to guests.[4]

The second reason was associated with the provision that when all other means of support failed, the brothers should go out and beg their bread, which called for a reasonably frequented thoroughfare close by. No cell was ever situated right on a main road but always two or three kilometres distance. Thus they were far enough away to ensure conditions of solitude and tranquility, yet close enough to be both of assistance to travellers and accessible for begging purposes. Grezillier has considered the possibility that the grandmontine cells formed part of the chain of monastic hospices which was established in the Middle Ages to cater for the needs of pilgrims and travellers. He has also proposed that the Grandmontines may actually have made themselves responsible for the maintenance of roads and the dredging of rivers in some areas. This would explain a somewhat obscure direction in the Custumal to brothers working with laymen outside the enclosure.[5] The cell of Etricor appears to have been deliberately sited at a point where the River Vienne could be forded during the summer months, but a ferry would have been necessary in winter. Presumably, the monks provided this service.

The Grandmontines frequently chose to site their cells near the borders of states, provinces, or, at the very least, diocesan or parish boundaries. Both Craswall and Alberbury are very close to the border between England and Wales. These hermit monks seem to have been determined to distance themselves as far as possible from centres of government, civil or ecclesiastic. This decision was almost certainly bound up with their almost paranoic horror of becoming involved in any kind of lawsuit. It is worth remembering that in 1124 an unpleasant quarrel with the Benedictines of Ambazac resulted in the community abandoning their original settlement at Muret. No doubt it was the memory of this unfortunate experience which prompted the compilers of the Rule to dwell so intensely upon the evils of litigation and give such lengthy directives on how best to avoid it.[6] Border country, well away from major urban centres, was likely to provide the most sparsely populated as well as the least attractive, land for settlement. The further they set themselves apart from the haunts of men, the less they risked involvement in legal processes.

Ground Plan

The ground plan differs little from any standard design for a monastery save that the grandmontines' cells were constructed on a greatly reduced scale with cloisters rarely

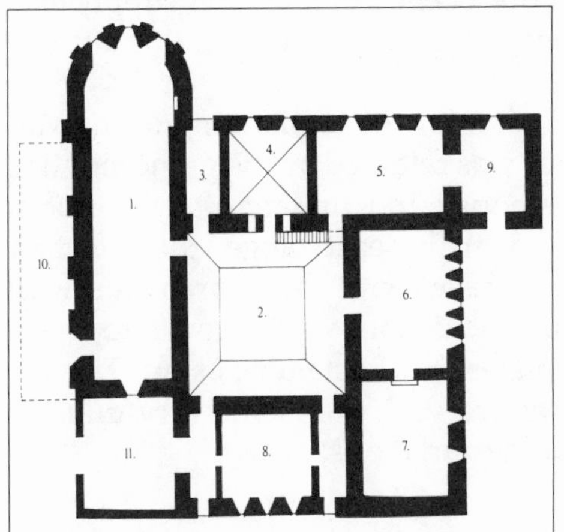

1. church
2. cloister with stairway to dorter over east range
3. cemetery passage (couloir des morts)
4. chapter house
5. undercroft
6. refectory
7. kitchen
8. guest lodgings
9. rere dorter
10. porticus
11. outer court

Typical Grandmontine cell plan.

exceeding twenty metres a side. They are usually roughly squared, although there are some rectangular examples, such as Comberoumal and Craswall. The church, the focal point of a monastery, normally assumes an air of greater importance than the conventual buildings around it. This is not the case in a grandmontine monastery, where it is barely distinguishable from the remainder of the buildings. It is always orientated in the usual way with the sanctuary to the east and is generally sited to the north of the cloister, although there are several exceptions. The reason why, in at least twenty cases, the south was preferred to the north is not readily discernible. In warmer climates, the Cluniacs and Cistercians more often than not constructed their cloisters to the north to render them cooler in the hot summer months. But several north sited grandmontine cloisters were built above the Loire, for example, at Chassay in the Vendée, Bois Rahier, just outside the city of Tours, Mathons Les Bonshommes in the Marne and Montaussan, Indre Loire. Badeix in the Dordogne provides a further outstanding example of a north sited cloister occurring in a region which is not particularly noted for the mildness of its winters. As was frequently the case with monasteries of other religious orders, the location of the water supply may well have been the key factor in determining this alternative siting of churches.

The usual monastic plan for the positioning of the various domestic buildings was retained by the grandmontine builders. The chapter house and undercroft with dorter over are always located in the east range, the refectory occupies the building parallel with the church; the west range, which was almost certainly given over to guest accommodation, completes the cloister enclosure. This being said, there were, as we shall see, some very unusual and strictly grandmontine variations.

Construction

Grandmontine buildings are always remarkably solid. The exterior walls are normally composed of enormous, finely cut ashlar blocks which are very carefully assembled in such a way that the joints are reduced to a minimum. In areas where suitable granite or limestone was not readily available, such as Montaussan, ragstone construction was substituted. Three interesting exceptions were: Loc Dieu, Pinel, and Francou in the Toulouse area where the traditional rosy warm brick of the region was employed. Unfortunately, Francou is the only one of these houses to have survived, and although it is in a very poor state of repair, it could still be rescued.

Wherever they settled, the Grandmontines always managed to site their buildings close to a convenient source of local stone, thus avoiding transport costs. St Michel de Lodève and Comberoumal are both exceptionally close to the quarries which supplied the stone for their buildings. The stone used for the walls at Craswall almost certainly came from a well-worked quarry just above the site. Here however, there is a strong indication from the large blocks of travertine lying amid the rubble in the interior of the church that this material was widely employed for the vaulting as well as window jambs and other sections of the interior. As there is no source of this material closer than Moccas, about ten miles from the site, the Craswall builders must have been faced with an exceptional and costly problem. However, the durability and resistance to weathering of travertine, combined with its lightness and the exceptional ease with which it can be worked, would seem far to outweigh any additional costs incurred through transporting it from a distance. To sum up, although grandmontine monasteries are always identical as regards plan, they reveal a tremendous diversity when it comes to fabric and colour, from greyish blue and milky shades of granite through all the various cream, yellow, and rosy tints of limestone and sandstone.

In conformity with standard twelfth-century practice, churches were built with inner and outer facing walls of massive stone blocks, the cavity between them being packed with rubble. This was bound with a mortar composition which has proved every bit as durable as roman cement. While the walls are invariably very thick, yet the thickness is always found to be proportionate to the weight of the vault. In churches such as Badeix, which is built entirely of granite, the walls attain a thickness of 1.90 metres, whereas at Fontguedon, where the local yellow limestone was employed, the maximum thickness is only 1.07 metres. In some cases, the exterior side wall of the building is thicker than its interior counterpart, which derives additional buttressing from the adjoining conventual buildings. Such is the case with the travertine construction at Villiers. Here, the north wall of the church achieves a thickness of 1.26 metres while that to the south is twenty centimetres smaller. In the case of granite churches like Badeix, both the outer and inner walls are constructed in identical fashion. Where limestone has been used,

The apse at Badeix (Dordogne).

however, the courses of the inner wall are more carefully aligned than those to the exterior and the blocks themselves have a rougher, grosser finish. The conventual buildings are constructed with the same stone and in the same way as the churches; the only difference is that their walls are less thick.

The efficiency and durability of grandmontine building methods is nowhere more apparent than at Rauzet, one of the finest of the surviving churches. It is situated on farm land in the department of Charente and has been left to fall into dereliction. The roof covering the vault was removed more than a century and a half ago and a whole forest of trees has taken root in the upper sections of the walls. This is subjecting the vault itself to continuous pressure and strain. Despite these odds, there has only been one major collapse in the apse and the nave vaulting remains miraculously intact. At Hauterive (Indre Loire), and Fontcreuse (Charente), the churches are currently in use as barns. Only the core material of the buildings survive, the facing walls having been stripped away so that the dressed stones could be put to alternative uses. Still the buildings themselves continue to stand, and at Hauterive in particular the walls have had to withstand the additional pressures asserted by the annual storage of grain.

GRANDMONTINE CHURCHES

Uniformity

Of the one hundred fifty churches known to have been built in the twelfth and thirteenth centuries, only sixteen have survived in a really good state of preservation, although there are a further twenty-nine in various stages of

The derelict church of Rauzet (Charente).

decay. Even the most dilapidated examples, such as Montaussan, abandoned deep in the forest of Amboise, reveal a remarkable uniformity as regards both plan and style. Without exception they comprise a single aisled, tunnel-vaulted nave, lacking transepts and terminating in a semicircular apse which is marginally broader than the nave.

The extent of this broadening varies between thirty-four centimetres at Aulnoy and one metre at Rauzet. The apse is pierced by three, equal sized, round-headed windows with unusually broad embrasures: the typical grandmontine triplet. The only other window in the building is located in the centre of the west wall and is constructed in exactly the same manner. The general appearance of these churches, with the exception of the enlarged apse, is akin to the little eleventh-century rural parish churches of central and western France. It is possible that these simple churches constituted the basic model for the oratories constructed by the early followers of St Stephen of Muret.

Dimensions

The length of grandmontine churches varies between twenty and approximately forty metres. Etricor is the smallest surviving example, 21.70 metres. It would seem that the smaller churches also represent the most ancient, for Etricor has been dated between 1148 and 1157. Comberoumal and St Michel de Lodève, the two best known and certainly the best preserved and restored, are considerably larger. Comberoumal measures 30.75 metres and Lodève, 27.50. Both can be dated between the years 1189–92. These three examples are all located well south of the dividing line formed by the River Loire. To the north, la Haye d'Angers was built around 1188 and reaches a total length of 37 metres. Near to the town of Dourdan, south of Paris, is Notre Dame de Louye which has the largest surviving church at 38.30 metres. Unfortunately its full extent cannot now be appreciated for a large portion of the nave was divided off and turned into living accommodation some time in the last century. However, the sanctuary and what would have constituted the monks' choir, have been faith-

The church of Notre-Dame de Louye (Essonne) is now beautifully restored as a chapel for a community of Ursuline sisters.

fully and beautifully restored to use as a chapel by the present owners, a community of Ursuline sisters. The church of the english priory of Craswall in Herefordshire was one of the last to be built; it achieves an overall length of 34 metres.

The Grandmontines remained strictly faithful to a nave the width of which was approximately one quarter of the length. In a church measuring thirty metres, the apse enclosing the sanctuary accounted for five or six metres of the total length. The nave was therefore between twenty-four and twenty-five metres by a width of six metres. In some cases, possibly where the master of the works decreed and the quantity of available stone allowed for a somewhat more refined and higher vaulting, the width was augmented accordingly. Something of this nature must have occurred at St Michel de Lodève, for here the nave measures 21.10 by 6.50 metres.

Departures from the Standard Church Plan

Any deviations from the standard grandmontine plan are exceedingly rare. Bandouille [Deux Sevres], which survives though in ruins, and Trezen [Haute Vienne], are the only known churches to have been built with square east ends instead of the traditional apse. Trezen was demolished in 1905 but is known to us from a photograph. To these two french examples we can add Alberbury in Shropshire, the nave of which has long since been razed. The choir was refashioned for living accommodation as late at 1875, at which time the east wall of the church was finally demolished. However, the extant elizabethan plan shows it to have had three single light windows in the grandmontine manner. (See p. 283). The nineteenth-century historian, Louis Guibert, visited and described the square-ended church of Trezen, completed in 1205 and proposed that an earlier monastic foundation may have existed on this site. It seems well within the realms of possibility that here the Grandmontines inherited a church which was built for previous occupants of another religious Order. This was certainly the case at Alberbury, which we know to have been built originally for a community of Arrouaisian canons from nearby Lilleshall Abbey, and this explains its ungrandmontine square east end. Bandouille was another late foundation, circa 1217, and as such it may represent a further case of a monastic hand-me-down.

Another outstanding departure from the strict grandmontine church plan is apparent at Chavanon (Puy de Dôme). Here, at the point where the break between nave and apse would normally occur, there is a pair of engaged columns on either side of the nave supporting a double arch. This is certainly the only surviving example of such an arrangement and there is no evidence for anything similar having existed elsewhere. The relieving arches which support the nave vaulting, at Louye, are of recent origin; almost certainly they were introduced in an effort to counteract the outward thrust of the walls. Similar arches at Desgagnazeix are part of much earlier remedial work; this church ceased to be monastic and became parochial in the sixteenth century. The construction of the western tower and doorway in 1880 not only altered the grandmontine appearance of the church out of all recognition, it also

View of Desgagnazeix (Lot) from the east.

weakened the vault of the nave. This called for considerable strengthening which lowered the height of the vault at the west end and necessitated the introduction of a reinforcing archway close to the juncture with the apse.

Vaulting and Elevation

This aspect of grandmontine churches reveals a pattern of uniformity equivalent to the ground plans. The naves are all tunnel vaulted with one exception, where rib vaulting was substituted. This was at Petit Bandouille, another late foundation dating only from 1226.

The springing of the vaults both of the nave and chancel is marked by a string course, usually quadrant shaped but a few chamfered examples exist. This was no mere decorative feature; it fulfilled the practical function of supporting the planks necessary for the construction of the vault itself. Only in the two aforementioned instances, Desgagnazeix and Louye, is the vaulting broken by reinforcing arches; all the remaining churches still depend on the thickness of the lateral walls for their support, although this is often supplemented by an irregular system of exterior buttressing.

The highly unusual covering of a nave with a continuous, plain vault is referred to in the earliest known edition of the Custumal, the only existing grandmontine text to speak expressly of buildings:

> Since all excess is inappropriate to our religious life, the church and other buildings of our Order should be plain and free from all forms of excess . . . The vaults of the churches should be plain so as to conform with the simplicity of our Order.[7]

It is the *voute plana*, the plain unembellished vaulting, which renders the naves of all grandmontine churches austere and yet at the same time both imposing and practical. But although the exceptional austerity of the Grandmontines caused them to reject any superficial artistic ornament, they were certainly neither blind nor insensitive to natural beauty. A consideration of the precise measurements of Comberoumal, one of the recently restored

The church of Puy Chevrier (Indre)

The church of Saint-Jean les Bonshommes Charbonnières (Yonne)

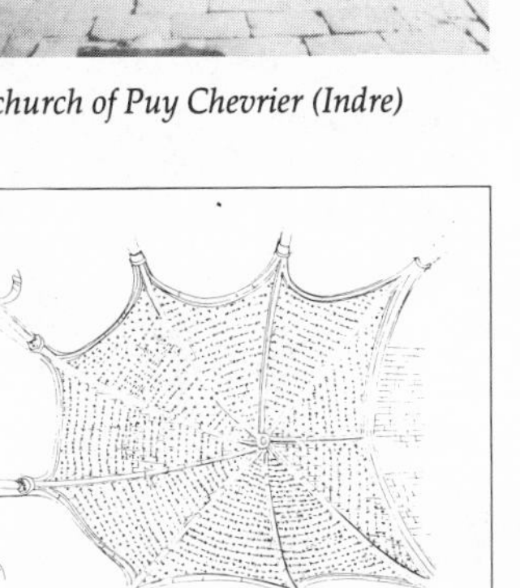

The apsidal vaulting at La Primaudière (Loire-Atlantique)

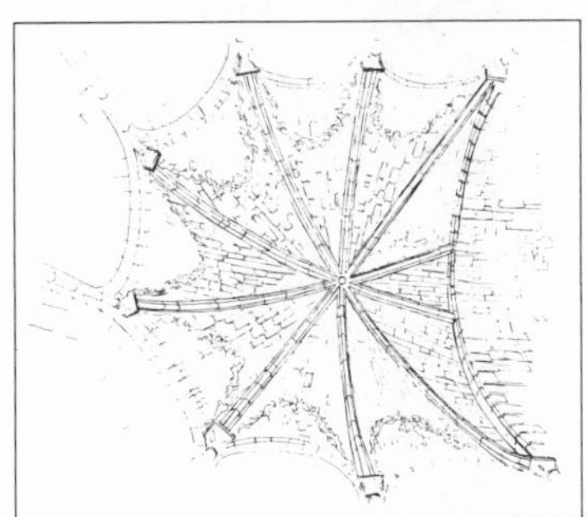

The apsidal vaulting at Bois d'Allonne (Deux-Sèvres)

churches, reveals that its height, at 10.68 metres, is nearly twice its width, at 6.40, and roughly a third of its total length, 30.75 metres. Add to this an illusion of even greater height created by the light which in the morning hours, floods the apsidal vault, plus the simplicity of the smooth, even stonework and an impression of immense soaring

The church at Comberoumal (Aveyron)

height is achieved. The use of so much fine quality dressed stone in raising the vaults of their churches to such generous heights does not appear to be in keeping with the extremes of poverty which we know the Grandmontines practised. The explanation may well be bound up with another aspect of natural artistry which they found to be acceptable—quite simply, acoustics. The raised vaulting may have been intended to improve the tonal quality of the chants by eliminating any unpleasant echo which a low barrel-vaulted ceiling might create. It is significant that at some time subsequent to its building, the church at Etricor had its vaulting raised by two metres along the nave and one metre over the apse. The operation was achieved by literally lifting the roof, heightening the vault and building up the walls with layers of rubble. This has a rather unhappy effect upon the exterior of the building. The cleanly cut slope of the original gable is still clearly in evidence and as the upper section has not been modified, it is disagreeably obtuse. As well as this, the upper courses of rubble stand out in marked contrast to the dressed stone which

The church of Etricor (Charente) from the north.

clads the remainder of the buildings. Such clumsy alteration must have been governed by hard economics rather than any artistic consideration, at least where the exterior is concerned. The work can only have been effected in order to bring Etricor, one of the earlier churches, into line with later buildings where the chants sounded so much better.

The fidelity of the Grandmontines to the *voute plana* is remarkable but it applies only to naves, the apses being an altogether different matter. A number of these are rib vaulted and present a certain richness of design. The surviving examples can be conveniently divided into two distinct types although all of them share the common characteristic of being both broader and higher than the naves to which they are attached. The first category involves those which are vaulted by means of a simple half cupola or semi-dome. The churches of Etricor, Puy Chev-

The apse of the church of Comberoumal (Aveyron)

rier, la Haye d'Angers, Badeix, Desgagnazeix Comberoumal, and St Michel de Lodève are all of this pattern. The apses in the second category are rib vaulted but they vary

The apse of the church of Notre-Dame de Louye (Essonne)

considerably as regards numbers and placement of ribs. Charbonnières, Louye, and les Moulineaux all have six, received on wall columns the corbels of which are positioned at a height equivalent to the window sills. A blind arcade of five arches reinforces the wall. Three of these arches enclose the windows while the remaining two occupy the space between the windows and the juncture with the nave. La Primaudière is somewhat more elaborate with nine vaulting ribs and seven arches fashioned in the enclosing wall. The inclusion of this pair of supplementary outer arches appears to have the sole purpose of increasing the depth of the sanctuary area, which if it were dependent on five, would only cover an area equivalent to that of apses designed with plain half cupolas. Eight of these ribs are received on the corbels incorporated into the columns of the outer arches, the ninth has no intermediary member but is received into the extrados of the nave vaulting at the key of the arch. At Bois d'Allonne and Breuil Bellay, this more elaborate style is taken a stage further, both examples having an additional, tenth, rib. As is the case at la Primaudière, there are seven supporting arches but the ninth and tenth ribs are both received into the extrados of the nave. The blind arcades surrounding these apses combined with three perfectly proportioned windows create a fine sense of harmony. Unfortunately, this has been badly marred at Breuil Bellay, where the remodelling of the sanctuary in the baroque style of the seventeenth century has involved the misguided decision to pierce a fourth window through the south wall of the apse. The clumsy, misshapen result detracts sadly from the original unity of the design but fortunately, a similar version is preserved at Bois d'Allone.

The two main categories of vaulting pattern outlined above would seem to correspond to both chronological and geographical considerations. The semi-dome variety predominates in the southern houses, whilst rib vaulting is found in the more northerly regions of France. The northern cells were mostly built later than those in the south so that it is possible as Dr Gaborit has suggested, that by the time the Grandmontines were building in and around the Ile de France, the architects of that region had discarded the fashion for semi-domes and were subject to the Gothic influence instead.[8]

The Apse

Why did the Grandmontines adopt the unprecedented design which allowed for the apse to be always marginally broader than the nave, and which they achieved by means of that curious reveal between the eastern sector of the nave and the sanctuary? The presence of this unique feature in areas as far apart as the Bas Pyrenees and Yorkshire, regions where architectural tendencies were quite different, suggests that it was one of the essential requirements imposed by the Order on the builders of its numerous cells. Dr Grezillier has proposed a symbolic reason for this design. Assuming that the church of the mother house, in company with the daughter houses, was single aisled and without transepts in order to accommodate the two hundred stalls spoken of by the sixteenth-century monk, Pardoux de la Garde, without considerable lengthening of the church, the choir itself was widened in respect of the nave.[9] The only flaw in this otherwise very plausible theory is that there is no means whatever of substantiating it. Pardoux de la Garde's description of Grandmont II contains several inaccuracies and it is likely that he also exaggerated the size of the choir.[10]

A more likely explanation for the unusual form of the grandmontine apse has been suggested by Dr Gaborit. This assigns it a role in practical architectural terms. The grandmontine church is composed of two distinct elements, the nave and an apse which is independently covered with a semi-dome. The semi-circular wall of this structure is boxed into the nave which thus provides it with considerable support. The chancel reveal could therefore have been purposely devised both as a buttress and to allow for the construction of the apse itself. It would have allowed for the positioning of the massive beams indispensable in the building of a hemispherical vault against the extrados of the nave vaulting already constructed.[11]

This theory has been reinforced by Cecil F. Wright, an architect and lecturer in architectural history who was responsible for the 1962 excavation of Craswall Priory in Herefordshire. He has suggested that the chancel reveal may well represent an aesthetic device which at one and the same time managed to solve some of the design problems which these churches involved. He enlarges as follows: The lateral walls of the nave had to be bulky enough to resist the outward thrusts from a very heavy and unsophisticated vault, devoid of any ribs or other devices which might resolve the load along lines of thrust and concentrate them on piers or buttresses. The semi-circular plan and hemispherical vault of the sanctuary would, in effect, hold itself together around the end of the building—to some extent—through the friction between stones under load both from the vault and the upper parts of the walls. Given that, certainly on this scale, a curved wall is more stable than a straight one, the thinner wall of the sanctuary would be quite stable and would also effect a saving in bulk masonry. As has been demonstrated in the sixteen intact churches which have survived, the apsidal walls have remained stable without the presence of conventual buildings or side chapels which would have provided additional support. Aesthetically, the apsidal east end has the advantage of being neatly accommodated within the robust structure of the church as a whole. Additionally, it provided a stop against which ribs could be neatly terminated as can be seen at la Primaudière and Bois d'Allonne, thus eliminating any need for further decoration (see p. 302). Finally, the reveal provided a convenient separation between the nave and the sanctuary which constituted a liturgical necessity.

From the other end of the argument, Mr Wright has asked how else, if the Grandmontines had not devised this

The apse of the church of La Primaudière (Loire-Atlantique)

The apse of the church of Bois d'Allonne (Deux-Sèvres)

sanctuary reveal, would they have solved the various design details outlined above without introducing much more decoration than they considered acceptable? In fact, he considers that the grandmontine apse drops neatly into the long family of architectural devices which serve both functional and aesthetic purposes and which have often been employed to contain or frame an element in design, in this case, the sanctuary.

It may be pure coincidence, but if the enlarged apse was devised primarily for a functional reason, the result of the design is nonetheless strikingly symbolic. While the curving, dark, cave-like structure of the nave accords with the self-negating ideals of these hermits, the bold soaring curves of the sanctuary flooded with natural light, presents a dramatic focus for their reflections upon eternity.

Normally the exterior of the apse is rounded to comply with the interior, although exceptions do occur. Breuil Bellay and la Primaudière are polygonal whilst Comberoumal, Desgagnazeix, Chassay and Bois d'Allonne all have flattened exteriors with three, sometimes five faces. According to the region, the exterior wall of the apse is flanked by flat buttresses or columns of differing number and design. Alternatively, as is found at Fontblanche, an overall thickening of the wall has been contrived with mortared rubble. This rises to just below the level of the window sills and is bevelled to carry off rainwater. The various methods of refining the exterior appearance of the apse appear to have depended entirely upon local usage and custom. In the Limousin columns are never employed, whereas in Poitou and Saintonge they are very much a feature of grandmontine churches.

Lighting

Far from proving insufficient, the four windows provided in a grandmontine church are at once adequate and practical. They are also responsible for the achievement of some very beautiful and symbolic lighting effects. Apart from the obvious theological equation of the apsidal triplet with the Trinity, when morning light floods the sanctuary it becomes an echo in stone of the psalmist's song: 'Praise and beauty are before him, holiness and majesty in his sanctuary.' For most of the day the nave remains in semi-darkness and its rounded vault is evocative of a cave, the traditional hermit's dwelling. The direct result of the carefully designed and positioned triplet and single west window is that the monk's day would have timed with a whole sequence of impressive and very moving lighting effects.

Seated in a grandmontine church at daybreak, one easily feels something of the spiritual elation which these hermit monks must have experienced when towards the close of their nightly vigil, the sanctuary of their church began to be suffused with radiant light. How appropriate the *Benedictus*, the Church's official morning song, would have sounded in this setting: 'God who visits us like dawn from on high . . . who gives light to those who dwell in darkness and in the shadow of death.'

The first rays of light penetrate the sanctuary through the northernmost of the three windows. As the morning wears on, more light infiltrates the central aperture at the same time as the original beam is moving slowly along the south wall of the choir. By late morning a crescendo of brightness is achieved with the light reflecting off the walls while the curving vault is transformed into an aurora of shimmering light. At a time which varies with the season, a natural spotlight beam illuminates the right side of the altar and then moves slowly across its surface. A dramatic climax is reached when a square of intense white light focuses directly on the centre of the altar. When the light withdraws from the east, the nave becomes a haven of shadowy coolness, as the sun makes its way around the cloister to penetrate the single west window in time to light the evening office of Vespers. As night approaches, a time which must have coincided with the celebration of Compline, a single shaft of light moves slowly along the north wall at the base of the nave. When the sun sinks to rest, there is an almost audible click as the beam which has been creeping along the window embrasure reaches the jamb and is abruptly extinguished. The ensuing twilight would have allowed the brothers just enough time to leave the church and retire to the dorter for their night's rest.

All four church windows are positioned very high up and their embrasures are exceptionally wide in respect of their apertures. They seem to have been meticulously calculated to direct the maximum amount of light into the interior in order to create the daily lighting sequence. This is by no means dependent upon conditions of brilliant sunlight, it is almost as effective even when the sky is overcast. The windows in the chapter house, refectory, and dorter are designed in the same way as those in the church only on a much reduced scale.

Doors

In the same way as windows, doors conform absolutely to the standard grandmontine pattern. They are always two in number. The one situated at the base of the nave in the side wall opposite the cloister is known as the 'doorway of the faithful'. As its name implies, it allowed occasional access to visitors. The earliest surviving examples are very simple in design. In the thirteenth century, however, some relaxation in the rules prohibiting ornament allowed for the introduction of shafts with mildly decorated capitals. Fontblanche provides the plainest surviving example, simply a narrow entrance through a single archway with a chamfered outer edge. Chassay, slightly more developed,

The lay entry of Fontblanche (Cher)

has two orders which are continuous through head and jamb. Châteauneuf progresses a stage further employing three, equally plain, orders. Etricor, the earliest surviving church, is nevertheless slightly more elaborate. It is of three orders, the outer being outlined with clean cut grooving. The centre arch is faced with a thick coiled moulding while the inner, has similar coupled moulding. At Comberoumal, the employment of twin shafts flanking the entry lends it an air of greater importance. Here, both the outer and central arches are carried on detached shafts the outer bearing cushioned and the inner, foliated capitals. Bois d'Allonne reveals a variation on the same theme, the outer and central orders here being elaborated with detached roll mouldings carried on slim shafts with decorated capitals. The most elaborate examples, however, can be found at le Breuil, St Michel de Lodève, Breuil Bellay, and la Haye d'Angers. These all have three ordered entries with their arches resting on imposts which are in turn supported on shafts with very simple capitals. La Haye is undoubtedly the most impressive with coiled moulding of the same diameter as the shafts outlining the archivolts.

The lay entry at Etricor (Charante)

In a cluniac or cistercian monastery, the monks' entry from the cloister is always an impressive portal broad enough to allow processions

The lay entry at Comberoumal (Aveyron)

The monks' entry at Le Breuil d'Autun (Côte-d'Or)

to pass through two abreast. In a grandmontine church it is contrastingly simple. Its extreme narrowness permits only one person to enter at a time and confirms the fact that the grandmontine liturgy included little in the way of ceremonial. It is invariably positioned one third of the distance along the nave and the area between it and the apse represented the monks' choir. The majority of the surviving examples are of one order only though a few slightly more elaborate versions do occur. At Comberoumal, a simple round headed aperture is charmingly framed in an exterior arch which rests on imposts borne by shafts with cushioned capitals. The well preserved example at le Breuil is all the more striking in that it represents the only surviving feature of a church which has been so badly mutilated as to be almost unrecognisable as a grandmontine church at all. It is of two orders, the inner incorporating a rolled moulding which rises from the imposts which rest on shafts with foliated capitals. Bois d'Allonne presents

The monks' entry at Bois d'Allonne.

by far the most elaborate example, however. Here the space allocated between the inner and outer orders is generously broad and is embellished with roll moulding supported on detached shafts bearing small but exceptionally fine foliated capitals. A chamfered hood mould emphasises the doorway and lends it a more imposing appearance. While there are considerable variations in the decorative details which are found to the exterior of these doorways,

The west end of the church at Bois d'Allonne (Deux-Sèvres)

the interiors are all, without exception, strictly regular, round headed, and totally devoid of decoration.

Just two exceptions to the grandmontine custom of siting the lay entry in the side wall of the nave have been gener-

The church and east range at Villiers (Indre-et-Loire)

ally accepted to date, Villiers and Puy Chevrier.[12] Certainly the present state of Villiers reveals a very convincing entry in the west facade. It comprises four orders of which the three outer arches are underlined with thick coiled moulding originating from shafts, sections of which have disappeared. A seventeenth-century plan shows, however, that this structure cannot be in its original position.[13] The plan, dated 1693, reveals that the nave at this time was considerably longer than at present and it also shows the lay entry in its customary grandmontine position. Although Monsieur l'Abbé Bourderioux attributes this to an 'inexplicable error', it seems inconceivable that the author of the plan should have committed so glaring a mistake. The most likely explanation is that the western sector of the nave was demolished possibly at the same time as the south range was remodelled in the eighteenth century. The entry was then re-erected in its present position.

The other grandmontine church which purportedly had an original west entry is Puy Chevrier. Even this is not entirely convincing, but unfortunately in this instance no documentary evidence which would support a case for subsequent remodelling has come to light. Nevertheless, the very appearance of the doorway is extremely odd quite apart from the fact that it is structurally unsound and, for a very obvious reason. The system of lighting the rear of the church, by means of a single window positioned in the centre of the west wall, called for a very long window indeed. This is not the case

The west end of the church at Puy Chevrier (Indre)

at Puy Chevrier, where a sizeable doorway inserted immediately under the window has shortened it in such a way that the width is wholly disproportionate to the length. This arrangement has rendered the entire wall unstable and its awkward appearance is totally at variance with the usual efficient and logical grandmontine expertise. The reduction of the area of masonry between the window head and the gables has created a weakness which has resulted in the wall cracking throughout its length. In fact, it would long ago have caved in altogether if remedial action involving the insertion of steel masonry pins had not been implemented. The awkwardness of the arrangement provokes the question; is this the original design as is generally thought, or a seventeenth-century transformation similar to that at Villiers? It certainly lacks the perfect symmetry implicit in the grandmontine design for windows and this is due to its having been shortened to allow a doorway to be inserted below. The work bears a remarkable similarity to the clumsily constructed fourth window which was pierced through the south wall of the apse at

The exterior of the porticus at Breuil Bellay (Maine-et-Loire)

Breuil Bellay in the seventeenth century. A further example of late grandmontine remodelling is apparent at Châteauneuf. Here a small, oddly shaped traceried window surmounted by a small oculus, has replaced the traditional long west window. Puy Chevrier could likewise have fallen prey to this desire for change.

Doorways inserted in the west walls of other of the churches, such as Breuil Bellay and St Michel de Lodève, all postdate 1772, when the churches fell into secular hands and were for the most part modified for use as barns and granaries. A western barn door, constructed at this time at Comberoumal, has been reblocked as part of the excellent restoration work carried out by the present owners of the site.

What can have prompted the Grandmontines to site their lay entries in this unusual position? Monks in general have always preferred the west sited entries which they used for ceremonial processions. Customarily, they formed up outside the church and progressed along the nave through the choir to the chancel. Considerable space was also required to the exterior of this doorway to serve as a stage for the clergy at specific solemnities, such as the lighting of the new fire at the culmination of the Easter vigil. Side entries are singularly unmonastic and are normally only associated with simple parish churches. This accords with the theory that the poverty-loving Grandmontines built in imitation of the simple rural churches of the Limousin, cradle of the Order.

A further explanation which has been proposed to explain this alternative siting is meteorological. Quite simply, because the west wind is so damp, the builders avoided opening doorways in that direction.[14] This is not a really satisfactory solution for it takes no account of the even more unpleasant effect of exposing the entrance to icy blasts from the north, particularly bitter in more northerly climes such as Normandy, Grosmont in Yorkshire, and Craswall located high on the Welsh Marches.

A more symbolic motive has to do with the lighting effects which the Grandmontines sought to achieve in their churches. A doorway simply could not be safely inserted beneath the exceptionally long and broad embrasured window necessary to light the church effectively at eventide. At least not without substantially weakening the entire wall and risking the sort of near disastrous cracking which, as we have seen, occurred at Puy Chevrier.

One obvious explanation for the unimposing entry to the church has to do with the porticus. Evidence for the one-time existence of such a structure can be found wherever the church, or part of it, has survived. Furthermore, its purpose is outlined in Chapter 51 of the Rule, which speaks of the manner in which the brothers should go out to the parlour to welcome visitors. Another reference to a parlour being provided alongside the church occurs in the *Life* of Blessed Hugues Lacerta. This mentions its existence at Châtenet, one of the earliest cells. Normally, the porticus would have consisted of a simple timbered structure with a pentice roof attached to the wall of the church and enclosing the lay entry. That these little annexes were nearly always built with very simple materials is evident from the fact that they have disappeared almost without trace. The only visible sign of their former attachment is the rows of corbels which were intended to support the main roof beam along with matching joist holes which would have received the rafters. All the surviving churches have retained some, if not all, of these corbels. Occasionally, some additional ones set into the west wall demonstrate that in certain cases the porticus was returned along it. A few of the churches had a stone built porticus but they appear to have been the exception rather than the rule. The only intact example can be found at Breuil Bellay. It is a curious structure, comprising a fairly long, quadrant vault which rests on an arcade, the arches of which were filled in at a later date so as to completely enclose the interior. The survival of this porticus has had the fortuitous effect of protecting the moulded archivolts of the doorway from weathering so that they remain in pristine condition. Remains of a stone porticus against the north wall of the church are clearly evident at Parc lès Rouen. There is,

The interior of the porticus at Breuil Bellay (Maine-et-Loire)

however, no way of knowing if this was the original or simply the replacement of an earlier timbered structure. Evidence for the former existence of a stone porticus has come to light at la Haye d'Angers. In the course of restoration work carried out by the brothers of the religious congregation which now owns the site, the area immediately to the north of the church was cleared and excavated to reveal the solid stone foundations of the walls of a building attached to the church and north chapel. A further possible example occurs at Chavanon. Here, a ruined stone structure alongside the north wall of the church is strongly reminiscent of the one at Breuil Bellay. A substantial mound of stone and rubble in the same position at Craswall indicates that this english house also had one of these rarer and more permanent stone parlours.

Buttressing

The sheer weight of the stone vault would have rendered the exterior buttresses, so characteristic of grandmontine churches, a very real necessity. French architectural experts have, however, found it almost impossible to determine which of these formed part of the original structures and which were added later to reinforce the buildings when it became necessary. The broad, flat examples found at Etricor, Charbonnières, Badeix, and Puy Chevrier quite obviously form an integral part of the original design. The enormous, cumbersome examples at Villiers, on the other hand, were almost certainly added when extra support to relieve the thrust of the vault was deemed necessary. In certain cases, Etricor being the most obvious example, the lay entry was pierced through an exceptionally broad buttress which has, in this particular case, increased the thickness of the wall from 1.25m to 1.60m. It extends six metres along the north wall to the angle where it is returned a further two metres along that of the west. The upper section tapers into the walls in three stepped sections surmounted by a hood mould. A similar though more refined version can be found at Bois d'Allonne.

The offset apses of these churches may well have posed problems of construction which could only be overcome by additional supports, for a further scheme of buttressing can sometimes be found against the nave, close to the apsidal juncture. The apse itself is not always provided with buttresses; in fact, the ones which are covered with plain semi-cupolas certainly do not have them. Rauzet, St Michel de Lodève, Puy Chevrier, Badeix, and Châteauneuf have no such additional support. A few are provided with alternative reinforcement in the form of columns; examples include Comberoumal, Charbonnières, Notre Dame de Louye, and Chavanon. Where the apses are rib vaulted, flat buttresses have usually been employed to strengthen them. The most notable of these are Bois d'Allone, Breuil Bellay, Chassay, and la Primaudière. In the last instance, the buttresses have been curiously capped with hanging tiles which taper upwards to the height of the gables. The effect is most unusual and has a decorative effect which seems out of character with a grandmontine church.

Church Interiors

In the absence of any material traces or verifying texts, it is not possible to discover the precise arrangements of grandmontine church interiors prior to the seventeenth century. We cannot know, for instance, whether any form of partitioning or screening was introduced to separate the monks' choir from the remainder of the nave. Plans dating from the seventeenth century reveal that the choir occupied the major section of the nave between the cloister doorway and the sanctuary. It further seems generally to

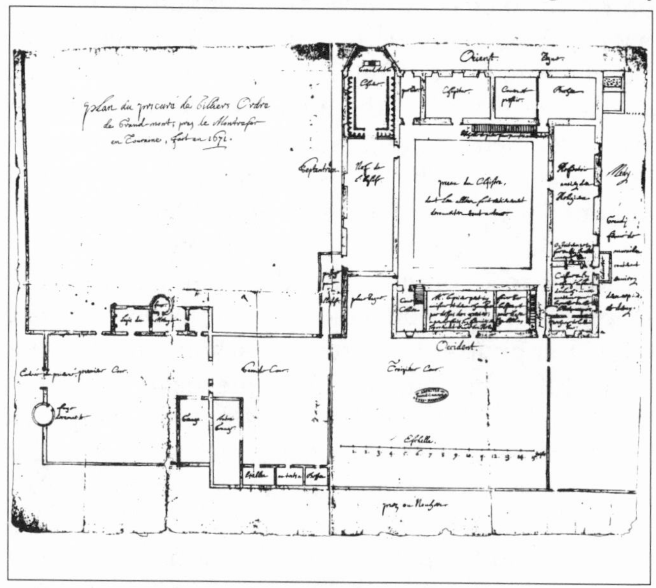

Seventeenth century plan of the priory of Villiers. Archives de l'Indre-et-Loire

have had two small altars arranged on either side of the entrance. Certainly, the piscinas which are frequently discovered fashioned in the thickness of the walls towards the base of the nave, indicate the existence of these altars relatively early in the history of the Order. They may have been included in imitation of the altars of St Martial and St Catherine which, according to Pardoux de la Garde, were erected at the entrance to the choir of Grandmont but which, Dr Gaborit has shown, were actually located at the base of the nave.[15] There can have been little call for additional altars before the close of the twelfth century, when we can in all probability associate their introduction with the marked increase in ordinations to the priesthood.

The monks' choir itself is referred to in verbal processes relating to annual visitations carried out in the seventeenth century as the *grand choeur,* while the sanctuary was known as the *petit choeur*. Given the exceptional narrowness of grandmontine churches, the stalls of the monks must have been set flush with the walls. This was certainly the arrangement illustrated on the seventeenth-century plan of Villiers which conforms to the usual monastic arrangement but on a greatly reduced scale. A single tier of eight stalls is set against the north and south walls, with a further pair on either side at the base facing eastwards. This particular plan also shows screening behind these eastward facing stalls separating them from the western sector of the nave. The only concrete evidence for any kind of partitioning having existed between the choir and nave before this date can be seen at Puy Chevrier. Here there are some holes in the wall of the nave which seem intended for the housing of a wooden beam. They occur approximately six metres from the base of the nave.

Within the sanctuary there is always a eucharistic aumbry fashioned in the wall to the left of the altar and a twin piscina facing it on the right. The arches enclosing these two niches are invariably round headed. No altars have survived though the one at la Primaudière is thought to be original. At Craswall, the base of an altar survives though the mensa has disappeared, in all probability removed long ago to be used as a salting slab. The only incidence of additional sanctuary furnishings can also be seen at Craswall. This consists of a fine and, in the grandmontine context, a very elaborate triple sedilia. It proves to be a very rare feature indeed for nothing of the kind has been discovered in any of the surviving french churches.

The ruins of the sanctuary at Craswall (Herefordshire)

In the latter half of the thirteenth century, some relaxation in the strict rules prohibiting ornament seems to have taken place and frescoes were introduced into these churches. Humbert de Romans writing at the time tells us moreover:

> In grandmontine houses the clercs devote themselves entirely to contemplation and divine worship in beautiful churches which have marvellously decorated altars.[16]

Humbert de Romans (d. 1277) was the fifth Master General of the Order of Preachers and himself preached to several grandmontine communities. A number of churches reveal traces of fresco paintings and a few have considerable sections covered with intricate and brightly coloured designs. At Châteauneuf, traces of a once very fine Virgin and Child are identifiable. Unfortunately the building is now abandoned and derelict with the result that damp and mould is rapidly obliterating all trace of it. The church of Montaussan lies deep in the forest of Amboise and, although in an appalling state of ruin, it too bears traces of a fourteenth-century Virgin and Child on the wall of the nave opposite the lay entry. Further traces of paint are still evident in the sanctuary.

Often, painted decoration simulates architectural features. At la Haye d'Angers the entire nave has been plastered and painted to represent cross vaulting. At Bois d'Allonne the voussoirs of the vaulting ribs of the apse have been coloured alternatively in prussian blue and ochre red, while the cells in between have been filled with a bold design in blue and red outlined with yellow ochre scroll work on a white background. The church at Francou in the south (Tarn and Garonne) reveals a particularly bizarre kind of ornamentation. It is one of the only three grandmontine houses which were built throughout in the traditional mellow brick of the region and the vaulting, arches, and columns in the chapter house have all been constructed in this material. The oddity consists in the fact that the brickwork of the church was completely plastered over, and then red and white paint was carefully and meticulously applied throughout to simulate brickwork.

The report of the 1962 Craswall excavation headed by Cecil F. Wright records that voussoirs of vaulting ribs uncovered in the north chapel bore traces of having been decorated with a serpentine brush line in red ochre on a white background. Evidence of what may have been quite extensive fresco work was discovered along the west wall of the chapel. Here, the careful removal of soil over an area of about three square feet revealed a similar design in red ochre and black on a white background. Mr. Wright describes it as having been 'very vestigial and suggesting some form of vine scroll'. Following this discovery, no further investigation was carried out in this area as it was rightly felt that there might be further valuable material requiring specialist examination. Certainly the serpentine and scroll design as well as the ochre red colouring described by Mr Wright would seem to bear a marked similarity to the grandmontine fresco work which has survived in some of the french churches, notably Bois d'Allonne.

The only grandmontine fresco work which can be dated with any precision is at La Haye d'Angers. In 1345, Pierre Roger de Beaufort, at the age of ten, received the priory *in commendam* from his uncle, Pope Clement VI (Avignon 1342–52). In due course de Beaufort became a cardinal and eventually had the distinction of being the last of the Avignon Popes under the name of Gregory XI. The fresco which he ordered for his commendatory church conveniently reproduces the rose of his cardinal's blazon. It must therefore date from sometime between 1355, when he was created a cardinal, and 1370, when he became pope.

Chapels

With very few exceptions (St Michel de Lodève and St Jean les Bonshommes at Charbonnières) grandmontine churches were dedicated to the Virgin and so there was no need to provide them with separate Lady Chapels. In the early years of the Order there were very few ordained monks residing in the cells, hence no need for extra Mass chapels. When in the thirteenth century it became customary to ordain the *clercs*, their obligation to celebrate daily Masses was easily catered for by the additional altars introduced into the nave. Several of the larger priories did, however, annex side chapels to their churches but only two intact examples survive at St Michel de Lodève and la Haye d'Angers. Others, such as Notre Dame du Parc lès Rouen and Bois Rahier lès Tours, are known to us from plans. There is some evidence in the form of marks of attachment in walls and foundation mounds to suggest that they were present in several other places besides.

The intact example at Lodève bears out the impression which can be gleaned from studying the ground plans of these additional structures where they existed. Their purpose has to have been strictly functional, for they were constructed with little regard for aesthetic values. The attachment of a rectangular structure to the north side of a semi-circular apse has a very awkward and unpleasing appearance.

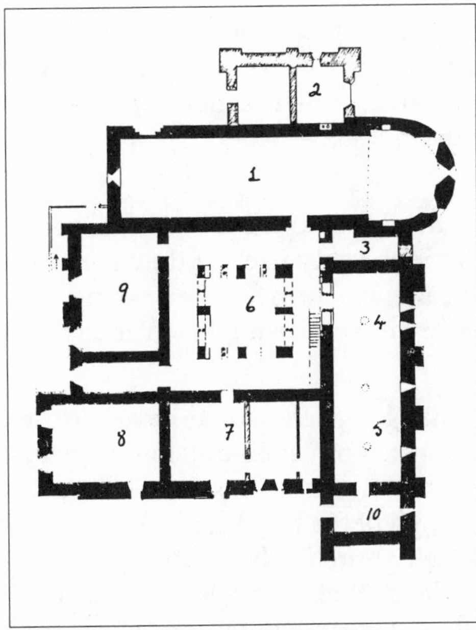

1. Church
2. North Chapel
3. Cemetery Passage
4. Chapter House
5. Monks' Day Room
6. Cloister with Stairway
7. Refectory
8. Kitchen
9. W. Range (Guests' Lodgings)
10. Rere Dorter

Over: 3, 4 & 5 — Dorter & Vaulted Chamber

Saint-Michel de Lodève, ground plan

What can have been the purpose of these ungainly chapel annexes? We cannot be altogether certain, although in most cases it would seem that they were intended to cater for the needs of the laity, especially women, who in no circumstances were permitted to worship in the church itself. Both at Lodève and la Haye, it is quite clear that it was the eastern extremities of the porticus which were transformed into chapels and neither communicates directly with the church alongside. In the case of Rouen we do have specific information as to the purpose of the chapel. It was built for the confraternity of St Catherine, founded in 1365. Just over a century later it was refurbished by Cardinal d'Estouteville.[17] As the chapel which formerly existed at Bois Rahier was also dedicated to St Catherine, it would seem that by the fourteenth century the Grandmontines were approving confraternities of oblates. This widely accepted monastic custom was absolutely forbidden to the Grandmontines by their Rule. This does, however add that such societies may be formed provided that all meetings be held well away from the monastery, and as long as the members did not expect the monks to send a representative:

> But if people express the desire to come and hold their meetings within your monastery itself, if they seek to breach the spiritual calm in which you are bound to dwell with God, you are not to permit this in any way whatsoever.[18]

Presumably the surviving chapels would have satisfied this condition, for they were both sited outside the actual monastic enclosure and had no direct means of communication with the main church of the monks.

All three of the english churches had side chapels attached to the north side of their chapels. According to Sir Alfred Clapham, they were a standard grandmontine feature built in imitation of the chapels at the mother house and were all dedicated to St Stephen. Neither assumption has proved to be correct. We now know that by no means all the french churches had additional chapels and the ones we do know of were certainly not dedicated to St Stephen. The north chapel at Craswall is extremely interesting in the manner in which it differs from its french counterparts. It could not be entered from the porticus but only through a doorway set in the north wall of the chancel itself. This certainly rules out any possibility of its having been used for the benefit of the laity.

A further strange anomaly is present at Craswall in the form of the so called South Chapel which intervenes between the church and the cemetery passage. It was discovered and partially excavated by C.J. Lilwall in association with the Woolhope Club in the early years of this century. They assumed it to be a sacristy.[19] Sir Alfred Clapham confirmed this assumption and gave the chamber a square east end on the plan which he published in 1926.[20] In 1962, Cecil F. Wright conducted a summer school field survey on

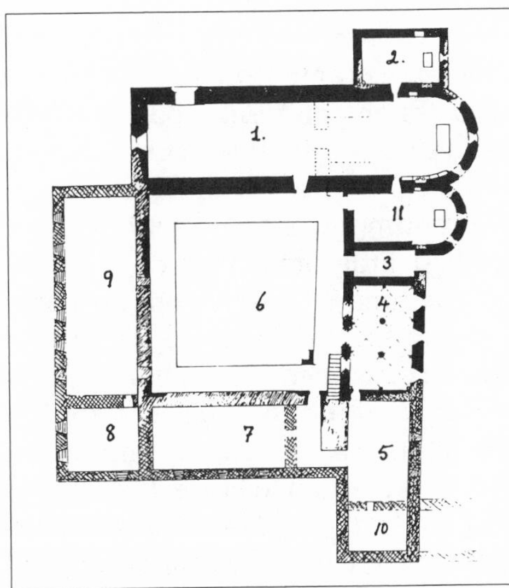

1. Church
2. North Chapel
3. Cemetery Passage
4. Chapter House
5. Monks' Day Room
6. Cloister with Stairway
7. Refectory
8. Kitchen
9. W. Range (Guests' Lodgings)
10. Rere Dorter
11. South Chapel

Over: 3, 4 & 5 — Dorter & Vaulted Chamber

Craswall priory ground plan

the site with students from the Liverpool College of Building. In an attempt to establish the precise plan form of this chamber, they cut trenches along the inside faces of the north and south walls. Matching breaks in both walls were discovered and identified as the typical grandmontine apsidal reveal. Further cutting uncovered a twin piscina fashioned in the wall and, beyond this, the commencement of the curve of an apse. Clapham's 'sacristy' was accordingly relabelled 'south chapel'.[21] In the light of this evidence it is no longer necessary to argue that the Grandmontines never made provision for sacristies in their church plans. The problem that does remain to be solved, however, is why the grandmontine builders should have provided at Craswall, and only at Craswall, such an unusually large chapel alongside a church which it reproduces in miniature. The 'chapel' is roughly one third the length of the actual church and this, by any standards, is exceptionally large for a simple mass or relic chapel. In fact, it is considerably larger than most cathedral chantry chapels. In practical terms, its builders set themselves a considerable problem attaching a smaller but identical circular apse alongside a larger version of the same structure. The result appears even more cumbersome and ugly than the rectangular chapel attached to the north side of the apse. A possible explanation is that this apsed chapel, which has no parallel in any other grandmontine monastery, was not a chapel at all but the first little oratory erected by the pioneer community. By the time it became both desirable and feasible to replace it with a larger and more impressive building, it is possible that it contained several burials. This was definitely the case with the first church at the mother house and it obliged the monks to construct Grandmont II alongside Grandmont I rather than disturb tombs. An alternative or parallel consideration is that the Craswall monks always intended to replace their first simple oratory with a larger and grander church. This being the case, the narrowness of the valley site would have prevented them from building it elsewhere and their only solution would have been to build the new church alongside the old.

Bellcotes

The original grandmontine building plans do not appear to have allowed for even the most basic of bell towers, as only one has survived and it has proved to be a much later construction. By the close of the twelfth century, some form of rudimentary bellcote must have formed part of every church building. One of the main bones of contention between *clercs* and *convers* concerned which group should be responsible for sounding the bell. The 'Privilege' of Honorius III, in 1217, afforded the Grandmontines the right to ring bells in times of interdict, which presupposes a bell big enough and loud enough to be heard outside the monastic enclosure. The only actual bell tower to have survived the centuries is at Fontenet in the department of Nièvre. Along with a perfectly preserved little apse the bellcote is all that has survived on this particular site, the nave having long since been converted into a house.

St Michel de Lodève incorporates an unusual and charming romanesque bellcote on the roof of the church. It appears to date from the twelfth century, but from the point of view of style it is more Spanish than French, being strongly reminiscent of the little bellcotes widely found in the Aragon region. Several churches have holes fashioned in the vaulting of the nave close to the cloister doorway which can only have been intended for the passage of a bell rope. Unfortunately in every case the bellcote itself has vanished. At Petit Bandouille sur Dives, the barrel vaulted chamber over the cemetery passage adjoining the church has steps fashioned in the thickness of the wall. These would have afforded access to the church roof at the position where a bellcote would have been located directly over the monks' entry. The very dilapidated church at Chavanon still retains a rusting and decrepit but nevertheless charming little bellcage in the same position. A recently restored example of what is probably a fairly typical example of a grandmontine bellcote can be seen at la Primaudière.

Conventual Buildings

By the close of the priorate of Etienne Liciac (1139–1163), the successors of the little band of hermits who left Muret for Grandmont were living more or less in accordance with the usual monastic arrangements. Gone forever were the primitive 'laurae', the rustic huts grouped around a simple stone oratory. It seems reasonable to question why the charterhouse system, so obviously more appropriate for hermit monks was not considered preferable to one which can only be compared with the traditional cluniac and cistercian arrangement. The only possible explanation must lie in the overriding grandmontine ambition to become the champions of an integral form of the eremitical life. Thus whilst they attempted to consolidate the early customs they had adopted from the desert fathers their anxiety to retain an individual identity precluded them from embracing the carthusian custom of near total seclusion in individual cells. Instead, they opted for buildings which, visibly at any rate, seemed to be in the traditional monastic mould but in which they might pursue a life style which, in its extremes of poverty, austerity, and simplicity, was poles apart from Savigny, Tiron, Aureil, or any other off-shoots of the benedictine or augustinian traditions. Despite these original aims, barely more than a century had passed before they were leading a life which was very similar to these other groups of reformed religious. The only permanent grandmontine departure from the monastic norm lies in their development of a singular and changeless style of architecture and one which survives as a solid testimony to their basic ideals.

In company with their churches, the domestic buildings of the Grandmontines were subjected to very little alteration or modification throughout the centuries. Two essential words described them: 'small' and 'regular'. They are small in that the church and conventual buildings grouped around a cloister form a monastic complex in miniature. They were built to house what seldom amounted to more than thirteen religious, three or four clercs and the remainder convers. They are regular in that they conform in just about every detail to the standard Grandmontine layout.

Cloister

Only one intact cloister remains, located at St Michel de Lodève. Constructed and vaulted almost entirely in stone, it casts little light on the appearance of grandmontine cloisters in general. The typical plan, however, allowed for an area more or less squared, although the church generally proves to be somewhat shorter than the east range. The roofs covering the arcades were obviously timbered, because the stone corbels which carried the main beam still remain firmly fixed in the walls of several of the surviving buildings. Substantial stone remains, segments of columns and capitals lying around in some of the cells indicate that the arcades themselves were frequently of stone. Most of the capitals which have been discovered are plain but some with simple foliate decoration have occasionally come to light.

The cloister garth at Saint-Michel-de-Lodève (Herault)

The most unusual feature of a grandmontine cloister is the positioning of the dorter stairway. It was always constructed against the wall of the east range, its first tread flush with the outer jamb of the doorway in the chapter house façade. The consistent grandmontine practice of placing the stairway against the wall of the cloister alley rather than inside the buildings, as was the usual monastic custom, has only one exception at Marigny (Indre and Loire). Here traces of an inside stairway remain in what was the east range building. We cannot be certain, however, whether this really constitutes the original arrangement or a subsequent modification. In cases where the stairway itself has been dismantled following the secularisation of the buildings, traces of its former attachment remain clearly in evidence along the wall. Additionally, a doorway, frequently blocked, can be distinguished at what would have been the head of the flight of stairs. So essential was it to the Grandmontines to retain the stairway in this particular position that at Craswall they preferred to raise the southern jamb of the chapter house and distort the entire façade in order to accommodate it rather than move it elsewhere.

The only possible reason for this unusual siting of a dorter stairway must have had to do with access to the church at night. Most monasteries, and certainly those of the Cistercians, were furnished with night stairways which descended from the dorter into one of the church transepts. As grandmontine churches lacked transepts, the most convenient and safest way of reaching the choir from the dorter in the dark would have been by means of a stairway which was sited directly in line with the entrance to the church. Also, the faint light afforded by the night sky must surely have been preferable to the pitch darkness of the interior.

EAST RANGE

Cemetery Passage

With the single exception of Craswall Priory, grandmontine chapter houses are separated from the churches by barrel vaulted slypes which have often been mistakenly referred to as sacristies. Dr Grezillier pointed out that as these passages have no direct means of communication with the churches they could not possibly have been intended for such a purpose. Unfortunately, in refuting one error he was inadvertently responsible for perpetrating another when he added that the Grandmontines had provided sacristies only in the case of their three english houses. This assumption was based on A.W. Clapham's plan of Craswall published in *Archaeologia* (1926) where the south chapel is labelled *sacristy*.[22] The passage is generally known in France as the *couloir des morts*, a name coined by the Abbé Bourderioux in 1959.[23] The term is highly appropriate for this corridor whose doorway opens directly into the monks' cemetery which was laid out alongside the apse close to the exterior wall of the range. There the Office of

The room over the slype at Chassay (Vendée)

the Dead was recited daily. The recessed niches with narrow stone ledges running along the base suggest that it was here that the brethren donned cloaks before filing into the cemetery itself.

A particularly remarkable feature of a grandmontine east range is the barrel-vaulted chamber which is always found directly over the cemetery passage. This little room is accessible from the dorter but not the church alongside. As all the surviving dorters have timbered roofs, this single stone covered room must have been intended for some very special purpose. The Abbé Bourderioux was not alone in thinking that it represented the corrector's quarters.[24] This seems an unlikely explanation however, as prior to 1216 the correctors did not exercise any particular authority and did not enjoy any kind of superior status. In addition, the rulings of General Chapters before the close of the thirteenth century, continued to uphold the Rule's requirement that even the prior of Grandmont himself sleep in the communal dorter.

J.B. Rochias was responsible for the suggestion that this chamber was used as a muniments room.[25] This seems equally unlikely because again the Rule expressly forbids the brethren to maintain archives, a prohibition which was not lifted before the papacy of Innocent IV (1243–1254). While it is true that this ruling was often transgressed, even in the late twelfth century, the possession of a few documents would still not have called for a room this size. Upon investigation, certain of these rooms have revealed caches secreted between the flooring and the vaulting of the passage beneath. These would have been accessible through trap doors and seem ideal for the storage of documents and small valuables. There is an example present in the ruins of Montaussan and another in the partially intact room at Grand Bandouille. Dr Grezillier has also described another perfectly preserved example at Puy Chevier.[26] However, close examination of the evidence in this particular case suggests that the so-called 'cache' is merely the result of alterations to the building which included new flooring. In all probability it dates only from the nineteenth century when the priory had long passed into secular ownership.

The two most plausible uses which have been widely proposed for the room over the slype are an infirmary or a night oratory. In the Rule, emphasis is placed on isolating the sick from worldly conversation although they are at all times to be 'comforted in God'. A chamber alongside the church in which the sick brother might lie and follow the offices would seem to be a very suitable arrangement. Alternatively, these rooms may have been used as night oratories at least in winter. Certainly with their barrel vaulted ceilings they seem like miniature versions of the church itself. This liturgical appearance is further emphasised in a few cases by small aumbries which have been fashioned in the thickness of their walls. At Grand Bandouille, there is a twin piscina in this position: evidence that the room was at one time furnished with an altar. Of course, this could well date from a time when communities were smaller and the original austerity of the monks had weakened to the extent that this room provided a somewhat cosier venue for the night offices than a large cold church. There can be little doubt that these rooms fulfilled a variety of purposes during their long history and in the absence of any conclusive evidence there is little point in speculating about their original purpose. In several of the surviving cells this room has been provided with an interior window which opens onto the sanctuary of the church. This has been used in support of the theory that the room was an infirmary and the window permitted the invalid to hear the services. While this may or may not have been the case in later times, it certainly could not have applied when the cells were first in use. None of these openings is constructed in the romanesque style favoured by the Grandmontines, and the clumsy manner in which they have been pierced through the massive wall blocks indicates that they were almost certainly inserted long after the completion of the building.

Chapter Houses

Twenty good examples of this chamber have survived, some of them in an exceptionally fine state of preservation. Chapter houses constitute the only area of a grandmontine monastery where the strict architectural rule of uniformity appears to have been considerably relaxed. A certain amount of artistic embellishment was also permitted with the result that they vary considerably both as regards style and ornament. Some, exemplified in Comberoumal and St Michel de Lodève, are simple squared chambers. Others,

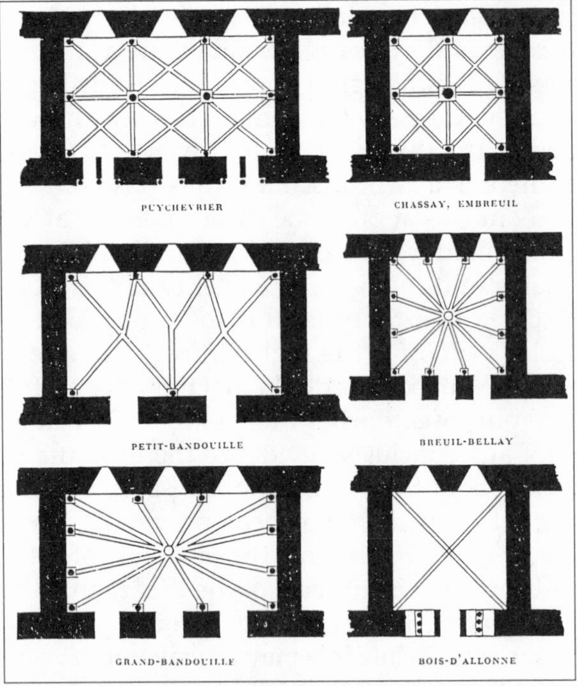

Chapter house vaulting reproduced from A. Grezillier 'L'Architecture Grandmontaine', Bulletin Monumental *121 (1963).*

such as Chassay, Montcient Fontaine, Epoisses, and Montguyon, are rectangular chambers divided into four bays and with vaulting dependent on a central column. There are also several six-bayed examples, Badeix and Puy Chevrier being the most notable although both have been extensively remodelled since they fell into lay ownership. The ruined chapter house at Craswall is unusually large and remnants of stonework show it to have been exceptionally ornate. Despite all these variations, Grandmontine chapter houses fall into certain relatively homogenous regional groupings. Lodève, Comberoumal, and le Sauvage are characteristic of those found in the south, while Fontblanche, Hauterive, and Villiers are typical of the central french variety.

Square Chambered Chapter Houses

Bois d'Allonne, centrally situated in the department of Deux Sèvres, is a good example of this type. The chamber is 6.50 metres squared and reaches a height of 3.80 metres. The vaulting is carried on a pair of diagonal ribs which rise from the ground at each of the angles. It is lit by two windows which have been so considerably enlarged that they have completely lost their grandmontine character. The portal has a rounded lintel which attains a height of 2.25 metres; the opening is only one metre wide. It is flanked by plain walls and the facade is completed by twin windows on either side of the portal. These are each divided by a row of three stout little columns with simple foliated capitals. The lintel of the doorway is raised slightly higher than those of the windows. Variations on this theme can be seen in the three southern chapter houses, Comberoumal, St Michel de Lodève and le Sauvage. In all three cases,it is the facades and not the interiors which vary. The window openings on either side of their entries are reduced to two and are separated from the doorways by a row of small columns. Comberoumal and Lodève each have three columns while le Sauvage has four. All three facades are set in a single rounded enclosing arch. Grand Bandouille is another of the single-celled variety, but differs considerably from those already described in that its vault is carried on twelve ribs which radiate outwards from

The cloister area at Comberoumal (Aveyron)

The chapter house facade and dorter stairway at Grand Bandouille (Deux-Sèvres)

the centre and are received on wall columns in the angles and corbels set into the faces of the walls. It is by no means excessively elaborate but considerably more so than others of the genre. Breuil Bellay, situated just to the north of Grand Bandouille in the department of Maine and Loire, has a similar arrangement with twelve matching ribs.

Rectangular Chapter Houses

The chapter house at Badeix is now divided into two rooms and used for a family dwelling but it nevertheless

The interior of the chapter house at Badeix (Dordogne)

The chapter house façade at Badeix (Dordogne)

provides a good illustration of this category. It totals twelve by six metres and is divided by two thick, central columns into six, groin vaulted bays. One of the capitals of these columns has a very rudimentary leaf design and the other bears an unusual tear-drop motif. The façade once consisted of a central portal with lightly pointed arch flanked by two rounded headed bays. These have now been partially blocked to allow for the insertion of casement windows and a farmhouse door. Francou, in the department of Tarn and Garonne, is similar in style although built of brick, and instead of central columns has square brick pillars with elegant engaged columns set in the angles. Puy Chevrier, in the department of Indre, is a further twin columned type. This, however, appears far lighter and more delicate than the previous examples. Here the vaulting springs directly from corbels set into the angles and wall-faces onto central fluted columns. Regrettably, the original grandmontine windows in the exterior wall have been squared in an attempt to modernise them. The façade is in excellent condition. Although it was filled in like the one at Badeix when the buildings were secularised, it has recently been unblocked and restored. While it is considerably more elegant and elaborate it nevertheless bears some resemblance to the facade at Bois d'Allonne. The twin windows on either side of the central portal area set in enclosed arches which rest on short columns with foliated capitals. Four bayed, single columned versions of this type

The chapter house facade at Bois d'Allonne (Deux-Sèvres)

of rib vaulted chapter house have also survived at Chassay, Embreuil, Montguyon, Montcient Fontaine, and Epoisses.

The latter two, however, have three bayed facades instead of just two.

East Range Undercroft

The remainder of the east range consists of a single long room. This is occasionally prolonged by the addition of a second chamber so as to project beyond the refectory range southwards in cases where the church is sited to the north of the cloister, as at Comberoumal, and northwards, whereas the reverse is the case as at Marigny. Normally in medieval monasteries this section of the range housed a monks' day room with a calefactory or warming room alongside. The Grandmontines, however, made no provision for warming rooms in their domestic quarters. The only chimneys and fireplaces which have been discovered are located in kitchens and west ranges, which were almost certainly intended for the reception of guests. The south and west ranges at Comberoumal, Villiers, Charbonnières, la Bellière, and Grosbois, to name but a few, all have fireplaces which are quite obviously later installations. In all probability they date from the time when these areas were refurbished as lodgings for the commendatory priors. Although several authorities have labelled this section of the east range *salle des moines*, it is debatable to what extent it was actually utilised as a community living room. In the first instance, it is always provided with fewer windows than are found elsewhere in the buildings, normally only three. And even these are considerably narrower than those provided in the refectory and dorter. The end wall, which forms the juncture between the east and refectory range, is always provided with a large doorway which leads either directly into the garden or into the range extension from which a further doorway opens to the exterior. It is generally supposed that this east range extension was intended as a storeroom for tools and agricultural implements and/or wood store.

Very little remains of the rere dorters which were sited at the extremities of east ranges. At les Bronzeaux and

Marigny, corbels which remain in the upper section of the end walls were certainly intended for the main beam of a timbered structure which would have housed this particular apartment. At le Sauvage, there is a large stone conduit running under the south and east ranges. The ground has caved in on the site of the rere dorter which has made the conduit accessible but highly dangerous. The excavations at le Pinel have revealed a similar drainage system which confirms that grandmontine plumbing was in line with the usual monastic arrangements. The great stone drain at Louye near Dourdan can be entered by a flight of stone stairs. It has an interesting post-monastic history in that it was used by the Resistance as an escape route for british airmen shot down in the area during World War II. At Petit Bandouille, the monastic water supply and drainage system have been utilised for irrigation.

At both Comberoumal and St Michel de Lodève the terraces built over the east range extensions are on the site of the rere dorter. The doorway to the latrines at the south end of the dorter at Comberoumal now gives onto a delightful sun terrace with magnificent views over the surrounding countryside. Alongside the doorway is a 'window' with a rounded head which almost certainly was originally fashioned as a lamp niche. This feature is generally found between the dorter and rere dorter of cistercian monasteries and was intended to hold a lamp to light the way at night. Doorways with corresponding niches are also found in the same position at Montcient Fontaine, Fontblanche, Marigny, and Chassay.

Dorter

This vast chamber conforms with the usual monastic custom in that it occupies the whole of the upper section of the east range. The only specific grandmontine variations are the inclusion of the small stone vaulted chamber at the end alongside the church and the cubicle system. Opinion varies considerably as to when the Grandmontines began dividing their dorters into individual cells or cubicles. Father A. Aussibal has noted that the number and emplacement of the windows in the dorter seems to indicate that the whole chamber was intended to be divided at the actual time of building.[27] Dr Grezillier had previously calculated the measurements of these cells as 3.30 x 2.65 metres, measurements which he derived mainly from his study of the cells of Badeix and Comberoumal.[28] The windows themselves are always constructed along the same principles as those lighting the church. Although the apertures themselves are quite narrow, they are broadly and deeply embrasured on the interior so that the maximum amount of light was directed into the chamber. Numbering in total thirteen or more, this amount of fenestration would have been unnecessarily generous to light just the one room. The fact that each individual cubicle would have been extremely well lit by a window both larger and distinctly more impressive than those found in the undercroft suggests that when he was not taking part in the offices in church, the Grandmontine hermit spent some time reading or meditating privately in his cell in the dorter.

The dorter at Comberoumal (Aveyron)

Refectories

This area of the monastery conforms with the usual monastic layout and is housed in the range parallel with the church. It never follows the cistercian custom which would have set it at right angles to the range. In most cases it occupies the southern wing of the monastic complex but in quite a few cases: Badeix, Chassay, Chateauneuf, Montaussan, Marigny, and le Sauvage, it is located in the alternative position north of the church.

When the Order of Grandmont was disbanded and the monasteries were sold for secular purposes, it was nearly always the south range housing the refectory which was utilised by the new owners for living quarters. Quite simply, a south facing aspect is always considered preferable for living purposes. Unfortunately, this has resulted in there being very few unmutilated examples available for study. Villiers, Marigny, Montcient Fontaine, Chassay, Comberoumal, and St Michel de Lodève provide the best surviving examples although the last two have been very greatly altered. Elements of the former refectory can also be identified at Fontblanche, Bonneraye, la Lance, Grosbois, as well as the ruins at Charbonnières. The major part of a refectory can also be discerned behind the modern cladding which conceals it at Louye. Most of the refectories were barrel vaulted and well-preserved examples can be viewed at la Lance and Montcient Fontaine. Chassay provides a rare exception in having been rib vaulted with two central columns. Nevertheless, the traditional grandmontine windows are in such striking contrast to the ribbed interior that they raise the question of whether this is indeed the original styling or a rebuilding possibly the result of a fire. The vaulting was dismantled as recently as 1949 when subsidence rendered it unsafe for the animals tethered beneath it. No doubt because Chassay has a north sited cloister and conventuals, the farming family who occupied the site for two centuries chose to make their home in the east range rather than the cold north facing building which they used as a cow shed. Happily, this rare example of a rib vaulted refectory is presently undergoing restoration.

The refectory at Chassay (Vendée)

The most outstanding feature of Grandmontine refectory ranges are the windows which are invariably scaled down versions of those found in the churches. At la Lance, they add tremendous character to what is now a family dining room. At Montcient Fontaine, the entire range of windows has survived and has been carefully cleaned and restored. It lends a rather strange grandmontine character to a very ungrandmontine function, for the refectory at Montcient is now the luxuriously furnished lounge of a prestigious golf club.

Kitchens

This apartment is invariably situated at the far end of the refectory, adjoining the west range. In the ruins of la Bellière in Normandy, it is still possible to make out the fireplace and chimney. Puy Chevrier, in company with Chassay, has had its kitchen used for stabling purposes for many years. The fine double serving hatchway is still clearly in evidence at Chassay while that at Puy Chevrier, temporarily lost to view beneath years of farmyard soil, has just recently been rediscovered. A further, lovely, example, with central rounded archway and flanking niches, forms a garden feature at a country house which was formerly the grandmontine cell of le Châtenet. Said to have been first founded in the lifetime of St Stephen of Muret, it was refounded by Abbot François de Neufville in 1576 to

The refectory at Montcient Fontaine (Yvelines) now a club house lounge

house grandmontine nuns. The present house, built on the foundations of what was originally the south range, incorporates this striking feature in the west wall. A further and very fine example of a servery is still in its original position at Comberoumal.

WEST RANGE

In general terms, the west range of a grandmontine monastery has always suffered the most, where it has survived at all, that is. Both Dr Grezillier[29] and Father Aussibal[30] are of the opinion that in some cases a western building may never have existed in the first place. However, in just about all of the sixty-two former grandmontine sites which have been considered for the present study, there is evidence in the form of mounds of rubble, or solid foundations beneath rickety outhouses, of a former building. Furthermore Frère Philippe-Etienne draws attention to the fact that according to the Grandmontine Custumal, the west range was actually the first of the buildings to be constructed when a new foundation was in progress. The reason for this was that it afforded the brethren shelter while they worked on the more elaborate construction which would become their permanent living quarters in the east range.

Father Aussibal's thesis which proposes that a west range was not present in every grandmontine cell is entirely dependent upon a seventeenth-century plan of Bois Rahier at Tours which, true to say, does not feature a west range. This is not to say that one never existed in the first place and, in fact, Frère Philippe-Etienne has proposed a very satisfactory explanation to account for its disappearance. The cell of Bois Rahier occupied a commanding position just beyond the southern sector of the city of Tours. In 1356, during the Hundred Years' War, the city militia purposely demolished the west building, overlooking the city, for fear that the English might capture and use it as a convenient position from which to launch a new attack on the city itself.[31] One might well ask why, when hostilities were ended, the building was not rebuilt. Most probably the explanation lies in the fact that by that time the priory was ruled by a commendatory prior who was not prepared to incur the expense that this would involve. Moreover, the greatly reduced community inhabiting the priory at this date almost certainly did not warrant an expensive rebuilding. That there was, without any doubt, a building in this position at some former time is clear from the same seventeenth-century plan. This shows a small section of the building adjoining the south range to the west. It also reveals that it was used to accommodate a stairway rising to the upper section of the south range which was adapted for the prior's lodgings.

In cistercian monasteries, it was always the west range which was allocated to the numerous lay brethren attached to the Order. The Grandmontines, of course, recognised no distinction between the two classes of monks and so the *convers* shared the same living accommodation as the *clercs* in the east range. Originally therefore, the grandmontine west range can only have been intended to house guests, a use suggested by the fact that wherever these buildings have survived, they are well segregated from the remainder of the monastery, presumably in an effort to safeguard the monks' privacy.

Of those houses which have retained some vestige of their west ranges, only six can be said to be in anything approaching good condition. Without exception they have been drastically rearranged, although the essential ground plan can still be distinguished. Basically, they consisted of a single large room with a passage at either end, each with doors opening to the exterior of the monastery and cloister respectively. The room itself had no communication with, and normally no windows looking onto, the cloister. A single upper chamber was reached by means of an internal flight of stairs located in one or other of the passages flanking the downstairs room. This was lit by only two windows, both set in the outer wall so that the cloister was not overlooked. This was the area of the monastery which was usually adapted in later times to house the commendatory priors. In an extant seventeenth-century plan of the priory of Boulogne, the modified west range has all the appearance of a fashionable country mansion. The pleasant formal gardens laid out to the rear confirm this impression.

CONCLUSION

The basic ground plan favoured by the grandmontine architects involving a church and three buildings grouped around a central courtyard, was not in itself unusual. The present study has attempted to identify those characteristics which are exclusively grandmontine and have no parallel in other religious orders.

In the first place, the churches are quite obviously unlike those which were designed and built by other religious of the period when the Grandmontines were building. Dr Grezillier has shown that although a few single aisled churches which also lack side windows were built in France in the early medieval period, few survived, and those which did were later subjected to extensive modification. Additionally, none of them can be dated prior to 1150 and, moreover, they all have square east ends and west entries. The Grandmontines alone retained the blind lateral walls throughout their history and with a few, rather dubious, exceptions, preferred to retain their main portal in its humble and lowly position in a side wall. Then there is that extraordinary and ubiquitous feature, the enlarged apse. This combines with the fanned out lintels of the apsidal windows to give grandmontine sanctuaries a distinctive character and unique quality. Neither is there any equivalent in other monastic churches of the porticus which enclosed the lay entries of grandmontine churches and which served the brethren as parlours.

In the layout of the conventual buildings, the unusual siting of the slype which separates the church from the remainder of the east range is remarkable. Monastic builders generally located such passages further along the range, well away from the church. But whereas the Grandmontines utilised the slype for the single purpose of gaining access to the cemetery, other communities of monks used it as a main thoroughfare to buildings set apart from the cloister area, such as the infirmary. Thus, they sited it as far away from the church as possible presumably to cut

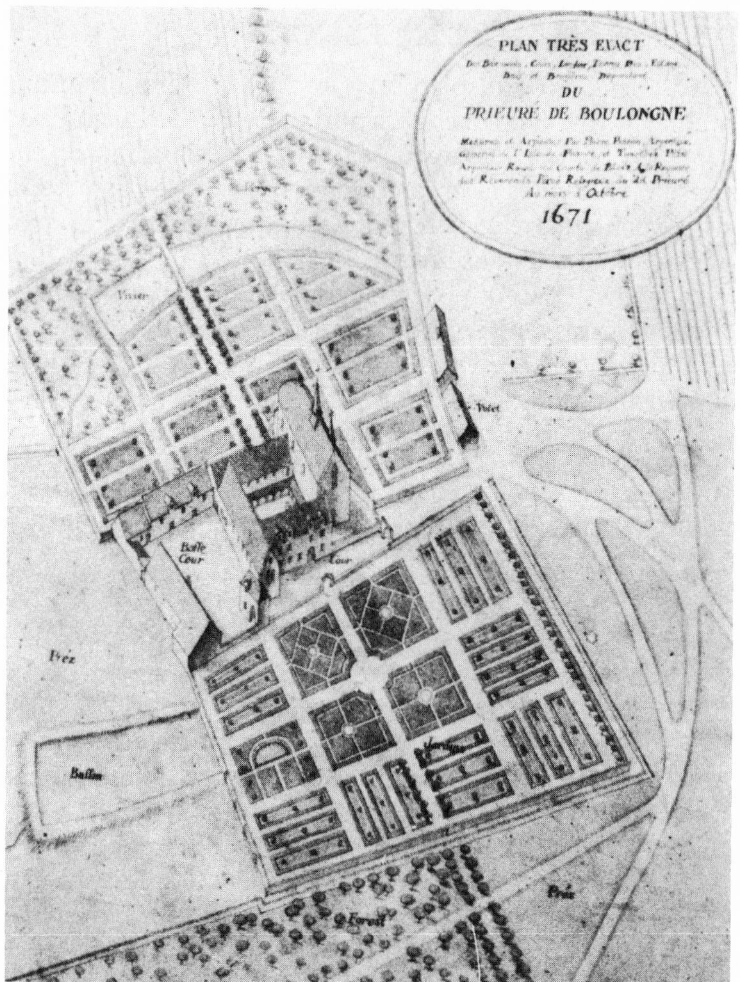

Plan of the priory of Boulogne (Loir-et-Cher) dated 1671 still in the possession of the owners, M and Mme Bège.

down on noise. A further distinctive feature is the positioning of the dorter stairway in the east cloister alley instead of the range building itself.

The grandmontine style of loop windows with monolithic lintels, fan shaped on the interior and tapering towards the apertures like miniature tympanums, are very distinctive. In fact, where a complete unbroken range of windows has survived as at Comberoumal, see p. 298, the grace and symmetry of the design is very impressive.

The accommodation of the lay brethren in the east range with the choir monks, instead of providing them with segregated quarters in the cistercian manner in the west range, is another outstanding grandmontine departure. Additionally, we have the simple arrangement of a single choir in church to accommodate both choir and lay brethren.

Finally, the Cluniacs and Cistercians habitually sited their various work rooms, guest lodgings, infirmaries, and farm buildings outside the cloister enclosure. By contrast the Grandmontines, initially at any rate, included all such offices including guest quarters within the tight little quadrangle which constituted their basic cell. In later times there is undeniable evidence that barns and outhouses were added outside the enclosure. Nevertheless, in the early years of the Order, agricultural implements would have been stored in the dimly lit undercroft which occupied the extremity of the east range furthest from the church. Bakehouses were sited at the juncture of the south and west ranges, judging by its presence in this position at both Comberoumal and Notre Dame de Louye. At Pinel the only site which to date has been subjected to thorough archaeological excavation, large silos for the storage of cereals have been uncovered under both the eastern sector of the south and the southern section of the east ranges.

Despite the introduction of more regular monastic customs to a limited degree before, but certainly after, the reconstitution of the Order in 1317, the spirit of the early hermits of Grandmont still lingers within these ancient walls. It has permeated the massive blocks of stone which remain as physical testimony to their ideals. It can be experienced even in the unlikely setting of the luxuriously furnished lounge bar of the country club now established in the former monastery of Montcient Fontaine. The Order of Grandmont is no more, but as the author Desmond Seward has observed: 'An inspiration which endured for seven hundred years cannot have been worthless. Indeed, at its best it was one of the heroic vocations of the Church'.[32] The architecture of these hermit monks symbolises and mirrors that particular and heroic blend of contemplation, austerity, poverty, and simplicity which has ensured the Order of Grandmont a distinctive place in the history of western monasticism.

NOTES

1. RG ch. XXX; Bec, SOG pp.83–84.

2. *Ibid*; p. 83.

3. Archives of All Souls' College, Oxford, Alberbury Collection No. 226, plate form made in 1579.

4. RG ch. XXXVI; p. 85.

5. A. Grezillier, 'Vestiges Grandmontains', *BSAHL* 86 (1963) 424.

6. See part 1 above, pp. 24–25 and 55.

7. Article 58; Bec, 'L'Institution, premier coutoumier de l'Ordre de Grandmont', *RevM* (1956) 25.

8. J-R. Gaborit, *L'architecture de L'Ordre de Grandmont*, 2 vols. Ecole des Chartes, unpublished thesis (1963).

9. A. Grezillier (above note 5) p. 422.

10. Pardoux de la Garde, description of Grandmont 2 in ms 1 Séminaire de Limoges Collection 81, Archives de la Haute Vienne ff 122–24. Cited Gui, *BSAHL* 25 (1877) 373–80.

11. J-R. Gaborit, (above note 8) vol. 1, ch. 4.

12. M. L'Abbé Bourderioux considers the doorway in the west facade at Villiers to be original: 'Vestiges Grandmontains Tournageaux', *Bulletin de la Société' Archéologique de Touraine* 32 (1959) 203. Dr Grezillier was of the same opinion; see 'L'Architecture Grandmontaine' *Bulletin Monumental* 121 (1963) 338.

13. Plan du Prieuré de Villiers, 1693. Archives d'Indre et Loire.

14. J-R. Gaborit, (above note 8) vol. 1, ch. 4.

15. Pardoux de la Garde, 'Description du lieu de Grandmont, cited Gui, *BSAHL* 25 (1877) p. 377. See J-R. Gaborit (above note 8) vol. 1, ch. 4.

16. 'De eruditione praedicatorum . . . ad Grandimontenses', Works of Humbert de Romans, Edition par Marguerin de la Bigne, *Bibliotheca*

maximum patrum 25 (1677) col. 467. Dom Jacques Dubois has discussed this work in his article 'Les ordres monastiques en France après les sermons de H. de Romans maître général des frères prêcheurs (mort en 1277)' in the Belgian review *Sacris erudiri* 26 (1983) 198–220.

17. J-R. Gaborit, 'Notre Dame du Parc, Église du Prieuré de Grandmont à Rouen', *Revue de la Société Savante de la Haute Normandie, lettres et sciences humaines* 53 (1969) 15–25.

18. RG ch. XX; Bec SOG, p. 80.

19. C.J. Lilwall, 'Craswall Priory Excavations', *Transactions of the Woolhope Naturalists' Field Club* (1908–1911) 39.

20. A.W. Clapham, 'Architecture of the Order of Grandmont', *Archaeologia* 75 (1926) 198.

21. C.F. Wright, 'Report on the Field Study in Mediaeval Architecture held in July, 1962 on the site of Craswall Priory, Herefordshire', *Transactions of the Woolhope Naturalists' Field Club* 38 (1964–66) 76–81.

22. A. Grezillier (above note 12) p. 343. For Clapham's plan see *Archaeologia* 75 (1926) p. 197.

23. L'Abbé Bourderioux, (above note 12) p. 204.

24. *Ibid.*, p. 207.

25. J-B. Rochias, *La Vie du Révérend Père Charles Frémon Réformateur de Grandmont*, pb. canon A. Leclerc, (Limoges: Ducourtieux et Goût, 1910) p. 50. This mentions 'un petit lieu vouté proche de l'église qui servait autrefois à conserver les chartes de la maison'.

26. A. Grezillier (above note 12) p. 348.

27. A. Aussibal, *L'Art Grandmontain*, (La Pierre-qui-Vire: Editions Zodiaque, 1984).

28. A. Grezillier, p. 348.

29. *Ibid.* p. 349.

30. Aussibal (above note 27) pp. 16 and 48, note 37.

31. Père J. Fouquet OMI and Frère Philippe-Étienne, *Histoire de L'Ordre de Grandmont* (Chambray: 1985) p. 126.

32. 'The Grandmontines—A Forgotten Order', *Downside Review* 83 (1965) 249.

ALPHABETICAL LIST OF GRANDMONTINE SITES

Many grandmontine site names have changed over the years and several have a variety of different spellings. To facilitate their location, the current versions have been employed as far as possible.

The number on the right refers to the French département in which the site is located. For additional information, consult the gazeteer which follows. This is arranged according to the French departmental numbering system. The letter which follows the departmental number corresponds to the location of the site on the map. For example, Aubepierres is located in Département 87 (Haute-Vienne) at the site marked A on the map.

1.	AUBEPIERRES	87	A
2.	AUBEVOIE	27	A
3.	AULNOY	77	A
4.	AURA VENTOSA	12	C
5.	AUTHON	28	A
6.	BABOEUF	33	A
7.	BADEIX	24	A
8.	BALEZIS	87	B
9.	BANDOUILLE	79	A
10.	BARBETORTE	85	A
11.	BEAUFEU	41	A
12.	BEAUJEU	69	A
13.	BEAUMONT	27	B
14.	BEAUSAULT	16	A
15.	BELLESELVE	24	B
16.	La BELLIERE	61	A
17.	BERCEY	72	A
18.	BOIS d'ALLONNE	79	B
19.	BOIS MENOU	82	A
20.	BOIS POUVREAU	79	C
21.	BOIS RAHIER	37	A
22.	BOIS SAINT MARTIN	28	B
23.	BOISSET	24	C
24.	BOISVERT	87	C
25.	BONNEMAISON	60	A
26.	BONNERAY	85	B
27.	BONNEVAL de SERRE	87	D
28.	Le BOUCHET	86	A

29.	BOULOGNÉ	41	B
30.	BREDIER	24	D
31.	Le BREUIL d'AUTUN	21	A
32.	BREUIL BELLAY	49	A
33.	Les BRONZEAU	87	E
34.	BUSSY	42	A
35.	CAHORS	46	A
36.	La CARTE	79	D
37.	CHAMPCOUTAUD	87	R
38.	CHARBONNIERES	89	B
39.	CHARNES	18	A
40.	CHARNIAC	19	A
41.	CHASSAY	85	C
42.	Les CHATAIGNIERS	36	A
43.	CHATEAUNEUF	18	B
44.	CHATEAUVILLAIN	52	A
45.	Le CHATENET	87	F
46.	CHAVANON	63	A
47.	CHENE GALON	61	B
48.	CLAIREFONTAINE	60	B
49.	CLAIREFEUILLE	37	B
50.	CLERY	45	A
51.	Le CLUZEAU	87	G
52.	COLOMBE	58	A
53.	COMBEROUMAL	12	A
54.	La COUDRE	45	B
55.	CRAON	53	A
56.	DEFFES (DEFFECH)	47	A
57.	DESGAGNAZEIX	46	B
58.	DIVE (PETIT BANDOUILLE)	79	E
59.	DIXMONT (L'ENFOURCHURE)	89	A
60.	LA DROUILLE BLANCHE	87	I
61.	La DROUILLE NOIRE	87	J
62.	L'ECLUSE	87	K
63.	EMBREUIL	17	A
64.	ENTREFINS	86	B
65.	ENTRUAN	79	F
66.	EPAIGNE	87	L
67.	EPOISSES	21	B
68.	L'ESPAU	36	B
69.	ETRICOR	16	B
70.	FAYS	39	A
71.	La FAYE de JUMILHAC	24	E
72.	La FAYE de NEVERS	58	B
73.	FAYET	63	B
74.	FONT ADAM	79	G
75.	FONT CREUSE	16	C
76.	FONTBLANCHE	18	C
77.	FONTENET	58	C
78.	FONTGUEDON	18	D
79.	FONTMORE	86	C
80.	FRANCOU	82	B
81.	GANDORY	16	D
82.	La GARDE en ARVERT	17	C
83.	GARRIGUES	47	B
84.	GRANDMONT	87	M
85.	GROSBOIS	03	A
86.	La GUERCE (La Barberandière)	71	A
87.	HAUTERIVES	37	C
88.	La HAYE d'ANGERS	49	B
89.	La HUBAUDIERE	41	C
90.	ISLE AUMONT	10	A
91.	ISSENGHI	71	B
92.	JAILLAT	23	A
93.	JARRY	17	B
94.	La LANCE	17	D
95.	La LANDE	33	B
96.	LIGNY le CHATEL	89	C
97.	LOC DIEU	82	C
98.	Le LOHAN	51	A
99.	LOUBERT	16	E
100.	LOUYE	91	A
101.	MACHERET	51	B
102.	MALGORCE	19	B
103.	MARIGNY	41	D
104.	MATHONS	52	B
105.	MERINIAC	47	C
106.	La MERLERIE	85	D
107.	Le MEYNEL	95	A
108.	MONNAIS	49	C
109.	MONTAUBERON	34	A
110.	MONTAUSSAN	37	D
111.	MONTCIENT FONTAINE	78	A
112.	MONTGUYON	53	B
113.	MONTESARGUES	30	A
114.	MONTMORILLON	86	D
115.	MONTUSCLAT	19	C
116.	Les MOULINEAUX	78	B
117.	MOULINS	36	C
118.	MURET	87	N

No.	Name	Dept.	Map
119.	OURSE (Ursia)	17	E
120.	PARIS (Collège Mignon)	75	A
121.	PETILLOUX	18	E
122.	Le PEYROUX	46	C
123.	PINEL	31	A
124.	La PLAIGNE (Plaine)	24	F
125.	POMMIER AIGRE	37	E
126.	POURRIERES	19	D
127.	La PRIMAUDIERE	44	A
128.	PRUNHOLS	43	A
129.	PUY CHEVRIER	36	D
130.	PUY GIBERT	19	E
131.	RAROY	77	B
132.	RAUZET	16	G
133.	RAVEAU	16	F
134.	La RIBEYROLLE	47	D
135.	ROCHESERVIERE	85	E
136.	ROUEN (Notre Dame du Parc)	76	A
137.	ROUSSET	87	O
138.	SAINT MICHEL de LODEVE	34	B
139.	SAINTE ROSE	32	A
140.	SAUMUR	87	P
141.	Le SAUVAGE	12	B
142.	SAUZAI	36	E
143.	SAVIGNY	02	A
144.	SERMAIZE	17	F
145.	THIERS	63	C
146.	TRAINS	77	C
147.	TREZEN	87	Q
148.	La TROUSSAYE	86	E
149.	La VAYOLLE	86	F
150.	Les VAYSSIERES	24	G
151.	Le VERDELAIS	33	C
152.	VIAYE	43	B
153.	VIEUPOU	89	D
154.	VILLIERS	37	F
155.	VINCENNES Bois de	94	A

ENGLAND

No.	Name	Map
156.	ALBERBURY Shropshire	B
157.	CRASWALL Herefordshire	A
158.	GROSMONT Yorkshire	C

SPAIN

No.	Name	Map
159.	ESTELLA	A
160.	SAN MARTIAL de TUDELA	B

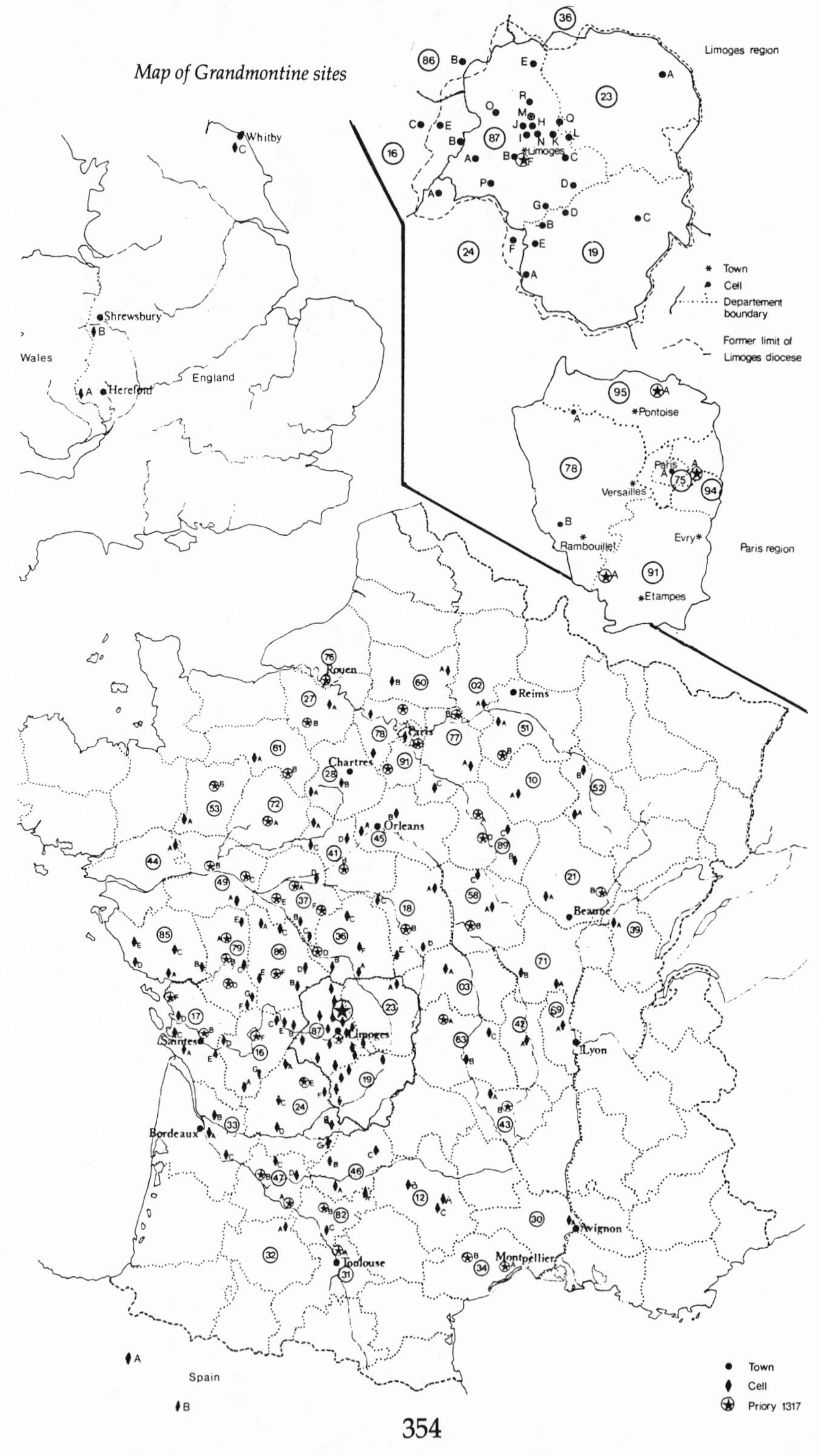
Map of Grandmontine sites
Limoges region
Town
Cell
Departement boundary
Former limit of Limoges diocese
Limoges
Pontoise
Paris
Versailles
Rambouillet
Evry
Etampes
Paris region
Whitby
Shrewsbury
Hereford
Wales
England
Rouen
Reims
Paris
Chartres
Orleans
Beaune
Limoges
Lyon
Saintes
Bordeaux
Toulouse
Montpellier
Avignon
Spain
Town
Cell
Priory 1317

GAZETEER

A list of one hundred fifty grandmontine sites was compiled by Dom Jean Becquet, OSB in 1982. Monsieur J-G Gabiron has since revised this and arranged the sites by order of département to help prospective visitors establish their precise location. This has been found to be very convenient and so it has been retained in the English version of the gazeteer which follows.

Additional historic information and documentary sources available for the study of each grandmontine site can be found in: J-R Gaborit, 'Architecture de l'Ordre de Grandmont,' Ecole des chartes, position de thèses, 1963, (unpublished thesis) Archives de la Haute Vienne.

The name and number of the département is listed on the left. Within each département, the sites are in alphabetical order. The first name in each address is that of the nearest commune followed by the full post code and canton in which the site is located.

Where a site is italicised this indicates that it was upgraded from a cell to a priory when the Order of Grandmont was reconstituted by Pope John XXII in 1317.

* An asterisk beside the name of a cell indicates that it is in an exceptionally fine state of preservation.

* An asterisk in the box devoted to 'present use' means that the site can be visited at any time. For the others it is necessary to obtain the permission of the owners in advance.

DEPARTEMENT		SITE		ADDRESS PROPRIETOR (where known)	REMAINS & CONDITION	PRESENT USE
01	AISNE	SAVIGNY	A	Seringes-et-Nesles 02130 Fère-en-Tardenois	Extremity of E. range with section of dorter over.	Farm
03	ALLIER	GROSBOIS	A	Gipçy 03210 Souvigny	Ruins of E. range. Refectory and kitchen housed in the S. range which is in a fine state of preservation.	*Farm Scheduled monument
10	AUBE	ISLE-AUMONT	A	Cormost 10800 St-Julien-les-Villas	Soil markings only can be identified	Situated on farm land.
12	AVEYRON	AURA VENTOSA Hermitage only	C	Castelnau-Pégayroles 12620 St-Beauzelay	Small hermitage fashioned in a cliff face. The outer wall with original window openings is extant.	*Situated on farm land.
		*COMBEROU-MAL	A	M. Mme. P. Bastide 12620 St-Beauzelay	Church, very well restored. E. range with dorter over in excellent condition. The S. and W. ranges have been considerably altered.	*Country house.
		Le SAUVAGE	B	Balsac 12000 Rodez	Ruins of E. range and refectory. The chapter house has retained its vaulting and façade in fair condition.	*Derelict and abandoned.
16	CHARENTE	BEAUSAULT	A	16210 Chalais	No visible remains	Situated on farm land.
		*ETRICOR	B	Col. Ragot Etagnac 16150 Chabanais	Church only but in very good condition.	Situated on farm land.
		FONTCREUSE	C	M. Guenery St-Coutant 16350 Champagné-Mouton	Ruins of nave with doorway half buried. Nothing else visible.	Situated on farm land.

DEPARTEMENT		SITE		ADDRESS PROPRIETOR (where known)	REMAINS & CONDITION	PRESENT USE
		GANDORY	D	Cherves 16370 Richemont (Cognac)	No visible remains.	Situated on farm land.
		LOUBERT	E	16450 Roumazières Loubert	No visible remains.	Situated on farm land.
		RAVEAU	F	Mr. & Mrs. Lewis Aussac 16560 Tourriers, St-Amand-de-Boixe	W. façade of church and section of west range. A stone-vaulted kitchen survives in the ruins of the N. range. Considerable amounts of worked stone lying about the site.	Situated on farm land.
		*RAUZET	G	Contact Mr. & Mrs. Fairbourn Combiers 16320 Villebois-Lavalette	The church remains in exceptionally fine condition considering that it has been lying derelict for years. Foundations of S. range clearly discernible.	*Situated on farm land. An attempt is currently underway to save this site.
17	CHARENTE-MARITIME	EMBREUIL	A	Breuil-de-Saintes, Grezac 17120 Cozes	E. range now incoporated into farming complex. Chapter house façade still in very good condition. The centre column has an exceptionally fine carved capital.	Forms part of farming complex.
		JARRY	B	Bussac 17100 Saintes	The monastic remains have been completely absorbed by the farm which was established on the site in the 17th c. Few visible Grandmontine remains.	Farm

DEPARTEMENT		SITE		ADDRESS PROPRIETOR (where known)	REMAINS & CONDITION	PRESENT USE
		La GARDE-en-ARVERT	C	17390 La Tremblade	No visible remains.	Situated on farm land.
		La LANCE	D	M. Mme. Luneau Breuil Magné 17870 rochefort	The nave of the church remains in good condition with exceptionally well preserved doorway. The refectory has retained 5 original windows.	Church = brn. Refectory range farm house.
		OURSE (de Ursia)	E	St-Germain-de-Vibrac 17500 Jonzac	No visible remains.	Situated on farm land.
		SERMAIZE	F	Nieul-sur-Mer 17140 Lagord	Nave of church with doorway well preserved. Extensive remains of conventuals but in very derelict condition.	Forms part of small holding on the edge of town.
18	CHER	CHARNES	A	Saint-Satur 18300 Sancerre	Part of church apse with vaulted slype alongside. Other distinguishable remains overgrown with vegetation.	*Derelict
		**CHATEAUNEUF*	B	Corquoy 18190 Châteauneuf-sur-Cher	Church complete but derelict. Fresco of Virgin and Child deteriorating. Ruined sections of E. range. Substantial mounds of rubble in cloister.	*Situated on wooded farm land. Derelict.
		*FONTBLANCHE	C	M. Mme. Huet Genouilly 18310 Graçay	Church and E. range with dorter over in fine state of preservation. S. range much modified for housing.	Country house

DEPARTEMENT		SITE		ADDRESS PROPRIETOR (where known)	REMAINS & CONDITION	PRESENT USE
		FONTGUEDON	D	Col. de Bonneval Thaumiers 18210 Charenton-du-Cher	Nave of church standing to half its original height is re-roofed and in use as a granary. Limited remains of conventuals.	Tenant farm
		PETILLOUX	E	18370 Châteaumeillant	No visible remains.	Grassed over
19	CORREZE	CHARNIAC	A	Louignac 19310 Ayen	No standing remains but considerable amounts of worked stone are lying about the site and have been incorporated in various farm buildings.	Forms part of farming complex
		MALGORCE	B	Saint-Martin-Sépert 19210 Lubersac	No visible remains	Not located
		MONTUSCLAT	C	M. Combartet Soudeilles 19300 Egletons	No visible remains	Forest area
		POURRIERES	D	M. Masgimel Lamongerie 19510 Masseret	No visible remains	On the border of a forest
		PUY GIBERT	E	19600 Larche	No visible remains	Situated on a plateau overlooking the valley of the Vézère

DEPARTEMENT		SITE		ADDRESS PROPRIETOR (where known)	REMAINS & CONDITION	PRESENT USE
21	COTE-D'OR	Le BREUIL d'AUTUN	A	M. Mme Sevry Thoisy-la-Berchère 21210 Saulieu	Nave of church much mutilated, in use as barn. The monks' entry remains in a very fine state of preservation.	Part of farming complex
		EPOISSES	B	Institut National de Recherche Agronomique Bretenière 21110 Genlis	E. Range only, much modified. The chapter house is in very fine condition.	*College of Agriculture
23	CREUSE	JAILLAT	A	Bord-Saint-George 23230 Gouzon	No visible remains	Situated on farm land.
24	DORDOGNE	*BADEIX	A	St-Estèphe 24360 Piégut	Church, including apse in good condition despite its use as stabling. E. range intact, chapter house especially in fine condition.	Farming complex. The chapter house is used for living accommodation.
		BELLESELVE	B	Tursac 24620 Les-Eyzies-de-Tayac, Sireuil	Extensive ruins of both church and conventuals.	*Abandoned on farm land.
		BOISSET	C	Saint-Aquilin 24110 St-Astier	The plan of the site still clearly evident from grassed over mounds and rubble.	*Grazing
		BREDIER	D	Queyssac 24140 Villamblard Bergerac	No visible remains	Not located

	DEPARTEMENT	SITE		ADDRESS PROPRIETOR (where known)	REMAINS & CONDITION	PRESENT USE
		La FAYE-de-JUMILHAC	E	24630 Jumilhac-le-Grand	The two wings of the château of Faye have absorbed the former E. range with its chapter house and the refectory which was housed in the S range.	Private house (visitors never permitted)
		La PLAIGNE (PLAINE)	F	Savigniac-Lédrier 24270 Lanouaille	Buildings dating from the 17th c. obscure the original monastic ground plan. Considerable amounts of worked stone and debris of earlier buildings.	*Situated on farm land.
		Les VAYSIERES	G	M. Martin Vitrac 24200 Sarlat	Considerable standing ruins of church and E. range. Other remains concealed by vegetation.	Ruin stands in the garden of a private house
27	EURE	AUBEVOIE	A	Aubevoie 27600 Gaillon	Soil markings only.	Grazing
		BEAUMONT	B	Le noyer-en-Ouche 27410 Beaumesnil	No visible remains	Grassed over
28	EURE-et-LOIR	AUTHON	A	28330 Authon-du-Perche	Part of the western sector of the nave remains and is in use as a barn. The W. range has been utilized as a farm house and has retained 5 original windows.	Forms part of farming complex
		BOIS-SAINT-MARTIN	B	Boncé-et-Montainville 28150 Voves	No visible remains: the present barn possibly occupies the site of the church.	Farming complex superimposed.

	DEPARTEMENT	SITE		ADDRESS PROPRIETOR (where known)	REMAINS & CONDITION	PRESENT USE
30	GARD	MONTESARGUES	A	30126 Tavel, Roquemaure	The church was sited to the south, but no traces remain. The N. range which housed the refectory still stands though much altered.	Forms part of farming complex
31	HAUTE-GARONNE	*PINEL*	A	Villariès 31380 Montastruc-la-Conseillère	Normally no visible remains but interesting excavation in progress.	Ploughed over
32	GERS	SAINTE-ROSE	A	32340 Miradoux	No visible remains.	Ploughed over
33	GIRONDE	BABOEUF	A	Farques Saint-Hilaire 33370 Tresses	The E. range is said to have been incorporated into the château of Sainte Rafine. No other visible remains.	Country house
		La LANDE	B	St-Emilion 33330 Libourne	The precise location of this site has not been established.	—
		Le VERDELAIS	C	Aubiac 33430 Bazas, St-Macaire	The central portion of the nave remains recognisably Grandmontine despite 17th and 18th c. modifications.	Farm use
34	HERAULT	MONTAUBERON	A	Préventorium. Faculté de Medicine 34100 Montpellier	Lateral walls of the nave, E. range—slype, chapter house and traces of undercroft.	Remains incorporated into the building, used as a clinic.
		**SAINT-MICHEL-de-LODEVE*	B	M. H. Bec Soumont et St-Privat-des-Salces 34700 Lodève	Church, N. Chapel, cloister and all three range buildings exceptionally well preserved although the exterior appearance of the building was altered when the site was secularised.	*Historic monument open to the public.

DEPARTEMENT		SITE		ADDRESS PROPRIETOR (where known)	REMAINS & CONDITION	PRESENT USE
36	INDRE	Les CHATAIGNIERS	A	Orsennes 36190 Aigurande	No visible remains	Not located
		L'ESPAU	B	Bel Arbre 36370 Bélabre	Foundations of church, rubble mounds and debris.	Situated on farm land.
		MOULINS	C	Beaudres-et-Moulins-sur-Céphons 36110 Levroux	Only a small chapel survives which may represent the former E. range slype.	Situated on farm land.
		**PUY CHEVRIER*	D	M. Mme. de Beauvais Mérigny 36220 Tournon-St-Martin	Church and E. range in a very fine state of preservation. Chapter house façade recently restored. The S. range has been much modified. Part only of the W. range.	Country house
		SAUZAI	E	Le Poinçonnet 36330 Ardentes	Rubble mounds and debris indicate the former ground plan.	Situated on farm land.
37	INDRE-et-LOIRE	*BOIS RAHIER*	A	Saint-Avertin 37170 Chambray-lès-Tours	This site has vanished beneath a suburb of Tours.	—
		CLAIREFEUILLE	B	37350 Le Grand Pressigny	Negligible monastic remains incorporated in 17th c. farm house. The cell, destroyed by the Huguénots was never rebuilt.	Farm
		HAUTERIVES	C	Yzeures-sur-Creuse 37290 Preuilly-sur-Claise	The nave and well preserved doorway and E. range have survived in reasonable condition and serve as barn and granary respectively.	Forms part of farming complex

DEPARTEMENT		SITE		ADDRESS PROPRIETOR (where known)	REMAINS & CONDITION	PRESENT USE
		MONTAUSSAN	D	Souvigny-de-Touraine 37400 Amboise	Extensive standing ruins of church and E. range. Site much overgrown.	*Abandoned on forest land
		Le *POMMIER-AIGRE*	E	Cravant-les-Coteaux 37500 Chinon	W. range only bearing 15th and 17th c. modifications.	Farm
		VILLIERS	F	Frère Philippe-Etienne Villeloin-Coulangé 37460 Montrésor	Nave (restored) and E. range. S. range modified in the 17th and 18th c.	Hermitage
39	JURA	FAY	A	Les Deux Fays 39230 Sellières	Traces of former monastic occupation have been identified in the house presently occupying the site.	Church Presbytery
41	LOIR-et-CHER	BEAUFEU	A	St-Marc-du-Cor 41170 Mondoubleau	Ground floor of W. range with well preserved slype.	Farm
		BOULOGNE	B	M. Mme. Bège Tour-en-Sologne 41250 Bracieux	Enclosure ditches and foundations visible as crop marks.	Farm
		La HUBAUDIERE	C	Sasnières 41310 St-Amand-de-Longpré	Foundations of church and associated debris. Traces of conventuals.	Situated on farm land
		*MARIGNY	D	M. Mme. Mettaie Lorges 41370 Marchenoir	E. range particularly dorter windows in fair condition. Also N. range which housed the refectory and kitchen. Fine servery. Water storage cisterns discovered under the cloister.	*Farm outbuilding. A modern house has been built on the site of the church

	DEPARTEMENT	SITE		ADDRESS PROPRIETOR (where known)	REMAINS & CONDITION	PRESENT USE
42	LOIRE	*BUSSY*	A	Bussy-Albieux 42260 St-Germain-Laval	No visible remains	Not located
43	HAUTE-LOIRE	PRUNHOLS	A	Cistrières 43160 La Chaise-Dieu	No visible remains	Not located
		**VIAYE*	B	M. Drouin Saint-Vincent 43800 Vorey, St-Paulien	E. and N. ranges have survived in reasonable condition although their upper storeys have been greatly altered.	Farm
44	LOIRE-ATLANTIQUE	*La PRIMAUDIERE	A	M. Hervé Juigné-des-Moutiers 44670 St-Julien-de-Vouvantes	The church is in a good state of preservation, recently re-roofed. The W. range was modified in the 16th, and again in the 17th c.	Country house
45	LOIRET	CLERY	A	45370 Cléry-St-André	No visible remains.	Situated on farm land
		La COUDRE	B	Chambon-la-Forét 45340 Beaune-la-Rolande	The church nave has been transformed into a habitation and an oven installed in the main doorway.	Farm house and outbuildings.
46	LOT	CAHORS	A	46000 Cahors	No visible remains.	Suburb of the city
		*DESGAGNAZEIX	B	Peyrilles 46310 St-Germain-du-Bel-Air	The church has retained its Grandmontine character despite the fact that it was adapted for parish use in the 16th c. The vaulting was reinforced when the bell tower was built in 1880.	*Church = parochial. E. range = presbytery

DEPARTEMENT	SITE	ADDRESS PROPRIETOR (where known)	REMAINS & CONDITION	PRESENT USE
	Le PEYROUX C	Issepts 46320 Astier	Extensive ruins partially concealed by vegetation.	*Abandoned on wooded hill-side.
47 LOT-et-GARONNE	*DEFFES* (DEFFECH) A	Bon-Encontre 47240 Agen	A farmhouse has been built into the nave of the church. There are no other identifiable remains except 300 metres to the south where there is an entry into a large cloacum.	Farm - known today as Sainte-Rose
	La *GARRIGUES* B	Saint-Pardoux-du-Breuil 47200 Marmande	W. range, now a small church. Some evidence of former monastic occupation in and around the modern house which stands on the site of the S. range.	*Parish church
	MERINIAC C	Miramont-de-Guyenne 47800 Lauzun	Debris	Situated on farm land
	La RIBEYROLLE D	Bias 47300 Villeneuve-sur-Lot	No visible remains.	Not located
49 MAINE-et-LOIRE	*BREUIL BELLAY A	Mme. Potez Cizay-la-Madeleine 49700 Doué-la-Fontaine	Church and original stone porticus intact but deteriorating. E. range in good state of preservation with chapter house intact. Exteriors of E. and S. ranges much modified.	Country house.
	**La HAYE-d' ANGERS* B	Brotherhood of St. Jean Avrillé 49240 Angers	Church and N. chapel well preserved and recently restored. The S. and W. ranges were rebuilt in the 17th c. Foundations of stone porticus recently excavated.	*Religious house. Church only may be visited.

	DEPARTEMENT	SITE		ADDRESS PROPRIETOR (where known)	REMAINS & CONDITION	PRESENT USE
		MONNAIS	C	Jumelles 49160 Longué-Jumelles	N. wall of church bearing some of the corbels which would have borne the main beam of the porticus roof.	Situated on the edge of a forest.
51	MARNE	Le LOHAN	A	M. Dailly Mareuil-en-Brie 51270 Montmort-Lucy	Enclosure ditches. Ruins of the refectory and part of the chapter house. Considerable debris.	Situated on farm land.
		MACHERET	B	Saint-Just-Sauvage 51260 Anglure	No visible remains	Situated on farm land
52	HAUTE-MARNE	CHATEAU-VILLAIN	A	Forêt de Chat 52120 Châteauvillain	W. range only partially preserved	Situated on farm land.
		MATHONS	B	Mathons 52300 Joinville	N. wall of sanctuary attached to E. range slype which has retained its vaulting. Ruins only of chapter house. Other foundation mounds and debris.	Forms part of farming complex.
53	MAYENNE	CRAON	A	Ballots 53350 St-Aignan-sur-Roë	E. range modified for use as farm house but chapter house in fair condition. S. range in very ruinous condition incorporated in outhouses.	Forms part of farming complex
		MONTGUYON	B	Placé 53560 Alexain, Mayenne	Apse wall (now woodshed) stands to about a third of its original height. Chapter house façade blocked but the interior is in a good state of preservation especially the central column and capital.	Forms part of farming complex

	DEPARTEMENT	SITE		ADDRESS PROPRIETOR (where known)	REMAINS & CONDITION	PRESENT USE
58	NIEVRE	COLOMBE	A	Montapas 58110 Châtillon-en-Bazois	Ruins of church and conventuals very overgrown.	*Abandoned on forest land.
		La FAYE-de-NEVERS	B	Sauvigny-les-Bois 58160 Imphy	Ruins of refectory with original window apertures. Debris.	*Abandoned in forest clearing.
		FONTENET	C	Corvol-l'Orgueilleux 58460 Varzy	Church incorporated into house. The sanctuary (retained as a chapel) is in good condition. Two later towers alongside.	Country house
60	OISE	BONNEMAISON	A	Choisy-au-Bac 60750 Compiègne	Vaulted refectory with two central columns, in use as a chapel since the 19th c.	Country house
		CLAIREFONTAINE	B	M. Mme Gromard Saint-Germain-la-Poterie 60650 Auneuil	Nave of church, the W. wall has retained its original window aperture. E. range slype in ruins. Rubble mounds indicate the remainder of the conventuals.	Disused tenant farm forming part of large country estate.
61	ORNE	La BELLIERE	A	La Bellière 61200 Mortrée, Argentan	Extensive standing ruins of both church and conventuals.	*Abandoned on farm land.
		CHENE GALON	B	Éperrais 61440 Mortagne-au-Perche	E. range incorporated in present house. S. range also but much altered.	Farm
63	PUY-de-DOME	*CHAVANON*	A	Comberonde 63460 Puy de Dôme	Church, lacking vaulting in very ruinous and dangerous condition. E. range, adapted for housing in the 18th c. and subsequently burnt out.	Forms part of farming complex.

DEPARTEMENT		SITE		ADDRESS PROPRIETOR (where known)	REMAINS & CONDITION	PRESENT USE
		FAYET	B	Yronde-et-Buron 63270 Vic-le-Comte	No identifiable remains, the site must have provided a local quarry as traces of ancient stone can be seen in the buildings of the farm.	Situated on farm land.
		THIERS	C	63300 Thiers	Of this, the last Grandmontine house to be built, (1650) only the stone porticus remains along with some low stone walls.	Feature of suburb.
69	RHONE	BEAUJEU	A	Blacé 69830 St. Georges de Reneins	Refectory with 4 original window apertures and other remains incorporated in the château of Grammont	Château and vineyard
71	SAONE-et-LOIRE	La GUEURCE (La BARBERANDIERE)	A	Colombier-en-Brionnais 71800 La Clayette	Foundations discernible.	Situated on farm land
		ISSENGHI	B	Saint-Agnan 71160 Digoin	Nave (in use as a barn) and E. range slype. Also parts of refectory.	Forms part of a farming complex.
72	SARTHE	*BERCEY*	A	Outillé 72640 Écommoy	Sections of E. range, wall of chapter house and the slype, which is intact and has been transformed into a chapel.	Private house
75	PARIS	COLLEGE MIGNON	A	Rue Mignon Paris 16	No remains	Built over

	DEPARTEMENT	SITE		ADDRESS PROPRIETOR (where known)	REMAINS & CONDITION	PRESENT USE
76	SEINE-MARITIME	*ROUEN* (N.D. du PARC)	A	Avenue de Grammont 76100 Rouen	Church in very good condition.	Parish church no longer in use.
77	SEINE-et-MARNE	AULNOY	A	Courchamp 77560 Villiers-St-George	Church has retained its vault but the apsidal roofing has been modified. Ruins of E. range include chapter house façade. The W. range, much modified, is the present farmhouse.	Forms part of farming complex. Church in use as a barn.
		RAROY	B	Crouy-sur-Ourcq 77840 Lizy-sur-Ourcq	Ruins of the church and W. range. Vaulted cellar and wells on site of S. range.	*Abandoned in woodland area.
		*TRAINS	C	Villecerf 77250 Moret-sur-Loing	Nave of church utilised for housing. E. range, especially chapter house in fine state of preservation. Remnants of W. range.	Farming estate.
78	YVELINES	*MONTCIENT FONTAINE	A	Sailly 78440 Gargenville, Limay	Nave and all three ranges in good condition though much restored and exterior façades modified. Refectory window apertures are original. Chapter house with central column and capital in very fine condition.	*Golf club
		Les MOULINEAUX	B	Poigny-la-Forêt 78120 Rambouillet	The apse of the church alone has survived.	In the grounds of château.

DEPARTEMENT	SITE	ADDRESS PROPRIETOR (where known)	REMAINS & CONDITION	PRESENT USE
79 DEUX-SEVRES	**BANDOUILLE* A	M. Boujin Chiché 79350 Bressuire	The nave survives in ruins. The E. range is in a good state of preservation especially the slype, chapter house and dorter stairway. Remnants of W. range also	*Country house
	**BOIS d'ALLONNE* B	M. Mme. Gerson Allonne 79130 Secondigny	Church and E. range in very fine condition.	Country house. E. range inhabited
	BOIS POUVREAU C	M. Paradeau Coutières 79340 Ménigoutte	No visible remains although remnants of stonework are distinguishable in a neighbouring farm.	Situated on farm land.
	La CARTE D	M. Babin Vitré 79370 Celles-sur-Belle	The monastery would seem to have been quarried to provide stone for the Château-du-Prieuré which stands on the site.	Château-des-Bonshommes
	*DIVE (PETIT BANDOUILLE) E	Saint-Martin-de-Mâcon 79100 Thouars	Ruins of nave. E. range in good condition. Also S.W. section of refectory range. Interesting entrance to cloacum also to S.W.	Tenant farm
	ENTRUAN F	Montalembert 79190 Sauzé-Vaussais	No visible remains.	Not located
	FONT ADAM G	Caunay 79190 Sauzé-Vaussais	No visible remains.	Not located

	DEPARTEMENT	SITE		ADDRESS PROPRIETOR (where known)	REMAINS & CONDITION	PRESENT USE
82	TARN-et-GARONNE	BOIS MENOU	A	Puylagarde 82160 Caylus	Fragments of worked stone and debris.	Situated on farm land.
		*FRANCOU	B	M. Galley Francou 82130 Lafrançaise	Nave of church in use as barn. The E. range is in a good state of preservation. The S. range, modified for housing has retained some original features including some window apertures.	Country house and leased farm.
		LOC-DIEU	C	Labastide-St-Pierre 82370 Grissolles	No visible remains	Situated on farm land.
85	VENDEE	BARBETORTE	A	Les Megnils-Reigniers 85400 Luçon	No visible remains, farm of recent origin occupies site	Situated at the edge of a wood.
		BONNERAY	B	Puy de Serre 85240 St-Hilaire-des-Loges.	S. range, in good state of preservation in use as farm house. Original window apertures. W. range (now a cowshed) has also retained grandmontine fenestration.	Farm
		*CHASSAY	C	Commune de Saint-Prouant Saint-Prouant 85110 Chantonnay	Church and all three range buildings in fine state of preservation having been recently restored to their former monastic condition.	*Conference centre and permanent grandmontine exhibition
		La MERLERIE	D	Château d'Olonne 85100 Les-Sables-d'Olonne	A field known locally as 'chapel field' almost certainly conceals the foundations of the church but there is nothing visible	Farm land

DEPARTEMENT		SITE		ADDRESS PROPRIETOR (where known)	REMAINS & CONDITION	PRESENT USE
		ROCHESERVIERE	E	St-Christophe-la-Chartreuse 85620 Rocheservière	The château of Grandmont has been built over the site and probably incorporates stone from the monastery.	Château
86	VIENNE	Le BOUCHET	A	Berthegon 86420 Monts-sur-Guesnes	No visible remains	Not located
		ENTREFINS	B	Mlle. Proust Adriers 86430 L'Isle-Jourdain	Site not readily identifiable	A 19th century oratory occupied part of the site.
		FONTMORE	C	Vellèches 86230 St-Gervais-les-Trois-Clochers	The S. and W. walls of the church have been incorporated into a barn. Parts of the E. and S. ranges have also survived. The W. range, used as the farm house has retained some of the original windows.	Farming complex.
		MONT-MORILLON (Grange only)	D	86500 Montmorillon	A large vaulted room.	Private town house.
		La TROUSSAYE	E	M. de Montjou Iteuil 86240 Ligugé	No visible remains	Woodland site
		La VAYOLLE	F	Marquis de Beaucorps Créquy Nieuil-l'Espoir 86340 La Villedieu-du-Clain	E. range in very poor condition. W. range somewhat better, in use as farm outhouse. A large cloacum has been uncovered on the site.	Tenant farm

DEPARTEMENT	SITE	ADDRESS PROPRIETOR (where known)	REMAINS & CONDITION	PRESENT USE
87 HAUTE VIENNE	AUBEPIERRES (Nuns) A	87600 Rochechouart	Mounds and debris overgrown.	Situated on farm land.
	BALEZIS (Grange only) B	Isle 87170 Limoges	No visible remains	Was situated on a plateau overlooking the River Vienne
	BOISVERT C	Bujaleuf 87460 Eymoutiers	Stonework incorporated in farm buildings.	Farm
	BONNEVAL-de-SERRE D	Sussac 87130 Châteauneuf-la-Forêt	Mounds and debris. Much stonework visible in the walls of neighbouring farms.	Forest land.
	Les BRONZEAU E	M. de Latour Saint-Leger-Magnazeix 87190 Magnac-Laval	S. wall of nave incorporated in barn. E. range intact, chapter house in fair condition. Dorter also intact. The S. range exists also but much modified.	Tenant farm house and outhouses.
	CHAMPCOMTAUD R	Folles 87770 Bessines-sur-Gartempe	Church intact but doubtful to what extent it can be considered Gandmontine as the site belonged to two other religious congregations in the course of its history.	Church adapted for housing.
	Le CHATENET (Nuns from 1576) F	Feytiat 87220 Limoges	The W. range has been incorporated into the present house. The monastic kitchen housed in the S. range has also survived. There is a very fine servery fashioned in what is now the exterior wall.	Country house. Visitors never permitted.

DEPARTEMENT	SITE	ADDRESS PROPRIETOR (where known)	REMAINS & CONDITION	PRESENT USE
	Le CLUZEAU G	Meuzac 87380 St-Germain-les-Belles	Soil markings only identify the site	Farm land
	Le COUDIER (grange only) H	Ambazac 87240 Ambazac	Building restored and in very fine condition.	Scheduled monument in private ownership and used for public functions.
	La DROUILLE BLANCHE (Nuns) I	Bonnac-la-Côte 87270 Couteix	No visible remains	Farm land
	La DROUILLE NOIRE (Nuns) J	Bonnac-la-Côte 87270 Couteix	Some stone work has been uncovered on this site, notably a finely carved boss.	Farm land
	L'ECLUSE K	Saint-Laurent-les-Églises 87340 La Jonchère-St-Maurice	No visible remains	Flooded by reservoir. The ruins are revealed every 20 years when this is drained.
	EPAIGNE L	Sauviat-sur-Vige 87400 St-Léonard-de-Noblat	No visible remains	Not located
	GRANDMONT MOTHER HOUSE M	Saint-Sylvestre 87240 Ambazac	Sections of perimeter walls and debris. Chapel of St John the Baptist built with stone blocks retrieved when the Abbey was demolished.	*The village has absorbed much of the site.

DEPARTEMENT		SITE		ADDRESS PROPRIETOR (where known)	REMAINS & CONDITION	PRESENT USE
		MURET	N	M. Mme de la Gueronnière Le Grand Muret 87240 Ambazac	Foundations, soil and rock markings.	*Situated in woodland area which forms part of a country estate
		ROUSSET	O	Vaulry 87140 Nantiat	Debris	Situated on farm land.
		SAUMUR	P	Les Cars 87230 Châlus	Foundations of S. range apparent. Quantities of worked stone.	Situated on farm land.
		TREZEN	Q	Les Billanges 87340 La Jonchère-St-Maurice	No visible remains	Situated on farm land
89	YONNE	DIXMONT (L'EN-FOURCHURE)	A	89500 Villeneuve-sur-Yonne	Ruins of the church. The W. range has survived but has been much modified	Country house
		*CHARBON-NIERES	B	Societé d'études d'Avallon Sauvigny-le-Bois 89200 Avallon	Church in very good condition. Ruins of E. and S. ranges well conserved.	*Scheduled historic monument.
		LIGNY-le-CHATEL	C	Varennes 89230 Pontigny	No visible remains	Not located
		VIEUPOU	D	Poilly-sur-Tholon 89110 Aillant-sur Tholon	Ruins of church and E. range. The refectory, rebuilt in the 18th c. remains in good condition.	Situated on farm land

DEPARTEMENT	SITE		ADDRESS PROPRIETOR (where known)	REMAINS & CONDITION	PRESENT USE
91 ESSONNE	**LOUYE*	A	Ursuline Sisters Les Granges-le-Roi 91410 Dourdan	Church well restored in very fine condition. E. and parts of S. and W. ranges, all in good state of preservation. The exterior façades have been remodelled.	Retreat house. May be visited by appointment in August.
94 VAL de MARNE	*VINCENNES*	A	94300 Vincennes	No visible remains	Parisian suburb.
95 VAL de OISE	*Le MEYNEL*	A	Maffliers 95560 Montsoult, Écouen	No visible remains	Situated in the forest of L'Isle-Adam
			GRANDMONTINE FOUNDATIONS IN ENGLAND		
HEREFORDSHIRE	CRASWALL		Mr. & Mrs. C. Richards Abbey Farm Craswall Herefordshire	Extensive standing remains.	*Scheduled historic monument
SHROPSHIRE	ALBERBURY		All Souls' College. Oxford. Tenant: Mr. R. Wilde White Abbey Farm, Alberbury. Nr. Shrewsbury	Chancel and N. chapel incorporated in farm house. Precinct moat and monastic fish pond discernible.	*Farm house
YORKSHIRE	GROSMONT		The Priory Grosmont, Nr. Whitby	No visible remains, site ploughed over	Farm land

APPENDIX

RENAISSANCE?

In 1979, the former grandmontine priory of Sainte-Trinité de Grandmont Villiers in the departement of Indre Loire became borne to a french priest desirous of living in accordance with the Rule of St Stephen. Père Philippe Permentier passed ten years of reflection and formation in the religious life before seeking permission from the bishop of Tours to follow in the footsteps of St Stephen and become simply Frère Philippe-Etienne, hermit.

With some assistance from an association of friends but mainly with his own hands, Frère Philippe has restored the church, rendered the south range habitable, and is currently working on the restoration of the east range which, like the church, was badly damaged when this former priory was taken over as a farm. For the past few years he has been sharing his solitude with two novices who are seeking to make profession as hermit monks of Grandmont.

Those who have not actually visited the 'hermitage' at Villiers might be forgiven for imagining that this is some kind of sensational project akin to those nineteenth-century romantics who donned robes and installed themselves as hermits in gloomy gothic ruins. The brothers at Villiers do wear religious habits and they do live in a partial ruin but their notions, far from being romantic, are distinguished by practical common sense. Their aim is to live their daily lives in accordance with the Gospel tradition. They are nevertheless wholly in harmony with the twentieth century. They dispense charity to those in need and hospitality to any who wish to visit them in their 'desert' in need of counsel or a few hours of prayer and quiet reflection. In company with their twelfth-century confrères they are determined not to be a burden on anyone and so they work for their livelihood and efficiently manage a small farm with dairy cattle. Like any responsible french citizens, they contribute to social security and pay local rates and taxes. They cheerfully admit to 'luxuries' which the twelfth-century occupants of the priory never even dreamed of; their priory is wired for electricity, and has a mechanised milking parlour and a telephone.

Of these latter day innovations Frère Philippe has observed: We have had to adapt our practice of the Rule to present day conditions but we must not lose sight of the fact that poverty consists in being content with the bare necessities and we must retain that spirit of abandonment to Divine Providence which was so dear to our founder and which is inherent in the Gospel, the first and only Rule for hermit monks of Grandmont.

THE PRIORS AND ABBOTS OF GRANDMONT

PRIORS

Saint-Etienne (Stephen) of Muret circa 1076–1124
Pierre de Limousin 1124–1137
Pierre de Saint-Christophe 1137–1139
Etienne de Liciae 1139–1163
Pierre Bernard 1163 -1170
Guillaume de Treignae 1170–1187 (resigned)
Gérard Ithier 1189–1198 (resigned)
Adémar de Friac 1198–1216
Caturcin 1216–1228 or 29 (remigned)
Elie Arnaud 1228 or 29–1238 (deposed)
Jean de l'Aigle 1239–1242 (resigned)
Adémar de la Vergne 1242–1245
Guillaume d'Ongres 1245–1248 (resigned)
Ithier Merle 1248–circa 1260 (resigned)
Gui d'Archer ?–1269 (resigned)
Foucher Grimoard 1269–1281
Pierre de Caussac 1281 or 82–1290 or 91 (resigned)
Bernard de Gandalmar 1291–
Gui Foucher 1291–1306 (resigned)
Guillaume de Prémaurel 1306–1312
Jourdain de Rapistan 1312–1316 (deposed)
Elie Adémar 1316–1317

FREELY ELECTED ABBOTS

Guillaume Pellicier 1317–1336
Pierre Aubert 1336–1347
Jean Chabrit 1347–1355
Adémar Crespi 1355–1378
Aimeric Fabri 1378–1385
Ramnulfe Ithier 1385–1388
Pierre Redondeau 1388–1437
Guillaume de Fumel 1437–1470 (resigned)

COMMENDATORY ABBOTS

Charles de Bourbon 1471–1477 (resigned)
Antoine Allemand 1477–1495
Guillaume Briçonnet 1496–1507 (resigned)
Sigismond de Gonzague 1507–1513 (resigned)
Charles de Carrest 1513–1515 (resigned)
Nicholas de Flisc 1515–1519 (resigned)
Sigismond de Gonzague (2nd abbacy) 1519–1525 (resigned)
François I de Neufville 1525 1561 (resigned)
François II de Neufville 1561–

FREELY ELECTED ABBOTS

François II de Neufville 1579–1596
François Marand 1596–1603 (resigned)
Rigaud de Lavaur 1603–1631
François de Tautal 1631–1635
Georges Barny 1635–1654
Antoine de Chavaroche 1654–1677
Alexandre Frémon 1678–1687
Henri de la Marche de Parnac 1687–1715
Rene de la Guérinière 1716–1744
Raymond Garat 1744–1748
François-Xavier Mondain de la Maison-Rouge 1748–1787

SELECT BIBLIOGRAPHY

The bibliography of the Order of Grandmont is mainly contained in the works of Dom Jean Becquet OSB (see below p. 386 and of J-R. Gaborit (see below under Art and Architecture.) There is a vast quantity of primary source materials distributed throughout the departmental archives of France. The largest collection of Grandmontine documentation is that of the former Seminary of Limoges now in the Archives de la Haute Vienne. Regrettably this collection is not available for consultation at present. However, the nineteenth century historian, Louis Guibert did have access to this material and much of it, especially the correspondence relevant to the suppression of the Order is reproduced in his work (see below). Chapter 7 of the present work is dependent upon this source.

Fundamental Texts

The Thoughts/Maxims of St Stephen of Muret compiled by Hugues Lacerta and others circa 1157: *Liber de Doctrina vel Liber Sententiarum*, PL 204: 1086–1136.

The Rule of Grandmont composed by the fourth prior of Grandmont, Stephen Liciac (ruled 1139–1163): *Regula Venerabilis Viri Stephani Muretensis*, PL 204: 1135–1162.

The Life of St Stephen which emerged between the years 1139 and 1163 and was supplemented circa 1190: *Vita Venerabilis Viri Stephani Muretensis,* PL 204: 1005–1076.

The *Speculum Grandimontis,* the work of the seventh prior of Grandmont, Gérard Ithier. Volume one, a compilation of the *Vita B* and appendices, the *Liber Sententiarum,* and the Rule, has disappeared but volume two survives in the Archives de la Haute Vienne. (MS 166) It includes a number of the treatises containing descriptions of grandmontine life and custom. These and other fundamental grandmontine texts have been published in the following works:

E. Martène and U. Durand, *Veterum scriptorum et monumentorum historicum dogmaticorum, moralium, amplissima collectio* 6 (Paris: 1729)

E. Martène and U. Durand, 'Antiqua statuta ordinis Grandimontensis', *Thesaurus novus anecdotorum* 4 (Paris 1717.)

All the above texts have been conveniently compiled and edited by Dom Jean Becquet OSB under the title: *Scriptores Ordinis Grandimontensis,* Corpus Christianorum, Continuatio Mediaevalis 8 (Turnhout, Belgium: 1968)

Early Eyewitness Accounts

Gerald of Wales	*Speculum Ecclesiae*; ed. J.S. Brewer, *Giraldus Cambrensis, Opera* 4 (London: Rolls Series, 1873)
Walter Map	*De Nugis Curialium* 1; ed., M.R. James, *Anecdota Oxoniensia,* Medieval and Modern Series, part 14 (Oxford, 1914)
John of Salisbury	Policraticus; ed. C.C.J. Webb, *Johannis Saresberiensis Episcopi Carnotensis Policratici sive De Nugis Curialium et Vestigiis Philosophorum* Book 8 (Oxford, 1909).

Geoffrey de Vigeois — *Chronica Gaufredi Coenobitae Monasterii S Martialis Lemovicensis ac Prioris Vosciensis coenobi*; ed., P. Labbe, *Nova Bibliotheca Manuscriptorum* 2 (Paris, 1657).

Jacques de Vitry — *Historiae occidental* cap. 19 (Douai, 1597). 5 Cited: J. Levesque, *Annales Ordinis Grandimontis* (Troyes, 1662) pp. 150–153.

Guiot de Provins — 'La Bible'; ed., J. Orr. *Les Oeuvres de Guiot de Provins* (Manchester: University Press, 1915).

Nigel Wireker — *Speculum Stultorum*; edd., Martène et Durand, *Veterum Scriptorum Amplissima Collectio* 6 (Paris, 1729).

GENERAL HISTORY

The best studies of the Order of Grandmont are the following thesis and series of articles by Dom Jean Becquet OSB:

— *Recherches sur les institutions religieuses de l'Ordre de Grandmont au Moyen Age*, diplôme dactyl. École pratique des hautes études (1951). Copy in the Archives de la Haute Vienne, Limoges.

Articles in the Revue Mabillon

- 'Les premiers écrivains de l'Ordre de Grandmont', *RMab* 43 (1953) 121–37.
- 'L'Institutio, premier coutumier de Grandmont', *RMab* 46 (1952) 15–32.
- 'Les Institutions de l'Ordre de Grandmont au Moyen Age', *RMab* 42 (1952) 31–42.
- 'Le Bullaire de l'Ordre de Grandmont', *RMab* 46–53 (1956–1963 *passim*.

- 'Bibliothèque des écrivains de l'Ordre de Grandmont' *RMab* 53 (1963) 59–79.
- 'Les statuts de réforme de l'Ordre de Grandmont au XIIe siècle', *RMab* 59 (1977) 129–43.

Articles in the Bulletin Archeologique et Historique du Limousin

- 'Saint-Etienne de Muret et l'archévêque de Bénévent Milon', *Bull* 86 (1957) 403–09.
- 'La Règle de Grandmont', *Bull* 87 (1958) 9–36.
- 'La première crise de l'Ordre de Grandmont', *Bull* 87 3e livraison (1960) 283–324.

also

- 'La liturgie de l'Ordre de Grandmont' in *Ephemerides Liturgicae* 76 (1962) 146–61.
- 'Étienne de Muret' in *Dictionnaire de Spiritualité* IV(1961) cols 1504–14.

OTHER HISTORICAL WORKS

Delisle, L.	'Examen de treize chartes de l'Ordre de Grandmont', *Mémoires de la Société des Antiquaires de Normandie* 20 (Caen, 1854).
Dereine, Canon Charles	'L'obituaire primitif de l'Ordre de Grandmont', *BSAHL* 87 (1960) 325–31.
Fouquet, J. & Frère Philippe-Etienne	*Histoire de L'Ordre de Grandmont* (Chambray, 1985).
Genicot, L.	'Présentation de Saint-Etienne de Muret et de sa pauvreté', *Revue Nouvelle* 19 (1954) 578–89.
Hallam, Elizabeth M.	'Henry II, Richard I and the Order of Grandmont', *Journal of Medieval History* 1 (1975) 165–86.

La Grassière, P.B. de — *Messieurs de Monneron Mousequetaires du Roi et l'Abbaye de Grandmont* (Limoges, 1979).

Lanthonie, A. — *Histoire de l'Abbaye de Grandmont en Limousin* (Limoges, 1979).

Lecler, Canon A. — 'Histoire de l'Abbaye de Grandmont', *BSAHL* 57–60 *passim* (1907–1911).

Levesque, Dom J. — *Annales Ordinis Grandimontis* (Troyes, 1662)

Palma, L. — 'La Povertá nell'Ordo di Grandmont', *Aevum* 48 (1974) 270–87.

Pellistrandi, C. — 'La Pauvreté dans la Règle de Grandmont'. *Études sur l'histoire de la pauvrete* ed. M. Mollat (Paris, 1974) 229–45.

Seward, D. — 'The Grandmontines — A Forgotten Order', *Downside Review* 83 (1965) 249–64.

The Seventeenth Century Reform

Becquet, Dom J. — 'Charles Frémon, *Dictionnaire de Spiritualité* IV (1961) 1504–14.

Rochias, Dom J.B. — *Vie du Révérend Père Charles Frémon Réformateur de Grandmont*, pb. Canon A. Lecler (Limoges: Ducourtieux et Goût, 1910).

The Suppression

Chevallier, P. — *Loménie de Brienne et l'ordre monastique, 1766–1789*, Vol 1: pp. 100–104; Vol 2 pp. 148–163 (Paris, 1960).

Guibert, L. — 'Une page de l'histoire du clergé franç ais au XVIIIe siècle, Destruction de L'Ordre et de L'Abbaye de Grandmont', *BSAHL* 23–25 *passim*. Reprinted in a complete volume under the same title (Paris and Limoges, 1877).

HISTORY OF THE GRANDMONTINE FOUNDATIONS IN ENGLAND

Rose Graham's work, 'The Order of Grandmont and its Houses in England' published jointly with Sir Alfred Clapham's article, 'The Order of Grandmont and its Architecture' *Archaeologia* 75 (1926), remains the definitive history of the Grandmontines in England. It was republished in *English Ecclesiastical Studies* (London: SPCK, 1929).

Craswall Priory (Herefordshire)

Wright, C.F. 'Report on the Field Study in Mediaeval Architecture held in July, 1962 on the site of Craswall Priory, Herefordshire', *Transactions of the Woolhope Naturalists' Field Club* 38 (1964–1966) 76–81.

Lilwall, C.J. *Something About Craswall Priory, near Hay* (pamphlet: Hereford, 1910)

— 'Craswall Priory', *Transactions of the Woolhope Naturalists' Field Club* 1902–1904, pp. 267–73.

— 'Craswall Priory Excavations' *Ibid.* 1908–1911, pp. 36–49.

Stallybrass, B. 'Craswall Priory, Near Hay, Herefordshire' (Report for the Committee of the Society for the Protection of Ancient Buildings). *Transactions of the Woolhope Naturalists' Field Club,* 1914–1917,pp. 49–52.

Shoesmith, R. 'Craswall Priory', *Archaeology in Hereford,* Annual Report of the City Archaeology Committee (1985–1986), pp. 26–28.

— 'Neglect and Decay: The Case of Craswall Priory', *Rescue News* – The Newspaper of the British Archaeological Trust 41 (1986) pp. 5–6.

Alberbury Priory (Shropshire)

Eyton, R.W. *Antiquities of Shropshire*,8 (London and Shifnal, 1858) pp. 66–110.

Chibnall, Marjorie M. 'House of Grandmontine Monks', *Victoria History of the Counties of England*, 2:Shropshire (London: University of London Institute of Historical Research, 1973) pp. 47–50.

Grosmont Priory (Yorkshire)

Atkinson, J.C. *History of Cleveland*, part II (Barrow-in-Furness, 1874) 200–202.

Brown, W. 'Description of Twelve Small Yorkshire Priories at the Reformation', *Yorkshire Archaeological Journal* 9 (1886) 213–15.

Fallow, T.M. 'The Priory of Grosmont', *Victoria History of the Counties of England* 3:Yorkshire (London: University of London Institute of Historical Research, 1913) 193–94 .

Kendall, H.P. *The Priory of Grosmont in Eskdale* (Whitby 1929).

Vickers, Noreen 'Grosmont Priory' *Yorkshire Archaeological Journal* 56 (1984) 45–49.

THE HISTORY OF SPECIFIC PRIORIES AND CELLS IN FRANCE

The archives and archaeological and historical societies of the various French departments contain a wealth of studies of individual priories and cells of the Order of Grandmont. The following list includes those which have been of some value in the preparation of the present work and is by no means exhaustive.

The name of the relevant department has been added in brackets after each work.

Bazin, P.	*L'Ancien Prieuré de Breuil*. Dijon, 1953. (Côte d'Or).
Bornet, Canon	*Le Prieuré de Notre-Dame-de-Clairefontaine ou des Bonshommes de l'Ordre de Grandmont près de Savignies, 1207–1791*. Beauvais, 1922. (Oise).
Bourderioux, L'Abbe	'Vestiges Grandmontains Tourangeaux' *Bulletin de la Société Archéologique de Touraine* 32 (1959) 199–223. (Indre et Loire).
Carre ''de Busserole, J-X.	L'Ancien Prieuré de Hauterives', *'Mémoires e de la Societe Archéologique de Touraine* 13 (1861) 188–92. (Indre et Loire).
Coutan, Dr	'La Chapelle de Notre-Dame-du-Parc, Prieuré de Grandmont à Rouen' *Bulletin Monumental* 92 (1933) 207–19. (Seine Maritime).
Darras, E.	*Le Prieuré Grandmontain de Notre-Dame-des Bonshommes du Meynel-lès Maffliers*. Pontoise- l'Isle-Adam, 1928. (Val d'Oise).
Farcy, Canon	*Une Page de l'Histoire de Rouen, le Prieuré de Grandmont des origines à nos jours*, Rouen, 1934. (Seine-Maritime).

Gaborit, J-R. 'Notre-Dame-du-Parc Église du prieuré de Grandmont à Rouen' *Revue de la Société Savante de la Haute Normandie* 53 (1969) 15–25. (Seine Maritime).

Garand, R. 'Essai sur le Prieuré Grandmontain de Bandouille en Bressuirais'. *Extraits du Bulletin des Amis du Vieux-Bressuire* 2 (1950–1951) 17–35. (Deux-Sévres).

Garriot, A. & Prêter, J.L. *Essai sur l'histoire de L'Abbaye de L'Ouye*. Dourdan (undated). (Essonne).

Guibert, L. *Le Monastère de Balezis*. Limoges, 1877. (Haute-Vienne).

Lerat, B. 'Une Charte inédite de Richard Coeur de Lion concernant trois prieurés de l'Ordre de Grandmont en Bas-Poitou', *Revue de Bas-Poitout* (Fontenay-le-Comte, 1944) 121–31.

Leveel, P. 'Grandmont-lès-Tours depuis deux siècles', *Bulletin de la Société Archeologique de Touraine* 37 (1972) 159–66.(Indre et Loire).

Moutie, A. *Receuil des pièces et chartes relatives au Prieuré Notre-Dame-de-Louye-lès-Dourdan de l'Ordre de Grandmont*. Paris, 1845. (Essonne).

Noirot, A.J. 'Le Prieuré Grandmontain de Vieupou, *La Vallée d'Aillant dans l'histoire,* IV (Aillant-sur-Tholon, 1976) 215–45. (Yonne).

Oury, Dom G. and Arnould, Canon 'Les Grandmontains de Bois-Rahier près de Tour, *Bulletin de la Société Archéologique de Touraine* 37 (1953) 245–61. (Indre et Loire).

Rey, D. 'Le Prieuré de Comberoumal en Lévézou', *Études d'archéologie grandmontaines*, Rodez, 1925. (Aveyron).

Rocher, C. *Le Monastère de Sainte-Marie-de-Viaye,* Le Puy, 1877. (Haute Loire).

Secret, J. 'Les Prieurés grandmontains du diocèse de Périgueux', *Bulletin de la Société Archéologique et Historique du Perigord* 82 (1955) 107ff.

Terre, M. *L'Ordre de Grandmont et le Prieuré de Saint-Jean-les-Bons-Hommes à Avallon.* Clamecy, 1951. (Yonne).

Vallette, R. & Charbonneau-Lucy, L. 'Un Monastère Oublié, le Prieuré de Grandmont au Diocèse de Luçon', *Revue du Bas-Poitou,* livraison 1 (1918) 18–27. (Vendée).

Vitalis, A. *Une page de l'histoire du Diocèse de Lodève, Le Prieuré de Saint-Michel-de Grandmont.* Montpellier, 1985. (Hérault).

Art and Architecture

Aussibal, A. *L'Art Grandmontain.* La Pierre-qui-Vire: Zodiaque, 1984.

Crozet, R. *L'Architecture de L'Ordre de Grandmont en Poitou, Saintonge et Angumois.* Angoulême, 1946.

Dion, A. de 'Note sur l'architecture dans l'Ordre de Grandmont', *Bulletin Monumental* 40 (1874) 560–74; 42 (1876) 247–65 and 310–29.

Gaborit, J-R. 'L'Architecture de L'Ordre de Grandmont', Unpublished thesis: École des Chartes, Paris 1963. (Copy in the Archives de la Haute Vienne.)

— 'L'Autel Majeur de Grandmont', *Cahiers de Civilisation Médiévale X*[e] *– XII*[e] *siècles* (Université de Poitiers, 1976) 231–46.

—	'Le Trésor de L'Abbaye de Grandmont', Unpublished thesis: École du Louvre. (Copy in the Archives de la Haute Vienne.)
Gauthier, Marie-Madeleine S.	'Coffret eucharistique provenant du trésor de Grandmont', *Information d'histoire de l'art* 9 (1964) 81–83.
	Emaux champlevés des XIIe, XIIIe et XIVe siècles. (Paris, 1950) 21, 29–30,70,72,74,77,88, 151.
Grezillier, A.	'L'Architecture Grandmontaine', *Bulletin Monumental* 21 (1963) 331–58.
—	'Vestiges Grandmontains', *BSAHL* 86 troisième livraison (1957) 411–424.
Guibert, L.	'L'école monastique d'orfèvrerie de Grandmont', *BSAHL* 36 (1889) 45–199.
Lecler, A.	'Les grandes chasses de Grandmont', *BSAHL* 38 (1891) 173 ff.
de Linas, C.	'Les Emaux de L'Abbaye de Grandmont', *Revue de l'art chrétien* 11 (1884) 341–43.
Souchal, Geneviève	'Autour des plaques de Grandmont: une famille d'émaux champlevés limousins de la fin du XIIe siècle', *Bulletin Monumental* 125 (1967) 21–71.
—	'Les émaux de Grandmont au XIIe siècle', *Bulletin Monumental* 120–122 (1962–1964) *passim*.
—	'L'émail de Guillaume de Treignac, sixième Prieur de Grandmont', *Gazette des Beaux-Arts* 3 (1964) 65–80.

GENERAL INDEX

CISTERCIAN PUBLICATIONS INC.

Kalamazoo, Michigan

TITLES LISTING

THE CISTERCIAN FATHERS SERIES

THE WORKS OF BERNARD OF CLAIRVAUX

Treatises I: Apologia to Abbot William, On Precept and Dispensation . . . . CF 1

On the Song of Songs I–IV . . . . CF 4,7,31,40

The Life and Death of Saint Malachy the Irishman . . . . CF 10

Treatises II: The Steps of Humility, On Loving God . . . . CF 13

Magnificat: Homilies in Praise of the Blessed Virgin Mary [with Amadeus of Lausanne] . . . . CF 18

Treatises III: On Grace and Free Choice, In Praise of the New Knighthood . . . . CF 19

Sermons on Conversion: A Sermon to Clerics, Lenten Sermons on Psalm 91 . . . . CF 25

Five Books on Consideration: Advice to a Pope . . . . CF 37

THE WORKS OF WILLIAM OF SAINT THIERRY

On Contemplating God, Prayer, and Meditations . . . . CF 3

Exposition on the Song of Songs . . . . CF 6

The Enigma of Faith . . . . CF 9

The Golden Epistle . . . . CF 12

The Mirror of Faith . . . . CF 15

Exposition on the Epistle to the Romans . . . . CF 27

The Nature and Dignity of Love . . . . CF 30

THE WORKS OF AELRED OF RIEVAULX

Treatises I: On Jesus at the Age of Twelve, Rule for a Recluse, The Pastoral Prayer . . . . CF 2

Spiritual Friendship . . . . CF 5

The Mirror of Charity . . . . CF 17†

Dialogue on the Soul . . . . CF 22

THE WORKS OF GILBERT OF HOYLAND

Sermons on the Song of Songs I–III . . CF 14,20,26

Treatises, Sermons, and Epistles . . . . CF 34

THE WORKS OF JOHN OF FORD

Sermons on the Final Verses of the Song of Songs I–VII . . . . . . CF 29,39,43,44,45,46,47

Texts and Studies in the Monastic Tradition

OTHER EARLY CISTERCIAN WRITERS

The Letters of Adam of Perseigne, I . . . . CF 21

Alan of Lille: The Art of Preaching . . . . CF 23

Idung of Prüfening. Cistercians and Cluniacs: The Case for Citeaux . . . . CF 33

Guerric of Igny. Liturgical Sermons I–II . . . . CF 8,32

Three Treatises on Man: A Cistercian Anthropology . . . . CF 24

Isaac of Stella. Sermons on the Christian Year, I . . . . CF 11

Stephen of Lexington. Letters from Ireland, 1228–9 . . . . CF 28

Stephen of Sawley, Treatises . . . . CF 36

Baldwin of Ford. Spiritual Tractates . . . . CF 38,41

Serlo of Wilton & Serlo of Savigny . . . . CF 48

** Temporarily out of print*

† Forthcoming

THE CISTERCIAN STUDIES SERIES

MONASTIC TEXTS

Evagrius Ponticus. Praktikos and Chapters on Prayer . . . CS 4
The Rule of the Master . . . CS 6
The Lives of the Desert Fathers . . . CS 34
The Sayings of the Desert Fathers . . . CS 59
The Harlots of the Desert . . . CS 106
Dorotheos of Gaza. Discourses and Sayings . . . CS 33
Pachomian Koinonia I–III:
The Lives . . . CS 45
The Chronicles and Rules . . . CS 46
The Instructions, Letters, and Other Writings of St Pachomius and His Disciples . . . CS 47
Besa, The Life of Shenoute . . . CS 73
Menas of Nikiou: Isaac of Alexandria & St Macrobius . . . CS 107
The Syriac Fathers on Prayer and the Spiritual Life (S. Brock) . . . CS 101
Theodoret of Cyrrhus. A History of the Monks of Syria . . . CS 88
Simeon Stylites: The Lives . . . CS 112†
Symeon the New Theologian. Theological and Practical Treatises and Three Theological Discourses . . . CS 41
The Venerable Bede: Commentary on the Seven Catholic Epistles . . . CS 82
The Letters of Armand-Jean de Rancé (A.J. Krailsheimer) . . . CS 80, 81
Guigo II the Carthusian. The Ladder of Monks and Twelve Meditations . . . CS 48
The Monastic Rule of Iosif Volotsky . . . CS 36
Anselm of Canterbury. Letters . . . CS 94,95†
Br. Pinocchio, Rule of St Benedict . . . CS 99
Peter of Celle: Selected Works . . . CS 100

CHRISTIAN SPIRITUALITY

The Spirituality of Western Christendom . . . CS 30
Russian Mystics (Sergius Bolshakoff) . . . CS 26
In Quest of the Absolute: The Life and Works of Jules Monchanin (J.G. Weber) . . . CS 51
The Name of Jesus (Irénée Hausherr) . . . CS 44
The Roots of the Modern Christian Tradition . . . CS 55
Abba: Guides to Wholeness and Holiness East and West . . . CS 38
Sermons in a Monastery (Matthew Kelty–William Paulsell) . . . CS 58
Penthos: The Doctrine of Compunction in the Christian East (Irénée Hausherr) . . . CS 53
The Spirituality of the Christian East. A Systematic Handbook (Tomas Spidlik SJ) . . . CS 79
From Cloister to Classroom . . . CS 90
Fathers Talking. An Anthology (Aelred Squire) . . . CS 93
Friendship & Community (Brian P. McGuire) . . . CS 95

MONASTIC STUDIES

The Abbot in Monastic Tradition (Pierre Salmon) . . . CS 14
Community and Abbot in the Rule of St Benedict I (Adalbert de Vogüé) . . . CS 5/1–2
Consider Your Call: A Theology of the Monastic Life (Daniel Rees et al.) . . . CS 20
The Way to God According to the Rule of St Benedict (E. Heufelder) . . . CS 49
The Rule of St Benedict. A Doctrinal and Spiritual Commentary (Adalbert de Vogüé) . . . CS 54
Serving God First (Sighard Kleiner) . . . CS 83
Monastic Practices (Charles Cummings) . . . CS 75
St Hugh of Lincoln (David Hugh Farmer) . . . CS 87

CISTERCIAN STUDIES

The Cistercian Way (André Louf) . . . CS 76
The Cistercian Spirit (M. Basil Pennington, ed.) . . . CS 3
The Eleventh-Century Background of Citeaux (Bede K. Lackner) . . . CS 8
Cistercian Sign Language (Robert Barakat) . . . CS 11
The Cistercians in Denmark (Brian P. McGuire) . . . CS 35
Athirst for God. Spiritual Desire in Bernard of Clairvaux's Sermons on the Song of Songs (Michael Casey) . . . CS 77
Saint Bernard of Clairvaux: Essays Commemorating the Eighth Centenary of His Canonization . . . CS 28
Bernard of Clairvaux: Studies Presented to Dom Jean Leclercq . . . CS 23
Bernard of Clairvaux and the Cistercian Spirit (Jean Leclercq) . . . CS 16
Another Look at St Bernard (Jean Leclercq) . . . CS 105
Women and Womanhood in the Works of St Bernard (Jean Leclercq) . . . CS 104
Image and Likeness. The Augustinian Spirituality of William of St Thierry (David N. Bell) . . . CS 78
William, Abbot of St Thierry . . . CS 94
Aelred of Rievaulx: A Study (Aelred Squire) . . . CS 50
Christ the Way: The Christology of Guerric of Igny (John Morson) . . . CS 25
The Golden Chain: The Theological Anthropology of Isaac of Stella (Bernard McGinn) . . . CS 15

** Temporarily out of print*

† Forthcoming